# Oakhurst
# Irregulars

# Oakhurst Irregulars

A Novel
by
Berton D. Garey

SLG BOOKS
Berkeley / Hong Kong

First published in 2008 by

**SLG Books**
PO Box 9465
Berkeley, CA 94709

Tel: 510-525-1134   Fax: 510-525-2632
Email: oak@slgbooks.com   URL: www.slgbooks.com

*I'd like to thank Kay Cavan, Janet Martinelli, Michael Garey, Dian Dunsay
and especially Regina Hartman for their thorough and thoughtful reading of
the early versions of Oakhurst Irregulars, and for their helpful suggestions. I'm
also grateful for the typos they found. It seems there is no end to them,
and they found many after I thought I'd found them all.
Any that remain must have grown overnight.*

Front cover photograph Berton D. Garey
Back cover photograph Sam Shaw/ © Shaw Family Archives
Book design and production by Mark Weiman/Regent Press
Color separation and printing by Snow Lion Graphics, Berkeley/Hong Kong

Library of Congress Cataloging-in-Publication Data

Garey, Berton D., 1944-
    Oakhurst Irregulars : a novel / by Berton D. Garey.
       p. cm.
    ISBN 978-0-943389-40-0
       1. Murder--Investigation--Fiction. 2. Children's secrets--Fiction.
    3. Nineteen fifties--Fiction. 4. Beverly Hills (Calif.)--Fiction.
    I. Title.

PS3557.A7148O19 2007
813'.54--dc22

                                    2007037664

Printed in Hong Kong

10  9  8  7  6  5  4  3  2  1

For George and Kenny,

Semper Fidelis.

For Josh and Grace and Ellis
Reason Enough

The fathers shall not be put to death for the children,
neither shall the children be put to death for the fathers;
every man shall be put to death for
his own sins.

Deuteronomy 24:16
King James Version

# Chapter 1

## *Seven Years and Counting*

## Monday, August 3, 1989

"I'VE GOT SOMETHING OF YOURS," he said.
It was the first Thursday of August, and hot by Berkeley standards, and my birthday had just come and gone. For just the flicker of an instant I pictured a birthday present overlooked. Then he added, "Or your brother's, anyway."

The words had a familiar ring. I couldn't place it, but the sudden slight ache and throbbing in my stomach told me I knew who this was. Before I recognized the sound of his voice, the hint of amused sarcasm brought a picture to mind and then the familiarity of the words sent my mind spinning.

"Are you there?" he said.

"Yes," I answered. "Detective Phillips, I presume?"

"Very good, cowboy. Very good. I'm impressed."

"I'm so glad. What is it you've got?"

Last time, it was the boxes of Marty's files pirated from my dad's apartment by Malovitch's thugs. I was thinking maybe I'd forgotten one and it had turned up.

"If it's another box of Marty's stuff, you keep it. It's been seven years and I try not to think about all that too much. I got out of L.A. alive and that's good enough for me."

"I wish it were that simple. You're going to have to come down here for a little chat."

I didn't say anything for several seconds. Examining my options. It had become second nature down there after Marty's death, but that was then. This was now, and I was out of it.

"No thanks," I told him.

My heart was beating a little faster and I felt a touch of lightheadedness.

"I could get a warrant. Have the Berkeley Police arrest and hold you. Would that be better? Right now it's just a little investigation. Let's keep it simple. I'm no more anxious to have you down here than I was the last time. But I'm here and the problem is here. It's an all-expense kind of deal. The Beverly Hills Police Department is going to pick up the tab. You can't beat that."

"Arrest me for what? What are you talking about? What've you got?"

"A cowboy belt."

"A what?"

"You know," he said, "a kid's cowboy belt. A fancy one with those rhinestone and silver deals around it."

"What makes you think it's Marty's?"

"Well, to begin with, it's got his name on it."

At first I was drawing a blank. But then, slowly, a picture of Marty's old belt came to mind. I hadn't seen or even thought about it in almost forty years. When Marty was fourteen or fifteen he gave it to me. I was seven or eight. It had had 'Goldman' in block gold letters on the inside of it and I remembered having added 'Kurt', or maybe just a 'K' with a writing attachment for a wood burning set I had. I wondered why Phillips hadn't said it was mine, but I really didn't care one way or another.

"Like I said, you keep it. I can't believe you're bothering me about some old belt. And threatening me. What in the hell do you think you could arrest me for? What in the hell is your problem?"

"Material witness. Co-conspirator. I'll think of something." His tone was playful.

"That's garbage. You do remember my younger brother's a criminal attorney, don't you? Why don't you call him and tell him how you plan to make up something to get a warrant. He'll love that."

"So maybe I've overstated it a little. I'd like you to come down here."

The sarcasm was gone now and his voice took on that official tone. "It's not so much the belt. It's what it's attached to."

I waited. He waited. I supposed to let me sweat or squirm, but I had no idea what was on his mind so I ended up waiting him out.

"There's a dead guy -a skeleton really- and the belt is around his neck.

I was quiet a long time.

"Any ideas?" he said.

When I didn't answer, he told me, "I've taken the liberty of making a reservation for you for next Monday morning. Southwest, Oakland to Burbank, 9am. Be on it. Second floor, 451 North Rexford. I'll expect you here by lunch. My treat."

I'd better call Nick, I thought.

# Chapter 2

## *Jacaranda*

IT WAS THE FIRST WEDNESDAY in June, 1951, the sixth of June to be exact, and things were going pretty good, I thought. In fact, I was sure this was going to be the best summer of my life. We shared a duplex with my grandparents on Oakhurst Drive. Our side was two bedrooms and it was too small for us, but it seemed to work okay. Nick was four and Marty was almost sixteen, really tall and skinny, more than six feet, so he seemed a lot older, and me, seven and three quarters, almost eight, and we'd been sharing a room with my sister, Sarah, except she turned eleven a couple of months before and crabbed about wanting to have a room without boys –any of us- but the best my mom and dad could do was to give her their room to share with Nick, which left them sleeping in what had been the dining room on a thing that for some reason was called a davenport.

It couldn't have been much past six. I was about to finish the second grade and then have the whole summer to get ready for the third. Sarah said it would never happen. She said I'd been lucky to get out of the first grade, but they'd never let me out, and I'd be a second-grader forever. We were broke a lot of the time, and there was a problem between my father and grandfather, they worked together, that caused a lot of yelling and arguing between my mom and dad, and a lot of it sort of worked its way down to us kids, but mostly, I thought things were pretty good.

The trick, I figured, was to stay out of the way.

Since Nick was too young to really play with and Marty was too old, and since Sarah could beat me up, I tried to stay away from her and her friends. So I was usually on my own, and as long as I left a message with someone about where I was, or would be, or when I'd be home, or got home before the six o'clock rule, or the before-dark-rule in the summer, no one had to worry. The good thing was, even by myself, there were lots of things to do and places to go.

Our street was lined with jacaranda trees, big old ones that reached from the parkway on each side of the street to the middle, forming a high-up tunnel, a canopy Pop called it, made of the green fern-like leaves. In June and July and August, the trees grew these pale purple trumpet-shaped blossoms that popped alive and you could smell them when the air was warm. All summer long they dropped to the ground, covering the lawns and the sidewalk and the street. New ones kept growing, so the trees looked full, until about the middle of September, they were done, and that was that. I loved it. I loved them. Sarah and her friends, or maybe Marty before her, had named most of the trees and I usually said hello to them as I passed.

I'd gotten up and looked over both pair of my Levi's to make sure I'd found the ones with the smaller holes at the knees. I used my belt to cinch them up at the waist. My pants were always bought too big because my mom figured I'd have room to grow and extra time before we had to buy new ones, but they usually wore out around the knees before that happened, so I needed the belt Marty had given me to hold them up. The belt had been too big too so he'd punched a hole in it to fit me, which left a lot of it hanging past the belt loop, so he cut off the extra. I rolled up the pant legs at the cuffs a couple of turns and took a white t-shirt that still smelled like bleach from the dresser Marty and I shared and found the thick socks that made up for the air or water that usually came through the holes at the toes of my sneakers and had a bowl of cereal and took the thirty-five cents lunch money my mom left on the kitchen table for me and slipped out through the back porch to the driveway. The screen door had a worn-out spring, so if you gave it a push, it would fly open and slam into the side of the house, whack hard enough to bounce back and bang shut. My mom said I drove her nuts when that happened, and even though I tried to remember not to, since I was usually in a hurry, it happened pretty often anyway. Two bangs for the price of one, Pop said, since his side of the duplex was far enough away so he didn't have to hear it. But I liked early mornings alone like this, so it was worth making extra sure that I eased the door open and closed with only the slightest bit of noise escaping from the spring.

I looked down the driveway to the left. One garage door was open and the garage was empty and the other was still closed, so that meant Pop, my grandfather, was up and out somewhere, and my dad was still asleep.

The whole street was quiet and empty. Almost no one parked on the street. You got to most of the garages behind the yards from the alley, except a few houses, like ours, had driveways to the street. It was early enough and still cold enough for some dew to be on the lawns. I walked up the street towards the railroad tracks that separated Lower Santa Monica Boulevard from Upper Santa Monica. I shuffled my feet so that my sneakers left two darker green paths on the grass next door. I tried to move mostly on my heels to keep the front of my feet off the grass, to keep the water away from the holes. When I got to the path from the sidewalk to the Courtyard, I tiptoed up the three steps to see if George Bowen was awake yet. If he was, his newspaper would be gone. If he was in the right mood, he might let me sit next to him on his front step while he had a smoke and tell me about the war. Mostly, he told me how they were Marines and helped each other. Kind of like the Three Musketeers. All for one and one for all. My friend, Allen, told me his father said the stories probably weren't true. He said all of the men on the block that had been in the war exaggerated their war stories, but Pop said if George said a thing, it was true, so I believed him, even if Allen and his father didn't.

The older boys on the block, not Marty, but some of his friends, Noel and Jackie and Paul, tried to get Kevin Doyle, who lived straight across the street from us, to tell his war stories because he won a medal on some island. Most of the time, he wouldn't talk about the war with anyone but George, but sometimes, if he'd been sitting on his front steps and smoking and drinking beer, he did. Marty said his stories were mean and gory, and Kevin was weird and smelled bad, and said I should keep away from him. At the Courtyard, there were three apartments on the left and three on the right and George's at the back. All of them still had the L.A. Times in front of their doors, so I went back to making tracks in the wet grass. I slid my feet and made a large double loop and then another, leaving a trail like a fighter pilot would in the sky. I crossed Mr. Avery's lawn and came to the thick hedge that ran from the third house up the street from us to the sidewalk. It was supposed to keep Mr. Sullivan's lawn private. He was older than my dad, but younger than Pop, so it seemed strange to me that we almost never saw him. Not outside anyway, but he'd be looking out from his front window for anyone on his grass or pushing through his bushes. If he spotted you, me mostly, he'd open the window and yell and say he was going to make sure your parents punished you, but since Pop owned our duplex and the complaining about something one of us kids had done came to him instead of my mom and dad, and since Pop didn't like Mr. Sullivan to begin with, he usually told Mr. Sullivan he'd look into it, but he didn't say anything to my mom or dad, so that was usually the end of it. I forced my way through in the same spot I'd gone through a thousand times before. I couldn't really remember how come I got started going through there, but I think it was Marty that had started the hole when he was little because he didn't like Mr. Sullivan either, and sort of invited me to keep it going when he got too big to do it. The hole was there where the branches and leaves had given up trying to grow from Marty, then me, going through. Pop didn't say anything about it, but whenever we were together and we drove past the bushes with the hole in them, he sort of snickered to himself. I made the tracks on his grass too. My sneakers were getting soaked and the thick socks were getting soggy, not so much from the holes, but from the top down through the canvas. Next was the Pink House.

An actor named Rathbone owned it. Marty and his friends called him Rathbutt, and said he used to be famous before the war. It was a huge place, not the house so much which was only a little bigger than others on the block, but the gardens. The lot was on what would have been seven or eight of the regular sized ones on the street. No one was supposed to know what was back there, because it was forbidden to go in, but every kid on the block had heard stories of an amazing garden behind the brick wall and iron gates. We also knew that you risked death if you even thought about going in there, and the guy that would kill you would be Iyama Osaka. He was supposed to be the gardener, and he did do the gardening, but we also knew that Rathbutt captured him during the war and let him live on the condition that he do all of the gardening and kill anyone who even tried to sneak in.

I knew what was back there because I'd been sneaking in for a couple of weeks. If I started for school before Marty and Sarah did, or a little after, I could get in and out without anyone knowing. And sometimes on my way home after school, too. It was the most beautiful place I'd ever seen, and in a way, it was all mine. I snuck in through a hole I'd dug under the fence where the bamboo patch came right up next to it along the alley. I used the trash can from the house next door to cover the hole. I had to check it pretty often, because sometimes the garbage men didn't put it back just right, and you could see the hole, but at least they didn't tell anyone about it, so that was good. Just inside the fence, with a little limb saw I took from Pop's garage, I cut a path for about twenty feet, to the middle of the patch, and made a hideout in the center about ten feet across. I used the cut bamboo to make a sort of floor mat for it. I'd also cut away just enough of the bamboo on the other side of my hideout so that I could squeeze through, and get close enough to see the rest of the garden without being seen by either Rathbutt or Iyama Osaka.

Pretty often, Rathbutt wandered around on the crushed rock paths that went this way and that through these large special areas like the rose garden part and the pond part and the bamboo patch and the flowerbeds and the rolling grassy hill with the shade trees part. He always walked slowly from place to place examining the flowers, or watching the fish in the pond, or sitting on little concrete benches that were here and there, reading the newspaper or a magazine. I couldn't stay long, but I almost always had the place to myself in the morning before school since he didn't get up early and Iyama Osaka, when he came, didn't come early either. He was there on Mondays, Wednesdays and Saturdays, usually not too early and not too late, so if I was careful, even on days he was going to be there, I could enjoy the quiet and warmth and sweet smells that filled the place all by myself. I didn't tell anyone. Not even Marty.

And you never saw Rathbutt in the neighborhood except for that once in a while Iyama Osaka would take his car out of the garage and drive it around from the alley for him, leave it running in front of the house, and Rathbutt would walk across the path from the house to the street and get in and never look at anyone and drive off. Marty said it was a 1937 Packard convertible, and he and his friends called it the Green Machine, and they all drooled over it.

I stood at the edge of the Pink House lawn. I thought about going around to the alley and into the gardens. I thought about continuing the tracks across the grass in front of me and then going around to the alley, and had decided to do that until I looked up and saw Rathbutt peeking out through a lifted up Venetian blind slat. He had the most unsmiling face in the world and he shook a warning finger at me. I made my way back to the sidewalk and the slat dropped back into place. Way too early for him, I was thinking, maybe he couldn't sleep. That was the end of my plan, so I continued up the street and was about to the middle of the Pink House when Iyama Osaka's old Dodge truck rattled up and stopped.

Why was he so early, I wondered? Why was Rathbutt up so early? What was going on around here? It ruined everything. I stared straight ahead and kept walking. Marty said if you looked at him wrong it might set him off and there was no telling what he might do. I could feel his eyes on me so I walked a little faster and tried not to look back when I heard his truck door open and close. I could tell by the sounds he was taking tools off the truck. When I had gone three more houses up, I looked back. He had taken a gasoline-engine mower down a ramp of wooden planks. He had other tools and a large canvas tarp laid out on the parkway, but he just stood there, not moving, with his hands on his hips watching me. I looked away and walked some more and then looked back again. He was still watching me! Then he walked across the lawn to the white iron gate in the middle of the brick wall. The wall was only four or five feet high, but there were wooden things attached to it that added another three feet or so, and they were covered with flowering vines, so you couldn't see in at all, except through the gate itself. With the gate open, he went back for the mower and other tools. When everything was inside, he closed the gate with a clank I could hear all the way up the block.

The way he just watched me! Brother, that was a close call! I couldn't wait to tell Marty. Sarah would never believe me.

I continued my trail making across the wet grass of the rest of the lawns until I came to the low chain link fence surrounding the front yard of the last house on the block on our side. I stamped my feet on the sidewalk to shake off some of the water that I'd collected and was about to cross the street and go through the thick mess of Oleander bushes to the railroad tracks when I heard puppy noises. I tried to look through the fence, but there was too much ivy covering it, so I climbed up a little to see over. On the front porch was a black ball of fuzz with a black nose and black eyes. It whimpered and yipped.

"Hey, doggie, over here!" I called.

It stopped making noises and looked all around for me.

"Over here!" I said again.

It finally saw me and came running over to the fence. Its butt wiggled like crazy and I walked along the fence until I found a gap in the ivy. He or she poked its nose through trying to lick my fingers. The door to the house opened.

"Snowball! Snowball, where are you, girl?" a woman called.

She was barefoot and had a lot of sort of blond, light brown hair going in all directions. She was holding a white terrycloth robe closed at her neck and sipped from a coffee mug.

"She's over here with me," I called to her.

She came down the path to the fence.

"Hi," she said in a soft, whispery voice. "Who are you?"

"Kurt," I told her. "I live down the street."

"What are you doing up so early? Are you all by yourself?" She noticed my t-shirt. "Aren't you cold?"

" No. I was just checking on things. I'm on my way to school."

"All by yourself? So early?"

"Yes."

"Does your mother know where you are?"

"Not yet. No one else was awake. Except Pop, and he was already gone before me."

"Are you going to be okay? How old are you?"

"Seven and three-quarters. Almost eight, really."

"That's pretty young to be out alone, don't you think?"

"No. I've been checking on things since I was really little. Sometimes I go to school with my big sister, though."

She had a pretty smile, I thought.

"Do you have time to come in the yard and play with Snowball?"

"Snowball!? How can you call her Snowball? She's black! Snowballs are white, for pete'sake."

She smiled and played with her hair and told me, "I know. But it makes me laugh to think about it, so Snowball she is! Do you want to come in and play with her?"

"Sure," I told her.

As I went back down the fence and through the gate, I asked, "Where'd you get her? From the Lesters?"

"Yes, Mrs. Lester, across the street. You already knew her dog had a litter, and she's giving them away?"

I nodded.

"Maybe you could get one too."

"Pop says we can't have any pets."

"Pop?"

"My grandfather. He's the boss of the house."

"I think that's kinda mean of him."

"Mostly he's nice…."

"I'm sure he is. Maybe he'll change his mind."

I shrugged, but I knew that wasn't gong to happen.

Once I was inside the gate, Snowball couldn't wait to jump up on my leg and then she kept licking my fingers. The woman handed me a rubber ball with a tin bell inside. I threw it for Snowball and she brought it back and dropped it and barked for me to do it again. After a while, she got tired and went to her water bowl and had a drink and laid down.

"Would you like some hot chocolate? I've got to get dressed and go to the set, but we could have a little hot chocolate first."

"Sure."

"Do you need to call someone? To ask them?"

"No, it's okay."

We went inside, but she left the front door open. We sat at a small round table in the kitchen.

"What's your name?" I asked her.

"Well, why don't you call me Norma?"

"Sure."

Another woman's voice boomed out, "Who'n the hell left the door open? Norma? It's freezing in here!" She came down the last stairs and poked her head into the kitchen. When she saw me, she was all smiles, and said to Norma, "Oh, excuse me. I didn't know you had a gentleman caller."

She was kind of heavy, and her face was puffy from it being early in the morning and she had a deep laugh that made her whole body kind of shake, but I wasn't sure what she was laughing about to begin with.

"Shelly, this is Kurt. He lives down the street. Kurt, this is Shelly. I'm just staying with her a while."

"As long as you want, honey. Mi casa es su casa."

Shelly reached out a hand and we shook. "Where's that little mutt of yours?"

"Kurt was throwing the ball for her. She's resting on the porch."

"Aren't you supposed to be on the set early?"

"I'm going. We're just finishing our hot chocolate."

"You go get dressed. I'll keep Kurt company."

"I guess I should go, too" I told them.

I headed for the door. Snowball wanted to play again, and she followed me, but I just petted her and went through the gate.

Norma called after me, "Come again, Kurt. You can come play with Snowball anytime.

"Maybe not so early, though, kid. Okay?" Shelly said.

The door closed. I picked up a couple of the jacaranda blossoms and put them in my pocket.

# Chapter 3

### *Not my Kind of Town*
### August 7, 1989

IT WAS A LITTLE AFTER ELEVEN when I walked into his office.

"I'd like to say it's good to see you," Phillips said with a little smirk as I sat down. "Flight okay?"

"Fine."

"Where's your brother? I thought you planned to have him with you."

"I thought I'd wait and see what's up," I told him.

No point in getting Nick involved if he's just blowing smoke.

He gave me a long dour look. Was I sure? It was unsettling. But then again, that's probably what he wanted. He looked good. Older, a touch of gray in his dark hair, but good. He was dressing better than before and he still had that air of liking what he did and knowing he was good at it.

"Pretty fancy," I said, looking around.

He smiled. "In a way, I have you to thank for it."

"How so?"

"Arresting and prosecuting those guys Malovitch and Wolf and Faustini. Salio. There was a fight over jurisdiction between downtown LA, and Santa Monica. The compromise was to let Beverly Hills take it. I was temporarily transferred here to work with their D. A. They asked me to stay."

"Glad I could help. Looks like the pay is better."

I nodded at his clothes.

He smiled again. "Much."

"So, about the belt. And the guy attached to it."

"I'll get to that." He looked at me for a moment. "I don't want to open old wounds…your brother and all…but I suppose that's unavoidable. I have a theory. Right now it's just that, a theory, and you're not going to like it, so I wanted to talk to you about it face to face. I don't want to make allegations I can't support, but here's the deal. They're digging a foundation for some project of fancy living units on Oakhurst. It's right up the street from where you lived as a kid. That much I know. I also know that your house, the duplex that used to be there, was torn down and a larger place was built on your lot and one north of it in 1954. Originally, the address you lived at was 431 North Oakhurst, right?" he asked.

He looked at me for confirmation.

I nodded. "My grandparents did. We were at 431 1/2."

"Your grandfather remained a partner in the new building. Until 1958."

That I didn't know.

"Then about nine years later that building and one to the south and another to the north were torn down and all four lots were merged to build what's there now. Are you familiar with it?"

"Sort of. Fancy apartments or condominiums or something?"

"Yeah, they have a doorman and an underground garage; the works."

"...there goes the neighborhood."

"It turns out the developers had hoped to do two projects of the same size at the same time: the one that's there now, and a second, by merging the old Rathbone property with the single lot that was between them and Rathbone's. But one of the trustees of Rathbone's property objected and the owner of the property at 437, in between, wouldn't sell, blocking them, so they had to settle for the one project on," he looked down at his notes, "429, 431, 433, and 435."

"So?"

"Your grandfather owned the lot."

I had no idea where he was going with all of this, and I suspected he wasn't too sure himself. But it was all news to me, and I had to admit, it had a slightly suspicious feel to it if nothing else. It must have showed, because he had a slight smile on his lips, like now we're getting somewhere. I must have been a little flustered by it all, because it didn't immediately dawn on me that Pop died in 1959, so he couldn't have been the owner of anything in 1967. I was about to point this out to Phillips, but he spoke first.

"Do you remember the house that was directly across the street from you? 432?"

"Sort of. It was a duplex, I think. Two stories."

It was uncomfortably hot in the room. No shortage of heat if the taxpayers are picking up the tab, I thought.

"Did you know that your grandfather had a half interest in it just after he sold your duplex?"

"No."

"Do you know where your grandparents lived after they sold 431?"

"They moved into an apartment a couple of blocks south. Still on Oakhurst."

"Why?"

"Why what? What do you mean?" I asked him.

"Why move into an apartment down the street when they just bought into the two unit place across the street? Or were partners in a newer fancier place where their duplex had been?"

"I don't know."

"Not even a guess?"

"Maybe the people living there had leases. Maybe the new places were too expensive. I don't know. I was nine or ten at the time. It wasn't anything to me."

"Do you know who owned the building before your grandfather?"

"No."

"Well, it turns out he was one of your grandfather's partners in the new building."

"Sounds like they traded partial ownership of the properties to get the new building built on our lot and the one next door."

"Maybe. Why didn't the guy tear down his own building and build the new one there?"

"How should I know? Listen, you asked me to come down here. You made it sound important. You hinted at an arrest warrant. How about getting to that? Or should I call Nick now?"

"I'll get there in a minute. Let me ask you a few more questions. Okay?"

"Right. Fine."

"Well, do you remember any of the people who lived there? Across the street?"

"Not really," I said, but as I said it, I had a funny feeling pass through me. I don't know if it showed or not, or if he noticed my hesitation, but a wave of discomfort passed through me that came out of nowhere, and I felt a little dizzy. A dank, dirty ashtray smell accompanied it. It made me want to be outside in the sun. I wanted some fresh air to get rid of the smell. I felt claustrophobic and too hot.

"You okay?" he asked.

"I'm fine. It's too hot in here," I told him.

He reached into his desk drawer and took out a plastic bag with the cowboy belt. It was Marty's, alright. He handed the bag to me.

"Familiar?"

"Yes."

He reached over to point out the faded gold letters spelling out Goldman, and the burned- in letter before it: M.

"M. Goldman. Marty Goldman," he said. So what I want to know is, how did it get around the neck of the guy they dug up in those gardens behind that house? You paying attention?"

I was examining the belt, puzzled, because the way I remembered it I'd burned my name in front of the GOLDMAN Marty already had on it not too long after he gave it to me. Or at least my initial, 'K'.

I looked up at him. "I don't know. Who was the guy?"

"We're not sure. He had on some dog tags, but they're pretty thrashed. Our lab and the Army guys are trying to figure it out. I hoped you could help."

"Have you talked to anyone else from the block?"

"Let's just stick with you for now."

"When did he die?"

"We think it was 1951 or '52."

"How did you determine that?"

"Forensics. That, and he'd been wrapped in a blanket or bedspread. It and his pants were pretty much gone, but there were coins in what was left of his pants pocket. The most recent date was 1951. So far, we know the guy was probably twenty-five to thirty-five. Probably slightly built, about five foot eight or nine. You remember anyone like that?"

I shook my head no because my throat suddenly felt constricted and words weren't going to come.

"Well, let me ask you this: Marty was about fifteen or sixteen then, right?"

"Right."

"And he was pretty big for his age. Tall and skinny, but strong, right? He was changing tires, doing a lot of physical work at the Standard Station at Wilshire and Cannon?"

The direction he was going finally dawned on me.

"What are you trying to say?" I didn't even try to keep the anger out of my voice. "I think we're to your theory now, right?"

"Did you know he was arrested around that time?"

"What are you talking about? He was only fifteen or sixteen. What for?"

"Assault and battery. Someone named Ron Baylor. Ring any bells? The charges were dropped and the records were sealed because he was under age, but we had 'em opened. Maybe a pattern here?" He had the little smirk on his face again.

I was at a complete loss, and he used it as a wedge, wasting no time to lay his theory on me. His look was steady and his tone unapologetic.

"Maybe your brother's suicide was out of guilt. Maybe he'd been carrying this around with him and it just got to be too much. That, and all the crap with Malovitch and Wolf and Faustini. Maybe it just got to be too much. So I've got two questions for you: who do you think the guy might have been, and why might your brother have offed him?"

"Fuck you," I said as I got up to go. "Fuck yourself."

He leaned back in his chair, clasping his hands behind his head.

"Think about it. And don't plan on going anywhere for a day or two. We'll talk again," he said in a convivial tone, then with a smile, added, "When you've had a little time to think it over. But soon. Maybe Il Fornaio this evening? About seven?"

I returned his smile.

"Fuck yourself," I repeated.

I looked at the clock on his desk. It was a little after noon.

"I'll be there at 1:30. I'll be leaving at 2:30. Leaving town. Either bring an arrest warrant, or a more compelling reason for me to stay."

When I was almost to the door, he asked, "When's the last time you saw the belt?"

"I'm not sure," I told him.

But it was coming back to me.

# Chapter 4

## *The Red Rider*
### Wednesday, June 6, 1951

I PUSHED THROUGH THE BUSHES and looked up and down the tracks. It had to be at least 7:30 by now. There would be a train at 7:45. I put two pennies on the track and lowered myself down the steel rungs into the switchman's box. It was about ten feet long and four or five feet wide, eight or ten feet on the north side of the tracks. It was really just a hole in the ground with walls and a half covered roof made out of railroad ties, and they were oily and smelly, but you could hide down there from the engineer as the train passed. The levers that moved the tracks were in there too. In fact, that's why they called it a switchman's box, so a guy that worked for the railroad, a switchman, he could switch the tracks. If he did, the train would go one way instead of the other. Anyway, they were much too hard to move unless you were really big, and besides, it was a rule that you could flatten coins and crush small rocks on the tracks, but you could never try to move the levers. I think Marty started that rule and everyone obeyed it.

I could hear Sarah and Juli and Jeryl Stern, and maybe Megan Weis, talking as they came to the top of the block and turned left onto Lower Santa Monica. I wondered if Allen was with them. I wanted to tell him about Norma and Shelly and Snowball, but not with the others there. Maybe it was better not to tell him. He'd tell Megan and she'd tell Sarah and then she'd be in charge of everything. Anyway, I couldn't see them through the bushes, and he might not be with them, so there was no point in missing the train and then end up having to walk to school with them.

It was only a couple of minutes until the train came. It wasn't going very fast, but it was loud and got louder when the engineer blew a warning whistle as he approached the crossing at Doheny. The cars clattered by and when the caboose finally passed I climbed up and looked for the coins. One penny had been flattened just right. The other had vibrated off the track before the engine had gotten there. I put them in my pocket and pushed my way through the Oleander bushes on the north side, and crossed Upper Santa Monica to the little park with the fountain.

It was an odd shape, not round and not really a polygon either, more like a combination of them both, with fancy details in the sandstone that went all the way around at the edge. There were large blue and yellow tiles, sort of Moorish, Pop said, on the floor. The water spurted high up above the upper level, then fell back and spilled over it, splashing into the lower part. Even when there was no wind, there was water in the air that wetted your face if you stood near. "I wish we could have one of Mrs. Lester's puppies," I said out loud, and tossed the two pennies into the water.

I walked along the crushed rock path through all of the sections of the Beverly Gardens Park until Rexford Drive and went right, on my way to Hawthorne Elementary School. When I'd gone as far as Carmelita, there were lots of other kids, some on bikes, some in groups walking. I thought about visiting the Red Rider at Bill's Bike Shop after school. My dad was matching the two or two and a half dollars a week I was earning, and together we were paying five dollars a week on a bicycle for me and we only had two more weeks to go. I wanted it so much I could taste it. Most of the kids I knew, mostly second or third graders, mostly northsiders, had bikes and rode to school. If I had a bike, I could go to Whalen's and the pet store and maybe stop at the Standard Station and see Marty and still get home before the six o'clock rule. Two more weeks seemed like forever. At least Bill, the owner of the bike shop, let me come in there and sit on it and pretend I was riding. Two or three times a week I went there after school. If I had any lunch money left over, or if I skipped lunch altogether so I would have some money, I would go to Whalen's Drug Store for a milk shake after a pretend trip to school on the Red Rider. I'd picture myself parking my bike in the rack and pretending I didn't notice everyone looking at how neat it looked and how new and shiny it was. I wouldn't have it in time to ride to school this year but my dad promised me we'd finish paying for it and I'd have it for third grade.

I walked through the gate to the lower playground. Allen was there at the bicycle rack arguing with Teddy Browner. There were some other kids putting their bicycles away, but mostly I noticed John Dolan was there too, away from the others, leaning against the chain link fence, his arms folded across his big chest. If you didn't know better, you might think he was fat, but really, he was stocky and strong. Way too strong. "I'm telling you she lives at the top of our street! On the corner. My dad says so!?" Allen was saying.

"That's baloney," Teddy said. "Why would she live on the south side of the tracks? That's not exactly the neighborhood for a movie star." He had a big smirk on his face, sort of playing to the crowd of boys watching, like he was the actor or something, especially since most of them were northsiders too.

I whispered to my friend, Gene Morelli, " What are they talking about?"

Gene was always quiet, always sort of moody, and didn't like getting involved in stuff like this.

Gene whispered back, "Marilyn Monroe."

"Who's she?"

He whispered back, "You don't know who Marilyn Monroe is? Geez! The movie star! Allen says she lives on your street."

John Dolan had a scowl on his face. He always did. He was almost two years older than I was and close to a year older than Allen. He should have been at least in the fourth grade, maybe even in the fifth, but for some reason he was only in the third. He was short for his age, but heavy and strong. He was always getting in fights and he usually won. Even when he fought with fourth or fifth or sixth graders, he won. And even if he didn't win, after a fight with him, the winner tried to stay as far away from him as possible. Allen told me he'd been kicked out of school a bunch of times, but his father was the assistant mayor or the mayor's friend or something, and he always got back in. Allen could beat me up and I knew he was afraid of John Dolan, so I didn't want to get too close to him, in case he got mad about something.

There were seven or eight other boys there now, all listening, but looking like they were caught between wanting to believe Allen and at the same time, thinking it couldn't be true.

"Have you seen her?" Eric asked.

"Not yet. She just moved in a couple of weeks ago," Allen said. "But she's there. My dad said so."

"Your dad!" Teddy Browner said, still acting for the crowd. "Mister multi-deck! My dad says they're never going to let him build that thing. Not in Beverly Hills!"

"He'll build it. You bet he will!"

Allen moved towards Teddy. They were just about nose-to-nose.

"It's just the crooked politicians like your dad that are against him. Because he won't give them payoffs! "

"Take that back!" Teddy yelled.

"Whose gonna make me? You?"

John Dolan came off the fence and crowded between them. Teddy Browner moved aside, relieved, if you asked me.

"Maybe I will," John Dolan said.

Allen looked at him. The trouble he was in showed on his face. He just stood there and said nothing. He looked down at the ground, mad okay, but mostly frustrated, afraid to say anything that would give John Dolan an excuse to start a fight, but not willing to be a chicken and take it back. He took a quick look around, hoping for help, I think, but these guys were northsiders, and that by itself made it unlikely. That it was John Dolan made it impossible.

"I think I had hot chocolate with her this morning," I said.

As soon as the words were out, I knew it was a mistake. Maybe being at the bike rack, the hope of having a bike of my own and actually belonging there with the bike riders made me do it.

Not that I wanted it, but now I had the floor, as they say. John Dolan forgot all about Allen. He spun around towards me, his face scrunched up in anger because I spoiled his big showdown with Allen.

"You're a liar," he said.

He marched over the few steps that separated us. He pushed Gene Morelli out of his way so he could stand right in front of me. He held his fist under my nose.

"How'd you like a taste of this?"

Gene Morelli, stumbled back half a step, but was still next to me more or less, not because he was going to be on my side, but more like he was frozen and couldn't move. John Dolan decided his still being there meant he was on my side after all. No matter how this turned out, he was going to hit somebody, and Gene was it. Only taking his eyes off of me for half a second, he hit Gene in the face, knocking him down and making his lip bloody. Gene started to cry. John Dolan turned back to me. I was on the verge of tears myself, the fear making my skinny arms and legs shake, and I was skinny even if you weren't comparing me to John Dolan. He pushed me and I stumbled back a step. I had tears in my eyes and my lip was trembling and my arms seemed like they were pinned to my sides, but I took back the step and stood directly in front of him again. I don't know why I did that. I shouldn't have, but I did anyway. He smiled, about to lower the boom, glad that I was making it easy for him.

Then the bell rang. We had five minutes to get to our classrooms.

"You're next," he told me, waving his beefy fist in my face, "I'll be looking for you."

I started to cry.

"What a baby!" he said as he walked off.

At lunchtime, Jimmy and Mini Marx and their cousin, Timmy, and Allen and Eric, all third graders, came out of the lower elementary building and down the steps and found me and Gene Morelli sitting on the steps in front of the kindergarten building. They wanted me to come with them to the lower elementary lunch tables and tell them all about Marilyn Monroe. But Gene and I were afraid that John Dolan would be there. I had already decided to skip lunch and save my lunch money for a milkshake at Whalen's and visit the Red Rider. And keep away from John Dolan. Allen stayed behind with me and Gene as the others went down the steps to the lunch lines to get their lunches.

"Did you really see her?" he asked.

"Yes, I promise. Only she told me her name was Norma. And the other woman's name is Shelly."

Allen wasn't as sure now. "The house on the corner? With the ivy on the fence? That one?"

"Yes."

"Then it's got to be her! You're so lucky! You actually went in?"

"I played with her dog, Snowball, and then we had hot chocolate and she had to get ready for work and I had to go to school."

"God, how come you're so lucky?"

He started off to join the others.

"I'm going to the bike shop and Whalen's after school. Wanna meet me there?"

"Sure."

"You wanna come?" I asked Gene.

"Can't. My dad's mad and I have to be home right after school."

"What did you do?"

"Nothing."

"Then why's he mad at you?"

"He's not mad at me." He thought about it a second. "I don't think he's mad at me. He's just mad about something. It's big trouble if you don't do what he says when he's mad. My mom says it's just better to do what he says, and he says to go home right after school."

"Is he going to be there?"

"No."

"Is your mom?"

"No, just Elaine, our housekeeper. Maybe Wes."

"Why maybe Wes? If he's not mad at you and you have to be home, Wes should have to be there too. Just because he's a little older, that's not fair. It's not fair to make you…"

"I don't care! That's just the way it is!" he yelled as he got up to go. He walked down the steps to the lower playground and the bike rack, no longer seeming to care where John Dolan was.

I stayed put.

At 3:10 the bell rang and we were free. I raced out of the lower elementary building and flew down the steps, past the kindergarten building and down the other steps to the lower playground and across to the bike rack and kept going out the gate. I was gone before anyone else even got to the playground. I slowed to a walk about half way down the block. A couple of minutes later a few kids on bikes started passing me, then Allen came up next to me on his bike and slowed to keep pace.

"What was she wearing?" he asked, wiggling his bike to stay balanced. "Could you see anything?"

I wasn't exactly sure what he meant, but I guess I had an idea, because I had a feeling of embarrassment all over me.

"A white robe," I told him, then changing the subject, "She got Snowball from Mrs. Lester. Jeez, I wish we could have one of those puppies."

"Me too," Allen said.

Just then Teddy Browner rode past us on the left side, riding his bike across the grass on that side and slapped me on the back of the head as he went by.

"That's for being a liar!" he said as he cut back to the sidewalk in front of us and raced down the block.

Allen took off after him. I took a look around for John Dolan, didn't see him anywhere, and called after Teddy, "You're a big chicken!" but let it go at that.

When I opened the door, the little bell attached to the top of it rang and Bill came out from behind a wall separating his repair shop from the bicycles for sale out front, wiping his hands on a rag. The bikes were in longs rows facing each other along the left and right sides of the narrow shop, leaving an aisle three or four feet wide down the middle. He saw it was me and waved.

"Going for a ride? It's up there, closer to the front," he said pointing. He went back into the shop. He'd moved things around so that there was a little more room on either side of the Red Rider in the row of bigger bikes along the right hand wall. It was a deep red, named for the comic book cowboy character. It had balloon tires and shiny chrome spokes with red reflectors, two to a wheel. It had big fenders to keep splash off and wide swept-back handlebars, and on them there was a chrome horn with a black rubber squeeze bulb that sounded like the Canadian ducks that hung out around the La Brea Tar pits. It rested on the kickstand. The bar that went from just below the handlebars to just below the seat, that made it a boy's bike, was not just a round tube like on most bikes, but was deeper, sort of wider from top to bottom, making room for the words, The Red Rider Special, written on both sides. The seat was wide and padded and had springs underneath. Every time I saw it, I was so happy with the thought that it was mine, or almost mine, I felt like I'd overflow. The waiting was so painful sometimes I couldn't go to sleep at night. I'd lay in bed and picture myself either here in the bike shop with it, or when I felt pretty sure that my dad and I would finally finish paying for it, and it would actually be mine, I'd picture riding it to school.

In September or October, I forget which, Sarah, Jeryl and Julie Stern, Allen and Megan Weis, Joanne Lester, Dick Goldsmith and Jeff Schumur and a couple of their little brothers and I had gone to Whalen's after school. We were going to start the Oakhurst Irregulars' Club. Well, Sarah was. She was always starting clubs. Mostly to have something to keep someone in or someone else out of. Usually me. But this time it was going to be Marylou because for some reason she'd become a mortal enemy, even though she was new on the block and really hadn't had time to do anything, except for that she always wore dresses, even on weekends. Maybe that was it, I thought, while I was waiting for the details. We sat on the stools at Ozzie's soda fountain, just inside Whalen's Drug Store, on the right. Ozzie was always talking about the war, his part of it anyway, usually to the older kids or adults, but if little kids were all he had, that would do. Sometimes it was scary, sometimes not. This time, there were some adults at the end of the counter, so he made our milkshakes and put the tall ribbed glasses and the cold steel mixing cans with the extra in front of each of us, and went back to the other end of the counter and continued with his story. Usually we'd listen to every word, but Sarah had a plan, so we tried to ignore Ozzie and listen to her instead.

"We fried those Japs to a crisp…" he was saying.

Kevin Doyle, the guy who lived two houses up from Allen and Megan, the weird guy from across the street from us, was at the pharmacy counter. It seemed like most of the grown-ups on our block had been in the war. None of them talked about it much, but at least when George mentioned it, it was about the men helping each other, and he left out the gory parts. Ozzie liked to tell the gory parts. I watched Kevin Doyle as he stood there listening to Ozzie. He shook his head and smiled his nasty smile and came over to the lunch counter and stabbed out his cigarette, then lit another one.

"Ozzie," he said sort of quietly, "you're so full of shit, I don't know whether to laugh or cry."

That stopped Ozzie cold, because it was Ozzie's Soda Fountain, and no one was supposed to interrupt him.

Ozzie had his hands on his hips and told Kevin Doyle, "Well, you can get your sorry butt out of here anytime, buster. The sooner the better!"

Kevin Doyle kept shaking his head from side to side. He put out the cigarette he'd just lit and lit another one. He started to leave, then stopped, then started again, then turned back. He just stood there. Then, out of nowhere, he just exploded, yelling at Ozzie, "You think that fucking war was a game? You think that was a good war? You ever stick your bayonet in someone, face to face, so close you can smell what he had for lunch? See in his eyes, he knows he's gonna die, but you do it anyway, before he can do it to you? You ever wipe the insides of one of your buddies off your face when he steps on a mine and explodes all over you?" He quieted down, but I could tell he wasn't done with Ozzie. "I don't think so." he said, "you mop-up army assholes came in when the rough work was done. You don't know a thing Ozzie. Why don't you just make the milkshakes and shut the fuck up."

It was so quiet I could hear the ticking of the clock on the wall behind Ozzie. His face was completely red. Finally, he said something back to Kevin Doyle.

"You were nuts before the war and during the war and you're still nuts. The war didn't do that to you. That's just you. Now get outta here and don't come back. I don't care who your father is, get out!"

Kevin Doyle stared at Ozzie, then dropped his cigarette in the milkshake canister that Ozzie had just made for one of his listeners. Kevin turned our way, heading for the door. His eyes grabbed onto mine as he passed. He had a weird smile. His fingers and fingernails were a yellow-brown color from the cigarettes and his teeth too. Allen grabbed my leg.

"Don't look at him!" he said through his teeth. "Look straight ahead. He killed lots of people in the war. They gave him a medal for it, but he went crazy anyway."

I watched as he stopped just outside the door and lit another cigarette, then walked away leaving a cloud of smoke hanging in the doorway. He always looked the same, like he'd just woken up and was wearing the same exact clothes from the day before, army clothes, and he smoked all the time. On the block, he would usually come outside and sit on his front steps and smoke a few cigarettes and watch us play around the neighborhood, then go back inside if there weren't any of the bigger kids out. With some of the older boys, Marty's friends from our block and Palm, the next street over, who seemed to like him, sometimes he played catch across his lawn and the neighbor's, between his house and Allen's, but mostly he smoked and watched the younger kids play. I don't think he had a job. Allen's mom said to stay away from him too.

"Let go of my leg," I told Allen, but he didn't. He seemed hypnotized, like Kevin Doyle had changed his body into the cloud of smoke left behind in the doorway.

"We'll be a secret army to protect Oakhurst," Sarah said, shooting me a look. "We'll report anyone who violates the blackout. Anyone who parks on the street at night or does anything suspicious. Especially Iyama Osaka." There wasn't any disagreement about the dangers of Iyama Osaka. "And anyone who's out of uniform."

Marylou.

"Let go of my leg!" I said, again.

"Quiet! If you can't pay attention, you can't be in the club. You'll have to leave."

I thought she meant if there were any more interruptions.

"You heard me!" she said, pointing to the door, making it clear she meant right then.

"That's not fair! Please, Sarah. Let me stay. "

"Outside!" she bossed me.

"I haven't finished my milkshake," I said.

She called to Ozzie, "Can Kurt take his glass outside?"

Without paying much attention to anything, Ozzie looked at me like I'd complained about my milkshake being Strawberry instead of chocolate or something, because he came down the counter and took my glass and the mixing can with the left-over and dumped them into the sink behind him, then walked back, looking over his shoulder the whole way at what was left of the Kevin cloud of smoke. He tried to start his story over again, but it looked like he'd lost interest in it, because he switched and began to tell the grown-ups how crazy Kevin Doyle had always been. I was going to tell him I'd paid for the milkshake and should have been allowed to at least stand in the doorway and finish it, but I could tell Kevin was still on his mind and he wasn't going to pay any attention to me, so I didn't. What a gyp! No Oakhurst Irregulars and no milkshake and Sarah pointing to the door again like things couldn't have worked out better if she'd planned the whole thing from the beginning. On my way out, the rest of the Oakhurst Irregulars gave me looks like they were sorry, but glad it wasn't them.

I hated when Sarah bossed me around, but leaving was better than having her beat me up, which she would have loved to do, especially in front of everyone. Ever since Pop started taking me with him places instead of her, she could always find an excuse to pound me. I wasn't sure where to go or what to do, but I was sure it wasn't fair and whatever the Oakhurst Irregulars were going to be, I should be in it. I wandered south on Beverly Drive looking in store windows. Three stores down I saw it. The most beautiful thing I'd ever seen. I was stopped by the bright chrome and shiny red paint like they were ropes that had lassoed me. I stood there more hypnotized than Allen had been in front of John Dolan, but in a good way, and I didn't care about the milkshake or the

Oakhurst Irregulars one bit. Next to it, a big sign said: Just in! The Red Rider Special! $79.99. Sorry, No Lay-a-Ways!

I went in. The ringing of the little bell above the door surprised me. I'd thought I could just sort of slip into the store and look at the bike close up and not have to explain anything. The bell changed all that. I had to decide between turning around and leaving, or telling someone what I wanted. At the end of the long line of bikes on each side of the narrow shop was a counter, and at it, a grown-up who turned out to be Bill, the owner.

"Hi," he said. "Can I help you with something?"

I looked over my shoulder and nodded at the Red Rider.

"Could I look at the bike in the window?"

"Sure," he said. "There's another one on the floor, down here. You want to sit on it?"

"Really?"

"Sure. Just be careful not to tip it over. Maybe keep one foot down."

"Yeah, sure, thank you!"

I sat on Red Rider for about an hour, pretending trips to school and from home to Whalen's and back, to the Farmer's Market and Gilmore Field, where the Hollywood Stars baseball team played, all the places I could think of. No one else came in the shop while I was there, and Bill was in the repair shop the whole time, behind a wall behind the counter, so my trips weren't spoiled by anything real, just me and the bike and my day-dreaming without any interruptions.

When he finally came out front again, he asked me, "What's your name?"

"Kurt."

"Well, Kurt, I'm Bill and Bill's Bike shop is about to close up."

I got off the bike about as slowly as I could, never taking my eyes off of it. It was the most beautiful thing ever.

"I take it you're ready for a bike. Would this be your first?"

"Uh huh."

"Well, you can tell your parents it's a good one. Solid, well built and safe. Bring 'em by to see it."

"I don't think we can afford it," I admitted.

He looked at me a moment, then smiled and said, "Well, you can come sit on it any time you want. How's that?"

I was embarrassed, but excited just the same.

"Thank you," I said, the little bell tinkling as I pulled the door open, then closed.

My interest in the Oakhurst Irregulars or Ozzie's war stories or the creepy guy Kevin Doyle all disappeared. The only thing I could think about was The Red Rider Special and how much I wanted it. I knew we could never afford it. A long time ago, Marty had bought a used bike with money he made mowing lawns in the neighborhood, and he still rode the same old bike to school and to his job at the Standard Station.

He was saving for a car, and he promised me I'd get his bike when he did, but that was a long ways off. Sarah had a bike that my dad got her at a police auction of lost and stolen bikes, and had told me when it was my turn we'd try to get one for me there too. But that wouldn't be the Red Rider! I went right past Whalen's when I left the bike shop without looking to see if the others were still there. I walked along Lower Santa Monica. I imagined riding it, just zooming along, dodging rocks in the street, looking out for the steel storm drain grates that sometimes caught your tires and flipped you over. That happened to a friend of Marty's and he broke some teeth, so you really had to be careful. And besides, if you went down, you'd probably scratch up the bike. No way that was going to happen to the Red Rider. When I got as far as Palm, I quit pretending to ride, and started to think about the seventy-nine ninety-nine. That might as well be eighty dollars, I decided, and if I could work for Pop, I might be able to make fifty cents or maybe even a dollar every Saturday. Maybe a dollar-fifty. I could help him wash his car and help him cut the lawn and collect dog poop for his compost pile and clean out the garage and rake the jacaranda blossoms and clean the leaves off the garage roof so they wouldn't plug up the drains. I could save the eighty dollars in…how long? I was doing the math in my head, figuring it out if it were one dollar was easy enough, but I wanted it to be a dollar-fifty, and that made it harder. I needed something to write on, so I crossed Lower Santa Monica to the railroad tracks. I found a piece of glass and sat down on the track and was scratching the problem into one of the dark railroad ties. Eighty divided by one and a half. I tried it a couple of times, but got confused, and started over. If I hadn't been busy with the math, I probably would have noticed the vibration, but I didn't. There was a bunch of noise, and it was making it hard to concentrate, and when I looked down the track I could see the train, but it was pretty far away, so I tried to ignore it and finish the problem. I just about had it, trying to figure the remainder and what it meant for how long it would take to get the Red Rider. We'd just started doing long division, and I wasn't very good at it. Always check your answers, that's what our teacher said, so I looked back at the scratches, the remainder, and was pretty sure it would take fifty-three and one third weeks. Fifty-four since I could only work on weekends. Geez, I thought, that's more than a year. That's when the whistle started blowing over and over, screaming until there was nothing else in the world. I looked up and saw sparks flying from the front wheels of the engine as they spun crazy backwards and the big round light on the front of the engine seemed like it was bigger than the sun and the vibration was jiggling me where I sat. The whistle became one long blast from the engineer, who was hanging out the window waving his arms at me. I could see his face and he was going crazy for sure. But he wasn't really that close and besides, I almost had it. I got up and stepped back from the tracks as the engine, getting pretty close now, and taking turns spinning its wheels backwards, then braking, then backwards again, slid past me, the sparks spraying across my knees. It didn't seem like that much of a close call, but the engineer seemed to think so, because when the train came to a stop about half a block down the track, he climbed down and came straight at me fast, yelling like a maniac. I knew I might be in trouble, so I ran.

I ran back up the tracks a couple of blocks hoping he'd get tired of chasing me and go take care of his train, but he didn't, and when I thought he was catching up to me, I pushed through the Oleanders and crossed Lower Santa Monica and went down the alley between Beverly Drive and Cannon. "God dammit, get back here, kid!" he called as he came through the bushes, but by then I was half a block down. There were some parking spaces behind the Beverly Hills Shirt Company store, and the back door was open. I went in and raced through the store and out the front before the surprised clerk guy could say anything. I took a much longer way home than usual.

"Can I ask Pop for a job?" I asked my mom when I got home.

Sarah was back from Whalen's doing homework at the breakfast-nook table. I thought I'd have a better chance without her around, but I couldn't wait. I could tell Sarah was listening, only pretending to do her homework.

"Why?"

The way she said it sounded more like no than yes, or even maybe.

We were in the kitchen and she was making dinner and Nick was wandering around, dragging his blanket by the same hand with its thumb in his mouth. Pop said he was too old for a blanket and sucking on his thumb or fingers and should cut it out, but my mom told him when Nick was ready, he'd stop. He was sort of in-between getting rid of it and not. Anyway, his mop of curly blond hair looked like Minnie and Timmy Marx's dad, Harpo, and he was crying about something and following her back and forth. So was I. I cut between him and her to get her attention and he changed to the louder crying.

"What's the matter, sweetie?" she said, picking him up. He was getting too big to picked up like a little kid, and it was hard for her, but he still liked it and it settled him right down.

"Kurt! You're right under my feet!"

"Can I? Please!"

"What? What are you talking about?"

"Get a job. With Pop."

The phone rang and she put Nick down to answer it. He started to cry again. "Hello," she said. "Nick! Stop crying! I'll pick you up as soon as I'm off the phone."

Nick kept crying, but he wasn't as serious about it, but, he waved his free arm to remind her he wanted to be picked up.

"Can I, please?" I begged.

"WHAT?!" she yelled at me. "What do you want?"

"Can I ask Pop for a job?"

"No! Leave me alone. Go outside. Can't you see I'm one the phone and making dinner and Nick is…"

"That's not fair!"

Sarah was smiling at me as she returned to her homework.

My mom said something into the phone as I ran out through the back door.

"And don't let the screen door slam!" she yelled at me.

I gave it the usual push and let it bang against the side of the house and fly back, slamming into the jamb.

"Dammit, Kurt!" I heard her say as I passed under the kitchen window on my way down the driveway.

It wasn't fair at all, I thought. Why can't I work for Pop and save the money for the Red Rider? Pop was the only one I could think of. I stood on the sidewalk at the end of our driveway, trying to decide what to do or where to go. When I looked up and across the street, Kevin Doyle was back from Whalen's sitting on his front steps smoking a cigarette. I went next door to the courtyard to see if George was home.

He had a cigarette in the corner of his mouth and the LA Times across his knees and his head tipped back to avoid the rising smoke. He sat on the lower of the three steps to his apartment. The smoke drifted up near his right eye, and he had it squinted almost shut. He looked up from the paper.

"Look who's here," he said to me. He folded the paper and reached around and put it down on the step behind him.

"Hi George."

"Why the long face? What's the matter?"

"Nothing."

"Must be something. You're usually pretty upbeat."

"My mom won't let me work for Pop and I need seventy-nine dollars and ninety-nine cents right away and I'm too little to get a job with anyone else and it's completely not fair!"

"Your grandfather?"

"Uh huh."

"Why not?"

"I don't know. But it isn't fair. I didn't ask for any money."

"What do you need so much money for?"

"The Red Rider Special. You can't believe how beautiful it is, George! Bill at the bike shop let me sit on it and I pretended to ride to school and Whalen's and to the baseball field and to see Marty at the Standard Station. It's so perfect and if I could work for Pop, I could save up the money in about fifty-four weeks and it would be mine and I could ride it to school and anywhere!"

George seemed to like talking with me until he saw Kevin Doyle coming up the walk into the Courtyard. His smile left and he told me, "It must be pretty close to your suppertime. Maybe you better be running along."

I was just getting started telling him about the Red Rider, and was disappointed at being bumped out of there just because the weirdo, Kevin Doyle, showed up.

"That guy's kind of weird," I whispered to George.

"He had a pretty rough time of it in the war," he whispered back. "He just needs some time and he'll be okay."

Kevin looked at me without much really looking at me, then at George.

"Got the ghosts today," he said. "It's a goddamn good thing that Jap isn't around."

"Come and see me tomorrow," George said to me, "I might be able to help you with your problem."

"Really?!"

"No promises, but I think something might work out."

"Geez, thanks, George!"

# Chapter 5

## *Il Fornaio*
## Monday, August 7, 1989

THERE WAS A COMFORTABLE SENSE of familiarity here. I imagined Vann waiting tables again, moving with that determined purposefulness of hers, and even if her job here had been a ruse, a way of keeping tabs on me for Ron Lawton, I took pleasure from the memory of it. I thought I'd gotten over hating this town. I thought I was content to forget about it and steer clear. But this morning, Phillips had given me a whole new place to start. It was busy, a steady stream of people having come in well past what had already been a busy lunch time crowd, and the hostess had had to start another waiting list, the people on it having drinks and sitting on bar stools at the high bar-like counter near the front windows while waiting. Phillips came in, looked around, spotted me at a table along the Dayton Way side. He brushed off the hostess and joined me. I'd been nursing a salad, bread, and a couple of glasses of Cabernet for an hour. I had hoped he wasn't going to show, now I was just hoping he wasn't planning on staying long. The waitress came to the table and he pointed to my glass.

"Let me have one of those," he told her.

From his expression, I knew Phillips knew he'd gone too far this morning. Or, at least, he wanted to back up a bit and squeeze a little cooperation out of me.

"Look, forget about my theory. I apologize. It's just one angle I'm working on. And at this point, I can't make you stay and I won't pretend I can. I got you down here under false pretenses, I'll admit that. But you're here and I think you can help. We can keep it simple. All I really want from you is to look at this block map," he said as he handed me a copy of the 1950 assessors map of Oakhurst Drive, "and try and put a name with as many of the houses on the block as you can. Kids you knew, adults you remember. Anything."

I looked at the map, thinking, his theory included, I didn't want any part of it. Everything else aside, even for a murder case, thirty-eight years seemed like a bit of a reach. I was willing to let those dogs lie.

"I know what you're thinking," he was saying, "but I just want you to try. You'd be surprised how some of it's going to come back."

The same thought had already crossed my mind. God, how I hated this town.

"Really," he said. "Just give it a day or two. Three at the most. There's a reason this is still important that I can't get into now. Just give it a try, okay?"

"You've already tried old tax records? Property tax records?"

"Yes. They threw out a lot of stuff in the sixties when they were putting old records on microfilm. But even with the names I've found, too often the owner wasn't the occupant. Or if they were, they're dead now."

"What about an old reverse directory? Wouldn't the Beverly Hills Police have had them back then?"

"All gone. When they microfilmed what they thought was worth keeping, they got rid of the rest. Old phone books and reverse directories were probably the first to go."

"And the phone company?"

"Same story. Just give it a try."

Without really intending to, I glanced down at the map, just for the hell of it, trying to locate our house, and after finding it, I located Allen's house and then the Courtyard and the Pink House. A few faces sort of floated through my mind. It was eerie. When I looked up, he was smiling, figuring he had me hooked.

"You're putting me up at the Beverly Hills Hotel, I presume? Room and a bath?"

He smiled. "Not exactly."

He pushed a key across the table to me. I looked at the name on the plastic id tag.

"The Pacific Hotel in Venice. For old time's sake," he said with a grin.

"And food?" I asked.

"We did a little better there." I was afraid to ask, so I waited for him to tell me. "You've got an open tab here at Il Fornaio. Breakfast, lunch and dinner The department will take care of it. If you go anywhere else, get a receipt and we'll reimburse you. I know I said I'd take care of lunch today, but I've got a meeting, so put this one on the tab too." He took a business card from his jacket pocket and wrote a number on the back, then handed it to me. "If you think it's important, call me at home. Otherwise, give me a call tomorrow morning and let me know how you're doing." He stood.

"Who else have you already talked to from the neighborhood?"

He looked like he wasn't going to say anything, just leave me with his rueful little smile. But he changed his mind and told me, "A lot of the adults from those days are gone. Dead. But a surprising number of the kids are too." He watched me a moment, then added, "I've talked to your sister, your younger brother, Megan Weis and one of her brothers. The short version is there's not much there. A few of the same names came up, but they all sort of remembered you as moving kind of freely through the neighborhood. That you had a few connections with some of the adults." He stopped and looked at me again. "I shouldn't say any more. I don't want to influence your recollections. Just give it a try. And it might be best if you didn't talk about it with anyone. See what you remember on your own."

"But before I leave, you'll let me know where things stand? What else you've learned, right?"

"We'll see."

"That's not much of an inducement."

"If I can, I will. That's as much as I can promise."

"But you're going to tell me why it's important. Why you're looking into this so long after it happened, right?"

"I can't promise."

We looked at each other and he knew the clarity of my memory, if I did remember anything, hinged on his doing better.

"Okay. Before you leave town, I'll fill you in on some of it. It depends on how far the investigation has gone. I can't compromise it, but I'll bend as much as I can."

"Fine," I said.

He stood with his hands on his hips, head slightly tilted, still not very sure I'd tell him anything. We left it at that.

When he'd gone, I went to the alcove in the back, near the bathrooms, where there was a pay phone and phone book. On the way down, I figured I'd see what Phillips wanted, deal with it, then call my dad and tell him I was in town and invite him out for dinner. But Phillips and his theory felt like a toxic cloud, a contamination that might spread, so I thought I'd just keep him out of it. I'd call him when I got back to Berkeley. Instead, I found the number for Lawton Security, called it and asked for Vann.

It hadn't worked out. I was sorry. She was sorry. Maybe we didn't try hard enough. Maybe I didn't, or wouldn't or couldn't, but in large part, it came down to my not wanting to live in L.A. and her not comfortable in Berkeley. We tried taking turns going back and forth, but after six months that got old, and still neither of us would give in. I'd like to be gallant and say it was all my fault. That she was more willing to make concessions than I was, which is partially true. But she's so damn stubborn. She's sweet and funny and warm and driven and pretty and athletic and a dozen other things I miss everyday, but good god, is she stubborn.

I'd given the receptionist my name, and after a moment on hold, she returned and said Vann was out and connected me to her voice mail.

"Vann," I began, "This is Kurt. I'm in town and…" before I could continue, she came on the line.

"How are you? How's Jason?" her voice seemed both expectant and reserved.

"He's fine. He just finished high school."

"Oh my god, has it been that long?"

"I'm afraid so."

"What are you doing here? You hate this town, remember?" she teased.

"I got a call from Phillips. Remember him?"

"Of course. He and I still trip over each other from time to time. What did he want with you?"

"Could we meet?"

There was a long pause. Her hesitation made me realize this probably wasn't a very good idea.

"I'd like that," she finally said. "When? And where?"

"How 'bout tonight at seven? Il Fornaio?"

"You're so completely predictable," she said. "I'll see you there."

# Chapter 6

### *Grasshopper*
### June 6, 1951

WHEN I LEFT BILL'S BIKE SHOP, it was 4:30. I expected to find Allen at Whalen's, but the soda fountain was empty. Of kids, anyway. Ozzie said he hadn't seen Allen, but with Ozzie, that could mean anything. He could have been there looking for me, and not seeing me, left. Or he might not have come at all. Or maybe he poked his head in and asked Ozzie if I'd been there. Ozzie would say something like, sure kid, you just missed him, whether he'd seen me or not. He knew most of us by name, but he didn't really pay much attention to us one by one -we were just his audience- unless someone was talking when he was telling his war stories, then he'd know exactly who you were and say your name, like, Kurt, I'm telling a story here. Am I telling the story or are you telling the story? and when you agreed he was telling the story and you got quiet, he'd continue, shooting a glance at you every once in a while.

I crossed Lower Santa Monica to the tracks and walked along the ties, trying to make it from one to the next without stepping between them, which meant I had to half jump. When I got tired of that, I stepped up on the track with my left foot, and onto the next tie with my right foot. Up down, up down, up down I went for two or three blocks until I got tired of that too. Mostly, I was thinking about the Red Rider, about Norma and John Dolan and wondering if Allen caught up with Teddy Browner. If he did, he probably pounded him good, and if he did, John Dolan wouldn't stop with Allen or Gene Morelli tomorrow. He'd pound me. And if he hurt me so much that I couldn't work at the car wash for George's friend, our neighbor Mr. Avery, where would I get the money to match my dad's? We only had two payments left. What if I couldn't work? That was completely unfair! I got so mad thinking about it, I even imagined me pounding him. Wouldn't that be something? Every once in a while I put a small rock on the track just for the heck of it, even if I wouldn't see them get crushed. Maybe I wouldn't go to school tomorrow. I could leave the house and pretend to go and sneak in the Pink House Gardens and hide in the bamboo patch. But I knew I couldn't avoid John Dolan forever. Then, out of nowhere, I knew he was going to hit me in the eye. I just knew it. If he hit me on my arm or chest, or even my chin, that wouldn't be so bad. Even if he hit me on my lips and they banged against my teeth and gave me a bloody mouth, that wouldn't be so bad since I was used to it from Sarah. But the idea of getting hit on my eye really scared me. What if it fell part way out? What if it was just hanging there and no one knew how to put it back? I wouldn't be able to see and they wouldn't let me work at the car wash and we wouldn't be able to make the last two payments for the Red Rider. The more I thought about it, the more I could feel the Red Rider slipping away. It started to seem hopeless. I was so close and now, all of a sudden, just because of John Dolan, I might never have it. It was making me dizzy because the more I thought about it, the more it seemed like there was nothing I could do. I couldn't ask my dad to pay the rest by himself. When my mom said I couldn't ask Pop for a job and when George said he might be able to help, I begged my dad to help me because I couldn't wait for the police auction, and they'd never have a Red Rider bike anyway and if I had to wait thirty-two weeks I'd die, but if I could pay half and if he would I could have it in just sixteen weeks, so every day for a week I kept telling him new ideas about how we could buy it and finally he and my mom argued about it and she said no and he said yes and we had a deal. But if I couldn't keep my part of the deal, then what? Why did John Dolan have to go to my school? Why did I have to say anything about Norma? I should have just kept quiet. But then, he would have pounded Allen and that wouldn't have been fair either. None of it was fair. On top of all that, I was hungry.

I'd gotten almost to Beverly Boulevard when the smell of the baking bread coming from the Wonder Bread factory on the south side of Lower Santa Monica made me kind of woozy. I hadn't had lunch because of John Dolan, and no Allen at Whalen's had left me with my thirty-five cents, so that meant I could go to Joseph's Hot Dog Stand at the car wash after a side trip for bread. I pushed through the Oleanders and crossed the street. The brick building was only one story high, but it was huge, and ran a whole city block long. It had milky windows facing the street and rows of saw-toothed shaped windows on the roof. The bricks were a brown-red, more brown than red, and it made the blue and white and yellow balloon-like circles and black letters spelling out WONDER BREAD stand out more. I walked along the sidewalk past the small entrance door to the driveway at the east end of the building. The giant gate was always open since they made bread and other baked stuff there all day and all night and that meant there were trucks coming and going all the time. I crossed the strip of grass between the sidewalk and the building to hide myself between the building and some bushes planted against it so I could see any trucks about to leave before they could see me. There were a dozen or so parked in the lot behind the fence east of the building, but none about to leave. I slipped through the gate staying close to the building and made my way down to the far corner and peeked around. There were six or seven trucks at the loading dock. Workers rolled tall metal racks filled with loafs of bread in the white wrappers with the red and blue and yellow balloons on them, into each of the trucks. I waited until the dock was clear, then raced up the steps and went through a door near the corner. Inside, the smell and the warmth in the air wrapped around me like a blanket. Just breathing it started to fill up my empty no-lunch stomach. There were long rows of lights that hung from roof beams that ran from one side of the building to the other. The roof windows lit the place up pretty well during the day, but they kept the lights on day and night anyway. I heard the hissing sound of rubber wheels on the smooth clean concrete floor coming towards me.

"Hi Kurt," Jesse said as he pushed a rack of bread towards the trucks.

"Hi Jesse."

He went past me like I worked there too. In a way, I did, because I'd been here millions of times and knew most of the day shift guys from after school, just before their shift ended, and some of the night shift guys from before school, if I came really early, just before they got off. I also knew the layout of the place. I knew where the dough mixers were, and the rising shelves and the ovens and the conveyor belt path to the sorting rollers, and the slicing and the wrapping machines. And I knew where the pastry section was. That was the best part, but it was too close to the doors that led to the offices. If I avoided the office guys that dressed up in suits, I could wander around as much as I wanted. But if they saw me, they'd make me leave. So the only time I could go to the pastry section was early early in the morning before the suit guys got there, or on weekends. My favorite was Helen. She would throw her arms up in the air when she saw me, smile her biggest smile and call my name, and say, "Kurt, boy, come to your brown momma!" and hug me to her so hard I couldn't breathe. Then she'd let me loose and make a big show of looking around to make sure there were none of the boss guys around, even though she knew they'd never be there that early, put a finger to her lips, widen her eyes like we were robbing a bank or something, and put two or three warm bear claws or a double cinnamon roll in a bag for me to take to school. They were usually the bent ones that came out of the oven shaped the wrong way, and I knew they'd throw them out if one of the pastry workers or I didn't take them, but sometimes if there weren't any of the bent ones, she'd give me some anyway, but either way, it was kind of a game we played. This time of the day, a trip over there was too risky, and besides, I wanted bread, so I went over to the sorting rollers, and Nina.

"Hey, Kurt, gonna help me out here, or what?" she said.

"Sure. But I can't stay too long."

"How was school?" she asked as we worked.

I told her about John Dolan and Allen and Teddy Browner. It was pretty noisy there at the rollers, and she smiled like she knew what I was saying, but I think she was being polite and couldn't really hear me. Also, she was sort of singing to herself as she worked.

The loaves of bread came from the ovens on a conveyor belt, hit the rollers in front of us and slowed down. Most of them were fine, but every once in a while, one would be damaged, twisted or bent in some way that made it no good for sale. It was perfectly good bread, only it didn't look like it was supposed to. Which made it perfect for me. For us, really. My mom was sort of embarrassed, like it was charity or something, but it was free and it was good, so I would bring home three or four loaves a week, which meant she didn't have to buy it. My dad would have been mad about it and said no, don't do that, if he'd known, but I didn't tell him and neither did she. Usually he'd just eat what was put in front of him, but every once in a while, she'd hand him a piece of toast that had an especially funny shape to it, and I watched her watch him looking at it. "You'd think those bastards could at least make it look like a slice of bread for all they charge!" he'd complain. My mom would shoot me a look when it seemed like I was about to laugh out loud, and I could tell she was about to laugh too, but it was our secret and we had to keep it. Marty and Sarah sometimes looked at some of their odd shaped sand-wiches and probably wondered, but I never told them and I don't think my mom did either. I liked that almost as much as the warm bread two or three times a week.

Nina and I stood by the roller table and eyed the loaves as they came past. If a loaf was too dark or too light or misshapen in any way, we'd grab it off the rollers and put it on the table behind us. On and on they came.

"How 'bout that one?" I asked her. "Looks too crooked to me."

"Pluck it," she said, and I did.

In half an hour we'd taken ten or twelve loaves off the rollers. The others had gone their way to the slicing and wrapping machines and then to the end of the belt where a woman named Joyce put them on the metal racks. Nina asked me, "Do you want one or two, sliced or whole?"

"One sliced, one whole, if that's okay. I like to make extra thick slices sometimes," I reminded her.

She put the misshapen one in the wrapping machine and handed it to me when it was done. She put the too dark one in the slicing machine, then wrapped it and handed it to me.

"Thanks for the help, Kurt."

"Thanks for the bread. See you later."

I went back out the way I'd come and headed for the hot dog stand at Avery's Car Wash at the Standard Station on the corner of Beverly Boulevard and Lower Santa Monica.

"Mustard and pickles and a coke, please," I told Joseph.

"Another mustard and pickle sandwich?" Joseph said. "You oughta eat better'n that. How 'bout a dog? I'll throw it in for an extra nickel. Naw, scratch that. It's on the house. How 'bout it?"

"No thanks, just the other stuff."

I had been coming here with Pop on Saturdays to get his car washed for years, and also a couple of days during the week after my stops at the Wonder Bread factory, so Joseph knew me even before I started working. And now I had a job here thanks to George Bowen.

I climbed up on one of the tall stools in front of the counter. It was 4:40 by the clock on the wall behind Joseph. The smell of the hot dogs and hamburgers on the grill brought a bunch of saliva to my mouth. For twelve cents I could get a large coke and as much mustard and sliced pickles as I wanted. I put the two loaves of bread on the counter and opened the one that had been sliced. I took out three of the warm pieces and spread as much of the yellow mustard on the up faces as I could fit. Then I covered each piece with dill pickle chips and put it all together in a double-decker. Joseph put a tall glass of coke in front of me. When I bit into it a glob of mustard fell to the counter.

"Jeez," he said, "put this under it."

He wiped the counter with a cloth and slid a plate in position to catch the next glob.

"Here, let me cut that for you. It's too big like that."

He took the sandwich from me, cut it in half, and put the halves on the plate.

"That's better," he said.

I was really hungry and the whole thing disappeared in no time. I finished the coke and wiped a lot of mustard off my fingers and mouth.

"See you Saturday," I said.

"You must be 'bout saved up for the bike by now, aren't you?"

"Only two more weeks."

"Well, you've earned it, kiddo. George said you'd work hard and you have. Mr. Avery says when you're bigger, you can have a bigger job if you want."

I hopped off the stool and grabbed the two loaves of bread. That would be pretty neat, I thought, but didn't tell Joseph one way or the other. Once I had the Red Rider, I might not need to work anymore. On the other hand, you never know.

"See you on Saturday," I said as I left.

"See you Saturday, Kurt."

When I got to the corner of Oakhurst and Lower Santa Monica I looked for Snowball in the yard, but she wasn't there. I was going to ask Norma if I could give her a little bit of the fresh bread. I opened the bag with the slices and took one out and tore it up and put the pieces in my pocket so they'd be there in the morning, when I'd try again. I was going to go right home until I saw a grasshopper on the sidewalk. He looked lost, so I decided take him with me and go around to the alley and sneak into the Pink House gardens and set him loose there. What a perfect place for him to live, I thought. When I picked him up, he didn't try to get away and he didn't squirm around in my hand, he just moved his leg once in a while. If he had, I probably would have dropped him and left him right where he was.

The alley was empty and I moved the garbage can to the side and crawled under the fence and into the back of the bamboo patch. I put him down in the clearing thinking he'd start jumping around looking for stuff to eat. But he just stayed there where I'd put him. It was probably five o'clock by then, and still sunny, but the clearing was completely shaded. Not cold, but not very warm either. I put the loaves of bread to

the side and took him in my hand again and wiggled through the trail
where I'd thinned the bamboo until I could see the sun on the crushed
rock path just in front of the bamboo patch. I was going to put him there,
thinking the warmth might make him feel more like jumping around,
but by the time I got close to the path, the whole rest of the place sort
of pulled me out of my hiding. It was warm enough and sunny enough
for the squawking of bluejays and buzzing of flies and bees to fill in the
spaces between the quiet. Even though it was a Wednesday, and Iyama
Osaka had been here in the morning, it was way past the time he'd be
working and the blinds on the back windows were closed, so Rathbutt
might be taking a nap or something. And since I had the bread pieces
in my pocket, I had something to feed the Garibaldi fish in the pond. I
squeezed out through the last of the bamboo and crossed the path and
made a dash across the grassy hill to the top where the pond was. It was
ringed by a flower bed with narrow lines of crushed rock for paths, like
the hour marks on a clock, so you could go right up to the pond without
stepping on the flowers. The pond was sixty or seventy feet across and
the Garibaldi could be anywhere, but if I sprinkled some breadcrumbs on
the water, it never took them long to come. I put the grasshopper down
on the sunny crushed rock at my feet and took a few pieces of the bread
from my pocket. I broke them into smaller pieces and tossed them a few
feet out from the edge. I checked and the grasshopper had taken a few
steps but he still hadn't decided to get going. The breadcrumbs floated
on the surface in an open patch of water surrounded by Lilly pads and
tall reeds and pond grass. Pretty soon a bubble broke through the surface
and sent a ring that spread wider and wider. Then another and another.
Then the head of the first Garibaldi, his big mouth open, swallowed one
of the bread pieces. He was all gold-orange colored. Then a gold and
white one surfaced and took a piece, then one that was black and gold.
They were all about three feet long, with thick bodies and really delicate
fins. They disappeared below the surface when the bread was gone. I
took more from my pocket and tossed a piece close to the edge. In just
about a second the gold and black one took it. He stayed near the surface,
circling the open patch of water, but came even closer when I put a piece
only a foot from the edge. He swung in close, then turned away just when
I thought he'd take it. He made two or three more passes, but left it. The
solid gold-orange didn't mess around and took it on his first pass. I took
another piece from my pocket and knelt down with my knees resting on
the narrow concrete lip that was the edge of the pond. I held the piece
between my first finger and thumb, just above the water. The solid gold
Garibaldi took one pass and rolled slightly on his side and looked right
at me with his big round eye, circled away and then came back up right
underneath the bread and took it out of my fingers.

"YIIIKES!!!!" I said out loud as I pulled my fingers back at the pinching feeling. It scared me more than it hurt, so I took another piece of
bread from my pocket and did it again. Only the big solid colored one
would take it from my fingers, so I threw a few of the remaining pieces

farther out for the other guys. When all the bread was gone, I turned to check if the grasshopper was still there. He was, but so were the tall laced-up boots of Iyama Osaka. I felt a pounding in my chest that moved up to my ears. I looked up but had to hold my hands in front of my eyes to see him because of the glare from the sun behind him. He was a just a silhouette, his wide cone shaped straw hat on his head, his eyes, his whole face, too dark to see. He wore a khaki shirt and khaki pants tucked inside the boots. He was short and stocky and his sleeves were rolled up to his elbows and I noticed the veins in his big forearms were thick, like little ropes running up from his wrists across the smooth brown skin to his elbows. Hanging from his right hand, almost touching the ground, was a machete. The handle was black and the blade was a blue–black color, but the bottom quarter of an inch was bright and shiny where it had been sharpened. The sun sparkled off of it. In his left hand, he held a rake. I could hear him breathing through his nose in little grunts, like he'd been running to catch me before I could get away. This was going to be worse than John Dolan, I thought. If he killed me and buried me here, no one would ever know. Suddenly the large coke didn't seem like a good idea. I was about to pee in my pants. I was so scared I couldn't breathe. All of the stories about Rathbutt and Iyama Osaka killing any-one caught in here were racing around in my head. I wished I listened to Marty. I started to cry, not out loud, but tears crowded up in my eyes and started plopping to the ground near my knees, making little wet spots on the crushed rock path. The pounding in my ears got replaced by the buzzing of the flies and bees around the pond, and then by the sound of tears, big round ones, hitting the ground in a steady hopeless rhythm. I was doomed. I wet my pants. The large coke kept spilling out of me, on and on. My fear got replaced by embarrassment and I wished he just kill me and get it over with.

He knelt down, placing the rake and the machete flat on the ground. He took off his hat and put it on the ground too. Then he carefully picked up the grasshopper and held it in the palm of his hand. He gently poked it with his finger. It didn't move. He looked at me to make sure I was watching. I watched everything, but mostly kept an eye on the machete. If he looked away for just a second, maybe I could make a run for it and get into the bamboo patch before he could grab it and cut me up. He was too big to follow me through my thinned out path and I could get out through the hole under the fence before he could come through the gate near Rathbutt's garage. And that way, I thought, I could get the loaves of bread too.

He tipped his head from side to side, examining the grasshopper and his mouth turned down, letting me know he was sorry or that it was too bad. When I looked at him, really looked at him, I saw his face wasn't mean at all. In fact, his eyes had a quiet, kind look, sort of sad, but not mean. Maybe because the grasshopper was dead. He took my hand and put the grasshopper in it and motioned to the pond with a tip of his head. My tears stopped. He put the hat back on his head and picked up the rake and machete, he looked right at me and winked and nodded his head just slightly and headed for the thicket of bushes and tall wild grasses on the garden side of the garage, seventy or eighty feet from the pond.

"Sorry," I said to the grasshopper.

I held the grasshopper just over the water until the solid colored Garibaldi came and took him from my fingers.

"Iyama! Get that boy!" Rathbutt yelled from the window overlooking the gardens. "He's by the pond! Look! Here's right there behind you!"

I raced for the bamboo patch, far enough to the left so that Rathbutt wouldn't see me disappear into it from where he stood. When I looked back, Iyama Osaka had his hand to his ear, then his hands were held up in a kind of helplessness, like he couldn't hear or didn't understand.

"Dammit, Iyama, behind you. He's getting away!"

Iyama Osaka looked around in every direction except towards me and the bamboo patch, saw nothing, and shrugged again, pretending to be unable to understand what Rathbutt was trying to tell him.

I got to the bamboo and scrambled to my knees and forced my way into the patch through the thinned stalks. I looked back and saw Iyama Osaka turn back to his work and heard Rathbutt slam the window shut.

I took the loaves of bread with me through the fence and put the garbage can back over the hole.

I came into our back yard through the alley and went to the square of ground between the back of the garage and the back fence, which was hidden from the house, and turned on the hose and sprayed myself until I was completely soaked. Then I rolled around in the dirt until you couldn't tell about the coke.

I pulled the screen door open harder than I meant to and it slammed against the side of the house and slammed back with a whack, but it really was an accident this time. Most times it was, but this time, even more.

"Kurt," my mom called, "I've told you a million times, don't let that door slam!"

"Sorry."

Before I was able to completely pull off the muddy clothes to the floor of the back porch, she came from the kitchen and saw me.

"What on earth have you been doing? You're supposed to wear those pants tomorrow."

"Sorry," I said again, holding up the two loaves. "I came through some sprinklers. But the bread is dry."

# Chapter 7

## *Ghosts*
## August 7, 1989

VANN AND I PLANNED TO MEET at Il Fornaio at seven and it was only two. I thought I'd drive over to Oakhurst and have a look for myself. It wasn't called Lower Santa Monica anymore, and the Wonder Bread factory was long gone, but I drove along what was now Civic Center Drive all the way to Oakhurst and turned right.

Shelly's house was the same as it was in '82 when I was here after Marty died. It was the same as it was the morning I met Norma. Same low ivy covered chain link fence, same flagstone path through the grass to the house, the same off-white stucco and red tile roof. If I rang the bell, I thought Shelly might just answer the door. Poor Norma, I thought. What a waste that was. I thought about our day at the beach, and about Marty and Sarah and my mom, completely tongue tied when she came to get me. I passed Jeryl and Julie's place and Kenny Lester's house and both were mostly unchanged, but as I went farther south, there were fewer of the duplex and four-plex buildings. I passed one on the right and remembered Donna Hooper had lived there. She was closer to Nick's age than mine, and I remembered her father hadn't ever been around because either he died in the war or was divorced from her mother. Divorce was pretty rare then, or at least rarely talked about, so he probably died in the war. Or maybe they would have said he did one way or another to avoid acknowledging a divorce. When I got to the hole in the ground that used to be the Pink House Gardens, it was clear the old days were gone. When Marty died and I came here, it was mostly unchanged. Just seeing it had given me a lift. But now, with dirt piles and a backhoe, drain rock and pipe strewn across the huge expanse of the block all the way back to the alley, it felt like an evisceration, a scorching of the earth. Phillips or his minions had strung yellow Crime Scene tape from one end to the other, side to side and front to back. It looked like the work had been stopped for at least a week. The building that stood where our house and the Courtyard and Mr. Avery's place had been, the one with the underground garage and doorman, was unchanged from the time of Marty's death, but across the street, the house where Allen and Megan and Wyatt had lived, was gone. So were the next two south of it, leaving a large dirt parcel surrounded by a six foot high chain link fence that started at the corner of Oakhurst and Beverly Boulevard and went all the way up to…to…to? I lost my train of thought.

The third house north of the Weis's had been occupied by someone my grandmother knew and liked well enough to rouse herself from what we were told in those days was one of her headaches, but what was more likely depression or a hangover of one degree or another, or both. My dad had had an older brother, her firstborn, who died when he was two. She'd taken him on a picnic, and they'd both dozed off. He woke first and wandered away to nearby train tracks and was killed . I sat in the rental car transfixed, seeing her coming out of the now non-existent house, emerging from the closely held secrets and mysteries of her existence in the shadows down the hall to her bedroom, from underneath the shadow of both her guilt and my grandfather's endless rebuke. Short, not even five feet tall, in a well tailored dress, a hat the size of a baseball cap without the bill, off to one side of her head, a little dark mesh veil stylishly covering her eyes. There would have been a lot of rouge and very red lipstick and dark nylons and shoes with heels cheating her height upwards an inch or inch and a half to just above the otherwise unattainable five feet. She'd have the kind of handbag that snapped shut at the top and would have had a million little beads or pearls or sequins glistening on the sides. She'd cross the street and stand there a step or two up the driveway from the sidewalk, poised for an outing of some kind. She'd call out, "You hoo! Miriam! You hoo!" in a high-pitched sing-song until Miriam emerged from the entrance to her house, which faced the driveway and the house to the south, instead of the street, emerged from the mysteries of her world, and together they would wait on the grass parkway near the curb for a cab that took them god-only-knows-where and for what. But I could now see Miriam clearly. She was much younger than my grandmother, who in the spring and summer of 1951 must have been about sixty-four, and I think she must have been a lot younger even than my mother, forty-two. I could see her so clearly and remembered she had a wonderful smile. When did I see her smile, I wondered, because seeing her and my grandmother waiting for the cab, they seemed to be holding each other up, weak with sadness or drink or both, and I knew the strength of that image, of that scene, was the result of seeing it repeated. There was something else about Miriam, something that was tickling and teasing the back of my brain like a sneeze that wouldn't quite come. Looking at the image more closely, even though Miriam was six or seven inches taller, it dawned on me it was Miriam being supported. She had a huge mane of cinnamon-red hair and unlike the tailored suits my grandmother wore, Miriam wore a cotton dress, cinched in at the waist, accentuating a Sofia Loren-like figure. But so sad. When had I seen the smile?

Someone was honking their horn behind me. I must have been there in the middle of the street for some time. I snapped out of my reverie and pulled to the curb and parked. I got out of the car and walked back up the street to the Pink House-no-longer-Gardens.

The length of the block, the old jacaranda trees that used to reach to the middle from each side and touch, had died and been replaced. The new, younger ones hadn't yet completed the trip, but they were pretty, their fern-like leaves a vibrant green, the lavender blossoms delicately colored. I crossed from the sidewalk to the yellow tape and ducked under it.

McDermott. It was Miriam McDermott. How in the hell did I know that? If I could find a way to confirm it, I knew it was going to be right.

After demolishing Rathbone's Pink House and removing the foundation and the garage and the pond and everything else, from a clean dirt surface they'd begun to lay a perimeter drain line. They'd worked their way around from the alley side near where the garage had been and gone clockwise until they came to what had been the bamboo patch. That's where they must have found the mystery guest, because the trench stopped there and had been widened to expose the unexpected obstruction. The backhoe was still lifted high up in its digging mode, resting in front on the flipped over bucket and in back on the rear extension arms, the hoe itself, poked into the pile of dug-up dirt off to one side. I wandered around the place. Maybe it wasn't quite as big as I remembered it, but it was huge anyway. Without meaning to, my mind drifted more into the construction project that had been undertaken than what had been there before, and I found myself thinking about what I'd design and build on a parcel this size. It was an interesting problem. I gave in to it and got lost in thought. When that had pretty much run its course, I figured I'd seen enough and was ready to go. I turned to duck back under the tape, when I heard or glimpsed or sensed, or at least imagined that I had, some sound or movement behind me, and when I turned to take a last look I was suddenly sucked into something like a rip-tide or a time-tunnel, and I was powerless to move outside its reach. It pulled me along and dropped me where it wanted.

There was a loud buzzing sound. The air was warm and the scent of the jacaranda blossoms was everywhere, stronger than I'd ever remembered it. The ground behind me, the parkway, and in the street the length of the block, was littered with them, but the trees of late August were almost emptied, having given up replacing them. In front of me, the gardens the way they'd been. I closed my eyes, or maybe I'd opened them. I was standing just inside the white iron gate. The bamboo patch was to the left. The grassy hill leading to the pond ahead and to the right, the rose garden, the colorful flowerbeds, the buzzing of bees and flies and dragonflies as they zipped over the water, all of it unchanged. The garage and back gate ahead and just slightly to the right, obscured by the tall wild grass and reeds. I kept trying to open my eyes or close them to change the picture, but no matter what I did, it was the same, it was the way it had been, exactly like before. I saw myself, just turned eight, without the usual manic energy, walking from one area to another. Not sneaking, not trying to avoid being seen by Iyama Osaka and Rathbone, numb to anything outside the small bubble of a world that surrounded him, just walking, starting for the pond, then heading for the garage instead. I, he, went in through the side door almost hidden by the wild grass in front and the ivy that hung down, covering most of the building from above. He had to push hard because the door had sagged and was resting as much on the concrete threshold of the little basement room as its hinges. He pushed the door closed behind him. I waited for what seemed like a long time for him to come out, and when he didn't, I wondered if I could go in. It seemed to make sense. I'd just make sure I was all right. I tried to take a step and couldn't. When I looked down, expecting to see my feet on the crushed-rock path, it wasn't there. There was nothing but blackness. When I looked straight ahead, the scene was restored. It was getting late, close to the six o'clock rule, and still he hadn't come out. It was getting dark and still I couldn't move. Finally there was the noise of the door scraping across the concrete as he opened and closed it. When he turned and I saw his face, my face, my heart sank. I hoped he could see me. I wanted him to. But his expression never changed, never engaged me, and I thought I must be a kind of ghost, just another ghost, dancing around the edges of his shell, trying to penetrate into his world, trying to break through, or he into mine, and I started crying. I was powerless to intervene, to help, and I couldn't walk away either, couldn't move, couldn't leave him locked inside himself so completely.

"Are you okay?"

It was Vann. It was dark and I'd been there much longer than I'd realized.

"I don't know," I said wiping away tears. "What are you doing here?"

"It's eight-thirty. You stood me up and I called Phillips and he said maybe you'd come here. What's the matter?"

"Ghosts," I said, and tried to let it go at that.

She put her arm around my shoulder and we walked back down the street to my car.

"Where are you staying?" she asked me.

"Phillips set me up at the Pacific Hotel," I smiled, "for old times sake."

"How sweet of him," she said. She looked down at the ground a moment, considering, then up into my eyes, direct, to the point, no uncertainty. Vann to a 'T'. "Come home with me."

When I raised my eyebrows in both mock and real surprise, she added, "I have a very nice guest room. I don't think you ought to be alone tonight. And besides, I'd like you to see my little house." She touched my arm. "And I miss you."

"Thank you."

She wrote down the address: 151 Hart Avenue in Santa Monica, not far from where Tina Cox's house was. Or at least, had been. Now there's a thought, Tina and Vann as neighbors.

"What?" she said.

"Nothing."

"With you, it's never nothing. What?"

"I was picturing you and Tina Cox as neighbors. Borrowing a little sugar, exchanging gardening tips, stuff like that."

"Yeah, right. I haven't seen her. I read about her once a couple of years ago. She quit practicing law and became a literary agent. I think she still lives in that house on Millwood Drive.

She handed me the piece of paper with the address, "Think you can find it, or should I drive slow enough for you to follow?"

I looked at the paper.

I'll find it. I've got a stop to make, but I'll be there before ten."

"Some things never change. Try not to get too sidetracked."

She kissed me on the cheek and walked to the car parked ahead of mine and got in. It was Tate's '65 Fury, still immaculate. I wondered how she'd gotten him to part with it. The deep rumble of the engine, the slightest chirp of rubber as she took off, her warm eyes in the rear-view mirror made me smile.

I got in the rental and started it. There was the distinct smell of Castrol in the air, probably from the Fury, but it triggered something else in me, and my gaze was drawn across the street to the house south of Miriam McDermott's. I saw it and didn't see it, my vision stalled again in a kind of trance, unable to focus. I smelled oily smoke and then pictured it in flames. I could see Max taking the lighter from the ashtray on the porch rail and lighting the pile of newspaper and cardboard and some greasy rags that were under the back steps, then running to the alley between Oakhurst and Doheny

I could always count on Max.

# Chapter 8

### *The Garages*
### Thursday, June 7, 1951

THE NEXT MORNING I got up at six and looked out the back window. It was as fresh and crisp as the day before. Marty was asleep, the covers pulled up over his head. My muddy pants were washed, but were still hanging on the clothesline in the back yard, and I was pretty sure there was no chance they'd be dry. So I had to wear the bad ones, the ones with the really big worn-out knees. I used the old belt Marty had cut down for me to cinch them up because they were too big too, but what really bothered me was that I could see my knees through the holes. Since they were way too long and I had to roll up the cuffs, and since they were just about used up anyway, I had this great idea. I got the big scissors from my mother's sewing basket and cut off the bottom six or seven inches from each leg, which made the length just about right. I cut the two rings of cloth open and flattened them out and measured them against the holes and cut patches big enough to cover. I turned the pants inside out and sewed the patches on the inside. That way no one could see my knees, and they wouldn't know the pants were patched! I thought it was a pretty neat plan, except when I turned them right side out again, the much darker cloth from where they'd been rolled up all the time showed through the white strings of what remained of the knees. It was better than having my knees sticking out, I thought, so I was pretty happy with it anyway. It was early enough to skip breakfast at home and stop by the Wonder Bread factory and see if Helen was there and maybe get a cinnamon roll for breakfast and lunch. I took my thirty-five cents lunch money and slipped out through the back porch.

I went through the back yard and checked the jeans on the clothesline just in case. Still damp. I went through our yard to the alley, planning to go to Beverly Boulevard and up to the factory, but instead, I headed towards Lower Santa Monica, hoping maybe Snowball would be in the yard. I passed the Courtyard garages, which were jammed up close to ours, and Mr. Avery's garage and then the Pink House garage. The gate next to the garage was open. Maybe Iyama Osaka forgot to close it, I thought, and decided to close it for him, but then out of curiosity, for the first time, I entered the Gardens on the path from the alley.

It ran along the side of the garage and past a couple of steps that went down to a room at the back of the garage but slightly below it. I'd never seen it from the garden side because the tall grasses and ivy hid it. I went down the steps to the door at the bottom. There were four panes of glass on the top half that were so dirty that even if I'd been tall enough

I wouldn't have been able to see inside anyway. I tried the knob and it turned, but when I tried the door, the top half wanted to open but the bottom was stuck because the door had sagged and was mostly resting on the concrete floor. I lifted on the knob and pushed at the same time and it popped open. It took a few seconds for my eyes to get used to the dark, but there was a little light that came in from a high up window on the wall that faced the gardens. Most of it was blocked by the ivy, but what got in was in those kind of bright shafts. It made the cobwebs and dust in the air sparkle. There was a slightly damp, moldy smell, but it wasn't too bad. There was a table in the middle of the room. It was covered with a thick carpet-like cloth that reached almost to the floor, and on it there were huge shiny broad swords! Seven or eight of them. And those things with a spiked ball on a chain attached to a handle to clobber someone with. I could see fine now, and against the west wall were two knights in armor on either side of a door that I supposed went into the garage. They were holding spears and standing at attention like they were guarding the door to a castle. On the door was a poster from a movie called, Robin Hood, with a picture of Rathbutt and another guy sword fighting. Below the picture in big letters it said, Starring Errol Flynn, and below that it said with Olivia DeHaviland and Basil Rathbone! There were crossed swords and shields on the wall next to each of the armored knights and next to that on the left side a cloth thing with a coat-of-arms. There were chairs and tables stacked along the wall under the window that looked like they came from a real castle. I tried to take one of the swords off of the table, but it was too heavy.

I heard footsteps on the path and someone clear their throat as they came towards the garage. How could that be? Rathbutt was never up this early and Iyama Osaka had been here yesterday. It was too late to make a run for the alley, so I dove under the table. I could see out through the space between the floor and where the bottom edge of the cloth hung. I could see Rathbutt's feet in slippers as he walked past on the path taking trash to the cans in the alley. On his way back he noticed the open door.

"What's this?" he said out loud, "Iyama's getting sloppy in his old age."

He came down the steps and started to close the door, then changed his mind and just stood there in the doorway. My heart was beating so fast and loud I was sure he'd hear it. Just because Iyama Osaka didn't kill me, didn't mean Rathbutt wouldn't. He put the empty wastebasket down and reached inside and flipped a switch that turned on a light bulb that hung down just above the table, and then he came over to it. I could see the white skin on his ankles and the little dark hairs just below the legs of his silky looking pajamas and the bottom of his maroon satin-y robe. Pop has one like that, I thought, and he's not even an actor. Rathbutt picked up one of the swords.

"Take that!" he growled, "…and that! Your band of scoundrels can't help you now, Robin of Loxly!"

I lifted up the cloth just high enough to see him as he stabbed and poked at one of the suits of armor until he was huffing and puffing. Then he stopped fighting with the armor and looked at himself in a tall dusty mirror that leaned against the wall from where it rested on the seat of an armchair. I moved around so I could keep an eye on him just in case he got really crazy. I could see him stand up straighter and suck in his stomach and slick back his hair. He raised the sword up and made a mean face ready to deliver the killer blow.

"Death to traitors!" he shouted, stabbing the wall next to the suit of armor. He pulled back and stood there for a minute with the sword in his hand hanging at his side. Then, he tossed it back on the table where it hit with a clatter against the others.

"I should have been Robin Hood! Flynn could have been Guy de Gisbourne!! Ahh, what's the use?"

He went to the door and picked up the wastebasket, turned out the light, and pulled the door shut tight behind him. I waited for a couple of minutes to make sure he was gone before tugging on the door to get out.

There was no one in the alley besides me, and no sign anyone had left for work yet because the garages were either open and I could see a car in them, or the doors were closed, with the lock in the hasp, locked. Then, farther up the alley, about two or three houses past the Pink House, a man came through his back gate and lifted his garage door, then backed his car into the alley and left it running while he got out and closed the door, then drove off towards Lower Santa Monica. When I got that far, I noticed he'd left the lock hanging in the hasp, unlocked. Probably to make it quicker and easier to put his car back in when he got home, I was thinking. At the top of the alley I saw Norma back out of the carport that went with Shelly's house. It was a little red car with wire wheels and no top and running boards on the sides like old time cars I'd seen sometimes in the parking lot at Carl's Market. She saw me and waved and waited for me.

"Hi!" she said, "you're up early again. Where can you be going so early?"

"Gonna get some breakfast," I told her.

Her hair was pulled into a short ponytail and she had a blue and white scarf that went over the top of her head and tied under her chin. She was wearing old gray sweat pants and a sweatshirt with the sleeves cut off above her elbows. He eyes were bright and she looked more awake than the day before.

"Is your name really Marilyn Monroe or what?" I said.

If John Dolan was going to pound me, I might as well know if it was fair or not. She frowned and looked a little sad.

"What gave you that idea?"

"Well, it's kind of complicated, but Allen said his dad said so, and John Dolan and Teddy Browner said it was impossible and John Dolan was going to hit Allen but I said I had hot chocolate with you and thought

Allen's dad might be right and then John Dolan said I was a liar and he hit Gene Morelli and then he was going to hit me but the bell rang."

"Whew!" she said. "All that because of what? Someone might be someone? Doesn't that seem crazy to you?"

"Yeah, I suppose."

"Can you keep a secret?"

"I think so."

"Well, I think you and I are going to be the best of friends and with my really good friends, I'm Norma. Sometimes I have to be Marilyn, but that's a kind of pretend. Do you understand?"

"I think so."

"So, the thing is, it's nicer if you and I can just be Kurt and Norma. That's the secret part. We just don't have to talk about Marilyn. Do you think you could do that?"

"Sure...I guess so...but..."

"What's the matter?"

"I don't want to lie to Pop or my mom or anything..."

"Oh no, sweetie, I don't want you to lie! No, never!"

"I know," I said, "I could just say you're Norma to me and that's all and not say anything else. If they think you're Marilyn, that's their problem."

"Exactly. That would be perfect. Do you think that would be okay?"

"Sure."

"Okay, then! Where were you going for breakfast?" she asked.

"Oh, up the street," I told her, remembering my plan about the cinnamon rolls.

"What's up the street? I was going to that little hot dog stand at the car wash for coffee."

"Me too," I said. "I work there."

"No!" she said. "Aren't you too young?"

"No, really I do! I wash the hubcaps and whitewalls on Saturdays so I can save enough money to buy the Red Rider bike at Bill's Bike Shop. You can even ask Joseph at the hot dog stand. He knows me."

"Hop in," she said, "I'll give you a ride."

I opened the little side door and started to sit down, but there was a book-like thing on the seat.

"I don't want to wreck your book," I said.

"Oh, don't worry about that," she said, "it's the script for Love Nest."

She tossed it on the floor.

"It's the film I'm working on," she said.

She sounded like she didn't like it much. When I sat down it felt like I was sitting on the ground.

"We're off," she said with a really pretty smile.

It couldn't have been seven yet, and there wasn't much traffic and there weren't any other cars at the gas station. The car wash was closed, but Joseph was there and open. Norma pulled the car up to the pumps and we both got out. Randy, the gas pumper who wore the regular white Standard Station clothes and hat, came out from the office.

"Fill it up, miss?" he asked.

She turned towards him and handed him two dollars, and said, "This will probably fill it."

When he saw her face, his eyes got wide and his mouth fell open. She smiled at him just a little as he took the money. I could tell he wanted to say something but couldn't get it out, and she seemed glad and headed for the hot dog stand before he could. When we sat on the stools in front of the counter, Joseph smiled at me.

"Who's your girlfriend?" Joseph said, winking at Norma.

"She's just a friend!" I told him. "Tell her I really work here on Saturdays."

"That he does, and he's doing a good job of it. So, what's it going to be?" he asked me, then he told Norma, "This kid eats nothing but pickle and mustard sandwiches. How 'bout a couple of hot cakes?"

"No thanks. Just hot chocolate."

I put a dime on the counter.

"Just coffee for me," Norma said. "Wouldn't you like something more, Kurt?"

"No," I said getting off the stool. "I'll be right back."

I ran across the lot to the Wonder Bread factory and through the gate and around the back and up the steps and went through the loading dock all the way to the pastry section. Helen was there.

"Thank god almighty!" she yelled when she saw me. "I thought I was goin' to go the whole week without a visit. Where you been?" she hugged me into her white apron.

"I was here in the afternoon yesterday, but in the morning I met a lady who moved into the house on the corner of our street and she has a dog and I played with him and it was too late to see you before school. She's with me now at the hot dog stand having coffee and I'm having hot chocolate."

"Well, then," she said in a whisper, "maybe you better take her a cinnamon roll or two and a couple of these bear claws just in case, how would that be?" She began to put them in a bag. "Let's put in another two rolls for lunch, okay?" She handed me the big white paper bag with four of the huge warm rolls and two bear claws so soft they bent in two over her fingers as she put them into the bag.

"That's perfect. Thanks, Helen."

"Any time, love. Have a good day at school."

When I got back to the hot dog stand my hot chocolate was waiting for me. Norma was sipping at her coffee and Joseph was over by the gas pump talking to Randy. I climbed up on the stool next to her and opened the bag and held it towards her.

"Smell!" I said.

She leaned over, took a peek inside, then closed her eyes and smelled.

"Oh my!" she said, "That's wonderful. Where did you get all that?"

"My friend, Helen. Over there," I said nodding. "Take one. I got plenty. You could even have two if you want."

She reached into the bag and got one of the bear claws, took a napkin from the holder in front of us and used it as a plate. She pulled it apart and ate it, licking her fingers and sipping at her coffee as I ate one of the rolls and drank my hot chocolate. We sat there like that another five or ten minutes, enjoying the quiet morning and sweet rolls. It was a pretty good way to start the day, I thought.

"I'd better get going," I said, looking at the clock on the wall in front of us.

She looked at the clock. "I've got a little time, would you like a ride to school?"

I wanted to say yes, and almost did, but I thought about John Dolan and Teddy Browner and even Allen and Sarah and Gene Morelli.

"No thanks. I've got a lot of time. Do you want another roll before I go?" I got off the stool and held the bag out to her.

"No thanks, sweetie, I'm stuffed. That was delicious. Thank you."

"Bye," I said.

All the way to school I thought about her and couldn't wait to tell someone, but I knew I wouldn't and that made it even better.

At lunch, I bought a milk and had a cinnamon roll and shared the remaining bear claw and rolls with Allen and Gene Morelli. Allen said he never caught up to Teddy Browner which was probably why John Dolan seemed to have forgotten all about Marilyn Monroe and me and Gene and Allen, and didn't bother us at all.

After school Allen and Gene and I walked down Rexford to Carmelita and along Carmelita two blocks to North Elm, Gene's street, and he went up towards his house and Allen and I went the other way, down to Santa Monica Boulevard and across the tracks to Lower Santa Monica to the alley between North Oakhurst and Doheny on Allen's side of the street. Sometimes on our way home from school, Allen and I would kind of poke around in other people's garages, mostly on my side of the block. There was all kinds of neat stuff in them. The garage between Juli and Jeryl's and the Lester's, Mr. Erwin's, was open. Lots of them up and down the alley usually were, but we'd never been in his.

"Look at this!" Allen said, already way in.

I stood at the mouth of the garage, but the sun was so bright on the outside, I couldn't see anything inside. Allen had started to take something off a shelf at the back.

"Help me! It's too heavy," he said.

"What is it?" I said from the alley.

"It's a model of an airplane, maybe a B-17 or something like that. Look! It's perfect! Just like a real one. It's made out of metal. And there's others. Come here," he insisted. "There's bombers and fighters too! This one's a P-38! And a B-29! And a P-47 and P51!"

Allen was pushing the first one back onto the shelf as I came into the garage one slow step at a time.

"Come on! Hurry up! There's no one around. Help me."

Together we took the first bomber plane off the shelf. He was right, it was really heavy. And it was perfect to the smallest detail. In fact, there were drawings pinned to the wall above the shelf for each of the seven or eight models, real drawings to make the real planes from. The wingspan was about three feet across, and it must have weighed thirty or thirty-five pounds.

"Mr. Erwin must be an engineer for Lockheed or Douglas or Corsair or Boeing or something," Allen said.

"Mr. Lester says Mr. Erwin was an engineer before the war and a test pilot during it."

"He must have flown every one of these!" Allen said.

"Mr. Lester was in a B-24," I told him.

We took them down one at a time and played with them, pretending to fly missions across the Pacific to Pearl Harbor, refuel, then go on bombing raids against any of the enemy held islands whose names we could remember, names and places I'd heard about from my uncle Buddy, or Allen's cousin, Big John, or George Bowen or even Ozzie. It took both of us to fly and land the planes on the garage floor. We were careful not to drop or scratch or do anything to hurt them, not just because they belonged to someone else, but because they were so beautiful. We made towns from scrap wooden blocks we found in a firewood pile on the south side of the garage, standing some on end and others on edge or flat to look like different sized buildings seen from above, the way bomber pilots and bombardiers would see them. Joanne Lester told me her father had been a waist gunner and armaments officer on a B-24, and Allen's cousin, Big John, had been a pilot of a B-29 and he'd told us about bombing runs he'd been on, so we knew all about it, and how they'd flattened lots of towns. We'd fly over making the engine noises and falling and exploding bomb noises and kick over the blocks, then set them up, and do it over and over again. It was getting late I could tell, because the light outside wasn't as bright, and the air was cooling off.

"We ought'a get out of here before Mr. Erwin gets home," I told Allen.

"I guess," he said, "but we should keep this one."

"Are you crazy? That's stealing!"

"Look how many he has. He'd never miss just one. Besides, they're out in his garage, aren't they? He probably never even looks at them."

I shook my head no.

"You're just being a baby! Sarah says you're a baby and you are! Come on," he said, "it's too heavy for me alone."

"No," I said, shaking my head.

He stood there for a second with his hands on his hips, waiting for me to change my mind, and when I didn't, he just looked at me like I was hopeless and he headed for the alley. I looked at the last plane we'd been playing with, the biggest and heaviest, the B-29, still there on the floor.

"Allen, come back! Help me put this away. Please!"

I didn't know how to get it back on the shelf by myself and I was afraid if I left it there, Mr. Erwin would come home and drive into the garage and run it over. That would be terrible! Then I thought, if that happened, I'd have to pay for it and it would probably take all the money for the Red Rider Special, and I'd never get it. And that was even worse. It was completely unfair. If I tried to lift it alone, I'd probably drop it and ruin it. Either way, no Red Rider. I was going to run away and had even gone out into the alley, thinking that if no one saw me they'd never know who was there, and they couldn't make me pay for it and I'd be able to get my bicycle. Allen was already about half way down to his house. I was going to yell for him to come back, but then I thought yelling would only get me caught. I looked back at the plane on the floor and just couldn't leave it there to get run over. Then I had a great idea.

I jumped up and caught the rope you used to pull the door down. I had to hang onto it just to get it started, and once it was started, it came down so fast I couldn't do anything to control it, so I just got out of the way and let it slam. Allen heard it and stopped. He ran back up the alley to me.

"What are you doing?! I could hear that all the way down there! You're going to get us in trouble! I'll help you put it away, but let's hurry."

We tried to lift the door but couldn't. Allen looked at me like it was all my fault.

"He's gonna come home and open the door and run it over anyway. You should'a helped me take it," he said.

"We could lock the garage," I said looking at the lock hanging in the hasp, unlocked.

"Don't be so stupid. He'd just unlock the lock and open the door, then run it over."

"Maybe he'd see it first."

"Maybe, maybe not," Allen said.

"How 'bout if we do this," I said, taking the lock from the garage across the alley and exchanging it for the one in front of us.

I wiggled the hasp into the jamb hole and snapped the lock shut. I started laughing, even with my fears about losing the Red Rider Special, it seemed sort of funny.

"Now let's see him run it over," I said, "let's see him even get in!"

Allen started laughing too. "You're crazy!"

I had the lock from Mr. Erwin's garage in my hand.

"Now what are you going to do with that?" Allen said.

I looked at the lock in my hand. I didn't want to steal it any more than the plane, but there it was.

"Do you still have that old red wagon?"

"Yeah, so?"

"Let's go get it."

"Why?"

"You'll see."

We raced down the alley laughing all the way to Allen's gate and into his back yard and found the wagon upside down, almost buried by ivy in a corner. He kept asking me what we were doing and I kept telling him he'd see. The wagon was dark with dirt and rust, but the wheels still rolled. We took it into the alley and I began collecting all of the locks that were unsnapped in their hasps from both sides. We skipped Jeryl and Julie's house and Mr. and Mrs. Lester's, but by the time we got to the top of the alley we had twelve or thirteen.

"If we hurry, we can get them from my side too."

"You want to steal locks, but you don't want that airplane? You are nuts!"

"I'm not stealing the locks."

"Then what do you want them for?"

"You'll see," I told him again.

We went around the corner of the alley onto Lower Santa Monica and past Shelly and Norma's house to the alley on the west side between Oakhurst and Palm. Almost every garage we passed had a lock just hanging there, but some we left alone, like Mr. Avery's and the Pink House and Courtyard garages. When we'd gone the length of my side, I mixed the locks up, stirring them with my hands until there was no telling which was which.

"Oh man, are you crazy, or what! You're not gonna do what I think you are, are you?" Allen said, his hand to his forehead. "Oh boy!"

The wagon wasn't nearly full, so I suggested we cross Beverly Boulevard and collect the locks from the next block too. We went down as far as Alden between Oakhurst and Palm and came back up the alley from Alden back to Beverly between Oakhurst and Doheny. The little wagon was really full and it was hard to mix the locks up, but together we stirred them around and then began closing doors and snapping the locks on every garage we passed on the way up to Lower Santa Monica. We made the trip all the way around again, ending back at Allen's gate. We must have swapped forty-five or fifty locks. Allen took the wagon back into his yard.

"See you tomorrow at school," I said.

"If you're not in jail!" he laughed.

It was close to five and people would be coming home soon. I couldn't wait to see it, but I wanted to see if Snowball and Norma were in their yard even more, so I went back up the alley to Lower Santa Monica and around the corner to Oakhurst. Shelly was in the yard throwing the little ball with the bell in it for Snowball. She saw me coming.

"Heya kid, how ya doin'?"

She looked me over.

"What's with the pants? You get shipwrecked or something?" she laughed.

I'd forgotten all about them until then, and all of a sudden I felt like I'd forgotten to get dressed or something and she'd caught me naked, and even though I wanted to explain, I couldn't say anything because I didn't really know what to say. She must have guessed that, because she said, "Well, it's a nice effect. Gives you a kind of rough and tumble look. I like that."

"Is Norma here?" I asked her, glad that the subject had changed.

"Not yet, but she should be here soon. You wanna come keep the mutt company until she gets here? I got stuff to do."

"Sure."

I went around to the gate and into the yard. She handed me the ball and went inside.

I'd played with Snowball ten or fifteen minutes when Norma tooted the horn at me and stopped along the Lower Santa Monica side coming from Doheny.

"Hi," she waved, "how was school? No problems about you know what from you know who?"

"I think he forgot all about it," I told her.

"Good," she said. "I'll be right there."

She drove around to the carport in the alley.

When she came back she was carrying an open cloth bag with a strap that went over her shoulder. She reached over the fence and put it on the grass, then came around and through the gate and sat down next to it. Snowball ran to her and jumped into her lap and wiggled her tail and licked her face.

"What a day," she said. "I just want a bath and some quiet. How 'bout you, Snowball?"

She laid back and held Snowball in the air above her. There was a honking horn coming from the alley. Then another. Pretty soon it seemed like there were horns honking everywhere.

"What in the world?" Norma said. "What is that?"

She got up and went out of the yard heading for the alley. I followed, a little behind.

When we got to where the alley met Lower Santa Monica, there were a few cars waiting to turn into it from both the east and west. They were beginning to back up into a line of three or four cars in both directions, and since the newcomers couldn't see what the hold up was, they got angry about it right away and honked their horns, which seemed to make the drivers of the cars closer to the alley honk more too. The car at the top of the alley was blocked by a car two garages down, where the owner was out of his car trying the key or combination of the lock in front of him. Except it wasn't his, and wouldn't open. Farther down the alley there were others making the same discovery, blocking cars trying to get into the alley from Beverly Boulevard. It was hard to see past all of the cars, but it looked like the same thing was happening between Beverly and Alden, but because Beverly was a pretty big street and busy most of the day, and especially busy at rush hour, the cars backing up were blocking traffic there. We could hear someone yelling what kind of a lock was on his garage and asking if it belonged to anyone, but there wasn't much chance of that since we mixed up the locks from all four blocks. The traffic on Lower Santa Monica was just about stopped because the cars trying to get into our alley from the east were now lined up past Oakhurst where they met ones trying to get into Allen's alley, from the west. The ones trying to get into Allen's alley from the Doheny side were starting to block the intersection near Carl's Market where Lower Santa Monica and Doheny and Upper Santa Monica and San Vicente all met. Boy, what a mess, I thought. It was great! No way the airplane would get run over! The amazing thing was all the honking. It didn't help at all, but that didn't stop anyone. The longer that they were trapped in the lines, the more they honked. Norma looked at me and smiled, running her hand through her hair.

"I've never seen anything like this. Have you?"

It was just a question, but when she looked at me, I had a funny feeling, like she knew I'd done it, and I just stood there looking at the ground and didn't answer. Then she looked at me in a different way, like now she did know. When I looked at her again, she was still smiling, but she was shaking her head too. I smiled at her.

Lots of the drivers had gotten out of their cars and come into the alley to see what was wrong, and when they found out, they went to their own garage and checked the lock. When they found it wasn't theirs, they joined the yelling back and forth trying to find the owner.

"I'll be right back," I told her.

I ran across Oakhurst to Allen's alley and saw the same thing was happening there, yelling and trying to identify locks and cars left in the street with driver's doors open. I ran back to Norma to report.

"They have the same problem over there," I told her.

"Do they really?" she said.

Shelly came through their back gate and the carport.

"What the holy hell's going on!? There're cars out front just honking."

She took a look up and down the alley and out onto Lower Santa Monica. She saw her neighbor fumbling with his lock, or at least the lock on his garage.

"Spence, what are you trying to do, start a riot? No one can get in until you guys quit blocking the alley. Fer Christ's sake, get a move on!" she called to him.

"I'd love to Shelly dear, but some sonofabitch switched the goddamn locks!" he said. His face was red and he was really mad. "If I could get my hands on him, I'd strangle the bastard."

Shelly started shaking with laughter and put her hand on Norma's arm and said, "Oh God, I wish I had a camera! This is beautiful! What an idea!"

Then the police cars came.

When I saw the first one trying to weave its way through all of the stuck cars west of Oakhurst, with its flashing lights, I didn't feel so good. My stomach hurt, sort of a pounding, and I thought I probably ought to go home.

"I'll see you later," I told Norma and Shelly. "I think I better be going now."

Norma said, "Be good, dear. Try to be good." She waved a warning finger at me, but she was still smiling.

Shelly was watching us.

"You mean," she started to say, but Norma put a finger to her lips and Shelly just reached out and sort of mussed up my hair as I was leaving and said, "You got a knack, kid, a real talent there."

I saw another police car stuck in the traffic at Lower Santa Monica closer to Doheny. The policeman was out of his car and took some giant bolt cutters from his trunk. He walked into the alley on Allen's side. Instead of going home, I decided to watch him. If he cut the lock off Mr. Erwin's garage with the plane on the floor, I wanted to make sure he noticed it and didn't run it over. I crossed Oakhurst and turned into Allen's alley. There were cars that had gotten into the alley but couldn't get into their garages and there were drivers standing around waiting for the policeman who was working his way down from side to side, cutting off the locks. When he cut the lock from the garage with the plane, Mr. Erwin lifted the door and started to go back to his car but stopped, maybe because he got a glimpse of it, and he turned back. He just stood there, looking in. Whew, I thought, he'd seen the plane. He looked down the alley, then up, right at me. If I'd just stood there, everything would have been okay, I think. I think it would have been okay to be standing there and watching. But instead, I ran. I got around the corner and ran past Mrs. Lester's yard on Allen's side of Oakhurst. She had the puppies out in the front yard. She looked up and saw me running past.

"Do you believe this, Kurt?" she said.

To be polite I stopped, but all I really wanted to do was get out of there.

"The noise is scaring the puppies. I've still got four left, Kurt. I know Sarah would like one. Why don't you ask your mom if you can have one of these little guys? There's one boy and three girls. Do you want to come in and hold one?"

"Not right now," I told her, "I've got to get home. I'll ask, but Pop says no pets and he's the boss of the house."

"Well, you tell him I said children should have pets, especially dogs. It gives them a sense of responsibility."

"I'll tell him," I said as I took off again down the block.

Rathbutt and George Bowen were standing together out in front of the Pink House, both smoking a cigarette. Rathbutt was tall and slender, except for a kind of potbelly, and his hair was slicked back and he had a funny long skinny nose, but he didn't seem as mean or dangerous as usual just then standing there like that. He was watching the whole thing and maybe because we hadn't switched his lock, he didn't seem to mind the noise all that much. George Bowen was much shorter than Rathbutt, and stronger looking, and he had a smile and a wave for me as I ran past them on the other side of the street, then crossed to our side in front of the Courtyard. Marty came up from Beverly Boulevard on his bicycle and pulled into our driveway just as I got there.

"Man, have you ever seen anything like this? It's the same all the way down to Alden! The cars are backed up everywhere because someone switched the locks on the garages. There's policemen cutting them off."

"Boy oh boy," I said. "It's the same thing up here," I told him.

After dinner, my mom went to get a few things at Carl's Market, leaving Sarah and Nick on the living room floor listening to The Shadow on the radio. I went into our room where Marty was doing his homework. I was supposed to study spelling words for the Friday test, and Marty was supposed to give me a practice test, but before we got that far, Sarah opened the door and said there was someone to see me. She had a big smile on her face.

Both of the policemen were tall and kept their hats on the whole time. The older one told me to sit down on the couch. Marty had come from our room, turned off the radio and was leaning against the arch that separated the dinning room from the living room, watching. I could tell that if I didn't have to go to jail, Sarah was going to pound me for making her miss The Shadow. She was still on the floor, her back against the big wooden Zenith radio, with her arms around Nick, who was between her legs. She wasn't sure what it was about, but having the police there asking for me couldn't get much better.

"When do you expect your parents?" the older policeman asked Marty.

"My dad won't be home until late. My mom should be back in fifteen or twenty minutes."

"We may have to come back to see them, but you tell them there was a problem in this neighborhood today," he told Marty.

"Sure," Marty said.

Then to me, "I'd like to ask you a few questions. Okay?"

I was trembling inside and trying not to let it show. I knew I was about to cry too, and trying not to made the trembling sort of run through me in shudders. In fact I was shaking all over.

"This is very serious, young man," he said, waving a finger at me.

"You should put him in jail," Sarah said, "he's always causing trouble around here."

"Not all the time," Nick said.

"Be quiet Sarah, it's none of your business," Marty told her. "What's he supposed to have done?"

"Someone collected locks from your alley and the one between

Doheny and Oakhurst all the way down to Alden and then switched them around randomly and locked the garages.

Marty looked at me, tried not to, but then burst out laughing. I was still scared, but smiled a little anyway.

The policeman looked at him, "It's not funny, son. Someone might have gotten hurt in the traffic mess it caused."

"Sorry," Marty said, still smiling. "What makes you think Kurt had anything to do with it?"

"Sounds like Kurt to me," Sarah said, then to Nick, "stop squirming."

Marty shot her a look.

"Well, doesn't it?" she said.

Marty ignored her and waited for the policeman to answer.

"One of the neighbors saw him in the alley and he ran from the scene."

"What time?" Marty asked.

"About five-thirty or five-forty."

"That's the time he's supposed to be home. Maybe he was just watching the commotion and then ran because he knew he was late."

The policemen looked at each other, considering the idea, but mostly they didn't seem to believe it

"Some of your neighbors are pretty mad," the younger policeman said. "What have you got to say?" he asked me.

If I spoke I'd cry so I just shrugged my shoulders.

"Did you do it?" the older one asked.

I shrugged again.

"Is that a yes?" the older policeman said.

"He's asking you a question, kid," the younger one said in an unfriendly voice. He moved a step closer and leaned down, his face close to mine. "And who helped you? You didn't do this alone. Tell me who was with you."

"No one," I lied.

"You know," Marty said, "I think my parents should be here if you're going to question him like this."

"What are you, his lawyer?" the younger one said. "Maybe we should just arrest him and question him down at the jail."

Tears started to run down my face. Even Sarah wasn't enjoying it now. Nick was pressing himself tight into Sarah's arms, not squirming any more.

"Maybe you should come back when my parents are here," Marty said, like that's the way it was going to be because he said so. "I'll tell them you were here. Do you have a card or something so they can call you?"

He walked to the door and held it open. The two policemen looked at each other, thought about it, and I guess, decided not to arrest me yet. As they got to the door the younger one, not much taller than Marty, and probably not more than eight or nine years older, leaned in close, pushing a business card under his nose.

"Be sure that they do."

When my mom got home, Marty told her about the visit. She kept looking at me while he talked. I could tell she was mad, but she seemed more sad or tired than mad. Sarah was back to Sarah and said they should have arrested me. While she was putting away the groceries, my mom called the police station and left a message. She told Sarah to help Nick get ready for bed. The phone rang and she answered it. It was my dad. She listened to him and her face got sadder. I could hear his voice through the phone next to her ear because he was upset and talking loudly and I think he was crying or something because she started crying too and she motioned for me to go away. I wanted to tell her I was sorry for the garages and locks, so I stayed there. As soon as she hung up with my dad, she told me to go and get ready for bed, but the phone rang again, and I stayed there. She listened without saying much, but when she looked at me, she closed her eyes and kept them closed so long I knew she just wished I'd disappear. She held her hand over the receiver and told me to go to bed again. I thought I should wait there in case she wanted to spank me when she got off the phone, but I was wrong because when she did finally get off, she said she was going to tell my dad about it and let him deal with me. She told me to go to my room and stay there. She looked tired and sad so I stayed there, so I could tell her I was sorry, but before I said it, she started yelling and yelling at me. I don't remember exactly what she was saying, but I don't think it was about the garages.

It was late when my dad got home. I think I was asleep and woke up or maybe I wasn't really asleep all the way, but they were talking loudly and I was just awake and when I looked over at Marty, he was awake too. He had his hands behind his head on the pillow and he was looking up at the ceiling, listening. My dad was crying about Pop and Bernie being bastards and not being fair and that they weren't strangers they were his family and something was his idea and Pop was taking it away from him and giving it to Bernie anyway. My mom was crying and telling him to lower his voice so he wouldn't wake us up, that it was Pop's business and there wasn't much he could do about it. And he yelled that that wasn't the point, that it was his father and his brother and she didn't understand, that his whole life Pop had been doing things like this to him no matter what he did or accomplished, Pop would ignore it or find a way to make it look like Bernie had done it or deserved it or should be in charge of it. His voice was loud and kept breaking with sobs, and the sound of it made me cry too, and when I looked at Marty, I could see there were tears running down his cheeks and then Sarah and Nick came into our room with Marty and me and Sarah got in bed with Marty and cried while Nick climbed in with me and fell asleep before I got the blanket over him. My mom said she knew that it hurt, that it wasn't fair, that Pop just wouldn't let him breathe. My dad got quiet and so, after a little while, my mom finally got around to telling him about me and the garages and that the police said we'd have to pay about seventy-five or eighty dollars for the ones they had to cut off and we didn't have the money to spend on something like that and what were we going to do? That I had to be punished and since Pop owned the duplex and the neighbors would probably bring their complaints about it to him, he'd have to deal with Pop about it, and it would make talking to Pop about the business and Bernie harder and what was he going to do? She said that if it had to happen it was better that it was me because Pop thought the sun rose and set on that kid, but then again, it's not the kind of thing Marty or Sarah or Nick would do in the first place, so we're back to where we started. Everything was quiet, I think because she was waiting for him to say something. He said he'd tell Pop he'd take care of the locks. She wanted to know how, but he said she needed to listen to him carefully. What, she said?

He told her that there was no other way. That Pop had told him Bernie would handle the new line. Always the same old thing: Bernie needs to do this or Bernie wants to do that and so he finds a way to take what I've done and give it to him and then treats me like I'm an outsider. But not this time! This is the end of it! My mom wanted to know what he was talking about, what was he going to do, and she sounded worried. Nick was asleep but Sarah and Marty were awake and listening. He told her he'd already done it and she said what, and he said he'd told Pop he was out and she said, oh god, and he said I've talked to Alice and Manny and they'll come with me, and she wanted to know where and for what and how? He said he talked to old man Schwartz who was going to loan him some money to start, that Schwartz had always been better to him than his own father, that for the five years he worked for Schwartz, Schwartz knew how much he did and appreciated it and wasn't afraid to let him know it. He said he should never have left Schwartz and agreed to come help when Pop asked him to.

My mom wanted to know if Schwartz was coming in as a partner and my dad said no, that he was tired of all of the liars and schleppers and didn't need the money, that it would be a loan and said that for my dad he always had a little tucked away. My dad said Alice worked on the designs of the new line with him, and Manny was the best cutter in the business and he'd bring three or four of the best girls on the machines and they'd have samples ready before Pop and Bernie. He sounded happy. Marty looked over at me and in the light of the moon coming through the window at the foot of his bed, I could see him smile at me and I smiled back.

My mom said don't you think you could talk to him, make him, but before she finished, my dad shouted, TALK?! WHAT TALK? I've tried to talk to that man all my life! He's taken everything I've ever done or had or made and given it to Bernie. I'm through! Don't you understand? They're not my family any more. He started to cry again, and she kept saying, shhhsh, and there there, and things like that. My mom said what if the line doesn't sell, we don't have much saved, and he said of course it will sell, I've got orders lined up and she said that those orders were for Pop because they know he can deliver. She said, what if again, but he didn't let her finish, and said, what if what if what if! Don't you know what I can do? Haven't I been doing it all along? Don't you think I can pull it off? You should be behind me, not trying to hold me back or tear me down! My mom said that's not fair, you know that's not fair. I'm just trying to be practical. Where will you work and how can you pay Manny and Alice and the girls and how can we live here right next door to Pop? And my dad said it will be alright, that he'd make it work, that he was going to rent space from one of the jobbers in the Bradbury and after the line was sold, he'd get a space of his own. But what can we live on my mom wanted to know. It was quiet for a while. Then Marty got out of bed and I heard him go into the kitchen where they were talking.

"I've saved almost eight hundred dollars so far for a car and college and I won't need it for another two years and besides, the car can wait. You can use it if you need to," he told them.

My dad started to cry again, but in a different way and said, "this is a son, this is a family. We'll make it work because we're a family!"

My mom said what are we going to do about Kurt and the garages and the locks? It was quiet for a couple of seconds and then my dad and Marty started laughing. What an idea my dad said, and Marty said you should have seen it! The whole neighborhood was jammed with cars and honking and people yelling back and forth trying to identify locks. It took the police more than an hour to untangle the mess. Some of the neighbors were really mad about it, but a few thought it was kind of funny. My mom said it's really not funny at all, but she was laughing too, and she said that kid is just wound up too tight, he drives me nuts, he's always got something he has to do that can't wait and he doesn't listen or ignores whatever you tell him because he's so intent on whatever it is and he's never still unless he's asleep. Where are we going to get the money, maybe Pop could loan she started to say, but my dad said absolutely not, we're not a bunch of beggars, we're not taking a thing from him, and Marty said take it from the eight hundred, and my mom said that was his money and even if dad used it temporarily, it shouldn't be wasted on some foolish prank. She said Kurt is going to have to do without a few things.

I figured the Red Rider Special was a goner.

# Chapter 9
## *The Way We Were*
### Monday, August 7, 1989

I GOT MYSELF TO ROBERTSON and went south to the 10 West. The traffic wasn't bad and in ten or fifteen minutes I was in Santa Monica parked in front of 81436 Ocean Avenue, the Pyramid Building, home of Marty's former law partnership, GOLDMAN, MARSHALL AND WOLFE. It may have been slightly morbid, but I found comfort there. There was no cemetery to visit, and even if there were, I probably wouldn't have gone. I never visited my mom's plot in the Valley. It was only a parking place for her bones. Her spirit was somewhere else. Even if they hadn't cremated him and scattered the ashes farther north in Malibu, I'd probably think of this stretch of the coast as his. It was as good a place to come as any, and between his having wanted to be here, to be near the beach at the bottom of the cliffs and across the Pacific Coast Highway, and the time I spent here in the days after his death, it's where I thought of as the home of his spirit. At the rate they were tearing down and changing things on Oakhurst, pretty soon there wouldn't be enough left for old memories to attach themselves to and they'd probably drift away like dispossessed ghosts. In the seven years since his death, I'd gradually come to believe he'd shot himself. I knew that Wolfe, a law partner at the time of his death, and Malovitch, a partner in his previous firm, and Marvin Perry, the head of Millennium Studios, had all tried to have him killed, the three of them separately planning and setting their plans in motion, but he'd beaten them to it. I was pretty sure, anyway. Which forced me to think about Phillips and his theory. I had a pretty good idea who they'd found buried in the Pink House Garden. I tried to avoid the thought, to keep it as far away as I could. Even when Phillips was fishing, I could feel it coming up like scum from the bottom of a foul, stagnant pond. I pushed it down and tried to keep it away, but standing there tonight, seeing myself going into the garage, seeing my face when I came out, I was pretty sure I knew who they'd found. But Marty? There's no way he could have done it. No way he would have done it and no way he could have known. Could he? I found myself once again looking for some place to start or some way to feel his presence, to intuit or divine a sense of him and the confusion at the end of his life. Was there any possibility Phillips could be right? That Marty could have been involved and the memory or guilt of it contributed to his suicide? That just wasn't possible. If for no other reason than to remove any doubt about a conceivable link to Marty I knew I'd have to stay in L.A. and see this through.

I needed to be here and I needed to think. Notwithstanding Phillips' theory, there was a connection to Marty in another context about this whole thing, and I hoped by being here at the beach I'd gain some perspective on it. A little clarity. None was coming. Not much anyway. I kept trying to sort and separate things, but they just ran together. Except I knew I didn't want to spend the night with Vann and have begin again what I hadn't been willing to continue before. I wasn't sure how Vann could help if I weren't willing to tell her everything, and I wasn't. I hadn't been before and I wasn't now. If I had, maybe we'd have stayed together. Some things stay secret or they don't. They have a corrosive effect in either case, and up to this point, I'd settled on it corroding only me. It always seemed a certainty that if I told anyone or looked into it any further than my own memories, no good would come of it and, possibly, much harm. Chacun son gout. Each to his own poison. Mine had been a solitary brew and I thought I should keep it that way. I couldn't fathom Phillips' reasons for pursuing this, but I knew he wouldn't let it rest until he knew who the dead guy was and why he was dead and why Marty's belt was around his neck.

I kept trying to persuade myself that if I just hung around a couple of days and told Phillips that nothing had come of it, that I really couldn't remember much, it would just fade away. But I knew that was dreaming. It was going to continue to fester in whole new ways, far beyond what it had already been for so long. And because that seemed a certainty, I knew it would be best if I could get a fix on it before he did. I didn't know to whom or where this would lead, but the only way I could keep some kind of control was to get there first. I couldn't see how to do it without Vann, but I couldn't see how I could do it with her. I thought about telling her only what Phillips had told me. Let her start from zero with the 1950 assessor's map and help me fill in names and track them down if they were still alive. If I stuck close to her and monitored her discoveries, maybe I could control what she'd know. If I could keep it strictly business between old friends, it might allow me my secrets and keep her far enough outside to avoid a repeat of our unhappy disintegration. It did also occur to me that this might be the time to free myself from my ghosts, an opportunity to rewrite the ending. Then again, probably not.

Vann's house was a little beach cottage only a block from the water, on Hart between Neilson Way and the Venice Promenade. It was elbow to elbow with the houses on either side, so close that if you stood between hers and the next one, you could probably reach out and touch them both. Hers had white wooden shingles, most likely redwood, that had been painted so many times since the house was built, sometime in the late twenties or early thirties, that the spaces that would have defined one shingle from the next or edges that would have defined the row above from the one below were just about filled, leaving only the impression of shingling. The houses were all well kept, all painted, many others also white, but just as many blue or green or yellow, the kind of colors and shades that had for some reason come to signify cheery little beach properties. They were close to the sidewalk, so there were no lawns or gardens to speak of, but decoratively placed driftwood or Abalone shells on the ground in the five or six feet between the street and the front steps. Some had a single-car attached garage to the left or right of front steps with a pair of the old kind of out-swinging hinged doors with multiple glass panes at eye level. The living rooms were usually above the garage in this arrangement, but because these houses were so small, most that had started out that way had long ago been remodeled to convert the garage to living space. Vann's was a compromise. Half of what had been the garage was open to the street, the Fury nosed into it to about the door handle, no doubt making it hard to get in or out, the rest reaching back just short of the sidewalk. The remainder had been incorporated into living space. The signs on both sides of the narrow street warned against parking between 8am and 4pm, the penalty, towing. Since so few of the houses still had off street parking, and because the street was so narrow, cars the length of the block straddled the curb, two wheels on the sidewalk, two on the pavement. I parked the rental like that behind the Fury, got out and locked it.

The porch light was on and there was light coming from the front room windows. I was about to go up the half dozen steps to the front door when the sound of the surf eased across the sand, the Promenade, and the short half block between me and the ocean. It wasn't ten yet, so I thought I had time to take a little walk down by the water. I debated asking Vann to join me, but decided against it. When I got as far as the Promenade, a concrete walking and roller-blading and bicycling path that ran for several miles from Venice to Santa Monica parallel to the water at the top of the sand, Vann was standing there, just starring at the reflection of the moon on the calm water.

When I approached, she briefly looked at me over her shoulder, then looked back to the water. She didn't say anything, but held out her hand. If I were going to take it, I knew I should have right away, but I hesitated, then took it. We stood there for a long time without saying anything. A couple of times she turned slightly to look at me. It seemed to be an appraising look, not urgent or imploring or demanding, just a look to get herself focused in some inner way. She squeezed my hand a little tighter. We took off our shoes and walked across the cool dry sand to the wet sand at the top reach of the little waves. It never ceased to amaze me how she knew when talking was not going to be useful. Few people ever learn that. Fewer women.

"I'm not going to let you rip my heart out again," she said softly.

We had the assessor's map spread out on a table on the Dayton Way side at Il Fornaio by seven the next morning. I had a café latte and toast and the apricot jam they made there themselves, and Vann, true to form, had enough food for a lumberjack. Pancakes, eggs, hash browns, coffee and grapefruit juice. Same girlish, lithe slim figure, maybe a little more womanly, curvy, but the same huge appetite.

She had me start by writing in the names of anyone I could remember on the block map, owners, parents, kids, first names, last names, nicknames. Anything. There were sixteen parcels on the east side of the street and twelve on our side because of the size of the Pink House gardens. The map had the assessor's parcel number and the street number of each lot. Just seeing the street numbers elicited fleeting visions of faces and voices, and in some cases, smells, cooking smells that seemed to be wedded in my mind to some of them. Where Phillips had relied on the phone company and old city records and failed because they'd modernized and destroyed much of it, Vann suggested going to outlying libraries, branches that would have had phone books and reverse directories throughout the years and been unlikely to have computerized or microfilmed them out of existence.

Looking at the map reminded me that something Phillips had said, or implied, didn't make sense. I hadn't commented on it to Phillips, but Pop died in 1959, a year after he'd sold his interest in the project that had replaced our duplex. If it had been 1967 when the developers had proposed building two of the huge projects, how could he have blocked them? And who was the trustee of the Rathbone estate who'd objected? And how had they managed to start now? When Pop died, Bernie swooped in and took control of the money left to my grandmother, trying to prop up the remnant of the bankrupted partnership with my dad.

By the spring of 1952 my dad had successfully put together a line of his own with the help of Manny and Alice, and with Schwartz' money and some of Marty's, and things were going pretty well. Through the last four months of 1951, I'd been chosen to answer the phone during daylight hours. "You just missed my mom" or "My dad won't be home 'til late", and my favorite, "you should try calling on the weekend", because the caller and I both knew that they wouldn't be at their collection jobs on the weekend, but there wasn't much they could say to me. Marty and Sarah would have sounded old enough to tempt the caller to leave a message, warnings and threats that this or that was about to be turned off or repossessed or turned over to a collection agency, or if they were a collection agency, spell out the dire consequences of our continued failure to pay up. Nick would have been way too young sounding, and besides, his interest in the phone had only reached the level of not really answering it, but picking it up when it rang to stop the annoying noise, then just leaving it hanging from the wall to the kitchen floor. I sounded sufficiently young that the caller wouldn't be too likely to leave a detailed message with me, but they could at least tell some supervisor they'd made contact with our deadbeat selves. But by the spring of 1952 the phone calls had stopped. Bills were getting paid, I had Levi's and sneakers without holes in them and my dad got a pretty cool car. Not new, but close, a two-tone pale blue and white 1951 Chevy. In the meantime, Pop and Bernie's business slowed to a crawl. Pop decided he'd had enough of manufacturing, and opened a little retail store in Pasadena. Bernie suddenly had nowhere to go, and not coincidentally, rediscovered his big brother and his family feeling. He begged and nagged my dad to bring him in. And of course, my dad did. Their partnership was called Sarah and Sulla, after my sister and Bernie's oldest daughter. For the next couple of years, they did well enough to become a threat to some of the bigger manufacturers in the L.A. area, enough of a threat to elicit offers to buy them out. And even though a recession in 1956 was squeezing them pretty hard, my dad had made use of the time the slowdown had forced on them to develop a new line and a new approach, offering more sophisticated designs for smaller sizes, something that hadn't been tried before, and one that he was convinced would elevate them into a much larger arena. But Bernie was getting panicky and wanted to sell while the offers were still on the table. Without my dad's agreement he couldn't. But what he could do and did, was to declare himself bankrupt and get the court to allow him to sell his half of the partnership to one of their suitors over my dad's objections. Since the buyer had no interest in continuing Sarah and Sulla, they objected to the routine borrowing of money for new lines, factoring money, and forced Sarah and Sulla into bankruptcy, which in turn left my dad deep in debt as well. He filed a Chapter 11 and spent the next ten years paying back everyone who'd loaned him a nickel or advanced him credit on material or labor. He sold shoes and drove cabs in addition to hawking the lines of other manufacturers. Bernie on the other hand, had filed for Chapter 13. What his creditors could get their hands on, they could have, but no more. Then when the smoke cleared a year later, he miraculously reopened and again began to do business as Sarah and Sulla, adding considerable insult to mortal injury. There are laws against hiding assets from a bankruptcy court, but what always comes to mind for me is the picture of my dad as Charlie Brown, forever believing Bernie will actually hold the ball for him, believing each time it would be different. When Pop died in 1959, Bernie's Sarah and Sulla was struggling, at a turning point, needing working capital to make it. The money left to my grandmother proved to be the difference. Bernie got her to sign it over to him to be used as factoring money, since his recent bankruptcy kept bank money out of his reach. By 1961 or '62, Sarah and Sulla was on sound footing. By 1963 my grandmother was dead, Bernie was making a lot of money, never offering to bring my dad in, or even repay the money he, and not Bernie, had spent taking care of their mother until her death. But I'd never heard about any property that Pop had an interest in at the time of his death. Even with my dad's estrangement from Bernie, it seemed like he'd have know if Pop, then Nanny, still owned property on the street. Especially since, as Bernie went through Nanny's money, she had to come to live with us. And when her confusion got to be too much, my dad and mom struggled to pay for her nursing home. I don't think Bernie helped at all, or at least not much. It seemed Phillips had a lot of this information already. Was it as incomplete as he wanted it to seem or was he just trying to bait a hook? Even if you couldn't find out who resided in a building, a title search would tell you the chain of ownership. Phillips must have already done that. He must know who owned what and when. The LA County Assessor's Office had archives that would be the place to discover the chain of titles. I was about to say so, when Vann spoke.

"The Long Beach libraries are great," she told me. "And Pasadena."

"Why?"

"They're big, they're old, and they're not used as much as the L.A. County libraries, so they don't have the budget to microfilm much. They don't like to throw anything away so they stick some of their branches with old phone books and plat maps to make space for the new ones. The branches don't bother to catalogue it, so it's not easily accessible, but it's there somewhere and it's surprising how far back some of it goes."

As I tried to reconstruct the neighborhood lot by lot, she watched, nibbling on my toast, since she'd finished everything on her plate. I penciled in names as fast as they came. Getting one would often trigger one next door or near by, or one in a duplex or four-plex would call up others at the same address. By the time she'd finished her breakfast and most of mine, I'd put one name or another to fourteen of the twenty-eight addresses.

"Not bad," she smiled.

"Not really so good, either," I told her. "Most of the buildings were at least four-plexes, and some had six or eight separate units. Ours was a duplex, and so were a few others, and I think there were a couple of single family houses, but there must have been close to a hundred separate families on the block. Maybe more."

"No wonder Phillips is sticking you with this."

"Probably."

She thought we'd find where there were overlapping jurisdictions there would be the possibility of duplicate records and the possibility some remained.

"I think both Southern California Edison and the L. A. Water and Power are going to be our best bet. I'd have thought Phillips would have tried there."

"He didn't mention it," I told her.

"You really think he just decided to let you do some of his leg work?"

"Maybe."

"But why? If this is important enough to make a fuss about after thirty-eight years and drag you down here, why not pursue it himself? Thoroughly. L. A. Water and Power is a pretty obvious place to start.

"I don't know."

"Or Southern Cal Ed. Do you know which one served your street?"

"No."

"Sounds like he wants you in this for more than just information from you, or to avoid the grunt work himself. Could he think you're involved? Not Marty, but you?"

The thought had crossed my mind, but I just shrugged, "With Phillips, who knows?"

"How old were you then?"

"If he's right about the date of the guy's demise, seven, almost eight."

"A little young to start a criminal career. Even for you."

She gave me a taunting, teasing little smile, but also seemed to be scrutinizing me a little more carefully. Her face still had that look of only partial transition from adolescence to adult, but more adult now than before. Her innocence and guilelessness were unchanged, but given our history, she knew better than to assume I'd provide her with some kind of full disclosure.

Last night, as we'd walked along the top edge of the damp sand watching the moonlight dance on the water, I'd told her about Phillip's theory. I told her I thought it was garbage. What I didn't tell her was that garbage or not, it put me in that same frame of mind I found myself in after Marty's death, that having been unable to protect him in life, I felt doubly compelled to somehow shield him after it. Whatever happened to the notion of rest in peace, I wondered? The frustration then had been almost unbearable. It looked like it wasn't going to be much better this time. She'd taken my hand a second time, looked at me without speaking, her silence an invitation to confide in her. It was one of those defining moments that come along every so often. Down one road was more of the darkness and secrecy that had accompanied me for thirty-eight years. Down the other, there seemed to be thin shafts of bright light just aching to break through. They say confession is good for the soul. I'd be lying if I didn't say I came close. It pained me, at least briefly, to know she knew she couldn't expect that from me. She had reason to be wary, and she was, even if neither of us liked it. My hesitation at taking her hand when I first joined her hadn't gone unnoticed and there wasn't any question about my sleeping anyplace but in her guest room last night. If anything were to change, it was up to me to change it, and I couldn't. Or wouldn't. All that notwithstanding, she radiated warmth and energy, her skin fresh and smooth and glowing as a ten year old's. Her hair was longer than before, shoulder length, shiny, silky auburn hair pulled back in a ponytail. Her green eyes sparkled and the dark brows and long lashes didn't need and weren't going to get makeup. She was wearing little gold earring studs that made me wonder how old she'd been when she'd had her ears pierced. She was thirty-four now, so she'd probably had them done for at least twenty years, only the way she played with them, rotating them absently, seemed like they were something new and still a little exciting. That's what I loved about her: she took pleasure and joy in almost everything. She had a limitless enthusiasm for things. I'd pretty much stalled out on the map.

"Ready to go?" she asked.

"Sure. Where to?"

"Let's try Water and Power first. If they still have the records we want, we may find both the names of owners and tenants, if the units in these buildings were metered separately. Let's go see."

I signed the check, included a generous tip, and made sure the wait-ress knew it was supposed to go on Phillip's tab. We headed for the door. I planned to go to the assessor's office alone.

We went down Robertson to the 10 East towards downtown. L.A. Water and Power was at 111 North Hope Street, which on the face of it seemed easy enough, so I followed the 10 to the 110 and got off at 6th Street. But after several unsuccessful tries at finding the right combina-tion of one-way streets, Vann's original suggestion that I stay on the 110 heading for the 101 where I'd cross Hope and be able to turn and be headed towards our destination without resorting to making it a tempo-rary two-way street, became the only reasonable solution. Just getting back on the freeway took five bucks worth of gas.

It was a fifteen story building on the west side of the street a couple of buildings up from the corner of 1st. I turned right and started to nose my way into the narrow winding drive down into the underground park-ing lot when I saw the rate sign. They charged six dollars each twenty minutes and had a one hour minimum. I almost put Vann through the windshield hitting the brakes. She took one look at me and rolled her eyes.

"You'll never find parking on the street," she said.

"I could try."

Someone was behind us trying to enter the garage, not willing to wait for the outcome of my indecision. They honked a good loud one.

"Yeah, and it'll be lunch by the time you do and there'll be no one around to help us. You can't back up now anyway, so just pony up."

"Somehow this is going on the tab for Phillips."

"Good luck," she said.

The receptionist, a good looking girl maybe twenty or twenty-one with a couple of text books on the left side of her desk, maybe a part-timer here and a student at UCLA or USC, had long blond hair and a little make up and clothes just dressy enough for the job and comfortable enough for class. She gave us the name of the guy in charge, Wu, on the 14th floor, Maps and Records. Only it wasn't open to the public without an appointment and the accompaniment of Wu or one of his staff, and to make matters worse, all of them were going to be in a staff meeting the whole morning. She told us this between calls that came non-stop through the switchboard in front of her.

"We could try the Pasadena Library and call Wu this afternoon and make an appointment for tomorrow," Vann suggested.

"Swell. We're here two minutes and have to pay for an hour."

We decided to split up and agreed to meet at Il Fornaio at seven, have dinner on Phillips and compare notes. I said I'd cover the recorder's and assessor's offices and call L.A. Water and Power to make the appointment with Wu and make a call to Southern California Edison. Traffic was the usual mess as I took her back to her place in Venice to get the Fury. As we crawled along the 10 West, we didn't speak much, but I was thinking how nice it was to be with her. I thought she was thinking the same thing.

In front of her place, she sat there in the rental scribbling down the street addresses for both sides of the block from the assessor's map. After a couple of minutes, my mind had already started making the trip back downtown to the assessor's and recorder's offices, and I was getting a little impatient with how long it was taking her. I was sort of tapping my foot on the accelerator, not revving the engine, but just tapping it. She looked at me with a sort of tolerant annoyance.

"Some things never change, do they?"

"What?"

She reached over with her left hand and hooked it around my neck and pulled me to her for a kiss on the cheek.

"Just cool your jets, buster," she said. As she got out of the car and closed the door, she reminded me, "Seven. Il Fornaio. Right? Not six. Not eight."

"Right."

She walked down the little half driveway, unlocked and squeezed into the Fury where the jamb prevented the door from opening very far, brought it to life with its telltale roar, backed out onto the street and headed for the libraries in Pasadena and Long Beach.

# Chapter 10

## *The Paper Route*
## Wednesday, June 6, 1951

I T WAS FIVE-THIRTY and the house was quiet. I found my lunch money and slipped out the back door, making sure it closed quietly. The air was almost too warm for this early and the sky was clear, the bright light shining through the feathery jacaranda leaves. Most mornings like this I would have turned my face to the sun and soaked it up, then tried to pick out the pattern of leaves that were silhouetted black against the pale blue, like animal shapes or shapes of continents or something. But for me the whole world might as well have been gray and cloudy and cold. I wanted to complain to someone, anyone, about how unfair it was going to be, but the locks had to be paid for, and there was no one else to blame but me. Well, maybe Allen. If he hadn't wanted to steal the plane, he could have helped me put it back on the shelf, and if we'd put it back, there wouldn't have been the chance of it getting run over, and if that wasn't a problem, I'd never have had to switch the lock on Mr. Erwin's garage, and if I hadn't switched that one, we'd never have switched the others. So, in a way, it was Allen's fault, but I knew that wasn't going to do me any good, so I figured I might as well quit thinking about it. With tomorrow's payment, we'd have paid about seventy-five dollars towards the Red Rider Special. I figured I'd stop by the bike shop and tell Bill the bad news after school. He'd been super nice to break his own rule about no lay-a-ways, and I just hoped he'd give us our money back. I was about to the middle of the Pink House lawn when I heard the horn toot.

"Why so glum?" Pop said. He was heading towards Lower Santa Monica and had pulled up to the curb next to me, his Oldsmobile facing the wrong way.

"You know," I said, not looking up at him.

"What in the hell were you thinking?" His face sort of crinkled up and he laughed through his nose in his funny way, but I could tell he was more mad than anything else.

I kept walking, not looking at him, and he kept rolling along next to me.

I shrugged.

"There's got to be more to this than just a prank, Kurt. I know you. You don't do things for no reason. You can tell me. Come on, get in the car. I'll take you to school."

"We'll get there too early."

"We can stop at Joseph's for hot chocolate. My treat."

"No thanks."

"I've heard from a lot of the neighbors."

I looked at him but didn't stop walking.

"And the police," he said.

I stopped. So did he.

"Are they going to arrest me?"

I said it pretty calmly. I was surprised it didn't make me cry when I asked, but losing the Red Rider Special had pretty much been the worst thing that had ever happened, so going to jail didn't seem like such a big deal.

"Not if we buy new locks," he said.

"You mean me," I said.

"No, we. I could loan you the money and you could work it off."

"Thanks, but I don't think so, Pop. Mom wouldn't let me. They're mad at you about Dad and Bernie and all that. That's why I got the car wash job in the first place. And now it's all for nothing."

I was about to cry and didn't want to so I started walking again.

"If your dad can't help you, let me."

"No! We're not a bunch of beggars!"

"Come on, get in. At least the hot chocolate will make you feel better."

"No! Just leave me alone!" I shouted at him.

He stopped following me. I kept going up the street and when I got as far as Donna Hooper's, I looked around. He was just sitting there in the car on the wrong side of the street. Farther down, I saw Kevin Doyle come out of Miriam McDermott's house, smoking a cigarette. He went barefoot across the driveway between her house and his and across the grass and up the steps into his.

On the playground, and near the bike rack, I stayed away from Allen and Gene Morelli and John Dolan and Teddy Browner. I stayed away from everyone, trying to figure out how to pay for the locks and still keep the Red Rider Special. There just wasn't any way.

It was our class's turn for the ceramics room and we were supposed to make anything we wanted out of clay, paint it with whatever color glaze we wanted and then it would get fired, and we were supposed to get it back before June 15, next Friday, only one week from today, because that was the last day of school before summer vacation. I had been pretty excited about it, but now I didn't care at all. I had had this great idea and I wasn't going to tell anyone. When I first heard that we were going to be allowed to make something, and I had my great idea, it was going to be for Pop, but even before he started causing so much trouble, I changed my mind, and planned on giving it to my Dad instead, because he'd made the deal with me to pay for the Red Rider, even if we were broke. Maybe it would cheer him up, I thought, even with all the Bernie and Pop stuff. When I wasn't dreaming about the Red Rider Special, I'd been dreaming about making the green horse. It was going to be like it was lying on grass, it's legs folded under and its head stretched out to munch.

We'd had to wait almost the whole school year until the eighth, seventh, sixth, fifth, fourth and third graders had had their turns in the ceramics room before it was our turn, and Miss Kendall told us to use the time to plan. She didn't want us to get in there and waste time. And she didn't want us bothering Miss Rimes, the ceramics room teacher, with a lot of questions or asking for help. She was not going to be the teacher of the class that wasn't prepared. Gene Morelli and Tony Wilde and the Marx kids were all making ashtrays for their fathers, and lots of the girls were making clay flowers or flowerpots for their mothers, and Betty Walcott was making a Giraffe, but no one was making a horse. And for sure no one except me was gong to make a green horse! That was the great part. There would never ever be another one like it! It made me laugh to think about it, but I didn't think it was funny, I just laughed because it was green for a reason. I would never ever tell why the horse was green, but I'd know. I supposed I did still care. Without the Red Rider, the green horse was all that was left.

I spent most of the morning before lunch making the body. Leslie Morrison came over once and asked me what it was.

"You'll see," was all I told him.

"Kurt! Stop talking! Pay attention to what you're doing! And you, Leslie Morrison!!" Miss Kendall yelled, "sit your fanny down! We've got just one day to finish up here. I don't want a bunch of half finished stuff from my class in the ceramics room over the summer, and neither does Miss Rimes!"

Miss Rimes was young and pretty and the older kids like Sarah and Megan Weis and their friends said she helped them a lot, and she didn't seem to mind at all, she even liked helping them, and I think she would have liked to help us too, but Miss Kendall had been at Hawthorne since before Marty was in the second grade, and had been just as mean when Marty had her and when Sarah had her, and would probably be just as mean when Nick had her, so people did pretty much what she said. If you didn't, she would make you hold out your hands and hit them with a wooden ruler. If you talked when you weren't supposed to, she would pinch the skin under your chin and bang your mouth open and closed until you bit your tongue. Marty told me all about that when he walked me to school on the first day of second grade. Miss Kendall wasn't going to be like kindergarten or first grade, he warned me. And sure enough, on that very first day, she hit Gene Morelli on the hands with the ruler because he didn't put his lunch away in the cloak room when he hung up his jacket, and I started to cry when Gene started to cry, and so did most everyone in the class, but I yelled at her, 'you're mean!', and she made me bite my lip and I got a bloody mouth when she tugged my chin up and down. Miss Kendall would have banged my chin up and down this time, except that Miss Rimes was there, and she never did it if another grown up was around.

When we came back from lunch, I finished the body and neck and ears, and Miss Rimes came over and knelt down beside me and said she liked my horse. She knew right away it was a horse.

"Don't tell anyone," I whispered to her. "I want it to be a surprise."

She smiled and whispered back that she wouldn't. Very quietly she asked me if I were going to make a mane and tail, and when I said yes, she showed me how to make the mane from a separate piece of clay that could be flattened out with a roller thing she brought over and how to scratch lines in to make it look more like hair, and roll another piece for the tail and scratch lines in it too. It worked! And then she brought over a little dish with water and a tiny sponge and held my hand and showed me how to smooth the clay where the pieces joined. It looked even better than I'd thought it would. It was two o'clock and we were supposed to clean up at two-thirty, so I knew I had to hurry and get the glaze on.

Miss Kendall was watching all the time Miss Rimes was helping me. She didn't say anything, but she had a really mean look on her face.

Everyone was finding the colors they wanted except me. There was a green, but it wasn't the right one. It was too pale. I checked the colors other kids were using, but no one had the green I was looking for.

"Kurt," Miss Kendall growled at me, not caring that Miss Rimes heard, "find what you're looking for and finish up!"

If I couldn't find the right color, the whole idea was ruined. I sat back down next to my almost perfect horse. No Red Rider, no green horse. I could feel tears start to drip off my face, and I wanted to yell that it wasn't fair, none of it, and I almost did, no matter what Miss Kendall would do to me, but before I could, Miss Rimes knelt down beside me again and put her arm around me and asked, "What color are you looking for?"

I didn't really want to tell her, and I wanted to stop the tears, but they kept coming and so I told her anyway, "It has to be dark green and there isn't any," I said.

It didn't seem to surprise her. In fact, she made it seem like the most normal thing in the world, and she said, "Of course. I think I've got just what you want. It's called Hunter green."

She went into the storage closet and brought out a brand new jar of glaze, the most perfect dark green, exactly what the horse was supposed to be.

"You're not really going to open a brand new jar of glaze, are you?" Miss Kendall said. "The school year's just about over. He can paint it something else."

"It's okay," Miss Rimes said. "I should have had it out anyway."

She opened the jar and put it on the table next to me and handed me a brush. I began to paint before Miss Kendall could stop me. Miss Kendall came over. Her lips were pressed together tight and when she saw it was a horse that I was painting, she couldn't stand it.

"That's the most ridiculous thing I've ever seen! A green horse! There's no such thing! Stop that! Stop painting that right now!"

Everyone in the class was staring at me. They saw the green horse and laughed and for just a second, I was embarrassed. But just as quickly, it went away. Miss Kendall put a jar of black glaze and a jar of brown glaze on the table next to me.

"You choose. Right now, or your horse doesn't get fired."

I took a long look at the green horse and tried to imagine it black or brown. There was no point to it if it was black or brown, and I shook my head, no.

"You've got ten seconds," she said, her arms folded across her chest.

I looked up at Miss Rimes and she smiled and said, "It's perfect like that. I think that's the best color for it."

"Not in my class. No sir! That thing doesn't get fired unless it's black or brown. What's it going to be?"

"Green," I said.

"Black or brown," she insisted, "this is your last chance, young man."

I sat there shaking my head, no, from side to side.

"Well?"

"It's supposed to be green," I yelled at her

"Don't you dare raise your voice to me!" she yelled.

She reached under my chin and grabbed. She didn't bang it up and down very hard, but just enough, and I started to cry anyway.

"Stop that!" Miss Rimes said.

Miss Kendall glared at her and at me and at all the other kids and boomed out, "Clean up everyone. Leave your pieces on the table for Miss Rimes. After they're fired, Miss Rimes will bring them to our class next Friday so you can take them home. But not this!" she said, pointing at my green horse. "I forbid it! Do you understand?" She looked right at Miss Rimes to make sure she understood.

Miss Kendall grabbed my green horse from the table in front of me and put it on a shelf.

"If you change your mind, let me know," she said to me, "it could still be fired before next Friday."

Back in our classroom when the bell rang, I stayed in my seat, letting the other kids get a head start out of the room. I went to the front of the class and stood across the desk from her. She ignored me.

"Why can't it be green?"

She looked up, her face all pinched and mean, but then she suddenly smiled at me, and I thought she'd changed her mind, and I was so happy, picturing the horse, dark green and shiny, giving it to my dad.

"Because I say so," she said.

When I went out the gate on the lower playground, there was no one else around and I was glad. I walked as slowly as I could, to make the trip to Bill's take longer, imagining riding on the Special one last time. If I couldn't have it in real life, I wasn't going to go sit on it and pretend any more.

I stayed on Rexford all the way to Upper Santa Monica instead of taking Camelita to Oakhurst and home. The light was red so I couldn't cross. I could have gone right, across Rexford, and walked along the Beverly Garden Park towards Beverly Drive and crossed Santa Monica later, but that was going to bring me closer to Bill's bike shop and the end of the Red Rider, so I waited for the light instead. It must have changed when I wasn't looking or something, because when I looked up it was going from yellow to red again and I had to wait all over.

"Hey kid, which way to Doheny? I'm lost this side of Santa Monica."

There was a guy who looked like he wasn't even much older than Marty in a banged up truck next to me stopped at the light.

I pointed to my left, "Way down there," I told him.

"How old are you?"

"Seven and three-quarters. Almost eight."

"Do you have a bicycle?"

"I was supposed to…" I started to tell him, but then just said, "…no," instead.

"Too bad."

"Why?"

"I'm the route master for the Daily Mirror in this area. I need some kids for paper routes. But you gotta have a bicycle. You're kinda small anyway. You got an older brother or neighbor might be interested?"

"A brother, but he's already got a job. What if I had a bicycle? How much money could I make?"

"It depends. Somewhere between fifteen and thirty dollars a month. You have to deliver seven days a week. Think you could do that? If you had a bike, I mean."

"I think so."

He reached out the window and handed me a piece of paper with his name and a phone number on it: Ron Baylor, Crestview 9-3653.

"If you can get hold of a bike, and your mom and dad say it's okay, give me a call. You look a little small, but we could give 'er a try."

"Thanks," I said, "thanks a lot!"

The light changed and I crossed Santa Monica and then the railroad tracks to Lower Santa Monica and went left towards home and away from Bill's Bike Shop. I was wondering who could loan me the money for the locks until I got paid from the paper route.

When I got to the alley I looked for Norma's car but the carport was empty. The fence had less ivy on the Lower Santa Monica side and I could see that Snowball wasn't in the yard, so I just headed down the street towards home.

"Hey Kurt! Come on over."

It was Mr. Lester. He and Mrs. Lester had the puppies on the lawn and the puppies were crawling all over them.

"We need some help playing with these guys."

I had other things on my mind, but playing with the puppies sounded good too, especially since Snowball wasn't around. As soon as I crossed the street and sat on the grass they started jumping all over me. Their teeth were small but really sharp and one guy got in my lap and bit my leg right through my pants and growled and tugged like he thought he could pull them off me or something.

"Owww!!! Cut that out!" I said, trying to push him away.

Mr. Lester grabbed it by the back of its neck and pulled it off and tossed it a couple of feet away, but it came right back and tried to get me again.

"Kenny, don't be so rough with them," Mrs. Lester told him.

"They're fine. Stop worrying so much. Kurt, do you have a few minutes? I'd like to show you something."

"Sure. I guess."

We left Mrs. Lester with the puppies and I followed him between his house and Mr. Erwin's to the alley. He opened his garage door and turned on a light and I followed him in. At the back were shelves a lot like those in Mr. Erwin's garage. He had two planes like Mr. Erwin had, with markings on them, one a B-24 and the other a B-29.

"You know what those are?" he asked me.

I was worried about the garages and the locks, but he shouldn't be mad because we'd skipped his. I wanted to go back to play with the puppies, or maybe just go home.

"Sure. Bombers. From the war."

"Those are killing machines, plain and simple. I know you think they're pretty neat, and I think I know what happened yesterday, and that's really your business, but I want you to know that no matter what anyone tells you or what you hear about the war, it's probably all, well, bull-manure. We flew those things and dropped down bombs and lots of people died, and there's nothing neat about it. John Erwin says you ran yesterday when he opened his garage. Said one of his planes was on the floor. Couldn't lift it back up?" he smiled.

I was looking down at the odd shape of an oil spot on the floor wishing he would stop talking about it. He put his hand on my head and tipped it back so I had to look at his face.

"I'm not mad at you and neither is John. In fact, he knows your switching the locks saved him from running it over, and he thinks that was pretty smart of you, but you shouldn't be in other people's garages, at least not without their permission. Right?"

"Right," I mumbled.

"If you ask, I'd let you play with these two, and I think John would too. But you have to ask. Okay?"

"Okay."

"The thing about the war is...well…" he stopped.

"What?"

"Never mind."

"What?" I said again.

"It was crazy. Crazy scary, crazy deadly, but crazy fun in a crazy way."

"Fun? How can a war be fun?"

He laughed, "That's just another part of the crazy, right?"

"Like what?"

"We can talk about it some other time."

"Ozzie says..."

"Forget what Ozzie says. He's full of shit!"

"That's what Kevin Doyle says."

"Yeah? Well, you should steer clear of that guy too. He's bad news."

"I do."

"Good. And as far as Ozzie goes, have a milk shake, a coke, a burger, but skip the war stories, that's my advice."

"Okay."

"So, what's happening about the locks?" he asked as we headed back to the front yard.

"I've got to pay for them and we can't afford it so I can't finish paying for the Red Rider Special and we're going to try to get the money back from Bill's Bike Shop to use for the locks. Except if I have a bike, there's a guy that said I could have a paper route and that way I could pay for the locks and have the Special!"

"Are you big enough for a paper route? That's pretty hard work."

"I've been working hard at the car wash. I think I could do it."

"How many locks are you going to have to replace?"

"I'm not sure. I thought we'd done forty-five or fifty, but the police told my dad it was fifty-five or sixty or so."

"Jeez, you really did it up right."

He smiled at me and messed my hair.

"You know the San Vicente Hardware store, down by Robertson?"

"I think so."

"Mrs. Lester's father, Pat, owns it. What if we got him to open an account in your name and give a new lock to everyone who needs one? Then you'd pay on the account just like anyone else with an account at his store. How would that be?"

"You mean it? You think he'd open an account for a kid?"

"I don't see why not. I can tell him you're good for it. You always pay your bills, right?"

"I don't have any bills, except the payments on the Special."

"And I bet you make those on time, right?"

"That's right! I do."

"So, I don't think there'll be a problem."

"That would be so great!"

We came out from the side of the house to the front lawn.

"I'll call him tonight, and let you know. What's your phone number?"

I told him and thanked him and couldn't wait to get home and call the route master guy.

"I gotta get home and call the guy about the paper route."

"Come play with the puppies again, Kurt, and bring Sarah." Mrs. Lester said. "So long, dear."

"Bye. Thanks, Mr. Lester, thanks a million!"

"Why don't you just call me Kenny?"

"Okay. Thanks, Kenny."

As I ran down the block on their side, farther down, across from our house, I saw a really long black Cadillac stopped in front of Kevin Doyle's house. The driver left the car running and got out and went to the door. He was wearing chauffeur's clothes, and when Kevin Doyle came out, he was wearing a fancy army uniform, and even from half a block, I could tell he was all cleaned up. When the Cadillac passed, Kevin looked right at me. Actually, more like right through me, like I wasn't there, just staring out the window in my direction. He was wearing an army hat and there were medals and ribbons on his chest and he was sitting in a cloud of smoke from his cigarette. There was another man in the back seat with him, but I couldn't see him very well because of all the smoke and because he was on the far side of the car away from me.

I ran the rest of the way home, crossed the street in front of Mr. Avery's place and turned into our driveway.

"Mom! Mom!" I shouted, pulling the screen door open. It slammed against the outside wall and bounced back behind me with a whack into the jamb. "I can still get the Red Rider! Where are you? Mom! It's going to be okay!"

She came from the hallway into the kitchen as I came in from the back porch.

"Kurt, stop yelling. Nickie's getting a cold and he needs some rest. He finally fell asleep. I'm sorry honey, but the money has to come from somewhere."

"It will!"

"I don't see how," she said not really listening to me.

She sat down at the breakfast nook and lit a cigarette.

"Listen!" I said.

I reached out with both hands and tried to turn her face towards me. She blew the smoke out of the side of her mouth to keep it away from me but at least her chin and eyes were in my direction now.

"Stop that, Kurt! That's really annoying," she said as she took another puff on the cigarette, "can't you let me alone for one minute?"

I let go of her face. I told her about the paper route and Mr. Lester's idea about the hardware store and the locks.

"See!? That will work, right? Won't that work?"

"I don't know," she said, sitting back into the nook with the cigarette. "That's very nice of Mr. Lester, but I don't think you're old enough for a paper route. You'd have to ride the bicycle in the street so soon after you got it and that doesn't sound very safe to me. I'm sorry, but it doesn't sound like a good idea at all."

"But MOM! That's not FAIR!! It would work! I know it would!"

"Kurt! Lower your voice! You'll wake up Nickie."

"But Mom, please!" I begged her a little more quietly, "please!"

Her look was closing the door on the whole idea.

"Dad would say yes, I bet he would," I said.

"He won't be home 'til late, you know that, and he'll be going out early tomorrow. Let's not bother him with this. Kurt, things are difficult right now. He's got enough to worry about. Let's just get the locks paid for and see about a bicycle later."

She reached out to pat my hand, but I pulled it back.

"BUT THAT'S NOT FAIR!"

I ran out through the back porch pushing the screen door out of my way as hard as I could. It slammed against the wall and snapped back into the jamb with a loud whack. I could hear Nick crying as I ran through our back yard to the alley.

I went up the alley as far as the garbage can that covered my tunnel. I was going to go into the Pink House garden, but just then Sarah and Megan and Allen and Jeryl and Julie and Joanne Lester and Jeff and Dick walked past the alley on Lower Santa Monica and Allen called to me.

"Where were you? We had a meeting of the Oakhurst Irregulars at Ozzie's."

He waited there for me, but Sarah and the others kept on walking. He came part way down and I went farther up the alley to meet him.

"Sarah says you can't have the Red Rider now because of the locks. Sorry," he said, and I knew he meant it.

I shrugged, "It's not your fault. It was my idea."

Even if he was the one that wanted to steal the airplane, I was thinking. But it didn't matter anymore. I just had to get the paper route! When we got back up to the top of the alley, to the carport at Shelly's house, he asked me, "This is the place where you saw her, right?"

"Right."

"Have you seen her again?"

"Yes."

"Why didn't you say so?"

"Look how much trouble it caused the other day."

"Well?"

"Well what?"

"Is she Marilyn Monroe or what?"

"She's just Norma," I told him.

"But...."

"Forget about it, okay?"

We came around the corner onto Oakhurst. Jeff Schumur and Dick Goldsmith were headed down the block home, but Sarah and Megan and Donna Hooper were playing with the puppies so Allen and I crossed over too. Sarah and Megan were playing with the one that bit me.

"Watch out for that guy," I told them, "he bites!"

"Probably just you," Sarah said.

Kenny Lester sort of whispered to me, "Is everything set?"

"No."

"Why not?"

"I don't know. My mom said she thinks I'm too little for the paper route. That it's not a good idea."

"That's too bad."

"You can say that again! It's not fair at all!"

"What?" Sarah asked.

"That Pop won't let us have a puppy," I said to change the subject.

"You can say that again!" she agreed.

The Cadillac turned the corner from Lower Santa Monica and passed us. Kevin Doyle looked out the window at all of us there on the lawn with the puppies and then looked away.

"That guy's really creepy," Juli said.

Jeryl and Megan and Allen never looked up from the puppies, but I sort of watched him pass.

Mr. Lester and Mrs. Lester looked at each other, and he shook his head.

"His old man's parading him around again. Gettin' every bit of mileage he can out of the poor bastard."

"Kenny! Watch your language in front of the kids. Sarah…why don't you try your grandfather one more time. One of these puppies would be such a joy for you guys. You too, Megan. Wouldn't you and Allen like to have one?"

"Sure, but until the Multi-Deck deal is done, my dad says no to everything. We have to take turns waiting by the phone for calls so he doesn't miss an important one. He'd never let us have a dog now. We might be outside playing with it and miss a phone call. Even if my mom has to go to the store or somewhere important, she has to wait until I'm there, or even him," she said, jerking her thumb in Allen's direction, "so there's someone by the phone. It's the biggest deal of our lives, so maybe after, we could have one."

"Well, they might not be here any more."

"You're not going to take them to the pound are you?" Sarah asked.

"No, dear. But we've got to do something with them pretty soon."

"You could take them to the Beverly Hills Pet Shop. Wouldn't they take them?" Megan said.

"They've got all the puppies they need right now," Joanne said.

"What's wrong with the pound?" I asked.

"You dope," Sarah said, "they kill them there!"

"Not right off," Kenny said. "Maybe after a coupla weeks…if no one takes them …"

"Kenny!" Mrs Lester said.

"We gotta go, Allen," Megan said to him. "The phone," she told Mrs. Lester.

We all left together, heading down the block. The puppy that bit me started to follow. He was the last of the boy puppies, all shiny-black with a white patch on his chest. He came a few feet off the grass onto the sidewalk and stopped. He barked for us to come back and play some more until Kenny scooped him up. Sarah watched Kenny and Mrs. Lester and Joanne take him and the others into his house.

"Why does Pop get to decide?! Why's he the boss? He's mean to us, he's mean to dad, he's mean to mom, I wish…" Sarah grumbled, but she didn't finish whatever she was going to say.

"Because it's his house," I said.

"You just shut up! Just because you're his pet, you're on his side!" she said.

"No I'm not! But it is his house."

"I ought to pound you."

She looked over her shoulder to where Allen and I were following and waved a fist in my direction.

"And since you missed the meeting of the Oakhurst Irregulars, you're out! Completely."

I was going to complain, but with the loss of the Red Rider and no paper route to save it and no chance for one of the puppies, and Miss Kendal trying to make me paint the horse another color, and maybe John Dolan still looking for trouble, that didn't seem to matter very much. Besides, I thought I already was. My not arguing about it wasn't what Sarah expected. In fact it made her more mad at me. She began muttering to Megan about what a troublemaker I was, and how much trouble I caused for everyone, from the day I was born, and how I wasn't wanted in the first place, that I was some kind of accident and my mom blamed my dad and if I didn't believe her I should just ask Marty. They'd been just fine without me, and now everything was a mess. She stopped and turned, and before I even saw it coming, she punched me in the mouth, banging my lips against my teeth. My mouth filled with blood and it dribbled down my chin. I was so shocked, I didn't even cry. So she hit me again, harder.

I cried.

"What a baby!"

"Why'd you hit me?!"

"Because you're nothing but trouble."

I wiped the blood from my mouth, and when I saw it on my hand it sent a wave of something through me, and I cried like I'd been run through with one of Rathbutt's big swords.

"Oh shut up!" Sarah said. "You make me sick!" She started walking down the block again.

Megan took a napkin from her lunch box and put it against my mouth. She found my hand and placed it against the napkin.

"Are you okay?"

I shook my head that I wasn't. I'd stopped crying but didn't really feel okay. Megan said she and Allen had to get home to the phone, so they left and followed Sarah down the block. I just stood there. The puppies were gone and Norma and Snowball weren't around and I didn't want to go into the Pink House gardens and for sure I didn't want to go home.

# Chapter 11
## *Jigsaw*
## August 8, 1989

I CALLED Southern California Edison, spoke with a guy named Gil Alexander who was in charge of their historical records, but found that their main office was to hell and gone in Rosemead, south and east of downtown L.A. There was a question of confidentiality that he said he'd have to resolve before letting me look at the record of accounts, and he'd have to get back to me, even though, as I pointed out, the records were thirty-eight years old and confidentiality seemed a bit of a reach. I thanked him and said it was easier for me to call him than the other way around, and that I would, tomorrow, which left me with the assessor's office and the recorder's office.

The recorder's office was more or less conveniently located on Broadway, only a block or so from the Bradbury Building, close enough to tempt me into stopping there to say hello to John Goodman and Bob Winters at Goodman Winters Callahan and Street, the probate lawyers for Marty's estate. They'd probably be just as glad not to see me, to let the complicated, convoluted, contentious, and for their firm, inordinately skimpy financial outcome of his estate, stay in the past. They occupied the same building, just one floor up, from the space my dad had had, first alone, then during the Sarah and Sulla days, with his brother Bernie. It had changed from the 1950's only in the type of occupants, no longer the assortment of small clothing manufacturers like my dad and a few others, or the salesmen in spaces just large enough for an office and tiny showroom. It was now a collection of upscale law offices, a few CPAs and even a couple of state Senators who had their LA offices there. Nick and I had spent a lot of time in the Bradbury on Saturdays, cleaning up the scraps of cloth and thread from the cutters and seamstresses off the floor, making a little money, but mostly playing in what was now an historic landmark. Even if I didn't stop in to see Winters and Goodman, it would be worth a trip down Broadway just to see the Bradbury. But as much as a little trip down memory lane attracted me, it was the assessor's office on Temple that should be the first stop. I'd start with each property address and trace the chain of title as far back as I could, then work whatever names I came up with through the recorder's office. I'd still have to dig deeper to get tenants names, probably from LA Water and Power or Southern California Edison, but this should get me started.

When I'd left Vann, it was a little before eleven. The traffic on the 10 East was approaching the noon hour gridlock. The twenty minute trip took forty-five. After a few misfires, I found the right combination of one-way streets and parked in a lot across the street from the Bradbury. I thought I'd walk the four or five blocks to the assessor's office, and if there was time, I'd make a stop at the recorder's office on the way back. In any case, I'd get to see the Bradbury Building coming and going, which made the walk worthwhile no matter what else came of it.

500 West Temple was an eight story concrete building that looked like something from the Soviet Union school of architecture, unapologetically ugly. The receptionist asked for my driver's license and wrote down the number and my name and address on a sign-in sheet, then directed me to room 205, Archives, on the second floor, the elevators or stairs to get there, behind her station at the back of the lobby. The indicator was pointing to the sixth floor and didn't look like it was going to move anytime soon, so I took the stairs.

With the exception of a small glassed-in office to the left of the stairs, the second floor was one huge room lit by rows of fluorescent lights. There were rows of map books and record books on shelves no more than five feet high. Most of the books were large and awkward and if the shelves had been any higher to allow them to stand on edge, instead of laying flat, they would have toppled off. There were four large flat tables for spreading out and examining the books, and also on each, a microfilm viewer. One of the tables was being used by a middle-aged woman with lots of make-up and jewels and even more perfume. There was also a card catalogue. A slender man with thick glasses and an embarrassingly obvious and thin comb-over, in shirtsleeves and clip-on bow tie, came out of the office.

"Can I help you?"

"I hope so. I'd like to trace the ownership of some properties on North Oakhurst in Beverly Hills. The four-hundred block."

"Do you have Tract and Parcel numbers?"

"Yes. From the 1950 Assessor's map book."

"Oh, good. What years?"

"1967 back to, say 1940."

He smiled. This was right up his alley.

"Present day, including 1967, back to '58 is going to be on microfilm. Before 1958, you'll have to go through the books." He nodded in the direction of the shelves. "If you have the assessor's map, there should be map book numbers on it below the tract numbers. Look those up in the card file and you'll find the number of the corresponding record books. There's a chart on the wall showing the layout of the shelves and location of the book numbers on the shelves. If you need any help, I'll be in my office."

"Thank you," I said.

I had a legal pad, a pen and plenty of time. If I could get the ownership and chain of title information here, and correlate it to occupancy from Southern California Edison's records, or LA Water and Power, I thought I'd be able to pretty well reconstruct the neighborhood. It was tempting to skip around and do the properties that I already had some recollection about, but I decided to be more disciplined and start at the beginning on our side of the block at Beverly Boulevard, and work my way up to Lower Santa Monica one place at a time to Shelly and Norma's, then down the other side, back to Beverly. For most of them, ownership and occupancy in 1951 would be enough. Others, like the Pink House and our place and the one across the street and the one next to the Pink House would be more complicated.

Our block of Oakhurst was described as Tract No. 31971, Map Book 854-21-22, Reference 4342, page 34 for our side, 35 for Allen and Megan's. At the card catalogue, I found the Deeds of Record for the whole block were covered in four books and two microfilm reels. I got the books from the shelves and checked out the film from the guy in the office.

I took out the little strapless wristwatch from my pocket and put it on the table. It was 12:45.

The building at 425 was on two lots and had been built in 1947. It was two stories high, and there were 18 apartments in it, no garage, but a parking lot in back adjacent to the alley. It was originally owned by Raymond and Claire Abrams, husband and wife. Their son and daughter took title in 1986. There were various loans recorded against the property, paid, refinanced and paid off again. I couldn't remember ever having known them back then, or their kids if they'd lived there themselves, or any of the occupants for that matter, except that, not completely coincidentally, that's where my dad was living now. After my mom died, he sold our house in the Valley and moved into an apartment there. It suddenly dawned on me that Phillips might have tried to massage my dad with his theory about Marty. Cop or no cop, I didn't think he'd be that low. It sent an uneasy shudder through me, but at least for the time being, I'd give him the benefit of my doubts.

The house next to ours, 429, had six units and had been built in 1948 with a fifteen year GI loan in the names of Harry and Berna Warner. They paid it off in 1963. There were no other recorded documents until 1967, when they sold to the Beverly Hills Development Group, which built the big new fancy building that straddles 429 through 435. I remembered the pathway into the old 429 was on the south side, the Beverly Boulevard side, and all of the units faced that way, away from us. There were dark bushes, maybe Oleander, that crowded the front of the building and the pathway, and thinking about it, I remembered the same bushes were also between our house and theirs and across the length of the property at the alley, thick and dark, an effective screen in all directions. It was a white stucco building, also two stories with black wrought iron railings and handrails. Three units upstairs and three down. I remembered lots of French doors and multi-paned windows. Whoever lived there must have kept pretty much to themselves. I vaguely remember people older than my mom and dad, but younger than Pop and Nanny. I don't know if any of them were the Warners or not, but no one in that building seemed to have much to do with anyone on the block. I had a few other memories of the place, none of them very good. Something to do with my paper route, but I couldn't put my finger on it.

Our place, Pop's place, had a richer history. 431 and 431 1/2, our duplex, had been built in 1928. It was first owned by Morris Cousins, then Russell and Mary Nockles, then Pop and Nanny. According to my dad, Pop had been out of town on a business trip when the house came up for sale in the spring of 1935. Nanny saw it, thought it was a good investment and bought it. Given the subordinate role in which we'd always seen her, that level of initiative seemed way out of character. On the other hand, she may have been a different woman in those days, before the depression took over. It's hard to imagine her as dynamic or forceful or savvy enough to have seen the merits of buying the place, but harder still to imagine her acting on it. My mother was pregnant with Marty then. I wondered if it had had any influence on her decision, especially since Marty was named after her firstborn, my dads' dead older brother. In any case, as the story goes, Pop came back, made a big fuss, but mostly fussed because he didn't see and do it first. That mortgage was paid off in 1954 and a new one was recorded for the larger place built on 431 and 433, our place and The Courtyard. Pop and Nanny, George Bowen and a J. T. Dolan were partners in the new building, a four story sixteen-unit place.

I checked 433 next. The Courtyard was built in 1929 and to my surprise, owned from the outset by George Bowen. He'd had a small loan that was paid off in June of 1939. He'd owned it free and clear until he partnered with Pop and J. T. Dolan in 1954. He remained on title as one of the partners in the Beverly Hills Development Group in the next phase, when 429, 431, 433 and 435 were merged in 1967. George died in February 1979, and in June his interest in the place was purchased from his estate by the partnership. I gave in to temptation and decided to skip around after all. I looked up 432. It was built in 1928, went through two short ownerships until 1931 when husband and wife, J. T. and Elizabeth Dolan bought it. There was a recorded Quit Claim Deed from J. T. Dolan to Betty Doyle in July, 1939 as a Life Estate, the remainder to J.T. Dolan. In May, 1954 it was changed by another Quit Claim Deed to Betty Doyle and Pop and Nanny, as a Life Estate, the remainder again to Dolan, then a Deed of Trust with Pop and Nanny and Betty Doyle on title together, ownership for the three of them as a Life Estate, the balance to J.T. Dolan. That was in June of 1954, when the deal to build where our house had been must have been completed. I assumed Betty Doyle was Kevin Doyle's mother, but wondered how and why she suddenly entered the picture, and why they'd used Quit Claim Deeds and why as a Life estate? I knew she and Kevin had been living there since before the war, probably renting from J. T. Dolan, but transferring title both to Pop and Nanny and Betty Doyle by Quit Claim seemed odd. If it were part of the package to get the new building built on 431 and 433, why not regular deeds?

In 1958, a year before Pop died, another set of Quit Claim Deeds transferred title back to J. T. Dolan from Pop and Nanny, leaving him and Betty Doyle on title. In 1960 she quit claimed the property back to J.T. Dolan, who held title alone. In 1980 there was an inter-family change of ownership filed by J.W. Dolan, taking title as a married man, his sole and separate property from the estate of J. T. Dolan.

I went back to our side of the street and found the chain of title to 435. It was pretty straight-forward: six units built in 1928, owned by Richard Clark until 1937 when Charles Avery, my Mr. Avery from the car wash, bought it. He owned it until 1967, when he sold it to the Beverly Hills Development Group. I already knew from the other deeds that he hadn't been a partner in the new building.

The chain of title for 437 was a shocker. It was a twelve unit building built in 1928, also owned by Richard Clark until April, 1935. He must have been a builder or developer, I thought. But after that, by Hiroki Osaka until May 4, 1942, when there was a Quit Claim Deed recorded in favor of James J. Sullivan. Sullivan took a $500 loan in June 1942, the Deed of Trust listing himself and wife as joint tenants, paid it off in June 1945, and held it free and clear until, in June 1954, Pop bought it, maybe with some of the money from the sale, or trade and sale of our place at 431. In any case, it too was transferred by quitclaim from the Sullivans to Pop. Nanny wasn't mentioned. In June 1954, since Pop was selling 431, and we were losing our part of it, 431 ½, we moved to the San Fernando Valley. In July 1954, Pop recorded a deed against it as the sole and separate property of a married man. But it was held as a life estate. The remainder to Iyama Osaka! So, when Pop died in 1959, the property would have automatically gone to Iyama, and it would have been Iyama, not Pop, that wouldn't sell to the Beverly Hills Development Group. How could Phillips know as much as he did, but still miss so much? Or was it just feigned as part of a strategy to suck me in? Hiroki Osaka had to be Iyama's father. I wasn't sure how I could confirm it, but it seemed a certainty. Two months ago, in June, Victor Osaka, Trustee for the Life Estate of Iyama Osaka, had sold 437 to Paragon Properties and Point Dume Associates, the current developers of his and the Rathbone property. Since Victor was acting for the Estate of Iyama, Iyama must be dead and Victor probably his son. If not, if he were still alive, he'd only be about sixty-six or sixty-seven.

I skipped to 434, across the street. Built in 1927, it was four units, two up and two down, owned by a succession of people whose names were unfamiliar, until in October 1951, Miriam McDermott took title with J. T. Dolan, a life estate for her, the remainder to him. That guy really gets around, I thought. In 1966, Miriam quitclaimed her interest back to J.T. Dolan. Like 432, title changed to J. W. Dolan in 1980 as an inter-family transfer, and was unchanged until 1982, when the Beverly Hills Management Corporation took title.

The next two properties on our side, north of Rathbone went through a series of ownership changes, but none of the names were familiar. 449 had a series of owners until 1947, when John and Irmi Hooper bought it, and held title as joint tenants. In 1950, the title was changed to Irmi Hooper alone. Apparently Donna's parents had divorced. The chain of ownership of 451 didn't produce any familiar names, but Spencer and Margaret Aduan at 455 owned the duplex next to Shelly and Norma from 1940 until 1978, when their son and daughter took title as tenants in common. I didn't remember them at all, and my only recollection of Spencer Aduan was that he'd been particularly upset about the locks. I also had a sort of hazy vision of him being older than my dad but younger than Pop, so his kids may have already been on their own back then. I couldn't remember who occupied the other half of his building.

Shelly Winters had owned 457 since 1948. The names of the string of owners before her were unfamiliar to me, but it looked like she still owned it.

Across the street from Shelly, at 458, an attractive eighteen unit building on an oversize lot, there were no familiar names from 1928 to the current ownership. Jeryl and Juli Stern's place at 454 had been in their father and mother's name from 1945 to 1955, but before and after, no familiar names. Theirs was a duplex, with them upstairs. I couldn't picture or remember anyone from the downstairs unit. Next door to them, to the south, was Mr. Erwin's place at 450. It was a six unit building and he must have just rented, because his name had never been on title, and the names that were, weren't familiar.

Kenny and Ramona Lester had bought the fourplex at 448 in 1945 with a VA loan. The building had been owned before the war, from 1932 until 1945, by Patrick Mahoney, and I remembered that Mrs. Lester's father, Pat, had owned the hardware store on San Vicente, so Mahoney was probably her father, and sold it to them after the war. In 1988 the title changed to Joanne Lester Stuckey, a married woman, as her sole and separate property. I was picturing the Lesters and the puppies on the lawn, and vaguely remembered Marylou in one of her usual pink or pink and white dresses, hanging back, wanting to play with them, but not wanting to get dirty. Maybe she lived in one of the Lester's other units, or maybe next door at 446. I couldn't remember her last name no matter how clearly I could see those dresses.

There was a string of owners for 446, a twelve unit building built in 1931. None of the names were familiar. 444 was six units, owned by Toby and Ellen Arnold from September, 1950 until June, 1986, when Marylou Arnold's name appeared on title, from June, 1986 to January, 1987 after an inter-family transfer. The name that followed, the Beverly Hills Management Corporation.

The next two properties going south, were 440, 438. Throughout the chain of title there were no familiar names. Between them, there were fourteen units. Without really thinking about it, I suddenly pictured, then knew, Dick Goldsmith and his parents rented one of the units at 440 and Jeff Schumur and his parents rented another. They were both a little older than Sarah, but younger than Marty. Sarah somehow drew them into the Oakhurst Irregulars. Why they put up with her being in charge of everything, I couldn't fathom, but they did. They followed her around like robot bodyguards, or more in keeping with the Oakhurst Irregular's, MP's. I remembered Robbie Ganz lived next door to Jeff and Dick, so his parents must have rented at 438.

There was a fairly long series of changes of title for 436, and no familiar names, until 1951 when the ubiquitous J.T. Dolan bought it. Again, in 1980, it passed through inter-family transfer to J.W. Dolan from the estate of J.T. Dolan. Then, in 1982, the Beverly Hills Management Corporation bought and still owned it. That brought me back to Miriam's place, then Kevin Doyle's, then the four empty lots on the corner of Beverly and Oakhurst. They were now owned by the Beverly Hills Management Corporation. But before, they had been 430, 428, 426 and 424. After earlier owners, all four had gone the familiar route of J.T. Dolan to J.W. Dolan to Paragon Properties. I knew Allen and Megan's parents had rented 428, one of the few single-family homes on the street. 426 was another single family house, but I couldn't remember anyone who lived there. I wasn't sure, but the way I remembered it, 424 always seemed like a big side yard and part of 426. It was gardened and there wasn't a fence or anything, so it didn't seem like a separate property, and I guess I just assumed it was all one.

Phillips had been right about the outcome of looking at the assessor's map. Things were coming back. The lines on the map depicting separate parcels, the house numbers and names I'd found were transformed into a street buzzing with faces and voices, cars coming and going, lawns being cut, sidewalks swept, adults yelling at the neighborhood kids to stay out of their yards and off their lawns, newspapers waiting to be picked up, the mailman and milkman coming and going. I was there again. A wave of apprehension swept over me. When you travel to a foreign land, you can get yourself inoculated against the obvious risks. Going back to Oakhurst Drive was going to be a hazardous trip, and there were no vaccinations that would help. I still wanted the information from Southern California Edison or L.A. Water and Power about occupants rather than just ownership. There were names and faces just out of reach. I could feel them, sense their presence on the block, but couldn't quite bring them into focus. This was not a trip I wanted to take, but instinctively I knew it would be better if I got there ahead of Phillips.

Looking over my notes, and the memories they produced, I wanted to know more about J.T. Dolan, J.W. Dolan, the Beverly Hills Development Group, the Beverly Hills Management Corporation, and Paragon Properties. And I wanted to know what was the driving force behind Phillips investigation. No matter what I remembered or what he suspected, thirty-eight years is a long time. Someone had more than just a passing interest in this, and whoever that was, they must be important enough for Phillips to take it seriously.

I took a look at my watch. Who says there's no such thing as time travel? Not only had I spent most of the day jumping around from 1989 to the 1930's, '40's and '50's, but it was 4:20 already. The recorder's office would have to wait until tomorrow. At least I'd get another look at the Bradbury, the late afternoon sun now turning the bricks a glowing burnt umber.

# Chapter 12

## *Miriam's Smile*
### Friday, June 8, 1951

I REFOLDED THE NAPKIN, trying to find a part of it not already soaked, but it was no use. My chin was dripping blood and my fingers were getting sticky with it. I ran my tongue up against the inside of my lower lip and felt the ragged edges where Sarah's punch had cut it against my teeth. I tried to push my tongue against the cut to slow the bleeding, but it just created a space where the blood could collect, and then I had to decide whether to swallow or spit it out. I didn't want to make a stain on the sidewalk, so I stepped onto the grass of the parkway, planning on spitting it out at the base of the nearest jacaranda tree. Maybe it would help the tree grow, I thought, like fertilizer, like the compost stuff Pop used on our plants from the pile he had on the side of the house. Then I thought that that would be even better, if I could hold it in my mouth long enough to get across the street and spit it in the compost pile. Except I didn't want to go home. I didn't know where I was going, but not home, that was for sure. A Yellow Cab coming down from Lower Santa Monica passed me and pulled to the curb on the wrong side of the street just a little ahead of the tree I was about to spit on. Miriam McDermott got out. She had on a pretty blue dress and nylons with the black line that went up the back of her legs, and a wide black belt that pulled the dress tight around her waist and made her chest look bigger and stick out more. Her hair was thick and red, not strawberry blond like mine, but like a cinnamon stick when you lick it, and it was held in back with a blue and white scarf tied in a fat knot. I held the blood in my mouth. I would have kept walking, so as not to spit near her, but I didn't think I could hold it much longer. As she got out, she smiled at me, turned back to the driver and paid him. I don't think I'd ever seen her smile before. The times she and my grandmother went places together, it seemed like they weren't having any fun or going to, because neither one of them smiled, so seeing it now, I could see that she had probably the most wonderful smile in the world. Her face had cheekbones and a chin that made you notice them, like they were carved out of skin-colored clay. The cab crossed back to the right side of the street on the way down to Beverly. She snapped her purse closed and then looked up. My mouth was so full it was beginning to dribble out between my lips. Kevin Doyle came out of his front door, still in his fancy uniform, smoking a cigarette. He started down the steps, but stopped when Miriam looked away from him and turned to me. He sat on the top step, lighting a new cigarette from the one he'd been smoking.

"My goodness! What happened to you? Are you okay?" she asked me as she knelt down in front of me and reached out and held my free hand.

I pressed the soaked napkin to my mouth as tight as I could, but it was no use. I pulled my hand away and turned toward the tree. I hoped the bark could use it, because I didn't get it neatly at the base of the tree like I'd planned, leaving a long red blotch a little higher than a dog peeing might have done. Gooey red saliva dangled from my mouth and attached itself to my t-shirt a little above my belt. I started to cry again, but more from embarrassment than from pain. Or maybe it was just the hopelessness of everything. Or her being nice to me.

"Can I walk you home?"

I shook my head no.

"You should go home. I'm sure your mom would make you feel better. Don't you want to?" She looked over my shoulder to Kevin Doyle, who seemed to be waiting for her to get rid of me.

I shook my head no again.

"Then let's go see your grandmother. How about that?"

"No," I said.

"How would it be if I cleaned you up a little first? How would that be? Would that be okay?"

I nodded yes. She led me by the hand and we crossed the parkway and went up the driveway between her house and Kevin Doyle's. He sat there on his top step, smoking and watching us, like he was mad about something, probably about her not getting rid of me, but then again, that's how he always looked. We walked to the entry of her building, which didn't face the street, but faced Kevin Doyle's place. There were front doors on either side of an archway for the lower front and back apartments, and stairs from the archway going up. At the top of the stairs were two more doors, hers to the left, the upper front apartment, and another to the right for the upper back one. When we got to the landing at the top, the other door opened and an old man and woman came out. She had a scarf over her head and he had a cane and snowy-white hair and his dark blue suit looked too big for him and they helped each other down the stairs, hanging onto the handrail and each other and smiling, acting like each step was a special occasion, like how I felt when we paid Bill at the bike shop the five dollars each week. Miriam opened her door and we went in.

We walked through the living room and dining room on the way to the kitchen. Her place reminded me of my grandmother's room at the back of their part of the duplex, dark and closed off from the rest of the world. The windows that faced the street, and the ones that faced Kevin Doyle's house, were all closed and there were shades pulled down and blinds that were tipped more closed than open and curtains that were pulled most of the way closed, leaving only a slit in the middle, so only a little yellow light sneaked through into the room from both directions. There was a lot of dark furniture with dark wood and dark colors on the couch and chairs and the rug was dark red. There was a piece of furniture with lots of drawers on the Kevin Doyle side of the room that was covered with pictures of Miriam and some man and one of them was a wedding picture. There were other pictures of the man by himself working on a car and another at the beach wearing a swimsuit, and another at the beach in the water but looking back towards the sand. There was another table on the street side that had pictures of the same man in his army uniform, some of them by himself, others with a couple of army guys together with their arms around each other. The smaller ones surrounded a bigger one in the middle. He was wearing a fancy uniform in it, and it had red ribbon around the edges and a Christian cross, like some people wear, hanging down from one side, and dog tags hanging down the other and a little dish with a burned down candle in front of it.

Miriam watched me looking at the pictures as we went through the room, but she didn't say anything. She pushed the swinging door to the kitchen open and held it for me. The kitchen had one window that faced Oakhurst and one that faced the next building up the street. They both had curtains on them, but the curtains were white and pulled back to the sides, so the room was filled with light. She sat me down at a little yellow table with a chrome strip around the edge in one of the four chairs around it. They had chrome legs and yellow plastic seats that matched the tabletop. The floor had small white tiles like at our house. While she was wetting a dishtowel at the sink I started to count the sides on each of the tiles. Six, just like ours. I noticed the black lines on her nylons that went up her legs were very straight. She wrung out the dishtowel and took some ice from her icebox and wrapped the damp towel around it. She wiped my mouth and chin and neck with a corner of it, and then put the cold towel in my hand.

"Try to roll your lip out like this and put the ice against it," she said, making her lower lip stick out and curl down towards her chin. She looked pretty silly like that and it made me smile.

"What?" she said, her green eyes going wide, "you think I look funny?" She wiped her top teeth dry with the back of her hand so that she could make her upper lip stick and ride high up by her gums and then flipped her lower lip down again. "How's this?" she said. It made me laugh out loud. She let her mouth go back to normal and sat in the chair across the little table from me, laughing. Her smile was so easy and relaxed, and just like when she smiled at me outside, I was sort of shocked to realize how young and pretty she was. She reached across the table and pushed the hair back from my eyes. She seemed pretty comfortable like that, like she wanted me to stay, so I didn't think about going anywhere. Especially since I didn't have anywhere good to go. We sat without saying anything for pretty long. I checked the dishtowel every once in a while, and pretty soon my mouth had stopped bleeding. "How old are you?" she asked me.

"Seven and three-quarters. Almost eight," I said through the dishtowel.

She stood and took the towel from me, with what was left of the melting ice in it, to the kitchen sink and began to rinse the blood out.

"I thought we'd have had a little boy like you by now," she said so quietly I wasn't sure if she was talking to me or just sort of saying it in her head but it slipped out. I could see the side of her face and see that the smile was gone. She was still very pretty, I thought, but the change made her look a lot older.

"Aren't you 'bout done here? Don't look like the kid's gonna die or anything."

It was Kevin Doyle.

She turned from the sink and looked at him like he was a burglar or something, not afraid of him, just surprised to see him standing there.

"Kevin, you can't just walk in here…."

"Christ, Miriam, you gonna fool around with this kid all night? He's got a home. He oughta go home now. "

I was sort of glued to the chair, afraid to say anything and get him mad or crazy, afraid to get up and go and have to pass right next to him, but also, I had a funny feeling about leaving her with him alone. He's bad news, I was thinking, just like Kenny Lester said.

"Kevin, not now. Please. Not now," she said, sounding tired and annoyed, looking away from him. "Just leave me alone. Please."

He shifted around and looked like he didn't know what to do or where to go. He just stood there looking helpless. I felt sort of sorry for him until he got mad and yelled at her. At both of us, really.

"Fuck you! Fuck yourself and fuck this kid and fuck your precious and completely dead Sean! Fuck you all to hell!" he screamed, pointing a finger at her, then me. His eyes had gone crazy and his yellow teeth looked like they belonged to a dog or a wolf or something. I was so scared I forgot all about my mouth and Sarah and the locks and even the Red Rider, and that's really saying something.

"Get out, Kevin, just get out," she said quietly.

She didn't seem to be afraid of him, but I was. He moved around where he stood, shifting from foot to foot, moving but not going anywhere, moving towards her and back, like there was an invisible chain that stopped him from getting any closer. He was making noises like growls or little cries that were stuck in his throat and wouldn't come all the way out. He was getting pretty crazy alright, and I thought he was going to hit her. Or maybe me. But just when I thought he would, instead, he started to sob and he looked like a little kid lost in a big store. He stood there, not knowing what to do, but then his face got mad again, and the next thing I knew, he exploded out of her apartment and slammed the door, and we could hear him yelling, "Fuckers, fuckers, motherfuckers all of you!" as he went down the stairs.

Miriam looked at me and said, "I'm so sorry you had to hear all that, honey. My god, you're white as a sheet." She knelt down next to me and put her arms around me and kept repeating how sorry she was. I was close to crying, but before that happened she started to sob and cry first, so I didn't. I held onto her and she held onto me and that sort of made us both feel better I think. So while we were like that, after a little while had passed, I started to wonder if Mr. Lester's father-in-law at the hardware store would let me pay him from the car wash money. It would take a lot longer, but it could work. And I was pretty sure Mr. Avery would let me keep working there. It could work. It could! I knew it would! Why didn't I think of that before? I could do that without asking anyone because I already had that job. It was perfect.

"Are you okay now?" I asked Miriam.

I wanted to get out of there quick and go see Kenny Lester in case he was going to tell the guy at the hardware store to forget about it, to ask him to ask the guy if the money from the car wash would be enough even if it would take longer to pay for all the locks.

She pulled back and laughed.

"Looks like you are," she said.

"You bet! I just figured something out. I think it's going to be okay now. Geez, I think it is."

She was smiling and looked young and pretty again.

"I'm fine now. Thank you."

"Great. I've got to go. Thanks for fixing my lip."

"You're completely welcome."

She took my hand and as we walked back through the living room to the door, I nodded to the picture of the man in the army clothes.

"Is that Sean?"

"Yes," she said.

"Sorry."

She knelt down and hugged me to her.

"If I'm feeling sad again, can I count on you to cheer me up?"

"Sure," I told her. "Any time."

She kissed me on the cheek.

Going down the stairs I was thinking I sort of loved her.

I ran down most of the steps, but when I got close to the bottom I slowed down, then stopped and peeked out from the stairwell checking for Kevin Doyle. He wasn't waiting there in Miriam's driveway between their houses like I thought he'd be, so I walked slowly towards the sidewalk expecting to see him sitting on his front steps but he wasn't there either. Whew, I thought, that's a relief!

It had to be five or five-thirty, maybe even close to six and I didn't want to go past the six o'clock rule and have my mom mad and say no to my new plan, so I ran up the street all the way to the Lester's house. Joanne answered the door.

"Is your dad home?" I asked her.

"He's out in the garage."

"Thanks," I said and turned to go.

"You should probably leave him alone," she said.

I stopped and turned back to her.

"How come?"

"Sometimes he likes to go there and be by himself. When he's sad," she added.

"Your dad? He's never sad!"

"Sometimes he is," she said, and I could see it made her sad too. "About the war. My mom says he was never sad before the war, and it would help if he talked about it, but he won't."

She shrugged, like that's all she could say and I could do what I wanted, but she'd told me and it was my problem now. I didn't want to bother him, but maybe I could cheer him up a little. I'd cheered Miriam up, at least a little. And it would be awful if he told the hardware guy it wasn't going to work out when it still could. I thought I'd check on him and see how it went. If he was really sad, I'd just tell him real quick it might still work and could we talk about it before he talked to the hardware store guy and told him it wouldn't. That would be okay, and then I'd get out of there and he could still be sad if he wanted.

I walked along the path between the Lester's house and the house between theirs and Marylou's. The path was narrow and the buildings pretty tall with plants on both sides of the path crowded in making it even more narrow and a little creepy. I didn't notice that before, but I sure did now. The side door was open part way, and even though the sun was still out, the buildings and plants made it a little dark back there, enough so that I could see light from a bulb slipping out. It was a two-car garage and the Lester's only had one car, so there was a lot of room where Mr. Lester sat on the floor, his back up against their Buick. He had his knees pulled up towards his chest and his forearms resting on his knees and his face resting on his arms, hiding it. I pushed the door open a little further and saw the B-24 was on the floor next to him on one side, and an open box, maybe a shoebox, was on the other side. There were some papers in it and some ribbons and metals, like the kind Kevin Doyle wore when he got dressed up in his fancy uniform. He looked up at me and tried to smile, but Joanne was right. I should have left him alone.

"Sorry," I said and started to pull the door closed.

"Kurt….it's okay, come back…come in."

I pushed the door open but held onto the knob.

"Really," he said, "it's okay. Come on in."

He rubbed his eyes with the heels of his hands and took a deep breath. He put the top on the box and the smile he smiled was more like his usual one.

"What's up?"

"I just wanted to ask you something about your plan. It'll only take a minute."

"Go ahead. I'm fine."

"Well, do you think the guy at the hardware store would still open the account even if I don't have the paper route but still have the car wash job? It would take me longer to pay him, but I promise I would. Do you think he'd go for that?"

"I think he might."

"Really? Really?!"

"I think so. How much can I tell him you'd be able to pay?"

"Two-fifty a week. More if I get the paper route. My mom says no, but my dad might say yes. So I might. I can't promise that, so two-fifty might be the best I can do. Although I was thinking about other jobs I could do during the summer, so it could be more, but at least the two-fifty from the car wash. What do you think about that?"

"I think he'll go for it. Can you stop by sometime tomorrow? I'll have an answer for you by then."

"Sure I can. That's great. Thank you."

I think it was good that I stayed. He didn't seem so sad anymore. But I was wondering about the stuff in the shoebox. He followed my look.

"Some stuff from the war," he said.

I didn't want to make him sad again, so I pretended I wasn't curious about it and told him I had to get home and he said goodbye and that was that and it wasn't even six yet.

# Chapter 13

## *Il Fornaio – Seven PM*
## August 8, 1989

VANN WAS AT A TABLE on the Dayton Way side sipping at a glass of red wine. It was seven on the nose as I walked in the door. I took the wristwatch I used as a pocket watch, the straps cut off, out of my pocket and held it aloft pointing to it. I put it on the table turned towards her.

"Pretty good, eh?"

"Unbelievable, really," she said.

She had a very pretty smile going, but it was from excitement, I thought, not my promptness or just the simple pleasure of seeing me. Maybe a little of that, I hoped.

"What?" I asked.

"I struck gold!"

"What?"

"First you." Apparently her discovery was going to dwarf mine.

I gave her a rundown, not so much on my recollections of people and events that went with some of the names that had cropped up on the title searches, but the convoluted ownerships of J.T. Dolan, Pop and Nanny, Elizabeth Dolan, Betty Doyle, Miriam McDermott, the Beverly Hills Development Group, the Beverly Hills Management Group and Paragon properties. And now, more recently, J.W. Dolan. I was about to speculate on it a little, but she was anxious to tell me about her discoveries.

The waitress came and we ordered. I ordered, she ordered and ordered and ordered. I was glad Phillips and the Beverly Hills Police Department was picking up the tab.

"How can you eat so much?" I asked.

"I'm eating for two," she smiled, looking down at the table.

My face must have fallen six or seven feet as the information registered, "You're pregnant?" I could hardly say the words.

She looked up into my eyes, into my discomfort, with a sly little smile and patted my hand, "No, dummy, I'm eating for you, too. You don't eat enough and I don't think Phillips should get off so easy." Then after a moment, "But I had you worried, huh?"

I just made a face at her, like, thanks a lot. This was a whole new side to Vann.

"So, tell me about the gold."

Salad and bread came and we started on that. I made a mix of the Balsamic vinegar and olive oil from the tall skinny bottles already on the table onto a little plate and dipped the bread in it, sipped my wine and downed the salad pretty quickly. I'd ordered a chicken something or other, but the bread and wine and salad was filling me up. Vann had ordered the salad, an appetizer and what I'm sure Phillips would tell me was more entrees than two people could possibly eat. She was working her way through the salad and appetizer and enough bread to bring the waitress back with a second basket. When she brought the entrees, I picked at mine a little, and when Vann saw I wasn't going to eat much of it, she motioned for me to push it her way.

"The Pasadena Library," she said as she swallowed, "hadn't thrown away anything in more than fifty years. Nothing! Like I thought, they kept everything that ever came through the door, if not in the main branch, then at the LaCanada branch in a huge basement. It would have been a treasure trove at both locations. Then, two years ago, they got some grant money to computerize and expand, and whoosh, they're dumping left and right to make space. No one knew anything about old phone books, old reverse directories, or old neighborhood association newsletters, where they'd gone or if they'd been destroyed. They were all very nice, but too young and not interested in anything but their new computer system and how nicely the transition to it had gone to give the old stuff any thought. Looked like another dead end until an older woman, a patron not an employee, told me the head librarian at the time fought to keep the stuff, lost, but wouldn't allow them to destroy it. She had everything that was slated for shredding transferred to the basement in LaCanada, then offered it to local historical clubs and used bookstores. They jumped at the chance to get it. I found this at Pegasus Books in LaCanada."

She reached down under the table on the floor near her feet and retrieved a stack of photo copies she'd made from the 1950, 1951, and 1952 Beverly Hills Reverse Directories. She placed them on the table between us.

"There are plenty of others going back to the early '30's if we need them."

"This is great," I told her.

"But it begs the question again about Phillips. He didn't try very hard. Why not? If it's important, why's he being so sloppy? It's not like him."

"The whole thing is pretty weird. But before I get too far into this old stuff, I want to talk to Victor Osaka and J. W. Dolan. From the look of things, they're both about my age and both still involved in the land deals that go back to the '50's on the block."

"John William Dolan?" Vann asked.

"Yes. He goes by J. W. on all the documents I've seen, but he's John William, J.T. and Elizabeth Dolan's son. On one of the intra-family transfers I saw, the D.O.B. was April 1941."

I didn't mention that I thought I knew him in a different context.

"If he's the same John William, he's the City Councilman who's running for mayor. Haven't you seen any of the campaign stuff? It's all over town."

"I hadn't noticed."

"Look out there." She nodded to the streetlight pole across Dayton Way. A dozen flyers taped to it announced, DOLAN FOR MAYOR, DOLAN FOR CHANGE, DOLAN FOR PROGRESS! TOGETHER WE CAN END THE INCOMPETENCE!

"They're all over town. Billboard ads, newspaper and radio and TV spots. It's a nasty campaign. Lot's of mud. Charges of influence peddling, conflict of interest. Mayor Tannenbaum is the darling of the movie crowd. He's distinguished, a decent sort of everybody's-grandfather-type. A little too easy going and resistant to change to suit the development crowd on the council and Dolan. The new City Hall and Public Service Building and the new downtown parking structure were pretty much forced on him by Dolan and the Chamber of Commerce."

As she was talking, I was remembering Ellis Weis's frustration trying to crack into the closed circle of Beverly Hills politics and development. Megan and Allen and their mom, Reggie, babysitting the phone, afraid to miss a call, a new deadline for another submission, a new condition that had to be met. There was a political campaign that summer too, I remembered, and it seemed like everyone on our block and up at the carwash had strong opinions about it, about the old mayor and the city manager and council and the guys trying to replace them. I couldn't remember much about it, but for Ellis it was important. His multi-deck project was finally approved, but on the edge of town, not in the prime location for which the city had originally solicited bids. Most, but not all of the crowd in control at City Hall, had managed to stay in office. They couldn't freeze Ellis out when it became increasing clear his bid couldn't be ignored, but they managed to substitute sites. Still, it was a terrific coup for him and his construction company. Even though it was one his best paydays ever, he was bitter about the unfairness and corruption of the process for years afterwards. I remembered Allen's accusation to Teddy Browner that his dad was a crooked politician looking for a payoff before they'd approve the project. I sort of liked Phillips. He might be an asshole in a lot of ways, but I respected what I thought was his professionalism. If there were a tug-of-war between candidates for mayor, and one side or the other was attempting to use the police department to sabotage the other, would Phillips really let himself be dragged into it? I didn't think so. I gave him more credit than that. But I was reconsidering.

"What?" Vann asked me.

"Do you think Phillips would let himself and the police department get used in a political campaign? A nasty one?"

"Where'd that come from?" she asked, a little shocked, but considering it.

"I was remembering some stuff from those days," I said, nodding at the pages from the old reverse directories. "The politics of the town. How there's this tension between the movie crowd that wants a nice, quiet enclave, a well run, efficient place with great schools, clean smooth streets and pretty parks, you know, just a place to live and raise families free of the special burdens of their notoriety, and the developers that want to capitalize on the enormous development value just having the movie crowd here brings to any project. There's always going to be a lot of money at stake. It must be quite a bonanza for the guys in the position to make the decisions. For the winners of the elections around here. Dolan, for instance. Or the current mayor. You think one side or the other might have found a way to make this investigation a part of the mud slinging you mentioned?"

She was shaking her head 'no', but still considering it.

"Geez, Phillips? I give him more credit than that."

"Me too. But maybe that's why he's hanging back. Pushing me into it. Maybe there's an investigation that needs to happen because they found this body, but he's trying to skirt the politics of it. Both proceed with an investigation and keep his hands clean at the same time."

"That's pretty good."

I raised my eyebrows, telling her I wasn't quite convinced that I was right, but not ready to dismiss the idea either. In fact, as I sat there, it started to feel right. She sat there thinking about it too.

"You could just confront him with it."

"I can just hear him," I said, imitating his voice, 'It's a murder investigation, cowboy, if that's okay with you. That's what we do around here. Not politics, just police work'."

"That's good. You could have a whole new career."

"I think before I just drop that on him, I'm going to make sure my J. W. Dolan is your John William Dolan. Find out more about Dolan and the current mayor, and Victor Osaka and the land deals."

We were pretty much done with dinner. The waitress brought the check. It was for a little over fifty bucks. I smiled, made the tip for ten more, showed it to Vann, signed it and told the waitress there was a tab opened for me by the BHPD.

"The Pacific Hotel?" she asked, a hint of a smile on her lips.

# Chapter 14

## Saturday, June 9, 1951

SUDDENLY I WAS AWAKE. My eyes popped open and I was awake, just like that, but instead of jumping out of bed and getting started like usual, I just lay there thinking. There were so many things that were going to happen today it was making my head spin. I had to go see Kenny Lester about the hardware store guy and find out if that was going to work. And if it was going to work, then the Red Rider was still mine and we'd have to make the second to the last payment. And I wanted to play with Snowball before I went to the carwash, and I wanted to play with the puppies before the Lester's got rid of them. The clock on Marty's desk said 6:15.

When I got home from Kenny Lester's the night before, it was still two minutes before six, so no one could get mad at me. My dad was home early, sitting at the kitchen table while my mom was making dinner. He was telling her things about the new line. She didn't say anything but just kept making dinner.

"It's going to be okay," he told her a bunch of times.

I came racing in through the back porch, trying to beat the six o'clock rule, the screen door whacking against the side of the house, slamming back into the jamb.

"Kurt! How many times," my mother began.

"Hi! How come you're home so early?" I said to my dad.

"I thought it would be nice if we could all have dinner together."

"Neat-o," I said.

"Neat-o," he repeated.

He pulled me to him and hugged me tight. The muscles on his arms were huge, and I could hardly breathe. He stopped squeezing and I sat on his knee.

"Especially since, you know…tomorrow…"

"What?"

He bent his head down close to my ear and whispered, "We're going to have to tell Bill at the bike shop…"

"No!" I interrupted him.

"I'm sorry, Kurt, but we're going to have to pay for those locks…"

"I know. But it's going to be okay. Really! Kenny Lester said…"

"I told you the paper route wasn't a good idea," my mother began.

"What paper route?" my dad asked.

"Kurt had this idea he could get a paper route if he had the bicycle and pay for the locks with the money from it. I told him it wasn't safe for him to be out in the street so soon after he gets the bike."

"No! This is a different idea. Kenny thinks it'll work! Really!"

"What about Kenny Lester?" my dad asked.

"Mrs. Lester's father owns the San Vicente Hardware store, around the corner from Carl's Market. Kenny said Mr. Mahoney would open an account for me and let everyone who had to have their locks cut off buy one from him and I could pay it off. I thought I'd need the paper route money to do it, but mom said no, and I told Kenny Lester it was no deal, but then I figured maybe he'd let me pay him from the carwash money even if it would take longer and he said yes! At least, maybe yes. He's going to ask Mr. Mahoney and tell me tomorrow if that's okay. That'll work? Won't it? Please!"

My mom said, "I don't think they're going to open an account for you, Kurt. And even if they did, there's not enough money from the car wash to pay for the locks in a reasonable amount of time. It's nice of Kenny to suggest it, but it makes our problem theirs, and that's not fair, is it?"

"But mom! It can work. Really. And without the paper route. You said no because of the paper route."

The Red Rider seemed to be slipping away again. She was shaking her head 'no'. I could feel the tears starting, but I didn't want them to come, so I bit my teeth together as hard as I could. Sometimes that worked.

"Kurt, go tell Sarah and Nick and Marty dinner's ready."

"MOM! That's not fair! It can work. It can! Why won't you ever listen?!"

I looked at my dad, begging him.

I whispered, "Please! I'll work really hard besides the carwash. I can do other jobs during the summer. I'll pay for the locks faster, I promise."

"Kurt…go get the others…" my mom said again.

She started putting food on the plates. My dad had his arms wrapped around me, pulling me into him. When she went back to the stove and had her back to us, he whispered in my ear, "Let's see what Kenny says tomorrow. If Mr. Mahoney's willing to open an account, that means he trusts you, and I know you'd never, ever, let him down, right? It's a little like me and Schwartz. When someone trusts you it's a big responsibility. You have to make good on it. Understand?"

"Yes."

" Let's keep this between us for now, okay?"

"Okay!" I whispered back.

"Go get the others now," he said.

As I got off his lap, my mom was looking at us and her lips were pressed together. I don't think she'd heard, but I don't think she had to. I was smiling when I went to call everybody to dinner.

Nick had come into me and Marty's room sometime in the night and climbed in bed with Marty and they were both out cold. Marty had to work at the Standard Station, but not until noon, so he was sleeping late. If he didn't need food or the bathroom, Nick could probably stay in bed forever. He could just lie there, and you could definitely tell he was thinking about things, whatever they might be, until someone got him up, or he got tired of thinking about them. I got dressed in the bad jeans since I'd be at the carwash, found a clean t-shirt, socks and my Keds. I tiptoed through the kitchen, looked at the clock on the stove, which said seven-ten, and went to the back porch and carefully opened and closed the screen door. Pop had the lawnmower flipped around backwards so the blades were lifted off the ground, pushing it down the driveway to the front yard with one hand, carrying the grass catcher in the other. He was wearing his old khaki work pants, some old black shoes and an undershirt. His arms weren't like my dad's at all. They were skinny and kind of wrinkly and pale white. My dad was six feet one-inch tall. Pop wasn't even close to that, and Nanny was really small, less than five feet, so it was funny that my dad was so big. Everyone said Marty was going to be big too. He was going to turn sixteen this summer, but he was already taller than my dad. Skinny, but tall. His arms were getting muscles from changing the big truck tires at the Standard Station, but mostly he was still pretty skinny, like Pop.

"You talking to me today, or you still mad?"

"I'm not mad at anybody."

"Well, that's a relief. Wanna help me? You could earn a little dough."

"Sorry, I'm not supposed to work for you anymore."

He frowned. "Well, you could keep me company, couldn't you? That's not against the law, is it?"

"Sure, for a little while. I got a lotta stuff to do today."

He put the catcher on the mower and started cutting the parkway. I walked along with him.

"Like what? You're working at the carwash today, aren't you?"

"Yeah, but not 'til ten."

"What else?"

I told him about the account at the San Vicente Hardware store. He stopped mowing and looked at me.

"You think you can handle that? That's a lot of responsibility."

"I know. I'll pay 'em every penny."

Pop messed up my hair.

"I bet you will. Lester's a damn good guy. So's Pat. I'm glad it's going to work out."

He started to mow again. We heard Iyama Osaka's truck rattling to a stop in front of Rathbutt's place.

"The Jap's pretty early today," Pop said.

I reached over and spanked his bottom one hit. He stopped mowing and looked down at me.

"What? What was that for?"

"That's not nice," I said.

"What?"

"Jap," I whispered.

"Oh for Christsake."

"Well, it's not," I said. "Besides, he's not even mean like everyone says."

Pop kept mowing and I walked along side him again. The grass catcher was almost full and he took it off the mower.

"Wanna dump this for me on the compost pile?"

"Sure," I said.

I took it to the south side of the house past the stucco archway and dumped the cuttings onto the pile he kept there between the pathway and the side of the house. When I came back with the empty catcher, he put it back on the mower and started to cut the grass in front of his side of our duplex.

He said, "You're right. That wasn't very nice. Or fair. He's not bad at all. And he's always been a hell of a hard worker. Even as a kid. His dad was okay with me too. Didn't deserve any of it."

I was going to ask him how could he know him as a kid or know the father when Iyama Osaka was a Japanese soldier in the war and Rathbutt captured him, but Mr. Sullivan came down the block walking his dog, one of those tiny hairy dogs with the pushed-in face that you can't see, except maybe the eyes looking out from underneath long eyebrows, the kind of dog that's always in the house, just like Mr. Sullivan himself. The dog was on a long leash that looked funny because he was so small. Mr. Sullivan came right up to Pop.

"Abe," he said to Pop, but looking at me, "is this the kid that switched the locks?"

I sort of shifted myself behind Pop.

"He's taking care of it, Sullivan."

"What kind of kids you raising here? I know they're your grandkids, but just the same, you own this place, you gotta exercise a little control."

"You don't have to make such a big deal out of it. You're gonna get a new lock."

"Yeah? Well, we'll see. And while I'm thinking about it, how about you keep these little bastards off my garage roof? The girl's the ringleader on that one. His sister. You talk to her. I swear, I'm calling the police next time. They're up there jumping from one garage to the next like it's a game or something. They fall off and break their necks, next thing I know, you're suing me!"

"Anything else?" Pop asked, making a face like he was getting pretty tired of this.

"Yeah, as a matter of fact, there is. Keep this guy off my lawn," he said, nodding at me again. "That would be nice. He's ruined the goddamn hedge. It won't grow back where he keeps going through it."

While they were arguing, the little dog started to hunch up to poop on our lawn. Pop gave him a little kick with his foot, interrupting the dog's plan. He ran around in a little circle, like he couldn't remember what he'd wanted to do.

"How about you keep that little hairball's crap off my lawn," Pop said, even though he liked to use it on his compost pile, "that would be nice for a change!"

The dog was whimpering, not so much from the kick, but because he still needed to poop and wasn't sure what to do about it or where. Mr. Sullivan scooped him up and leaned in close to Pop's face and growled, "Don't you dare kick my dog, old man. You're not too old to get a little ass-kicking of your own!"

Pop let go of the lawnmower. He didn't seem to care that he was shorter, thinner, and older than Mr. Sullivan.

Just then my dad came backing his car out of the garage and down the driveway. He stopped with the back wheels just onto the street and the front wheels on the sidewalk. He took one look at Pop and one look at Mr. Sullivan and another at me. I could tell me he was still mad at Pop and didn't want to talk to him, so he asked me, "Is everything okay here?"

I shifted my look down at the sidewalk so I didn't have to see the look on either one of their faces. I felt bad for Pop, but I knew he'd been mean to my dad, so I felt bad for both of them.

"I guess," I said. I looked up at him.

"Come here," he said, "close."

I went up to the car and stood right next to his open window. I got up on my tiptoes and he leaned out the window slightly so he could whisper to me.

"This is for you to give to Bill with your two-fifty from the carwash if things work out with Mr. Mahoney. I've got to get downtown now and I won't be back until after the bike shop's closed." He smiled at me and pulled my head closer and kissed me on the forehead. He looked at his watch. "Christ, I'm already late. Look, if it doesn't work out, this has got to go for the locks, understood?" He handed me the money and I shoved it into my pocket.

"Yes. Thank you, daddy."

"Well, I'm betting on you. If anyone can make it work out, I'm confident you can."

My dad took one more quick look at Pop and Mr. Sullivan, then backed the rest of the way onto the street and drove towards Beverly Boulevard.

Pop had been standing there with his hands on his hips watching me and my dad. He watched as my dad drove off, then turned back to Mr. Sullivan.

"Sullivan, you're a disgrace. You're a thief, a liar, and a two faced plain no-good schemer. In every goddamn way. You know it and I know it, and everyone around here knows it. If I can't kick your ass, and I think I can, Dave will. You want Dave to hear you're calling his kids 'little bastards'? Have you ever seen Dave lose his temper? Really lose his temper? It's not a pretty sight. We won't find enough of you to make half a meal for this little crap machine of yours," he said, nodding towards the dog.

Mr. Sullivan must have seen my dad lose his temper sometime, because as soon as Pop said it, his face changed and he didn't seem as mad any more. In fact, all the time my dad was there, Mr. Sullivan looked like he was trying to be invisible. He didn't apologize, but he didn't stick around much longer either. He started walking up the block and sort of called out over his shoulder, "Just remember what I said!" But it looked like he'd lost interest in the whole thing.

Pop stood there with his hands still on his hips with that funny posture of his that reminded me of Jack Benny, someone we saw on Pop's TV when he invited us over to watch, then smoothed back his thin black hair. I noticed how his glasses magnified his eyes and his face was smooth shaven, even on a Saturday morning. He just stood there until he was calmed down and ready to mow again.

"Pop?"

"What?"

"How could you know Iyama Osaka or his dad from before the war? Rathbutt captured him during the war and made him his gardener and ordered him to keep people out of the yard. So how could you know him?"

His laughed his funny snort of a laugh.

"That's ridiculous. Who told you that?"

"All the kids say so. The older kids too."

"No, that's a bunch of baloney. The Osakas used to live on the block. Before the war, the old man, Hiroki, owned the house where that jerk Sullivan lives. Iyama was twelve or thirteen when we moved here. I don't know, maybe fourteen."

"What didn't they deserve?"

"None of it."

"What?"

"It's complicated."

I thought he was going to explain it to me, but instead, he just made a face and shook his head and kept mowing. He was thinking about it, I could tell, or maybe he was thinking about my dad, but he wasn't going to tell me, so I walked along side him for a little while longer.

"I'll see you later, Pop."

"Where you off to?"

"Up the block. Maybe play with Snowball…one of the Lester's puppies that a lady on the corner on our side got from them."

"Okay, buddy, see you later. Keep away from that jerk, Sullivan. I'd hate to see your dad go to jail for pounding him."

"You think?"

"No, don't worry…I'm just kidding."

"Whew! That's a relief. We got enough trouble around here."

I walked up the block past the Courtyard, took a look in, but didn't see George on his front step, so I kept going. I was going to go through Mr. Sullivan's hedge just for the heck of it, but since he was probably sitting in his living room, watching out the window, just waiting for me to do it, I thought I should skip it. At least this once. But then I thought maybe I could run through so fast he wouldn't even see me. That would be pretty neat. I was standing on Mr. Avery's lawn, sort of warming up, making the kind of revving up noises a race car does, getting ready to blast through the hedge and across Mr. Sullivan's lawn and back to the sidewalk before he could even get the window open even if he did see me, when Mr. Avery came out his front door.

"Good morning, Kurt. Ready for another day at the salt mines?"

"Salt mines? What salt mines?"

"The carwash," he said. "You're working today, aren't you?"

"Of course."

"See you there." He nodded at the hedge. "Knock a few branches off for me," he said.

He walked towards Beverly Boulevard. It was only four longish blocks to the carwash and he always walked. He stopped to talk to Pop and they both watched me as I revved up and dashed through and back to the sidewalk clean as a whistle. If Mr. Sullivan was in his living room, he must have missed it. I waved to Pop and Mr. Avery and headed up the block. I was thinking it was pretty neat that I'd gotten through so fast he didn't even see me. But then I thought, maybe he did see me but was scared my dad would pound him if he complained. I was thinking about Sarah always telling me she was going to pound me for something and it made me feel sort of sorry for him. It took the fun out of it too. Maybe I'd let the branches grow back for a while and then I could just start over.

Snowball was in the yard and Norma was standing in the doorway, watching her, with a cup of coffee in her hand. She was wearing Levi's and a sweatshirt with the sleeves cut off all the way up to her shoulders, with a t-shirt underneath it. She had on the kind of fancy low white tennis shoes like they wear on sailboats, the kind lots of the northsiders wore. Teddy Browner said he had a sailboat, but I'm not sure I believed him. He was such a liar about everything, and even if they were rich, a sailboat didn't seem possible. I bet Norma didn't have a sailboat and she wore them, so I think Teddy Browner just wore the shoes without the boat.

"Hello," she said. "Isn't it a beautiful morning?"

"You're right, it is," I said, thinking about my dad's two-fifty in my pocket and a pretty good chance at getting the Red Rider, "because it looks like…well, it just is."

"Want to come with me and Snowball to Carl's Market? We need a few things."

I couldn't wait to check with Kenny Lester about the hardware store deal, but it was still pretty early and he might not be up yet and this would kind of be like playing with Snowball.

"Sure," I told her. "But I've got to be at the carwash by ten."

"I don't think it's even eight yet. We've got plenty of time."

She took the coffee cup back into the house and came out with Snowball's leash in one hand and a big cloth bag in the other.

"Why don't you put this on her," she said, handing me the leash and putting the bag over her shoulder. "You can walk her. She likes you."

Snowball didn't like the leash though, not one bit, because as we walked out the gate she was pulling backwards against it so hard her head was cocked sideways and her ears were being pushed forward by her collar, making her face scrunch up. She kept growling in a puppy voice and trying to get her head turned so she could bite the leash.

"Geez,' I said, "she doesn't like being on the leash, does she?"

"Not very much. But it's part of her training. Shelly got me a book about it. She'll get used to it."

We crossed Oakhurst, walking along Lower Santa Monica. Snowball was making me drag her just about the whole way, past Allen's alley to the corner at Doheny, then across Doheny. Norma tied Snowball's leash to the door handle in front of Carl's on the Doheny side, but we walked down Doheny a little and came in through the door on the parking lot side. When you came in that way, you were entering through the liquor store part of Carl's and were going to see Big Max whether you wanted to or not. If I came in with my mom or dad or Pop, he was okay, but if I came in alone, he was a crab for sure. There were huge racks of magazines and newspapers on the wall that separated the liquor store from the market, with the ones Marty called girlie magazines on the top shelf that we weren't supposed to know about or see, but they were right there and we could see them anyway. They were too high to reach, but even kids my age could see them. They were really really weird, like the one called Natural Fun, with people on the cover, men and women, playing volleyball together without their clothes on. Lots of others that were weird too, but I thought the volleyball one was the weirdest. The shelves ran from the Doheny side of the building to a little ramp up into grocery part. Past the ramp on that wall, and coming all the way back around to Max's counter, the walls were filled with shelves of wine and booze, but mostly booze for boozers, Marty said. Big Max was usually behind the counter with his back to the parking lot wall. The phone was always ringing in there, and even if all you wanted to do was buy just one coke from the big case filled with soda bottles and ice water that was to the left of Max's counter, you had to wait until he got off the phone. You could stand there with the bottle dripping and have your money all ready, and he'd puff on his cigar and write things down and hang up and tell you you were dripping all over his floor, but the phone would ring again and he'd start writing down more things and he'd forget all about you. The sodas were five cents, but you had to give him three cents extra for a deposit on the bottle. You got the three cents back when you returned it, but sometimes if I didn't have enough money for the coke and the deposit, I'd just drink it there. If the phone rang enough, it was okay, because, like I said, he sort of forgot about you. But if it was quiet, he'd make sure you drank it quick and left.

"Hiya, kiddo," Big Max said to Norma. "Everything comin' up roses?"

"Sure, Max. You know my friend, Kurt?"

"You betcha. You're Abe Goldman's grandson, right? Got some brothers and a sister, right?"

I nodded.

Big Max always had a short soggy looking cigar in the corner of his mouth and he kept it moving around as he talked. His tongue kind of came out of his mouth to play with it, which is probably why it was so soggy. Sometimes it was lit and sometimes not. But I'd never seen him without it. He was short and stocky, a little like George Bowen, but a lot heavier, especially around the middle. I don't know why everyone called him Big Max, because he wasn't very big, but his arms were what I always noticed. He had a tattoo of a mermaid on one forearm and a ship's anchor on the other, really big, dark tattoos, and his arms looked really strong. He didn't have any hair on the top of his head, but lots of frizzy hair around the sides. If he didn't have a customer at the counter, he was always reading a newspaper that Pop said was about racehorses, but Big Max called them ponies.

Norma and I walked up the wooden ramp into the market. The floors in Carl's Market were made out of wood too, dark and worn, especially in the middle of the aisles, so you could tell people had been coming and going for a long time. They were the color of the saddles on the little horses at the Beverly Ponyland, dark brown and just slightly shiny. Benny, the vegetable guy, saw Norma and smiled.

"Hi, sweetie, how are you?"

"Fine, Benny, and you?"

"Can't complain. Wouldn't do any good if I did, now would it? Kurt, smell this. They just came in."

He took a peach from the table behind him and held it under my nose. It smelled so good my mouth started to fill up with saliva and had that funny silvery taste all of a sudden.

"Ain't that something? This one's on the house." He rubbed some of the fuzz off of it against his apron and handed it to me. "Go on, take a bite."

I bit into it and some of the juice ran down my chin. It was tart and sweet, and it wasn't mushy at all, but a little crisp, like an apple.

"That's great!" I told him, "I'll tell my mom to get some."

"See?" he said to Norma, "one free peach and I'll sell a dozen!"

Maybe when we weren't so broke, I was thinking, but I didn't say it. He was putting out fresh heads of lettuce for the Saturday shoppers from three boxes stacked on top of each other on the floor next to him. Benny was small and really skinny and was always friendly and in a good mood. He had gray hair that was slicked back like Pop's, but not as much of it. He wore glassed that had thin wire things that went over his ears, but across his face, the glass part was attached to the wire stuff with screws, so there weren't any frames. He had a tattoo on his arm too, but it was just a bunch of numbers. He knew the names of all the kids in the neighborhood and was nice to them even if they came in the store without a grown up. Marty said he was in the war too, but you shouldn't ask him about it. His squad had gotten captured by the Germans and sent to a prisoner of war camp, but they didn't put Benny in with the other soldiers. Instead, they sent him off to a different prison for almost half the war where he almost died. Marty said he just wanted to forget the whole damn thing.

Norma put a few of the peaches in her cloth bag, a head of lettuce and some tomatoes. We wandered around the store and she got a can of coffee, a quart of milk and a loaf of bread.

We ended up at the meat counter on the San Vicente end of the store. The butcher was Carl. Pop said he never acted like the owner, like a big shot or anything, just took care of the meat counter and let Benny and Big Max and Jan do their jobs. He was a pretty big guy, bigger than my dad and about the same age, but heavy, like one of the wrestlers Pop liked to watch on his TV. He had sandy colored hair that was thinning, but the thing I always noticed was his face was as red as the bloody meat all around him. He was cutting up pieces from a huge chunk on a big wooden block table. The top of the block was slightly dish-shaped, so most of the blood collected there beneath the chunk, and only a little of it fell to the sawdust that covered the floor.

"What's really good today, Carl? I want to surprise Shelly with something nice."

Carl looked up from his cutting, wiped his hands on his bloody apron, and smiled.

"Well, we got some New Yorks that don't get any better. We got some lamb chops this thick," he said, holding his thumb and first finger about three inches apart, "tasty as can be. And..."

"Mmmmm," Norma said, "the lamb chops sound perfect. Let me have the two biggest ones you can find!"

"You got it."

He poked around in the pile of lamb chops in the refrigerator case between us, then took two pieces and put them on the scale. He tore off a piece of the white butcher paper from a roll on top of the case and wrapped them up and wrote the price on it with a black crayon and handed it to Norma.

"Let me know what you think," he said.

"They look wonderful. Thank you, Carl."

We went up and down another two aisles and Norma looked at a few things and took them off but then put them back on the shelf. We went back through the store to the cash register where Norma emptied all the stuff in the bag onto the counter and Jan, Carl's wife, rang them up and placed them to her left, where Norma put them back in the bag. Jan sort of leaned in close to Norma and whispered.

"Carl said I shouldn't bother you, but I just can't help myself," she said, "could I have your autograph? I just love your work. I just know you're going to be the next Carol Lombard!"

"Of course. That's so nice of you to say."

Norma looked at me and smiled, and sort of shrugged as Jan pushed a piece of paper and a pen across the narrow counter. Norma wrote, To Jan, your friend and neighbor, Marilyn Monroe. Jan was so excited she didn't notice the money Norma was holding out to pay for the groceries. She looked at the paper with Norma's signature and seemed hypnotized by it. Past her, I saw Big Max was standing at the top of the ramp leaning against the jamb of the opening between the liquor store and the market, his arms folded across his chest, his wet stump of a cigar moving from one side of his mouth to the other, his tongue wetting his lips.

"Fer Christsake, Jan, take her money so she can get outta here," he said, shaking his head and walking back down the ramp.

"Oh…yes…I'm so sorry," Jan said, taking the money and making change.

Norma and I went back through the liquor store. She turned to the east wall shelves, which were mostly wine, and asked over her shoulder, "Max, can you suggest a nice red wine to go with these lamb chops?"

The phone was ringing, but for once Big Max didn't answer it right away, actually, not at all, which was pretty weird. His voice was gravelly, and his lips were shiny brown from the cigar juice, but his eyes seemed to light up at the chance to help her.

"You bet, honey. One way or another, I got just the thing."

He came out from behind the counter and stood next to her at the wine shelves.

I sat down at the bottom of the ramp finishing the peach, nibbling off the last of the little strings from the pit. A couple about my mom and dad's age came in from the parking lot and saw Norma and kept looking at her over their shoulders as they went past me into the store, whispering to each other about did you see who that was? I think Norma noticed them noticing her, but pretended she didn't. The phone kept ringing but Big Max ignored it.

"We got the cheap stuff, but you probably don't want that, right?"

"Right," Norma said.

"Then we got your run of the mill stuff, not bad, but not really good."

He looked at her and she shook her head no. He smiled, like he already knew that wasn't going to do.

"We got the good stuff right here, and the very good stuff up there," he said pointing at one of the higher shelves. He looked at her again. She seemed a little uncertain.

"Just to give you an idea," he said, "the good ones run four or five bucks a bottle. This other, well, eight, ten, even twelve bucks a throw. Some a little more. All depends on you."

"I think a pretty good one this time. I'll save the very good one for a real occasion."

"Like winnin' an Oscar, right?" he winked at her.

"An Oscar. Wow, what a thought!"

"Well, you get the Oscar, a bottle of the best in the house is on me."

"That's so sweet," she said. "But just a good one this time, okay?"

"Gottcha. Now, here's a cabernet I think you'll like."

He ran his hand along the shelf until he found what he was looking for. The phone rang again.

"If you need to answer the phone…" Norma said.

"Naw…they'll keep. Probably save 'em some dough if I don't pick it up."

They took the wine to the counter and Big Max rang it up and Norma paid him.

Kenny Lester came in from the parking lot. He saw me and Norma and said hello.

"I thought I recognized Snowball out front. She behaving herself?" he asked Norma.

"She's wonderful," she said, "I just love her. Thank you so much."

"Thank you. I just wish we could find homes for the last couple. Maybe you can help me talk Kurt into taking one of them."

"I don't think he's the one that needs talking into," she said. "It's Pop you've got to work on, right?" she said to me.

"I wouldn't bet on it. He's pretty much made up his mind."

"I bet if Miss Monroe asked him to let you have one, he'd let you."

I shrugged.

She laughed and told Kenny, "I think that would be a little…awkward. I don't think I should interfere."

"Maybe you're right, but I bet it would work." Then he said to me, "Kurt, Pat says he'll open the account for you. You wanna walk over there with me and meet him?"

"Sure, that's great!"

Norma looked at me.

"About the locks," I said.

"Kurt's gonna take care of it," Kenny Lester told her.

"I didn't do her garage," I said.

"He was very selective," Kenny told Norma, "he didn't do ours either."

They both laughed.

The three of us walked out into the bright morning sun. There were a few cars in the lot now. When we came around to the Doheny side, Snowball started wagging her tail and yipping as soon as she saw us, pulling the leash so tight Norma had a hard time untying it. She set the bag on the ground and untied Snowball and put the bag over her shoulder.

I asked Norma, "Can you get back home okay with Snowball and the groceries?"

"Sure, Sweetie, I'll see you later. Don't work too hard."

"But I'm supposed to," I told her.

Kenny Lester and I walked around the corner to San Vicente, past the Motion Picture Arts and Science building that we weren't supposed to know Pop owned, but we did, and one block farther to the hardware store. Mr. Mahoney was putting some shiny metal trashcans out on the sidewalk up against the front of his store next to several wheelbarrows already there.

"Hi Kenny. This the kid?"

"Pat, meet Kurt. Kurt, Pat."

Pat Mahoney reached out to shake hands. He was a little younger than Pop, but seemed a lot younger. His skin was tanned and his arms were solid, more like my dad's. His hair was thick, a mix of black and gray, but curly and wild like my uncle Buddy's hair. You could hardly get your hand through Buddy's hair.

"You got a wicked sense of humor, Kurt," he laughed. "Kenny told me all about it."

"Well, it's not so funny right now," I said.

"How many locks you think you're gonna need?"

"Fifty or fifty-five. Sixty at the most."

"You really covered some ground, didn't you?"

"I suppose."

"Well, it is pretty funny, and Kenny told me you were trying to keep John from running over one of his models and all, so it was pretty clever too. But I'm glad to see you're taking responsibility for it. That's important. Right?"

"Right," I said.

"Well, here's the deal. Locks like that, either combination locks or key locks sell for a buck fifty. I get 'em for sixty-eight cents apiece. I'll let you have up to seventy-five of them for seventy-five cents each, including tax. Worst case, you gotta shell out fifty-two bucks and change. If you can pay two-fifty a week, you'll have it taken care of in about twenty-two weeks. How's that sound?"

"That's great. Thank you. I won't let you down, I promise. And I might be able to pay more than the two-fifty a week. Maybe."

"Well, the two-fifty a week will be fine. If you can pay it off faster, that's fine too. Kenny said you might like to start the week after next."

I looked at Kenny.

"So you can finish off paying for the bike first," he said.

"That'd be perfect."

Mr. Mahoney reached out to shake on it.

"You just leave a note at all of the houses that had the locks cut off and tell them they can charge one lock to the Kurt Goldman account at the San Vicente Hardware store. Let's give them to the end of the summer to do it, say, September 15th. After that, they're on their own."

He went inside and came back out and handed me a stack of about eighty business cards from the store. He took one of them and began writing on the back. He handed me the card.

"You can copy this on as many cards as you need."

He'd written: good for one lock until September 15, 1951. Kurt Goldman account.

"So, get those cards out there and we'll see who shows up. Probably
be a week or so before too many of them have cashed in anyway. We
gotta deal?"

"Yes, thank you."

"I think were all set, then."

"Thanks, Pat," Kenny Lester said.

"Thank you," I said again.

Kenny and I headed back towards Carl's Market.

When we got to where Doheny and Lower Santa Monica and San Vicente met, Kenny said, "You wanna go over to the little park for a bit?"

"Sure," I said.

The sun was really bright and the air was getting warm even though
it couldn't have been much after 9:00. It was going to be hot at the carwash, I was thinking. Kenny just sat there and let the sun shine on his
face. He had his eyes closed. I noticed how square his jaw was, and that
his eyes were deeper in his face than on most people. He wasn't too
big, about the size of my uncle Buddy, who said he was six feet tall, but
couldn't be, because he was a lot shorter than my dad, and my dad was
six feet one inch. Kenny was younger than my dad for sure, but it was
hard to tell how old he was. He didn't seem old, not any particular age
at all, really, just not young. He was good looking, a little like that Errol Flynn guy from the Robin Hood movie poster in Rathbutt's storage
room. There was a small breeze and the water splashing from the upper
part of the fountain down to the lower part made a mist in the air that
drifted over us and cooled things down. It was nice, except that once in
a while drops would get you instead of the mist and it was like someone
with a squirt gun. Kenny reached into his pocket and took out one of the
medals that had been in the shoebox.

"I'd like you to have this," he said. "The others, too, if you want them.
They're just too much a part of the crazy. The sooner I get rid of them
the better."

He laid it between us where we were sitting on the sandstone rim of
the lower part of the fountain. It was pretty neat, all right, a shiny cop-
per-colored medal with the design of an airplane propeller attached to a
ribbon with five stripes, a fat and skinny blue stripe, and a fat and skinny
white stripe on either side of a little red stripe in the middle. I didn't
reach for it. I didn't say anything either. It was going to be such a perfect
day, the start of what I knew was going to be a perfect summer, and I
didn't want to ruin it by saying anything that would make him sad again,
especially after he'd helped me with the locks.

"It's okay," he said, "you can touch it."

I sort of pushed it with my finger, but didn't pick it up.

"Do you know what that is?"

"For something good you did in the war?"

"That's what it's supposed to be for. It's the Distinguished Flying Cross," he said.

"Neat," I said, but I could see from his expression that it wasn't to him.

"Before the war, Mrs. Lester and I thought we'd have more kids. I thought I'd have a son. After the war...well, the thing is, I don't have a son and it doesn't look like I will. I used to think I'd give it to my son. I'd tell him it's a reminder that there's nothing good that comes from war except the friends you make and feeling that comes from taking care of each other. Not a damned thing else. Even if you live through it, the war keeps on eating you up unless you can think about your buddies and all the crazy, funny stuff that happened."

"What funny stuff?"

Kenny was smiling his regular smile now. He had a really good laugh, the kind that makes you laugh too, even before you've heard anything funny that he was going to say.

"It's not the kind of thing I'd tell Joanne, and her mother really doesn't want to hear anything about the war, anyway. I thought I might tell you."

"I guess."

I was thinking about Ozzie's stories.

"I know you're a little young, but before you get too caught up in the war stories from guys like Ozzie, or what you hear from the older kids that remember the war from the radio and newspapers, I wanted to make sure you know it's not a game. No one wins."

"I thought we won."

"No one wins, Kurt."

He looked at me and smiled. He picked up the medal and looked at it in his palm and closed his fingers around it.

"I think we should wait until you're a little older. I don't know what I was thinking."

He closed his eyes and let the sun shine on his face. He was smiling and I figured he was thinking about some of the funny, crazy stuff from the war. Better than thinking about the crazy nasty stuff like Ozzie was always talking about. In a minute or two, he opened his eyes. I was still sort of thinking about the Distinguished Flying Cross in his hand. He stood up.

"We should probably get back," he said.

"I'd like to hear about the crazy funny stuff," I said.

"Mrs. Lester would skin me alive," he said, "but there are some pretty funny stories you might get a kick out of."

"When could you tell me?"

"Oh, I don't know. Sometime," he said.

I was sort of disappointed that he wasn't going to tell me right then, now that I knew his stories wouldn't be like Ozzie's.

"Sometimes the guys that I work with at the carwash mention the war.

And a lot of the customers sit around at the tables with Mr. Avery, or just with each other, or with Joseph, while their cars are being washed, and even sometimes way after the cars are done, and talk about the war," I told him.

"Oh yeah?" he said.

"It's true. Really," I said.

I looked at his closed hand.

"Would it be okay if I kept it to remember your helping me with the locks?"

He smiled, putting his hand on the top of my head. "That would be perfect," he said and handed me the medal.

It was about 9:20 and I told Kenny I was going to walk along Upper Santa Monica to Beverly and the carwash. It was six long blocks, and I figured if I hurried maybe I could stop at the Wonder Bread factory, help a little, and get something to eat before I went to work.

"Maybe I'll see you there," he said. "My car could use a good wash."

"Neat," I said.

He cut across Upper Santa Monica and disappeared through the Oleander bushes heading for the railroad tracks to Lower Santa Monica and Oakhurst.

# Chapter 15
## Wednesday, August 9, 1989

IF THE PACIFIC HOTEL were the same as it had been, I still didn't know it yet. I slept at Vann's again. In the little guest room. Not a bad guest room, but a guest room just the same. I wasn't sure which one of us was more annoyed. Or more relieved. There's something about Vann that deserves to be loved so completely and openly and faithfully that it makes me cringe at my inability to do any of those things. In my defense, without being too defensive, I've done that with Jason, my son. My mental mantra has always been, the one thing I want him to know for sure in this life is how much I love him, and for him to take pleasure in it. I've even managed to get it beyond the confines of my interior musings and say it out loud to him. It wasn't even that hard. But the idea of actually feeling that kind of unqualified love for another adult, let alone saying it, is beyond me. There's this looming sense of betrayal, of resignation, of blackness that's so palpable, so immediate, so unreasonable and inescapable, that even Vann's sweetness and goodwill couldn't penetrate it. So it makes me both grateful and incredulous and slightly ashamed that she has feelings for me and entertains the notion that whatever feelings I communicate to her, mostly by osmosis, are worthy of her consideration. Maybe it's true that a man should know his limitations, but he doesn't have to wallow in them. That wasn't for me and I didn't plan to. It didn't seem likely that I'd escape or outgrow those limitations anytime soon, and my business down here was really limited to Phillips and the dead guy, so I thought I'd just focus on that. None of which escaped Vann.

When we came through the door into her little house at the beach, the playful smile on her lips at Il Fornaio had changed. She seemed resigned. Annoyed too, but mostly resigned. She pointed to the pillow and blanket I'd folded up and left at the end of the couch this morning.

"You'll have to remake the bed, but you're all set. Let me use the bathroom first, then it's all yours."

She reached up with both hands and cupped my face, smiled a little sadly, and pulled me to her for the kind of kiss that leaves you thinking about it for a long time. I stood there, thinking about it. She went into her bedroom. She came out a minute later wearing only a man's t-shirt, which came to mid-thigh. It reminded me of the first night in the Pacific Hotel when she wore one of my t-shirts to bed. I sort of wondered whose this was. I tried to banish the thought. It wasn't any of my business. The light caught the reddish highlights of her dark auburn hair, the ponytail gone now as she brushed it on her way to the bathroom. She raised her eyebrows in a little greeting as she went from the bedroom to the bathroom, but it was just by way of acknowledging my presence, not inviting any response.

"Good night," she said, leaving the bathroom door open and the light on for me, closing the bedroom door behind her. I was still thinking. As usual, uncertain, slightly annoyed, mostly with myself, not her, but with that old all too familiar feeling of having let something important slip away.

We took separate cars and got to Il Fornaio at seven. The traffic on the 10 East was at its usual crawl even then. As she was about to get in it, I'd asked Vann how she'd ended up with the Fury. I asked if Tate was all right. I told her that was a car I thought they'd have had to either bury him in or pry from his cold dead hands. She gave me a funny look and just said, "another time," and let it go at that. I thought she would have told me if he were dead or in jail, so that was some comfort, but I had a uncomfortable mixture of apprehension and relief. There were the usual early morning half-a-dozen regulars, a couple of them I even recognized from my early morning trips here in the days after Marty died. We again took a table on the Dayton Way side about half way down, spread out the photocopies of the reverse directories Vann had scored at the bookstore in LaCanada. The waitress came and we ordered. Vann would be eating from now until noon, I thought. I had a latte and toast. She had the breakfast menu, or most of it.

I put the assessor's map in front of me and started to go through the listings from the 1950 reverse directory pages. It would have been nice if there'd been listings by addresses, but that would have been too easy. I didn't think there were, or at least I'd never heard of old reverse directories by street address, which made L.A. Water and Power or Southern Cal Ed's records all the more attractive. These were by phone number. The good news was that in fifties most neighborhoods in Beverly Hills and West L.A. had distinct prefixes. Ours was Crestview, so you dialed 'CR' and the numbers. It covered an area about twelve or fourteen blocks square. It was large, but manageable. By scanning down a page of the copies, I'd spot the Crestview prefix, check the address for the 400 block of Oakhurst and underline it all the way across the line to the name. The light pouring through the windows was good, which made the job easier. It was going to be hot, but for now, the crisp brightness was welcome. Vann ate and ate as I checked and underlined. It went pretty well. The waitress had come and gone several times with more coffee and had left the check twenty minutes before. There was no guarantee that everyone on the block had had a phone, but one by one I was finding street addresses and names, many of them familiar. or familiar sounding, anyway. By the time Vann was winding down, I'd filled in names next to addresses on the assessor's map for about two thirds of the buildings on the block. With the names of the adults, names of kids I'd forgotten about came to mind. If Phillips had his way, I was going to be a walking bonanza for him. But I still planned on getting wherever this was heading before and without him. At least until I knew what or who was pushing his investigation.

I checked my little pocket watch. It was 8:30. The recorder's office would open at 9 and I wanted to go there alone. Vann watched as I filled in names on the assessor's map.

"We've got this phone book thing on discs at the office. I might be able to match up some of the names you're coming up with to people still in the county. Actually, it covers all of California, Oregon, Washington, Arizona and New Mexico. It searches pretty fast."

"That's pretty cool."

"When we're looking for a missing person or someone on bail who's skipped, it comes in handy. The drawback is it can produce too much information. People with the same name. But mostly it's a big help."

"I want to go to the recorder's office. Maybe you could start running these names and see what you come up with?"

"Sure."

"I don't think you'll find anything for Iyama Osaka or his father Hiroki, but you should for this Victor Osaka guy. He just sold 437 to Paragon Properties in June. You ought to be able to find him, don't you think? "

"Most likely. Where should we plan to meet? And when? And are you going to call Phillips with any of this?"

I was thinking about Victor Osaka. If Iyama had refused to sell 437 for all these years to J. T. Dolan, or any of the companies he controlled, or to Paragon Propterties, which I assumed J. W. Dolan controlled now, then it seemed pretty clear Iyama died, Victor inherited and sold. I was picturing Iyama, the muscular arms with the rope-like veins, the smooth brown skin, the conical straw hat and the tall boots. When I looked across the table at her, Vann was waiting for an answer, but I hadn't heard her.

"What?" I asked.

"Some things never change. I'll look for Victor Osaka first. I'll run these other names and see what comes up. Where should we meet and when? And are you going to call Phillips with any of this?"

"Good questions, all," I said, refocusing on her. "Let's meet back here at three. And no, I am not going to call Phillips. If he contacts you, just tell him I'm working on it like he asked. If he wants to know how it's going, tell him it's going. Period."

"He'll know something's up. If you're still here, still looking into it, avoiding him, he'll figure you're onto something and want to know what it is."

"Well, good. Let him want all he wants."

I smiled as I signed the check, putting the breakfast on Phillip's BHPD tab.

"He wanted me here and here I am. He'll just have to wait a little bit longer. While you're at it, would you see if you can find an address and phone number for your John William Dolan. I'm assuming he's the J. W. Dolan on all these property transfers and the son of J. T. and Elizabeth

Dolan. If he is, I'd like to speak with him."

"You think he's going to talk to you? He's a councilman running for mayor. He's a little busy now."

"I have the feeling he might find the time."

Instead of gnashing my teeth stuck in the East 10 traffic, I took Wilshire Boulevard all the way across town. It was slow but steady. From Rampart Street going east, most of the signs were in Spanish, most of the people dark, most of the businesses like something in Juarez or Tijuana. The area looked vibrant and poor, entrepreneurial and lethargic, third world and other world. The jacarandas throughout the city had become legion, no longer gracing just a few streets like Oakhurst, but running like a common thread from Beverly Hills to downtown L.A., and becoming an ad hoc forest around, and especially in, MacArthur Park. Wilshire ends at Grand. I found the right combination of one-way streets pretty quickly this time and parked in the lot across the street from the Bradbury. I walked the two blocks to the recorder's office.

It was an old brick building, not as compelling as the Bradbury, but nice. It was four stories high on the west side of the street. The top floor had six large arched windows, both taller and wider, but similar to the ten on the fifth floor of the Bradbury. They faced the street and must have been floor-to-ceiling, or something close to it, since they were ten or twelve feet high. The brickwork forming them stood in relief to the adjacent courses, and the sills were an attractive use of sandstone slabs, also like the Bradbury, sloping steeply towards Broadway.

Inside, the lobby was grungy. The marble floors and marble wainscoting, a nice touch in their day, were poorly maintained, dirty and chipped. Not even a half-assed attempt at clean, just plain dirty, I thought. The wide stairway to the left of the counter had a nice ornate brass railing and balusters, but it had been left to find its own way from the last century to this, the finely cast details lost to years of neglect and an accumulation of dirt and oxidation. The ceiling here had obviously been dropped down from the original, now yellowed acoustical tiles and buzzing fluorescent lights. A sign on the counter instructed you to sign in, get a badge and go to whatever floor contained the records you wanted. This floor had fictitious business names, business licenses, marriage licenses, divorce and birth and death records for the last two years. Old birth, death, divorce and marriage records were on the fourth floor. I signed in, was handed a badge that had my name and the date on it, pinned it to my shirt and headed up the stairs. There was a door no larger than that of a small closet next to the steps and buttons on the wall that suggested it was an elevator, but even if it were, I thought I'd rather walk. My slight claustrophobia, not the "Out of Order" sign hanging on the knob was the deciding factor. Even if it had worked, walking probably would have been faster. The marble steps had that nice worn-in-the-middle aspect that I normally liked so much because it created a link, a connection to the thousands of others that had come and gone over the ninety or a hundred year life of the building, maybe looking for clues to their own dead guys, their own links to a past they too probably had thought was dead and buried. Whatever I was going to find, I had the feeling it was going to leave me straddling the past and present in a way that would leave my footing in both uncertain. I had the feeling I was heading for a fall, a nasty one, that this was going to spin out of control, but instead of dread or apprehension, as I got closer to the fourth floor and some answers, I had a growing sense of, first relief, then exhilaration. Go figure.

The stairs arrived at a marbled mini-lobby at the fourth floor landing. The marble shone. The neglected brass handrail coming up the stairs merged with the railing surrounding the landing and it too was not only clean, but polished, the details of the castings clearly defined. Just beautiful. Everything was clean and well kept. Light from the six huge arched windows, which, as I'd suspected, did come to within a foot of the floor, poured in, illuminating every detail of one of those miracles of nineteenth century self-confidence in design and craft. The room occupied the whole fourth floor. It had to be eighty feet along the Broadway side and at least sixty feet deep. The ceiling was about fourteen feet high, the windows reaching to within two feet of it. But it was the oak woodwork that caressed you and touched your senses. All of them. There was a distinct hint of tannic acid, a slightly spice-like smell, and there was warmth that you could feel radiating from it as the sunlight that poured into the room with such crisp and sharp abandon through the huge windows was absorbed and reflected back into the room, softened, quieted, steadied and made golden. On all four exterior walls, the pale glazed tan brick was visible, interrupted by three-side fluted oak columns from floor to ceiling on twenty-foot centers, probably encasing the steel columns of the super-structure. But the real glory was the ceiling itself. There were three rows of two each of the fluted oak columns, but here in the open, four-sided, supporting an elaborately subdivided, and alternatively recessed, oak paneled façade, creating about four-foot squares. I assumed the oak columns and the lower portion of the crisscrossing squares were concealing the interior structural steel posts and beams. At every meeting of a vertical and horizontal plane, against the recessed panel, there were wonderfully detailed quarter-round oak moldings with carved rings around smaller carved circles around a small round dot the size of a pea, mitered so cleanly and tightly, they looked like they grew there. Other moldings that capped the top of the columns where they met the ceiling had an alternating square notch pattern, like the top of a rook in a chess set. At the center of each of the twelve squares that were formed by the rows of columns, there hung from a five-foot cast brass pendulum, a brass and glass light fixture about three feet in diameter with a cluster of ten oversize bulbs. Even without the bright light coming through the windows, the room would be well lit. I was aware, too, that the wood was not only absorbing and re-working the light, it was filtering and softening the sound. The room was at once overwhelming and calming, and only served to enhance my sudden sense of liberation.

"Hello," a man said to me, "do you need any help?"

I had been standing there transfixed. When I focused on him, he smiled at my having been so absorbed. He looked to be about sixty, small, wiry, good looking, probably of Japanese descent, with a mane of thick black and gray hair just over his ears, and small round spectacles low on his nose. He was wearing a dark blue shirt under a black sport coat, a dark charcoal tie, Levi's and comfortable looking loafers. He looked like he should be a professor of architecture or architectural history at UCLA, but he had on a badge that pegged him as Tad Matsumoto, Head Clerk, Archives.

"Beautiful, isn't it?"

"Just amazing, " I said. "From the outside, I thought it was just a poor step-cousin to the Bradbury, an imitator, but this…." I said, taking in the confident quiet grandeur of the room, "…is wonderful."

"Same designer as the Bradbury. George Wyman. This came a little later, and without Louis Bradbury as a patron. He died just before the completion of his building at 304, so Wyman was at the mercy of Bradbury's wife and children here. This is a similar, but simpler use of the steel super-structure, the glazed brick and sandstone. No dramatic skylight, but these windows," he smiled proudly.

"Why the hell have they left the lower floors to fall apart? It's criminal. Especially when there's this."

"It is. The Bradbury has landmark status. Unfortunately, this does not. You probably noticed the drop ceilings on the first floor? Same thing on two and three. They're like this underneath. Not in as good shape, but restorable. I'm on a committee that's been trying to get this building declared a landmark too. So far, without success. No money and not enough interest from the county and opposition from a developer who'd like to see the recorder's office relocated then pick this up for a song."

"Wouldn't he want the landmark status, at least after he bought it on the cheap? Wouldn't it make the building much more valuable?"

"If it were to get landmark status, the value would skyrocket, but there'd be restrictions on restoration and upgrades, making it much more expensive to develop. The seismic work alone would be expensive, but under the landmark guidelines, it would be prohibitive, making the financial outcome for a developer, iffy. There'd also be restrictions on who the occupants could be, which might be the kiss of death for it as a commercial project. He's very influential. He's got the county thinking that if they don't have the money to restore it themselves, maybe it's better off in his hands to restore it outside of the landmark restrictions. Better than using it until it falls apart. Maybe they're right. My feeling is he wants to pick it up cheap, restore it outside the landmark guidelines, rent it to the highest bidders, then turn around and get landmark status when he's done. It wouldn't be the same building, but it would be the best of all worlds for him. The building would be worth a fortune, the improvements and type of tenants grand-fathered in, the value only enhanced by the belated landmark status."

He looked resigned.

"So why this one floor then?"

He smiled.

"I've enlisted the volunteer help of some architecture students from UCLA and USC. We got a little grant money from some admirers of Wyman and alumni of the architecture departments of both schools. We're all hoping that by restoring this room, we can generate enough interest to get the landmark status without turning it over to a commercial developer. We've been working on it weekends for six years."

"And?"

"Dolan's still got the inside track. Unless there's a change of heart, or some extra money is found in the county's budget, we're scheduled to be out of here in 1992. The building would be put on the market 'as is', which is exactly what he wants."

"Dolan? Not J.W. Dolan?" I asked, not even trying to keep the surprise out of my voice.

"Yes, the Beverly Hills councilman. Do you know him?"

"I've come across the name linked to Paragon Properties and The Beverly Hills Development Corporation and The Beverly Hills Management Group. Same guy?"

"The one and only."

"And he's the same guy, the councilman?"

"Yes, why?"

"He's a large part of the reason I'm here. I came to research connections between him and a J.T. Dolan and Elizabeth Dolan and some others. And those development companies. They were all involved in convoluted ways with multiple properties on the block where I grew up."

"I've done a little background research on him myself. Maybe I can be of some help."

Three hours later, and half a dozen trips between the first and fourth floors, I'd learned plenty.

# Chapter 16

## *Saturday at The Carwash*
## June 9, 1951

WHEN I GOT TO WHERE Upper and Lower Santa Monica met Beverly Boulevard, I could tell that it wasn't too close to ten yet because Joseph hadn't put the stools in front of the counter or the tables and chairs out on the side of the hot dog stand, which is what he did just before he was ready to open. He usually opened later on Saturdays and Sundays, at the same time the carwash opened, but not all the time, depending on how he felt, I guess, so I knew it was probably only about nine-thirty or nine-forty at the latest and I'd have time to go to the Wonder Bread Factory. Joseph looked up and saw me and waved. The other carwash guys were already there. Jackson and William had on their tall rubber boots and were filling buckets with soapy water and getting the blue cloth rags laid out on the worktable, ready to go. Maurice and Dennis were standing at the counter waiting for Joseph to finish pouring coffee so they could have coffee and one last smoke before things got crazy. Mr. Avery wouldn't let them smoke anywhere near the gas pumps, anywhere on the whole lot, really. They had to go onto the sidewalk, so they always got their coffee and then, if I were around, like at lunchtime, they said to me "smoke 'em if you got 'em, and don't be leavin' no butts out there on the street," and laughed like I might really smoke too. I knew they were just joking me, but every week they said it like this time I might actually do it. Jackson and William and Maurice and Dennis had all been in the war too, Mr. Avery said, in a special part of the Marines just for Negroes. They didn't tell stories about the war like Ozzie or Kevin Doyle or even funny crazy stories like Kenny Lester was going to tell me, but they mentioned it in different ways. Like when it got really hot and the carwash was especially busy and there wasn't any time to stop and take a break or have a smoke or even get a coke from the hot dog stand, and so maybe Jackson would say something like, "We gonna die for sure today!" and Maurice would say, "War didn't kill your sorry ass, no carwash is gonna!" and the others would say, "That's right, brother, amen to that" and then as soon as there was a little break one of them would call out, "Smoke 'em if you got 'em" and look around for me and say, "You too, little brother, you too!" and they'd all laugh and go out to the sidewalk. They smoked a lot. Once, Dennis's hand slipped off the washrag as he was sloshing soapy water on the fender of a car and he cut his wrist on a sharp edge just inside it. I was right next to him because my job was washing the hubcaps and whitewalls on all the cars, and the blood spurted out like it'd been shot from a squirt gun right onto my t-shirt. It reminded me of the fountain at the park near Carl's Market, shooting up into the air and dropping down, except here it mixed with the soapy water on the ground. At first he didn't seem to know what happened. He just looked at the cut and watched the blood spraying out. Then, all of a sudden he started yelling, "I'm hit! Christ, I'm hit! Oh Jesus, I'm hit!" and he dropped down on his knees and couldn't seem to move or do anything. William and Jackson and Maurice ran over and Jackson wrapped a clean washrag around his wrist and Maurice took off his belt and tightened it around Dennis's upper arm so tight that the bleeding stopped. Almost stopped, anyway. They huddled around him and kept looking every which way, first at the sky, like what had cut him had come from up there, and then around the whole lot, looking this way, then that, making sure to protect him from whatever they could, until Mr. Avery came and snapped them out of it and put Dennis in his car and took him to the emergency room at Saint John's Hospital They came back a couple of hours later and Dennis had a big bandage around his wrist and said he was fine and had a smoke with Maurice and Jackson and William out on the sidewalk before they all left for the day.

I went past the carwash the half block to the driveway of the Wonder Bread factory, then tiptoed down it and peeked around the corner to see the parking lot and loading dock. The dock was full of trucks, six or seven of them, and there were still lots of trucks in the lot waiting for their turn to be loaded. Saturdays were always busy, but this was pretty late for so many trucks to still be there. At least there wouldn't be any of the boss guys to chase me out. I went straight for the pastry section and Helen. She worked Saturdays from five in the morning until noon, and I thought she'd still be working. I pushed the swinging doors open and there she was.

"Hiya sweetie, how are you?"

"Good, how're you?"

"Good baby, really good. Lookin' forward to getting' offa my feets pretty soon, but I'm real good. Gonna take the grandkids to the beach this afternoon. Oughta be nice. Maybe I'll dip these big hot feet in all that cool water. Won't that be nice? How'd your girlfriend like the Bear Claws the other day?"

"Helen! She's not my girlfriend. Just my friend. She loved them. Thanks again."

"You're welcome. Gonna be a hot one at the carwash. Got somethin' in your stomach yet?"

"I was hoping you had some of the bent up Bear Claws."

"Well, of course we do, even if we gotta bend them a little our own selves. You want to take your black brothers a little somthin'?" she asked me.

'Sure," I said, "they're all there having coffee and smoking."

"You give 'em each one of these, and tell 'em to be good to each other, and especially good to you. Hear?"

She hugged me and I was off.

I could feel the heat coming up through my tennis shoes from the blacktop, and not just because they had the holes in them. It was going to be burning hot today, but I kept thinking about getting paid and going to the bike shop and giving Bill the five dollars. That would be cooler than dipping my feet in the ocean, I thought.

"Want a hot chocolate to go with that?" Joseph said, nodding at the bag from Helen.

"Too hot. How 'bout just a glass of cold milk?"

"You got it."

The clock on the wall behind Joseph showed a couple of minutes before ten.

"You want a Bear Claw? Helen gave me a bunch of extras for the guys."

"Sure, thanks."

I took one out of the bag and put it on a paper plate he'd set on the counter. He poured the milk and I put a nickel on the counter.

"Your money's no good here when you're working', pal," he smiled.

"Thank you."

William and Maurice and Dennis and Jackson came back from the sidewalk and I gave them each a Bear Claw. They gobbled them up in about one bite and licked their fingers and thanked me. I told them what Helen had said.

"You thank her for us, hear?" Jackson said.

"I will," I told them.

There hadn't been any boots at the carwash that were my size, so Mr. Avery had gotten the smallest ones he could find at the Beverly Hills Hardware store at Canon and Wilshire and kept them in the storage room where he kept all that kind of stuff, and said they were just for me, every Saturday. Even if they were the smallest, they were still way too big and when I walked, my feet started moving before the boots did, but they were better than working in my leaky tennis shoes, that was for sure, so I put them on, tucked my jeans into them, got a bucket with the soapy water and a clean rag and the brush for the whitewalls and took my place along the white stripe that came in off the driveway on the North Elm Street side of the lot where the big sign was that said, Carwash $1.75, Tuesday--Friday 10 a.m to 3 p.m. Saturday-Sunday 10 a.m. to 4:30 p.m., Closed Mondays. It directed cars to us carwash guys. There was a rope across the driveway between two posts that kept the cars off the lot until it was time to open. There were already eight or nine cars lined up. Jackson took the rope down and the first six cars came onto the lot and stopped at boxes painted onto the blacktop, three on each side of the white line.

When we would first open, Mr. Avery himself would greet the customers as they got out of their cars and he'd take the money for the wash. Later, Maurice was the greeter, but Mr. Avery usually hung around and steered customers over to Joseph's Hot Dog Stand, where they could wait out of the sun. Besides the stools at the counter, on Saturdays, there'd be half a dozen round tables set up between the hot dog stand and the Alden Drive side of the lot. They had wrought-iron legs and glass tops with shade umbrellas on posts that stuck down through a hole in the middle and four or five chairs around each one. Most of Mr. Avery's customers were regulars, guys that came every Saturday morning, or maybe every other one, but often enough so they knew each other pretty well, and knew me and Maurice and Jackson and Dennis and William and especially Mr. Avery. They laughed and joked a lot, had coffee and cigarettes and hot dogs and cokes while they sat at the tables and told stories. Mr. Avery never made them go to the sidewalk to smoke. Most of them stayed a long time, way after their cars were already washed, so Jackson or Dennis would come up to them and hand their car keys back and they'd move it out of the way, or they might ask Jackson or Dennis to do it, so others could get in for a wash. Pretty soon the lot was full of sparkling clean cars parked all over the place, with the North Elm Street side still full of cars waiting to get in and the wash area full of cars being washed and just about any other space on the lot about to be filled up with even more clean cars. That's what I mean by crazy Saturdays. It got so busy I wouldn't have any idea what time it was and the next thing I knew, Mr. Avery would be handing me my two-fifty. All of us carwash guys had our favorite customers, some of them because they gave tips, which was extra money just for doing our job. Maurice and the others put the tips in a big pickle jar that Joseph gave them that they kept at one end of the hot dog counter, until at the end of the day, they divided it up. They offered me a share of it too, which I thought was pretty nice of them, but I said they should keep it because they did the hardest work, but really, I didn't want it because it seemed like stealing to me. I was already getting paid by Mr. Avery, so taking the tip money didn't seem right. Anyway, my dad said the Negroes and Mexicans had it pretty hard making ends meet in this town, so I thought they should just divide it up themselves.

The fourth car on the lot this morning was Pop. The third was Bill Boyd, Hop-a-Long Cassidy! His name was really William, but he said I could either call him Bill or Hop-a-long. I'd told Gene and Allen and Jeff Schumur and Sarah and some of the others from the Oakhurst Ir-regulars that I saw him every Saturday, and they could come see him too, if they stayed out of the way, but they didn't believe me. At least Sarah said she didn't and Jeff Schumur and Robbie Ganz agreed with her. Why would a big TV star come to a little carwash in our neighbor-hood? I couldn't think of a reason, but here he was, so he must have had one. Gene believed me, but he said his father would probably say no and maybe get mad on top of it and it wasn't worth it so he never came, and I know Allen believed me, but said he thought Hop-a-Long was for little kids, so he never came to see him either. I knew he was really for little kids too, but it was fun to see him anyway. He and Pop were friends, just from the carwash, I think, and they'd find a table together and talk while we washed their cars. Pop had a '48 Oldsmobile that was really nice, a powder blue, four-door V-8 with a Hydramatic, but Bill Boyd's car was just amazing. It was a brand new, 1951 Cadillac convertible. I supposed it had a big engine and some kind of a Hydramatic too, and it was a very pretty dark red, with white leather seat covers, and the kind of whitewall tires where the white part was extra wide, but the best part was, on the hood, where the Cadillac gizmo should have been, there were huge horns instead. Not the kind you honk, but real horns, like from a cow or bull, because he was a cowboy. I told them, all of the kids in the neighborhood and the Oakhurst Irregulars, it was worth coming to see Hop-a-Long just for that, but only Marty showed up to see it. He said he thought it was pretty silly, kinda cool, but mostly pretty silly. I thought so too, but Bill Boyd was also very nice and didn't make a big deal because he was Hop-a-Long. Well, in a way he did, because every week, at least every Saturday when I saw him, he wore all black outfits with white pearl buttons and a big white cowboy hat and white boots with a curvy design made out of red and green rhinestones set in silver rings. But he was nice. He'd take off the hat and put it on the table and run his hands through his hair, which was completely white. He looked older in person than he did on TV, and fatter, and I wondered about his horse having to carry him around everywhere. He didn't like to have the top up at all, I guess, because even at the carwash it was down, which meant that Maurice and Dennis and Jackson and William had to work especially carefully not to get water or soap on the inside. It didn't make any difference to me, because hubcaps and whitewalls were just hubcaps and whitewalls no matter what car they were on. Some of the fancier cars, like Pop's and Bill Boyd's, had skirts that hid most of the back wheels. They were made to fit so they'd look like just a part of the back fender. At each end of the skirt, along the bottom edge, there were two little levers that you had to twist one way or the other, and that unhooked something that let the skirt come off. The only problem was the levers could be stuck, or sometimes even if I got the lever to turn, the skirt wouldn't unhook and come off and I'd have to get one of the other carwash guys to help me, but usually I could do it myself. There was a special table just for them and either I'd put them there or whoever helped me would, and then they'd be washed separately and put back on the car, for sure by one of the others, because they were heavy and hard to get into the right position, and if you didn't do it right, Mr. Avery said you could really scratch things up. Maurice had a little whiskbroom that he kept in the back pocket of his overalls, and he jumped into the first car and swept it out. In his other back pocket he had a spray bottle with some kind of cleaner in it and he sprayed and he wiped down everything until the whole inside was clean and smelled good. As soon as he was done Jackson was wetting the first two cars with clean water from a hose with a spray nozzle on it. As soon as he finished, Dennis and William started sloshing soapy water and rubbing every inch and especially the chrome parts while I did the hubcaps and whitewalls on one side, then the other. While we did that, Jackson was already wetting down the next two cars, Pop's and Bill Boyd's, and first Maurice, then me and Dennis and William started in on them while Jackson rinsed off the first two. Maurice took clean blue cloth towels and began to dry off the first two cars, and Jackson helped him. And that's how we did it. All day long. By noon, we must have done twenty-five or thirty cars, but they were still lined up on North Elm like we hadn't done any. It was like that every Saturday. They just kept coming and coming. My hands got absolutely clean and pink and completely wrinkled, and my arms got so tired I could hardly lift the brush for the whitewalls, but the cars just kept coming. Finally, Mr. Avery came over and said we should take a break for lunch. We finished the six cars that were in the boxes along the white line, dried them and made them sparkle, and Maurice put the rope back up across the driveway. You could tell that the drivers who were about to be next were a little mad because everything came to a stop when we had lunch, but most of them were good sports about it and came over to the lunch counter and had something to eat while they waited. I could see the clock behind Joseph and it was almost one-thirty. There was one more of the Bear Claws from Helen, but I didn't really feel like that for lunch. Maurice and William and Dennis and Jackson had brought sandwiches in paper bags, as usual, and got cokes from Joseph and went to the North Elm side and down the block away from the carwash for what they called their 'sit-down' on the grass of the parkway under a tree in the shade. It was probably an Elm tree.

"You look pretty beat, buddy. Maybe you oughta take my seat here." It was Kenny Lester. He got off a stool and let me have it.

"Thanks," I said. "I'm pooped. Did we wash your car?"

"About fifteen minutes ago. You guys do nice work. It looks great." He pointed to the pale yellow Buick across the lot to the Beverly Boulevard side. We'd gotten so busy I didn't even notice him or his car.

"What's it gonna be?" Joseph asked me.

"The usual," I told him, "and a coke please."

"This kid don't eat nothin' but sweets from the factory there, or pickles and mustard sandwiches," he said.

But he got me the pickles and mustard. The pickles chips were on a paper plate and the mustard was a brand new jar he put in front of me. He kept working hamburgers and hot dogs around on the grill. The smell of them was making me a little dizzy. The guy next to me left, and Kenny took his seat.

"You get yourself some bread there this morning, or just the Bear Claws?"

"Rats!" I said, "no bread."

"You want white or wheat or rye?"

"This is fine," I said.

While he was talking to me, Joseph took a hamburger off the grill and put it on the bottom of a bun and put pickles, tomatoes, cheese and lettuce on top of the meat, spread some mayonnaise and a little mustard on the top bun, put it on a paper plate and handed it to Kenny. He put a coke in front of me and another in front of Kenny. I took a spoon from a glass full of silverware in front of me and scooped a blob of mustard onto the plate, licked the spoon clean and took one of the pickle chips and dipped it into the mustard and ate it.

"Why don't we share this?" Kenny said to me. "I don't think I can eat it all. And besides, you gotta eat if you're going to work."

The hamburger smelled so good I had that silvery taste at the back of my mouth from a lot of saliva getting there all of a sudden. I thought about it. Pop and Bill Boyd were still there at the same table, not very far away, talking. Pop was watching me. When he saw that I saw him watching me and Kenny, finally he smiled and waved. I waved back. Kenny looked to where I was looking, saw Pop and nodded hello.

"No thanks," I said. "This is fine."

"See what I mean?" Joseph said working the grill some more. He kept making hot dogs and hamburgers and handing them across the counter to a steady stream of guys whose cars we'd already washed or ones we'd have to after lunch. The stools were all full and there was someone at every one of the chairs around tables and a bunch of guys standing and all of them were eating and drinking stuff that Joseph made, so it was the usual crazy Saturday for him too.

Which reminded me.

"You were in the war, right."

"The duration, plus six, kid."

"So was Kenny."

"Yeah?" Joseph said. "What branch?"

"Army Air," Kenny said. He took a knife out of the silverware glass and cut the burger in half. He started eating the first half and sipped at his coke. I had another pickle dipped in the mustard and nibbled at it.

"Action?"

"Yes."

"Bad?" Joseph said.

"Some, some not. You?"

"All bad. Made it through all kinds of ugly stuff without a scratch, then towards the end, got shot and nearly lost my feet to frostbite at the Bulge. All bad. Europe?"

"No, the Pacific."

"Now that's the life," Joseph said. "If you gotta have someone shootin' at you, at least you oughta be warm. We used to tell each other if we got outta there alive, we'd sign on for after the war if we could just go to the Pacific and be warm. Geez, we were so damn cold. We used to cram together huggin' like a bunch of kids on a campout. Good guys, though. Took care of each other. Didn't all make it back, but it wasn't for lack of trying."

"Amen to that," Maurice said. He and the other guys were back from their North Elm sit down for another coke.

Joseph refilled his, then Jackson and Dennis and William's.

"You too?" Kenny said.

"Only reason we here," Jackson said. "Took care of each other."

The four of them were crowded in close to me and Kenny, surrounding us on the stools.

"Only reason I'm here," Joseph said. "You ever heard of the 761st? The Black Panthers?"

"No," Kenny said.

"Well, we were the 106th Infantry in the Ardennes, near Saint Vith, north of Bastogne. Three regiments, the 422nd, 423rd and 424th. Our lines were thin since no one expected anything would come our way, about a third the strength you'd normally have for a front that size. So, on December 16, outta nowhere, all of a sudden we're getting' pounded, beat up by artillery, tanks, 30 calibers, our units scattered to hell and gone, not even sure where the lines were anymore and afraid of shooting each other. The 424th was south of us and managed to pull back and get the hell out of there before it was too late. The Krauts are trying to run right through us, coming in waves, first close, then really close, hand-to-hand and you can see they're crazy-eyed and wild. Later, we figured they musta been on drugs. But that was later. At the time, all we knew it was like fighting demons. They just keep coming. Killing didn't even seem to stop them. Three days of it and we've slowed them down but the 423rd gets overrun and has to surrender. One whole regiment gone, just like that. We're giving up a little ground, but making them work for it, but were pretty much up shit creek, alone, almost surrounded and running out of everything. We're hanging on, but hoping for some help and then we hear the 101st is fighting their way in to reinforce us, but next thing you now, they get as far as Bastogne and they're trapped too. They hadn't brought much with them, not much food, not much medicine, so they're in as bad a shape as we are. We're running out of ammo, all but surrounded, getting pounded day and night, it's unbelievably cold, and the weather's so bad there's no chance for air support or a supply drop. A couple of days before Christmas and it looks like were completely fucked…" Joseph looked at me, "sorry, kid…looks like we've had it. You can't see twenty feet in front of you for all the fog and snow and trees. We get orders to reposition ourselves, tighten up, get the healthiest guys and ammo in position to hold off another surge. I saw a couple of stragglers and yelled to them we were falling back to a mound fifty yards to the rear. They didn't seem to hear me, so I yelled at them again. They turned towards me and started shooting. They were Krauts! Forty feet away! Walking around the place like they owned it or something. I got it in the side, not too bad, but bad enough. I returned fire, a couple of my guys heard and came back and we drove them off. The next two days weren't as bad for us, but we could tell Bastogne was getting a pretty good dose. By Christmas I didn't know which was worse, the Krauts looking to finish us, the wound in my side, or my freezing feet. A couple of my guys kept my wound packed with snow and that helped, but we'd pretty much used up everything we had holding them off 'til then. We figured the next serious run they took at us, they'd overrun us for sure. The day after Christmas we could feel the rumble of half a dozen tanks, and thought that was that, but they were coming from the south, and it was the sweet ugly sound and smell of Shermans. They forced themselves between us and the Krauts, pushed the Krauts back with canon and 30 caliber fire, cut them off from their supply lines by taking a stretch of the Houffalize-Bastogne Road, and kept them off balance most of the day until more of Patton's 3$^{rd}$ showed up. When the crew of the M4 closest to me popped open their lid and these black faces poked out like muddy prairie dogs, my first thought was they was just guys covered with dirt and diesel. Then this guy here says, 'You just gonna lie there bleedin', or you gonna offer us Black Panthers somethin' to drink?' Smiles that big tooth smile of his."

"Amen, brother," Maurice said. He reached across the counter and he and Joseph shook in this way they had, not shaking hands, but instead, going past each other's outstretched hands and grabbing each other at the forearm. Jackson and Dennis and William put their hands on top of Joseph and Maurice's locked arms.

"A little prayer for Raymond," Maurice said.

They bowed their heads.

"Raymond," Maurice said.

"Amen," they all said.

They stepped back. Maurice looked at Kenny.

"Raymond was the fifth man in our crew. Killed a few days later."

Kenny nodded. He used his elbow to shove the paper plate with the second half of the hamburger in front of me.

"I'm full," he said.

Joseph was standing right in front of me. He pushed the paper plate a little closer.

"Hate to see my cookin' go to waste. Why don't you at least nibble on it?"

I looked around and couldn't see anything except the overalls of the carwash guys and now another eight or ten guys who'd come up surrounding us too, standing there listening to Joseph. The hamburger still smelled good so I picked it up and dipped a corner of it into the blob of mustard on my plate and took a big bite. A couple more and it was gone. That and the coke and I didn't feel dizzy anymore. Joseph was done with his story, but no one left. They were drinking coffee or cokes and eating, but they just stayed there standing around, some in the sun and some in the shade of the little awning thing over the stools on the front side of the hot dog stand, like they were waiting for something and didn't want to go until it happened instead of getting their cars, or going back to the tables they'd been at, or saying anything.

"Thanks, Kenny," I said, "that was good."

Kenny smiled at me but he was watching Joseph.

"Amen," Maurice said again as he nodded to Joseph. Then to Kenny, "You see any of them island girls? They got a good dark skin on 'em? Right?"

"Not dark as you," Jackson said. "Now you just dreamin'."

"Dark enough," Maurice said to Jackson. "You musta seen some island girls, right?" he asked Kenny.

"Yes. Some," Kenny said, smiling.

"I knew it!" Maurice said. "And they was dark?"

Kenny laughed.

"Yeah, pretty dark."

"See," Maurice said to Jackson, "I told you. If we coulda' just got the hell out of France!"

"We did get outta France," Dennis said. "That's all the getting' out I needed."

"Amen to that," William said.

It was about quarter to two on the clock behind Joseph, so we still had fifteen minutes before we had to start again.

"Tell me just one story about the island girls before we go back," Maurice said.

Kenny thought for about just one second, and said, "How about an island girl and a pig?"

"A pig?" Dennis said.

"Just so long as the island girl and the pig ain't the same one," Maurice said.

"No, a pig and an island girl," Kenny said.

"That's good. That's good," Maurice said, "tell us 'bout that."

"Our crew trained together in Fairfield, outside Sacramento. Just a bunch of dumb kids. Same crew from beginning to end."

"Never lost anyone?" Dennis asked.

"No, not really. We had a replacement once for two weeks, dumbass son-of-a-bitch almost got me killed, but our crew went through it, came through it together. We ended up in the 5th Air Force, 380th Bomb Group, 528th Bomb Squad in Darwin, Australia. In the month before we were assigned to the 380th, we went from California to Hawaii to Canton Island to Guadalcanal to Australia then to Port Moresby in New Guinea. They had us flying from one base to another of the three in New Guinea and back to Australia and back to New Guinea and back to Australia again for a month. Finally we were assigned to a field in Darwin. Once we got settled there, we went on long missions to the Phillipines and back. We had a lot of time on the ground because the turnaround time was so long that they'd give you extra down time to rest, which was nice. We'd get drunk with the Aussies, look for girls, swim in the clearest, warmest water you can imagine. You could almost forget there was a war on. Then the damn Marines took Mindoro and we got moved. Shitty little strip carved out of the jungle, hardly room to get in and out. We were flying shorter missions, and more of them, so less time on the ground. Not much time for anything but flying, dropping bombs, coming back to reload and do it again. The brass had it pretty nice though, comfortable quarters, girls from the nearby village cleaning their tents, cooking, stuff like that."

"Stuff like that," Maurice said, with a big smile to Jackson and Dennis and William. "That's what I'm talkin' about!"

Kenny said, "With all the trips we were making, when we were on the ground, all we wanted to do was get drunk and sleep. Maybe find an island girl."

"See?" Maurice said.

"Our C.O. was some sixty-day wonder, thought the war was going to be the start of a big military career he'd parlay into something political back home, so he wanted everyone in uniform, wanted us to fly extra missions so we'd run up some record numbers, wanted everyone's tent regulation, the whole ball of wax. He didn't go up at all, but he'd volunteer us for special runs, then when we finally had some down time, he turn our tent upside down with his damn inspections. It was hot, so unless we were flying, I seldom got out of my shorts and a t-shirt, pair of sandals I got off a native from the village. He'd say, 'Lester, if you don't put on some khakis instead of that rat's ass t-shirt and those shorts, I'm gonna court martial you.' And I'd tell him, 'So do it. Quit threatening me. I don't like getting shot at. I don't like flack coming up through the floor trying to take my balls off. I don't like you and I don't like this war, so do it or shut the fuck up.'"

Kenny looked at me for just a second and sort of shrugged and smiled, like he'd apologize or something later.

"And he'd just walk away saying something like, 'And clean up your goddamn tent! It's a disgrace! We got almost a hundred flight crews, and you guys are the worst. The absolute worst! I've never seen such a bunch of pigs.'"

"So the village that was closest to the strip made this hooch from some fruit or other that grew on the trees around there and we'd trade for it."

"What about the girl?" Maurice asked.

"I'm getting there," Kenny said. "We just wanted to get drunk and stay drunk and be left alone when we were on the ground. But our C.O. was serious about the inspections. Especially if we had visiting brass on the island, he'd make sure to throw a surprise inspection to impress them, and if a crew's tent looked good, so did he, and if it was bad, like ours, he'd threaten to subtract flight hours, which also made him look good, since he'd be squeezing extra flights out of us. You know what that means?" Kenny asked Maurice.

"No," William answered before Maurice could.

"When we got to 275 hours of combat flight time, we were supposed to go back to Honolulu. No more getting shot at. So if he subtracted hours, we'd have to fly more missions."

"Could he really do that?" Dennis asked.

"He could do any goddamn thing he wanted!" Kenny said.

"So, what'd you do?"

"Well, at first it didn't seem to matter. We weren't close to the 275, and none of us figured we'd live that long anyway, so we didn't worry about it. But as we got closer, at around 220 hours or so, it started to

seem more important, like we might actually get there. He'd already subtracted twenty hours, so we kept the place a little cleaner. Not much, but
some. I even started wearing my khaki pants. Sandals, no shirt, but the
khaki pants. When our crew had a little over 250 hours, they announced
that the number was being increased to 380 instead. We figured, fuck
'im, we'd never live to see 380, so why bother with the tent or regulation
clothes."

"And the girl?" Maurice and Joseph said at the same exact time, and
looked at each other and laughed.

"She was about seventeen. Pretty as can be. Wore a little thing here,"
he pointed to his waist, " and a little thing here," he said pointing to his
chest, "and flowers in her hair. Built real nice. Just pretty as can be."

"All right, now," Maurice said.

"Her cousin, or some damn thing, a little older, maybe twenty-four or
twenty-five and a couple of her friends, all around the same age, were
cleaning the headquarters tent and the tents of the administrative officers.
Did a little cookin', a little laundry, a little of this and that, if you know
what I mean…" Kenny said, sort of looking at me, then at all the guys
standing around listening to him. "They hung around most of the day and
most of the night too."

"This an' that!" Maurice said. "I know what you mean. I surely do!"

I didn't, but I thought maybe Kenny would tell me later, when he
wasn't in the middle of the story.

"The village had an old diesel generator that probably dated back to
the 'Twenties to run a few electrical circuits in the main lodge, a sort of
communal building. But they couldn't get fuel for it anymore. So we
worked out a deal where we'd steal some from our supply depot, with a
little help from the supply sergeant, him getting some of the hooch, and
trade it to the village for the booze. The problem was getting them the
fuel and getting us the hooch. Since the C.O. was so determined to have
us keep the tent clean, we just happened to mention there was a girl in
the village, not one of his girls, because that would've killed the deal,
but another girl, that was willing to come clean for us, if that was okay
with him. He thought it was great. So we arranged for her to come once
a week. We snuck her in at the back of our little tent village where all
the flight crews lived when we were on the ground. She could have just
walked in the front gate, past the MP's, since they were used to seeing
the other girls come and go, but to carry the hooch in and the diesel out,
she needed this little cart that was pulled by the biggest fucking pig you
ever saw. She'd have a couple of gallons of the hooch under a blanket,
come to the back of our tent from the edge of the jungle and we'd unload
the hooch, load her up with the diesel, and off she'd go."

"Off she'd go?" Maurice said. "Of she'd go? What's that about?"

Kenny laughed, "Well, she was really kind of innocent. Pretty and
sweet, but more like a kid sister."

"Man, she might be someone's sister, but she weren't your sister!"
Maurice said.

"No," Kenny said, "but still…"

"Tell me there's more," Maurice said, "please, tell me there's more!"

"There's more," Kenny said. "So, to make it look good, in case the C.O. was paying attention, she'd stick around sometimes. She didn't clean or anything. Maybe she'd give you a haircut, take you down to the river and wash your hair, get rid of all the loose stuff, sort of give you a bath. That was pretty nice."

"Pretty nice?" Dennis laughed, "any you guys remember the Krauts givin' us a haircut and bath?"

"She'd turn the pig loose from the cart if she was going to hang around a while. So, this one time, she'd given a few of us haircuts, and we'd been splashing around in the river for an hour or two. The hooch was unloaded, the diesel loaded and hidden under the blankets, and she was ready to go, but we couldn't find the pig. Our whole crew was outside looking high and low, but no pig. Not down by the river, not at the edge of the jungle, hadn't wandered on to the runways. Nowhere. So of course, that's when the damn C.O. shows up with some visiting brass. Three of them. We can see them going into the tents of some of the other crews, and we're all just willing them away, hoping they won't get all the way down to us. But he sees all of us outside together, like it's an invitation or something, and he also sees the girl and figures we've just had our tent cleaned, so he skips a couple other tents and comes straight for ours. "Lester," he says, "what have I told you about being in uniform?" I'm wearing khaki pants, the sandals and no shirt. He says it with a smile, like we're pals. He starts bragging to the visiting brass about what a good crew we are, how many missions we've flown, how many extra mission hours he's added for our sloppy dress, gives me and Jack Banks, our pilot and aircraft commander a big wink, like were all buddies and it's a game we're playing, him subtracting hours, us flying the extra missions, ack ack punching holes through our plane, zeros coming at us like mosquitoes, just one big joke, and so on, until one of the brass says, "It's pretty fucking hot out here, Colonel, let's inspect this tent and find something cold to drink. How's that sound?" And the C.O. smiles his suck-up little smile, and says, "Just fine, sir." They all have a nice little laugh and duck into the front part of our tent. It's sort of like a living room, divided off from where our cots are. Our C.O. stays outside with us while the brass go in. Next thing we hear, "Colonel, get in here!" The smile goes off his face and he ducks into our tent. We sort of follow him in. It wasn't any better or worse than usual, but it wasn't exactly regulation. The brass stood there silently demanding an explanation. Our C.O. takes one look around, turns beet-red and begins yelling at Jack, "Commander Banks, what's the meaning of this?! Are you in charge here, or is Lester? You guys have been bad in the past, but this is unbelievable! I've never seen such a mess! How can you live like this? You guys live like a bunch of pigs! Hell, a pig would be ashamed of this! This is the worst goddamn pigpen I've ever seen! I demand an explanation!" He's yelling pretty loud, and suddenly we hear a few startled grunts, and just then the pig comes roaring out of the back part of the tent where he'd been sleeping, the three visiting officers are screaming for their lives like they're in the middle of a stampede of water buffalo, the pig's tearing through the place, running in circles, crashing into the chairs and our little table, scattering everything that's already scattered all over the place, knocking one of the visiting brass into our C.O. and they both go down, and the pig charges right out the front, squealing all the way."

Joseph and Jackson and Dennis and William were laughing so hard they were wiping tears out of their eyes. So were most of the guys that were standing behind us. Maurice was laughing too, but I could tell he thought he'd been going to hear more about the girl. He looked at the clock behind Joseph and nodded at us carwash guys that it was time to go back to work.

"That's some crazy stuff, guy," Dennis said to Kenny Lester, and they shook hands; then Jackson and William and then, shaking his head and laughing, Maurice, who said to Kenny, "There's got to be more about the girl. Right? Right?!"

"Maybe another time," Kenny said, smiling.

The others, who'd been standing behind us in a half circle, came up and shook hands with Kenny. They were all smiling and looked pretty happy, Kenny too, and on top of it, they all had clean cars.

Kenny Lester's war was funny-crazy alright and I wanted to hear more of his stories.

Jackson took the rope down again from across the driveway on the North Elm Street side so the next group of six cars could come in. But just when he did, and before the first six cars in line could take their places in the boxes along the white line, a big black Cadillac convertible cut in front of all the waiting cars, honking and honking its horn. It was as big and fancy as Hop-a-Long's, but without the cow-horns. The top was down and I could see it had dark red leather seats and was being driven by a chauffer with a uniform and hat, and in back was Kevin Doyle, all dressed up in his special army stuff with the medals and ribbons pinned on, with two other older guys in the back seat with him. The car had fat red and white and blue paper ribbons attached to it, and signs on the back and both sides that said, DOLAN FOR MAYOR. The man in the middle must have been Dolan, because he made a big deal out of smiling and waving. He had the kind of smile Pop said an alligator smiles just before the first bite. When the car came to a stop, he stood up, waved some more, and acted like everybody had been waiting for him. Kevin Doyle looked pretty crabby, mean as usual, but mostly uncomfortable and unhappy, and I kind of felt sorry for him. Dolan motioned for everyone to gather around him. Me and the other carwash guys stood with our buckets and brushes and rags with nothing to do. Mr. Avery came out of the office.

"J.T., to what do we owe the pleasure?" he said.

"Avery, it's no secret this country's struggling to get back on its feet."

His voice was way too loud, and I could tell he wasn't really talking to Mr. Avery. He was what Pop called a blowhard, planning on making a speech to anyone who had ears, as Pop always said about blowhards.

"It's no secret lots of our boys, good, brave boys who did their duty for all of us, are out of work." He looked at Kevin. "Even some of our most decorated heroes. It's a crime! It's no secret that from Washington, D. C., right on down here to Los Angeles, California, we got a bunch of leaders that don't understand that to build a country back up, you got to BUILD!"

By now there was a pretty good crowd gathered around his car. Some of the people who were next in line had gotten half out of their cars, listening, but mostly angry that first lunch, now this guy, was keeping them off the lot. The sun was beating down hard and it was definitely hot and getting hotter. Mr. Avery had the same look for this Dolan guy that he'd had for Mr. Sullivan, like he didn't want to be mean, but didn't like him much, either. And besides, you couldn't wash cars and make any money if some blowhard was bringing everything to a stop.

"But here in Beverly Hills, we've had the benefit of a majority on the city council and a mayor who know the value of development. This good man here, your mayor and mine, F. Britton McConnell, has been fighting the good fight!" The other man waved to the crowd when his name was mentioned. "He's done a hell of a job, but there are those on the council who've fought him at every turn. This same bunch of do-nothings, know-nothings, this same little gang that's been fighting to hold back our city council and this mayor, are looking to take over. He's tired of it! He's sick of it! And I don't blame him. He's stepping down, and I'm stepping up! I'm doing this for all of you! Especially those of you who put on a uniform and fought for this great country, like my boy Kevin, here, we owe it to fight right here on the home front, to fight for you and to put you and America back to work. To build America! That's my goal. It's no secret that I'm a developer. I'm a builder! If we lose City Hall to those who can't see the right way to proceed, we're lost! Someone's got to step up and show them the way. I'd rather attend to my business, but this city needs me. If you think for one minute, my opponent and current councilman, Dean Olson and his gang, if elected, god forbid, are going to support development, my friends, you got another think coming!"

"Dolan," Kenny called out, "You've said your piece. I think you should get your car washed or get the hell out of the way!"

"Who said that?" Dolan said, the smile gone from his face. "This is serious business!"

"I did," Kenny said, going right up to Dolan's car.

Kevin Doyle's eyes had gone from unhappy and bored to angry and looking for a fight. They dug into Kenny, then they drifted over to me. I was thinking he was thinking about the locks and so was I. He shifted around and lit a cigarette, and it looked like maybe he was going to jump out of the car and fight with Kenny. Kenny just looked at Dolan and Kevin Doyle. He didn't seem to care what they might do. But Kevin

Doyle kept staring at me, like he could burn me up with those mean eyes. First Maurice, then Jackson and Dennis and William had put down their blue washrags and moved up close behind Kenny.

"J. T.," Mr. Avery said, "we need to wash some cars now."

Mr. Dolan could see he'd pretty much used up his welcome. The chauffer started the Cadillac, and slowly backed up.

Kevin Doyle had a nasty smile on his face and there was a cloud of cigarette smoke hanging around his head that followed him as the car moved. He waved a warning finger at me.

Maurice looked at Kevin, sort of puzzled, then at me, then back to Kevin. He looked at William and Jackson and Dennis. When he turned back to Kevin, he wasn't smiling. He waved the same warning finger at Kevin.

# Chapter 17

## *Dolan for Mayor*
### Wednesday, August 9, 1989

WHEN I LEFT the recorder's office I had the feeling I knew where this was going to go. Tad Matsumoto had done his homework on Dolan and had been able to guide me to the information I wanted. At least most of it.

The offices for the Beverly Hills city councilmen were in the new City Hall on North Rexford, a nicely done art-deco building, part of the same complex of buildings that housed the police department. It was a little before one. The morning had started out sunny, clear and mild. While I'd been in the recorder's office, it had become one of those Southern California days where the sun beats down with a vengeance. Heat seemed to be coming from off the sidewalk and parked cars. Even the huge glass windows in the storefronts mirrored it back, magnifying it as I drove past. There was no escape from it. It may have accounted for the lack of activity in general, and the unusual abundance of parking in particular. It may have also accounted for my rashness. At least that's my story and I'm sticking to it. I found a space and parked. There were police cars parked in spaces reserved for them. There were other official vehicles from Building and Planning, and Health and Safety, and an assortment of meter maid carts. I'd decided to just confront Dolan. No real plan, no list of particulars ready to throw in his face, no series of questions, the answers to which I would have already known, as Nick might do in a cross-examination, bless him, but just a sense of here I am, here you are, and what are you going to do about it? It seemed like a good idea at the time.

"Hey, Cowboy, you comin' to see me? I was beginnin' to worry a little."

It was Phillips. I'd almost completely forgotten about him.

"As a matter of fact, no," I told him.

"You don't know how much that hurts," he said.

His sardonic smile was working nicely and it seemed he was prepared to forgive me.

"Then whatcha doin' here?"

"I'm here to see Mr. J.W. Dolan."

Or maybe not.

"Whoa there, hoss," he put his hand on my shoulder, more symbolically restraining me than actually holding me back. But if I pulled away, I had the feeling he'd get more insistent.

"Just what kind of trouble you lookin' for now? How 'bout we go up to my office and you fill me in on what you've remembered from the parcel map? How's that sound?"

He was smiling again, pretty sure of himself.

"What about my appointment with Dolan? You want me to just stand him up?"

"Jesus Christ! You' made an appointment with him?"

I smiled and shrugged.

Phillips' hand dropped to his side. His smile faded. He had this funny look on his face that seemed to acknowledge that he'd brought this on himself by forcing me into his little investigation. He wanted to say something to dissuade me, and his agitation seemed to confirm some of my suspicions about the politics of his investigation, but he recovered a bit and shrugged.

"Well, aren't you just the loose canon?" he said.

"Could be," I said, as I headed for the entrance.

Dolan's secretary wasn't about to just usher me into his office for an impromptu conference. She made it clear how busy he always was with his business and civic responsibilities, and now with the election, seeing him without an appointment was impossible. The phone kept ringing, she'd answer, take a message, promise Dolan would return their call, and come back to me. Making an appointment, it seemed, was also impossible. She consulted her calendar. She flipped through August, September, October, November and even December shaking her head no, no, no. A couple of calls must have been important, because she told them she'd put them through as soon as his line was open, and put them on hold. At least I knew he was here.

"Maybe early next year," she said, "after the election and after he gets settled into the Mayor's office."

She smiled. Apparently, Dolan was a shoe-in.

"I'm only here for a couple of days," I said. "I'd hate to speak with Mayor Tannenbaum and Councilman Salter and not with Mr. Dolan."

According to Tad Matsumoto, Salter was a councilman allied with the current Mayor, Tannenbaum, running against Dolan to replace him.

That got her interest.

"Just what is the nature of your business?" she asked, a little more pointedly now.

The phone continued to ring but now she ignored it.

"I'm working as a consultant for the Beverly Hills Police Department in a murder investigation. My participation is only quasi-formal, but they insisted I fly down here and help, and I thought if I were getting cooperation from Mayor Tannenbaum and councilman Salter, I could expect the same from Mr. Dolan."

"A murder investigation? What are you talking about? What could Mr. Dolan possibly know about something like that? Just what sort or cooperation did you have in mind?"

"I really can't get into the details of the investigation. I understand that you're his gatekeeper. You have your job to do."

I took the little watch out of my pocket. It was almost 1:30.

"I've got to see the mayor and Mr. Salter soon," I lied. "If you could mention the name, Kevin Doyle, to Mr. Dolan, I think he might like to talk with me."

She just stared at me. The phone kept ringing and flashing.

"I won't be anywhere where I can be reached, but I could call a little later to see if he's been able to make time for me. Okay?"

"Sure," she said, her smile a tight little line across her face. "I'll let him know you were here."

"Thank you," I said, taking two of councilman Dolan's cards from the little holder on her desk. I wrote my name on one and gave it to her. I kept the other.

As I was exiting the City Hall building, before the heavy brass and glass door could ease its way closed, Phillips was behind me pulling it open again.

"God dammit," he said, "you know who just called me? Do you have any idea what you've done?"

I hadn't been out of Dolan's office for more than five minutes tops. It had to be some kind of record, I thought.

He was panting like maybe he'd been on the phone, had to get off as fast as he could, politely excuse himself from Dolan, so he could run and catch up to me before I got too far away.

"Dolan, perchance?"

"God damn right, Dolan! What's this about you going to see the mayor and Salter? Are you out of your mind?"

"Hey, you asked me down here. You had questions for me. You had a theory. Well, now, I've got questions. I've got a theory."

"Yeah, like what?" he demanded.

"It's not to the discussion stage yet."

"It's not to the discussion stage?" he repeated. "God dammit, you've managed to completely compromise my investigation, that's what you've done, and it's not to the discussion stage? God dammit!"

He stood there glaring at me, his arms no longer waving around, but settling, hands on hips, his finely tailored suit jacket open. He was panting slightly, his lips pressed together, his nostrils flaring in and out with each exaggerated breath. He had on a very nice tie and his belt was tasteful and they both looked expensive. Here he was, at the top of his game, doing his detective thing in Beverly Hills, great pay, nice clothes, probably a fine automobile, maybe a girl friend that made heads turn, hell, maybe two, in a town that was truly civilized, all this, and incongruously, a face contorted in frustration. Not the calm, deliberate, slightly sardonic fellow I'd come to know and expect. I might have even sympathized with him because it didn't seem fair. But I have to confess, I was enjoying it. If nothing else, as payback for his theory.

I was about to suggest his investigation was compromised the minute he'd let the politics of the town enter into it, but I wasn't ready to throw that in his face just yet.

"Anything else?" I asked him. "Nice tie, by the way."

He stood there forcing himself to slow his breathing and calm down.

"God damn it, I should have known better," he said, shaking his head at his own lack of foresight. "I don't know what I could have been thinking. I should have known better."

He was talking more to himself than me, but it was serving his purpose. I could see him regain control.

"Look," he said, "tread lightly with Dolan. You don't know this guy or what you might be getting yourself into with him, and you don't really want to. He's probably going to eat you for breakfast, but that said, if you become some kind of nuisance to him or the mayor or Mr. Salter, I'm going to have to take some action, so watch yourself. I know I brought this on. I brought you down here an' all, but I want to know what you're doing. I want to know what you've remembered, who you've remembered and what your little theory is. When can we sit down and talk about it?"

"It won't be long now," I told him. I didn't really have a clue when that might be, but added reassuringly, "I'll be in touch."

I thought it was a nice parting line, sort of closing the discussion on my terms, until he added with a hint of both doubt and impending doom, and that rueful little smile of his, "I hope so. I surely do."

It was almost two and I was supposed to meet Vann at Il Fornaio at three. I could have walked there, but since the heat had seemed to scare off the traffic, I figured I'd find a parking place easy enough over there as well, and I did.

It was cool inside, not crowded, the lunch crowd having come and gone. Maybe a dozen stragglers, leaving the waiters hovering with too little to do. I found a table on the Dayton Way side and waved off the waiter when he approached. What they weren't going to make on me, they'd make up on Vann. I was looking out the window, seeing and not seeing Dolan's campaign posters across the street. It had been about twenty or twenty-five minutes since I'd left his office. Either it was enough time or not. I went back to the little alcove that led to the bathrooms and the pay phone between the men's and women's, took his business card from my pocket and dialed.

Dolan's secretary had undergone an attitude adjustment, and said, "I'll put you right through."

"Who the fuck are you and what the fuck do you want?"

No hello, no how are you, no candy and flowers or dinner invitation.

"Thanks for taking my call, councilman. I'm here helping with the investigation of…"

"Phillips says that's a load of crap. Who are you and what do you want?" he interrupted.

"As I started to say, I'm here at the invitation of the Beverly Hills Police Department. Insistence, really. Specifically Phillips. He twisted my arm to get me down here to help and now…"

"…now you think you're going to twist mine?"

I was picturing him as he talked. A tough customer, a sort of Jimmy Hoffa type, smoothed over just enough to pass himself off as either a man of the people or the best friend the Chamber of Commerce ever had. In either case, he seemed like the kind of guy who played by his own set of rules, and rule number one was, there are no rules. I was hoping he'd already had breakfast.

"About Kevin Doyle," I tossed out there.

There was complete silence. It lasted so long I thought maybe he'd hung up and I hadn't heard the click. I was about to say something to see if he was still there when he spoke.

"Where are you?"

"Il Fornaio, on Beverly…"

"I know where the fuck it is. Don't move. I'll be there in ten minutes."

Apparently, I'd struck a nerve.

It had only been about five minutes when he came through the door like he owned the place. Maybe he did. He owned a lot of everything else in this town. He came straight at me like I was the only one there. Either Phillips or his secretary had given him a description, or like Hoffa, whom he did resemble, he knew a candidate for cement shoes when he saw one. He pulled a chair out and sat down. It seems our phone conversation had been introduction enough.

"Right now I've got only one question for you: who put you up to this? Salter? Tannenbaum?"

He was stocky like Hoffa, but looked strong, like he found time to lift weights regularly, and instead of the slicked back hair, he had a fairly well tamed mop that was thick, brown and gray and styled by Beverly Hills' finest, no doubt, but he was no dandy, nor trying to be. No gaudy rings or chains or anything even slightly declasse. His suit was at least as expensive and well fitting as Nick's, and that's saying something.

"Neither," I said. "Phillips. Period."

"So, where'd you come up with the name? Phillips hasn't mentioned it."

"Phillips keeps you informed on an investigation in progress?" I said with mock surprise.

"That's none of your business. Where'd you come up with that name?"

"I suppose you're referring to Kevin Doyle?"

"You're goddamn right I am!" he said, his beefy fist pounding the table hard enough to jiggle a little water from my glass onto the crisp, white tablecloth. "Have you spoken with Phillips? Does he have the name?"

"No, not yet. At least not from me." I shrugged.

Who knows what Phillips does or doesn't have, I was thinking. He relaxed just a little, as much as a guy like this ever relaxes. He sat back, surveying me.

"So, now we're back to the part where you think you're gonna twist my arm, right? Let me guess. As you see it, there's an election coming up, you've got something you think might be a little problem for me and there might be a little money to be made if you make it go away. If you go away. Am I getting the picture?" he smiled.

He seemed to have it all figured out. He was putting it in terms he was familiar with and could handle. He was doing some mental arithmetic and seemed to conclude the numbers were workable. I was just a cost of doing business. And a temporary one at that. His look, and Phillips' warning made that pretty clear. I had the feeling this guy wasn't going around kissing babies to get elected. If he had to get rid of me, he'd be doing the math on how many votes it would cost. Nothing more.

"Not at all," I assured him.

"Then what?!" he demanded through clenched teeth. "I don't have fucking time for this! You told my secretary you've met with Salter and Tannenbaum. Or are going to. Which is it?"

"I haven't met with either of them, yet," I told him.

"So they don't have the name, either?"

"As far as I know, not yet," I said, a little too unreassuringly.

"If I find out you're working for or with Salter or Tannenbaum…"

He didn't finish the sentence, but he didn't really have to. I felt a shudder run through me. Just below the surface, the guy barely bothered to conceal an ocean of churning, roiling anger. The cement shoes didn't seem so funny all of a sudden.

"As far as I'm concerned, it's got nothing to do with the mayor or Mr. Salter."

"I don't believe you!"

"But I can't speak for Phillips."

"You leave Phillips to me. Let's stick with you. What's this got to do with you? What's your angle? I suspect you already know what Kevin Doyle is to me. What's Kevin Doyle to you?" he growled at me.

"Who's Kevin Doyle?"

It was Vann. A little early, but just in the nick of time as far as I was concerned.

Dolan nearly jumped out of his seat. He'd been so focused on me that just the sound of her voice shocked him and brought back the rest of the world. His face went through a few changes, settled on affable candidate for mayor, and he stood to greet her.

"John William Dolan, young lady. Nice to meet you." They shook hands. He looked at me and pointed a warning finger. "We'll talk again." Then to Vann, "Got to run."

He strode confidently and commandingly to the door and out. He looked very mayoral. It was on his way to the door that I noticed he had an oddly shaped cowlick at the back of his head.

She sat down, keeping her eyes on the retreating Dolan as he left the cool and relative calm of Il Fornaio for the sun-baked sidewalk of

Beverly Drive.

"Isn't this still the same day as this morning? How did you manage it?"

"What ?"

"Get a meeting with Dolan. Get Dolan to come to you. And obviously, get him pretty pissed off. Even for you, that might be some kind of a record."

"All in all," I said, "I don't think I'm going to vote for him."

"Who's Kevin Doyle? And why does the name bother Dolan so much?"

Therein lies the tale, I was thinking. But would I tell it?

"Before we get to that, how did you make out with the names?"

"Iyama Osaka is alive," she smiled. "Victor is his son."

"You talked to him?"

"Victor, not Iyama. Iyama's pretty sick. Victor and his wife want him to move into the city closer to them, but he won't. He's got a little place at Point Dume and won't budge. The best they've been able to do is convince him to keep a nurse around weekdays."

"How sick?"

"Very. Liver cancer."

"What did you tell Victor?"

"Not much. Just that you used to live on the 400 block of Oakhurst when you were a kid and would like to talk to both him and Iyama, if it's possible. I gave him your name and he said he'd talk to his father. We can call later and see what's up, or he may leave a message at my office. Either way, we should know by tonight."

"That's great. Anything on any of the others?"

"Didn't you mention that Phillips said something about a lot of the others on the block being gone? Dead? Even an unusual number of the kids?"

"Yes," I said, "why?"

"Even with a quick rundown, I've found three suicides among kids that lived there. Didn't make it out of their twenties."

She looked at me for a minute without saying anything, letting it sink in.

"Not counting your brother," she added, apologetically.

# Chapter 18
## *The Luck of The Red Rider*
### June 9 & 10, 1951

I WAS SO TIRED I could hardly lift my arms anymore, and when I did, my shoulders hurt so much I didn't think I could do another hubcap or whitewall if my life depended on it. We must have washed sixty-five cars. Maybe more. Towards the end, I even thought about holding the brush for the whitewalls with my teeth because on top of my shoulders hurting, my hands kept cramping and I had to pry my fingers open just to switch between the brush for the whitewalls and the soapy rags for the hubcaps. Usually Mr. Avery or Maurice put the rope across the driveway at four-thirty sharp and we'd finish washing the cars that had already made it onto the lot, but because that Dolan guy was beatin' his gums, that what's Maurice called it, Mr. Avery didn't put the rope up 'til five-thirty and there were still cars in all the boxes on the lot waiting to be washed and even more on the street. When that happened, Mr. Avery gave anyone in the street line a ticket good for one free wash, sort of an apology for them waiting and waiting and not getting onto the lot to get washed, but that didn't help us, because it was late and we still had to wash the cars already on the lot and then clean up and put everything away. The boots, the rags, the buckets, hose down the lot, clean and put away the work tables. All of it. At this rate, I'd never make it to Bill's Bike shop on time. On weekdays, he closed at four-thirty and on Saturdays he stayed there 'til seven, but even if I left right this minute, I might not make it.

Finally we were done and everything was put away and Mr. Avery came out of the office to pay us. He gave Maurice and Dennis and William and Jackson their pay in envelopes. I could see the clock on the wall behind Joseph. It was six-thirty and I really wanted to get going.

"There's a little something extra in there fellows. Sorry you had to stay so late."

"No problem, Mr. Avery. Got to do what we got to do. That right, boys?" Maurice said.

"That's about the size of it," William said.

"You good with that, little brother?" Maurice asked me.

"That's about the size of that for me too," I said.

Mr. Avery handed me my two-fifty.

"Joseph and the guys say you haven't been sharing in the tip jar."

"Well, that should be just for the regular workers," I said. I didn't want to say the part about the Mexicans and Negroes having a rough time of it in this town. "You don't owe me anything extra. Really. This is fine."

"Well, I'd feel better if you'd take this. For working late and all the tips you should have had a part of."

He held out a five dollar bill, two ones and a fifty cent piece. He was smiling at me and so were the guys and Joseph too.

"If we hurry, you could still make it to the bike shop and you could pay off the bike this week. Start on the locks next week. I can give you a ride over there, if you like," Joseph said.

Kenny Lester must have told him. Or maybe Mr. Avery.

The money was just sort of hanging there between us. I didn't really think I should take it, but I really wanted to anyway. So I did.

"I was beginning' to worry," Bill said as I came in. The little bell rang when I opened and closed the door. "I was just about to leave."

"Guess what!?" I said.

"What?"

"I'm going to pay off the bike tonight! Can you believe it?"

"That's great. A week ahead of schedule. How'd you manage that?"

"Some extra work at the carwash and stuff."

"Well, let's go get it. Are you going to be okay to ride it home?"

I hadn't thought of that. I was pretty sure I could, but it would be awful if I fell and scratched it up. Or if a car hit it and banged it up bad.

"Maybe we should go out back and you could practice a little. I can give you a few pointers. That is, if you need them."

"Let's do that. Just in case," I said.

Bill locked the front door and we went back to the cash register at the counter and he rang up the ten dollars I gave him. He took the paper work for the lay-a-way from a drawer beneath the register and stamped both copies, PAID IN FULL. It was one of the prettiest things I'd ever seen. I kept hearing it over and over in my head, even though I didn't seem like I was saying it, just someone in my head reminding me that after all this time, the Red Rider was paid for and was all mine! He handed my one of the copies.

"Congratulations, Kurt. That's quite an accomplishment."

He reached out and we shook hands.

"With every new bike I sell, I like to give my customers one of these."

He handed me a silver thing.

"What is it?" I asked him.

"Don't any of your friends use them? Kids with bikes?"

"I don't think so."

"It's a clip to keep your pants' leg away from the chain so it doesn't get caught or get greasy."

"Neat," I said.

"I always wear one," he said. "I ride my bike from home to the shop and back most days. It comes in pretty handy."

"Thanks you."

"You go get your bike and follow me out the back."

I got the Red Rider and carefully moved it from the line of bigger bikes on the right hand side of the shop and carefully rolled it down the aisle towards the back. The line of shiny new bikes on each side seemed like lines of soldiers standing at attention in their fancy uniforms, saluting me and the Red Rider like we had done something special and were going to get a medal or something for it. In a way, we had. I should have kept track of all the hubcaps I washed and all the whitewalls I scrubbed. I should get a medal for that, I thought, but the Red Rider was better. It was just the best! Or maybe the other bikes were just saying goodbye to the Red Rider, like he was being transferred to a different unit. I passed the counter and came into Bill's work area. It was clean and neat, with most of the tools hanging on hooks on the walls with outlines drawn around them so it was easy to find them and put them away again. There were a couple of stands with clamps that were specially designed to hold a bicycle up in the air so Bill could work on it, and hooks on the stand where tools hung ready to be used. Off to one side, there were a bunch of bikes with white tags tied to the handle bars with the name and phone number of the owner so Bill could call them when their bikes were fixed and they could come get them. There were hooks on the ceiling and bikes all over the place hanging from them upside down. The whole place seemed like a secret upside down forest where bikes grew. Bill took his bike down from a pair of the hooks. It was a skinny bike with the tubes for the frame like spaghetti and the tires tall and narrow. The handle bars were funny too, turned down and circling back, and the seat looked like it would hurt your butt. Bill leaned his bike against one of the repair stands and wrapped his pants leg tight around his shin and slipped the clip on to hold it in place. I put the kick stand down so I could let go of the Red Rider and tried to do the same thing, only the clip didn't fit me and just slid down towards the top of my shoe and stopped at the rolled up cuff.

"Here, let me fix that," Bill said. He put the clip in a vise on his work bench and with some long nosed pliers bent the clip into a smaller circle.

"Try that," he said.

It worked.

"Okay, then, we're all set."

We rolled our bikes out the back door to the parking lot behind his store and the ones on either side of it. He locked that door too and we were all set. There weren't any cars out there at all, not on his lot, or in the alley either, or in the lots across the alley for the stores that faced Canon, so we had a lot of room to practice.

"Why's your bike so skinny?" I asked him.

"It's a racing bike. They have bicycle races in Europe through city streets and this is the kind of bike you use."

"Did you ever race there?"

He smiled. "Sure did. I was stationed in Italy after the war."

"Did you ever win?"

"Came pretty close a couple of times. More fun than you can imagine," he said.

It must have been, because just thinking about it had him smiling and shaking his head.

"Neat," I said.

"It sure was."

He stepped over his bike and showed me how you'd bend over and ride low to keep your body from pushing extra air and slowing you down. He leaned his bike against the wall and held the Red Rider steady for me so I could get on.

"Let's start with some big circles and just peddling," he said. "You ready?"

I didn't tell him, but I was kind of scared. The bike seemed higher outside than it did in the store, and a lot more wiggly that just sitting on it with the kickstand down.

"I'm ready," I said.

He gave me a push. I was so shocked to be actually riding, I forgot all about pedaling. When I got as far as the alley, the bike was slowing down and started to wobble.

"Pedal! You've got to pedal!" Bill yelled.

So I did, and the Red Rider took off like a rocket and before I knew it, I was across the alley and across the parking lot on the other side and the back door of Hartzman's Jewlry store was right in front of me and coming up faster than I could believe.

I heard Bill yelling, " Turn! Turn!" then, "Use the brakes! Use the brakes!"

While I was thinking about it, wondering where the brakes were, I crashed into the door. If I hadn't been holding on so tight I would have gone right over the handle bars and smacked into the door myself, but I didn't want to let the Red Rider fall, so as soon as the door stopped me, I jumped off still holding onto the bike and kept it from falling.

Bill came running over.

"Are you okay?"

I was completely okay, but I was checking to make sure the Red Rider was. It looked okay too.

"Sure," I said, "that was great!"

"Haven't you ever ridden before? Besides in the store, I mean?"

"Not really. But I've watched my big brother, Marty, and his friends, and kids at school, so I sort of know how."

"Well, you did fine, but you need to steer and use the brakes. Do you know how to use the brakes?"

"No. Not really."

He showed me. It seemed easy enough, but I wished he'd showed me about ten minutes sooner. We tried again, this time straight up the alley, so there weren't any buildings in front of me. When I got close to Lower Santa Monica, I stopped so's not to go out into the street. Bill was running along side to make sure everything was okay and it was. I came to a nice stop using the brakes and jumped off to keep the bike from falling over. It was hard to turn around, but I did by sort of dragging the bike sideways a little at a time and then we went all the way down the alley to Burton Way. We went up and down the alley a few more times, but by then Bill was getting tired. So first he showed me how to get started without a push from him. And once I could do that and could pedal and stop whenever I wanted, Bill said we should do some turns. He took some small cardboard boxes from a dumpster down the alley and placed them in a pattern and told me to try and go on one side of one and the other side of the next one, weaving back and forth until I got to the end where he'd made sure I had a lot of room to turn all the way around and do the same thing on the way back. After a few trips and a few times I bumped into the boxes, I did it up and back with no mistakes. It wasn't dark yet, but it was getting there and I knew I might be in trouble since it was not only after six, but had to be getting close to eight. Since the car wash had stayed open late, that part would be okay, but eight o'clock was still eight o'clock.

"I think I better be getting home," I told him.

"Well, I think you've pretty much got it now," he said.

"Thanks, Bill. I didn't know I'd need so much help just to get started. It looks so easy when everyone else just does it."

"They had to learn too," he said. "Let's ride along together to your house. Make sure you get there okay. You've got to be really careful in the street. Watching for parked cars coming away from the curb and cars coming out of driveways and alleys and from cross streets. There's a lot of ways to get creamed if you're not careful."

"I'm going to be so careful, you wouldn't believe it," I said. "I don't want the Red Rider getting all scratched up. Especially not on the first day, so you don't have to come home with me. I think I'm okay now."

I wasn't completely sure, but I thought I was, and besides, he'd already stayed pretty late helping me.

"You probably are, but everyone should have someone with them on their first ride in the street. And it's going to be dark soon."

"Okay," I said.

There wasn't any point in arguing with him if that's what he wanted to do.

The most amazing thing ever was how fast we got to Oakhurst. I'd walked home from Whalen's Drug Store and Ozzie's Soda Fountain a million times before and I knew how long it takes. Believe me, I do. But in practically no time, we were turning the corner from Lower Santa Monica onto my street. I could hardly believe it, one minute we were leaving the alley between Beverly and Canon onto Lower Santa Monica and the next minute we'd turned and passed Shelly and Norma's house, then Rathbutt's place, Sullivan's, George's, then our driveway, just like that! I came to a pretty good stop, jumped off again to keep the Red Rider from falling, then put the kickstand down.

"Well done," Bill said. "When you're a little taller, you'll be able to straddle the bar and won't have to jump off like that. But for now, that's a pretty good technique."

Just then, Marty came up the street from Beverly Boulevard on his bicycle.

"Man, where have you been? I've been out looking everywhere. Mom is going nuts. Do you know what time it is?"

"Well," I said, "we had to stay late at the carwash because that Dolan guy showed up looking' for votes."

"We know all about that," he said, "Mom called Mr. Avery. But that was an hour and a half ago."

"I know, but look, I got the Red Rider!" I said.

Marty reached out and rubbed my hair.

"Pretty neat, squirt. Mr. Avery said you'd gone to the bike shop, but man, eight-thrity?"

Just then my mom and Sarah came onto the front porch. Sarah had that look like she couldn't wait to see what my punishment was going to be.

"Do you know how worried I've been? Do you know what time it is? Don't you know how worried we were?" my mom said.

"I'm afraid it's my fault, Mrs. Goldman," Bill said. "He came to pay off the bike and I got a little carried away giving him a riding lesson. I'm sorry. I should have suggested we call you from the shop."

"Kurt knows what time he's supposed to be home," she said, but she was smiling, and said, "But I guess this is a big enough occasion to bend the rules a little. That's a beautiful bike, Kurt. Congratulations. You've earned it."

"That's all?" Sarah said. "That's it? Boy is that not fair! I can't believe that's all you're going to do to him."

"Sarah, mind your own business," my mom said, then, "Have you eaten anything?"

"Well, I had part of …" I was going to say part of Kenny Lester's hamburger, but all of a sudden that didn't seem like such a good idea, like we were a bunch of beggars or something, so I just told her, "lunch at the car wash."

"How can you have part of lunch?" she asked.

She didn't seem mad, so I just shrugged.

"Well, that had to be seven or eight hours ago. Come on in and get cleaned up and I'll fix a plate for you."

"You're going to feed him? The kitchen's all cleaned up," Sarah complained. "I was home on time and did my chores cleaning up after dinner and you're going to let it get messed up just to feed Mr. Quarter-to-nine?! That's just…" Sarah couldn't find the right words and just threw up her arms at the unfairness of it and stomped back into the house.

The Red Rider was bringing me luck already. I knew there was no way I could have been this late and had dinner too. And no extra chores or punishment.

"Kurt's going to clean up the kitchen after he eats," my mom said loud enough for Sarah to hear too.

"Big deal!" she said.

Even so, the whole thing was about as lucky as it could get.

"Bill, have you had dinner yet? We've got plenty of pot roast and potatoes and green beans."

"No thanks, Mrs. Goldman. My wife's waiting. I'm already pretty late myself. I'm just hoping she hasn't sent out search parties for me too. Good night, Kurt. Don't be a stranger. If you stop by the shop in the next couple of weeks, I can show you some places to oil, and how to clean it and generally maintain it. And don't forget, that bike's got a one year warranty, so if anything isn't just right, bring it in and I'll fix it."

"Thanks Bill. For everything, all the way from the lay-a-way to the riding lesson," I said.

"Good night," he said, and off he went.

Marty looked at me and the bike and mom going back in the house to make me some dinner for me and shook his head.

"You lead a charmed life, squirt. That's all I've got to say."

We walked our bikes down the driveway to the garage and Marty made room for the Red Rider so my dad wouldn't run it over by accident when he came home. Marty started for the back door, but I couldn't stand to leave it. It was so dark it was hard to see, but not so dark that I didn't know it was there. It was there!

"Come on, squirt, don't press your luck," Marty called to me.

I was so hungry I couldn't believe it. I don't think I ever ate as much as I ate the first night of the Red Rider. I ate a huge dinner and I made the plate for my dad and put it in the icebox for when he got home, and I scraped out the pots and ate every last speck of food from them, then cleaned the table and washed the pots and dishes and put everything away. It was endless, like the carwash all over again, but this time I knew the Red Rider was mine and it didn't matter at all. It was just a few steps away and it would be there in the morning and the morning after that and the next and the next one after that forever. I wanted to wait up for my dad to get home and take him out to the garage to see it and tell him about paying it off a week ahead of time and Bill giving me a riding lesson and how I could start to pay for the locks sooner, and I was going to wait for him on the living room couch, and my mom said I could, but the next thing I knew it was morning and I was in my own bed.

My eyes popped open and there I was. The clock on Marty's desk said seven o-four. I couldn't believe I'd slept so late. When I looked around, it was the same room. I don't exactly know what I expected, but something. There was the same Marty sleeping late because it was Sunday. The same quiet house because no one was up yet, same everything, but nothing was the same! Nothing would ever be the same. I wanted to jump out of bed and get dressed and run out to the garage and just say hello to my bike. But I didn't. I just stayed in bed thinking about doing it. I wanted to go out there so bad it almost hurt. It did hurt, but I didn't budge. I forced myself to just stay there until about ten minutes had passed and I couldn't stand it anymore and I leaped off my bed like there was a snake in it and ran down the hall and through the kitchen and out through the screen door. It slammed into the side of the house, but I spun around so fast I was able to catch it before it could smack closed. I eased it shut, then ran down the driveway to the garage. My dad had left his car just outside of the garage last night and there was a little morning dew on the top of it and on the back windshield. He was standing there with a rag in his hand, I suppose to wipe it off, but he just stood there in front of the car looking into the garage, looking at the Red Rider.

"Isn't it incredible?" I said. "Isn't it just incredible!"

He turned around and he had tears in his eyes.

"It is," he said.

He knelt down next to me and put his arms around me and hugged me to him.

"So are you." Then he laughed and said, "You should probably put some pants on," because I was in my underwear, which came as a complete surprise to me.

Marty didn't have to work at the Standard Station until one-thirty and he didn't really have any homework because the next week was the last week of school before summer vacation and all he had to do was study for some tests, so he said we could take a ride together to Gilmore Field. It was Family Day and The Hollywood Stars were playing the Los Angeles Angels in a double header. There'd be a huge crowd trying to get both teams to go crazy because Marty said they didn't like each other much to begin with and because they'd almost gotten into a fight the last time they played. The first game started at ten so we could catch some of it at the back fence, what the kids called the knothole club. You were allowed to stand there and watch from behind left field through knotholes in the fence, and if someone hit a home run over it, all the kids would scramble for the ball, because whoever got it could bring it around to the front and they'd let you in for free for the rest of the game if you gave the ball back. Marty invited Sarah to come but she said never with him, meaning me, but by the time Marty and I had our bikes out of the garage and down to the sidewalk, she must have changed her mind, because she was already there with a bunch of the Oakhurst Irregulars: Allen and Megan, Jeff Schumur, Dick Goldsmith, Jeryl and Julie Stern and Joanne Lester. Even Robbie Ganz, who was pretty strange, and if Sarah let him be in the Oakhurst Irregulars, then it was even more completely unfair that I couldn't be.

"Just don't expect me to talk to him," she said, jerking her thumb in my direction.

"Boy," Allen said, "that's got to be the neatest bike I ever saw!"

"Pretty cool," Jeff Schumur said.

Robbie Ganz said so too.

Sarah was getting annoyed with all the attention I was getting, or at least the attention the Red Rider was getting.

"Let's get going," she said, starting down Oakhurst.

The others followed her.

Marty told me to go ahead of him so if I had a problem, he'd see and help me. My mom had even given us money for cokes, so we could stop at The Farmer's Market, which was right next to Gilmore Field, during the game or before we came home. We followed Sarah and the others to Beverly Boulevard, which was easy enough. There weren't any cars coming or going on Oakhurst at all, and not too many on Beverly Boulevard either, since it was only about nine-thirty or so, and Sunday on top of that, but I'd never realized how big it was. When you crossed it on foot, all you had to do was wait for an opening between cars and run like heck across the four lanes, six if you counted the parking lanes on each side, and there you were. But on a bike, you had to stop at the stop sign, then start up again, and by the time you quit wobbling, there were cars that came out of nowhere from Doheny about to run you over, so you might have to stop and wait and then do it all over again. Sarah made a big show out of signaling for the left turn we all had to make onto Beverly, but I knew she didn't do it all the time like you're supposed to when she rode to school. I was going to try it, but knew if I took one hand off the handle bars, that would be the end of me, so I didn't. When we got to Beverly and Doheny it was easier because there's a light there and all we had to do was wait for our turn and go. The good thing about going to Gilmore Field was that it was a little bit downhill all the way. You just kept going and going and hardly had to pedal. Every once in a while Marty would yell to me, " Are you okay?" and I'd yell back, "I'm fine," and we'd keep going. I was sure people on the sidewalk were looking at how neat the Red Rider was, but I couldn't tell for sure since I couldn't take my eyes off the street in front of me, or off the parked cars that might pull out from the curb or driveways or cross-streets, like Bill said, and cream you. We passed the Beverly Ponyland at Robertson. In a car, you hardly smelled it at all, but on a bike, you really got a whiff in a big way. I would have held my nose with one hand, but just like signaling for a turn, I knew that was a bad idea. We got to Beverly and Fairfax in about fifteen minutes and could have just turned right to the Farmer's Market on Fairfax at 3rd, but Marty wanted to avoid all the cars parking in the lots between the Market and Gilmore Field, probably because I was new to riding and there would be cars coming and going every-which-way with people going to the game or maybe just the market. So he yelled to Sarah and the Irregulars to keep going, and instead, we stayed on Beverly until we got to North Stanley and then everyone turned right and came around behind to the empty lots at the back of the baseball field. There were already about eight or ten kids there trying to get the best knotholes for themselves. I was for sure the youngest kid there, and Sarah was the only girl, except for the Oakhurst Irregular girls with us, but she'd been there lots of times before with Marty, or with some of the Oakhurst Ir-

regulars before they called themselves that, and I'd heard from Allen that
Megan had said there weren't too many of the boys that knew her who'd
say anything to her about her being a girl. I wasn't the only one who'd
gotten a bloody mouth for saying something she didn't like or when she
was in a bad mood, so even though these boys were about her age and
height, they probably knew her, because they let her pick the knothole
she wanted. Marty was so much taller than any of the kids there, when
he found a knothole he liked, no one else could have used it anyway. And
I was shorter than everyone, so when I found a good one, nobody cared
either. There was a little pushing and shoving between some of the others
over whose knothole was whose, but no fights, and without much fuss,
we all had practically perfect knotholes and I knew it was because of the
luck of the Red Rider.

The game started right on time and almost right away Marty was telling us, and the other kids that we didn't know, to keep an eye on the
Angels' pitcher, Joe Hatton. It looked like he was throwing at the Stars.
Marty said there was bad blood between the two teams anyway, and it
might just boil over today, especially if Hatton kept that up, and wouldn't
that be something if we got to see it! The game was pretty much fun to
watch, but it was getting hot and the sun was beating down from straight
above us and there wasn't a piece of shade big enough for an ant. It even
hurt to look at the Red Rider because the glare of the sun off the shiny
paint and chrome stabbed me right in the eyes. I was thinking about the
money my mom had given us and the cokes. Marty and Sarah had come
to games together before and were used to it, I guess, because they never
took their eyes away from their knotholes.

"You guys getting thirsty?" I asked.

"I knew he'd be trouble!" Sarah said to Marty. She turned to me, "If
you get your coke now, you'll just have to pee. Then what? Huh? Then
what are you going to do? Make one of us miss some of the game while
we try to find you a bathroom? Man, are you trouble in triple!"

"I just asked," I said. "I can wait."

Marty checked his watch. "It's still pretty early. It's almost the fourth
inning and it's only eleven-twenty. We've got plenty of time. How 'bout
you go for the cokes, but use one of the bathrooms at the Market first,
then get the cokes and come back. Can you do that?

"Sure," I said. "Pretty much the same as Carl's."

"Pretty much," he said, but he had his faced pressed up against the
knothole again. "Oh man," he said, "another one of those, and it's a rhu-
barb for sure!"

He reached in his pocket and gave me the thirty cents.

I asked Allen if he wanted to come.

"I don't want to miss the fight, if there is one," he said. "I'll get a coke
on the way home."

"Don't forget to pop the tops," Sarah said. "It'd be just like you to go
all the way over there and back and forget to open them and then we'd
have to go all the way back."

"I know what to do. Leave me alone."

"Boy, I wish I could."

Marty saw me looking at the Red Rider standing there on its kick-stand.

"Don't worry," he said, "I'll keep an eye on it. It'll be here when you get back," he said, pressing his face to the fence again.

I was worried just the same.

It seemed like an endless walk and took much longer than I thought it would to go all the way around the ball park to the back side of the Farmer's Market, but boy, was it worth it. After all the sun behind the left field fence, and the hot dusty walk, the inside of the Farmer's market was cool and clean and smelled good. The floors were wet because there was a guy washing them down all day long to make sure the place stayed cool and clean. There were lots of fruit and vegetable stands, and a bunch of different food sellers too. The place was huge, much bigger than I remembered from the couple of times I'd come here with Pop. You could get hot dogs or hamburgers or fancy sandwiches and salads or Mexican food and all kinds of other stuff too, that is, if you had the money for it. There were several different bakery tables and all together the smells alone were enough to either fill you up or make you dizzy, and I wasn't getting filled up the least little bit. So instead of thinking about that, I asked a lady where the boys bathroom was and she told me and I used it and then found a seller with coke in bottles instead of the other guys selling less of it in a glass for more money. I got the three cokes and started to leave, but when I looked around, I couldn't remember which way I'd come in. I started down one long aisle and finally came to a set of big doors, but it looked like Fairfax in front of me, so I knew I'd gone in exactly the wrong direction. All I had to do was turn around and go back the way I'd come, which seemed easy enough, but when I'd walked pretty far in that direction, there were so many people all around me, I got turned around again trying not to drop the three cokes when some people bumped into me, and lost track of which way was which and even worse, I couldn't even see Fairfax anymore and there were aisles not only to the front and back, but ones going off to each side and they all looked pretty much the same. It's a good thing I was so thirsty, because I decided to drink my coke right then, which made a lot of sense, partly because I was so thirsty, but also I'd have less to carry back to Marty and Sarah, but even more important, when I chose which one I was going to drink, I realized I'd forgotten to pop the tops loose. Sarah would have murdered me for that. I couldn't find the place where I'd bought them, but there was a counter at a Mexican food seller's place and the woman saw me looking around and asked if I was lost and I said yes, but I only meant lost like I couldn't remember which way was which, but she thought I meant lost and she said, "don't worry, I'll call the police", so when she turned to pick up the phone, I ran away through the crowd of people. I'd had enough of the police about the locks and could do without them any more. I didn't really run away, because running wasn't possible since the Market was so crowded by then, but I managed to escape anyway and when I stopped to see where I was, I was right back to the place where I'd bought the cokes! How lucky is that, I was thinking, and I knew exactly why. So I popped the tops and walked slowly down the aisle drinking mine while I was still inside and found my way to the back of the Market where I'd come in in the first place. By the time I got to the fence, Marty said it was almost the end of the sixth and we'd have to go when the inning was over. He told me Hatton had thrown a couple of close ones at Kelleher in the fourth, and Kelleher had charged the mound, but the umpires and two policemen from the stands had calmed things down. I handed him his coke first and Sarah hers, after I carefully lifted off the top for her, making sure she knew that I knew that she knew I'd remembered to pop them. I found my knothole and started watching the game again, and that's when it happened.

Joe Hatton popped Frank Kelleher right in his back.

"Here it comes," Marty yelled, "here it comes! Kelleher and Dahlke are going after Hatton!" and they did, running to the mound and wrestling Hatton to the ground. Then the Angels first baseman jumped into it, pulling Kelleher off Hatton and they started slugging each other. Before all of the other players could get into it, the umpires and the managers from both teams pulled them apart and settled things down again. Almost as soon as they started to play again, the guy on second tried to steal third.

"There goes Beard!" yelled one of the kids we didn't know.

Beard was the guy trying to steal third, I guess.

"Oh, man!" Marty said. "He really laid his spikes into Franklin!"

Franklin must have been the Angels third baseman. Even from where we were, we could see he was bleeding on his arm and chest. He threw off his glove and went after Beard, and that's when all the players from both dugouts charged onto the field and everyone was hitting everyone else. I couldn't see how they could tell who to hit, but they seemed to know, because it just went on and on. There had been only a couple of policemen in the stands before, but someone must have called the police station or something after the trouble in the fourth inning, because now about twenty of them came down onto the field. Instead of helping calm things down, it just made the fight bigger, like there were three teams instead of just two. The policemen were hitting the players and the players were hitting each other and the policemen, so what was the good of that? Finally the fighting slowed down. Mostly, I think, because they were all getting tired. Several player had gotten spiked during the fighting and left the game. When things were pretty much under control, the policemen divided up and half of them sat in the Angels dugout and the other half sat with the Stars. When the sixth was over, Marty said he had to get going.

"Are you going to stay and watch the end of the game?" he asked Sarah.

"Yeah," she said, "but I'm not takin' care of him," she said, nodding towards me.

"You wanna stay?" he said to me.

"Sort of," I said. One coke wasn't going to be enough to get through a whole game in that sun, and not even close for a double-header, but this was probably as close to being in the Oakhurst Irregulars as I was going to get.

"Sarah, he can stay if he wants to and you'll look after him. Especially on the ride back. I'm making it your responsibility. Understand?" He looked at her until he knew she knew he meant it.

"Say it," he told her.

"Okay, okay already. I get it!" she said.

"See you guys later," Marty called to all of us as he got on his bike. Then he said to me, " Pretty nice outing for your first day with the bike, huh?"

"Perfect," I said. "Thanks."

A little later, the Stars catcher, Malone, came up and fouled three in a row along the third baseline into the stands. The next one might have been a homer, which would have been good too, but at the last second it drifted foul too, though the important thing was it made it over the fence right behind me. All I had to do was turn around and pick it up, which I did. When I turned around and held it up to show Sarah and the rest of the Oakhurst Irregulars, one the other kids tackled me and pulled it out of my hand.

"Hey! That's mine!" I shouted at him. "Give it back!"

"Make me," he said, taking off for the entrance and a free ticket to the rest of the first game and the whole second one.

I got up started to chase him. He was older and bigger and faster than me, and was pretty easily getting away, about to turn the corner around the fence, when Sarah caught him by his shirt collar and pulled him down. There was a cloud of dust as they hit the ground together. They were wrestling on the ground with Sarah trying to pull the ball out of his hands and him hanging onto it, tucking it tight against his stomach with both hands, kicking at her to force her away. Sarah got to her feet first.

"Hand it over," she told him. "That's my brother's."

By then the Oakhurst Irregulars and the friends of the kid and I had caught up to him and Sarah.

"Like heck it is!" he said, getting to his feet and noticing for the first time it was a girl facing him.

"Keep it Jimmy" his friends told him. "You got it fair and square."

"The heck he did," Allen said. "Kurt got to it first and had it in his hands. That makes it his."

It looked like Allen and this other guy were going to start a fight about it and the rest of the Oakhurst Irregulars and the guys friends were standing around looking like they just couldn't wait for someone to start something so they could all get into it too.

The kid with the ball, Jimmy, dusted himself off and told Sarah, "Out of my way, girlie. I've got a ball game to go to."

His friends thought that was pretty funny.

"Give it back to my brother," she said. "I'm not going to ask you again."

"Good," he said, smiling to his friends.

He pushed her aside and took what he thought was going to be the first step to get past her and on the way to the ball park. Sarah's punch came so fast and hard it was a blur. Jimmy went over sideways and backwards and hit the ground in a heap. Both of his hands went to his mouth, which was already leaking blood between his fingers and the ball rolled off next to him into the dusty dirt. Sarah bent down and picked it up and dusted it off. She tossed it up and down a couple of times and then handed it to me.

"Here," she said. "Try to hang onto it."

"Thanks, Sarah."

"What the heck. It's Family Day, right? Besides, if Marty found out I let a jerk like that take the ball away from you, I'd never hear the end of it."

The Stars won the game 2-0, but we heard later they lost the second one. Since there were so many of us, one ticket wouldn't have done us any good, and even though I could have gotten the free ticket and used it for a game some other day, I thought it would be better to keep the ball as a souvenir of my first day with the Red Rider and Family Day. By the end of the first game it was really hot, and everyone was tired of standing at the fence anyway, so Sarah decided we should just go home.

I put the ball down the front of my shirt and we got on our bikes and headed back the way we'd come. It was a lot harder going home. What had been an easy downhill ride now seemed like an endless uphill one. Bill had put the seat down as low as it would go, but even so, my feet just barely reached the pedals. On the way home from his shop and to Gilmore Field it didn't matter much since I hardly had to pedal, but uphill, I had to push as hard as I could, and at the bottom of each push, my foot was barely on. I started out in front, like when Marty was with us, but pretty soon, one by one, the Oakhurst Irregulars passed me. Sarah stayed behind me, but kept complaining she could hardly stay up going this slow, telling me how much trouble I was. Allen said he'd stay back with me, so Sarah raced past to catch up to the others, then got out in front of them.

We'd ridden like that for a few minutes when Allen called from behind me, "Did you see that punch?"

"Too fast," I said between breathes, struggling with the bike, wobbling a lot.

"Where'd she learn to fight like that?"

"I…don't…know, but…she…gets…lots…of…practice…on…me."

"What are you going to do when you get home?"

"Get…the…cards…from…the…hardware…store…ready…and…

pass…them…out…to…the…houses…that…need…new…locks," I puffed.

"Want help?"

"No…thanks."

# Chapter 19

### *Hannah Aduan-Mercer & Iyama Osaka*

### **August 9, 1989**

## "WHO?" I ASKED HER.

Vann looked at her notes. "Perry Arnold. Joey Schumur. Ronnie Ganz."

They were the younger brothers of Marylou Arnold, Jeff Schumur and Robbie Ganz.

"I think we're going to find others, she said.

"What makes you think so?"

"These three showed up in the thirty calls I made. Their dates of birth are all close. Close to yours, by the way. Some a little older, some a little younger, but all born in the middle of, or late 1943 to the end of 1945. And from the people I've already talked to, it sounds like there were quite a few other kids around the same age on your block. Just applying the percentages, it seems likely there's going to be more. Any ideas?"

I was trying to picture some of the younger brothers and sisters of the kids Sarah's age, because besides Allen, most of the kids I knew were her age, not mine. But I remembered Joey Schumur. Very curly dark hair, overweight, soft, baby-fat body even at six or seven. I couldn't picture Marylou's brother, or Robbie Ganz's either.

"Any ideas," she repeated.

"Maybe."

"Like….?" she said, a touch of annoyance in her voice.

"I don't know. Just maybe. Before we get to that, did you find anyone else? Any of the adults whose phones I listed?"

She pressed her lips together, the touch gone, the annoyance now all on its own.

"Miriam McDermott. Shelly Winters. Stephen Aduan and Hannah Aduan-Mercer. A few others. Which again raises the issue of Phillips being sloppy or lazy or deceptive. Or some combination of the three. Especially if he mentioned an unusual number of the kids being dead. How would he know that? Who's he talked to if he hasn't pursued any of the records you and I have?"

"It's a mystery," I said, "but, Miriam? She's alive? Where is she? And Shelly?"

Vann looked over her notes again, her annoyance sort of hovering over us.

"Miriam's in Corte Madera. That's up by you, isn't it?"

"Across the Bay, in Marin. My god, Miriam McDermott."

"I talked to Shelly Winters's personal assistant. She doesn't live on

Oakhurst anymore, but she still owns the building at 457. She lives up on Coldwater Canyon, near Mulhuland. The phone for the house next door to hers was listed to Spencer Aduan. He died in 1978, but his son and daughter, Steve and Hannah, still live in Southern California and still jointly own it. He lives in Silverlake, she lives in Pacific Palisades."

"Nice work," I said.

She was waiting for me to get back to the percentage issue she'd raised.

"When do you think we could call Iyama? Well, Victor at least."

She looked at her watch. It was about 3:45.

"We could give it a try now. Let me call my office first to see if he's called and left a message."

She went to the phone in the alcove in back. I sat there trying to picture Marylou's little brother, Perry, and Robbie Ganz's brother, Ronnie, among the gang of kids running around on the block just before dinner, or just after, or maybe playing in one of the thousand games of hide-and-seek Sarah organized, games that lasted right up until dark, or sometimes just a hair past, as we tried to finish the game but beat the six o'clock rule, or before dark rule, or whatever governed at their houses. I couldn't. But it did bring back the larger number of kids than I'd so far remembered. Some of those hide-and-seek games must have involved eighteen or twenty of us. I tried to picture them, Perry and Ronnie, as unhappy young adults. Without trying too hard, I could feel their fear and hopelessness, a nagging despair that takes whatever fresh new wind that's filled your sails and leaves you becalmed but not calm, isolated and agitated, out to sea so far that sinking beckons like a siren song. Like a homecoming. A chance to start fresh. I could feel all that and weep for them, knowing that without Max, I might have sought those waters myself. I came back to Phillips. I couldn't see how he would know about an inordinate number of early deaths of kids on the block unless he had talked to and gotten information from someone who'd lived there. He's said he hadn't. Unless that were a lie, the only sure connection I could see was to Dolan. He hadn't lived on the block, at least as far as I knew, or at least when we did, but he was the only link I was sure of, that and Phillips' apparent willingness to share information from his investigation with him. If he'd never lived on the block, technically at least, Phillips wouldn't be lying. It had to be Dolan, I concluded. But how or in what way would he be familiar with the arch of those lives? Simplicity itself: The Beverly Hills Management Corporation and Paragon Properties. In following the chain of titles on the properties, the progression was from an owner, or owner as a life estate, the remainder to J.T. Dolan and then The Beverly Hills Development Group while J.T. Dolan was alive. When J.W. took over, the names had changed only slightly to the Beverly Hills Management Corporation, and their development arm, Paragon Properties. J.W. Dolan would have had the opportunity to be in touch with the owners and their children and or successor owners from those days to these.

"We're all set," Vann said.

"What?"

"Victor Osaka? Remember? Where do you go when you do that?"

"I was sort of floating around," I said. Can we go see Iyama?"

"Yes. Victor will meet us at his father's place sometime after seven. But not too late. He gets tired easily and usually goes to bed by nine. I also called Hannah Aduan-Mercer. Pacific Palisades is on the way, so I thought we might talk with her too. Okay?"

I was still floating around, not all the way back yet.

"Okay?" she repeated.

Her annoyance was all set and ready to go when she looked at me. She sat down.

"You okay?"

She took my hand.

I couldn't picture their faces, but I could see Perry Arnold and Ronnie Ganz, I could feel them being sucked down and swallowed by dark cold waters, far from shore. I could feel the undertow pulling at me.

I shook my head no. It was the best I could do.

Vann wanted to eat before we left Il Fornaio, but I thought we should get going. If she got started, it'd be dark before we got to the beach. Given the state of things between us, I was thinking I'd surprise her with a late, if not certifiably romantic, dinner at Gladstone's after we'd talked with Hannah Aduan-Mercer and Iyama. Besides, it wasn't quite four-thirty and we might be able to beat some of the rush hour traffic. Apparently, down here, rush hour was now an all day affair. We went up Beverly Drive to Sunset then crawled west along Sunset in an ocean of big Mercedes sedans, Jaguars, Porches, a few Aston Martins, an occasional DeLorean and the ubiquitous Mercedes sport coupes. We crossed over the 405. Traffic began to thin after Barrington. I tried not to think too much about Marty when we passed Saltair Drive. Not much escapes Vann. Nothing, really. When we passed his street, she put her hand on mine. It helped. I supposed Roberta still lived there. My first thought was, fuck her. Then I relented a little, thinking, okay, just a pox on her. But I continued to play with it, and settled on either fox her, or maybe a fox on her, combining the two in what I thought was a magnanimous gesture of goodwill and letting bygones be bygones. I thought it was sort of funny, nothing that Vann would find too amusing, but Nick would like it. But almost as quickly, I changed my mind. Nasty as she was, and probably still is, I should just let it go. Completely. May all her days be happy and healthy, I tried. I could tell I didn't really mean it by the way it sounded in my head. So I settled on, may she go her own way and find what she seeks and get what she deserves. That seemed non-denominational or maybe agnostic enough. Vann continued to hold my hand, but was awfully quiet, even for her. She'd always had a fine sense of when to talk and when not to, and I'd been glad not to up to now. But I was feeling better. I was going to tell her about my current progress in the human relations department, supposing she was either quiet or maybe a little mad about dinner delayed. Or my changing the subject and ignoring her question concerning the early deaths of so many of the kids. Or maybe....

"Kurt, I want to help you, but I'm not going to stumble around blindfolded and in the dark again," she began. "You've got to decide if you trust me. I don't care that you don't trust people in general. I know that about you. But do you trust me? Can you? Will you? Whatever it is... whatever...however you're connected to Phillips' dead guy, whatever it all has to do with you...you know I love you. I care about you. But I can't be this close and this far away at the same time. I won't. Can you understand that?"

I didn't think she was expecting an answer. I took it more as a rhetorical question.

"Dammit!" she said.

Or not. She let go of my hand.

"Let's talk to this Hannah woman and to Iyama Osaka. Whatever we find out we find out. But if you can't let me in, that's the end of it for me. Fair enough?"

I nodded.

"In words, please. Even one syllable ones will do. Fair enough?" she repeated.

"More than fair," I said.

We dropped back into our own thoughts, moved with the much thinned traffic past UCLA, then through the little Pacific Palisades shopping district and finally started the drop down the hill to the Pacific Coast Highway. Vann knew her way around here.

"Take a right up there at Palisades Drive," she said.

"What did you tell this Hannah woman?"

"Just that you lived on the block in the late forties and early fifties and would like to talk to her."

"Did you mention Phillips? Or anything about his investigation?"

She gave me an exasperated look.

"No."

She directed me through a series of winding little streets until we came to the end of Vista Pacifica where it swung around, facing west.

Hannah and her husband had a nice place, the only place on the cul-de-sac, high enough up the hill to have a wide, dramatic, sweep of the water view. It was probably about an acre, mostly flat, carved unceremoniously out of the hill in that devil-take-the-hindmost way they have down here of rearranging nature to suit themselves. On a more positive note, on a clear day you could imagine you were seeing Japan just where the water and sky became indistinguishable, and you might be right. The house was late fifties, early sixties Eichler, or a reasonably good copy. Slender post and beam construction, framing lots of glass framing expansive views. A shallow pitched roof. Stark, clean, crisp. So was Hannah. The front door had been left open, maybe for us, maybe to let a little more of the evening breeze slip in, but I rang the bell anyway. She came to greet us with a pair of barbeque tongs in one hand. She was about sixty, tanned, fit and looked like she made a point of staying that way. She was wearing running shorts and a tank top. Barefoot. If you didn't see her face, which was very nice, just not that of a twenty-eight year-old, you might have thought she was, or not too far from it. Her husband wasn't home yet. She led me and Vann through the house and out to a yard on the south side that also overlooked the water. She had a barbeque going, a couple of nice thick steaks that had been on just long enough so the smell was intoxicating. There was a platter with several more on the left side little wing-like table attached to the barbeque. There was a green wrought-iron table with a glass top and four matching chairs to the left and closer to the edge of the yard. Four places already set.

"It's no trouble to throw a couple more on," she said nodding towards the steaks.

"Thank you, but we're supposed to meet someone else a little later."

"Bill likes to eat as soon as he gets home," she half apologized. "In any case, by the time we get started talking, the steaks will be done. Why not just talk over dinner?"

"She's right," Vann chimed in. "Otherwise, we're either going to delay their dinner, and ruin those steaks, or be hovering over them while they eat."

So much for Gladstone's, I thought. I'd had a fleeting vision of dinner there with Vann as some sort of refuge, an oasis after talking with Hannah and Iyama Osaka. I'm not sure why, or what I'd expected from it, but without really meaning to, I'd attached some importance to it and was disappointed it wasn't going to happen. The smell of the steaks and the carnivorous look in Vann's eyes made that clear.

"Fine," I said. "Thank you."

"Don't look so glum," Hannah said, patting my arm, " you're going to love the steaks. I promise. I'm very good at this. Why don't you two take a look around the house and the yard, if you like. This is just the nicest time of day. Isn't it?"

Vann and I wandered around the yard, looking through the floor to ceiling sheets of glass into the house at the various rooms, all laid out to capture the panoramic view, and avoided talking about anything. We ended up sitting on the soft thick grass watching the sun move lower towards the water. Bill got home about ten minutes later. Hannah knew her man, knew the traffic, had it all timed to a 't'. He was shorter than she, a little heavy, balding, but had a dynamic and friendly energy about him. They kissed like they meant it. It started out a little one, puckered lips just going to touch, but then she threw her arms around his neck and made it clear she was thrilled he was home. It seemed genuine and very nice. She leaned slightly to whisper to him. He looked around and greeted us.

"Hello, there," he said. "Bill Mercer."

He came over to us, Hannah a step behind. Vann and I stood and shook hands with him.

"You got it?" she asked him in something of a stage whisper.

"Of course."

He and Hannah exchanged a smile. He handed her a little paper bag.

"This is for you," she said, reaching into the bag and showing me a Master combination lock, unable to contain her glee.

Vann looked at it, puzzled. It took a moment for it to register with me too, but it did, and I couldn't help smiling at the gesture.

"You can't imagine how long I've waited to do this!" she said. "It's been something of a contest..."

"More like sibling rivalry, I'd say," Bill teased her.

"...maybe," she said, "but more of a race to fulfill a promise, between me and Steve, my brother. Which one of us would get to do it. He'll just die when I tell him I've met you!"

Vann was looking around for an explanation.

"Never heard the story?" Bill asked her.

"No."

"It's legend with the Aduans."

"My dad, god rest his soul, wanted so bad to do this himself. He made me and Steve promise if we ever met you, we'd give you back the lock. Not the lock of course, but a lock."

Vann looked to me for an explanation.

"When I was about eight..." I began.

"Oh no you don't," Hannah said. "I get to tell her! Wait just a few more minutes and dinner will be ready and we can talk and I'll formally present it to you," she said to me.

The steaks were perfect. That and the tossed salad, some sourdough and a little cabernet and I was willing to forget all about Kevin Doyle, J. T. Dolan, J. W. Dolan and Phillips. All of it. Just listen to Hannah telling Vann about the garage doors and the locks, watch the sun ease itself towards the water and let everything else go.

The story had taken on a life of its own in her family. Steve and Hannah were both in college in 1951 when I'd switched the locks, their mother and father, Spencer and Margaret Aduan, living in the lower part of the duplex they owned next door to Shelly and Norma. The retelling of it had become a part of the family's Thanksgiving ritual until their father's death in 1978. Each time he told the story, Hannah told us, there were more cars piled on top of each other and it took the police longer to sort it all out than in the previous telling. She said her mom pooh-poohed it, but her father always claimed he and some of the others who'd been locked out formed a vigilante group, a sort of commando unit, and scoured the neighborhood for the ringleader who'd organized the whole thing, swearing they'd kill the bastard when they got their hands on him. He'd gotten into several arguments with Shelly, convinced she knew who was behind it, only she wouldn't say. She just kept telling him to settle down and get a grip. When the police told him it was a kid, me, he was dumbfounded. He couldn't believe it. He'd imagined his enemy, steeled himself for battle, and now, it turns out it was a kid. "But some-how," Hannah said, "he was able to convince himself that that was as bad or worse. How could a kid be so irresponsible? What kind of kids were being raised around here? What kind of people raised them? Was this what the country had gone through four years of hell for? What kind of country had we become? Kenny Lester and John Erwin had tried to explain the situation to him. They told him about the model plane, how you were trying to save it, but he just wasn't about to accept any excuses for such behavior. It made him crazy for reasons he couldn't explain and didn't understand, but completely out of proportion, as my mom would remind him every Thanksgiving."

"Then you showed up at the front door with this little card in your hand from the San Vicente Hardware store. Dad said later, he couldn't believe how small you were. He said he took the card, read the back of it about a free lock, looked at you and just started yelling. He said you had tears in your eyes but just stood there letting him yell and yell. He said he didn't even remember what he'd said twenty minutes later. My mother heard him and came to the door not knowing what to expect, but certainly not you. She said she put her hand on his shoulder and told him to stop, but he didn't. He couldn't. Shelly was in her front yard and heard him too. She saw you standing there and charged over and put her arm around you. 'Fer Christskes, Spence,' she told him, 'stop it, just stop it, you're scaring him to death.' But you told her, 'It's okay, he can yell at me if he wants too,' then you told my dad, 'I just wanted to apologize and say I hope you'll go get a new lock.' Dad said you just stood there with the tears running down your face, waiting to see if he wanted to yell any more, and when he didn't, you said, 'sorry' and left. Shelly stayed there for another ten minutes reading dad the riot act, calling him every name she could think of, which, if you knew Shelly, must have taken at least ten minutes. Every time dad told the story he cried. He said he saw you on your bicycle delivering papers and working at the carwash on Beverly Boulevard to pay for the locks and it just killed him that he'd yelled at you. It just killed him."

Hannah was laughing, but she had tears in her eyes.

"When he was telling the story about all the locked garages, all the cars backed up everywhere, the honking and yelling and police cutting off the locks, he made it very, very funny. The whole thing, telling it, it just delighted him. And to cap it off, he'd hold his hand up about this high," she said, demonstrating, "and remind us and our guests just how small you were. As the laughing died down, he'd pause, waiting for everyone's attention, and then he'd tell us all how he'd yelled at you. Every time. 'I can't believe I did that,' he'd say, his eyes starting to tear. 'I'm so thankful for all of you, for all of us, for having come home, safe, for our being here together and being good to each other. I can't believe I did that. I'm so ashamed.' And the tears would be running down his face. It was sort of his Thanksgiving prayer. Every year. A kind of atonement. He made me and Steve promise, swear an oath, that if either of us ever met you..."

She took a deep breath, wiping away tears, "Rest in peace, dad. Sorry," she said, and handed me the lock.

"Kevin Doyle," I said a little later. "Do you remember him?"

"Of course I do," Hannah said. "Mom and dad bought the duplex on Oakhurst in 1940. I was twelve, Steve was ten. I think Kevin was eighteen or nineteen. Maybe twenty. He was sort of weird."

"Weird how?"

"I don't know, just creepy. We heard from neighbors that when he was young, he and his mother and father had lived together as a family, there down the block...weren't they right across from you?"

"Yes."

"...they'd lived there from the early thirties until his parents separated, a little before we got there."

"What was so creepy about him?"

"It's hard to put your finger on. He just sort of always hung around. He didn't work. Didn't go to school. And he wanted to play with kids our age."

"Play?"

"You know, like play catch with kids. Like he was their big brother or something"

"You don't think it could have been because he was an only child?"

"Maybe, but still, he was definitely weird. And mean. He had this mean streak. Oakhurst was the kind of street where parents felt their kids were safe. We played 'til dark or after and no one gave it a thought. I remember your brother, Marty, during the war, he must have been six or seven, marching up and down the street with some old metal army helmet strapped on his head, a cut-off broomstick for a rifle, bony knees sticking out from below his khaki shorts, never sneakers, he always wore hard shoes and dark socks. He was going to win the war single-handedly. Boy, I don't know where that came from, but I can see him so clearly."

She was smiling at the image, but it then it dawned on her, "I'm sorry," she said, reaching out to touch my arm. "That was stupid of me. I read about his death."

"No," I assured her, "it's good to hear things like that. He was eight years older than me, so I only know him at that age from pictures. But you were saying about Kevin Doyle? Mean. How so?"

"Right. Kevin. You know how some bigger kids like to bully little kids? Push them or poke them or trip them when they think no one's looking? That was Kevin. As safe as the neighborhood was, my dad saw him around, talked to him a couple of times, and came to the firm conclusion that we should steer clear of him. He made it clear to me in no uncertain terms, it was my responsibility to bring Steve inside if Kevin were around. "

"How old were you then? And Steve?" Vann asked her.

"This was just before the war, probably June or July of 1940, so I was twelve, Steve, ten."

"And Marty?" Vann asked me.

"He turned five a little later that summer," I told her.

"When the war came, my dad was really a little too old and already had two kids, but felt it was his duty to serve, so he volunteered. With everything else on his mind, it still was important enough for him to remind me about Kevin. As it turned out, it didn't matter since Kevin joined up too."

I asked Hannah, "How big was Kevin?"

"Not very. Maybe five-eight or nine. Not skinny, but slender. Think Frank Sinatra when he was young, and you'd have a pretty good picture of him. Except a little more muscular and without even an occasional smile. And he had these mean narrow eyes."

"What's this about?" Bill asked me, becoming a little uncomfortable with the tone of the conversation.

"The short version is, there's a murder investigation under way in Beverly Hills. While digging the foundations for a new project on the old Rathbone property, they found a skeleton. The police don't know who it is yet, but I think it's Kevin Doyle."

"Really?" Hannah said, her hand going to her mouth in surprise. "But what makes them think it's murder?"

"You mean, other than the fact that the body was buried in someone's back yard?" I teased.

"Well," she smiled, "yes, other than that."

"There was a leather belt around the neck," I told her.

"Well, that's certainly a clue, isn't it," she said with an amused nod to Bill, patting him on the knee.

She was beginning to enjoy the whole thing like it were a parlor game. For a time there, so was I. She had an infectious warmth and humor, an unmistakable and genuine goodwill. Bill was a lucky man, I thought. They both were. I looked at Vann. She was enjoying them too.

"Then, all they have to do is find the owner of the belt!" she said, and leaned over to give Bill a little kiss on the lips, like, that's that. She'd wrapped up he whole case and we hadn't even had dessert yet.

"They have," Vann told her.

"No!" Hannah said. "Really?"

"It's his," Vann said, smiling at me.

"When do they think this happened?" Bill asked.

"1950 or '51," I said.

"And you were how old then?" Hannah asked, smiling.

"We've been through this," Vann said, getting to what was becoming her favorite part. "Seven or eight. A little young, even for him."

She and Hannah shared a laugh, until the timetable sank in and Hannah's smile faded.

"1951? That's the summer you switched the locks, isn't it?"

When it comes, it comes out of nowhere. No warning, no creeping sense of unease. Just, not there, there.

"Indeed," I said, unable to stay seated. "I left something in the car. I'll be right back."

"Are you okay?" Vann said.

"Fine," I said.

As I headed through the house, I knew I'd let this go too far, too fast, and I wasn't ready. Then again, I'd probably never be. That all too familiar sense of suffocating had engulfed and overwhelmed me. All this fresh ocean air and I can't breathe, I thought. A hell-of-a-note. Pace yourself, buddy-boy, pace yourself. First things first. Breathe. Then breathe some more. That would be a start. There was nothing in the car I wanted or needed, but after standing next to it for a minute or so, I felt better. The strange tunnel-like, slightly blurred yellow vision was dissipating. I could feel the air washing over and into me. I was okay. Again. But I wasn't sure I wanted to see Iyama tonight. I wasn't sure I could. There's only so much ocean air, and right now, it didn't seem like enough. On the other hand, Phillips couldn't be this stupid. If he didn't know about Hannah or her brother, he would soon enough. If he didn't have Kevin Doyle's name yet, he would. And Miriam's? And Shelly's? Even Iyama. Dolan would know these people, or know of them, and whatever Dolan was worried about or wanted to hide, he seemed to think he was both using and could control Phillips to that end. I knew I needed to get there first, and Iyama was next. Suck it up buster, I told myself. Postponing it would only allow Phillips to close the gap between what I knew and could find out and what he did. Unless I was kidding myself about being a few steps ahead of him. Since I couldn't know for sure, I'd assume it until it proved false. I went back through the house. Hannah and Vann had cleared the table and had brought coffee and a pretty mean looking cake.

"Get what you needed?" Vann asked me.

"What?"

"Whatever you went to the car for?" she reminded me.

"Right. Yes. We should go pretty soon. Iyama probably doesn't want to be up much longer."

"Oh, my god. Iyama?! Not Iyama Osaka?" Hannah said.

"Did you know him?"

"Of course. He's alive? And you know where he is?"

"We're going to see him when we leave here," I told her. "He lives at Point Dume."

"You've got to be kidding! He lives there? So close? I can't believe it!"

"What's so shocking about Iyama being alive and out here at the beach? He's only about sixty-six or sixty-seven. He's sick, but you didn't know that. Did you?"

I had a sudden flash of paranoia, Phillips or Dolan or both, pulling strings behind the curtain, contacting and talking to everyone just ahead of me, so that they all knew each other and knew everything there was to know about all of it, but were putting on an act to misdirect and deflect me.

"No. I haven't even heard his name in thirty-five years."

I looked at her face for some telltale sign of duplicity while she poured the coffee, then started to cut the cake.

"What?" she said, looking up at me, a little smile on her lips, the kind that had deceived and undone the resolve of men since the dawn of time. She was either a very good actress, or like Vann, genuine to the core. I was going with genuine.

"So what's so surprising about it?"

"Sit down, Kurt. Have some cake and coffee. There's a lot more to tell about Oakhurst back then, and a lot of it won't go down easy. You've heard of Manzanar?"

I took out my little pocket watch out. It was six thirty-five. The sun was still inching its way lower and I figured we could get to Point Dume in about fifteen or twenty minutes this time of the day. If we left by seven or seven-fifteen, we should get there pretty close to the time Victor said he'd meet us, and not keep Iyama up too late. I took the cup of coffee Hannah was handing me and sat down.

"Nedlam's Bakery down in the Village makes this. The best damn German Chocolate cake in the world," Bill said.

"Enough to take the bitterest taste out of your mouth," Hannah said with a sigh.

And so it was. Almost

# Chapter 20

### *The Skies Are Blue and Clear Again*
### June 10 & 11, 1951

WHEN ALLEN AND I GOT as far back up Beverly Boule-
vard as Robertson, I'd had it. I couldn't push the pedals anymore. I got
off the Red Rider and started to walk it. It was only about six blocks back
to Oakhurst. They were long city blocks, but only six or maybe seven of
them.

"What are you doing?" Allen said. "It'll take forever if we walk our
bikes!"

"You can go ahead. I can't pedal any more."

Sarah and the others were long gone by then.

"Jeez, come on, just try to ride a little longer," he begged, "I don't
want to leave you, but I gotta get home too. Megan and I are supposed
to stay by the phone."

"I can't!" I said. "Just go. I'll be okay."

"You sure?"

"I'm sure."

"Okay," he said, "I'll see you later," and he took off.

After about two blocks, I wasn't so tired any more, so I tried to ride
again. I was more wobbly than before, but if I went slowly, I thought I
could make it home okay. I sort of wobbled away from the parked cars
a little too far into the traffic lane and heard the sound of tires screech-
ing and a horn honking. I wanted to look over my shoulder to see, but
couldn't do that and balance too, and I wanted to tell the driver I was
sorry, but I'd have to stop to do that, so I just yelled, "Sorry!" and kept
going. When she passed me I could see her lips moving but couldn't hear
what she was saying, which was probably good.

When I got home I was really tired. I parked the Red Rider on the
sidewalk and looked it over. No scratches and not even much dirt from
the lot behind Gilmore Field. I planned on washing it at the end of the
day, after I rode around the neighborhood delivering the cards from the
hardware store.

I went down the driveway and through the back porch into the kitchen.

"Mom?"

No answer.

"Sarah?"

No answer.

"Nick?" I yelled, just for the fun of it, like he might be home alone.
No Nick either.

Well, wherever everyone was, I hoped they were having as much fun as me. The idea of passing out the cards had seemed terrible. It would be so embarrassing I had even been thinking about getting up really early and sneaking out of our house and doing it at four-thirty or five so no one would see me. But now, it didn't seem like a big deal or such a bad thing since I was going to be on the Red Rider doing it. I got the cards from our bedroom and took a pen and a fat rubber band from Marty's desk and went out through the front door to the porch. I sat on the bottom step where I could see the Red Rider if I wanted and I began to fill out card after card the way Mr. Mahoney had shown me. It wasn't as hot now anyway, but the jacaranda trees were like a big pale green net strung over the street, keeping some of the extra heat away, so it was ''bout as good as it gets', which is what Maurice said a lot. It was quiet too, no one coming or going, no cars, no people walking up or down the sidewalk, just me and the Red Rider and the cards and pretty soon I was done. Now all I had to do was put one on every door whose garage lock we'd switched. I'd switched. It hadn't been part of my plan at all, in fact, it was so far from it I'd never even have thought of it by myself, but when I looked at the Red Rider and got the happy feeling just seeing it gave me, it was like it was talking to me and I could hear it as plain as anything, telling me I should apologize to them all.

So that was the new plan. I'd start next door and work my way down Oakhurst on our side, cross Beverly Boulevard down to Alden, then come back up all the way to Lower Santa Monica, then down our side again and home. I put the rubber band around most of the cards and dropped them down the front of my shirt. I put about ten in my pocket. I rode the Red Rider on the sidewalk to the house next to ours and put it back on its kickstand.

Since it had six apartments and only two garages, I didn't know who I should give a card or apologize to. I went up the walkway through the open gate between the dark green bushes. There were three apartments upstairs and three downstairs and they all had double glass doors that were divided into lots of small windows that faced towards Beverly. Upstairs, on the little balcony that ran in front of them, there was a pair of the doors that were opened out and pushed all the way around until they were against the wall for the middle apartment, which pretty much would have opened up their whole living room to anyone walking by, so I thought maybe that must be why they grew the bushes so thick. I climbed the stairs slowly, trying to think of what to say to whoever was there. I thought maybe I'd explain about the model plane and Allen not helping me put it back on the shelve, but decided that part didn't matter, especially to these guys a block away, so I'd just say, sorry, and leave it at that. I figured I might as well get it over with, so I ran up the last few stairs.

"What's all that racket?" a man's voice yelled.

It only took him about two seconds to poke his head out of the open doors and look my way. I stopped there right where I was. He was wearing glasses and had part of a newspaper in his hand.

"We don't want any!" he said, waving the paper at me once like he was shooing away a buzzing fly. Then he turned and went back in.

I heard a woman's voice saying, "Harry, who are you yelling at?"

"Some kid," I heard him answer.

"Well, what does he want?"

"How should I know!"

"Oh, Harry, for pete'sake."

I stood there not sure what to do. Maybe I heard the Red Rider wrong. Maybe it meant I should be sorry, but should just leave the cards in the mailbox or something. That was probably it. I turned to look behind me. From up here on the balcony I could see just over the tops of the bushes so I could see part of the handlebars and most of the front wheel. I waited to see if it had any more ideas, but it was quiet. I must have heard it wrong. I was all set to go back down and leave a card in the mailbox that was on the gate post.

"Can I help you?" a woman said.

I turned around. She was older than my mom, but younger than Pop and Nanny.

"I'm the kid that switched the locks on the garages," I began.

"Oh?"

She turned back into the room.

"Harry, I think you'll want to hear this."

"Fer Chrisskakes, Berna," I could hear him complain. "What?"

Then he was standing beside her.

"What?" he said.

"You're Abe's grandson, next door, aren't you?" she asked me.

"Yes mam."

"He switched the locks," she told him.

All of a sudden, he looked like he was going to explode, or maybe come after me, or both, but she put her hand on his arm. She had a nice smile and it didn't seem like she was mad about the locks at all. I stood there waiting to see if he was going to yell at me or tell me to get out of there and when he didn't I took a card out of my pocket and held it out towards them. I didn't want to get any closer to him, just in case, and I wanted to say sorry, but my mouth wouldn't open. The woman must have read my mind I think, because she asked me if I was trying to say something.

"I'm sorry," I finally said. "Here," I said, wiggling the card a little, "this is for a new lock at the San Vicente Hardware store."

The woman took the few steps towards me and I handed her the card. She looked at it front and back.

"You arranged this?"

"Mr. Lester up the street helped me, and Mr. Mahoney, his wife's father, he owns the store. He opened an account for me, so all you have to do is take the card to his store and he'll give you a new lock."

"And you're going to pay for it?" the man asked me.

"Yes, sir."

"Well, that's very responsible of you, isn't it, Harry?" she said, poking him.

"I suppose it is," he said. "That was a pretty nasty trick you played, but I'm glad to see you're making good on it. You going around to everyone on the block?"

"Everyone whose lock I switched."

"It's pretty hot out," he said. "Would you like a Coke? Go get him a Coke, Berna."

He still sounded sort of crabby, but he was being pretty nice, and it was hot, so I said yes. His wife brought me the Coke and had already popped the cap. I stood there and drank it in about ten seconds, and handed her the bottle so she could get the deposit back. I thanked them and went back to the Red Rider.

I worked my way down to Alden, crossed over, and started back up on the east side of Oakhurst. Some people were home, some not. If they weren't, I'd leave the card tucked between the door and the jamb where they'd be sure to see it. I was surprised at how many of the people who were home, weren't too mad about it. It was about half and half. Either way, I'd apologize and give them the card and some would scold me and a few yelled, but all of them thanked me for the new lock. A few people had already bought new locks and didn't need the card, so that was pretty good because I wouldn't have to pay for as many.

I parked the Red Rider in front of 344 and started up the walk.

"I see you got your bike," someone said.

I turned around and saw it was the paper route guy.

"I just got it yesterday." I told him.

"Isn't it a little big for you?"

"A little, but I'm getting used to it."

"I'm still looking for a few delivery boys. You interested now that you got the bike?"

"I am, but my mom didn't like the idea."

"Why not?"

"She thought riding in the street so soon after I got the bike was too dangerous."

"But you're riding in the street now. Right?"

"I suppose."

"So what's the difference?"

"I don't know."

"Well, I've got a route all laid out in this neighborhood. Forty-two papers. It could be all yours."

"How much would I make?"

"Well, that's a little hard to say. You'd have to deliver six afternoons a week and Sunday late mornings. If you could handle that, you might be able to add some extra customers to the route and make a little more. You know, friends or neighbors or family."

"More than what?" I asked him. It seemed like he should be able to figure it out.

"Like I said, it's a little hard to say, exactly. If you can do it, we can talk about that later. Do you still have my number?"

"Yes."

"Why don't you talk to your mom again and give me a call if you can do it. And tell her once a month you've got to collect from your customers. You can do that on any of the last four days of the month. Most of the guys do it with their Saturday delivery. And at least once a month we have subscription nights. You'd have to do that too."

"What's that mean?"

"It means I pick you and the other route boys up around six, take you to a nice neighborhood, and you go from house to house and see if they'd like to subscribe. If they do, you get a credit. If you get enough credits, you can get some pretty nice prizes or some bonus money. You'd be home by nine."

"Does that have to be part of the job?"

I didn't really like this going door to door stuff much.

"It does. Call and let me know. Otherwise, I've got to keep delivering this route myself until I find someone. See you," he said and drove off towards Beverly.

I went up the walk to 334. There were three steps up to a small covered porch with 334A to the left and 334B to the right, across from each other. The door to B was wide open and I could hear music. It was still pretty warm out, so that's probably why the door was open. I couldn't remember if there was more than one garage for this place. I didn't want to leave extra cards around and end up buying more locks than I'd switched. On the other hand, since some people had already bought their own, I figured it would probably come out about even. I rang the bell for B.

Next to Norma and Miriam, the most beautiful girl I'd ever seen came to the door. She was wearing shorts and a t-shirt and she was barefoot. She had long black hair with red in it, the color of a dark cherry, and her teeth were perfectly white.

"Hi," she said. "Who are you?"

I forgot. I just stood there. I couldn't remember anything.

"What's your name?" she said, kneeling down so she didn't tower over me, then shifted so that she was sitting on her heels. "My name's Julie."

She reached out and we shook.

"Kurt," I finally said.

"Sharon," she called over her shoulder, "we've got company. The cutest little kid."

Sharon came and she was almost as pretty as Julie. Sharon had her hair wrapped in a towel and was wearing a short white terry cloth robe. It only came to her knees and her legs were dark and smooth and shiny. She must spend a lot of time at the beach, I thought. She had a script in her hand, like the one Norma had had in her car.

"So, what can we do for you, Kurt?" Julie said.

"I switched the locks on the garages and I'm sorry and you can get a new one with this," I said, handing her one of the cards.

She read it. She looked at me, and her eyebrows sort of squeezed together.

"Switched what locks? What for?"

"It's a long story," I told her, "but the police had to cut off a lot of locks and I'm going to pay for the new ones."

"Just the little mischief maker, aren't you? How are you going to pay for them? If you don't mind my asking, that is."

"I work at the car wash up on Beverly on Saturdays and I might have the paper route for the Daily Mirror in this neighborhood. Might," I said.

"That's pretty industrious of you. Aren't you a little young for all that?"

"No, not really. I just finished paying off my bicycle, see," I said, pointing it out to them there on the sidewalk, sort of bragging, really, "so the paper route's possible now."

"Well, you should give this to Morrey," she said, standing up and nodding at 334A. "He's our landlord and it's his garage. We park on the street."

"Oh. Okay," I said.

She had the card in her hand and I didn't want to ask her to give it back because it seemed like Indian-giving. But on the other hand, I didn't want to pay for a bunch of people getting free locks for nothing, even if they were as beautiful as she was. I'd just have to trust her, I thought. Anyway, if she didn't have a garage, she didn't need a lock, so it would probably be okay. I turned to the other door and knocked.

"Oh," she said, "he's out of town until next week, but you can leave it with us. We'll give it to him."

That solved both problems.

"Thank you," I said.

"If you get the paper route, let us know. If you need more customers, we could subscribe," Sharon said, looking at Julie to make sure.

"Of course we would," Julie said.

I was trying to decide which one was prettier. It was just about a tie, but I thought Julie was. Sharon was close, though.

"Is that for Love Nest?" I asked, looking at the script she had in her hand.

They both laughed.

"Don't I wish! No, I'm just auditioning for a bit part. Even if it gets made, no one will ever see it," Sharon said. "We are both actresses, though."

"Yes we are, oh yes we are!" Julie teased with Sharon. "But what do you know about Love Nest?" she asked me. "Next, you're going to tell us you're a producer? A car washer, a paper boy, and a producer, right?" she laughed. "I love this town."

"A producer? Me? No. I don't even know what that is. My friend, Norma, has a script like that for Love Nest. She has a job on it."

"Norma?" they said at the same time, looking at each other. "Norma?! You know Norma? You're friends with her?"

"Sure," I told them.

Their eyes got wide and they started laughing and acting silly. They grabbed each other and sort of danced up and down like I'd told them they'd won a new Cadillac or something. I figured they probably knew Norma sometimes was Marilyn Monroe.

"She lives up the street from me with her friend, Shelly. We have breakfast together sometimes at the carwash," I bragged again.

"Shelly Winters?"

"Breakfast with Norma. She lives with Shelly. I don't know her last name, but she works on movies too."

"Do you think you could introduce us her sometime?" Sharon said, with a big smile. "To Norma?"

I wanted to say yes because they were both being so nice to me and were so excited about just the idea of meeting Norma, but, really, I wished I'd just kept my mouth shut.

"I don't think I should," I said. "Sorry."

I could see by their expressions that I'd spoiled their fun, but it didn't seem like the kind of stuff Norma wanted, and now, because I'd been bragging too much, first about the Red Rider, now Norma, I'd made a whole new mess.

"Sorry," I said again.

"Well," Julie said putting her hand on my shoulder, "sometimes when you're friends with someone that's famous, you have to protect them a little. That's very gallant of you. When we're famous, I hope you'll be as protective of us."

"I will," I promised them.

Still, they both looked disappointed and I felt bad, like I'd ruined everything. George Bowen said the fastest way to end good fortune is to brag about it. He was right.

"Hey," Sharon smiled, "buck up, kiddo." She messed my hair and bent down and kissed my cheek. "You're right. We're just a couple of struggling actors and got a little too excited about a hero of ours. Next time you see her, tell her we admire her and love her work. Can you do that?"

"Sure," I said. "I should get going. More cards to deliver," I told them.      "Be sure and tell us if you get the paper route so we can subscribe," Julie said.

"I will. Bye."

After another eight or ten houses and about twenty cards, I crossed back to our side of Beverly and realized Kevin Doyle's place was coming up. Just thinking about him I could smell cigarette smoke in the air. It was only my imagination, but it was like he could appear and disappear like some kind of ghost, using the smoke to come and go through like a magic curtain. I thought about skipping him, but knew I couldn't. I thought about tiptoeing up to his door and putting the card in either the mail box or between the door and jamb. I even thought about giving the card to Miriam and asking her to give it to Kevin. I hadn't switched her lock, and I knew she and Kevin were sort of friends, so she'd probably do it for me. I was pretty sure she would, anyway, but I could hear Pop's voice in my head, telling Mr. Sullivan, 'he's taking care of it', so I knew there was no escaping it. I had to do it, and that was that.

I parked the Red Rider right in front of his walk for a quick getaway if I needed one. If he started yelling again, like he had in Miriam's kitchen, I was going to make a run for it. There was a note over the door bell that said, 'out of order, knock', so I did. It took pretty long before he opened the door, but when he did, the room behind him was so dark there was nothing at all to see except him, and he looked bad. Not mean or angry bad as usual, just bad, like he'd been sick and could barely get out of bed to answer the door. He smelled bad too. Not only the cigarette smell, but something else. I didn't know what, but whatever it was, I wanted to get away from it and from him. He looked at me like he wasn't sure what I was, not like he didn't know who I was, but what I was. I had the feeling I didn't make any sense to him at all. I handed him a card.

"I'm sorry for the trouble I caused by switching your lock," I told him. "This is for a new one."

He looked at the card, flipped it over, then back.

"Okay," was all he said.

Then he shut the door very gently. I went back to my bike and was about to get on when Miriam's window opened and she called down to me.

"Pretty cool bike, Kurt. It's all yours now?"

"It sure is, and ..."

I was about to tell her that I'd paid it all off yesterday, every last penny, but remembered not to just in time.

"Good for you. Wanna come up for a coke to celebrate?"

"I'd like to, but I've got to finish giving out these cards for new locks at the San Vicente Hardware store. You, know…for the locks I switched that had to be cut off."

"That was quite a show you treated us to. Don't tell anyone I said so," she kind of whispered, "but I thought it was pretty inventive. And funny too, especially since you didn't switch mine. As a Catholic, I was particularly honored to be on your special Passover list," she said, joking me. "See you later," she said and closed the window.

The rest of the apologies and card passing out went pretty well. All except for the guy next to Shelly and Norma's place. He was really mad and yelled a lot, so much that Shelly heard him and came over from her yard to make him stop, but I'd already decided way before I'd even gotten that far, no more bragging about the Red Rider or Norma, no more complaining about Allen, even inside my head, and if someone wanted to yell at me, that was probably fair. I didn't like it and he sort or scared me, but all in all, it was fair. It was nice of Shelly to want to help me, but sometimes you have to pay with more than just money. George Bowen said that too, but he was talking about the war.

It took about three houses after the guy next to Shelly and Norma before my eyes stopped crying. It wasn't me so much, but my eyes wouldn't stop and I couldn't make them, so I just tried to pretend they weren't. In a way, it might have even been a help, since even if they wanted to yell at me, the people at the next couple of houses could see my eyes were already crying so they didn't have to yell and try to make me. Mr. Sullivan's was the last one on our side whose lock I'd switched, so he was going to be my last stop. I hoped he wouldn't be home. I knew he'd complain about the hedge and the lock, and to tell the truth, I was sort of tired and didn't want to hear about it, even if it was fair. On the other hand, I wanted him to be there so I could hand him the card in person and prove that what Pop said was true, even though he didn't believe it, that I was going to take care of it and get him a new lock.

From the outside, Sullivan's place didn't look as big as it turned out. It was two stories high of course, but if anything, our lot was a little wider than his, so the width of his building was about the same as ours from the front. But when I'd gone up the steps, I discovered the front door was really just an entry door into the building. There were buzzers and mailboxes for twelve apartments. How come I didn't know that, I wondered? I'd always thought it was strange that he had six garages, and I'd switched the locks on all of them, but I never saw anyone besides Sullivan around, so I thought the whole place was just his house. There weren't any kids there that I knew of, so maybe that's why I didn't pay much attention to it, except for the bush. Anyway, inside, there was a hallway that was way too dark. Mr. Sullivan's apartment was the first one on the left. There were two more on the left, three more on the right, and stairs that went to the second floor and six more up there, I guessed. There was a glass door at the end of the hallway that let some light in, but not enough to take away the creepy feeling I got being there. I could see the back of the garages through that door, so he didn't have a back yard at all. That's how they fit the twelve apartments in.

I took the cards from the inside of my shirt and counted out six, put the rest back and knocked on the door. No one answered and boy, was I glad. I bent over and as I was sliding the cards under the door, it opened. I stood up and there he was. He didn't look happy to see me. Not happy at all. His mouth was all scrunched up and moving like he was already talking to me, sort of grumbling really, but the words hadn't come out yet. If anyone was going to yell at me, I thought, Mr. Sullivan would make the guy next to Norma and Shelly look like Howdy Doody. It looked like my eyes had finally quit crying a little too soon, because they were just going to have to start up all over again.

He looked at me, then down at the floor at the cards. He bent over

and picked them up. He counted them. He looked at me, then back at the
cards, flipped them over and read about the new locks. He put them in
his shirt pocket and slammed the door. I just stood there for a second or
two, surprised and relieved.

"Sorry, Mr. Sullivan," I shouted through the door.

I rode by the Courtyard as slowly as I could without falling to see if
George was sitting on his step. He was. If I were going to brag to anyone
about the Red Rider, I wished I'd saved it for him, since he helped me get
the job with Mr. Avery in the first place. I thought I could thank him and
just show him the bike and how neat it was without it being bragging.

He had the whole Sunday LA Times spread out at his feet, taking sections from a pile on the left and putting them on a pile to the right when
he finished with them. He was wearing his tan army khaki pants and an
undershirt with ribs running up and down, like the ones Pop wore on Saturdays, and black shiny shoes, and like always, a cigarette in the corner
of his mouth, his head tipped a little sideways so the smoke missed his
eyes. There was a tattoo high up on his arm I'd never seen before. When
I got closer to him I could see it said, Semper Fidelis below a round ball
with an anchor and above it, Gung Ho.

"What's that mean?" I asked him, pointing at it.

He looked to where I was pointing. He didn't answer right away. He
smoked some more and sat there thinking and smoking, a section of
paper drooping in his hands.

"Semper Fi is the Marines' motto. It means always faithful, always
loyal. Gung Ho is Chinese for 'Work Together', or 'Work in Harmony'.
I was in a group of Marines called the Raiders. That was our motto."

He saw the bike.

"Hey, the man's got some wheels," he said nodding, towards the
Red Rider and putting away the section of the paper he'd been reading.
"Good for you."

"I don't want to brag, but George, it's the neatest bike ever! That's not
bragging, it's just plain true!" I told him.

"You bet. I think that's about the prettiest bike I ever saw. How's she
ride?"

"Like a dream, George, just like a dream. I'm still just getting used to
it and I just barely reach the pedals, so I wobble a lot, but it's the most
perfect thing ever. Thank you for getting me the job at the car wash."

"I just helped get you in, but you've proved yourself by working.
That's the important thing. Avery's glad to have you. You're gonna keep
working there, now that you've got the bike?"

"I want to anyway, but I've got to, to pay for the locks," I told him. "I
just finished handing out cards for people to get new ones at the San Vincente Hardware store. Mr. Lester's wife's father owns it and he opened
an account for me and anyone that needs a new lock can go get one and
charge it to me and I pay it off."

"Kenny told me about that. Well, you're doing the right thing. You'll

have 'em paid off in no time and after that, it's smooth sailing all the way
to the bank," he said, his hand was making a motion like a boat going
through easy waters. "How'd it go? Anyone give you flak about it?"

"A few."

"Yeah? Like what?"

"Oh, you know, stuff about it was mean or irresponsible, stuff like
that? But that's okay."

"Nothing worse?"

"Not really."

"What's that mean?"

"A couple."

"Kevin Doyle? Sullivan?"

"No, neither of them. Just some others, but it's okay. Really."

"You're sure?"

"Yeah," I told him. Then, "You're sort of friends with Kevin Doyle,
right?"

"Well, I try to look out for him if I can. Why? He didn't bother you in
some other way, did he?"

"No. I thought he'd be one of the people who'd want to yell at me,
but he didn't."

"What'd he do?"

"Nothing. He wasn't mean or angry or crabby like usual, he wasn't
anything at all."

"Well, that's good, isn't it?"

"I don't think so, George. He looked like he was sick or something.
And he smelled bad."

"I'll look into it. Thanks for letting me know."

"Sure," I told him, then I asked, "Have you see my mom and Nick or
Sarah around?"

"No. No one home?"

"Nope."

"Well, you can hang out here with me 'til they get back if you like.
I'm just going to work my way through the rest of the paper. Want the
funnies?"

"No thanks. I think I'll take a practice ride to school and back. You
know, to get ready for riding there tomorrow. But you know what?"

"What?"

"I saw the paper route guy again, and the paper route's still available."

"What paper route?"

"Well, I met this guy the other day who's the new route master for
the Daily Mirror around here and he needs some delivery boys. I didn't
have the bike then and it looked like I might not ever get it and even if I
did, my mom thought it was too dangerous for me to be a paper boy on
a bicycle that I'd just started riding, so that was the end of that, but I've
got the bike now and he's still got the route and said I could have it if
my mom said so. With the paper route and the car wash, I could pay for

the locks in no time. And then, it's just smooth sailing all the way to the bank," I joked him, doing the same thing with my hand that he had.

"That's an awful lot of work," George said. "I know you could probably handle it, but that wouldn't leave much time for having any fun, would it?"

"We're out of school after next week. I'll have plenty of time for the paper route and the car wash and fun," I told him.

"Sounds like you've thought it all out. I hope your mom sees it your way, then."

"I don't know about her, but I think my dad will. That might do it."

"Well, good luck with it. And have a nice ride."

I rode past our driveway to see if Pop's car was in the garage or if there was any sign of Sarah or my mom or Nick. Still no one. I figured Sarah and the rest of the Oakhurst Irregulars were probably meeting somewhere. I turned the bike around and was about to head up the street when Allen called from his front porch.

"Where're you going?"

"I'm going to take a practice ride to school. Wanna come?"

"Can't," he said, jerking his thumb over his shoulder, "the phone."

"Okay, see you later."

"Watch out for parked cars and driveways."

"I will."

I got as far as Kenny Lester's place. He was sitting on the bottom step smoking a cigarette.

"I can see why you wanted that bike so bad. It's a beauty," he said.

"Thanks. I think so too. Did you tell Joseph about the garages and the locks and stuff?"

"I may have mentioned it," he smiled.

"Well, thanks, because...well, just thanks. I got the cards all passed out, so that's that."

"Good. We'll just wait and see who shows up. How many did you hand out."

"Sixty-eight."

"Could have been worse," he said. "I saw you coming up the street. You having trouble reaching the pedals?"

"Not too much...well, maybe a little."

"When I was a kid, we had a fix for that."

"You did?"

"Sure, we'd just tape some wooden blocks on the pedals until we grew a little more. Wanna try it?"

"It won't mess up the bike, will it?"

"No. They'll come right off when you don't need them anymore."

"Okay."

He came out to the parkway and held the bike and had me sit with my leg down as far as it would go when the pedal was at the bottom. Only the front part of my foot reached. Kenny held my foot in a more comfortable position and checked to see what it would take.

"Let's go see what we've got," he said, and I followed him down the side of his house to the garage. He found a board that looked about right to him and took a hand saw off a peg-board and cut four pieces from it and put the saw back, then he sanded the fuzz off the edges. There was friction tape on his work bench and he grabbed it.

"This should do it."

I followed him back to my bike. He had me hold two of the pieces on each side of one pedal while he wrapped the tape tightly around them. Then we did the other side.

"Try that."

I got on the bike and rode up the street a little ways. It was a miracle! I could reach easily and push harder without struggling or wobbling. It was like a whole new new bike all over again!

"That's great," I yelled to him. "What a great idea!"

"I thought that might help."

"I'm going to take a practice ride to school. It'll be easy now. Thanks!"

"Have fun. And watch out for parked cars," he called to me, "you know, someone opening their door. Be careful."

"I will. Bye."

I got to the corner and turned left on Lower Santa Monica. When I'd gotten almost to Maple, Norma tooted at me coming from the other way. She stopped and so did I.

"Oh sweetie," she said, "no wonder you were so excited about getting that bike. It's just beautiful."

"Thanks. Kenny Lester just put some blocks on the pedals so I can reach them better. It really works great."

"Where're you off to?"

"I'm taking a practice ride to school. That way when I want to ride there tomorrow and my mom says it's too soon, I can tell her I've already done it and it worked out fine."

"Sounds like a good plan. Where's your mom now?"

"I don't know. I was at a Stars' game with Marty and Sarah and some other kids and then we came home and I passed out the cards for the garage locks and when I was done no one was home, so I'm taking the practice ride."

"How'd it go with the cards?"

"Okay."

"Just okay?"

"Yeah. And guess what?"

"What?"

"I met some actresses that wanted me to tell you they like your work."

"Oh?"

"I sort of mentioned I knew you, but I only said Norma, not Marilyn Monroe, because Sharon had a script like the one you had in your car for Love Nest and I asked her if hers was for Love Nest too, but it wasn't, and they asked me what I knew about Love Nest, and I said you had a job on it, and they seemed to know that Norma meant Marilyn, so…"

She laughed, "Don't worry, honey, that's fine. If it comes up, well, it just comes up, right?"

"Right," I said.

"Anyway, that's very sweet of them. Did you get their names?"

"Julie and Sharon."

"Well, if you see them again, thank them for me, and tell them if they really want it and don't give up or get discouraged, they'll get their turn."

"I will. If I get the paper route, I'll see them a lot. They said they'd take the paper if I was going to deliver it."

"So will I!" she said. "Have a nice ride, and be careful."

"I will. Bye."

When I got to where Beverly and Lower Santa Monica and the railroad tracks come together it was a mess. Cars in all directions. Taking turns going through the stop signs like they were supposed to, but I couldn't tell when it was my turn and every time I thought it was and started to go, the light would change at Upper Santa Monica and a whole new wave of cars turned onto Beverly and I had to wait all over again. I wanted to turn right onto Beverly, cross the tracks and Upper Santa Monica, then left and go to Rexford, but I could tell you could get killed doing that, so finally, I decided I'd just cross Beverly to the car wash and show my bike to the carwash guys. Show, not show-off, I reminded myself. On Sundays, when I wasn't there, Jackson and the others had to take turns doing the hubcaps and whitewalls and their regular jobs too, so they were especially tired at the end of the day. They had already finished cleaning up and were on the parkway on the North Elm side under their tree having a smoke.

"Man oh man, ain't that a beauty!?" Dennis said.

"Sure is," Jackson said. "So that's what you been workin' for?"

"Uh huh," I said.

"What's those doo-hickies?" Jackson said, pointing at the blocks.

"My friend, Kenny Lester, the guy you were talking to yesterday about the pig and the girl, he put them on so I can reach the pedals better."

"Ain't that fine," Maurice said. "You tell him I still want to hear more 'bout the girl. He can save the pig for Jackson, here," he laughed, and he and Dennis slapped hands.

"Only pig I wanna see is at a barbeque," Jackson said. "Joseph seen your bike yet?"

"Not yet."

"You should go show him. He was almost as excited 'bout you gettin' the bike as you were," Dennis said. "He's still cleanin' up over there."

"I will. See you guys next Saturday."

"Ride your bike to the wash, and we'll give it a nice once over," Maurice laughed.

Joseph hadn't put the stools away yet. He was still cleaning the grill, but everything else was cleaned up.

"Hi."

He turned around. I put the Red Rider on the kickstand.

"Hiya, kiddo. Wow. Boy oh boy, I'll bet you're just in heaven, eh?"

"That's about the size of that," I said. "Isn't it great?"

"Sure is. Taking it for a test drive?"

"Yeah, sort of. We went to the Stars game and I rode it down there. Then I rode it around our neighborhood and now I'm on my way to school to practice for tomorrow." I didn't want to tell him about being afraid to cross Beverly and Upper Santa Monica but he already knew.

"I saw you trying to get across the street. That's a pretty nasty corner, but if you press the button for the pedestrian crossing, it makes the signals change. Then you can go."

"I should have thought of that!" I said.

"Well, give 'er a try when you're ready to go."

"I will. Want me to put the stools away?"

"Naw, you go have fun on your bike."

"I want to. Really."

"Well, if you're sure, thanks."

He handed me his keys with the one for the storage closet separated out. It didn't take very long and I had them put away and the closet locked up again.

"See you next Saturday, Joseph," I said, giving him the keys.

"See you, kiddo."

The buttons worked like a charm. The light changed a few seconds after I pushed it and I rode in the crosswalk over the tracks and then to the far side of Upper Santa Monica, but instead of going left to Rexford, I went up North Elm instead. Maybe Gene was home and would take a ride with me to school and back, just for the heck of it. It was uphill, but with the pedal blocks, it wasn't a problem at all. I sailed along, zipping past house after house until I crossed Carmelita and was half way up the block and almost to Gene's house when I realized I hadn't stopped at the stop sign. Yikes! What if a car had been zooming along Carmelita? That could have been the end of me and the Red Rider and on the first day! I was going to leave that part out for sure when I told my mom about my practice ride to school. Besides, that's what practice is for, I thought. When I got to Gene's house, I put the bike on the kickstand and started up the path to the door. I'd never noticed before, but the path was made out of yellow bricks, and it didn't go straight to the door, it sort of wandered around from side to side, like a snake curving one way, then the other, through the front yard garden and finally to the steps and the porch. It was kind of neat, but I could see where people, probably Gene and his brother Wes, had made a short cut going straight for the door from the sidewalk, squishing flat the little mossy stuff that grew between the bricks and on each side of the path, before the real flowers in the flower beds popped up. Gene had never said anything about it, but I wondered if his mom was thinking about the yellow brick road from the Wizard of Oz when she made the path. I thought it was sort of funny if she did it on purpose, and even if she didn't, since a lot of people would think of that anyway, but funny or not, it reminded me that I hated that movie because of the little flying monkeys. When I was three or four, Marty took me and Sarah to see it at the Beverly-Canon Theater. When it got to that part, I got so scared and cried so much that he had to take me out to the lobby and stay with me until the movie was over. He was mad at me about that for a long time even though my mom let him go back to see it with kids his own age. He still teased me about it sometimes. Gene's house was huge compared to ours. And since ours was really a duplex, that was saying something. It was two stories high and white with dark green trim around the windows and front door, and the door was dark green too. This was what the northsiders called the real Beverly Hills. Even though our address was in Beverly Hills, they said if you lived below the tracks, it wasn't really Beverly Hills. I knew that wasn't true, but I couldn't argue with them about the difference. I turned to look across the street, both up and down, and it was the same everywhere. Huge, nice houses, the yards all taken care of by gardeners, I bet, and fancy cars in the driveways, and quiet. I thought our street was pretty quiet, nice too, really, especially because of the jacaranda trees, but this was like a whole neighborhood of Rathbone gardens. I could hear bees buzzing. I saw a butterfly bumping from flower to flower and could almost hear the thump of his wings against the air, it was that quiet. I turned back to the door and was about to knock when it flew open and Gene's father charged past me yelling about something. It was like I'd fallen into a noise pit. He ran right over me and down the steps and got into his Buick in the driveway and started it and backed into the street and burned rubber off the back tires as he roared off towards Sunset. I could hear him yelling from the time he flattened me until he was half a block away. So much for the quiet real Beverly Hills, I thought. Gene's mother had been sort of running after him, I think, because she almost stepped on me.

"Oh my god," she said when she saw me, "are you okay?"

Her eyes were all red and there were tears in them, but she wiped them away and helped me up.

"I think so."

Gene and Wes were right behind her. They both looked like they'd been crying too.

"What are you doing here?" Gene asked me.

"Boy, that Buick really moves," I said.

"Thank god for that," Wes said.

"Wes!" his mother warned him.

"Well, it's about the only good thing..."

"Wes!!" she stopped him right there.

"What are you doing here," Gene said again.

I think he was embarrassed that I saw the whole thing, whatever it was.

"I got the Red Rider yesterday. I thought maybe you'd want to come with me. I'm taking a practice ride to school. Wanna?"

"No thanks."

"Why don't you go, Gene? Dinner won't be ready for another forty-five minutes. If would be good for you to get out of the house for awhile."

"Yeah, but dad said...."

"It'll be okay...."

"But what if he comes back and I'm not here? What then?"

"Don't worry, he'll settle down," she said. "What's your friends name?"

"Kurt," Gene said.

"Kurt, would you like to join us for dinner after your ride?"

"No thank you. I'm not sure where my mom is, so I should get back pretty soon, before she does."

"Well, you guys have a nice ride. That's a very nice bike, Kurt."

"Thank you."

Gene went down the driveway and got his bike. We rode up North Elm to Elevado and over to Rexford and down to school. Gene didn't say anything the whole way and neither did I. When we got to Hawthorne, we went to the lower playground and put our bikes in the bike rack and sat on the ground up against the fence next to them. The sun was behind us, just barely above the tops of the houses on the other side of Rexford, so we were in the shade, but there were some big kids, maybe eight or ten of them, probably about Marty's age, playing basketball on one of the far courts, and the sun was still on them. They all had their shirts off and their skin was red and wet from the sun, but they looked like they were having fun.

"I hate him," Gene said quietly. "I wish he'd just died in the war."

He tried not to, but he started to cry. I wanted to say something to make him feel better, but I couldn't think of anything, so I just sat there, but I was wondering how his father could have been in the war since Gene was my age and I was born in 1943 and the war wasn't over then. My dad had two kids already by the time the war started, so they didn't want him, then me and Nick came on top of that. Wes was Sarah's age, so Gene's father could have gone to the war a little after Wes was born, but it didn't seem like he would have gone after Gene was born, because there wasn't that much of the war left, and he'd have had two kids too. Then again, no one knew exactly when the war would end, so maybe he joined up after Gene was born after all. I wanted to ask Gene about it, but it didn't seem like a good time, so I didn't. But looking at Gene sitting there crying, it made me think about the grown ups who lived on Oakhurst and the guys at the car wash, all of them, Joseph and Maurice and Jackson and Dennis and William and all the guys who came to have their cars washed and stayed to talk about the war and Kenny Lester and George Bowen and Rathbone and Iyama Osaka and Gene's father. Even Kevin Doyle. No matter what anyone said, what Kenny Lester said was right. War was a mess and no one wins.

"We better go," Gene said. "I should be there when he gets back."

He looked at me like he wanted to explain something but there just wasn't any way to do it. Like he'd have to speak in a different language and I wouldn't understand.

"My friend, Kenny Lester, says no one wins a war," I told him, "it just messes up everything."

Gene sort of smiled at me and we headed back towards his house.

When I got home it was a little before six. Marty was in our room studying for his finals. He told me dad had come back and taken Sarah and Nick and my mom downtown so she could do some bookkeeping for him. Marty was going to make dinner for the two of us. Mom and dad and Nick and Sarah would get something to eat across the street from the Bradbury.

My eyes popped open and I looked at the clock on Marty's desk. Six o'clock. Monday, June 11, 1951. I promised myself I was going to remember that day forever. Because I could ride to school, I had more than plenty of time. My mom and dad and Sarah and Nick had come home a little after seven, and they all seemed to have had a good time helping with whatever he had them doing and then having dinner at the Deli across the street from the Bradbury Building, because everyone was in a good mood. So when I told them I wanted to ride to school and that I'd taken a practice ride with Gene Morelli and that Kenny Lester had put pedal blocks on the bike so I could reach better, they just looked at each other and said fine. I didn't have to argue them at all. The luck of the Red Rider strikes again, I thought, but didn't tell that to anyone because of the no more bragging rule. I took the thirty-five cents off the kitchen table and just eased the screen door open and closed. I looked down the driveway to the garage and there it was, okay, not a dream, but real, and really mine. It made me so happy I just laughed. The sun was behind me shinning on the bike making the chrome so bright I could hardly look right at it. My dad had put it directly behind his car and said that would be its place. I was worried that if he was in a hurry and left before me some morning he might run it over by accident, and I made him promise me he'd be careful, and he did.

I walked it to the sidewalk.

"Heya, Kurt. nice bike."

It was Pop. He was sitting on the front step on his side of the duplex.

He was dressed up and ready to go downtown, but looked like he didn't really want to.

"I passed out the cards for the locks yesterday, so that's that," I said, hoping to cheer him up.

"I heard. Good for you. I knew you'd take care of it. So, how's the bike?"

"Better than I even imagined, Pop. It's the best."

"Well, enjoy it, but be careful."

"I will. You going downtown?"

"Yeah," he said, and got up and came over to me and the Red Rider Special. But it still looked like he didn't want to go.

"Well, try and have fun," I told him.

He laughed his funny snort laugh and messed up my hair.

"Thanks. I'll try."

He headed down the driveway to get his car. I took off for the Wonder Bread Factory and Helen.

It was before seven for sure, so I knew the office guys wouldn't be there yet and I didn't have to sneak in. In fact, I rode right down the driveway and through the gate. I thought it would be funny to park the Red Rider at the loading dock and get Helen to come outside and see it parked with all the big trucks that were already there, but I figured a driver might not see it and might back in and run it over by accident, so I didn't. I parked it by the steps instead, out of the way, where it would be safe. There were half a dozen trucks at the loading dock and lots of the metal rolling racks with bread and baked stuff being loaded into them by the drivers and some of the inside workers. I only recognized Jesse. He looked like he was sleep-walking, loading stuff from the racks to the trucks so slowly and with his eyes just barley open, but when he saw me and the bike, he perked up.

"Wow, that's gotta be brand new!"

"I just got it Saturday."

"From workin' at the car wash?"

"Uh huh."

"Dios, mio, it's a beauty. You enjoy it, hear?"

"Thanks, Jesse. Is Helen here?"

"Yes. She's gonna be all excited you finally got it."

I walked with him back inside as he rolled the empty rack to refill it. We passed by the sorting rollers and Jesse leaned in close and yelled to Nina over the noise.

It was too noisy to hear anything anyway, so Nina just gave a thumbs up sign and waved at me.

When I got to the pastry section Helen pretended she didn't, but I could tell, somehow she already knew.

"How's my white sugar?" she said with a big smile. "Anything new to report? Anything you wanna tell your black momma?"

"I got the bike!" I said.

"NO! You don't say!? Is it here? Can we go see it?" she said, making a big fuss, like it was a surprise.

"Sure. It's out by the loading dock. But you knew, didn't you?"

"Who, me!? How would I know somethin' like that, honey? Tell me now, how would I?"

"Did Jesse tell you?"

"No, sweetie," she confessed, "I had a cup of coffee with Joseph at the car wash early on this mornin' and he happened to mention it."

She grabbed one of the big white bags and put in a couple of cinnamon rolls and a bunch of bear claws, wiped her hands on her apron, and put her arm around me.

"Let's go see that miracle on wheels," she said to me, then over her shoulder to the other women in the pastry room, "you girls just have to stay here and keep things goin'. I'll tell you all 'bout it when I get back."

She was joking me around as we walked back through the factory, asking me things like did it have both wheels or just one and did the tires have air in them or did I have to pay extra for that and a bunch of other things, but when we got to the loading dock, she stopped and looked at it. She shook her head and made a clicking sound with her tongue. The sun was shinning right on it like it had been in our driveway, and the chrome was so bright it made me squint my eyes.

"Oh my," she said. "I can surely see why you wanted it so bad. If I could be your age again, I'd want somethin' like that so bad it would hurt!"

She gave me a big hug, kissed the top of my head and handed me the bag.

"You think you can get this under that skinny little t-shirt of yours? You gonna need both hands to ride that thing."

"Sure," I said, stretching the collar my shirt wide enough to drop the bag in. "See?"

"Well, you ride safe, hear?"

"I will. Thanks, Helen."

I headed for the hot dog stand at the car wash. Norma was there on a stool at the counter having coffee with Joseph. Both of them waved as I came onto the lot. I pedaled as fast as I could and came roaring up and hit the brakes, kind of showing off, but it was fun, and I hadn't tried it before, so it seemed like a good time, only the brakes took hold better and faster than I thought they would and the back wheel skidded around and I lost control and just about went over the handlebars, then sort of flopped this way and that trying to hang on so the bike wouldn't get hurt. I didn't exactly crash, but I knocked over the two stools on the end, and would have hit the ground, but the counter and the two fallen over stools underneath held me and the Red Rider up.

I don't know if she originally jumped off her stool to help me or to get out of the way, but Norma got to me about the same time I came to a stop against the counter and helped un-wedge me from between it and the bike and the stools.

"Are you okay, honey?" she said. "You've got to be more careful! You could really get hurt."

Joseph had jumped over the counter.

"Take it easy, tiger," he said. "There's a speed limit posted around here somewhere."

He pulled the bike up while Norma got my leg unstuck from it, then he pulled the stools from underneath me while she helped me to my feet. I moved the bike away from the counter and put it on the kickstand and checked it over. No damage. That was lucky. I was okay and so was the Red Rider. Lucky, lucky, lucky.

"Sorry," I said, starting to laugh, even though I was trying not to, "it sort of got away from me. Boy, that baby really moves, huh? It's even faster than I thought."

"You're laughing now, but I wish I had a picture of your face when you hit the brakes. Your eyes were about this big," he said, making a wide eyed scared face.

I was laughing partly because, really, it had been so much fun. Even the almost-crash. But mostly because the pastries were flattened against my chest. I took the bag out from my shirt.

"Any one want a bear claw or cinnamon roll? Really thin ones?" I said, handing the bag to Norma. She took a peek inside.

"I can't tell for sure, but I think they're either bear rolls or cinnamon claws now. See how they're squished into each other?" she laughed, "but they smell good. Can I have one?"

"Sure," I told her, "you too, Joseph."

I sat on the stool next to Norma. Joseph went back behind the counter.

"Don't mind if I do," he said, taking one from the bag. "You show Helen the bike?"

"Uh huh."

"Hot chocolate?"

"Just cold milk, please."

He put a big glass in front of me and I put the nickel on the counter. He looked at it, then at me, smiled and pushed it back.

"Your money's no good here, pal," he said.

"Yeah, but I'm not working today, so I should pay," I said, pushing the nickel back to his side of the counter.

"Well, let's just call it even for the..." he looked at Norma, "what did you call it?"

"A bear roll or cinnamon claw," she said, pulling off another piece, then eating it and sipping her coffee. "They're even more tasty like this! Maybe you should tell Helen about your invention, and they could make them this way," she said.

I didn't know if she was joking or not, but they were good all squished together.

"Whatever they are, let's call it even, okay?" Joseph said.

"Like William always says, I'm good with that," I told him.

"Okay, then," he said.

"How'd your practice ride to school go?" Norma asked me.

"Fine."

"So your mom and dad let you ride, just like you planned?"

"Uh huh. I could hardly believe my luck. They didn't even make me argue them."

We sat quietly eating the rolls and drinking the milk and coffee. A few cars came in for gas, and a few customers came over to the counter for coffee and a few recognized Norma and said hello and tried not to be too nervous or talk too much when she said 'Hi' back, but most of them did anyway, but other than that, it was quiet and nice, just the three of us there.

"Oh my," she said, looking at the clock behind Joseph, "I've got to go."

She got off the stool and sort of gulped down the rest of her coffee and licked the sticky stuff off her fingers.

"You be careful. No more speeding around, especially in the street with all the cars, okay?"

"Sure. I just had to try it out. See how fast it could go. But now I know," I told her.

"Okay. Bye. Bye Joseph."


I used the crosswalk buttons again and the lights changed so fast the cars going east and west along Upper Santa Monica had to stop so suddenly their tires screeched. I got across Beverly and Upper Santa Monica easy as can be. As I was riding up Rexford, looking at the fancy houses of the northsiders, thinking about taking the Red Rider to school for the first time, at least the first time with kids there, putting it in the bike rack with all the other bike-riders, I realized that I had it and none of them did. Even if they lived in big houses with gardeners and maids and all that stuff, I was pretty sure I had the only Red Rider Special in the whole school! I was wearing the better pair of jeans that only had small holes at the knees, and my sneakers had holes right where the bottom part of my big toe was, but I just didn't care, because I had that feeling again that I always got just thinking about the Red Rider, happy all over, and at first I thought it was from knowing it was finally mine, but it was different this time. It was even better. I had the greatest feeling in the world, because all of a sudden I knew I was free to go wherever I wanted. Wherever, whenever. At least, before six or before dark, but I could just go places. I wondered how long it would take to ride to Will Rogers State Beach in Santa Monica. I could ask Marty how far it was. Maybe not. If I asked him, he'd know I was thinking about going there and if he told my mom or dad, they'd probably say no, and then I couldn't go, so if I didn't ask him, he wouldn't have to tell and they wouldn't have to say no, and I could just go. If I went to one of the other gas stations where Marty didn't work, they'd probably know and then I could do it like a math problem. After I found out how far it was and then figured out about how fast I could go peddling at a good steady speed, then I'd just divide? Or maybe multiply? I wasn't sure which, but whatever, I could figure out how long it would take each way and how early I'd have to leave to get back before six or dark and how long I could spend there. All of a sudden, the endless math practice sheets we did in class and all the homework I did was paying off and I wasn't even in the third grade yet. I was trying to picture where the other gas stations were, thinking if I left school right at 3:15, I could stop at the bike shop and ask Bill about how fast a bike goes with a kid my size peddling, and then go to a gas station. I could ask Bill how far it was, but he might want to let my mom and dad know I was thinking about it too, so the gas station seemed like the best plan. There was a Texaco station at Rodeo and Wilshire! That's where I'd go.

I got to Carmelita and there were lots of kids walking and riding to school coming from both directions and turning up Rexford towards Hawthorne. There were also a lot more cars because some of the kids got driven to school. If fact, the street was actually sort of plugged up with the whole mess of them. I got nervous from all the cars passing by so close to me and I began to wobble and bumped into the curb, then went farther into the street than I meant to trying to get away from the curb and a car honked at me and I hit the curb again.

"Is that a Red Rider?" someone called to me.

I didn't know who it was and I didn't want to try and look over my shoulder because I had enough trouble already, so I just yelled, "Yes," and that was that.

"Neat!" whoever it was yelled back.

At the bike rack the Red Rider was the best bike of all. When I parked it in one of the spaces with the bars that went up and down to hold the front wheel, I wanted to keep it away from the other bikes so it wouldn't rub and get scratched, so I put mine in the end spot. That way, there could only be a bike on one side of it instead of both. A kid I didn't really know very well, a third-grader named Paul, put his bike next to mine. He did it very carefully, I think, because he could tell mine was new, and maybe he could tell I was worried about it.

"That's a beauty," he said as he looked it over, then headed for the classrooms.

Gene Morelli and Leslie Morrison and Allen Weis all got there about the same time. Allen and Gene had already seen it, but Leslie hadn't and he made a big fuss over it. So did Ricki Freeman, and he was friends with Teddy Browner, so I thought that was pretty nice of him. Then Teddy Browner and John Dolan and a few other bike riders showed up and parked their bikes too. I was glad the space next to mine was already taken. You could bet Teddy Browner or John Dolan wouldn't have been any too careful about it. Teddy Browner looked at the Red Rider and then at Gene and Leslie and Ricki. He didn't even consider me and Allen because we were southsiders.

"Is that yours?!" he said to Leslie.

Leslie shook his head no.

"Don't I wish!" he said.

"Yours?" he said to Gene.

Gene shook his head no. Teddy looked at Ricki, who sort of nodded at me at about the same time I said, "It's mine."

Teddy swung around and looked at me and made a face. I could tell he didn't believe me, but it was John Dolan who said it.

"You're a liar."

I shrugged.

"I got it Saturday. It's mine, alright."

"Not from Bill's?!" Teddy asked.

"Yeah, Bill's on Beverly Drive."

"How could you have? My dad tried to buy it for me a bunch of times but Bill kept telling him it was already sold...months ago. How could you buy it on Saturday?"

"I've been paying it off a little every week since the middle of March," I told him.

"That's not fair! Bill's says no lay-a-ways for the Red Rider. It says so right in the front window! We could have paid cash!"

I shrugged again.

"Wait 'til I tell my dad Bill put it on a lay-a-way, and for...."

It seemed like he couldn't think of anything bad enough, but he finally settled on the usual thing.

"A dirty southsider!"

He wasn't happy with that because it didn't seem bad enough, I suppose, so he added, "...a dirty, hole-in-the-knees southsider!"

On any other day, that would have for sure embarrassed me or at least bothered me. But not today. The thought sort of floated through my head, 'what the heck, I'm good with that', like William was always saying. And besides, these were my better jeans. If I were wearing the bad ones, he'd really have me. I thought that was kind of funny, and I must have been smiling.

"What's so funny?" he said, getting madder.

"I'm good with that," I told him, "besides, these are my good jeans. You should see the other ones."

Anyway, I didn't know what he was so mad about. I was sure Bill could probably just order one for him if they wanted it that bad and had the money to pay for it. It didn't seem like such a big deal to me. But I wasn't about to tell that to Teddy Browner. I thought it would just make him madder, if possible, and I didn't want to spoil what looked like might be just about a perfect day. Teddy was quiet, but I could tell he wasn't finished with the whole business yet. Then, all of a sudden, he sort of exploded and kicked the bike rack. He was about to kick the Red

Rider, but Ricki Friedman wouldn't let him. Even though Ricki was his friend, and not really mine, he stopped him. He was bigger than Teddy, and Teddy was sort of a chicken anyway, so when Ricki pushed him away from the bike, he didn't start a fight with him about it.

"Why don't you get your dad to order one? I'm sure Bill could get one for you in no time," Ricki said in a friendly way, like he hadn't pushed Teddy at all, and was just making a friendly suggestion.

"Why don't you mind your own business?" John Dolan said, and just like that, Ricki knew he was in trouble.

Ricki was younger than John Dolan, a little older than me, but younger than John. Even so, he was a lot bigger, but with John, that didn't matter. Ricki stood there. He didn't seem to be afraid, which sort of amazed me. I was, and John wasn't even about to hit me. It was more like he knew he was going to get pounded and couldn't do anything about it, and sort of figured that's the way it goes sometimes.

John Dolan stood right in front of Ricki, pushing his face into him, actually, only trying to, because his face didn't come up past Ricki's chin. He had his fists all balled up about to lower the boom. When Ricki didn't move, John just smiled at him and quicker than anyone could see it coming, turned and hit me in the mouth. Just like with Sarah, my lip banged into my teeth and I could feel the blood filling my mouth and leaking out between my fingers and down my t-shirt. Twice in one week had to be a record. I was so surprised I didn't even have time to cry. I might have and probably would have, except, almost as fast, he turned and kicked the Red Rider.

So much for my perfect day.

He started to look back to see everyone's reaction with this big nasty smile on his face, but before he got all the way turned around, I jumped on his back and wrapped my arms around his neck, choking him. Later, Allen told me I was yelling something at him, but I didn't remember any of it. Anyway, my weight up high around his shoulders tipped him over, and as he was falling, he was using his hands to try to break my hold, so when we fell, there was nothing to stop the fall except his head hitting the blacktop with a big thump, because on the way down, I twisted sideways and landed on top of him instead of under him. I hit him seven or eight times before Ricki and Allen Weis and some of the others pulled me off. Either someone called Mrs. Brasserri, the playground teacher, or she just saw the trouble and came over, but by the time she got there John's face was bloody and I was still yelling at him while he was trying to sit up. He looked like he didn't know where he was or what had happened. Gene Morelli told me later that I told John Dolan if he ever touched the Red Rider again there was more where that came from, but I didn't remember that either. I did remember that I checked the bike and it looked okay.

Mrs. Brasserri marched both me and John to the nurse's office and stood there with her arms folded across her chest and the usual scowl on her face while the nurse looked us over. John's face was a mess and he had a cut on the back of his head that the nurse said was going to need stitches, so she gently and carefully cleaned him up first and sent for his mom. I had to sit there with the blood leaking out of my mouth until she was done with him, then she gave me some ice in a cloth and told me to hold it to my mouth while she looked at some scrapes on my arms and elbows and knuckles. I thought she was rougher about it than she had to be, scrubbing them about as hard as she could with Hydrogen Peroxide, but she finished and that was that. Mrs. Brasserri took us both to the principal's office and had us sit on benches on opposite sides of the door in the front part, where the school secretary's desk was, while she went into the principal's office and reported the whole thing to him. I suppose the idea was to keep us apart so we wouldn't fight anymore, but I wasn't looking for any trouble, and for once in his life, it looked like John wasn't either. He could barely keep his eyes open. I was still holding the ice against my mouth, turning the cloth to a new place every once in a while, trying to find a place that wasn't bloody yet, and every time the secretary asked me something and I answered, the blood oozed out of my mouth in gooey strings and landed with the ones that had gone before right onto my t-shirt. She made a face like she was completely disgusted. Heck, I wasn't too happy about it either, but she was the one asking the questions. I just wanted to go to my class, but it didn't look like that was going to happen any time too soon. The secretary tried to call my mom, but she wasn't home, so she told me to just sit there and she'd try again in a while. Then Mrs. Brasserri came out of the principal's office and stopped in front of John and asked him if he was okay, and even though he nodded, no, she said fine, and left. Then the next thing I knew, I could hear the principal talking on the phone, probably to John's father, because he kept saying, 'yes sir' and 'I'm so sorry, sir' and things like that. He said something about the troublemaker was going to be suspended, meaning me, but that was crazy and I wanted to yell at him through the open door that John Dolan was always starting trouble and he started this, but I was sure the principal already knew it and he just had to act sorry because John's father was some kind of a big shot. Then John's mother got there. While she was fussing over him, the principal came out of his office and gave her a lot of the so sorry stuff and they both kept looking at me like I was the worst person in the world. The way she looked at me almost made me cry. I'd never been to the principal's office before for anything, good or bad, but most times when someone was sent here, it was because they'd done something bad and the principal was the guy who figured out the punishment, so when we left the nurse's office and Mrs. Brasserri said she was taking us here I was surprised just the thought of it didn't make me cry. Now her. Up down, up down like a roller-coaster. Then I thought about my mom and dad not needing any more trouble just now, and thought a call to them from the principal so soon after the locks was going to be more than they could stand and they might take the Red Rider away as a punishment on top of whatever the principal punished me with and that would be rotten, but picturing how hard my dad was working trying to make everything work out and how hard my mom was working trying to help him, if they had this fall on them on top of everything else, even if it wasn't fair, along with the no more bragging rule, I made up another one while everyone in the room was busy hating me: no more complaining. I was going to try to have a perfect day, every day, no matter what. Me and the Red Rider. I was going to try and stay out of the way and not get into trouble, and not complain about the punishment if I did get in trouble, even if it wasn't fair. Even if it was completely unfair, like this. If my mom and dad didn't take away the Red Rider for too long, I was going to convince my dad to let me call the guy about the paper route so I could pay off the locks faster. I was sitting there remembering what an amazing feeling I'd had riding to school this morning, feeling so free. No matter what anyone did or said, I was going to keep that in mind from now on. I was free to at least try to have a perfect day from now on.

"Aren't you going to take him to the emergency room?" the principal was saying to John's mom.

"J.T. wanted us to wait until he got here," she told him.

John had been sitting there quietly, like he was half asleep or something, his eyes still sort of dopey looking, but almost as soon as his mom mentioned his father, he started to complain that his head hurt and he wanted to go.

"Can't he just meet us at the hospital?" he said, crying.

That was one for the books, I thought. John Dolan crying. No one would believe me if I told them. If he hadn't kicked the Red Rider, I'd almost have felt sorry for him. I even did, a little. Then his father showed up. Actually, he sort of burst into the room, not only scaring me, but the secretary and the principal and even John's mom. The odd thing was, I was pretty sure I'd seen him before, somewhere. I wasn't sure where, but somehow, I knew I'd seen him before this.

"God dammit, John, I don't have time for this crap!"

He looked at John and John's mom with this mean, nasty look that I'd seen on John so many times, like they'd made him come down here, and ruined whatever he'd been doing, and like with John, somebody was going to pay for it. Then he looked at me.

"Is this..." he said, pointing at me, laughing like I was the most ridiculous person in the world, not just the worst person, but so ridiculous that he couldn't even believe that I was the cause of him having to come down here and ruin his day, but he wasn't laughing like it was funny, not even close, more like the whole thing was so unbelievably stupid it was making him crazy. He put his face close to mine. I was about to cry, but at exactly that moment I had this funny thought drift into my head that John's dad was so scary that if I didn't start crying right then, which I was sure I was about to do, I might never be scared of anything else enough to cry about it, ever again, and just that thought made me not cry. My eyes were leaking a little bit, but I didn't think it really counted as crying. I wasn't sure I'd ever try to explain it to anyone, but I sort of wished I could tell Marty.

"This scrawny little piece of crap knocked you around?!" he yelled right in my face, but the question, if it was really supposed to be a question, was aimed at John, who was crying a lot now. The principal tried to say something about getting the stitches at Saint John's emergency room, but John's father told him to keep out of it, and he did. He didn't look happy about it, but he stepped back. He was small and had glasses and a bow tie and not very much hair and didn't seem like the kind of guy who liked to get into fights or even arguments, and John's father was like a big version of John, not too tall, but thick and strong looking. He made the principal look like a skinny dressed up kid. John's father kept looking right at me but was still talking to John when he said, "If you can't handle something like this, you're no better than that hopeless sonofabitch brother of yours. You understand me, buster?"

John didn't answer right away. This time too, it didn't seem like the kind of question you were really supposed to answer, but that's not the way John's father meant it, I guess, because the next thing I knew, he was out of my face and right into John's. He grabbed John's shirt and pulled him up off the bench and said, "You listening to me?"

"Yes, sir," John said, crying.

"And stop that crying. You're acting like a baby. A coward and baby. Hopeless. All of you, just hopeless!" he yelled.

He let go of John's shirt like he was completely disgusted with him.

"Get him stitched up," he told John's mom. Then he turned to the principal. "Just what kind of school are you running here? What's your plan of action for this one?" he said, jerking his thumb over his shoulder at me.

"I'm going to suspend him."

"For how long?"

"Today through Thursday. Friday's the last day of school and he'll need to be here to wind up the year."

"That's it? Four days? My god, he rips my kid's head open, and that's it? He should be out of this school permanently!"

"The bang on the head was an accident, Mr. Dolan. The boys were both fighting. Both of them. As I understand it, John was the instigator."

"That's a load of crap."

"Mr. Dolan, we've had this discussion before about John. Many times. On the other hand, I've never seen Kurt Goldman in my office. Ever. Not once."

"You seem to be forgetting who you're talking to."

"No, I'm not. As a courtesy to you, I'm not suspending John. He may be out a few days in any case. But I do not intend to let you bully me"

"When I'm mayor, you can bet your ass I'll be making some changes around here."

"That may very well be," the principal shrugged and John's father stormed out the same way he'd stormed in.

And that's when I remembered him. The guy with Kevin Doyle in the convertible at the car wash. He'd been all smiles then, so he seemed like a different person.

"Would you step into my office," the principal said to me.

He said it in a pretty nice way.

"Yes, sir." I said. "Should I leave this or bring it with me?" I asked holding up the bloody rag. The ice had melted and it was dripping water and blood.

"Sandy," he told his secretary, "would you please go to the nurse's office and get a new rag and ice, please."

"Yes, sir," she said.

She handed me a bunch of kleenex to wipe my hands and mouth with and told me to throw them in her wastebasket. Then we went into his office and he told me to sit in the big wooden chair in front of his desk.

"I'd like to hear your side of this," he said.

I explained about the Red Rider and Teddy Browner and Bill's Bike shop and even told him about the locks and that I was paying them off and I'd stay away from school but I hoped he wouldn't have to call my mom or dad, because they had enough trouble without this.

"Well," he said, "it makes a lot more sense, now that you've explained it to me."

He started writing something when his secretary came back in and handed me the new towel and ice. My lip had almost stopped bleeding, but the cold felt good anyway.

"Take this note to your mom," he said. "It says you got in a fight defending your bike from a senseless attack, and you and the other boy are going to have a cooling off period the rest of the day. It might be a good idea if you cooled off tomorrow, Wednesday and Thursday as well, but I'll leave that up to you and your parents. It's not a suspension at all, so I won't call them. You could come back to school tomorrow, or wait until Friday, get your report card and any art projects or end-of-the-year projects or papers you want to keep and say goodbye to your friends for the summer. Does that seem fair to you?"

"Yes. Completely. Thank you."

"Okay, then, I guess were done."

He stood up and reached across the desk to shake hands with me.

Only five days of school left before summer vacation and I was getting kicked out for four of them. Or at least sort of kicked out. Since he said it wasn't really a suspension and wasn't going to call my parents, and since he was only suggesting I stay away from school the next couple of days, I figured there was no point in worrying my mom and dad about the whole thing at all. All I had to do was figure out what to do for the next couple of days instead of going to school. Since he called it a cooling off period, that gave me a great idea

I'd go to the beach.

It gave me a funny feeling to walk out of the principal's office, out of the building, down the steps, past the kindergarten building and down the steps to the lower playground and bike rack with no other kids around. Not one. I couldn't decide if it felt bad or good, because I couldn't decide if it was a punishment or a vacation. It felt like both, which was strange, but that changed as soon as I saw the Red Rider waiting to take me to Will Rogers' State Beach.

I rode on the sidewalk all the way down to Carmelita, then got into the street and took Camelita about six blocks over to Bedford and down to the Texaco station at Brighton. They had a map on the back of the door between the office and the repair shop and it had a red dot where the station was, so it was pretty easy to see how far it was from there to the beach. I counted and recounted because it's pretty easy to loose track since the streets and print were so small, but it was at least forty blocks. I asked the attendant how far it was in miles and he said seven or eight, which didn't seem too bad, and I asked him how fast he thought a kid my size would go pedaling at a steady speed and he said seven or eight miles an hour. So an hour each way. It was only about ten-thirty, so if I got to the beach by eleven-thirty I could stay for at least two hours and get back around the time school would be getting out. I could even use my lunch money for something at the Gert's Foot Long Hot Dog Stand. I was trying to picture the different ways my mom drove when we went to the beach. I knew you could go all the way out Wilshire and end up at the Pacific Coast Highway south of Will Rogers', but it was a huge street and there was a lot of traffic all the time, so even though that's the way I remembered best, it didn't seem like a good idea. Sometimes we went on another, smaller street. I searched the map looking for it. None of the names sounded familiar. It had a grass strip down the middle that separated the cars going in one direction from the ones going the other way, and me and Sarah, and Nick played this game where we'd try to be the first to spot the house with the fancy garden with the fake white swans in the yard. It was part of the deal that we had to be quiet when we passed the Veterans Cemetery out of respect for the guys that died in the war. My mom's older bother, Kurt, the guy I was named after, died in the war and was buried there, so when we passed the row after row of white crosses, I always wondered which one was for him, but I never asked because my mom was usually crying by then anyway, so we'd just be quiet and wait to spot the swans. Whoever saw them first could end the silence and shout, 'white swans, white swans!, and they won. By then my mom had stopped crying about uncle Kurt, so yelling was okay. Most of the time Sarah won, because she had a better idea of where it was even before we got there. I followed Wilshire on the map to where it crossed Sepulveda and saw the big chunk on the map that said Veteran's Administration, which was the hospital and cemetery. Wilshire passed through there and on the far side as you left, you could go straight on Wilshire or turn right and get on San Vicente. That was it! San Vicente! I followed it on the map all the way to the ocean. There was some little street that was really steep going down and when we got there, my mom always pretended it was a cliff and we were falling off. From the back seat, it seemed like we really would, but Sarah got to sit up front, so she never fell for it. That little street led to another and pretty soon you came out at the corner where Gert's Foot Long Hot Dog Stand was, right at the Pacific Coast Highway across from Will Rogers' State Beach. I was pretty sure I'd recognize the little steep street, but even if I didn't, the ocean was going to be right in front of me one way or another, so it would work out either way. I went back out to the Red Rider.

"Got it all figured out?" the station guy asked.

"I think so," I said.

"Go west, young man," he said and laughed.

That's what I planned to do because that's where the ocean was, so he didn't really need to tell me that, but he was just being friendly, so I said, "I'm good with that."

# Chapter 21

### *The Journey of*
### *Iyama Osaka*

WE HADN'T REALLY been kicked out of Beverly Hills, it just
felt that way. What began as our dispirited retreat from the deep, cool,
manicured green of even southside Oakhurst, to the hot, flat, parched and
barren San Fernando Valley, our own little Diaspora, was softened and
changed into a kind of adventure by the fact that we'd own the house;
that it was brand new, a part of the post war housing boom that sent LA
sprawling in every direction, made possible for us by a VA loan that
was somehow finessed and transferred to us through one of my mother's
brothers' service during the war; and that, eventually, we'd each have our
own room. Nick and I would have to share a room until Marty started
living full time close to UCLA, but there was at least the realistic ex-
pectation that it would happen. One of the biggest changes that resulted
from the move was that when we lived in the Valley, we went to the
beach at Zuma. Out the Ventura Freeway, through the West Valley to
the barren rolling hills of Calabasas in the kind of heat that threatened
even the most reliable car with overheating and vapor lock, then over
the broken rocky mountain on Las Virgenes Canyon Road to the Pacific
Coast Highway. There, the only semblance of commerce was a gas station, drugstore, soda fountain included, and tiny country market. The
rest of the trip north to Zuma was a trip to the end of the world. Maybe a
little past. The beach clubs, the screened sands, the umbrellas and beach
chairs of the Santa Monica beaches might as well have been on another
planet. If you came up from Venice and Santa Monica on the PCH, civili-
zation ended at Malibu, and even Malibu wasn't all that civilized in those
days. Zuma was the wild west of beaches. No stores, no hot dog stands,
no surf shops or beach wear stores, no real estate offices or commercial
development of any kind. Just the four lane ribbon of badly worn and
poorly maintained blacktop with the chalky hills and scraggly brush on
one side and the sand and big blue on the other, an outpost graced with
only two lifeguard stations for a three or four mile run of beach, and
those mostly for show, since county lifeguards were seldom there on
duty, at best, only a handful of days and only at the height of the summer. If the huge waves and pounding surf were a threat to swimmers and
body surfers' safety, Santa Monica was always there waiting. Zuma, and
a little farther to the north, Leo Carillo Beach for the board surfers, were
wild, untamed, beautiful and so remote that compared to Santa Monica,
they might as well have been private. And just a little south of Zuma, in
keeping with the feel of this stretch of coast, was the well kept non-secret

of Point Dume. It was an enclave then too, not for the rich and famous, but a mixed group of slightly befuddled, slightly forlorn and wished-to-be forgotten fringe characters. There were a handful of beat up house trailers, a few of the old, rounded Airflows, and some of the rectangular ones, all unhappy looking, all up on railroad-tie or concrete blocks, wheels off or just tires flat, going nowhere ever again, home to some of the leftovers from the war that couldn't find their way all the way back into jobs and wives and kids, alive enough to watch the waves roll in and listen to the sound of the surf, maybe watch the moonlight reflected on the water at night, pick up checks from the VA and hope to make it to the end of the month. There were a few artists, mostly old guys living in scattered shacks, and there were even three simple but nice little houses, occupied by equally private and unknown refugees from other times and places and lives. They were the unofficial royalty of Point Dume, based on the relative permanence and sophistication of their homes, right down to the running water, from wells, but running water nevertheless. All of the dwellings so far from each other you wouldn't know any of the others existed, so far that if there were any sense of community, it was more figurative than literal, more from a shared need to be left alone than from any shared experience or common purpose. It was to southern California what Bolinas has become to northern California, a not very well known, not exactly secret, not exclusive, but definitely not talked about retreat for the kind of eccentrics that have no interest in outsiders knowing anything about them. Point Dume Road wasn't paved then. If you didn't know where it was, you'd miss it as just another dirt and crushed rock driveway off the Pacific Coast Highway leading to some ramshackle property or another, the kind of places with an old rusty truck or car or two up on blocks, weeds swamping whatever well-intentioned, long-ago and long forgotten effort had gotten it up there in the first place, where the beauty and majesty of an expanse of ocean almost limitless was framed by the half-assed and ill-conceived projects of screwballs that had every intention of finishing them, but never would. If it weren't far enough off the highway and hidden by the contours of the land and the flourishing eucalyptus and oak trees, it would have been well on the way to becoming the kind of eyesore Ladybird Johnson had in mind with her Beautify America program. But the collection of aging artists and shell-shocked veterans and a few younger surfers that lived there in the late fifties and early sixties, seeking only to be left alone, had given way to the smart money that saw the coast as a commodity. Where there had been no commercial development before, there was now nothing left undeveloped.

Vann and I came down the hill from Pacific Palisades and went north on the PCH. It was mostly unchanged to Malibu. Above Malibu, where Las Virginas Cayon road comes down to the highway, the little settlement with the drug store and soda fountain, where my mom and Sarah and Nick and I used to stop for hot fudge Sundays on the way back from Zuma, was now a serious shopping mall, upscale in every way. It was

done in the faux Spanish-Mission style popular throughout Los Angeles
and Orange counties, terra cotta colored stucco and red tile roofs, Mexican pavers everywhere, and generously sized fountains splashing water
indiscriminately, water stolen, no doubt, from us up north. But at least
you could still steal a glimpse of the ocean as you drove past. Even the
shoppers walking through the mall, if that's what it was, couldn't help
being reminded there was an ocean there just beyond all the shops and
merchandise. Not so the rest of the way to Point Dume and Zuma.

Every inch of land had been developed with as tacky a collection of
shops, storefronts, houses, apartments and small offices that made the
distressed and disintegrating Van Nuys to Burbank part of the eastern San
Fernando Valley look good. It assaulted my eyes and put a knife in my
heart. What the hell happened to the Coastal Commission, I wondered.
Wasn't it created to avoid just this? To Vann, this was either old news or
she'd never seen it the way it had been. In either case, she seemed unper-
turbed. My agony was compounded by having missed the Point Dume
Road turn because I was looking for and expecting to see the old dirt
road and had been watching carefully for it, which focused my attention
on the non-stop ugliness of mile after mile of this mess all the more.

"You passed it about a mile ago," Vann said in answer to my muttering about where the hell it was, only partly under my breath.

"Where?"

"That big gate with the security booth," she said.

"You're kidding me."

"I thought you knew where you were going, or I would have said
something," she shrugged apologetically.

Most of the software companies in Silicon Valley and even Berkeley were fond of calling their facilities campuses, I guess to make their
freshly minted college-graduate employees feel more at home and not
threatened by the notion that they were out in the real world now. And
we'd passed the Pepperdine College campus that overlooks the ocean on
the way up the Pacific Coast Highway from where we'd hit it coming
down Sunset, so thinking the gate and security booth was one or the
other or something similar made sense. At least to me. The idea that
Point Dume had become a gated community, especially in the midst of
all this sleazy development, didn't quite register. Then again, the idea
that someone, or a group of people, would see the beauty and inher-
ent value of Point Dume was being wasted on the rag-tag collection of
residents left over from the fifties, sixties and early seventies was probably inevitable. And what better way to avoid all the tacky stuff out on
the highway than to gate off their little oasis. You couldn't even get a
glimpse of the water all the way from Las Virgenes Canyon Road to a
little before Zuma. The only thing that was still the same was the sign
at the entrance to the parking lot at Zuma, except with all the garbage
surrounding it, it seemed ironic and sad, like the sign for the decrepit Fun
House at the Santa Monica Pier, the fun long since gone. The beach and
water still looked pretty good, though, I thought. I turned around at the

entrance to the parking lot and headed back towards Point Dume.

"Slow down," Vann said, "it's coming up pretty soon."

"I thought that was something like Pepperdine, or maybe some company with an ocean-side campus."

"Not hardly," she said. "Johnny Carson and Barbra Streisand and a lot of other celebrities live here now. The really big stars that don't need to be close to town."

We pulled up to the security gate and the guard came from his booth.

"Can I help you?"

"We're here to see Barbra," I said.

I gave Vann an aren't I cute look. She rolled her eyes.

The gate guy just frowned, looking down at the clipboard in his hand. Apparently Barbra hadn't told him we were coming. Vann leaned across me so the guard could see her face.

"He's kidding," she said, "we're here for Iyama and Victor Osaka on Cliffside Drive."

"Kurt Goldman?" he asked.

"Yes," Vann answered for me.

I was still holding out for Barbra.

"Take Point Dume Road all the way down to Cliffside, then left to the end. It's the little house on the cul-de-sac."

"Thank you," Vann said.

It was seven-forty and the sun was about to finally ease itself into the water, making deep red and purple and orange streaks across a turquoise sky, setting the clouds on fire. The water was a blue-black, the briny smell of it strong and satisfying. Privacy is a funny thing, I thought. Even inside the gated Point Dume Road, the residents, secure in the exclusivity of their estate sized parcels and the knowledge that their neighbors were equally, or almost equally famous, still found the need to wall themselves off from each other. There were a lot more houses and residents now, some impressively nice houses, but even without the masonry and stucco walls or wooden and shrubbery fences, they'd no more see each other than the old artists and surfers and vets did twenty or thirty years before. All they'd managed to do was chop up what had been an expansive meadow, making clear who owned what, but losing the more compelling sense of vastness and open space and open ocean. I liked the feel of the place with the shacks and beat up trailers better.

Cliffside ran north and south, the last quarter of a mile untouched meadow on both sides of the street. When we came to the cul-de-sac there was only one house, one of the three royalty places from the old days. I can't say I really remembered it specifically, but it seemed familiar anyway since it and the other two were so unlike the trailers and shacks from those days. They'd made an impression that stuck. Iyama's place was no more than a thousand square feet, a rectangle maybe twenty-five feet deep and forty feet long, the long side facing the water. It seemed to sit on a lot of land, because not only was there nothing even close to it. There were no fences or landscaping to define or separate his property from anything even remotely near by. That whole last quarter mile might be his, I thought. If it was, it made the Rathbone property look pretty chintzy by comparison. I bumped over the crushed rock driveway and parked behind what was probably Victor's new Porsche. It still had the dealer's name where the license plates would go. The recent sale of 437 North Oakhurst came to mind. The house was fifty or sixty yards off the street, oriented so that it faced the water, nothing but wild flowers and tall grass between it and the edge of the cliff and the water below, maybe two hundred yards away. The plain on which it sat was seventy or eighty feet above a rocky beach. When the sound of our tires crunching over the rock driveway was gone, the sound of the surf pounding the beach below replaced it. The colors of the sky were darkening, but even though it wasn't dark yet, some of the brighter stars were already beginning to sparkle. As we approached the front door, on the far side of the house, the south side, to my left, I could just make out the back end of a pick-up truck parked there. Before I knocked, I went to take a look.

"Where're you going?" Vann said, waiting for me at the door.

"Come see this," I told her, motioning her over.

It was Iyama's truck, probably a 1937 or '38 Dodge. It had been painted and restored and looked better now than it had in 1951.

"Iyama had this truck back when he did the gardening on the Rathbone property," I told her. "Same truck. Amazing."

"Some things don't change," Vann said, smiling.

I wasn't sure if she was referring to the truck or my penchant for little side-trips, but she took hold of my hand and gave me a little kiss on the lips, so I didn't care which it was.

The front door was set back from the plane of the wall, creating a little sheltered area about four feet square under already generous eaves. There were a couple of pairs of well-worn sandals and some old work boots, most likely Iyama's, and what were probably Victor's shiny black businessman shoes. I took my sandals off and placed them next to Victor's. Vann took her sandals off and put them next to mine.

The door had been made from some thick redwood planks held together by steel straps running across both top and bottom and diagonally, bolted frequently. The exterior walls were made from the same material. There was a wrought iron thumb latch on the door, but no knob or lock. There was a brass knocker about the size of my fist, the shape of dolphin, and I rapped it a couple of times. Victor answered the door.

"Kurt?" he said extending his hand.

"Yes, and this is Vann."

"Yes," he said, "we spoke on the phone. Konbanwa. Good evening. So nice to meet you. Come in please."

As they shook hands, he bowed slightly. He noticed we'd taken off our shoes.

"Our custom," he said. "Thank you."

"At our house too," I told him.

He was about my age, maybe a little younger. He wore a nice fitting business suit, crisp white shirt, dark charcoal tie and dark socks.

From his dress and the Porsche and his general demeanor, he seemed like a guy with one foot firmly planted in two very different cultures, doing justice to both.

As he ushered us in, I could see the edge of the door. The planks were a full two inches thick. Beautiful stuff, and it had been used everywhere. Clear, almost burgundy colored redwood. The house was small but felt bigger since only the bathroom, on the right and to the east, was a separate room, accessible through doors from both the main room and the sleeping area, which was on the west and opened to the big room when three shoji-type panels were slid east along grooves cut into the floor, and above, in another grooved redwood top plate as an upper guide. To the left, on the east side was the kitchen, and to the west of it a dinning area, a table and four chairs. The rest of the house, the whole middle of it, was the living room with a couch, coffee table and an old ornate potbellied stove up off the floor on a raised concrete slab about four feet square, a stovepipe rising straight up and through the roof. The concrete had been darkened with lampblack and polished so that the pebbles were revealed in a homemade smooth as glass sort of terrazzo. The front wall was redwood post and beam in five sections about eight feet long, maybe seven feet high to the top plate, the middle three sections, closed off from the outside by huge redwood-framed sliding glass doors on two wooden tracks, one in front of the other, just outside the wall. The tracks allowed the doors to slide and stack either left or right in front of the fixed panes in front of the kitchen and sleeping areas, so that all three middle sections could be opened up to the ground level redwood deck, and beyond, to the wildflowers and tall grass, and beyond that, the ocean. The floor itself was parquet. Not the usual little flat squares, but thousands of end cuts of the redwood 2x8's stood on end, packed together tightly and sanded and oiled, like a butcher's block. The whole house was single wall construction, the vertical redwood planks with a vertical shiplap or rabbit joint, like those the door was made from, forming the only barrier between the outside and inside. The roof was a shallow pitched gable with a 6x12 ridge running north and south, supported at the two end walls and then intermediately by two pair of doubled redwood 4x12's resting on the east and west walls, dividing the length of the room and the span of the ridge in thirds. There were 4x8 redwood rafters on six foot centers with the same 2x8 planks over them, a little lighter in color, like they'd been sanded or planed, making a nice contrast with the darker ridge and support beams and the rafters. Not a shred of insulation in the single wall construction, and almost certainly none in the roof above the planks, under the roofing. The potbellied strove must get a workout in the winter, I was thinking. The few light fixtures were handmade Japanese lanterns done as wall sconces, the wiring hidden behind redwood moldings. It had a cool and quiet and peaceful feel, simple, elegant and charming. Distinctly Japanese. Someone had put the pieces together and breathed life into them, giving them a soul, knowing the soul would live on in the house, keeping it alive and well as the wood continued to breathe on its own. Tad Matsumoto would love it.

"Beautiful, isn't it?" Victor said.

"It's perfect," I said. "Iyama did this?"

Victor smiled. "No, not really, though he helped. It was my grandfather, Hiroki. After Manzanar."

He motioned for us to sit at the dining room table.

"My father is resting," he said. "Before I see if he's ready to get up, could you tell me please what this is about?"

Vann and I sat at the table facing the ocean. Victor sat to my left, his back to the south wall. The sliding door closest to us was open, the sound of the surf pulsing like a healthy heart beat, like it was the heartbeat of the house gently beating in rhythm with the ocean. The last of the red was leaving the sky so that only various shades of purple remained against the darkened turquoise background, making even more sparking stars visible. Crickets began to chirp. If there were any more to the world than this, you wouldn't have known it. Wouldn't have needed to know. Again, I wished we could leave it there.

"You recently sold 437 North Oakhurst to Paragon Properties, right?"

"Not exactly. I sold it on behalf of my father to a joint venture with Paragon Properties."

"Joint...?" I began, then remembered, "...ah, yes...Point Dume Associates."

As I said the words, only then did it dawn on me that he was Point Dume Associates.

"You?" I asked.

"Yes," he said.

"So you know work on the project there was stopped."

"I'm aware of it, of course," he said.

"And why?"

"I'm aware of that, as well. And your interest in this is?" he asked me.

"Detective Phillips asked for my help."

"You're with the police? I thought you had grown up in the neighborhood."

He looked at Vann, troubled, like maybe she'd deceived him.

"I did. I'm not really with the police. I'm just helping Phillips. I lived on Oakhurst at the time they think the body they found was buried there. Your father worked for Mr. Rathbone then."

"I hope you're not suggesting there's some connection to my father," he bristled.

"I'm not suggesting anything. We're trying to determine who was buried there. Why and how will follow."

He seemed only slightly mollified, but at least he hadn't asked us to leave.

"The question that first comes to mind is, why now?"

"What?"

"It seems Iyama has been set against selling the property for a long time, first to the Beverly Hills Development Group and J. T. Dolan, then Paragon Properties, and John William Dolan. So, why now?"

"I don't know. Maybe because he's sick. He gave me power of attorney for the Oakhurst property and the acreage here at Point Dume two years ago. He's not specifically aware of the project nor of the stoppage. And he's neither well nor interested enough to oversee a development of this kind. It's what I do."

"With Dolan?"

"As it happens, this time, yes. It's the first time he and I have been involved in a project together. His family, their development companies, have wanted to make this project happen for a long time. My father's property was the key."

"Don't you think Iyama would assume Dolan would jump at the chance? Something he's worked pretty hard to prevent all these years."

"Perhaps."

"I mean, giving you power of attorney would be an invitation to Dolan, wouldn't it?"

"Perhaps."

"So, again, I can't help wondering, why now?"

"I wouldn't presume to speak for him."

"What kind of developing have you done? If you don't mind my asking," I added.

"For the past ten years, I've developed sites here at Point Dume. On behalf of my father, of course."

"Geez, how much land does he own here?" Vann asked.

Victor looked at her with a strained smile. It was none of her business, his look said, but he was too polite to say so, and he seemed to realize she'd asked innocently.

"Hiroki had seven acres surrounding this house. Over the years, my father added to that. At one time, he owned two hundred-eighty acres, not all of it contiguous. He was prevailed upon to sell some of the non-contiguous property to the Point Dume Realty Group for the improved road, the security gate and several of the properties developed closer to the highway. When he saw what they were doing with it, we formed the Point Dume Associates to better control the direction development would take."

"How on earth did he get almost three hundred acres here?" Vann asked him, incredulously.

Victor smiled a modest half apologetic smile on behalf of his father.

"In part, because at the time, no one was interested in it or wanted it. There was no demand, so no market. But my father saw the potential for it, and began buying parcels when they became available. That and thanks to your grandfather," he smiled at me. "You're Kurt Goldman, correct?"

"Yes."

"And your grandfather was Abe Goldman?"

"Yes."

"It was your grandfather and Charles Avery and George Bowen who prevailed upon Mr. Sullivan to sell them my grandfather's building at 437. They returned it to our family."

It only partially explained Pop's sole and separate property dealings and use of Quit Claims. I wondered about the how and why of it. Hannah's story about Manzanar had been a start.

"What's that got to do with Point Dume?" I asked him.

"Hiroki was grateful to the three of them, as was my father, but after Manzanar, Hiroki wasn't the same man. Did you know he was a medical doctor? Trained first in Japan, then in this country? A doctor and surgeon? He came here in 1920, just twenty-four years old. By the early thirties his practice in Japantown was thriving, and because his reputation was spreading outside of Japantown, many of his patients were whites. He bought 437 North Oakhurst in 1935. Can you imagine how proud he was? To come here on his own, such a young man, and make a place for himself and his family in this country? To own a building in Beverly Hills? In 1935, when they moved to Oakhurst, my father was not yet thirteen. He was the oldest of Hiroki's four children. He was expected to become a doctor also. Manzanar changed all that.

"How did my grandfather's help in getting the building back help with this?" I asked him.

"Rents from the North Oakhurst property paid for the acquisition of land here."

"Rents?" Vann asked.

"Did you know my father left Manzanar to fight with the 442nd? That he was actually discharged from the army before his father and mother, his two little brothers and a sister were released from their imprisonment at Manzanar, in November, 1945? Can you imagine such a thing? And it was Hiroki who was shamed. Can you imagine that? He had done nothing wrong, nothing at all, and he and his family were treated like criminals. His son is wounded in the war fighting for this country, and he is ashamed. Too ashamed to speak with Mr. Sullivan about the building on Oakhurst. Too ashamed to be seen by whites. Too ashamed to practice medicine, ever again, even within the Japanese community. If Mr. Rathbone had not been kind enough to employ my father after the war, I don't know what would have become of them. That was no small thing in those days. Hiroki was a defeated man. He wouldn't leave the apartment they all shared in Japantown. My father supported them all, helping to put his brothers and sister through UCLA, until they were old enough to help support their parents. My aunt finished her undergraduate work at UCLA in 1954. She went to UCLA Medical School. We credit your grandfather with that as well," he said with a slight smile and bow.

"How's that?"

"When your grandfather and Mr. Bowen and Mr. Avery arranged for the return of 437 to our family in 1954, Hiroki wouldn't consider living there. Since there were twelve apartments in the building, my father and uncles and aunt each occupied one until they were ready to move on. I lived there from 1954 until I graduated high school in 1964. My father, acting for the whole family, rented the remaining eight apartments. The income from them paid for medical school for my aunt and helped start the construction business my uncles formed. It also paid for the land here. They, my father, and my three cousins, their sons, and I, comprise Point Dume Associates. Your grandfather, Mr. Rathbone, and Mr. Bowen also helped my father buy this property for Hiroki. It was one acre to begin with. Do you remember the actor, Alan Hale? He was a friend of Mr. Rathbone's. His family had owned this property from before the first World War. When Mr. Rathbone asked him, he agreed to sell the original one acre site to my father. Later, after this house had been built and the one acre parcel had been paid off as agreed, he offered the remaining six acres he owned and my father purchased that as well. Hiroki put all his energy and creativity into this house. It was his way of purging himself of the disappointment and pain of Manzanar. It was his way of remaking his world, at least a part of it, so he could understand and be at peace in it. My father helped with the construction, as did my uncles, but it was Hiroki, working alone most of the time, that brought it to life. The rest of the land came in chunks here and there from time to time. With Hiroki living here, first on the one acre, then the seven, it was assumed our family would buy more if it were offered, so it became routine for families that had held land out here for years, who decided they were ready to sell, to offer it to Hiroki. My father really. They offered and he bought. The rents from 437 being the engine that kept things moving."

He looked at Vann to make sure her curiosity was satisfied. It seemed to be. But not mine. Not quite.

"My grandfather sold our duplex at 431 to Dolan, J.T. Dolan, in 1954. Actually, he traded it for a partnership in the building that was built on our property and the one George Bowen owned on the north side of us. I assume he and my grandfather used part of the money from that transaction to get your family's building at 437 back from Sullivan."

"I know nothing about that," he shrugged.

"Well, assuming they did, I would have thought they would have purchased it from Sullivan and there would be a grant deed and maybe a deed of trust if there had been a mortgage involved."

"I have no knowledge of that, either."

"Well, they didn't. They got it back from Sullivan by quitclaim, the same way Sullivan got it from your grandfather. My grandfather held it as a Life Estate, with the remainder to Iyama, so when he died, it went directly to Iyama. Any ideas?"

"None," Victor said. "It's all very interesting, but I have no knowledge of it."

"Sullivan," Iyama grunted, standing next to the shoji doors by the sleeping area. Victor rose to help him to the couch, but Iyama steered him to me and Vann. We both stood. He bowed slightly and shook hands with us.

"Ilasshai," he said.

"Welcome," Victor translated, as he helped Iyama to the couch and sat down next to him. "I'll translate for you. He hasn't used English in the last ten years."

Iyama may have moved slowly and in pain, but he looked vital. His arms still had the rope like veins and muscles of a younger, healthier man. His hair was mostly white, and it had been allowed to grow, pulled back into a short ponytail. He wore a loose fitting pair of overalls, no shirt underneath, so his tan smooth skin looked like that of a little kid in the too large, loose fitting outfit. His bare feet were a particularly dark tan. When he'd made himself as comfortable as he could, he nodded his thanks to Victor. Victor spoke to him in Japanese. I heard my name and Pop's. Iyama nodded, his eyes closed, his breathing becoming more regular after the exertion of the trip from the sleeping area. Iyama's eyes opened and he patted Victor's hand and shook his head no, he was okay.

"Sullivan was a thief," Victor translated as Iyama began, his voice soft but steady and determined. "When the FBI came to take us away in May, 1942, it was Sullivan who hovered like a vulture waiting for a meal he knew was coming. He smiled his false smile and said how sorry he was, but it was clear he'd had it all planned out. There had been rumors since February about what the President's Executive Order 9066, and later 9102, would mean. By March, there were reports of Japanese being taken from their homes. Sullivan was shrewd enough to be prepared. He had the quit claim ready and five-hundred dollars in his hand. The agents gave us only a few minutes to gather what we could, then marched us out of our home one by one. My sister first. Twelve years old, and an agent took her forcefully from my mother's grasp and escorted her outside and had her stand by the curb. She was very brave. I remember her dress. It was blue with small white flowers on it, and she had a shiny black belt that matched the black shoes she wore. Her socks were so white against her skin. They were new, I think. Next they took my two brothers. They were fourteen and sixteen. Then my mother. They told me to help Hiroki look around to make sure he had everything he wanted. As though you could choose an item or two in the five minutes they gave you from a life you'd lived for forty-five years. That's how old he was. Forty-five. I was nineteen. 'We've done nothing wrong! We're Americans!' I protested, but my father silenced me. 'Iyama,' he said. 'Enough. It will be okay.' But he knew it would not. The agents took me to the curb with the others. We stood there and watched while the FBI agents walked him down the front steps. He held his head up, but his eyes were blank. Dead. There was a crowd that had gathered, but none of our neighbors spoke up for us. I could tell some of them felt bad, but no one spoke up. Not Mr. Rathbone, not Mr. Bowen or your grandfather or Mr. Erwin, all good neighbors to us and we to them. But no one told the FBI we were Americans too. No one told the FBI my father had set a broken leg for their child, or eased a dislocated shoulder back into place or come to their house in the middle of the night for their emergencies, no one told the FBI we were their neighbors and not a threat. We were allowed to take only one suitcase each and the clothes we were wearing. We might never be back. We might not live. We had no idea what was in store for us. My mother, my brothers, my sister were crying and Hiroki blamed himself for failing us. He was shamed from the first knock on the door. What could he do? Standing there with the whole neighborhood looking on, he signed the paper Sullivan held out to him. He took Sullivan's money and thanked him. He thanked that thief because he knew that five-hundred dollars might be the difference between our surviving and not. If he hadn't been responsible for us all, he would have ended his own life right there on the parkway. In many ways, his life did end there."

Iyama sat silently, his eyes closed and rested. His eyes opened and he looked at Victor. Then me. Then Vann.

"There was one," Victor translated again when Iyama resumed. "There was one of our neighbors who spoke up and tried to stop them. Begged them to stop."

"There was? Who?" Vann asked, wanting even a shred of goodness to shine through the bleak recitation.

Victor translated Vann.

"Kevin Doyle," Iyama said to her.

Then he resumed in Japanese and Victor translated "He was my friend. He stood up for us. He yelled at the FBI men and he yelled for the neighbors to help us. When no one would lift a finger, he cried and swore at them all. He had always been a little strange, sometimes a little out of control, but now he was acting crazy-wild. The neighbors were embarrassed by him...for him, and for us too, but no one listened to him and no one helped. I could tell it was only further humiliation for my father and mother, but I was grateful to him and proud of him for speaking up. Before the war, when we were younger, we had been friends, and now he stood up for us and tried to help when no one else would."

Iyama looked at me. Then he spoke a few words to Victor, ending with a pat on his hand.

"English," Iyama said. "English."

Victor seemed surprised as he reported it to us.

"He says there's no need to translate any more. He may not have spoken English for a while, but he hasn't forgotten how." Victor smiled. "My son will be shocked and pleased to hear it. Iyama speaks only Japanese to his grandchildren."

"You don't think I remember you, do you?" Iyama asked me.

"Do you?"

"Of course. You came into the garden from under the fence. Into the bamboo. Many times."

"Yes!" I said in amazement.

He held his left hand palm up and pushed an imaginary something with the first finger of his right hand.

"The grasshopper," he said, and smiled. "It was his time. Do you remember?"

I nodded, speechless. Iyama's breathing was coming in short labored puffs through his nose.

"It was his time," Iyama said with a tired sigh, his eyes closing.

I nodded again, remembering. He sat quietly for a few moments.

"It was his time and I buried him," he said, eyes still closed.

I was puzzled. That's not how I remembered it.

"No," I said, "I fed him to the Garibaldi. Don't you remember? The big solid colored orange one."

Iyama opened his eyes and smiled at me, shaking his head.

"Kevin Doyle," he said. "It was his time. I killed him and buried him in Mr. Rathbone's garden."

Then, ever so slightly, he winked and nodded at me. Vann and I sat there, speechless. Victor seemed stunned. None of us had the remotest idea what to say or do. Iyama sat there quietly, breathing shallowly, resting. Then he tugged on Victor's shirt sleeve, pulled Victor closer and whispered to him. Victor went to the kitchen area, stood on one of the chairs from the table and took what appeared to be a shoe box off the top of the cabinet above the highest shelf. He took an envelope from it and returned to Iyama. Iyama looked at it for a moment, running his hand across it like he was dusting it off.

"For you," he said, extending the envelope towards me.

# Chapter 22

## *Gert's Foot Long Hot Dog Stand and Joseph's Too*
## June 11, 1951

I DISCOVERED THE FUNNY thing about riding a bicycle is how far you can go without getting tired, but how tired you can get all of a sudden after you've gone pretty far. Even when the ground is almost perfectly flat. From the gas station at Brighton and Bedford about half way to the Veteran's Administration on Wilshire, which was mostly flat, I felt fine. There were cars everywhere, cars that raced past me coming so close I could feel the wind they made, and parked ones pulling out in front of me, and cars coming out of parking lots and turning corners and changing lanes so they could turn right and none of them seemed to care if they ran me down or not. It was scary, okay, but the worst part was by the time I was getting close to the VA, my legs hurt and my feet were getting cramps so that my toes kept curling down on their own, without any orders from me. I had to stop every once in a while and sort of bounce on the front part of my foot to make them go back. When I got to the place where Wilshire went through the cemetery and I could see all the white crosses behind the chain-link fence, I knew I could just follow it straight to where I'd turn right and end up on San Vicente, but instead I went through the gate along a little skinny road where the grass came right to the edge of the pavement with no sidewalks. At first I thought it was going to be a huge mistake, because the ground wasn't as flat and I had to pedal a lot harder, and my legs were already complaining and I was probably only half way to the beach and I'd still have the trip all the way back even if I survived the rest of the trip there. But as soon as I made it up the first little hill, it got flat, so that was good. But better was the quiet. Even with Wilshire so close, it was quiet. And then there were the crosses. When we drove past, it always seemed like there were too many to count, just row after row, and we were busy being quiet for my mom and uncle Kurt, but being in here was different. The dark green grass and the white crosses weren't just too many to count, they were endless, like stars on a really clear night. In a car you zipped by, and that was that. On the Red Rider, I was in the middle of them and they went for as far as I could see in every direction and I knew I'd be riding for a long time before I'd be through them all. At the base of each cross was a flat plate with the name of the dead guy and when he was born and when he was killed. Uncle Kurt was buried here somewhere, and even though I'd never met him, he was sort of real to me because my mom said things about how he'd done this or that when they were kids or before the war or sometime during his life. But I'd never thought about all the other crosses. All of them with other guys underneath, real to someone, just dead. I imagined Kenny Lester or George Bowen or John Erwin under one of the crosses. It would be like that, I thought. Someone I knew could have died in the war and I wouldn't have known them, like they'd just been erased or something. I wished I could find uncle Kurt's cross and say hello to him. Tell him my mom missed him. But I could be here every day for a year and might never find him, so I didn't try. I just sort of said it in my head to all of them.

I wound through the cemetary road and finally came to the other side. I could see San Vicente across a long, slightly downhill stretch of more green grass and white crosses. It was a smaller street than Wilshire and I thought the rest of the ride would be easier, and it was. And I discovered another funny thing about bike riding. After you get really tired and your legs and feet hurt and you think that's as far as you can go, another time comes after that and you feel pretty good again. I was tired, but along the divided part of San Vicente, with the grass strip down the middle and not very many cars in either direction, I felt like I could just keep on riding for as long as it took. And since I was watching for the white swans it made the time pass by faster, and when I finally saw them, it made the trip, so far, worth it. I stopped, not really to rest, well, maybe a little, but mostly to see them up close. They were much bigger than when we drove by in the car, bigger than I thought they'd be, and their faces had black and yellow markings I'd never seen before. They were so big a kid my size could sit on them and it would look about right, like they were going to take you on a trip. Just up and fly away with you riding them. They were at the edge of a yard that made Rathbone's look tiny. There was no driveway into the yard, so I figured the house must face another street north of San Vicente. The swans were on the San Vicente side of a grass area bigger than Rexford Park, probably ten times bigger than Rathbone's place. The house was white and had a red tile roof like ours, but that was where it stopped being anything even remotely like ours, or even anything like the fancy houses of the northsiders. I was looking at the back side of it, and it was pretty far away, but even so, I could see a huge swimming pool and a house so big at first I thought it might be something like the Beverly Hills Hotel up on Sunset, but I didn't think so, it was all just one house for one family. It looked like it was three separate parts connected by glassed-in hallways and the whole thing curved in the shape of part of a circle around the pool, so big and spread out it was impossible for me to imagine who could live there. One of these days, I thought, I'm going to find out. If Norma was getting famous in the movies and she lived on Oakhurst with Shelly, who could live here and what could they do to make enough money to afford it, I wondered? Even someone like John Dolan's dad, trying to be mayor and all, there was no way he could live here. Or Teddy Browner's dad or even Gene Morelli's. They all made a ton of money, but I thought this must be as impossible for them as their houses, or any of the houses of the northsiders, were for us.

I got back on the Red Rider and headed for the beach. It was flat and easy all the way to 7th Street, but I went past it by accident. It doesn't take the steep drop close to San Vicente, so when I knew I was getting close to the ocean, I started looking for likely streets and it didn't seem very likely, but about three blocks past it San Vicente ends and there's a railing that looks down a big drop to the streets below, on about the same level as the beach, so I knew I'd passed it and had to go back. 7th goes for about two blocks flat as can be before you get to the steep part, and the name changes to Estrada Drive, but brother, when you get there you know you've found it. It drops like the rollercoaster at the Santa Monica Pier, just like you've fallen off a cliff. I tried pushing back on the brakes, but that wasn't slowing me down enough. In fact, I was going faster and faster and that wasn't the worst part, because on top of going too fast, the road wasn't straight. That would have been just too easy. It had a big curve, and it was coming up and if I didn't slow down, and right away, it would curve and I wouldn't and I'd end up crashing into something, I wasn't sure what because I was afraid to take my eyes off the road to see what it would be, but probably someone's house or garage or a parked car or something. It got to the point where I was about to yell, "I can't stop!!!!" but there wasn't anyone around to hear, so there wasn't any point to that, but I was yelling anyway, not words, just a long scream, like on a rollercoaster, except there weren't any tracks to keep you going where you were supposed to. So I stood up on the pedals in the braking position, balancing my body as well as I could, and it worked! I was finally slowing down, but the back wheel was completely stopped and was just skidding and I could smell the rubber burning, not on fire, just getting hot and smelly, and the next thing I knew, the bike began to wobble. If I kept that up I'd lose control completely and that would be as bad as going too fast, so I invented a way of standing on the brakes and then shifting my weight forward for just a second so the wheel could turn, and then braking again, sort of like the train engineer had done when he was afraid he was going to run me over on the tracks. It was part skid, part roll, and it worked. By the time I got to the curve, I was going slow enough to sit back down on the seat and make the turn and continue down. It was a huge relief until I realized I was going to have to do it all over again because the hill was steep for a long time and there was another sharp curve coming up. When I finally got to the bottom I was a nervous wreck, but at least not a wreck wreck, so all in all, I thought the whole thing had been a success.

Near the bottom, Estrada became West Channel Road, which is one-way for a couple of blocks. The other way was across a divider with grass and trees. All the streets around there at the bottom of the hill had small houses on small lots with lots of trees, so it was shady and cool, and almost flat, and that was a relief too after the hill. After about five or six short blocks the two parts of Channel came back together and I could see the Pacific Coast Highway in front of me. And on the corner, Gert's Foot Long Hot Dog Stand was right there where it was supposed to be.

I had my thirty-five cents lunch money, and it was a good thing. I could have eaten about a dozen of the foot-longers, that was for sure.

"Why ain't you in school?" Gert said, looking up from wiping the counter between us as I came in.

She knew me and Sarah and Nick pretty well because my mom brought us to Will Roger's State Beach almost every day during the summer year after year and the three of us collected empty soda bottles people left on the beach and cashed them in with Gert for three cents each. It drove my mom and Marty nuts that people left them scattered all over the place when there were trash cans you had to pass on the way to the parking lot, but we were just as glad they did, because we could almost always make enough for a hot-dog, a coke and share an order of fries. If it was a busy day and there were lots of people at the beach, we might make enough for hamburgers instead.

"I got the day off," I told her.

"You got it, or the school's off for the day?"

"Just me," I said.

"Hmmm," she said. "What about your brother and sister? They off too?"

"Nope, just me."

"Your mom bring you out?"

"Nope. Just me," I told her.

She stopped cleaning the counter.

"That don't sound good," she said.

She didn't keep after me, but I guess she was still thinking about it, because a few seconds later she stopped cleaning and looked at me.

"So how'n the hell'd you get all the way out here?"

"I rode my bike."

The way I said it might have sounded like bragging, but that's not how I meant it so it didn't count against the rule, I thought.

"No!" she said, "I don't believe it."

And I could tell she didn't. She wasn't just saying it like someone might to make you feel like a big shot if you were bragging and they were sort of going along with you. It wasn't like that at all, and not just because I didn't count what I said as bragging, either. She just plain didn't believe it.

"It's true, okay. Wanna see my bike?"

"You rode all the way down here from what, West LA?"

"Beverly Hills."

She rinsed out the rag she'd been wiping with, rung it out and put it on the counter. She washed her hands and used the wetness to smooth back some hair that had worked its way out of her ponytail.

"How long that take?"

I looked at the clock on the wall behind her. It was almost close to one. Yikes, that's not good, I thought.

"A little more than two hours," I said, thinking about the trip back. I would barely have time to eat.

"Well, I supposed you must be starved. What'll it be?"

"A foot-longer and a coke," I said, putting my thirty-five cents on the counter.

"Comin' right up."

She moved one of the very long hotdogs with some silver tongs from the cooler part of the grill to the middle where the flames made the fat drip and catch fire in little bursts. The smell was even better than at Joseph's, I thought, then felt a little bad, like that was being mean to Joseph, but he'd understand if he knew how hungry I was. I was much hungrier than I ever was even at the end of a really busy day at the carwash. She put the coke in front of me. I meant to just sip at it, but I finished it before the hot dog was ready. The hot dog was twenty cents and the coke ten, so I didn't have enough left over for another.

"Refills are free for bikeriders," she said.

"Boy, am I glad," I said. "I don't have any more money after the nickel there, and that's for you," I told her. I hadn't planned on that originally, but since she was giving me another coke, it seemed like a good idea.

"Ain't that nice," she said with a smile.

A few other customers had come in while I was eating, not too many because it was a weekday and summer vacation hadn't started for any of the schools I knew about, so there just weren't too many people at the beach yet. In a week or so, that would completely change, and you'd have to push yourself between people just to get in the door. The little room would be filled with people and all of the stools at the counter would be taken and the four inside tables too, and there would be people standing outside yelling in orders to Gert, and all the outside tables with the umbrellas over them would be full. How she ever kept it all straight amazed me, but she did. When it was busy like that during the summer, it was good she had a helper, an old guy named Pete. He was nice enough, but he hardly ever said anything. He didn't really have to because Gert talked and joked with the customers the whole time she was cooking and serving. Pete went from table to table cleaning up, swept the floor and got drinks and chips and fries for the customers who wanted them and worked the cash register. He smiled and seemed friendly enough, he just didn't say much. He came in and sat at the stool next to the empty one next to me. He nodded hello and smiled at me. I couldn't tell if he remembered me or not. He sat with his hands folded in front of him on the counter. He didn't ask, but Gert put a cup of coffee in front of him. He didn't put any sugar or cream in it. His hair was kind of long and a little gray, and pulled back into a ponytail. The skin on his face and neck and arms was a deep reddish tan, probably because he was here at the beach so much. He had a tattoo on the lower part of the arm that was closest to me. It looked a lot like the one Big Max had, and my uncle Buddy too. Buddy was in the navy during the war and got his tattoo when he was in Hawaii. It was a hula girl wearing a grass skirt, but without a shirt on top. Max and Pete's looked like the same girl.

"Do you believe it?" Gert asked Pete. "This kid rode his bike all the way out here from Beverly Hills."

I'd put all the mustard the little bun could hold and some pickle relish and I started by munching the ends of the hot dog where they hung past the bun on both ends. The hot dogs were a foot long, but maybe Gert couldn't find buns that matched because the ones she had were the regular size. A few sips of coke and I was working my way through the main part and next thing I knew it was gone and I was almost finished with the second coke too. After a while, Pete looked over to me and his eyebrows went up a little.

"That so?" he said.

"Uh huh," I told him.

"You come out Wilshire?" Gert asked me.

"Only as far as the Veteran's Cemetary. I came on San Vicente the rest of the way."

The seats on the stools could spin and Pete rotated on his to face me. I could see the steam coming up from the cup of coffee resting on his knees. It smelled good.

"San Vicente don't go through. How'd you get down?"

"That steep street."

"Estrada?" Pete said.

"That's it," I said. "Boy, was that scary!"

"Good god," she said, "you could get yourself killed comin' down that thing!"

"You can say that again. I didn't think I was going make the turn, but it worked out okay."

"How you think you're gonna' get back up there?" she asked me.

I hadn't thought about that. Plus it was getting late.

"I suppose I'll walk the bike up the hill back to the flat part."

That was going to throw my whole schedule off.

"I better get started," I told her. "I want to get back by three-thirty."

Gert looked over her shoulder at the clock. It was one-thirty five.

"That ain't too likely. Maybe Pete here could help you out," Gert said.

Pete didn't seem to know what she had in mind and so he didn't say anything.

"Right?" she sort of pushed him.

"What?" he said.

The expression on his face didn't change much no matter what. He either sort of smiled or sort of didn't. Right then, he sort of didn't.

"Throw the kid's bike in the back of your truck and give him a ride back to San Vicente. You can do that, right?"

"Sure. Why not?" he said, the sort-of-smile back. "You ready to go?" he asked me.

"I'm ready, but you don't have to. Really. If I get started now, I think I can make it back in time."

"Why push your luck? This way maybe you'll be back a little sooner. Nothin' wrong with that. Right?"

"Right," I said. "Thank you." Then to Gert, "Thanks, Gert."
"See you summer-time soon, kiddo."

Pete took one look at the Red Rider, then me.
"New?" he said.
"I just got it Saturday."
"Nice," he said, and very carefully put it in the back of his pick-up. It was sort of like Iyama's but probably older. He noticed me looking at it. "Don't look like much, but it runs real nice."
We drove up West Channel to the one-way part and then up the steep hill on Estrada. He was right. His truck went right up smooth as can be. When we got to the flat part, 7th Street, I pointed to the first corner.
"This is good. It's flat again. Thank you."
"Might as well take you back. I'm not doin' anything else."
"You don't have to, really. I can ride."
"Don't have to, but 'sokay with me. Okay with you?"
"If you're sure."
He just nodded and turned left when we got to San Vicente.

Pete seemed to know his way around, so when I told him North Oakhurst near Beverly Boulevard, he just went the way he wanted and that's where we ended up even though it was different from the way I'd come. He took a lot of side streets, I suppose to stay off Wilshire for as long as possible, then finally on it to Upper Santa Monica to Beverly Boulevard to Oakhurst, just like that. He turned onto Oakhurst and I pointed to our house and he pulled up in front of it with his truck on the wrong side of the street next to our curb. He looked at his wristwatch.
"Two-o-five."
"That's great. Thanks, Pete."
He nodded. We both got out and he took my bike out of the back and put it on the sidewalk on the kickstand for me. He got back in the truck and started it. The street was empty except for us, since it was too early for kids to be home from school and none of the dads would be back from work yet, so I had the whole block to myself. I was still pretty tired from the ride to the beach and thought I'd put the bike away and maybe go up to Rathbutt's place and take a nap in the bamboo patch. Pete took off for Lower Santa Monica.
"Bye," I shouted after him.
His arm came out of the window and he waved as he drove up the street and that was that, until Kevin Doyle came charging out of his house and across the street. I was still waving at Pete and didn't seem him coming 'til he was right there. He grabbed my shirt and spun me around.
"You little fuck," he screamed at me, "what did you say to Miriam?"
His eyes were wild and crazy looking and he shook me a few times to make sure I was paying attention. I was so startled, then so scared, the two cokes seemed like a much worse idea than the one I had when Iyama

scared the pee out of me. I was too scared to cry. It was there, but it wasn't going to make it out. In fact, I could hardly breathe. But I was trying to think of the last time I'd said anything at all to Miriam. I couldn't really get a hold of it in my head, but it didn't seem like whatever it was would get him so crazy, but it was Kevin Doyle, and with him, crazy was mostly normal. Time seemed to be moving more slowly, like his words and movements were just oozing towards me. He started shaking me harder, yelling louder, and his face kept getting angrier, but it didn't seem like it was happening to me. It seemed like he was a long ways off. And it got quiet. He was still yelling, I think, because his mouth was moving, but I couldn't hear it. It was happening to someone else. Then as suddenly as it began, Kevin Doyle was jerked away. My t-shirt tore as he moved backwards, but at least he wasn't shaking me any more. Then the sound came back. Kevin was making a lot of noise, but it wasn't from yelling at me, it was struggling against Pete, who had him from behind, the arm with the hula girl across Kevin's throat and his other hand locking the hula girl wrist under Kevin's chin, pulling him back against his body. Kevin struggled for a while then started to go limp, then as he slumped down, he grabbed Pete's leg from between his own and pulled up on it. It sent Pete flying backwards to the ground with Kevin landing on top of him. Kevin must have been faking to fool Pete, because he was full of crazy energy again. With Pete down, he punched him in the face so many times and so fast I couldn't have counted them if I tried. Then he put his own arm across Pete's throat and was pushing so hard Pete's face was turning purple, and he wasn't faking it. Kevin kept shifting around so more of his weight was pushing down on Pete. Then it was like I was waking up from a dream, a nightmare really, and I grabbed Kevin's hair and tried to pull him off, but he didn't budge. His head bent back a little, but it didn't stop him from pushing down on Pete's throat. Before I even saw his hand move, he reached around and knocked my legs out from under me. When I tried to get back up, someone pushed me aside. It was George Bowen. Just like that, he had his arm around Kevin's neck and was pulling him off Pete. Small as he was, George was strong enough to make Kevin's whole body move where he wanted it to. But to make sure he came, George was also pulling and twisting on Kevin's ear. And to make sure Kevin didn't try the same trick on him, George kicked at the back of Kevin's knees every once in a while as they backed up to collapse them. That way, Kevin couldn't get close enough or keep enough balance to reach back for George's legs like he'd done with Pete. Pete started coughing and choking and tried to sit up but he couldn't and just rolled sideways. He kept coughing and tried to wipe the blood from his mouth and face, smearing it really, but at least the right color was coming back. George pulled Kevin all the way back onto our lawn. He had choked him enough to put him to sleep. When he was sure Kevin was done fighting, he laid him down on the grass.

"You okay?" he asked Pete.

Pete was up on his feet now, bent over, with his hands on his knees, leaning sideways against Mumps, the jacaranda on the parkway next to our driveway, spitting gooey blood at the base of the tree. What he really needed, I thought, was Miriam.

"Think so," Pete said.

Just then, Maurice and William and Dennis and Jackson came down the driveway carrying a bunch of yard cuttings for the compost pile, wrapped up in big canvas cloths, the way Iyama did it. They took one look at Kevin on the grass, Pete against the tree and me and George.

"You okay?" Maurice said to me.

I nodded yes. If I said anything, I knew I'd cry.

"What's goin' on?" Jackson asked George.

"Who're you guys?"

"Kurt works with us at the carwash. That's who. You got a problem with that?" Maurice said.

"Not yet," George said.

"So what's goin' on?" Jackson asked again.

"That's what I was about to ask him," George said, nodding to Pete and lighting up a cigarette. He offered one to Pete and put the pack back in his shirt pocket. They both seemed to feel better as soon as the smoke hit them. George looked at the carwash guys, took the pack out and offered them a smoke. The four of them each took one and lit up off of George's cigarette and stood there waiting for someone to say something.

"How come you guys are here?" I asked.

"We met your grandpops at the carwash the other day and he asked if we had time to trim them big bushes and a coupl'a trees for him, so here we are," Jackson said.

George asked Pete, "What was that about?"

"Don't know," Pete said, wiping at his mouth. "I dropped the kid off and started up the street. Next thing I see in the rear-view, this bum's runnin' across and's shakin' the hell out of him," he said nodding at me. Pete shrugged, because that's all he knew. "Mean little bastard. He serve?"

"Raiders, in the South Pacific. You?"

"Navy. Subs. You?"

"Raiders, too."

Pete looked at him, trying to settle down, taking another puff on the cigarette. I could see his hands were shaking as he lifted it to his mouth. George was steady as can be. Like he'd been reading the Sunday paper or something, except it was Monday.

"I thought I was a little old when I went in," he smiled at George.

"You do what you can. I turned forty a little after Pearl. I was in pretty good shape, had some skills and the Raiders were a good fit."

Pete nodded at Kevin.

"I've known Kevin since he was a kid. He followed me in," George said. "When they were putting the Raiders together, he asked me to recommend him. He joined us a little late into the training in San Diego, so I tried to look after him out there. He'd go from scared to death one minute to a wild man the next. He ended up saving my life and a bunch of others.

Got a Soldier's Medal for it. All in all, he had a rough time and he's not adjusting very well to being back. I try to look after him."

"He's a nut case," Pete said without any anger in his voice. "I've seen a lot of them. The war just brought out the worst in them."

George just shrugged and kept smoking. Pete put out his cigarette against the bottom of his shoe and put the butt in his pocket. They shook hands.

"Thanks," Pete said, getting ready to go. "Fellas..." he said to the carwash guys.

"Glad I was here," George said. "Not too many ever walked away after mixing with him. Theirs or ours."

"Like I said, a nut case," Pete said.

He got in his truck.

"So long, kid."

"Sorry, Pete."

"Not your fault, kid, but I think I'll tell Gert it's her turn next time," he smiled.

He slapped the side of his truck a couple of times and took off.

George looked at me, then at Kevin.

"Did he say anything?"

"Something about what did I say to Miriam," I said.

George just stood there looking at me, like there was something I could tell him, but I couldn't.

"I didn't say anything," I said, trying not to cry, trying not to let it be complaining either.

I started to cry anyway. Whatever was too scared to get out before wasn't waiting a second longer. Maurice put his arm around me. The others looked like they wanted to help too but didn't know what to do.

"Sorry," George said, kneeling in front of me and holding my hand. "I'm afraid I did. I'll make sure he stays away from you, okay?"

"Okay," I said.

"You got that right...you don't know how right you got that," Maurice said to George.

"Amen to that," Jackson said.

I looked at Kevin Doyle there on the ground. He was starting to move and I didn't want to be there when he woke up, except he was at my house, and I was too tired to ride my bike anywhere, anyway. And that reminded me about my plan before he showed up, but I figured the nap idea was pretty much shot now too. Thinking about it, it actually seemed sort of funny. It wasn't, but it seemed funny, in a way. I pictured myself sneaking into the bamboo patch and taking a snooze, maybe sleeping with one eye open in case Kevin Doyle came looking for me. The tears were still coming down my face, and I was still scared, but the whole thing seemed sort of funny and unreal and crazy. It helped that Maurice and Jackson and Dennis and William were there. But it was more like with John Dolan. I'd spent so much time worrying about him pounding me and being afraid of him, and now, after today at school, it didn't matter anymore. He might pound me or I might pound him. We'd both have to take our chances. Right now, wherever he was or whatever he was doing, he might be worrying about me cracking his head open again. It was an accident and I wouldn't do something like that on purpose, but he couldn't be sure, so in that way we were sort of even. With Kevin Doyle, I couldn't see how we'd ever be even, and I couldn't count on the carwash guys or George Bowen to be around to protect me, so I just wished he'd die. I didn't want to spend my whole life being afraid of him or worrying about if he was going to be crazy or not. I stopped crying.

"You might want to go inside for a while," George said when he saw Kevin moving around.

"Uh huh," I said.

"Naw," Maurice said, "I think Kurt needs to be here a little more. That okay with you, little brother?" he said to me.

"I suppose," I said.

George seemed about as uncertain as I was, but he was keeping an eye on the whole situation from what I could tell, so I thought it would be okay.

Kevin's eyes opened and at first he didn't seem to know where he was or what had happened. I didn't know what he remembered or didn't, but as he looked around, he had that lost look again, like in Miriam's kitchen, like a little kid that got lost in a big store. He started to sob and put his hands over his face, and cried for a little while. Maurice and George and the other carwash guys were looking at each other and didn't know what to think and neither did I, but almost as fast as he started, he stopped. He looked around and his eyes began to focus, which was bad enough, but worse, it was on me. And he got that crazy look again. He didn't try to get up, but he pointed his finger at me. Maurice knelt down between me and Kevin, at the same time pushing Kevin's finger, then his hand, then his whole arm down to the grass with his knee and held it there. Kevin's eyes tried to hide from Maurice's. They got mean looking and came back to me again, but Maurice grabbed Kevin's jaw in his hand and made Kevin look into his face.

"Remember me?"

At first Kevin's looked afraid of Maurice, but that didn't last very long.

"Get your fucking hands off me you fucking nigger."

Maurice looked at Jackson and Dennis and William.

"Doncha love it when they talk like that?"

George was tensed up and I could tell he was only going to let this go a little more, even if Kevin was crazy, he was his friend. Sort of, anyway. Maurice seemed to know that and when he and George looked at each other and their eyes came to an agreement without saying anything. I could tell by the way George was standing and smoking, relaxed again.

Kevin's eyes tried to move away from Maurice's, but Maurice wouldn't let them. He held Kevin's jaw with one hand and a handful of hair on the top of his head with the other and forced Kevin to look at him.

"Remember me?" Maurice said again, "From the carwash?"

"Yeah. Right," Kevin said.

He was recovering from the hold George had knocked him out with and his eyes were getting wild, but with the four carwash guys there and George looking like he wasn't going to help, he seemed to know he didn't have much of a choice.

"This kid's off limits. Do you understand?"

"Sure. Whatever you say," Kevin said, but in a way I knew he didn't mean it.

"Keep away from him. If he's out on the street you go back inside. If you're outside and he shows up, clear out. That clear enough?"

"Fuck you," Kevin said.

Then, in a flash, he pushed forward, head first into Maurice's face, before Maurice could move out of the way. William grabbed him from behind, but Kevin swung his legs in a circle knocking William down. All of a sudden, it seemed like Kevin all by himself could wipe out the whole bunch of them and then he'd get me. Maurice's mouth was bleeeeding all over the place, and I felt bad for him, especially since he was trying to protect me, but if Kevin got past all of them, I was doomed. Kevin was on his feet and had gotten himself ready. All four of them, and George too, were going to stop him, but he didn't seem to mind. In fact, he had this crazy smile on his face, like that was the best thing in the world. Maurice wiped his mouth, then wiped his hand on his pants, leaving a dark streak. He motioned for William and Dennis and Jackson and George to step back.

"Whatever it takes, you gonna learn this kid's off limits."

For such a little guy, compared to Maurice, actually compared to any of the carwash guys, except for maybe Dennis, who wasn't that much bigger than he was, Kevin acted like he wasn't afraid of anything or anyone, which made him even more scary. He attacked Maurice like he didn't have a doubt in the world he could pound him. But he was wrong. Maurice knew what he was doing, and after what seemed like a long time, but I think was only a minute or two, or three at the most, Kevin's face was bloody and swollen and his eyes were just slits. There were cuts on his cheekbones that would probably need stitches, much worse than the one on the back of John Dolan's head. Maurice didn't get hurt much at all after that first smash in the mouth. Kevin was down on the grass again and panting and had been beaten, but I thought he was the kind of guy that would never give up until he got even or got dead. As soon as he had the chance, he'd be after Maurice. If not today, some other day, and if he couldn't beat him in a regular fight like this, he'd probably sneak up on him from behind. He raised up on his elbows enough to get his upper body off the grass. He was a mess, but he looked around until his eyes, puffed up as they were, found mine, and he smiled that nasty smile to let me know it wasn't over for me either, not yet. Maurice followed his look, just like he had at the carwash. He looked back at Kevin, then at George.

"If anything happens to this kid," he said to Kevin, but also so that George knew it too, so that George had to either object or agree, "they ain't gonna find 'nough of you to pick up with a sponge. I don't want no nothin' on him, no scratch, no bump, no bruise, no mean word, not a nightmare 'cause of you. You got that?"

"Sure," Kevin said through his bloody mouth and banged up face, but he looked at me again and even through his swollen, puffy eyes, I knew it was another lie and my heart sank.

The good thing was the principal didn't call my parents so there wasn't any talk at all about taking the Red Rider away from me. And the better thing was my dad said he'd thought about it and I could try the paper route. My mom made sure everyone in the family knew she thought it was a bad idea, but agreed I could try it. I called Ron Baylor that night and he said he'd come to meet with me and my mom and dad on Sunday around three to go over some of the details and rules, but they said they couldn't because they were going to be downtown working on the line so Marty said if we could do it before he had to go to work at the Standard Station at two, he'd do it and Ron said that would be okay, so it was all set for one-thirty.

Another good thing was that when Pop came home to pay the carwash guys, and saw Maurice's swollen mouth and a few other signs of his fight with Kevin, who'd already gone back into his house, like bumps and cuts and his shirt was torn and the wipe of blood on his pants, and asked if he was okay and what happened, and Jackson and Dennis and George told him, he kneeled down in front of me and held one of my hands in his.

"Are you okay?"

He had a look more serious than the one when he was mad at Mr. Sullivan. I said that I was.

"Are you sure? That little bastard isn't going to get away with this."

"I think we got it pretty well covered, Mr. Goldman," Maurice said.

"How's that?" Pop asked him.

Jackson said, "Maurice made it clear Kurt's off limits. He's got to steer way clear of the kid. If he don't...we're gonna make him wish he had."

Pop looked at George.

"You think that'll do? With Kevin? You think that will do?"

Just the way Pop said it made me afraid all over again.

"I'll make it clear to Kevin too. It'll be okay," George said.

"It's got to be for sure," Pop said. "Unless we can say for sure, when his dad finds out, there's going to be trouble."

"Do we have to tell him?" I asked Pop.

"He should know," George said to me and Pop both.

"He'd want to," Pop agreed, looking at me, giving me a chance to say something about it.

In one way, the idea that my dad might get really mad and kill Kevin Doyle seemed like a good one, but if he did, they might put him in jail, even if Kevin had it coming, but also, I thought, what if Kevin killed my dad? Small as he was, after all his army training Kevin knew stuff my dad didn't since he wasn't in the war, and strong as my dad was, he might. And even if nothing that bad happened, just talking about what happened would bring up Pete and how come he gave me a ride, and how come I was at the beach in the first place, and then John Dolan and the Red Rider and the principal's office and just like that, they might take the bike away even if I didn't really get suspended, just cooled off. So to keep my dad out of jail or from getting killed and also having to worry about some new thing at school that wasn't really a problem anyway, I begged Pop not to mention the whole thing, that my dad had enough to worry about without this. He and George and the carwash guys talked about it and finally Pop decided for now that would be okay, but if Kevin Doyle bothered me in any way, I had to tell someone and for sure they'd have to tell my dad about this one too.

"Okay," I agreed.

So when my dad said I could call Ron Baylor about the paper route, I didn't mention anything about Kevin Doyle, John Dolan, Pete or the beach. I was dying to tell my mom I'd ridden all the way to Will Rogers' State Beach to prove I could do the paper route, but besides being a bad idea because then they'd know about everything anyway, it would have probably been bragging on top of it, so I didn't.

It was six fifteen on Marty's clock and the start of what might be a perfect day. Might. Marty was out cold. Not a sound from Sarah or Nick yet and I hadn't heard my dad starting his car, so he and my mom were probably still asleep too. I got dressed, took the thirty-five cents off the kitchen table and headed for the Red Rider. I could go to school or I could keep cooling off. I wasn't sure which one I wanted to do. All I knew was the sky was clear, the jacarandas were all set to get serious about blooming and I was going to have the paper route! I walked the bike down the driveway to the street and pedaled up the block. The whole length of the block, no one was around at all. When I got close to Lower Santa Monica, Norma called to me.

"Hi!" she said. "Want to play with me and Snowball for a while before school?"

She was still in pajamas sticking out from under the same white terry cloth robe from the first morning.

"Sure," I told her.

"How did the bike ride to school go?"

"To school was fine. At school wasn't so good."

"Why not?" she said, her face all worried. "You didn't have an accident, did you?"

"No."

I told her about John Dolan and the Red Rider, his stitches, his mother and father and the principal. I also told her about the cooling off period and going to the beach. I'm pretty sure I told her the part about going to the beach without bragging, at least I tried not to. I just told her. Sometimes something might sound like bragging, but it's not really.

"My goodness, that sounds like a long ride there and back."

"Actually, I got a ride back. This guy Pete, a friend of Gert's, put my bike in the back of his truck. He was only supposed to give me a ride back up the big hill, but he ended up bringing me all the way back to Oakhurst."

I didn't tell her the part about Kevin Doyle.

"That was sure nice of him," she said.

"Boy, you can say that again, especially since...," I started, but stopped. "Anyway, I might not go to school today. More cooling off," I smiled at her.

She laughed and said she was hoping for a cooling off day too because she was waiting for a call that might mean she didn't have to go to the set because there was a problem with the script and the producer and writer couldn't agree and so they might not be ready for the actors yet, and while they were cooling off, she might get her first day off in almost two months and would I like to go to the beach with her if she did?

"Yeah. You could meet Gert. She makes these foot long hot dogs that are the very best."

We played with Snowball, who barked about a thousand times for one of us to throw the ball with the bell in it so she could chase it, barking and chasing for ten minutes, until Shelly came out in a ratty looking pink robe and pink slippers, with her hair going in all directions.

"Got the Crack-of-Dawn Club meetin' this morning, eh?" she said.

"Sorry, did we wake you?" Norma asked her.

"Naw," Shelly said, sipping her coffee, coming off the porch and down the path to us. "I had to get up early this mornin' to see what the hell kind of mischief this guy was gonna get into today. I'd hate to miss it."

She put her arm around my shoulder and sort of whispered to me.

"You okay?"

"I'm fine."

"I mean about Spence, next door. All his yelling. You okay?"

"I'm fine. Thanks," I whispered back.

"What?" Norma said.

"Just a little somethin' between me and the lockmaster, here," she joked me, messing my hair.

"You two have secrets?" Norma laughed. "Oh my goodness, Shelly, I think you're getting all soft and cuddly. This may open up all kinds of new roles for you!"

"It's just a little somethin' me and the kid are gonna keep to ourselves for a while, right?" she said to me. "When he's ready to tell you, that's up to him."

Norma watched her go back inside, then looked at me. I thought she had a hurt look, like I was keeping a secret I should be sharing with her, since we were friends and all, but just as quickly, she smiled and said, "I'm glad you and Shelly are getting to be friends. She's a wonderful person. Sometimes she acts crabby, but underneath, she has a heart of gold. She'd do anything for a friend. She really would."

She looked at me again and her face got more serious.

"I hope you know I would too?"

"Sure I do."

"Okay then," she laughed. "I should go get dressed."

"Wanna meet me at Joseph's? I'm going to go see Helen at the Wonder Bread factory and then have hot chocolate there," I told her.

"I'll come have coffee with you for sure," she said. "If I'm off, let's go to the beach. If not, just the coffee, and back to the salt mines for me, okay?"

"Okay," I told her.

Helen wasn't there. On my way back to the pastry section, Nina waved me over and told me one of Helen's grandkids was sick and her daughter couldn't stay with him and Helen said she would, so she took the day off. I started to leave, but Nina said Marie was there and they were bound to have some of the misshappen bear claws and cinnamon rolls if I wanted some. Without Helen, it wasn't the same, so I just thanked Nina, and said I wasn't really hungry anyway. Nina took one of the twisted loaves of white bread off the sorting table and put it into a bag.

"Here honey, you take this in case you get hungry later," she said.

"Thanks."

I got hot chocolate at Joseph's. I thought about a mustard sandwich, but that didn't sound very good for breakfast, so I just ate chunks of the warm bread and sipped at the hot chocolate. It hit the spot just right. Norma's little red car came zipping onto the lot and she waved to me and Joseph. She parked and got out and came over to the counter out of breath like she'd run here all the way from Oakhurst.

"Hi, sweetie. Sorry, no beach today. They called and I've got to get over there. They just called and I'm late already! How's that for starting the day?" Then she said to Joseph, "Just coffee, black, please."

"You got it."

He poured her a cup and she stood there blowing on it and sipping and blowing some more.

"Want a chunk of warm bread? Smell it," I said, holding the loaf up to her.

"Mmmm, I'd love some," she said, "but I'll have to take it with me. I've got to run!"

I pulled off a big piece of the bread and handed it to her. She smelled it again, took a bite and another sip of the coffee, put the mug down on the counter with a dime and gave me a kiss on the top of my head.

"They promised I'll be off on Sunday. Maybe we could go to the beach then?" she asked.

"Maybe. But I'm supposed to meet with the paper route guy at one-thirty. Me and Marty because my mom and dad are going to be downtown working."

"How about if we go to the beach early and get back by one or one-fifteen? That would work, wouldn't it?

"Sure. That would be great."

"Well, you ask your mom and dad if that's okay, and I'll come by around eight-fifteen or eight-thirty to get you, okay?"

"Great."

"Take the mug with you, if you like. Bring it back when you can," Joseph suggested.

"Thanks, I think I will."

"Here," he said, handing her a dish towel. "You can make a holder out of this on the passenger side floor. Keep it from tipping or spilling."

"What a great idea," she said as she headed back to her car, sipping at the coffee and nibbling on the bread.

She got back in and settled the mug on the floor and put the chunk of bread next to her on the passenger seat and zipped out as fast as she'd come in.

Joseph was smiling and shaking his head, "Going to the beach on Sunday with Marilyn...." he started, but finished with, "...Norma. Kid, you got some luck. And if there was a way you could save those little kisses of hers, they'd be worth a fortune some day," Joseph said, joking me. "How come you're thinking about the beach today? No school?"

I told him about the Red Rider, John Dolan, going to the beach, even Kevin and Maurice. The whole thing.

"That guy riding with Dolan?"

"His name's Kevin Doyle and he lives across the street from us. He's friends with George Bowen, Mr. Avery's friend. That's how I got the job here."

"Yeah, I know, and I know George. And I know a little about Kevin Doyle. He's Dolan's kid from his first marriage. A nut case, but he won some medals in the Pacific, and Dolan's milking it for every drop he can for his campaign."

"That's what Kenny Lester says."

"The guy in here last Saturday?"

"Yeah, he lives up the street."

"He seems like a real good guy. But you stay away from Doyle."

"I want to. Believe me, I do."

"So, what's your plan? Cooling off or school?"

He leaned down on the counter, crossing his forearms, getting comfortable, like we were going to have a big discussion about it. I dipped a chunk of the soft bread into the hot chocolate and held it up, catching the drips in my mouth, then eating the soggy part before it had a chance to fall off. I looked at the clock on the wall behind him. It was only seven forty, so I didn't have to decide right away. It would only take about ten minutes or less to get to school on the Red Rider. If I was going to the beach with Norma on Sunday, and I just went yesterday, it seemed like a pretty long ride two days in a row. On the other hand, if I went to school today, I'd have to go tomorrow and Thursday as well as Friday. I didn't think the principal would let me cool off yesterday, go to school today, and then maybe cool off again tomorrow or Thursday, so I figured I was better cooling off today too so I could decide what I wanted to do tomorrow and Thursday. That made more sense. I'd dripped a few drops of chocolate while I was thinking about it and Joseph wiped them up almost as fast as they hit the counter.

"More cooling off," I told him.

"Gonna go to the beach again?"

"I don't think so," I said, not really knowing where I'd go.

But I got that same feeling from yesterday morning, like a wave washing over me, lifting me up and carrying me with it like the body surfing Marty was trying to teach me. It wrapped around me and I was happy, just like that. John Dolan and Kevin Doyle, the locks, Mr. Sullivan, none of it could ruin that feeling. I was free to go wherever I wanted. I could ride and ride and ride. I wished Norma had a bike too. Maybe she'd come for a ride with me sometime. Maybe not as far as the beach, but Roxbury Park would be nice and it wasn't too far. She could do that, I bet. I must have been day-dreaming, because the next thing I knew, I heard my name.

"Kurt," she called.

I turned around and saw Miss Rimes in her car at the gas pump. Randy had started to fill her tank and was washing her windshield.

"On your way to school?"

"Yeah," I said.

What a gyp, I was thinking.

"Probably best," Joseph said, shrugging. "Sometimes things just sort of steer you one way or another."

"I suppose."

Miss Rimes got out of her car, paid Randy, and came over to the hot dog stand.

"One coffee, please," she told Joseph, "cream and sugar."

Joseph put a full steaming hot coffee mug on the counter and slid the little cream pitcher and the glass jar with the sugar cubes and a teaspoon in front of her. She didn't sit down, so it looked like she was just going to drink it quick and get going to school.

"You know this guy?" he asked her about me, but I could tell he wanted to hang around because she was pretty, maybe not as pretty as Norma, but almost as pretty as Julie and Sharon, even if Joseph didn't know them, and also with Miss Rimes, you knew right away she was nice, and I could tell Joseph knew that too.

"He's one of my favorite students," she said, messing up my hair, "stubborn about hanging onto his own vision, no matter what. A real artist in my book."

"A teacher, huh?" Joseph asked, wiping to clean the counter in front of her, but it was already about as clean as it was ever going to get.

"Art," she said. "Mostly painting and clay work with the kids."

"And for yourself? You look like the artist type as much as a teacher type. What's it you do for yourself?

Miss Rimes seemed pleased that he asked, because she lit up, like she was going to tell him she just got a Red Rider or something. She sat on a stool next to me, but it seemed like Joseph was the reason. From the look of things, she might be late to school.

"Bronzes," she said. "Clay to bronze. I love it! I've even sold a few pieces."

"You have? That's great. Good for you," he said.

"There's a gallery on Canon that lets me sell on consignment. The real problem is the foundry expense. My god, you have no idea what a foundry wants to cast bronze these days. Even with the discount I get through the school, I'm lucky if I can do three or four smallish ones a year."

"Three or four a year's pretty good, really. That and teaching. That's a good chunk of work."

"As much as I love teaching and the kids, I'm looking forward to summer as much as they are. I'll have time to work as much as I want. Then there's only the problem of the foundry."

"Maybe that's not too big a problem," Joseph smiled at her.

"What do you mean?"

"One of the carwash guys does some casting himself. He's got his own little foundry in an old warehouse. He can't do very large things, but he might take on a few small or medium size pieces for you."

"Really? That would be wonderful."

"Who?" I asked.

"Dennis," he said to me, then more to her, "he sculpted before the war. Says he had a great art teacher at Washington High. He wanted to do it professionally, make a career for himself as an artist, but the war came along and changed all that. Now he's here with the other guys washing cars most of the time. He does odd jobs too, trying to hang onto the scrap yard and warehouse his dad left, and sculpting when he can. He does it mostly to focus. Chase the ghosts away. I think he's good. Better than good, Very good. Maybe that gallery would take some of his stuff on consignment too? If you thought it was good enough, that is."

He looked at Miss Rimes. She was listening to every word. It seemed like they'd been friends for five years instead of five minutes, like they had some kind of connection from before this morning. I'd never seen Joseph talk so much or show much interest in anyone, not even some of the pretty women that came in for gas or a carwash and had a hot dog and coke at his stand, and there were lots.

"I can't make any promises, but if it seemed like it might be worthwhile, I could help him set up a meeting with the owner. Then it's up to the work."

"That's fair enough. I know he'd appreciate the opportunity. Think you could do that?"

"I'd be glad to."

He looked at me.

"Did you know Jackson plays the sax? Saxaphone? And William plays drums?"

"No," I said.

"Who are Jackson and William," Miss Rimes asked.

"I work with Maurice and Dennis and Jackson and William here at the carwash on Saturdays washing cars. They're the main carwash guys. I'm the helper."

"That's how he got his bike."

He nodded to the Red Rider.

"Good for you, Kurt. What a beautiful bicycle."

Miss Rimes looked at the Red Rider. From her look I guessed she hadn't heard about yesterday and John Dolan or his stitches or anything about me and the Red Rider, and besides, she was more interested in Joseph.

"And you?"

"What about me?" he said.

"Any artistic impulses?" she smiled.

"I blow a little horn. Before the war I thought I'd do it professionally. Now, mostly in a little combo with Jackson and William and a guy named Greg on piano. Just for the hell of it."

"To chase ghosts?" she said.

"Maybe. Who knows. Sometimes things just steer you one way or another," he winked at me.

"Where do you play? I'd love to come hear you guys sometime."

"Mostly The Albertine...a few other jazz clubs in Watts. Nowhere you're likely to have heard of. Once in a while a club in the Bay Area. They seem to like us up there."

"Watts?" she said.

"Watts," he repeated.

"Is that...safe?" she asked him.

"Safer than lots of places were in Europe," he joked her. "We're playing Saturday night, if you're really interested. You could meet Dennis. He'll be there. You could talk to him about casting."

"I'd love to, but I have to confess, I'm a little worried about driving there. By myself."

"How 'bout if I drove you?" he said.

"Would you?"

"Sure. Maybe we could have a little dinner before. Nothing fancy."

"Hot dogs?" she teased him.

"No. But I bet you've never heard of Flint's, have you?"

"Flint's?"

"See," Joseph said to me, smiling, "she's never heard of it."

"Neither have I," I admitted.

"Best barbeque in the world. Their ribs, some salad, maybe a beer and we'll call it dinner. How's that sound?"

"Wonderful," she smiled.

She wrote down her phone number and an address on a napkin and handed it to him.

"What time?"

"We'll get done here around six. How 'bout I get you at seven, we eat and get to the Albertine about eight, eight-fifteen?"

"It's a date," Miss Rimes said.

"I guess it is," Joseph said, sounding like he was more surprised by it than anyone, even though he'd asked her. He had this funny look, like he'd forgotten where he was or what he was doing.

"Gosh," she said looking at the clock behind Joseph and standing up. "It's eight already. I've got to run. You too Kurt," she said to me, "better give that bike a workout."

She reached across the counter to shake hands with Joseph. He didn't seem to know what to do. He looked at her and then her hand, then at her again. He was just standing there.

"Shake hands, Joseph," I said, "or she's gonna be late for school."

"Right," he said, wiping his hand on his apron and shaking with her.

"See you Saturday, Joseph."

"See you Saturday. What's your name?" he asked.

"Miss Rimes," I told him.

"Colleen," she said.

"See you Saturday, Colleen," he said as she headed for her car.

"See you at school, Kurt," she said.

"See you at school, Colleen," I said, joking her as she was getting in.

"See you at school, wizenheimer!" she said, waving a finger at me.

# Chapter 23

"CASE CLOSED," VANN SAID, looking at me, putting Iyama's letter back in the envelope. It said he'd killed Kevin Doyle and buried him in Rathbone's garden. That it was unavoidable. It was dated October 14, 1951, signed by him and witnessed by Kenny Lester.

We'd just turned right off Point Dume Road through the gates and were heading south on the Pacific Coast Highway. She said it like a statement, without the irony of a verbal question mark, but she was too smart not to include it subtly. Until she knew why Iyama said it was his time, Kevin Doyle's time, her instincts as an investigator told her it was much too easy.

"Not hardly," I said.

"What makes you think not? Iyama's old, he's sick, maybe he's ready to get it off his chest. He has nothing to lose. What's Phillips going to do to him? What's anyone going to do?"

That made sense, but she was playing devil's advocate, and more importantly, to her, giving me the opportunity to confide in her. Tell her why I'd thought from the beginning it was Kevin Doyle buried there. What Kevin Doyle had to do with me. And the cowboy belt. Why Iyama's confirmation told us who was buried there, but not how or why he ended up in Rathbone's garden. Why it was his time. She gave me an opening you could drive a truck through. But I didn't. I was trying to sort through the picture Hannah had painted of Iyama and Kevin Doyle the day the FBI came. The strange and unlikely bond between the two teenagers for almost five years before that day, isolated from the world around them for different reasons, but coming to rely on each other for companionship and friendship. Iyama with one foot in the old culture of his father, the other precariously resting on the rich, white, rarified world of Beverly Hills, and the hope of following his father into medicine, and added to that, the responsibility of helping guide his brothers and sister through that same divide. And Kevin, as Hannah described him, even before his parents divorced, scared, weird, friendless. A loner. The kind of guy no one wants to be around. And after, all that and angrier to boot. Somehow Kevin accepted Iyama's foreignness and Iyama Kevin's weirdness. They'd each filled a need for the other. It'd seemed to Hannah that it was Kevin who relied on the friendship more than Iyama. But Iyama's grad2itude for Kevin's defense of him and his family made it clear to me the need was mutual, the bond deeper than anyone would have guessed. Which made the change all the more inexplicable. I remembered Kevin talking with George Bowen, referring to Iyama as the Jap, and it made me think now that fighting in the Pacific against the Japanese had pushed the weird and disturbed Kevin over the edge, past the bond, that after the war, Iyama was just another Jap. I couldn't remember having ever seen them standing together in front of Rathbone's talking or even acknowledge each other with a wave or a shouted hello all the time Iyama worked there. Kevin was willing to spew his feelings about Iyama the Jap as though he'd never known him. Then again, Kevin was Kevin. Weird, ugly weird, to say the least.

Vann was waiting. Some fools are born, others made. I could say in all honesty, I was both. Not exactly a badge of honor. Vann looked at me for a long time, waiting. Giving me as much time to decide as I needed. More than fair. When I didn't say anything, she did.

"Drop me at my car."

"Okay," I said.

We drove in silence all the way down the coast. She looked out her window at the reflection of the moon on the water. It held her attention all the way to Sunset. On Sunset, whatever was out her window then did too, enough, at least, so she didn't have to look at me. I tried not to think about what I'd just done. Not done. I busied myself with thoughts of Shelly Winters and Miriam McDermott. Particularly Miriam. I wanted to talk with her. When we got back to Il Fornaio, I pulled up along side the Fury and was about to parallel park behind it.

"Don't bother," she said matter-of-factly.

"I'll call you tomorrow," I said.

"Don't," she said getting out of my rental. Then, "Hang on a second."

She got out, opened the driver's door on the Fury, reached in, took a file folder and came back around and handed it to me. I put it on the passenger seat. When I turned back to her she had tears in her eyes. She bent down and pulled my face to hers. It was long, passionate and probably the sweetest kiss I'd ever experienced.

"So long, you jerk," she said.

She got in the Fury, started it and pulled out in front of me where I was doubled parked a little back of her space. There was the slightest chirp of rubber as she took off. As far as I could tell, she didn't look back.

It was a little after ten. I parked where she'd been parked and went into Il Fornaio. I ordered a glass of Cabernet, a basket of bread and mixed some of the balsamic vinegar with olive oil on a little plate. I dipped the bread, sipped the wine and opened the file folder.

In Vann's very neat script, her notes on Hannah and Steve Aduan, Shelly Winters, Iyama Osaka , Joanne Lester Stuckey and Miram McDermott lay before me. She'd found addresses and phone numbers for all of them. There were others, maybe worth pursuing, maybe not, but I thought these might be enough. As much as I wanted to talk to Miriam, Joanne Lester Stuckey still lived on the block. I remembered from the title searches I'd done that ownership had passed to her just last year, so

Kenny and Ramona must both be gone. I hadn't noticed that she actually lived there. Somehow I'd gotten the impression she'd inherited it, but lived somewhere else. I looked at my little pocket watch. It was ten-twenty. I convinced myself that it wasn't too late to call. If I didn't, I might miss them in the morning unless I called really early, so this was probably better. I went back into the little alcove with the phone. It rang twice and a man answered.

"I'm sorry to call so late," I began.

"You should be," he said. "I've got to be up at five."

"I'll call back tomorrow."

"I won't be here after five-thirty. I'm up. Who are you? What do you want?"

"Well, I was actually calling for Joanne. Joanne Lester?"

"Oh, fer Christ sakes," he said.

I could hear him calling to at least another room in the house, if not to another house on the block.

"Joannne! Pick it up! It's for you!"

He waited for about five seconds and repeated it.

"Joanne!! It's for you!"

There was a click sound as she picked up an extension and a bang as he hung up his.

"Hello?"

"Joanne Lester?" I said.

"Yes...Lester-Stuckey, now. Who's this?"

"I don't know if you'll remember me, but my name is Kurt Goldman. I used to live down the block from you. On the other side? My sister, Sarah, is about your age. Do you remember us?"

"Yes, I think so. The name is familiar. How nice to hear from you."

"I'm sorry to call so late, but I was afraid I might miss you if I waited until tomorrow morning. Tell your husband I'm sorry."

"I will. He's got to get up early. We're expecting a big delivery in the morning at the store, so it's all got to be brought in before we open at nine and then inventoried."

"What store?" I asked her.

"Ed and I bought my grandfather's hardware store on San Vicente. Do you remember it?"

I laughed.

"I do indeed. It was my first credit account."

"Really?"

"Your father convinced your grandfather to open an account for me right about the time I turned eight."

"The locks!" she laughed. "Of course! Now I know exactly who you are. We've laughed about that whole episode for years. Pat loved to tell us about your coming in with two-fifty or three dollars a week or some-times more and paying off the locks people had charged. He got quite a kick out of it. You worked at the carwash and a paper route, right?"

"Yes," I said. How long have you been back on the block?"

"Since 1980. Even before we bought it from Pat, Ed and I were coming in from the Valley everyday to work in the store. We ran it for him. But Tarzana's in the LA school system and we hated it. We couldn't afford to buy anything over here, and after we bought the store, things were even tighter. In 1980 mom and dad let us have one of the downstairs units. In 1984, mom and dad offered to transfer title to me before their deaths if they could live in one of the downstairs unit and we paid them about what they'd lose in rent from the upstairs two. We converted the two upstairs units into one large one. Until their deaths in 1988, they and another tenant were downstairs. Our kids go to Hawthorne and Beverly High now. How's that for coming full circle?"

"Nice, actually."

"Well, I don't suppose you called about that."

"No, not really. You know about the construction at the old Rathbone property, right?"

"Yes. I can see it out our front window if I look across and down the block a little."

"Do you know why they stopped?"

"I heard," she said.

"Well, I'm sort of helping Detective Phillips with his investigation."

"Are you a policeman?"

"No. I got to know Phillips after my brother, Marty, died. Phillips contacted me about this because I lived on the block and he thought I could help. He hasn't contacted you?"

"No."

I thought that was pretty shoddy work, or part of some larger machination. With Phillips, who knew?

"What do you do? Normally?" she asked me.

"I design and build houses...in the Bay Area...mostly in and around Berkeley."

"That sounds pretty satisfying. Do you like it up there?"

"I love it."

"Do you have any children?"

"A son, Jason. He's seventeen now."

"God, the time flies. And Sarah?"

"She lives up north too. She has a daughter. About nineteen."

"Didn't you have a little brother too?"

"Yes, Nick. He's down around Laguna Beach. A criminal lawyer."

"I was sorry to hear about Marty," she said.

"Thank you," I said

"Ed and I have two boys and a girl. We started a little late. They're sixteen, fourteen and eleven now. It's so nice that they can go to school here. It's such a relief."

She paused, then, "So, now that we've covered the basics, how is it that you think I can be of help?"

"Do you remember Kevin Doyle?"

She was quiet a long time.

"Joanne?"

"Yes," she said finally, "all too well. My dad used to refer to him as 'that sick sonofabitch'. That was far too kind."

"Why?"

"Why?" she said, like the list was so long she didn't know where to begin. I pictured her throwing her free hand up, letting it come to rest on the back of her head, trying to find a place to start. It took a long quiet stretch for her to decide.

"Why?" she said again, "Ask Perry Arnold. If you could."

"I remember the name."

"He was Marylou's little brother. Do you remember her? They lived two doors down from us."

"Yes."

"He was the sweetest little kid you could imagine. It just breaks my heart to think about it, especially now that I have kids of my own. They moved because of it."

She didn't want to say the words and I didn't need to ask, but by not asking, she'd assume more than I wanted her to.

"What?" I said.

Her voice choked, like she couldn't get it out. Then determined, she said, "That miserable rotten bastard molested Perry! That's what! Can you imagine? Perry couldn't have been more than six or seven! Believe me, if my dad had known, Kevin Doyle never would have gotten off this block alive."

"When?"

"Nineteen fifty-one or two," she said, " I don't know exactly," her voice starting to waver again.

"How did you find out?"

She started to sob, then said, "Excuse me a second."

She put the phone down. I could hear water running, maybe at the kitchen sink. Maybe washing her face, I thought. When she came back he voice was tight.

"Marylou and I were best friends," she said, regaining control. "When they moved, they just picked up and left. She was my best friend and I never heard from her again, at least not for the next thirty-odd years. Then, a couple of years ago, her parents transferred title to her so she could have the income from the rentals, but she didn't want any part of it and sold the building. I saw her then. She told me about Perry. He never got over it. Never got past it. He just sort of, I don't know...Marylou said, '...floated around...until he drowned'. Not literally. He killed himself with pills just after his twentieth birthday."

I was curious if she knew about Joey Schumur or Ronnie Ganz, but decided if she did, she did. If not, she didn't need to.

"I've got to stop now," she said, starting to cry.

"I'm sorry," I said. "It's late, and all this is upsetting, I know. I'll let you go. Thank you."

"You're welcome."

She paused. The connection sank in.

"My god! You think it's Kevin Doyle!"

"Yes," I told her.

"Good," she said. "If it is, then the bastard didn't get off the block alive."

"I don't think he did."

She was quiet a moment. "I think I have something for you."

"What?"

"I know I do. Something from my dad. I'd forgotten all about it. He wanted you to have that old cigar box with his medals from the war. He put your name on it and said if I ever ran into you or someone in your family, I should give it to you or them. He didn't make a big deal about it, but I know it would please him."

There was a long pause.

"You know what?"

"What?"

"God, now that I think about it, he said if there was ever a problem at Rathbone's, I should open it. I'd forgotten all about that, too. Can you meet me either here or at the store tomorrow?"

"Sure," I told her.

"I come home around noon for a lunch break. If you don't think that will work, we could just plan on your coming by the store. There's a cafe next door, The Play's The Thing. Do you know it?"

"Not really, but I'll come to the store. We could go have coffee there."

"Any time after about ten-thirty. Ed and the kids and I should have things under control by then."

"The kids?"

"All three of our kids work in the store, weekends, vacations, especially during summer vacation. I used to work for Pat during the summers myself."

"I'll see you tomorrow after ten-thirty."

"See you then."


I slept poorly. I'd gone up the stairs to the second floor of the Pacific Hotel. It was late and I was tired and my head was swimming with memories of Oakhurst and the summer of 1951. I wish I could say that's what troubled my sleep. I wish I could say the same dignified, slightly dissolute looking clerk was still there at the hotel, but he wasn't. It might have shifted my perspective enough to alter my thoughts as I struggled to drift off. The place was enjoying a slight revival and had been spiffed up considerably, the beach at Venice once again becoming fashionable, the Hotel's prospects rising along with it. But he was gone, and the current clerk, along with the Hotel, was slightly more upscale, a quiet fellow, efficient and unremarkable. Kevin Doyle didn't trouble my sleep. I didn't dream of Kevin Doyle or anything related to him. I never did. When those waves washed over me it was always during the day, always triggered by something concrete, something I identified with him, but not him, not me, maybe someone like me, similar events maybe, ones I might read about in the paper, or even problems completely unrelated, but substantive enough to churn my secret places, lift the muck off the floor of that hidden pond. It came and went as it had this evening at Hannah's place. No, I knew my troubled sleep had little or nothing to do with Kevin Doyle or Oakhurst. It was beginning to register on me I'd probably never see Vann again. Some fools are born, others are made I reminded myself. Others, magically, stubbornly, make and remake themselves.

The San Vicente Hardware store was mostly unchanged. The floors were still wooden and worn. The windows seemed larger though, and if the skylights had been there before, I didn't remember them. If they'd been added, they were a nice touch, along with the larger windows, letting in enough additional light to alter what had been a friendly, but dingy ambience. The store was weighted more to the kind of household things you'd expect to find in a hardware store, but it was a big change from the old days, where shovels and wheelbarrows and saws and drills and rubber boots and garbage cans dominated. I wondered if it was just a sign of the times, or Joanne's influence.

A kid, a boy about sixteen, tall, slender, dark-haired and very good looking, with the same chiseled features I remembered on Kenny Lester, greeted me.

"Can I help you find something?" he said, his voice on the edge of cracking with each word.

"Is Joanne here?"

"Yes," he said. "She's my mom. Can I tell her who you are?"

"Kurt Goldman," I said.

He went to the back of the store. Most of the aisles were filled with plastic boxes stacked two or three or four high, the shipment of new items waiting to be inventoried and shelved. There was a girl and another boy, younger, sitting on two of the boxes, a third box open in front of them, the boy checking items off a list on a clipboard as the girl read to him from the box's packing list. They looked up at me and said hello as I wandered down the aisle, browsing. Joanne called to me from the other end of it.

"Kurt?"

"Hi. Is now a good time?"

"Perfect. I could use a break."

"What about us?" the little boy moaned, but with a mischievous grin.

"What about you? You guys only started an hour ago. Dad and I have been here since five-thirty. Back to work!"

"Mom! How 'bout we come for a coke?" the girl said.

"How 'bout later?" Joanne said. Then to me, "Let's get outta here before they go on strike. You kids should be able to get through this aisle before lunch if you don't fool around, so get busy."

They turned their attention back to the boxes. The older boy started shelving the items the younger ones had inventoried.

The Play's The Thing was a cafe-restaurant right next door to the hardware store. If it had been here long, I didn't remember it. I asked Joanne.

"There are two small playhouses nearby. One on Melrose, the other farther down on San Vicente. This opened to cater to the theatre crowd. They do an okay business for breakfast and lunch and dinner, but they count on the late-night theatre goers to stay alive. It used to be a tile shop. Almost no one else remembers that."

We sat at a table on a platform to the left of the entrance, raised a step above the main floor level, in a little niche with a floor to ceiling bay window, putting us almost on the sidewalk. Joanne got coffee, I got a coke. She reached down into a large shoulder bag she'd placed on the floor by her feet.

"Here," she said.

She handed me the cigar box. It had my name on a piece of paper scotch-taped to the top. The lid was also scotch-taped closed. Before I opened it, I asked her, "Do you remember the time I came to your door and your dad was out in the garage? You warned me he was sad?"

"No, not really. That happened pretty often. He'd go out there and look at the medals, think about the war and his part in it. Dropping bombs on people. He always tried to act like the war didn't have any effect on him. He'd done his job and that was that. Then he'd go out to the garage."

"He was sorting through this box, looking at the medals. The next day he gave me one."

"I didn't know that," she said.

"He told me no one wins a war. He made a real point of it. Made sure I understood. I thought a lot about that and him during the Viet Nam war while I was in college."

"Sounds like dad."

"I kept the medal to remind me of his help with the account at the hardware store. One was all I needed then. It's still enough. Wouldn't you like to keep the rest for yourself or your children?"

"He must have had his reasons," she said with a shrug.

I looked at her, asking without asking, if she was sure. She shifted her glance, and I had the feeling she would have liked to pass them onto her kids. I opened the box. Along with the other medals I'd seen, there was an envelope. I looked at her.

"What?"

"There's an envelope in here."

"There is? I've never looked inside, since he'd put your name on it."

I took the envelope out. Kurt G. was written on it and underlined.

"You've never seen this?"

"Nope."

I sat there, transfixed. The medals, the envelope, the touch of Kenny reaching across thirty-eight years. It was both disturbing and reassuring.

"You're going to open it, aren't you?" Joanne said, expectantly.

"Sure," I said.

I read it, then re-read it. I handed it to Joanne. She read it out loud.

"To whom it may concern- If it ever comes up, if there's ever any question about it, I killed Kevin Doyle. I'm sorry it turned out that way, but it was unavoidable. I buried him at the south end of the Rathbone property. If anybody needs to know, I swear this is true. Signed, Kenny Lester. Witnessed by, Maurice C-something. Dated October 14, 1951."

Joanne looked up at me with a troubled, confused mixture of fear and awe and satisfaction in equal measures. She held the letter out to me.

"What does this mean?" she asked.

"I don't know," I told her.

"Who's Maurice whoever?"

"I'm not positive, but I'm pretty sure he's one of the guys I worked with at the carwash."

"How would my dad know him?"

"They swapped war stories there at least a few times that I remember, maybe more. And he worked for my grandfather occasionally, doing yard work, so he was around on our block sometimes."

"I suppose," she said uncertainly.

"Last night, I spoke with Iyama Osaka. Do you remember him?"

"Of course I do. I didn't know he's still alive."

"He's sick, but alive. He lives out at Point Dume. His son, Victor, is one of the developers of Rathbone's property. With John Dolan."

"I knew about Dolan. What about Iyama?"

"He told me it was Kevin's time. That he killed Kevin and buried him in Rathbone's garden."

"How can that be?" she said, even more confused now, touching Kenny's letter.

"Iyama's letter was witnessed by your dad."

"My dad hardly knew Iyama. I don't understand. I don't understand any of it."

We both sat there looking at Kenny's letter, thinking about it and Iyama's confession. After a long minute, Joanne's apprehension seemed to melt away and was replaced with what I took as a measure of pride. She smiled ruefully at me.

"Whatever. If they could have killed him a dozen times, it wouldn't have been enough. Do whatever you have to with this," she said, pointing at the letter. "My dad wanted you to have it, to use it in whatever way was necessary. I just have one request."

"What's that?"

"I would like to keep the medals for my kids, as a reminder of who their grandfather was. Not so much in the war, but in life. If this comes out, I want them to know no matter how unpleasant, he did his duty as he saw it. He was a good man."

Amen, I could almost hear Maurice saying.

"Amen," I said, "Amen to that."

Joanne and I sat there quietly, thinking. She sipped at her coffee. I finished the coke, then started chewing the ice cubes.

"You know what's funny?" she asked me.

"What?"

"I never thought about it much until now, but my mom noticed the change in him. She joked about it."

"What?"

"He started going to the carwash almost every Saturday and she kidded him that we had the cleanest Buick in town. She didn't say it, but we both knew he didn't go out to the garage much anymore."

Joanne went back to the store. I wandered over to the little park with the Moorish fountain, where Doheny and Upper Santa Monica and North Oakhurst all met, just above the tracks. Where Kenny had given me his Distinguished Flying Cross. Then I wandered along the Beverly Gardens Park to Rexford and back. I hung around the fountain for a long time. I snoozed under a shady tree on the thick grass. I slept but didn't sleep. Dreamed but didn't dream. Basically, I pissed the rest of the day away.

"What a nice surprise. I was hoping I might run into you this morning," he said.

It was Phillips. It couldn't have been much past six-thirty. Pretty early for a cop I was thinking, especially a detective. I was betting it was something of a first for him. All dressed up in his five hundred dollar suit, showered and shaved and combed. He looked like he was headed for a Chamber of Commerce meeting to give them his department's statistics on the dropping crime rate, guaranteeing a warm welcome. I was at my usual table on the west side of Il Fornaio, on the Dayton Way side, the LA Times spread out before me. I had coffee, their homemade bread and jam and a large grapefruit juice. I'd been reading an investigative piece by Evan Morris: 'Office Autopsy - Successor to Flamboyant Noguchi Target of Mismanagement Charge'. It looked like Morris had first uncovered, then pursued the case himself, until finally the District Attorney's Office had been shamed into taking it up. I thought the morning was going to be a quiet, pleasant, maybe even a reflective time. I didn't want to try to focus too hard on Kenny's letter or Iyama's confession. I didn't want to force it. I wanted to let it simmer a while. I thought that if it did, some explanation would come, some intuitive notion would light the way. Eat a little, read the paper, let it happen. With Phillips in my face it wouldn't. He'd want to discuss it to death. He'd want an answer, an explanation, at least a theory, being a great one for theories and all. But he fooled me.

"'Bout time we wrapped this up, eh cowboy?" he said. "You've done your part. Raised a little hell, covered a good chunk of ground, stirred things up a bit," he said, giving me a look of clearly mock annoyance, letting me know all was forgiven, "found out a little of this and that. A little weak on the sharing part, I gotta say, but all in all, you did okay. All I could ask for. I'm going to talk to Victor Osaka later this morning, but given the circumstances, when I lay it out before the D. A., I don't think it's going to go much further than that. The old guy's sick. It's thirty-eight years old. So, no point, really. 'Bout time you got back to that up-north wine country. Right?"

"Berkeley," I corrected him. "We drink the wine but don't grow it."

He shrugged. Close enough.

He might be ready to wrap it up, but I wasn't.

"You've spoken with Victor Osaka? Did he call you?"

I couldn't imagine that he would have. I figured he'd try to protect Iyama as best he could.

"No, not yet," Phillips hedged. Like I said, later this morning."

"Then how do you know about Iyama?"

"I'm a detective, remember?" he said, irritably.

He was a detective here at six forty-five in the morning with information that I and Victor only learned last night about nine. He was a hell of a detective alright. I assumed it probably helped that Victor was in a partnership with Dolan, the would-be mayor, and for my money, the driving force behind the investigation. I could see Victor looking to protect Iyama through the influence of Dolan. It not only made sense, it seemed to be working if Phillips was right about the D.A.'s office. Phillips stood with both hands on the back of the chair across the table from me. It's true I hadn't invited him to sit, but it'd never stopped him before. Then it dawned on me he didn't want to. He didn't want to extend this business by the length of time a cup of coffee might take. His irritation had passed and he was back to his nice easy going smile. This wasn't a murder investigation his look suggested, it was merely an intellectual exercise, like a hypothetical chess problem on an imaginary board. We'd fooled around with it long enough and now it was time to go back to real work, whatever that might be. Not quite, I was thinking. There was the inconvenience of having a second confession. He probably wouldn't consider it a big problem, since he seemed to be in such a forgiving mood, but all the same, if you're investigating a murder, it might be good to at least examine and sort out conflicting, mutually exclusive confessions. Just for the heck of it.

"Sit down Phillips," I invited. "I'd like to show you something."

He had this exasperated look like I was making this more complicated than it needed to be. Like all I had to do was finish eating, get on the plane, and we were done. Simplicity itself.

"What?" he said. Without sitting.

His posture said he'd stick around maybe another minute, a minute and a half tops, but that was it. And that long only to humor me. So we could end on a positive note.

I took a copy I'd made of Kenny's letter out of the little file folder Vann had given me. I flipped it around so it faced him and pushed it across the table. He read it. He looked up at me. His face was serious.

Troubled. Annoyed.

"Who's Kenny Lester? Who's Maurice...what's this last name?"

"Kenny lived on the block. Maurice worked at the carwash at the Standard Station that used to be at Lower Santa Monica and Beverly Boulevard. Sometimes he did odd jobs for my grandfather. I don't know his last name. I can't read it either. Sit down. I think you're going to be here a while. Would you like coffee?"

"No."

"You might as well. You're paying for it."

He sat and signaled the waitress. She poured him a cup.

"Waffle, two eggs over easy, orange juice and a small fruit bowl," he told her.

"Our tax dollars at work," I said.

"Not yours, buddy."

"True."

"So, who's Kenny Lester? A little more detail."

"First, let me ask you something."

"Shoot."

"You're a pretty good cop. Thorough. Are you really being this sloppy or is there outside influence...pressure on you?"

His expression hardened. He didn't like the question and it didn't look like he was going to answer, but I was glad I'd asked, to put it out there for both of us to think about.

"Kenny Lester," he said. "How do you know him? How did you get this letter? Did he give it to you? And where is he? I'm going to have to talk to him."

"You can't," I said. "He died about a year ago. A little more. He left this with his daughter for me. She still lives on the street. You just missed that?"

"God dammit! Why is everything so complicated with you? This is ready to go away, all set to, and it should. But that's just too simple for you, right?"

"It is what it is. You said you'd tell me what was behind the investigation before I left. You want me to go. Tell me what this is about and I'll consider going. Otherwise, I'm not nearly done."

"If I tell you it's time for you to go, you go. Got me?" he said through clenched teeth, leaning half way across the table.

"You think the D.A. is going to let this just fade away if there's two confessions? Thirty-eight years or not, you don't think it will pique his interest? Just a little?"

I was bluffing. The last thing I wanted was further outside scrutiny. That seemed to be the case for Phillips as well, and I assumed Dolan too. He thought about the alternatives and decided he had to tell me something. It was up to me to decide if it was true or not, regardless of how complete or incomplete.

"This goes nowhere. Understood?"

"Of course," I said too quickly.

He looked at me to make sure I wasn't being a smart ass.

"I mean it. Nowhere."

"As long as you're not pulling me into some conspiracy to obstruct justice, okay," I agreed.

The possibility didn't seem so far-fetched. His look told me he was skirting the edges.

"Dolan owns this property. He's been trying to develop it for ages, and now, with Osaka involved, it's a go. He's also a councilman running for mayor, pushing a more aggressive development program. There's a lot riding on this election for a lot of people, and there's a lot of resistance to him, to his approach. To his style. He has a talent for making enemies. A body shows up and it's pretty clear it didn't get there on its own. It's murder. An old murder, but murder. I can't say I'm completely convinced, but I don't think he's trying to obstruct anything. He's looking for a little damage control, given the delicacy of his position. The current mayor, Tannenbaum, and councilman Salter, both hate him, but don't want an investigation to look like a witch hunt to de-rail his candidacy. Have it backfire on them and win the election for Dolan. They ask the department to extend him every reasonable courtesy. Every reasonable consideration. That's what I'm trying to do. That's why you're here. Then Victor Osaka confirms Dolan's worst, and believe me here, private fears, the dead guy's almost certainly his half-brother, Kevin Doyle. Dolan never mentioned the name to me until Victor called him with it last night and he called me. I knew nothing about Doyle, who apparently disappeared in the summer of 1951. It seems a certainty that both the coroner and the Army guys are going to confirm it. So, for your information, before Doyle's name came into it, I was trying to quietly, discreetly, conduct an investigation. Look into it without calling too much attention to it. I figured with you poking around, it would be below the radar. It wouldn't raise the interest of any of his enemies, or god forbid, the press. If I were too involved, it would. As a citizen, as someone who'd lived on the block, you could poke around without setting off too many alarms. I must have been out of my mind."

"And now?" I asked him, pointing to Kenny's letter.

"I won't ignore it. I can't ignore it. But I'd like to proceed with caution. I don't plan on voting for Dolan, but I agree with Salter and Tannenbaum that he's done nothing to get swept up in some thirty-eight year old mess, just because it involves his half-brother on property he's developing now. Hell, he couldn't have been more than ten or eleven back then. So, can I count on your...discretion?"

The expression on his face and the way he said it made it clear he thought it was probably a waste of time to even ask, but he felt obliged to go through the motions.

"For now, anyway," I promised. "But I'm not leaving just yet. I need to know more."

"You and me both, cowboy."

He looked at me appraisingly.

"Did you know this Doyle guy? Do you remember him?"

"Yes," I said. "Both."

"And?"

"And nothing," I said, trying to ignore the wave of lightheadedness that swept over me like sudden carsickness. "He lived across the street from us...with his mother, I think."

I wanted to close my eyes for just a moment, to let it pass; with Phillips there, the best I could manage was a few controlled breaths. It helped.

"Anyway, I've got a few more people I'd like to talk with. When I have, you and I can talk again, okay?"

"Sounds familiar," he smiled." What about this Maurice guy? Is he still around? Still alive?"

"I haven't a clue," I said, but I planned to find out.

Phillips shrugged, then began to buzz through his breakfast in earnest. He wolfed it down like he was already late for an appointment, but it wasn't even quarter past seven when he finished eating, so I doubted that. He stood, spooning some of the Olalaberry jam on a last piece of toast, stuffing it in his mouth, taking a few last sips of coffee, careful not to drip anything on his crisp white shirt, his tie or freshly pressed suit.

"Later, buddy. I'll let you take care of the check."

He gave me a big stage wink.

"Gotta run."

He took the linen napkin from the table and performed a last clean-up wipe at the corners of his mouth, then carefully wiped his fingers and tossed it on the table and took off. In less than a dozen purposeful strides, he was out the door and gone.

It was suddenly peaceful in Il Fornaio again, just the early morning hum of the regulars before they headed to offices or stores walking distance away. I don't think it had been anything other than that for anyone in there. It's not like Phillips was shouting or raising any kind of ruckus, but for me, there was a definite ease that returned as I saw him disappear across Beverly Drive, heading for Rexford and the police station. I looked at my abandoned LA Times and thought maybe I could get interested in it again, at least enough to return to my plan of not really trying to think about Kenny or Iyama's letters. But it was no use. Their faces, and Maurice's, filled my thoughts. Especially Maurice. The day he'd fought with Kevin Doyle on the parkway and our front lawn. I tried, but couldn't remember having ever seen him and Kevin on the block at the same time again. Not just in a confrontation, I couldn't remember Maurice or any of the carwash guys on the block even one other time that Kevin was around. When would he have been around Kenny? When would he have been available to sign Kenny's letter? It didn't exactly seem like the kind of thing Kenny would have brought to the carwash and asked Maurice to witness for him. I wanted to find him, but for the life of me, I couldn't think of his last name. I'd probably never know it. Nor any of them. They were just Maurice and Dennis and Jackson and

William, the carwash guys. The Standard Station and the carwash were long gone. I looked through Vann's notes to see if she had found a listing for Mr. Avery. Nothing. If he or someone in his family had old employee records from the Station, I might have found Maurice's last name that way, but no such luck. If I knew Joseph's last name, I thought, that might open up something. If I could find him, or his family, if he had one, that might lead to Maurice, or at least Jackson and William, since they'd played together. But I didn't have any idea what Joseph's last name was. Then the name, The Albertine, hit me. The name of the club he and Jackson and William played in Watts. It was a long shot, but I didn't have much else. I went back to the alcove and the phones and phone books. In the business listings there was an Albertine Cafe on Ottis Avenue. Maybe not a jazz club, but the same name had to be more than coincidence. It was Friday, it was just about seven and if it was a breakfast place, they should be open. It was worth a try. When someone picked up the phone, it was clear they'd been open for awhile and did a great early morning business if the noise level was any indication.

"Albertine's" a woman yelled over the noise. "Can't hear you. Probably won't be able to. We're open 'til 3. Serve breakfast all day. 1106 Ottis, near Firestone. Come on down. Gotta go."

She hung up.

Might as well, I thought.

# Chapter 24

## *Lucky Dog, Lucky Horse, Lucky Days*
## June 12-18, 1951

JOSEPH WAS RIGHT. Sometimes things just steer you one way or another and you go and that's that. Since Miss Rimes had showed up at the carwash, that pretty much forced me to go to school on Tuesday. Since I was going to be there Tuesday, it would have looked funny if I tried to cool off on Wednesday or Thursday, so that was how I got my horse.

It must have been about eight-fifteen when I came through the gate to the lower playground and coasted up to the bike rack. The playground was noisy with kids playing kickball and dodge ball and three or four groups of girls jumping rope. Miss Brasserri had her arms folded across her chest with the silver whistle she blew at the slightest sign of trouble, or when it was time to put away the balls and jump ropes and go back to class. The whistle was sparkling in the sun, hanging around her neck on a rawhide necklace, resting about halfway down to her waist, where she could get it quick if she needed to. It was sunny and I could smell the blacktop beginning to heat up. Everybody that needed to put their bikes in the bike rack must have already done it because there wasn't anyone else there besides me. The good thing was there were two empty spaces at the end, so I could park the Red Rider one space away from the nearest bike again with nothing at all on one side, and hope no one parked in the remaining space. When I turned around Gene Morelli and Leslie Morrison were right there.

"Boy oh boy," Leslie said, "John Dolan's a goner!" He moved his hand, palm down, about waist high, parallel to the ground, like that's the end of that.

"He died?"

Geez, if there was trouble about the locks, this would be the end of everything.

"No, nothing that bad," Gene said, mumbling through his swollen mouth. "His mom came to school at the end of the day and got all his end of the year stuff. He's not coming back until next year. You really put the KABOOM on him!"

"It was an accident!" I said.

"Yeah," Leslie said, "maybe the bang on his head was, but boy, you went after him like Sugar Ray Robinson! Boom, bang and stay away from the Red Rider! Man, I didn't know you had it in you."

"Neither did I."

"Weren't you scared?" Gene mumbled some more.

"I was too mad. I forgot to be," I said.

"Well, it was a sight to see," Gene smiled.

His smile was lopsided because his mouth was puffed up on the side where John Dolan had hit him, which was also why he was mumbling so much. Just then, Miss Brasserri blew the whistle and we knew it was time to go to class. I bet the neighbors around Hawthorne just loved that. About ten times a day she blew that thing. They could probably hear her all the way down to Santa Monica and up to Sunset. But that wasn't my problem. I didn't have any. Not really. This might just be the perfect day. No John Dolan, no suspension, nobody mad at me, and the Red Rider sparkling in the sun just waiting to take me somewhere. I couldn't see how it could get any better.

Miss Kendall was pretty crabby, but there wasn't anything new about that. She kept giving me dirty looks, like she was dying to say something about me and John Dolan, but she didn't. That surprised me, but I just considered it good luck and chalked it up to the Red Rider. She had folders with our names on them and she passed them out and we were supposed to go around the room and take down anything on the walls or in the work baskets that belonged to us. Then we had quiet reading time. There was a little library in our classroom with twenty or thirty or forty books, but if we couldn't find anything we wanted to read, we could raise our hand and ask to go to the school library. She usually said yes, unless she wanted to be especially mean, then she'd say no, and if you couldn't find anything you wanted to read in the classroom, she'd yell at you to hurry up and find something and sit down. Pretty soon it was lunch time and we got out of there. I wished I could have just kept cooling off. The last days of school were boring. There wasn't enough to do, but we had to be there anyway. It would have been much better to be on the Red Rider, free to go anywhere, maybe even to the beach again. I wanted to tell Gene about going to the beach, but one thing would lead to another, and I didn't want to tell him about Pete and Kevin Doyle and the carwash guys or any of it. I just wanted to forget about the whole thing. So I didn't. Besides, it would have been hard to tell him without it being bragging. Even if I was careful, it's the kind of thing that's going to sound like bragging no matter what, so that was another reason for not mentioning it. Lunch came and went.

When we were back in the class room, Miss Kendall was waiting for us. So was Miss Rimes.

"Hurry up and get into your seats!" Miss Kendall yelled.

She clapped her hands a couple of times.

"Hurry up!" she said again.

When we were all seated, she told us to pay attention, Miss Rimes had something to tell us. She looked at Miss Rimes, giving her permission to talk. Miss Rimes smiled at us.

"I've got some good news for you. All of your clay projects are done. They're ready now, so you don't have to wait until Friday. Miss Kendall is going to bring you down to the art room before the end of the day and you can get your pieces.'

Great, I thought. Everybody but me. I looked at Miss Kendall. She had a little smile on her face, and she dipped her head towards me, sort of a nod, like, I warned you. See? This is what you get. I made myself think about the Red Rider Special instead, about how free it made me feel and it worked. I smiled back at her. I knew the horse was supposed to be green and so did Miss Rimes and so did she. She could look at the unfired green clay horse forever for all I cared. She could even throw it away. I made it and painted it green. I did what I told myself I wanted to do, all except for giving it to my dad, but if she wouldn't fire it green, it wouldn't be the horse I wanted to give him anyway, so it didn't matter. If she wouldn't let Miss Rimes fire it, that was that. I had other things to think about.

"What are you smirking about, young man?" she crabbed at me.

"Nothing," I said.

"If you think I'm going to change my mind and let Miss Rimes fire it, you've got another think coming!"

"The truth is..." Miss Rimes began, but Miss Kendall interrupted her.

"The only truth this boy needs to know is who's in charge. And it's not you and it's not him. Am I clear?"

"Yes, mam," I said.

Miss Rimes didn't say anything, but she didn't like Miss Kendall yelling at her either.

Another funny thing was, even Miss Kendall didn't seem so scary today. After yesterday with John Dolan and then Kevin Doyle, I wasn't sure what would be any more. I must have been still smiling, even though I didn't mean to.

"You wipe that smirk off your face! I'm not going to warn you again!"

"Yes, mam," I said, but then a giggle leaked out.

I couldn't help it. It had to be the worst time for the giggles, but I had them and they were sticking to me like glue. It kept getting worse and pretty soon I was laughing so hard my eyes had tears in them and I could hardly see, so I didn't see her coming. She pulled me out of my chair so fast my feet didn't touch the floor right away.

"I want you to go to the principal's office! Let's see if you think that's funny!"

"Yes, mam," I said, still laughing as she pushed me out the door into the hallway. Threw me, was more like it.

Two days in a row to the principal's office. If it wasn't a record, it was only because John Dolan probably had it. I felt like I should be crying, but I wasn't. I was still sort of giggling. About half way down the hallway, Miss Rimes caught up with me as I poked along, wondering what I could tell him, especially after he'd been so nice about John Dolan's head.

"Can I walk with you?" she said.

"Sure," I said. "Did she send you to the principal's office too?"

"No," she laughed, "she didn't."

She leaned down close and sort of whispered to me.

"But I did fire your horse. It's a beautiful, shiny green," she said, "just the way it's supposed to be."

"You did?!"

"I most certainly did! I'm not going to let her bully me around. Even if she's been at the school longer than anyone else, that's no excuse for the way she acts. I intend to tell that to Mr. Brody. You let me talk to him first."

"I'm good with that," I told her, relieved.

When we got to the principal's office, we went in together but I let her do the talking. She said something to the secretary, Sandy, who told me to sit down where I'd been yesterday. At least she was smiling at me today, like we were friends now. Miss Rimes went into Mr. Brody's inner office. I could hear her voice but couldn't see her, and the voice by itself didn't sound much older than Sarah's or Megan Weis's, so she just sounded like another kid in the principal's office trying to explain why she got in trouble but how it wasn't really her fault, except, after about the first minute where her voice was raised and sounded mad about Miss Kendall, it started to sound more like Kenny Lester telling the carwash guys about the pig in his tent, because both she and Mr. Brody were laughing at the way she was describing it. She was in there only a few minutes more. When she came back out she was smiling.

"Mr. Brody said maybe you could use another cooling off day. He said maybe we should both cool off the rest of the day. How about them apples?"

There wasn't much left of the day to cool off for, but we both thought Mr. Brody was pretty neat. She was going to go back to the art room and make sure everyone's pieces were out on the tables so when Miss Kendall and the other teachers brought their classes down to collect them, everyone could find their stuff. She said she'd sneak the horse out before Miss Kendall got there with my class and she'd get it to me somehow.

"Want to meet at the carwash?" I suggested.

I didn't say it, but I was thinking about Joseph.

"We could do that, I suppose," she said, turning red.

"I suppose, too," I said, and headed for the Red Rider.

"Aren't you the one," she smiled. "I'll meet you there in about twenty minutes."

Even though it was only about two-thirty, and school wouldn't be out for another forty minutes, Joseph didn't seem too surprised to see me. There weren't any cars at the carwash, and the guys were just hanging around, waiting for a car to wash or for three o'clock so they could clean up, whichever came first. Jackson saw me and waved. I waved back, parked the Red Rider, and pulled up a stool.

"Trouble at school?" he asked, wiping the counter.

He looked me over, checking to see if I was okay, and seeing that I was, he wasn't worried about whatever it was.

"A little," I said. "I got the giggles at the wrong time, and Miss Kendall, my teacher, she's mean to everybody, not just me, but a lot to me, got mad at me and Miss Rimes, so the principal thought we should both cool off a little more."

Joseph stopped wiping, and looked up.

"Colleen?"

"She's gonna meet me here in a few minutes."

"She is?"

He couldn't hide the smile any more than I could've stopped the giggles.

"Uh huh," I joked him, "she might even have time to say hello to you."

"Hmm," was all he said, but he couldn't shake off the smile.

A couple of minutes later, she pulled into the station. She sat on the stool next to mine and handed me a thing wrapped up in newspaper.

"Go on and open it," she said.

She and Joseph looked at each other kind of gooey-eyed.

"Hello, again," she said with a big smile.

"Nice to see you so soon," he said, trying not to smile so much.

I carefully ripped the masking tape away from the newspaper and spread the paper back onto the counter, one part after another, until the package was open, and the green horse, a perfect shiny dark green, seemed to be looking at me as much as I was looking at him. Like we had just discovered each other, just been introduced, but both of us knew we were going to be friends. It was so perfect! I knew he would help my dad feel better about his fight with Pop. He could hold the horse in his hand and it would make him feel better. I knew it.

"Thank you," I told Miss Rimes. "It's for my dad."

"You're welcome," she said. "I'm sure he'll love it. It never should have been a problem in the first place."

"Problem?" Joseph asked her.

"Oh, Miss Kendall objected to the color. Ordered me not to fire it unless Kurt painted it brown or black. Can you imagine that? Ordered me, like I'm supposed to be afraid of her. But he refused, bless him."

She messed up my hair.

"Is that why you got kicked out of school? You fired it anyway?"

"Kicked out?" she looked at me, surprised, "did you say I got kicked out?"

"No, just told to cool off, that's all, I swear!"

"Just kiddin' her," Joseph said to me. "Just teasin'."

"No," she said, her finger to her lips, so he'd know to keep the secret. "Miss Kendall doesn't know I fired it. I snuck it out of school on my way to cool off."

"But you're not afraid of her," Joseph said.

Miss Rimes smiled, "No point in looking for trouble."

It must have been three by then because the carwash guys had cleaned

264                          Berton D. Garey

up and came over to the hot dog stand for coffee. Maurice's mouth was
puffed up from Kevin's head smash, but otherwise, he looked normal.

"You okay?" he asked me.

"I'm fine. How 'bout you? You okay."

"I'll be eatin' soup for a coupla days, but I'm good."

"Colleen," Joseph said, "this is Maurice, and Jackson and William
and Dennis."

They all shook hands.

"Colleen's Kurt's art teacher," he told them. "I told her you might
help her with some casting," he said to Dennis.

"You sculpt?" Dennis asked her, sort of lighting up.

The carwash guys pulled up stools and Joseph poured them coffee. I
had a coke and so did Miss Rimes.

"Who did this? This is damn good," Dennis said about my horse.

"I did," I told him.

"You did this? You ever think about castin' it?"

"What's that mean?" I asked him.

"We'd make a mold from this, fill the mold with brass so hot it's a
liquid, and when it hardens, you've got a brass horse. Maybe make a
bunch of them. This has a real nice feel to it."

"I think so too," Miss Rimes said.

"That sounds pretty neat, but would that mess it up?"

"Naw, we'd make a plaster casts from this. Since it's fired and got a
nice smooth hard surface, it'll clean up like new. Wanna try it?"

"But then there'd be two or maybe more of them, right?"

"Right," he said with a big smile, like that would be the neatest thing
in the world.

"I don't think so, then."

"How come?" he said, his face wrinkled up.

"I want my dad to have the only one."

"I agree with Kurt," Miss Rimes said. "Some things are meant to be
one of a kind."

"I'm good with that," Dennis said, nodding. "That makes sense. What
kind of stuff you doin'?" he asked Miss Rimes.

"Mostly busts, a few figures."

"How big're your figures?"

"Two feet, sometimes three," she said.

"That's no problem. I can do up to 'bout eight feet tall, twelve or
thirteen hundred pounds. Got anything ready to go?"

"I do!" she said all excited.

"Dennis," Joseph said, "she sells her stuff on consignment in a gallery
here in Beverly Hills. They might take a look at your stuff."

"That right?" Dennis asked her.

He shrugged, like that might be nice, but it wasn't a big thing. But
his eyes got wide and he had a hopeful look, like a kid, probably like I
looked when I first thought I had a chance for the Red Rider, only he was
trying to hide it and I couldn't because I was a kid.

"It's the deWitt on Canon. If I think James even might be interested, I'll ask, and then, all I can promise is he'll look at your work. I know he'll do that if I ask. After that, it's the work that's got to speak to him. I'd like to see it before I ask him, if that's okay with you."

"Fair 'nough. That would be real nice of you. When you'd like to see my little foundry? You could see some of my stuff then, too."

"Well, Kurt and I are supposed to be cooling off the rest of the day," she said, smiling at me.

"That'd be fine. Me and the others'll be taking the bus back downtown. Be home in an hour or so. The foundry and my house're all on the same the block. It's an old warehouse and yard my dad had before the war for his scrap metal business. During the war, they added the foundry and made cast parts for the shipbuilders in the yards at LA and Willmington and San Pedro. I could meet you there in an hour and a half?"

"How about if you guys all piled in my car and I gave you a ride?"

The guys looked at each other and smiled, shaking their heads no.

"That'd be nice, but maybe not a real good plan," Maurice told her.

"Why not?" Miss Rimes asked.

"Don't want to get lynched before dinner," Jackson laughed. "Got a real good dinner on tonight. Be a shame to miss it."

"It's not that bad," Dennis said.

"Maybe not for you," Jackson told him.

Dennis made a face and shrugged.

"He's half eye-tie," Jackson told Miss Rimes.

"What's that?" she asked.

"His dad was Italian," Joseph told her.

"Not that it done him much good," Maurice laughed, "he may not be as black as me, but they stuck him in the Panthers without a second thought, now, didn't they?"

"Yeah, yeah, but we's coffee, he's with cream," Jackson said, "'sides, look at that little thin nose. You don't find a nose like that too often downtown."

I didn't know what they were talking about, except for the part about Dennis wasn't as black as the other guys, but Miss Rimes did, I guess, because she looked liked she felt bad she'd said the wrong thing or something, but Joseph tried to cheer her up.

"Just the way it is. Sometimes you got to make allowances."

"But it's not right," she said.

"Thanks just the same. You wanna meet me at the foundry?" Dennis asked.

Miss Rimes looked worried.

"How 'bout if we go down together?" Joseph asked her. "I know where it is, and I could accompany you."

"But you don't close here until four, right?"

"Right, but maybe I could use a little cooling off too," Joseph said.

"How 'bout you, Kurt?" Maurice asked me.

"Yeah," Dennis said, "You like to come down to the foundry? You might not want to cast the horse, but there might be other stuff you'd like to cast later on. Might be you could get a little work from time to time helping me there. Whatcha think?"

I looked at Joseph and Miss Rimes and Maurice. They all seemed to think it was a good idea and so did I. If it worked out, I could pay off the locks even faster than I'd promised Mr. Mahoney.

Joseph told Miss Rimes that I lived just a couple of blocks away and that I could drop off the Red Rider at home and then go downtown with them.

"You better ask your mom if it's okay," Miss Rimes said.

I told her no one would be home and I told her about the six o'clock rule and that it would be okay, but she said I couldn't go unless there was someone at home to tell, so I figured the whole deal was off, but she and Joseph said they'd follow me home anyway and we'd see.

I wrapped the horse back up in the newspaper and put it down my shirt and rode down Beverly to Oakhurst. They'd given me a head start, so I got to our driveway about a block ahead of them. I was hoping Pop would be there and I could tell him, but his side of the garage was open and his car was gone. It was close to the time Sarah would be getting home from school, but telling her might not be good enough for Miss Rimes anyway, so that wouldn't help, and she wasn't here yet even if it would be good enough. And Marty wouldn't be home for at least two or three hours. Miss Rimes and Joseph pulled up to the curb next to me, on the wrong side for the way they were pointed.

"Anyone home?" Miss Rimes asked me.

"No," I said. "I guess I can't go."

"Sorry," Miss Rimes said. "I'd love to take you, but someone should know you're with us."

George Bowen came down the Courtyard walk, puffing on a cigarette, his head sort of tipped to avoid the smoke trying to get into his eye.

"I could tell my friend, George Bowen. Mr. Avery's friend," I reminded Joseph.

"That would be good enough for me," Joseph said.

He explained to Miss Rimes about Mr. Avery, then George.

"George!" I called to him.

He waved.

"Could you tell my mom or dad or Marty or Pop I'm going downtown with Miss Rimes, my art teacher and Joseph from the hot dog stand?"

"You are?" George asked, coming over.

Miss Rimes and Joseph got out of the car.

"Howya doin'?" Joseph said, shaking hands.

"Good. How 'bout you?" George asked him.

"This is Colleen Rimes, George. Colleen, George, Kurt's neighbor and Mr. Avery's friend."

They shook hands too.

"Dennis, one of the guys that works the carwash for Mr. Avery, has a little foundry downtown. He does some casting and Miss Rimes, Colleen here, is a sculptor and Dennis might do some casting for her. We're headin' down there to take a look, and we'd like to take Kurt with us, but we wanted to leave word for his parents. We'd have him home by five-thirty, quarter to six. Think you could do that for us?"

George looked at me.

"You okay?"

"Fine."

"I mean from yesterday."

"I know. I'm fine."

"I told Kevin it was me who spoke to Miriam. He won't bother you. I'm sorry Kurt."

"He better not," Joseph said. "Maurice's pretty worked up about it."

"It'll be okay," George told him.

"It's okay. Really," I said.

"What is?" Miss Rimes asked.

"Nothing," I said. "Could you tell my mom or dad or Marty? Please?"

"Sure," George said. "Glad to."

"Thanks, George," I said. "I'll be right back," I told Miss Rimes and Joseph. "Don't go without me."

I put the Red Rider in the garage, in another new place where I was even surer my dad wouldn't accidentally run it over when he came home, than ran to the screen door, through the back porch to me and Marty's room and hid the horse under my bed so I could surprise my dad with it later. When I ran back to the sidewalk, Miriam poked her head out the window and called to me.

"Where're you off to?"

"Watts, to see a foundry," I called to her.

"Watts? Really?" she said. Then, "Who's that you're going with? Does your mother know?"

"Miss Rimes, my art teacher and Joseph from the carwash hot dog stand. George Bowen already knows."

"Okay, then, have a good time."

"Thanks. Bye."

She waved and I waved and I got into Miss Rimes car and we were off

It seemed like we drove for a long time, but it couldn't have been that long because I figured we must have left my house by three-thirty and Joseph was telling Miss Rimes the traffic wasn't too bad for four o'clock. We drove all the way down Beverly Boulevard until it turned into East 1st Street downtown, and when we got to South Central, Joseph told Miss Rimes to turn right. We drove and drove and drove. It was like counting since we started at East 1st and kept going through all the numbers. I didn't start keeping track until the forties, but they were all there alright, the fifties and sixties and seventies and everything else all the way to the hundreds. My dad was right about one thing for sure, the

Negroes and Mexicans had it pretty rough in this town. The houses were pretty beat up and needed a lot of fixing. The lawns were cut and some houses even had flower beds, but you could tell right away, Beverly Hills was a million miles away, even our south-of-the-tracks part of Beverly Hills. Since my dad and Pop split up, money was always even more of a problem at our house than it had ever been. Things were getting better, but I knew we still had a big problem about it, but down here, you could tell things just went along, probably not getting a lot worse or a lot better, kind of bad day after day, without much hope for a change. Like being thirsty all the time and knowing there wasn't any water around. We drove down South Central all the way to East 107th Street.

"Left here, Colleen," Joseph said, "then left on Zamora."

Almost as soon as we turned on 107th we turned left again on Zamora and in half a block Zamora Avenue became Zamora Circle, a big oval street in front of us, like a popsicle with a stick on the top and bottom. We were coming in from the bottom stick and could go to the left or right around the oval, which surrounded this one huge lot that filled the inside, all of it inside a chain-link fence. Or we could go straight ahead through a big gate with a sign over it that said, Zamora Iron Works and Foundry.

"This is it," Joseph said, and had Miss Rimes pull in through the gate.

Dennis' foundry was a giant building, beat up looking, made out of the kind of metal in sheets that had grooves running up and down. The same metal was used on the sides and the roof. It had lots of rust spots, some of them bad enough to be holes all the way through, but Dennis kept the whole place neat and un-junky. There were piles of wood and steel of all kinds and sizes and shapes, all neatly organized. Joseph pointed the way after we went through the gate, and Miss Rimes drove around to the far side and parked. The sliding door into the place was big enough for a tank to drive through, but had been left open just enough for us to walk in without bumping. Next to it was a regular door, but that was shut and locked with a chain and padlock. Inside was like an enormous cave, only pretty well lit with big windows in the roof that let a lot of light in, like at the Wonder Bread Factory. The roof seemed like it was about a mile up. The walls were probably twenty feet high before the roof came down to them, and there were a bunch of steel beams that ran across the width of the building at that height, and others that ran the length of it. There were chains and pulleys on rollers that could lift and roll and move heavy things to just about anywhere inside the place, using the steel beams like railroad tracks. The floor was dirt, but packed so hard it might as well have been concrete. It was dark and smelled like a lot of oil had become a part of it over the years. On the right, about halfway down to the far wall on that side, was the furnace where Dennis melted whatever metal was being cast. It looked a lot newer than the rest of the place. About in the middle were several big flat steel tables, some of them looked like they were work tables to make the molds, others just work space to put things together or take them apart. There was a drill press and a lot of different kinds of power saws and drills and other electric and hand tools on racks, sort of organized like the tools in Kenny Lester's garage. Dennis didn't see us because he was welding something. There was a blue-white light that came and went in flashes along with a sort of hissing, sizzling sound.

"Don't look right at the light," Joseph said to me and Miss Rimes. "It can hurt your eyes. Take a look at that," Joseph told us, pointing to the far left corner of the building. It was dark down there, and the bright light from the welding torch made it even harder to see into the darkness, but what we were looking at was a tank.

"It's an M-4, like the one the guys had during the war. They got it in a surplus yard for five hundred bucks. I don't know why they bought it or what they plan to do with it, but you could climb in, if you want," Joseph said to me. "You too, Connie," he joked with Miss Rimes.

"I don't think so," she said.

"Can I really?" I asked.

"Sure," Joseph said. "Just don't bang your head on anything. It hurts. I know," he said, "I've banged mine more than once."

I ran down to the far side of the building to the tank. It was both bigger and smaller than I imagined a real tank would be. I'm not sure why I thought it would be bigger, even though it was huge anyway. I climbed and wiggled my way up onto the track and from there climbed onto the flat part below the big gun barrel. It looked like you could knock down just about anything with it. The trap door on the top was flipped open and I poked my head in. It smelled like gasoline and old garbage cans and was so dark I couldn't see anything. When I looked back to Joseph and Miss Rimes, Dennis had stopped welding and was standing there with them.

"Pee-yew!!!!" I yelled to the three of them. "I'm not going in that thing. It stinks in there!"

"War is hell, buddy," Dennis yelled to me.

I climbed back down and joined them at one of the big steel work tables. Dennis explained how he went about casting, depending on the size and shape of whatever it was. He told me the kind of mess that needed cleaning up after casting and asked if I'd like to work down here with him.

"It's too far, even for the Red Rider," I said.

"Well, if your mom and pops say it's okay, we might figure something out 'bout the transportation. Think you'd be interested?"

"Sure, I'd like to," I said, but I couldn't really see how that would work.

"The smelter looks practically new," Miss Rimes said, "and I see it can go with either gas or electric."

"Good eye," Dennis smiled. "Henry J. himself bought it for my dad."

"Kaiser?" she said, surprised.

"The one and only. Stood right about where you are and said they'd install the best available equipment if dad would shift his primary production to brass castings for the shipyards he and Todd, Seattle Shipbuilders, were going to open as emergency yards in 1940. They built eight ways at the San Pedro, Willmington and the LA docks, as the California Shipbuilding Corporation. Kaiser bought out Todd in 1942, but the yards continued to make ships right up to the end of the war. My dad was one of the hundreds of small sub-contractors who made it all work. That Kaiser was a genius. Found guys and yards like my dad's and organized them into a war effort. Just an amazing guy. I don't think we'd have won the war without him."

"I agree," Miss Rimes said. "I've read about some of the things he accomplished. I don't think he's gotten the credit he deserves. Is your dad still alive?"

"No, he passed. Heart attack, two years ago."

"Sorry," she said.

"It's a big hole in the world," Dennis said.

Past the furnace was a separate room. The door had a lock and a padlock. Dennis opened them both and reached in for the light switch. He let us go in past him, but then he stood there, just barely inside the door. Dennis had been busy, okay. There were shelves with the molds for fifty or sixty pieces, and thirty or thirty-five finished bronze pieces, some just heads, faces really, others, whole bodies. Some, I had to admit, I wasn't at all sure what they were, but none of them looked like real people, but you knew right away that's what they were supposed to be, in a way. If they had been too real they would have looked like they were supposed to be someone special. This way, it was more like the idea of a person or the idea of a face. They were hard to look at because they hurt. Not scary-hard to look at, but painful-hard to look at. Pain dripped out of them, like if you needed a picture of pain, they'd be it. I thought of Kenny Lester sitting on the floor of his garage, crying. I didn't want to, but I thought of Kevin Doyle, too. Not the usual crazy Kevin Doyle, but like he looked just before he got crazy with Ozzy at the soda fountain, more pain than he knew what to do with and it spilled out all over Ozzy.

Miss Rimes felt it too. She looked like she was trying not to cry. She turned to look at Dennis and then back at his work. As she moved slowly past, she put her hand on most of them.

"I'll talk to James," she said.

"Thank you," Dennis said.

We went back into the big part of the warehouse and sort of wandered towards the outside while Dennis locked up the sculpture room and met us by the big door.

"If you've got time, there's somethin' else you guys oughtta see. All of you, but especially you, Kurt. Think you're 'bout to go to heaven," he smiled.

"What's that?" Miss Rimes asked.

"The Towers," Dennis said.

"What towers?" I asked.

"The Watts Towers," Joseph said. "You ever heard of 'em?"

"Some strange guy building some strange something or other?" she said.

Dennis laughed, "That's one way to describe him. I like to think of Sabato as a small sculptor makin' a huge piece. He's been working on it every day for thirty years."

"Why's it taking him so long?" I asked.

"You got to see it to understand," Dennis said.

"Let's go," Miss Rimes said.

We all jumped in her car, me and Dennis in the back, Joseph and Miss Rimes in front, and took off for a new adventure, except it was only a few blocks away.

"You can pull up over there," Dennis said, pointing. Miss Rimes parked the car and we all got out. I wasn't sure what we were looking at, but whatever they were, they made me smile. They made me happy just to look at them, but sort of helpless and dizzy at the same time. Miss Rimes too. She stood wide-eyed and smiling, amazed by them, wanting to say something, but too shocked to speak. Her hand had gone up to her mouth and covered it. She kept shaking her head from side to side, unable to believe what she was seeing. But there was one thing I knew, I had the same feeling about them I did about my horse, small as it was. I could tell someone had done the thing they'd decided to do and it turned out, was turning out, the way they had wanted. Whatever it was, whatever it was supposed to be, that's what it was. Whatever people might think it was supposed to be was okay, too. It might be a little or a lot different from the idea of the guy that made them, but I bet that didn't matter to him. He'd done what he'd started out to do and probably knew people wouldn't be too sure about them, what they were for or why he'd done this or that, but they would make people feel good no matter what, and that would be good enough.

"I don't know what to say," Miss Rimes said finally, laughing and throwing up her hands at the same time. "What?" she asked Dennis, "Who?"

"They're the Watts Towers. Sabato, 'Sam' Rodia, has been working on them since 1921, and has been coming to our yard for scrap metal, parts, gears, castings, casings, anything he thinks he can use, since he began. It's his gift to the neighborhood. To the country. He came here from Italy in 1890 when he was a kid, ten or eleven years old. He loves this country. Says he wants to do something 'big' in return. He and my dad used to poke through the scrap metal together sometimes, having a smoke, talking Italian, maybe have a glass of wine late in the day. He keeps pretty much to himself since my dad died."

Miss Rimes looked at me and Joseph.

"My god," she said, "I've heard of them, but I had no idea."

Then she looked at me.

"You know how determined you were to have your horse green? Because that was the way it was supposed to be?"

"Uh huh."

"Well, meet another stubborn, gifted, generous artist. This is what art can be. Should be."

She looked like she was going to cry again.

"I thought you'd like it," Dennis said.

"See up there?" he pointed. "That's Sam."

Dennis shouted to him.

"Hey, Sam. Howya doin'?"

A little guy way up called down to us.

"Good, when it ain't too windy. Get's windy uppa here and I feel like I'ma gonna blow off!"

"Hang on, old man...you hang on!"

"Who's a old man? Who you callin' old man?! Le's see you come uppa here and do this! Tha's what I'da like to see! No! You betta stay down onda the ground where you safe."

He looked really small. Not much bigger than me. At first I thought it was because he was so high up, but then I began to think it really was because he wasn't much bigger than me. He was standing on a scaffold that didn't look very strong, but he seemed to think it was okay. He looked down on us, took off this big straw hat he was wearing and wiped the sweat off his face.

"Who's a the pretty girl? She comma see me? Tell'er toa come back later, 'cause I'ma busy now," he laughed and put the hat back on and returned to his work.

"What a character!" Miss Rimes said.

"But he's got pretty good eyes," Joseph said, "for an old guy."

Dennis smiled at that. "That he does," he said.

On the way back to his warehouse, Dennis told us that after World War I, Watts used to be a mix of Italians, Jews, Poles and a few blacks and Mexicans. The shipyard jobs brought a lot more Negroes from the south, and most of the little houses we were passing had been built to house them. After the war, most of the Italians and Jews and Poles had moved, leaving Watts almost all Negro.

We dropped Dennis back at the warehouse and headed back to Beverly Hills and that's how Joseph and Miss Rimes had their first date and I got my green horse fired for my dad right out from under Miss Kendall's nose, and Dennis started being a famous sculptor and I maybe could have another job. If it wasn't a perfect day, it was close.

Joseph and Miss Rimes dropped me off a little before six, so I was okay with the six o'clock rule, and anyway, I figured George told someone. I went down the driveway to the screen door and back porch. I could see Pop's car was in the garage and so was my dad's, and that was a surprise. I opened and closed the door as carefully as I could. No point in getting my mom mad at me when, so far, it had been such a good day. My mom was cooking dinner, Nick was on the kitchen floor sounding

out words from a book about Paul Bunyon and Sarah and my dad were
in the living room listening to something on the radio. Boy, was that a
sight! My dad home this early, going to have dinner with us, and reading
the paper and listening to the radio! I couldn't remember the last time
even one of those things had happened, much less all of them at once.

"How come you're home so early?" I asked him.

He put the paper aside and I sat on his knee.

"I wanted to see you guys. I'm going back downtown after dinner, but
I thought it would be nice if we could eat together."

"That's great," I said as he hugged me. "Is Marty home too?" I
asked.

"Shhhhhhh! Can't you ever be quiet?" Sarah said, "we're trying to
listen to the Shadow."

"He's in your room, studying," my dad whispered. George said you
went downtown with your art teacher. What's that about?"

"I'll tell at dinner, okay?"

"Okay," he said. "How'd the rest of the day go?"

"Like what?" I said, a little worried.

"School," he said.

"Oh, that. Fine."

"Except for the cooling off." Sarah said. "Let's not forget that!"

"What's that about?" my dad asked. "Sarah said you were told to
leave school."

"I told you, he got kicked out for talking back to Miss Kendall."

"Kurt, is that right?" my dad asked me.

"Sort of," I admitted.

"That doesn't sound like you. What happened?"

"Sounds like him to me," Sarah said.

My mom came into the living room.

"Dinner's ready. Kurt, go get Marty."

"Then tell us all about getting kicked out of school!" Sarah said.

"Sarah, mind your own business. We'll talk about it soon enough,"
my mom said.

"On second thought, what's to tell?" Sarah said, "He's just Mr. Trouble."

"Sarah, lay off," my dad told her.

I went to get Marty.

"Hiya squirt. Busy day, eh?"

"Yeah, sort of. Dinner's ready."

He flipped the book over and headed for the kitchen. I stood there
looking at my bed, trying to figure out when would be the best time to
give my dad the horse, during or after dinner. With or without everyone
else around. Before or after I had to tell about the cooling off. And if
Sarah knew about the cooling off today, I wondered if she knew about
yesterday? And if she did, would I have to tell about John Dolan and
the bike, the stitches in his head, going to the beach and Pete and Kevin
Doyle and Maurice? Man, I thought, it's amazing how all of a sudden an
almost perfect day can just fall apart. On the other hand, I couldn't really

expect there'd be another time when my dad would be home for dinner with us, at least probably not very soon, or around late enough in the morning so I'd see him then, so I wanted to do it tonight, so I could do it in person and not just leave it somewhere with his name on it for him to find, but if there was a big deal about the cooling off and if one thing led to another, that might completely spoil it. Then I thought, like Joseph said, sometimes you go where things push you and see what happens. I left the horse under the bed and went to the dinning room.

"Who wants to tell about their day?" my mom said as I sat down.

"I say let's start with Kurt getting kicked out of school." Sarah said.

"Be quiet, Sarah," my mom said, "we'll get to that."

"Cooling off isn't the same thing. Besides, Miss Rimes had to cool off too."

"Who's Miss Rimes?" Marty said.

"The art teacher," Sarah said. "She's really young and pretty and nice. And a great teacher."

"Why'd she have to cool off?" Marty asked.

"Miss Rimes was in our class to tell us our projects were ready to be picked up from the art room, and Miss Kendall was being bossy and mean and I got the giggles and she got mad and sent me to the principal's office."

"That's you. What about Miss Rimes?" Sarah said.

"She didn't like Miss Kendall bossing her around and she came to the principal's office and pretty soon they were laughing about it, and next thing I knew, she came out of his office and said we we're both supposed to cool off."

"That doesn't sound like getting kicked out," Marty said. "If they'd kicked him out, Mr. Brody would have called one of you," he told my mom and dad.

"I would think so," my mom said.

"Well, what about yesterday?" Sarah said, annoyed that the Miss Kendall thing hadn't done the trick.

I figured the almost perfect day was about to go right down the drain, and with it, the Red Rider, the paper route, paying off the locks faster, all of it. When things go bad, they don't poke along, it was more like a cliff showed up out of nowhere so everything could just fall off.

"What about it?" my mom said, first looking at Sarah, then me.

The way she looked at me, it seemed like she already knew. When I looked at Sarah, I could tell that she did for sure. She had this look like, let's see you get out of this one. Maybe she'd already told my mom, maybe not. Either way, that feeling of hopelessness hit me and I didn't know where to start. I could tell I was about to cry, but that would have been a big waste of time, and besides, Sarah would love it, so I didn't. It wasn't fair, any of it, and if Mr. Brody didn't think I was bad, why was the rest of the world about to squish down on me? I was about to tell how John Dolan kicked the Red Rider, just to sort of give everybody the picture before I had to tell them about his stitches, but before I did, Sarah smiled at me.

"Kurt rode his bike into Beverly Hills yesterday," she said, folding her arms across her chest.

I looked at her, shocked and relieved and grateful, and she gave me a little smile.

"So?" my dad said, "he's a bike rider now,"

"So what? What's with you?" Marty said. "Jeez, he's got a new bike, he wants to ride it."

He looked at me, "You were home before six, weren't you?"

"Yes," I said. "Completely."

"So what's the problem?" Marty asked her.

"None, I guess," Sarah said, acting like she was disappointed no one would get mad at me, but really, just acting.

Marty told about some stuff at school and reminded me he had to work on Sunday, so if we were going to meet with the paper route guy we had to be done before one forty-five.

"That reminds me," I said to my mom and dad.

"What?" my mom said.

"Norma from up the street invited me to go to the beach with her on Sunday. Before the paper route guy. We'd go early and come back in time to meet with him. Can I go?"

"Who's Norma?" my dad said.

"A lady who lives with Shelly at the top of the block on our side. Norma got one of the Lester's puppies. Snowball."

"Snowball?" Sarah said, "they're all black."

"That's the joke," I said.

"How do you know her?" my mom said.

"I've played with Snowball on the way to school a few times, and a few times we've had hot chocolate at the hot dog stand together, so I know her pretty well."

"That sounds fine," she said, "just make sure you're back so you don't keep Marty waiting."

"Okay. I won't. Thanks."

"Why does he get to do everything?" Sarah complained.

"And what are you doing Sunday morning?" Marty asked, but he already knew.

"Yeah, yeah," Sarah said.

"What?" my dad asked.

"She and her gang are going to the Stars double-header."

"And you weren't going to let me go?" I complained right back.

"You're out of the Oakhurst Irregulars, remember?"

"Oakhurst Irregulars?" my dad asked.

"A club Sarah started so she could kick me out," I said.

"Sounds good to me," she said.

"Sounds par for the course," Marty said.

"Well, that's not fair either," I said, but I didn't really care.

We finished dinner and had root beer floats for dessert.

Marty cleared his dishes and went back into our room to study. Sarah and Nick went into the living room to listen to the radio. My mom and dad were in the kitchen sort of smooching before he had to go back downtown. I went into the living room.

"You knew didn't you? About John Dolan?"

"Sure," she said.

"How come you didn't tell?" I asked her.

"You may be a mess of trouble, but John Dolan's a nasty jerk and had it coming. I didn't believe it at first, but about ten people told me it was true. I wouldn't have believed you had it in you."

She shrugged, "As much trouble as you are, I couldn't let you get punished for that. Besides, since Mr. Brody didn't suspend you...."

"Thanks."

"So, what did you do yesterday?"

"I rode the Red Rider to Will Rogers's State Beach."

"I don't believe you!"

"Really. I did. You could ask Gert at the Foot Long Hot Dog Stand."

"Shhhhh! I'm trying to listen," Nick told us, and put his blanket against his cheek.

My dad came into the living room and kissed everyone goodnight and headed out to the garage for his car.

I raced into our room and got the horse from under my bed.

"What's that?" Marty asked.

"Just something for daddy."

I went out the front door and got to the sidewalk as my dad was backing down the driveway. He stopped when he saw me standing there.

"That was nice having dinner together," he said.

"This is for you," I said and handed him the wrapped up horse.

"What's this?"

"It's the only one in the world," I told him. "When you're sad about Pop, it'll make you feel better."

He opened the package. He looked at the green horse, and sort of rubbed his fingers over it.

"It's terrific."

He closed his eyes and held it against his forehead. Then he opened them.

"I can tell," he said, "it's going to work."

He smiled and leaned out the window and kissed the top of my head.

# Chapter 25

## *Sabato's Spell*
## August 10, 1989

THAT OLD JOKE, you can't get there from here, must have been about Los Angeles. No matter where you had to go, there were three million people who wanted to get there too, and they all seemed to have had a ten minute head start. It was seven twenty-five and the 10 East was jammed. I'd gotten on at Robertson figuring I'd go to the 110 South, get off at Firestone and poke along until I found Ottis. The poking along began on Robertson before I even got on the 10 and got worse when I did. I decided the crowded surface streets and stop signs and red lights would be better than the parking lot the freeway had become. Nick, traveling from one courthouse to another down here, was in this kind of traffic a lot. How he kept his mind was a mystery. I got off at La Cienega and made my way across town to South Central, then headed south to Firestone. Ottis was about three miles east. 1106, The Albertine Cafe, was three doors down from the corner. I found parking easily and, just before I went in, noticed from a carved stone plaque just above the entrance, that the building, red brick accenting sandstone blocks, had been built in 1924 as a Masonic Temple. The windows to the street had been cut into the brick sometime later, but nicely done in a tall thin pattern, leaving columns of the brick to divide them and support the two floors above, probably apartments now. There were six of the windows on each side of the entrance, two feet wide, probably six feet high, the remaining columns, maybe sixteen inches wide, between them. Above the Masonic plaque, there was a large sign that said, The Albertine Cafe, Breakfast and Lunch 6am to 3pm. Below that, Jazz Thursday-Friday-Saturday Nites. If someone had been waiting for the chance to use the word, cacophony, this would be it. Noise came from every direction, from every conceivable source. Early as it still was, the jukebox, at full volume, had Aretha Franklin singing, Respect. Dishes were clattering, cooks were banging pots and pans, customers were shouting over each other and the rest of the noise to be heard, and the three waitresses were shouting over all of it to the cooks. Add to that, the busboys tossing plates and glasses into the little plastic containers on top of their carts, yelling a warning to the waitresses, "behind you" or "comin' through!" Straight ahead was a counter with fifteen seats. Left and right of the door were ten or twelve tables, and past the tables on the right side was another room, a set of double doors open, not set up for breakfast or lunch, but with thirty little tables with two or three chairs each, all facing a small raised stage.

I'd barely sat down on a stool at the counter when a waitress stood in front of me. Her name tag said Al. She was pretty, a little heavy, maybe forty-five or fifty, and sort of looked like Aretha before she started getting really big.

"What's it gonna be, honey?" she said as she poured coffee into a white mug in front of me.

"Just coffee," I said, figuring asking for de-caf at this point would only get us off on the wrong foot.

"We got the best omelets in town. Ham and cheese; onion and tomato, you name it. Put some meat on your bones," she smiled.

"No thanks, just the coffee."

She looked at me.

"No way you come all the way down here for our world famous coffee. Right?"

"I was hoping to find someone."

She smiled thinly, the coffee pot in one hand, the other on her hip.

"Well, we all hopin' to find somebody, honey. The thing is, is you in the right place?"

Her eyes swung around the room, across the forty five or fifty people there, in an exaggerated gesture, then back to me, sort of a reminder of where I was. Who I was. What I was. If there was another white person in the place, it would have to have been the dishwasher, because I didn't see one.

"Maybe," I said.

"Al, more coffee over here!" someone shouted above the noise.

"When I'm good an' ready," she yelled back. "I'm busy. You was sayin', honey?"

"Maybe. A friend of mine used to play here with a jazz combo. It was a long time ago, but I was hoping to find him. Or his family, or someone who knew him. He'd be in his early seventies now."

"Black man?"

"White."

"Only one white man ever play here. You talkin' 'bout Joseph."

My heart jumped.

"You remember him?" I asked, incredulously.

"Don't take much memory, honey, he the only white man ever play here. Still is. Maybe once, twice a month, he and the ol' gang shuffle in here, show the young guys what jazz oughta be."

"He's still around? Still playing here? That's great!"

"He don't live 'round here, but he play from time to time. Where you know him from?"

"He had a hot dog stand at a carwash on Beverly Boulevard when I was a kid, a little after the war. He talked about playing here and the name stuck with me."

"What you lookin' him up for now?" she said, a little suspicion creeping in.

"Actually, I was hoping to find someone through him, a friend of his, a friend of the guys he played with. Are Jackson and William still playing with Joseph?"

"William gone, done passed, but Jackson's still playin'. Who you lookin' for?"

"Their friend, Maurice."

"Maurice been gone quite a while, now."

"How do you remember them all so well?"

"Don't take much memory, honey. They be comin' in here every mornin' for probably fifty years. Sometimes they bring the wives, the kids, the grandkids. Have some food, some coffee, some chat, then go 'bout they business, and be back the next day."

What she was saying suddenly dawned on me.

"Are any of them here now?"

"Like I said, Joseph don't live 'round here, so he ain't one of the mornin' regulars. But that's Jackson over there," she said pointing to a table with two old men, two young men, and three kids.

Jackson had put on weight, lost a lot of hair, and what was left was gray and crowded his ears, but he still had the twinkle in his eyes. Even from across the room, a kind of ease shown on his face, in his posture and his general bearing. Whatever he'd been doing all these years had agreed with him.

"Don't be shy," Al said, "gowahn over an' say hello."

"Jackson!" she yelled over the noise, "got a friend of yours here to see you!"

"Well, tell 'im to come on over!" Jackson yelled back in our general direction.

I don't think he saw me, he was just inviting whoever over.

"Gowahn," Al said, motioning me with the coffee pot. "Take your cup," she said, topping it off, "save me the trip."

I slid off the stool and headed towards Jackson's table. When they saw me, the other older man, the two younger men and the three kids, there was an air of uncertainty that pervaded their table. Also, the nearby tables, the far away tables, the whole place. Just because I'd sort of been playing cop the last few days didn't mean I was one, but the sudden chill in the room awarded me an honorary badge. When I got to the table, two of the kids never looked up. The third, the youngest, a girl maybe three or four, flashed me a huge smile, and then brightly said hello. The two younger men looked at me more or less defiantly. The other older man shifted his eyes to me and away from me in an ongoing uncomfortable dance. On the other hand, Jackson, even though he had no clue who I might be, smiled warmly.

"Let's get you a chair," he said. "This one free?" he asked the people at the next table, simultaneously reaching behind to take an unused one from their table.

"It's all yours," the woman at the table said.

"Sit on down," Jackson said to me.

I sat. I sipped at my coffee, the general hostility in the room, coupled with the caffeine, making me a little nervous. Jackson was having none of it.

"So, you lookin' for me? Here I am."

His smile was huge and friendly. He reached over and patted my hand, leaned in close and confided, "Don't worry, you okay. We ain't lynched a white man around here in quite a while!"

"Grandpa!!!" one of the two boys, said.

Jackson laughed, and so did the two younger men.

"Geez, dad!" one of them said. Then to me, "Don't let the old man rattle you. I'm Thomas Jackson, Jr., this is my brother Dave, and his two boys Jeff and Lincoln. This little beauty is my Tanya."

He reached over to shake hands. The two boys, maybe eight and ten, sort of mumbled hello. Dave shook hands too.

"This old fool's uncle Carl. On my mom's side," he told me, as if that explained all I needed to know about him.

The older man nodded hello, but didn't offer to shake hands.

"Now you know who we is, who you?" Carl said, his eyes fixed on me, only to shift away when I looked at him.

"Kurt Goldman," I said to Carl. Then to Jackson, "I don't know if you'll remember me, but I worked with you and Dennis and Maurice and William at the carwash."

"Good god almighty!" Jackson said. "You the skinny little red-head kid got the bicycle! I remember you! Pickle and mustard sandwiches at Joseph's hot dog stand, right?"

"You've got a hell of a memory," I said.

"What you been doin' all these days?" he asked me.

"I've been designing and building houses in the East Bay. The Berkeley Hills near the UC Campus."

"Nice up there. Me and Joseph and William, God rest him, and ol' Greg, sometimes played Yoshi's up that way. You know it?"

"Sure. It's sort of an institution. I wished I'd known. I'd love to have seen you. Any chance you'll play there again?"

"Not likely. They aimin' at a younger croud."

"He's bein' modest," Dave said. "A few good places, like Yoshi's, still know the real thing. Try 'n' coax these ol' guys outta their caves to show the younger crowd what it's supposed to be. The trick is to get these guys on a plane. Don't none of 'em like to fly. 'Specially Joseph."

"Why's that?"

Dave looked at Jackson.

"Gowaahn," he said, "you runnin' on pretty good, don't stop now."

Dave shrugged, "His wife died in a plane crash."

"That's the truth," Jackson said. "Didn't get married 'til he was nearly forty, then lost her in the first year. Been somethin' of a ree-cluse ever since. Ol' man Avery, you 'member him, doncha?"

"Sure," I said,

"Well, he din't have no kin. Left Joseph the whole thing, the station, the carwash, the hot dog stand. 'bout nineteen sixty-five. Done just fine with it, then the Mercedes dealership wanted that corner, and all of a sudden, Joseph's doin' better than fine, only he don't go nowhere, don't see no one, don't do nothin' but write a little music, practice a lot, hang out sometimes with Dennis and his family down here. Kicked in a bit for the Center."

"Dennis? He's still around here?"

Jackson shared a laugh with his sons, grandkids and uncle Carl.

"Oh, he's around! You ain't heard of him?"

"No."

Jackson, Jr. said, "Dennis Zamora? Zamora Gallery? Zamora Fine Art? Man, he's big. His stuff's in galleries all over the world. Rich people been collectin' him for a long time now."

"Deserves every bit of it," Jackson said. "Stayed true to hisself and the neighborhood. Didn't take the first big money train out. Could've, and no one'da blamed 'im. He half white to begin with, you know? Italian, anyway. He and his white woman coulda picked up and shut down the old warehouse and yard and been long gone. But they didn't. Stayed and raised their kids. Them and Joseph built the center. Really gave the neighborhood a boost. That's right, he deserves every bit of it."

I was picturing Dennis' work. It was exciting to think he'd made a place for himself with it.

"What center?" I asked.

"You ever see the ol' Iron Works and Foundry? From his dad's days?" Jackson asked me, "That whole block of Zamora Circle?"

"Just once."

"Well, first he got a few pieces in a gallery in Beverly Hills. Sold 'em right off. Then a few more, pretty soon, there's a bunch a people wants his work. After they get married, his wife sort of managing things. Real smart girl. Only lets the one gallery show his stuff. Pretty soon, New York galleries tryin' to get a piece of the action, but she say no. Next thing, the New York crowd makin' special trips out here to get their hands on somethin'. Next thing you know, they've turned a part of the old warehouse into a little gallery, so now the New York and European guys 're comin' to Watts if they want an original Zamora! How's that, sound!? Make 'em come right here to Watts, if they want somethin'!" Jackson said, banging the table for emphasis.

"Pretty cool, if you can make 'em come," I said.

"Oh, they come alright!" he said.

"So what's the center?" I asked.

"Center's the Zamora Center for the Arts," Dave said. "They turned the whole property into the Zamora Gallery, the Zamora Community Arts Center, the sculpture garden and the rebuilt Zamora Iron Works and Foundry. They have after-school programs for kids and seniors, anyone, really, who wants to learn just about any kind of art work."

"I paint!" Tanya said.

"The boys, here, they both doin' a little clay. Pretty good, too," Jackson, Jr. said, rubbing the head of the older boy.

"Their older boy, Sabato, and the girl, what's her name?" Jackson asked.

"Caitlin."

"That's right, Caitlin. She and Sabato run the gallery and art center. Dennis and Colleen kinda keeps tabs on things, but mostly he does his own work back in the foundry. She supervises the art classes and teaches a few herself."

"Colleen?"

"His wife," Jackson said. "White girl."

"Colleen Rimes?"

"How'd you know that?" he asked me. "Man, I ain't heard that name in a long while."

"She was my art teacher at Hawthorne Elementary School. I sort of introduced them. Actually, I introduced her to Joseph. Joseph introduced her to Dennis."

"That's where he gone wrong," Carl mumbled.

"Well, they been together for three kids and an arts center. Looks like it workin' out okay," Jackson smiled.

"And they live around here?"

"Sure, all but the younger boy, Hunter. He gone to Europe a few years back. Don't see much of him, but the rest of the family on the north end of the property. Built a coupla nice houses. Got a nice yard and garden. Some big bushes keep it private from the rest of the Center. They in here most mornin's. Girl's married and got two of her own. Sabato's not married, is he?" Jackson asked.

"Nope," Jackson Jr. said.

"Didn't see none of 'em today, though. You never did say how or why you look me up."

"Maurice signed a document, witnessed it for a friend of mine who left it behind. I was hoping to find him and ask him about it. I didn't know or remember any of your last names. Joseph had mentioned The Albertine, and the name stuck, so here I am."

"You know Maurice's gone?"

"The waitress, told me," I said, motioning towards her.

"Good man, Maurice was. Kinda guy makes the world a better place."

"What happened?"

"Couple 'a punks trying to loot a store, beat up the ol' guy who own it durin' the Riots, and he tried to stop 'em. Got his head smashed with a brick for his trouble. Just like him. Jump right in and try to make things right. Always doin' that. Just didn't work out that last time. Anyway, he and Dennis were pretty close. Go see Dennis. Maybe he know somethin' 'bout your document. He be glad to see you anyway."

"I will," I said.

"Miss Zamora'll be there in the afternoon, the older boy said. She teaches the clay class."

"You 'member how to get over there?" Jackson asked.

"No, not really," I said

"Over t' the Towers?" Jackson tried.

"I remember them, just not exactly where they are."

He took a napkin and drew me a map and pushed it across the table. "In '75 they was gonna tear 'em down. You hear 'bout that?" he asked me.

"No. Why?"

"Said they was a hazard. Might fall and hurt someone. Can you imagine? The one beautiful thing down here, and they gonna tear it down. The neighborhood wasn't havin' none of it. Hired an engineer to prove the city was wrong. Joseph and Dennis were in on that. Got 'em declared a landmark and created a little non-profit group to raise money and keep 'em tuned up."

"Y'oughta drive by," Dave said. "Colleen and Dennis takes the kids from the art center classes there every so often just to get 'im thinkin' 'bout what art can be. Ain't that right?" he said to his boys.

The boys smiled, going to exaggerated eye-rolling trouble to let me know they'd heard all this more than once before. Dave didn't miss it.

"So? It's true, isn't it?"

"Right, dad," Jeff said.

"It's too early for the Gallery or Center to be open, but Dennis and Colleen always up early. Maybe give 'em a call first," Jackson said.

He wrote their phone number on the little map he'd drawn. Jackson and I traded a few memories about the car wash. About ten minutes later, Jackson, Jr. and Dave excused themselves, reaching out to shake hands again.

"Good to meet you, Kurt," Dave said. "The old man's told us a lot about the ol' days at the carwash. Makes it a little more real to hear some of it from you." Then to Jackson, "Later, dad. You guys be good," he said to the boys.

Jackson Jr. bent over and kissed Tanya.

"Bye, sweetie," he said.

They took off for work, leaving Jackson in charge of the three kids who were getting restless and wanted to go.

"We gotta go. Good to see you, Kurt. You know, after the war, workin' in the carwash an' doin' odd jobs, that wasn't no part of my plan. I been pretty lucky since then makin' a living with the music, not just with Joseph, either. I've recorded with some of the best. But every so often, I remind myself, Mr. Avery was a real decent man, and workin' with Joseph and the guys and the little red-headed kid, you gettin' us sweet rolls from Helen at the Bread Factory, well, those were pretty good days too, all in all. Yes they were," he said, reflecting on it. "You take care of yourself," he said as we stood.

We shook hands and he and Carl and the kids headed for the door.

It was only about eight-twenty, so I took myself on a side trip to the Towers. As I drove, on the streets, on the corners and in the doorways, there were men and women in their late twenties, thirties and forties, going nowhere, doing nothing, expecting even less. Some loud angry

exchanges, snippets of conversation overheard as I passed. Others, be-
wildered, disheveled, wandering aimlessly, items of clothing missing or
forgotten, likely by-products of a drug or alcohol habit. Some, quiet and
inward looking, standing or sitting comfortably on the step of a store-
front, a low retaining wall, maybe examining the course of their lives,
maybe just drained of all interest in thinking about it, falling into a coma-
like acceptance of the kind of grinding despair that sucks the very life
right out of you. Firestone back to Willmington, down to 108th, then
the frontage road along the Southern Pacific tracks to E 107th and there
they were. The walls and gate were more impressive than I'd remembered. The Towers seemed smaller, but more dramatic, maybe even more
beautiful. They seemed less a part of the neighborhood than some magic
garden that had grown when no one was looking. There was a box on the
gate that held flyers announcing hours they were open, a little history,
and contact numbers. One of them, I noticed, was Dennis's. The area
around the Towers was well-kept, but most of Watts had gone to hell. It
gave the Towers a different feel. Before, they'd been this miracle of creativity, this flower rising from the junkyard of war and dislocation, from
the ad hoc attempts to build new lives in a changed and changing world,
they were an affirmation that no matter what, there's a spirit and energy,
a drive in humans, that regardless of their circumstances, makes them
want to express love and joy in some form that can be shared. That's how
the Towers had struck me before. That's how Miss Rimes had helped
me see them. Now, they had more of an alien presence. Still beautiful,
still awe inspiring, but a reminder that some distant lands, some distant
worlds may be out there, but for too many, unreachable. Jackson and his
sons, his grandchildren, seemed hopeful and energetic and ready to find
that strange place where energy and creativity come together and make
life an adventure. But in general, Watts was far more desolate and beaten
down than I remembered it. There was a palpable lack of energy. A lack
of hope. It was that that made the Towers seem out of place. They had
always been a celebration of hope and energy and goodwill and creative
whimsy, but now, an unintentional slap in the face to this place so devoid
of them. I stood looking at them, saddened, wishing I could see them in
the old way. They seemed like space ships about to take off and leave all
this behind. Aliens who'd come, touched down with high expectations,
inspired a few, presided over the unraveling, and were ready to blast off
out of here. Or, on a more positive note, maybe they were the last gasp,
the last vestige and a reservoir, waiting for the neighborhood to find them
again. To find itself again. Maybe that's what Dennis and Joseph hoped
for the Center.

It was a little after nine. I found a pay phone and called Dennis.

"Hello?"

"Dennis, this is Kurt Goldman," I began.

"I know. Jackson called a little while ago. Where are you?"

"A few blocks away. At the Towers."

"Well, come on over. Colleen can't wait to see you."

The chain link fence was gone. The whole of Zamora Circle had been transformed into something akin to the Beverly Gardens, the little strip of parks that ran along Upper Santa Monica from the Arabesque fountain at Oakhurst, block after block, to Rodeo. Well groomed, nicely laid out, winding in and out of the buildings so that it was hard to decide whether it was a park with well placed single story buildings, or buildings, nicely crafted and purposely unimposing, cleverly mitigated by the park-like garden that snaked through them. There was something so well thought out and natural about the way the property had been developed that I got the feeling the idea of it, the beauty of it, might spread, like an aggressive ground cover, throughout the blighted Watts. I entered where the old gate had been, where Zamora Avenue approached the bottom of the circle, but now there was a beautiful heavy-timbered trellis that spanned the twenty foot width of the driveway, fourteen feet or so above it. It reminded me of the Green and Green fraternity on Piedmont Avenue in Berkeley, with its redwood timbers fastened with wrought brass straps and pins. It was an elaborate piece, but age and a nice conception had softened it, that and the mature wisteria, allowed it to just be without too much fanfare. There were jacaranda trees in every direction. The driveway snaked first left, then right to a parking lot for twelve or fourteen cars, partially hidden by the landscaping. There were bike racks too, enough for at least twice the number of cars. I parked and followed the curving brick path to the first group of three buildings. All of them were a basic post and beam construction on slabs, walls mostly glass between the posts, floor to plate height. I was thinking, if Eichler had gotten it right, it would have looked like this. If Zak, the guy who'd gotten me interested in designing and building had cared more about craft, it would have looked like this. If Eichler and Zak had met and decided to work together....I decided to give it a rest. The upshot was, it was well done. The Zamora Center for the Arts was carved into an irregular shaped black slab of granite about four feet square, tipped back from vertical, the footing that supported it buried, which made it look both solid and strong, and also like it was delicately balanced, resting only on the thick ground cover with its little bright red flowers. Since the walls were almost all glass I could see the first building was used for painting and sketching, two dozen easels ready and waiting. Inside were several big wooden cabinets along the far wall with wide flat drawers, and art supplies on top. There was a little office just inside the entrance with a desk and chair and phone and computer and file cabinet. The whole thing was probably twenty-four feet deep and fifty feet long. The next building, to the left of the first, was for clay work. It was bigger, probably sixty feet square, glass walls and lots of skylights, and had six huge work tables about eight feet square with two stools on each of the four sides. The tops were marble or granite. Three electric kilns stood side by side on the far side, then sturdy metal shelves with projects in various stages of completion, then more shelves with glazes and other supplies. The third building was the biggest, the new foundry. It was sixty feet by about eighty, two stories high. It had skylights but few windows, and those were small and made opaque by a Flemish glass, so it was impossible to see in. It was a hundred or hundred and fifty feet from the other two buildings, partially hidden by a cluster of jacaranda tress and more of the mature wisteria crawling across trellises attached to the redwood siding, but I knew it was the new foundry because Dennis had rescued the sign from the old one, cleaned and refurbished it, and attached it along the ridge of the new building's roof. Zamora Iron Works and Foundry. From behind it, I could see a more or less straight road that cut through to the east side of Zamora Circle, probably to allow easy deliveries of steel or other big and awkward materials. Or to truck away finished pieces. Whatever its purpose, it was the only straight piece of road or pathway on the property.

The brick path that had brought me this far continued past the foundry, but narrowed to half the width it'd been. It continued for about sixty feet past the far side of the foundry then passed through a thick hedge of Oleander that had become an eight foot high wall separating the Art Center from the two houses Dennis and Colleen had built for themselves and their family. Both houses had a distinctly craftsman, northern California feel to them, the whole Art's Center did, and I wondered about its origin. The private part of the property occupied a third of the original site. The entrance through the hedge was like a small tunnel, since the hedges were not only tall, but had grown five or six feet thick. When you emerged, you were in a garden of little rolling hills or mounds that reminded me of Rathbone's place, a pond at the top of one to the right, beds of bright colored flowers on another, roses on a third and another larger pond half surrounded by thin reedy bamboo on the left, the brick path meandering through it all. The two house faced each other from the left and right. The Oleander, besides dividing the property across its width into the two-thirds Art Center and one third private part, continued along both sides of Zamora Circle, surrounding the houses to the top of the property, where between them, there was another wider driveway-tunnel through to the street where Zamora Circle ended and Zamora Avenue continued east. The driveway came just through the Oleander, then split left and right into the respective garages of the two house. I was trying to decide which one was Dennis's when the front door of the house on the left opened and he came out onto the porch, a cup of coffee in his hand.

"God damn!" he said, smiling. "Good god damn! Lookit you now!"

Colleen came out through the open door and stood next to him, her hand resting on his shoulder, huge smiles on both their faces. Dennis was healthy looking, still very handsome, still thin, lean, but muscular in a wiry way. His light coffee colored skin was tight and youthful. Only his hair showed the years. Where he had it, it was still full, but gray at the temples. The real change was that it had receded, making his forehead more pronounced. Amazingly, Colleen didn't look much different than she had thirty-eight years before. She was older, deeper laugh lines around her eyes, her skin less tight than that of the twenty-five year old

I'd known, but the glow, the energy and vibrancy were undiminished. They looked so happy together it was almost shocking. Embarrassing. How was it some people could couple so well? Fulfill each other so completely and with such gentle passion? I might try to forgive my shortcomings and content myself with the idea it probably wasn't all that easy all the time for them either, but one look at them and I knew that was nonsense. I supposed they had to work at it, but the fruit of their efforts was a sight to see. I wondered how Joseph felt about it.

A slightly distressed, but still pretty snazzy Shelby AC Cobra rumbled in through the driveway hedge and turned left and parked in front of Dennis's garage. The driver revved it a little before shutting down. He slicked his thick wavy black hair into place, then pushed his sun glasses back onto his head. He was very good looking, maybe mid-thirties, tan, maybe from riding around in the open car a lot, and had a tall, slender, athletic build. He got out and came along the brick path between the houses.

"Hello," he said to me as he took the side stairs to the porch two at a time. He went right up to Colleen and kissed her on the cheek.

"Hi mom. Dad. Who's this?" he said nodding towards me.

"Sam, meet Kurt. He's a friend of your father's and mine from waaay back!"

I walked up the front steps and joined the three of them on the porch. The air was a little warm, but the lush greenness of the garden, the shade from the trees and hedges was extending the morning's cool. Sam and I shook hands. I held out my hand to shake with Dennis, but he pushed it away and threw his arms around me.

"Man, you don't know what a treat this is!"

He hugged me a couple of times in rapid fire succession and as soon as he turned me loose, Colleen hugged me, then kissed me on the cheek.

"What a pleasure," she said. "What a wonderful surprise and absolute pleasure to see you! Would you like some coffee?"

"Maybe half a cup. I just had some at The Albertine Cafe."

"We're usually there mornings," Dennis said. "but we been waitin' for this guy for an hour," he said as we sat in chairs on the porch.

"Havin' trouble with the machine," Sam said nodding to where he'd parked the Cobra. "Bad fuel pump, I think."

"Nice wheels," I said. "When I was a teenager, a friend of mine used to work for Shelby in Santa Monica when he first got started. He wanted a few of the cars on the street, sort of advertising, and since Allen lived in Beverly Hills, he got to drive one to and from work. I got a few rides back then and it's still my favorite car of all time. A classic."

"See dad? A classic! That's what I told you. Be worth a fortune some day."

"Yeah, well, we'll see about that. Got to keep it runnin' first. That'd be good for a start."

Colleen came back out from the house with my coffee and one for Sam.

"Sam is short for Sabato. Remember the name?" Dennis asked me.

"I might have in any case, but I just came from the Towers. The flyer by the gate had his name on it."

"Sam's fine," Sam said.

"Nothin's wrong with Sabato," Dennis said. "There's magic in it."

"I know, I know," Sam laughed, then to me, "we been livin' under Sabato's spell our whole lives. Not that that's a bad thing," he added quickly patting his dad's knee, "lot of love, lot of art always flowed from it. Just look around to believe it. Just, not everybody's gonna understand."

"Kurt met Sabato the same day your mom did," Dennis said to Sam. "You felt the magic in him, didn't you?"

"I did. But it took root because Miss Rimes, Colleen, made me see the connection between being stubborn about what you want from a project, and the energy and creativity and passion and joy you bring to it. That's what I learned at the Towers."

"You had that already. The Towers just brought it into focus. What are you doing now?" she asked me.

"I design and build houses in the Berkeley Hills," I said, "I think of it as sculpting on a large scale."

"I knew you'd find some way to express yourself. That's wonderful. Isn't it, Dennis?"

"It is. I hope you've been gettin' what you want out of it. The feelin' you want."

"I do. I love it."

"Nice," Sam said. "The art sort of skipped me."

"You're art is in making things happen. You and Caitlin do what we couldn't. He and his sister make this place work. He's got a real talent for organizing, planning, making things run. Maybe not the car, but everything else," Dennis teased.

"Nice to meet you, Kurt," Sam said, standing. "Speaking of making things work, I should get going."

Colleen took Dennis's hand as they watched Sam walk through the garden along the path until he disappeared through the hedge.

"Seems like a great guy," I said.

"He is. So's Caitlin. I called her. She's going to stop by on her way to the Center and say hello.

"Jackson said you were lookin' to find Maurice. Somethin' about somethin' he signed?"

"Right. He witnessed a letter written by a friend of mine. A guy who lived on my block."

"Who's that?"

"Do you remember the name Kenny Lester?"

Dennis eyes got a little wider but he didn't say anything.

"Remember the guy at the carwash that told the story about the pig and the girl?" I tried.

"That's one you never told me," Colleen teased him.

Dennis smiled and patted her hand.

"I do," he said to me, with a half smile, but then his expression got more serious. "Hang on a minute."

He went into the house.

"Hi, honey," Colleen said to the woman coming up on the porch. "Kurt, this is our daughter, Caitlin, and her girls, Grace and Emma."

I stood to shake hands with Caitlin. The girls were about two and three. Caitlin was stunning. Where Colleen was pretty and Dennis was handsome, their kids, at least the two I'd met, were exceptional. Taken separately, Caitlin had slightly exaggerated features: a too wide full mouth, slightly oversized teeth, a straight, thin nose with a little extra width at the bottom, thick honey colored blond hair that seemed to have a life of its own. Blue eyes that bordered on purple. Taken separately was one thing. Taken together, quite another. Both the little girls were going to be gorgeous as well.

"Hi grandma. Who's he?" Grace said, pointing at me.

"He's a friend from when grandma was teaching at Hawthorne. He was one of my favorite students."

"Mom's used you as a sort of model of stubborn determination when she thought we were giving up or caving in too easily on something," Caitlin laughed. "We been hearin' about you and your green horse since we were kids. I feel like I grew up with you," she laughed. "Well, the horse at least."

I looked at Colleen, who smiled and shrugged.

"Did you tell him about Hunt?" Caitlin asked.

Colleen rolled her eyes in mock embarrassment.

"No. But I suppose you're going to."

Caitlin looked at Colleen.

"Go on. You can't stop now."

"Mom named my little brother, Hunt, Hunter, sort of after you," she said.

I wasn't sure what she meant.

"Hunter Green? The color of your horse?" Caitlin said.

I looked at Colleen. She nodded, a little sheepishly.

"It was one of those things that just stuck with me," she said. "It defined something for me."

"For Hunter, too," Caitlin said. "Hunter's the artist. The guy that has to go his own way, no matter. I've got to go. Nice to meet you, Kurt. Take care. Thanks mom, Noemia will be here by ten for the girls."

"Bye, honey," she said to Caitlin.

Caitlin headed through the garden, then disappeared through the Oleander tunnel. Dennis came back.

"You missed Caitlin," Colleen said.

"I'll see her at the Center, later. Here," he said, "sorry, but after Maurice died, I read it."

"Girls, why don't you go into the garden and pick a few flowers for the kitchen table."

"Okay, grandma," Grace said.

Emma, the younger one, seemed willing to go anyplace or do anything with her big sister as long as she could keep her first two fingers in her mouth. When they'd gone, I looked at the letter. It had my first name on it. I opened it.

"To whoever needs to know- I had to kill that little bastard Kevin Doyle from across the street from Abe Goldman's house on Oakhurst. Couldn't be helped. Buried his sorry ass in that big garden up the street."

It was signed by Maurice Cook. Witnessed by Kenny Lester. Dated October, 14, 1951. I read it twice. I looked up at Dennis. He was staring straight ahead.

"What is it?" Colleen asked.

I passed Maurice's letter to her.

"Sorry, honey," Dennis said. "I didn't want you to worry 'bout this. Goes way back."

She read it, then in a troubled voice asked, "What's it mean. Is this true? Could it be true?"

"I don't believe it. Never have," Dennis said, his eyes beginning to tear.

"That's just after I met you," she said, reconstructing the time frame in her mind.

"He wrote it. He signed it. That's true enough. Gave it to me two or three years before he died. Said to give it to you or the police if the occasion ever arose, if there was ever any trouble at that big garden up the street from you, but I didn't believe it then and don't now. Just not him. Makes me hurt thinkin' he kept somethin' like this to himself for so long, whatever it's about.  But I don't believe it. I don't believe it," he said wiping at the tears

Colleen held his hand.

"Neither do I," I said.

I took the originals of the letters from Kenny Lester and Iyama Osaka from my shirt and handed Kenny's to him. He opened and read it. He looked up at me, somehow seeming both relieved and not too surprised. I handed him the letter from Iyama. He opened and read it too. His mouth turned down, his eyes widened. He handed them to Colleen.

"I knew it. I just knew it," he smiled.

"They're protecting somebody," Colleen said, "but who?"

# Chapter 26

## *Me and You, Big Blue and The Paper Route Too*
### Sunday, June 17, 1951

I DIDN'T HAVE ANY swim trunks that fit so I cut off the legs of the worst pair of jeans. I figured since school was over for the year, even if we were still broke in the fall, maybe I'd make enough money between the carwash and paper route so I could buy a new pair before the third grade, after paying off the locks. The locks came first, but maybe I could get the new jeans too. Maybe. Anyway, I needed something to wear to the beach, and an old pair of Marty's trunks would be floating around Santa Monica Bay after the first wave hit me, so that wasn't worth thinking about. It was a little after seven-thirty and I was sitting on our front steps waiting for Norma. It was sunny and warm already, a perfect day for the beach. I'd had some cereal and a glass of cold Ovaltine and a piece of bread, so I was pretty full. I had on the cut-offs, a t-shirt and my holey tennis shoes without socks. The rich guys at the Santa Monica Beach Club did that, especially if they had a boat. They wore low cut white tennis shoes with no socks. Mine were black and high tops, but it was sort of the same. I had a towel rolled up and all ready. My mom had left me fifty-five cents on the kitchen table for lunch, even though it wasn't a school day, which I thought was pretty nice since money was still a big problem. I thought everyone was still asleep, except for my dad, who I'd heard backing down the driveway before I even got out of bed at six, but then I heard the door behind me open and Nick came out. He was wearing his underpants and dragging his blanket with him. He started to put his fingers in his mouth, but changed his mind, maybe because of Pop, I thought. He sat on the step next to me and sort of leaned his head against me like he was planning on going back to sleep right there.

"How come you're up?" I asked him.

"I woke up."

He let his head rest against my shoulder and closed his eyes. I'd been thinking about taking a walk around the block, maybe going into the bamboo patch at the Pink House, but, what the heck, I could just as well stay put and let Nick snooze against me. Norma wouldn't be here for an hour. That's when the door opened across the street and Kevin Doyle came out looking for his LA Times. He was wearing some striped pajamas and slippers and an old dirty looking robe. His hair was all messed up and there was a cloud of cigarette smoke floating around his head, following him as he walked. I tried to sit very still, hoping he wouldn't notice me. No luck. He picked up the paper from his walkway and spotted me right off. He stood there just staring at me. Even from across the street, I could see his face was still puffed up from the fight with Maurice. He put the folded paper under his arm and took the cigarette out of his mouth holding it with his thumb and first finger and made a big gesture of tapping it with the middle finger of the same hand so that the burned up ash part dropped off. He was looking at me, at us, really, tipping his head from side to side with a funny look like I was supposed to know what he was thinking, or at least guess. As the ash fell to the ground he smiled, like it was a message or a clue, only I didn't get it. But the nasty smile was enough. He was telling me he wasn't going to leave me alone. No matter what George said, or what Maurice had told him. I had been holding my breath for a pretty long time without realizing it and I let it out and took a few gulps. I was still afraid of him, but I didn't know what I could do about it without it getting to be a big problem for someone, like maybe my dad or Maurice, so, like with John Dolan, there wasn't much point in spending a lot of time worrying about it. That didn't make me feel much better, but it was better than nothing, I figured. I took a look down to where Nick was snoozing against my shoulder. When I looked up, Kevin Doyle was smiling as he turned and walked back up his steps and went inside. Nick was sound asleep.

I sat there for about twenty minutes and then couldn't take it any more.

"Nick, wake up!" I begged him. "You're killing my shoulder."

He stirred and moved but didn't wake up. I moved around like I was going to stand up, sort of bumping him around like it was an accident. Finally he opened his eyes, looked around and seemed surprised we were outside.

"Where's mom?" he said.

"She's still sleeping I think."

"I'm hungry."

"Come on in and I'll make you some Ovaltine."

"Hot."

"You know I can't. I'm not supposed to use the stove by myself."

His mouth started to pout and I was afraid he was about to launch in to his air-raid siren crying.

"Please. You can make it hot."

"Nick, I can't. If I do, mom probably wouldn't let me go to the beach. I'll make it with extra Ovaltine. How's that?"

"Hot's better," he said, but he didn't seem to care much any more.

We went into the kitchen and I made the Ovaltine for him. I made him a piece of toast to go with it. He sat at the table in the kitchen nook and sipped at the chocolate and took bites of the toast. Then he put the blanket to the side and started dipping the toast into the Ovaltine until it was so soggy part of it dropped off onto the table. He picked it up and put it in his mouth leaving behind a little puddle on the table. He seemed happy enough, so that was that. Then Marty and Sarah came in.

"What a mess," Sarah said. "You better clean it up before mom sees."

"Anybody want an egg?" Marty asked us.

"I do," Sarah said.

"Me too," Nick said.

"Kurt?" he asked.

"No thanks."

Marty started frying eggs for the three of them.

"I'm making hot Ovaltine. You want some, Nick?" Sarah asked him.

"Yes."

"Marty?"

"Yes."

She didn't ask me, but I didn't want any anyway.

"Sure you don't want an egg, Kurt?" Marty asked me.

"No thanks. Norma'll be here pretty soon."

My mom came into the kitchen and saw Marty and Sarah had things going and started making a pot of coffee. Her eyes were so bad and her glasses were so thick it made her eyes look extra tiny, and on top of that, they were practically closed anyway.

"How's everybody?" she said.

"Fine," Sarah answered.

"Good," Marty said.

"I'm hungry," Nick said.

"It's coming," Marty told him.

The eggs were sizzling and Sarah poured the hot Ovaltine into the mugs that said Sleeping Beauty on them for the three of them and my mom made a bunch of toast with butter and plum jam and took it all out to the dining room table.

"There's a little Ovaltine left over if anybody wants it," Sarah said.

She wasn't going to pour it for me, but I could have it if I wanted, so I changed my mind and poured it into a mug. I got about half a cup, which was fine with me, since I'd already had some cold. I took a piece of the toast too, mostly because of the plum jam. The five of us were at the table munching away when there was a knock on the front screen door. Nick and I had left the real door open. It was Norma.

"Good morning," she called through the screen.

"Hi," I called. "I'm all ready."

I jumped up and grabbed my towel. My mom jumped up too, but so she could pull the Davenport together and make it look like a couch, even though it was up against the wall of the dinning room.

"Come in," my mom said, smoothing the spread.

Norma opened the screen door and stepped into the living room. She was wearing sandals and cut-off jeans and a red and white checkered blouse that was tied in a knot below her bosom, showing part of her stomach. She had a scarf tied around her head that matched the blouse. Her hair was in a pony tail and she looked normal, which means no make up. My mom hadn't gotten more than two feet from the dinning room table, heading towards the living room, when she knew. I had my towel and was ready to go right then, but that wasn't going to happen. Marty started sputtering like he forgot how to talk.

"You're Marilyn! You're Marilyn Monroe! You are, aren't you?"

"She can't be," Sarah said. "That's impossible."

"No, it is her!" Marty insisted.

Nick looked at her with a little interest, but not much, and went back to eating.

"Settle down, you guys," my mom said. Then to Norma, "Are you?"

"Kurt and I have settled on Norma. I hope you will too," she said, shaking hands with my mom.

Marty and Sarah were out of their chairs and hanging around just behind my mom like they wanted to touch her to see if she was real.

"I'm ready," I reminded her.

"Hold on," Sarah said, "I want to get my Brownie."

"Oh no you don't," my mom said. "She's here as Kurt's friend and our neighbor. You're not going to take pictures."

"Why not?" Sarah complained.

"Because I say so," my mom said.

"If you'd like to take a picture, that's fine, but how about if we all take one together? Wouldn't that be better?" Norma said.

"That would be so cool!" Sarah said.

"Well, maybe we could all stand on the step and your friend George would take it. We just said hello out front. He's on his walkway, having a cigarette."

"Could we mom, please?" Sarah begged.

My mom looked like she wanted to as much as Sarah did. Marty was too shocked to say anything more. He kept looking at her like he was dreaming, but couldn't figure out whether he wanted to wake up or not. Nick was done eating and came over and wrapped his free hand around my mom's leg. Sarah ran to get her Brownie camera.

"Excuse me for just a minute," my mom said.

She went back to her bedroom, Sarah's bedroom now, but the closet was still for her and my dad, and came back wearing black pants and a white blouse. She'd combed her hair. Marty noticed and made a run for the bathroom to comb his. When they were all done we went out on the porch. George was still there and waved. If we were ever going to get out of there, I figured I better go ask George if he'd do it.

"No problem," he said, leaning down to whisper to me. "Good lookin' girl. You know how to pick 'em."

I knew he was teasing me, but still, she was. First Marty, then Norma, then Sarah and my mom stood on the bottom step. Me and Nick stood just below them in the middle. George took the picture.

"Take another, just in case," Marty said.

"Take three," Sarah said.

George took the pictures and handed the camera back to Sarah.

"Thanks, George," I told him.

"Glad to help," he said going back to the Courtyard.

"It was nice to meet you, George," Norma said.

"Nice to meet you too. I've heard a lot about you and your wonder-dog, Snowball, from this guy."

"You should come up and meet her sometime. Shelly too."

"Shelly?"

"My friend Shelly. She's sharing her house with me for a while."

"Maybe I will," George said.

"We should get going," Norma told me. "Nice to meet you, Mrs. Goldman."

"Call me Lara," my mom said.

"Call me Marty," Marty joked. "Call me anything you like! Just call me!"

Norma smiled and shook hands with Marty.

"Now he'll never wash it," Sarah said, then, "Bye."

"Bye," Norma said and touched her cheek.

She bent down in front of Nick.

"Bye, sweetie," Norma said.

Nick watched her from behind my mom's leg, like he was figuring something out. With him, you could never tell what until he decided to say something about it. Which might be never.

We got in her little car and she started it and off we went.

"Wanna stop at the Hot Dog Stand for hot chocolate? My treat," she said.

"It might not be open because today he opens when the carwash does."

"Let's go see."

"Okay, but I already had a bunch of stuff. If you want to try for cof-fee..."

"Want has only a little to do with it, Sweetie. I've got to have some coffee, that's closer to it."

We pulled into the station right in front of Joseph's stand. It wasn't open yet since it was Sunday and only about eight-thirty, and he hadn't even put the stools out yet, but as soon as he saw us coming, he had a cup on the counter and was pouring it for her.

"You guys off to the beach?" he asked. "Kurt, you want hot choco-late?"

"No hot chocolate, yes to the beach," I told him.

Norma put two of the sugar lumps in and a little cream, stirred it and took a sip.

"God, I need this," she said.

"Take the cup if you're in a hurry. You can always drop it off later."

"Thanks, Joseph," she said, putting some coins on the counter.

We got back in her car and crossed Lower Santa Monica to Upper and out to Wilshire.

"Wanna see the white swans?" I asked her.

"What swans?"

I told her about the fancy big lawn with the swans on San Vicente.

"I don't know that way to the beach. Are you sure?"

"Sure I am. I rode my bike there the other day."

"All the way to the beach?"

Uh oh, bragging and telling something I wanted to keep secret. Oh brother, I thought. Nice going.

"Uh, yeah," I said.

She looked at me like she didn't believe me, which was good, sort of, except I didn't want her to think I bragged and lied. That would be even worse than just bragging by itself.

"It's sort of a secret, okay? I really did. That's the truth, believe me. That's not bragging, just the way things worked out. But I only went one way since me and the Red Rider got a ride all the way back home in Pete's truck. He's a friend of Gert's from the Foot Long Hot Dog Stand."

"I suppose I shouldn't ask why it's supposed to be a secret?"

"It's sort of like the difference between Marilyn and Norma. It's just better that way."

She nodded, like she understood completely, which was a big relief.

When we got to where Wilshire went right, along the VA cemetery, I was thinking about Uncle Kurt again. I thought about my mom and how it would be to have a brother or sister, to grow up with them, be friends with them, and have them dead all of a sudden. I tried to picture Marty or Nick, even Sarah, suddenly gone, and it made me ache inside. No wonder my mom wanted us to be quiet when we passed. It was a chance for her to say hello to him in her head. To pretend he was somewhere, maybe not where she could see him, but close enough to hear her thoughts.

"This is San Vicente," I told Norma. "You have to go left."

She looked at me.

"What's the matter?" she said, "I'm not going to tell your secret."

"I know."

"Then what?"

"My mom's brother is buried here somewhere. He died in the war."

"Oh, I'm so sorry."

"I'm named after him, but I never met him."

We drove along without talking. When we were getting close to where I thought the white swans were, I told her, and I began to watch for them more carefully.

"There they are!" I said, pointing.

She saw them too and pulled over.

"They're beautiful!" she said, "and so big. If they were real, you could fly away on them."

"I thought of that too when I rode here the other day."

"Is this a park?" she asked me.

"No, I think it's just the back yard of that house way over there. It must be on one of the streets behind San Vicente. See how big it is? Who could own a place like that?"

"I could think of a few," she laughed.

"Really. Like who?"

"Some of the producers and directors I've met. Some of the older guys in the business. The Marx brothers. Cary Grant. Katherine Hepburn. Some of them could."

"Not you?"

Her head went back and she laughed that really nice laugh of hers, "Not me. Not yet, anyway."

"I don't think the Marx brothers could, either. I know Timmy Marx and Jimmy and Minny and they live on the northside, but nothing like this."

"Well, I don't know who'd really want to even if they could afford it. It's just too big to think about."

We got back in the car and headed for the little street that dropped down the hill.

"This is it," I said when I saw 7th Street. "Turn right here. And get ready to fall off a cliff."

She just laughed but when we got to the steep part, her eyes got wide and she squealed like we were on a rollercoaster.

"Wheeeee!" she said all the way down the hill as the little car zipped around the curves, zoom, zoom, zoom until, in no time, we were all the way to the bottom and West Channel.

"That was fun," she said. "I'm going to come to the beach this way from now on."

"And it takes you right to the hot dog stand, see?" I said, pointing to Gert's up ahead and to the left.

"I see," she said. "You're not hungry yet, are you?"

"No, I just had breakfast."

We came to the stop sign at the Pacific Coast Highway, Gert's on the left, a beach store on the right, where they sold swim suits and sandals and fins and goggles and sold or rented beach umbrellas and rafts and surf boards, and right in front of us, across the highway, what Marty called the Big Blue. It was one of those perfect days with the white foam of the rollers coming in, the smooth blue slope of waves just forming and bright spots of white hot light from the sun bouncing off the water, looking like chunks of mirror scattered all around. It couldn't have been much past nine, so the parking lot was empty and Gert hadn't opened up yet, and if I hadn't cut off my jeans, I would have been out of luck since the beach store wasn't open either. We had the whole beach to ourselves. I'd never ever been the first person, the only person, on the beach. Norma parked close to the wall that separated the parking lot from the sand. There was a little rail on top of it that me and Marty usually climbed over and jumped from, down to the sand, instead of walking around to either end where the steps were. But since Norma probably wouldn't want to jump, I didn't either. It might have been fun, but it would have been showing off if not actually bragging, so a kind of bragging anyway, so I just took my towel and walked with her to the stairs closest to The Beach Club, which was a private club just south of Will Rogers State Beach.

There was a huge chain link fence that ran all the way from the parking lot to just a little above the wet sand. It was maybe twelve or fifteen feet high, with green wood slats to keep it private. To keep us out, really. I wasn't planning on telling Norma, but I'd been sneaking in for years and years, usually taking Nick with me, so we could shower just like the club kids, and get clean and dry before going home. Marty wouldn't do it because he was afraid he might bump into some of his friends from school who actually belonged to the Club, but Sarah did. My mom pretended she didn't know where we were going when we headed over there, but she was glad to have us clean and dry and not complaining about being sandy and scratchy on the drive back. The sand had been screened and you could see the tracks where the old army jeep dragged a big square steel frame with heavy wire screening to clean up any junk left the day before. We walked towards the water leaving the only footprints on the whole beach.

"It's perfectly clean!" Norma said. "Isn't that nice?"

"I've never been here this early before. I've never been the first one. Look. There aren't even any footprints. They probably just finished screening it in the last hour or so. By the middle of the day there's cigarette butts and coke bottles and wrappers from people's lunches. It's amazing what a bunch of pigs people can be," I told her. "Here they are at this beautiful beach with the white sand and the clean blue salty water, and they leave their garbage. Can you believe that? What really kills me, well, my mom and Marty, because they taught me about it, is there's trash cans about every fifty yards. Like it would kill them to put the trash in the trash can!"

"It's nice your mom and Marty are teaching you to care about it."

"Well, we come here almost every day during the summer, so it's sort of our beach. It's not as fancy as The Beach Club over there, but it's like it's our beach club. Me and Sarah collect coke bottles and cash them in at Gert's for the deposit. We can usually get a hot dog and coke and sometimes fries just from one trip across the sand to the parking lot. Pretty good, huh?"

"Really?"

"Really, it's true. The bad part is the sand is so hot that while you're looking around and collecting bottles, your feet get fried. Marty says he's getting too old to do it, and since he's working at the Standard Station, he can just buy a hot dog whenever he wants."

An old army jeep, painted red with a white cross on the door and seven or eight lifeguards piled in, came along the wet sand from the south. When they got to the first of the lifeguard stands on the public beach, after the beach club side of the big green fence, one of them jumped out and took his float thing, and climbed the ladder to his station and opened it up. The jeep took off up the beach to the next stand and dropped off the next guy and the next and so on until the stands all had guards for as far as I could see.

Me and Norma spread our towels out and got comfortable. The lifeguard tower wasn't very far from us, and once the lifeguard had opened it up and taken the wood and cloth chair from the inside and put it outside, he sat there with his feet up on the rail looking at the water to see if anybody needed saving, but since we were the only ones on the beach, it was really a waste of time. Since he didn't have anything else to do, I guess it didn't matter much, but pretty soon he realized it, because he started looking around and spotted us. Maybe not me, but Norma for sure. He waved. She had her sunglasses on, and I think she'd closed her eyes, but it was hard to tell. She didn't wave back, so I think her eyes must have been closed. The lifeguard waved again, so I waved back so he wouldn't feel bad, like we were ignoring him or something, when really, Norma's eyes just happened to be closed. In fact, from her breathing I was pretty sure she'd fallen asleep. I was getting a little bored of just sitting there so I went down to the water. It wasn't very cold, just chilly, when it first touched my toes. I tiptoed out until I was up to my waist.

"You know how to swim, don't you?" the lifeguard yelled to me.

"Yes, I do."

"Okay," he said, "but be careful. I'll keep an eye on you just in case."

"Okay. Thank you."

When the first wave was about to smack me, I dove under and came up on the other side. I wasn't very far out and the waves were pretty small, but I thought I'd try to body surf anyway. Marty had been teaching me. Half the time I ended up getting tossed around with water up my nose, but when I did get a ride, it was the most fun thing in the world. You'd slide down the face of the wave, angling your body this way or that to try and stay in it, really to stay in front of it, and when you got to the bottom where the new wave crashed into the water already ahead of it, you either got crunched and tumbled, or made the change from heading down to heading foreward. If that happened you'd done it. You zipped along until the wave ran out of power, or until you lost control and got tumbled anyway. Either way, it was the most exciting thing in the world. Next to the freedom of the Red Rider, that is, but close. It was sort of like flying and made me jealous of the seagulls. Anyway, Marty and his friends would stay in the water all day, wave after wave, ride after ride. If I got three or four or five good rides in a whole day at the beach out of maybe a hundred tries, I figured it'd been a good day. The lifeguard had come down from his stand and was watching me from the wet sand.

"There's a raft here if you want to blow it up," the lifegurard called to me. "Someone left it behind yesterday."

"No thanks."

Marty thought rafts were cheating and so did I. But Norma might like it.

"Maybe for my friend," I said.

"That's not your mom?" he asked me.

"No, just a friend."

He was looking over his shoulder to where Norma was snoozing on her towel.

"Not your big sister?" he asked.

"No," I said, "I told you, just a friend."

"Let's go ask her if she wants the raft," he said.

"I think she wants to snooze some more. She hasn't had a day off in a long time. Here they come," I said.

I could see there was another set of waves forming just a little farther out than I'd been or usually tried for, more like the ones Marty and his friends rode. With the lifeguard right there, I thought it would be a good time to give it a try. I swam out, ducked under the first one which was all set to break right on top of me, and came up behind it and saw the next one was a monster. I had this funny feeling like I wished I were on the towel on the sand next to Norma, but at the same time, I had the feeling like seeing the Red Rider for the first time, wanting it, but almost afraid to imagine it could be mine. This wave was mine. Or at least, that's what I thought. I got myself turned around and took a few strokes to get moving ahead of it. All of a sudden it just lifted me up, and instead of being about three or four feet above the water below, I was at least ten. Maybe only eight, but probably ten. I tried to go backwards but it was too late. The wave kept lifting me higher and higher and when it couldn't get any higher, it held me there for a minute to make sure I could see just what a mess I'd gotten myself into. I could see the lifeguard, but he couldn't see me because he was looking at Norma, hoping she'd wake up, I suppose. I started falling. Just before I was going to hit the water below, I took a big breath of air. Marty said that was important. I also closed my eyes, which was my idea, not Marty's. It seemed like it took forever to get from so high up in the air to the water below, but when I did, kaboom!, it was like being caught up in the biggest washing machine or cement mixer in the world. I got tumbled and twisted and flipped around so much I had no idea which way was up or down, and I could feel the water was thick with sand and little pebbles churned up from the bottom, wherever that was. Finally my right leg touched down, even though I would have guessed that that was sideways. I brought my left leg around to join it, and got ready to push off. I still had air, and Marty said it was the most important thing to time the push right. You had to wait until most of the churning stopped and the power of the wave had gone past you. When you could feel that, you were ready. If you messed it up, you could be in big trouble. Things had calmed down and I got my feet ready and my knees bent and when it felt about right, I pushed off as hard as I could. My eyes were still closed. With all the sand and pebble that had been churned up into the water, I probably couldn't have seen anything anyway even if they were open, but I was planning on keeping them closed until I felt air. It seemed like it was taking too long, and I started to worry that I hadn't pushed hard enough, or the water was too deep for my push to take me to the surface. My push kind of ran out of gas, and then it was more like I was floating up. I wiggled my legs and pulled with my arms to move through it and I could feel I was going up even though I was still being pushed and shoved in other directions at the same time, but the problem was I wasn't sure how much longer I could hold my breath. Finally, I got to the surface. I opened my eyes and took a breath, and was thinking that was a close call, but just as I got the first little taste of air, I could feel I was being lifted again. The next wave had already gotten there. I'd never had to try it before, but Marty called these doubles, or if things got really ugly, triples. That's where there wasn't time to do anything but get a little air and make yourself go down, not up, to try to keep from getting churned and tumbled twice or three times in a row. If that happened you could drown! Simple as that. If there was a bunch of waves that were big and powerful and kept you churning, the best you could do was to wait for the right time and grab a little air and duck below the worst of it. You had to try to find the bottom and wait. Even if you had to do it a bunch of times. The second wave seemed bigger than the first, but I got under it before it could lift me and crash me down. I could feel it trying to suck me up and forward, but I used my arms to pull myself down, and it mostly passed over. I opened my eyes. The water was clouded with lots of sand and pebble, but this time at least I knew which way was up because I could see the brightness of the sky above the water. That was the good part. The bad part was it looked a long ways off. I was crouched, ready to push off again, but I was being moved forward in little hops along the bottom, trying to keep my balance, to keep my feet ready to push, to keep the wave from tipping me over or sideways so I couldn't push when the right time came. I pushed and swam as hard as I could. I got to the surface easier this time and was able to get more air. When I got a look at where I was, I couldn't believe it. I wasn't in front of Will Rogers State Beach any more. I was down by the Beach Club, way past the green fence. No Norma, no lifeguard, because somehow I'd gone sideways. And the waves weren't pushing me any closer to shore. I was still farther out than I'd ever been before even after the two monster waves. I looked back and sure enough another one was coming. The good thing was I'd had a chance to get lots of air. The bad thing was I was getting tired. I remembered one of Marty's friends talking about a riptide taking him half way down to Venice Beach and he had to walk back. That was more than a mile. He said you'd drown if you tried to fight it. You just had to let it take you and after a while it leaves you alone and you can get out and walk back. I figured that's what I was going to have to do, but the part about getting tired would be a problem no matter where the riptide left me. I needed to get closer to shore or I was a goner. Ducking below this one wouldn't be much help if I was too tired to push up through it for air. It was sucking the water from all around, pulling me backwards and up. Not just up, but up and up and up as it formed itself into the biggest one yet. If I'd had a camera I could have probably taken a picture of the Beach Club roof, that's how high up I was. Before it had finished getting as high as it could, I started swimming as hard as I could to stay in front of it, not just let myself get lifted to the top and thrown crashing down and crunched again. The next thing I knew I was slidng down the face of the wave at a hundred miles an hour. The wave wasn't breaking straight ahead, it was curling and breaking on my left, continuing to form to my right, so I aimed a little that way. I could feel that if I angled too much, I'd just get rolled over, so I aimed back a little more straight ahead. My chest was just skimming down the surface, with a spray of water shooting off each side like from the front of a speed boat, until I got to the bottom of the face and there was a crash behind me and instead of getting crunched, I got squirted forward going even faster than before. I was going so fast that when me and my wave would catch up to the little ripples in the water in front of me, I sort of bounced over them, bump bump bump without even slowing down, like a car going so fast it just skipped over speed bumps. Finally, the wave slowed down and so did I and I began to feel the white foaming part slip around and past me. I put my feet down and could feel the bottom. I was in. I tried to walk to the wet sand, but my legs were rubbery and I was sort of dizzy. Boy, what a ride. No wonder Marty and his friends stayed in the water all day!

"Are you nuts!? Are you okay?!

It was the lifeguard. Even when he saw I was okay, he kept yelling anyway.

"Are you out of your mind!? Those are monsters out there! You're not big enough for those."

He was running towards me through the shallow water, running and splashing, towing his red float thing behind on its little rope. I was almost out of the water by then, about knee deep, and if I hadn't been so dizzy, I'd have already been the rest of the way out, but he was set on saving me now, anyway, and I could see why. Norma was running in my direction too, a little ways behind him. He grabbed me and lifted me up.

"Are you okay?" he repeated.

"Sure," I said. "Put me down. I'm okay."

"Kurt!" Norma called, "are you alright?"

I waved to her. He didn't put me down until Norma got there.

"That was the best ride ever!" I told them both.

"That was way too big for you, buddy, way too big. I'm sorry," he said to Norma. "I lost track of him." Then to me, "I thought I saw you come up for air, then you were gone. Man, did you give me a scare."

"I was trying to duck the churning," I told him. "Did you see that ride? Did you see it?"

"I saw it. I was holding my breath the whole time."

"Me too. Man, I can't wait to tell my brother."

"Oh sweetie!" she said. "You nearly gave me a heart attack! I thought the fall on the wave before would kill you! Then you disappeared under all that water and I thought you were going to drown! You were under so long and I couldn't see you and I was so scared! You have to be more careful. Promise?"

"I'm fine," I said.

"Promise!" she insisted.

"Okay, I promise. But did you see the ride? On that last one?"

"I saw it."

"Pretty neat, huh?"

"Pretty neat, for sure."

Wanna come in the water?"

"We're in the water," she said.

"Only your feet."

"That's enough for me," she said.

"Why not give yourself a little rest before you go back in?" the lifeguard said. "And not so far out the next time, okay?"

"Okay."

"I need some coffee," Norma said. "I'm exhausted. Aren't you hungry after all that?"

"I'm starved," I said, "and it can't even be close to noon."

Norma looked at her watch.

"It's quarter to eleven. Will the hot dog stand be open now?"

"I think so," I told her. "It's supposed to open at ten."

"Perfect," she said, calming down from the excitement of me almost drowning. "Let's go across the street see about some coffee and those foot long hot dogs."

The sun had been beating down a bunch while I was in the water, and we had to run across the sand to keep from getting our feet fried. Norma had grabbed her sandals when we passed our towels, and she held them to her chest as we ran, but I'd forgotten my sneakers, so my feet were getting burned from the hot sand and then the hot, rocky, pebbly parking lot too. When we'd crossed the sand, Norma stopped to put her sandals on before she crossed the parking lot. I just ran ahead to get it over with, to get to the concrete curb, which I knew would be a little cooler. I waited for her there. When she reached me, she held my hand and we waited for a few cars to pass, then crossed. There was a small crowd at Gert's. Six or eight people at the outside window, ordering things to go, or maybe just to sit at the outside tables under the umbrellas.

"Let's go in," Norma said. "I'd like to get out of the sun. I think I'm getting burned. Do I look red to you?"

"Yeah, a little."

She watched as I poked a finger on her shoulder, held it there for a second, then took it away. There was a white spot surrounded by red. It took a few seconds for the finger print to turn the same red as the skin all around it.

"That's not good," she said.

"Why not? Does it hurt?"

"No, not yet, anyway. But we're not done filming. If I'm a different color tomorrow than I was yesterday...."

She made a face, like she'd get in trouble.

"Well, we can't worry about that, can we? Wouldn't help if we did, so we might as well not, right?"

"I suppose," I said.

We went into Gert's. There were people at all of the tables and there was only one stool open at the counter.

"Get up and give the lady and the kid a seat," Gert told a guy about to take a bite out of his hot dog. "Go on, you been campin' on that stool too long already. Give the lady a seat!"

"Oh no," Norma said. "He doesn't have to get up on my account. Kurt, you sit here," she said, touching the empty stool.

The guy with the hot dog could see me, but he had to turn around a little to see Norma. When he did, his eyes got wide and his mouth hung open with the big bite of hot dog just sitting there, looking about ready to fall out onto the counter. He tried to say something, but the hot dog was about to fall, so he closed his mouth. He got up and nodded at the stool. "You fit yasef dow," he mumbled, his eyes bright and excited.

"Thank you," Norma said.

Everybody in the place was looking at her. She smiled like that was okay, sort of, hello to all of you, so now eat your hot dogs and me and Kurt are gonna have coffee and hotdogs too.

"You guys never seen a good lookin' dame before? What about me? Huh? You don't go droolin' all overyerselves fer me, so knock it off! Actin' like a bunch of kids! Worse than that, like tourists!"

She smiled at Norma then at me, and leaned in close and sort of whispered, as much as Gert ever whispered, "Kid, you got a lot of surprises in you, don't you? You nearly get Pete killed one day, now this. Peter ain't gonna believe it."

"Where is he? Is he okay?"

"He's hurtin', honey, but he's okay. I'm glad he was there to help. So is he. Don't you worry about it."

"What's wrong with Pete?" Norma asked. "I thought he just drove you home."

"Things got a little out of hand," Gert began

Norma looked worried about whatever it was and Gert was getting all set to tell her about the whole thing, but before she did, she looked at me and changed her mind.

"Well, it was one of those things," she said, wiping the counter, then turning back to the grill. "I'll let Kurt, here, tell you when he's ready."

She began moving the foot longers around, taking ones that were cooked and putting them on a cooler part of the grill and moving new ones onto the hotter part.

"What are you guys havin'?"

"A foot longer and a coke for me," I said.

"Coffee and a foot longer," Norma said.

She said it too quietly.

First Shelly, now Gert, I was thinking. I could tell Norma was trying not to mention it if I didn't want to talk about it, but it seemed like she wanted me to want to tell her since we were friends. Especially since Shelly knew one thing and now Gert knew about something else. They were starting to add up, like she was the only one I wouldn't tell things to, which wasn't true, but I could see how she might think that. The problem was, if I told her about this, she might feel like it was her responsibility or something to tell my mom or dad, and that would be a real mess, or if she didn't, she'd probably feel bad about not telling when she thought she should, so it was one of those times where no matter what you do you can't win. Either of us. At least if I didn't tell her, she wouldn't know and wouldn't have to decide about telling or not. That was something. On the other hand, we were friends. I decided to tell her the Shelly one. Gert put our food in front of us and we both started to eat.

"That guy, Spence, next door to you guys?"

"What about him?"

"He yelled at me. That's what Shelly was asking about."

"He what?"

"About the locks. I was giving out the cards from the San Vicente Hardware store so people who'd had their locks cut off could get new ones and saying I was sorry."

"And?"

"He started yelling at me. Shelly heard him and came over and made him stop. It's okay, though."

"It's not okay! How could he do that? There's no excuse for that. That's just mean."

"Well, I didn't like it, but I thought it was sort of fair. He was mad about the locks and I shouldn't have switched them around, so I figured we were even. Anyway, that was what Shelly was asking me about."

She sipped at her coffee and nibbled on the foot longer, thinking about things. I was afraid she was waiting for me to tell her the Gert one, but then she put her arm around my neck and pulled me over to her and kissed the top of my head. So I figured that was that for now.

When we finished eating it was eleven-thirty.

"If it's okay with you, I think we should head back. I've already had too much sun."

"That's fine. That one big ride was worth fifty more little ones."

I put all the money I had on the counter. The foot longer was twenty cents, the coke a dime. That left twenty-five cents for Gert. It would have been nice if I had enough money to pay for Norma's stuff too, but I didn't, and I didn't think she'd mind that she had to pay for her own. She had a pretty good job.

"Why don't you let me pay this time? You always get the sweet rolls or warm bread in the morning."

"Yeah, but that's free."

"Still," she said, "you treat me. Now it's my turn."

I thought about it for a couple of seconds. It was almost the cost of a lock to Mr. Mahoney at the hardware store.

"Okay," I said, and took the money off the counter before Gert could see me taking it back.

Norma put a dollar on the counter. That paid for her food and mine and probably a better tip for Gert.

"See you later, Gert," I said.

"So long, kid. See you soon. Nice to meet you...."

"Norma," Norma said.

"Norma," Gert repeated. "Close enough."

We crossed back to the beach and got our towels. I would have liked to sneak into the Beach Club for a shower, but Norma had had too much sun and I could tell she was worried about it, so I just dusted the sand off my feet and the cut offs in the parking lot and put my sneakers on and we got into the car and took off. Besides, the sneaking in part might embarrass her the same way it did Marty. The sun was really beating down by then and in the little convertible there was no getting away from it. My face and shoulders felt hot and my arms and legs did too. Even the back of my hands and my fingers did. When we'd gotten back up the steep part of Estrada to the stop sign at 7th Street and San Vicente, Norma pulled over to the curb. She put her scarf back over her head and tied it under her chin, put her sunglasses on, and left the car running while she got out and took a sweat shirt from the trunk and put it on too. The sleeves had been cut off, so it didn't cover her arms completely, but it was better than nothing. It was really way too hot for all that, but her skin was getting redder and redder and she probably figured it was better to sweat a bunch than get burned any more. My nose and the top of my ears were already beginning to feel tingly, like they'd had too much sun too, but since I wasn't in a movie, it didn't matter. The traffic was a lot heavier now, but most of it seemed to be heading towards the beach, so we zipped along. When we turned onto Oakhurst and she pulled to the curb on our side, facing the wrong way, like Pete had. I took a quick look across the street, just in case.

"Gosh, that was fun. I wish I knew when I'd have a little more time off so we could plan to do it again." she said. "Maybe Shelly could come too."

"Sure, but where would she sit?"

"You could sit in her lap, couldn't you?"

"I suppose."

"Well, we can work all that out. The important thing is we had fun. Right?"

"Right. And thanks for the hot dog and coke," I said as I got out of the car.

"My pleasure, sweetie. Good luck with the paper route," she said and waved as she drove up the street.

When I turned towards our house, Marty and Pop were there on the front porch, watching.

"Hi," I said. "You wouldn't believe the wave I got! It was ten or twelve feet high. Really! The lifeguard even called it a monster. I rode it all the way in," I said, showing them with my hand. "All the way. You gotta believe me because it's true!"

"Kurt, I'd believe anything," Marty said. "If I live for a hundred years, I'd believe just about anything, except that your first words after spending the morning with Marilyn Monroe at the beach would be about a wave."

Ron Baylor got there right at one-thirty. It was too hot in the house even with the front door open, so me and Marty and Ron sat on the top step of the porch. Marty didn't say much after hello. He took one look at the guy and got quiet. He was listening to every word Ron was saying, but he just didn't say anything back. Not until the end. Ron Baylor talked and talked, and boy, did he talk fast. If I was supposed to remember everything he was saying, all the rules and responsibilities and the special way everything had to be done, I was doomed before I'd even started. I thought I was just supposed to ride around and throw papers on people's lawns or front porches. You just about had to be a grown up for all this. He said I was about to become a small businessman, like I'd been waiting to hear that all my life. Pop and my dad were having a hard enough time with their businesses, so how was I supposed to do it? I was getting sort of scared, like maybe I should just forget the whole thing. But the trouble with that was it would slow down paying off the locks, and besides, even though I'd didn't really brag, I did kind of make a big deal out of how I was going to get a paper route, so I'd sort of trapped myself. If nothing else, I'd get to ride the Red Rider a lot, so that was something good. Marty had a funny look on his face when Ron finally looked like he was done talking.

"You didn't say how much Kurt would make," he said.

"Well, that's a little hard to say," Ron told us.

Ron shrugged, with the sort of smile that was supposed to make Marty think his question had been answered, and that was that.

"Why?" Marty said.

Ron frowned, like he didn't have to explain anything to anybody, but especially to some kid who wasn't even going to be the actual paper boy. When Marty just sat there waiting for an answer, Ron gave him an annoyed look.

"It's complicated."

"Well," Marty said, "let's look at it this way: people pay for the paper, right?"

"Yeah...."

"How much?"

"It depends..."

"On what?"

At first I thought Ron was going to get up and leave. He sat there thinking about it, I'm pretty sure, but I think he really wanted to get rid of doing this route himself, and I was his only choice at he moment.

"On whether they take just weekdays and Saturdays or Sundays too."

"Okay," Marty said, "I get it. Do most people do one or the other?"

"It's about even," Ron said.

"And you're going to charge Kurt for each paper you distribute to him, right?"

"More or less."

"What's that mean?"

"The Sunday papers cost more."

"How big is the route?" Marty asked him.

"What is this, the third degree?" Ron complained.

"Just trying to help you figure it out," Marty smiled, without meaning the smile. "How many deliveries on the route?" Marty said again.

"About forty."

"About? I thought you'd been doing it yourself."

"I have."

"So, you must know how many customers the route has, right?"

"Forty-two."

"That's pretty big isn't it?"

"About average?"

"Really? I have friends that used to deliver the Times, and the biggest was thirty-four. Thirty four Sunday papers gets awfully heavy. Forty-two, even for big kid, would be tough."

"Like I said, not everbody takes the Sunday."

"Even so, forty-two weekday papers, six days a week and maybe twenty Sunday papers.....that's a lot."

"Well, that's the route."

"What are the boundaries?"

"Roughly, Lower Santa Monica to Burton Way, Doheny to Rexford."

"That's big. Any deliveries ouside that?"

"A couple," Ron admitted.

"How many and how far?"

"Six or seven."

"Which?"

"Seven..."

"How far outside?"

Ron seemed to be getting fed up with the whole thing, and instead of dancing around, he decided to just answer.

"Two are down by Dayton Way, one down to Clifton, another east of Doheny and three up around Carmelita."

Just listening to all this was giving me a headache.

"It looks like you've scraped together a lot of strays into this route, a lot of deliveries that aren't convenient for any of the surrounding routes, making this one too big and way too spread out."

"Well, that's the route," Ron said, standing up, like we should just take it or leave it.

I knew which one I was going to vote for. He might have been twenty-four or twenty-five, but probably not. More likely twenty-two or three. He knew Marty couldn't be more than seventeen or eighteen, and letting a teenager argue him into telling things he was trying to hide was making him mad. If he knew Marty was only fifteen, about to be sixteen, it would have made him go nuts, I bet. On the other hand, he still seemed to be hanging on to the idea of getting rid of this route, so he stood up like was going to leave, but he didn't go anywhere. When Marty didn't say anything, finally he did.

"What if I get rid of the seven outside ones? That cuts the area and makes it thirty-five."

"It's still a big area. Spread out."

"Yeah....well..."

"So, how much do the papers cost Kurt, and how much does he charge the customers?"

"Eight cents weekdays, ten cents for the Sunday."

"'Is that to Kurt or the customer?"

"The customer."

"And Kurt?"

"Five and six."

"So he makes roughly seventy-five cents a customer per month for the weekday and Saturday deliveries, and another sixteen cents a month for the Sunday?"

"Sounds about right."

"So, if the route is down to thirty-five, and about half that on Sundays, that would be approximately twenty-seven dollars for the guys without the Sunday, and another two seventy-five for the ones with. Right?"

"You're the Einstein, buddy. Whatever you say."

Boy, did he have that right! Not only was Marty doing all the math in his head, he thought of all these questions to ask in the first place. I thought all I needed to know was the addresses to throw the papers to.

"Well, I'm sure you have other routes about the same size, so they must make about thirty bucks a month. Right?"

"Yeah, about..."

Thirty bucks a month? I'd be rich! With the car wash added in that would be forty bucks a month. Summer was three months long, so three times forty. That had to be more than a hundred. I'd figure it out exactly when I had some paper and a pencil, but it had to be at least that much. The paper route was starting to seem like a good idea again. A great idea! Marty looked at me.

"That sound about right to you?" he asked me.

I nodded that it did, trying not to smile, but what I was really thinking was, I'm rich!

With that, Ron was ready to wrap up the deal.

"I'll get you a route bag and rubber bands and the delivery addresses. Maybe the genius here," meaning Marty, "can help you plot out the route."

He went to his truck and got the stuff. He also brought a copy of yesterday's Saturday paper.

"You fold them like this," he said.

He was kneeling and had the paper in front of him, showing me how to put my thumbs on top, the other fingers underneath, with the paper facing you, like you were going to read it. Then you folded the right side over to the left, and the left side over that to the right, so it was in thirds, and you slipped a rubber band over it. He did it in about half a second. He took the rubber band off and unfolded it so I could try. It was harder than it looked. Getting it in thirds was the hard part, because if you didn't, it was sort of sloppy and the rubber band didn't go on very well, and there was no way you could throw it from your bicycle without it coming apart and making a mess, he warned me. I tried a few times without much luck.

"Keep practicing. You'll get better," Ron said. "Just keep in mind, every complaint about the paper not being delivered, or being delivered late, after six weekdays or after two on Sunday, or wet or muddy or flying apart because it wasn't folded right, and you're out the whole five cents for the weekday and Saturday, and six cents for the Sunday. Got it?"

"Uh huh."

Marty was back to watching and listening to him.

"I'll drop the papers off every day at one p.m. right there on the parkway," he said pointing. "By ten on Sunday. If you fold them right where I drop them, you won't have to carry the full bag when it's the heaviest. Just do it there, stand them up in the bag like this," he said, showing me, "about seventeen front and back, and then you can slip the bag over your shoulders, stand up, get on your bike and you're ready to go."

It sounded easy enough. With only one paper in the bag it wasn't heavy at all, but it hung down below my knees. The other problem was my shoulders weren't wide enough, or the neck hole was too big, because even with just the one paper, the canvas bag was drooping down to the middle of my left arm, and sort of cutting into my neck on the right side. With another thirty-four papers, it was going to be a big problem. I'd seen the Sunday paper a thousand times and it never seemed like a big deal, but all of a sudden, I could picture seventeen or eighteen of them in the route bags slipping down around my waist. And how could I pedal? The whole thing started to seem impossible again, but at the same time, the idea of thirty dollars a month jumped into my head, and I figured I'd give it a try. Even if it was going to be a lot harder than I'd thought, thirty bucks was thirty bucks.

"You can go collecting any of the last four days of the month, but Saturdays when you're delivering are the best. It slows the delivering way down, but people are usually home hanging around, so you're less likely to miss them and have to come back, and they probably just got paid on Friday, so they should have the money. You all set, then?" Ron said.

"Wait a minute," Marty said.

"What now?"

"What's that supposed to mean?"

"What?"

I was wondering what too.

"What do you mean, 'they'll probably have the money'. What if they don't?"

I hadn't thought of that.

"He's responsible," Ron said.

"You mean if someone stiffs him, he still owes for the papers?"

"You got it."

"So, you're saying The Mirror Company, and their official representative, the distributor, you, are making the delivery boys, a bunch of kids, responsible for deadbeats?"

"Yeah. That's the way it works. The delivery boys're sort of independent contractors."

"That doesn't sound right to me," Marty said.

"Well, that's the way it is," Ron told us.

Ron looked at me again.

"So, we all set?"

"I guess."

I looked at Marty. He had this look like he had a bad feeling about the whole thing, but if I wanted to try, what the heck?

"Okay, then," Ron said, shaking hands with me, turning to go.

He didn't shake with Marty.

# Chapter 27
## *For Love Or Money*
## August 10, 1989

"IT'S OBVIOUS they're protecting someone," Phillips said.

He folded the copy of Maurice's letter I'd given him and slipped into the inside pocket of his very finely tailored suit jacket. The guy was definitely a fashion plate, giving nothing away to the Beverly Hills doctors, lawyers and agents that surrounded us. The place was packed with the late lunch crowd or maybe guys calling it a day a bit early, or maybe some of both.

It was a little after three, the Dayton Way side of Il Fornaio, my usual table. Yeah, yeah, I'm predictable. Sue me.

"You went to detective school for that? The question is who?"

"They're protecting someone alright, and I'm pretty sure I know who."

He looked at me for a long ten-count without saying anything.

"You do? Are you going to share, or are you hoping to send me back to Berkeley before we get to that?"

"I've been ready for you to go back to Berkeley since you first contacted Dolan," he said with a wry smile.

He was eating a big late lunch, no doubt because it was going to end up on my tab. The department's tab, anyway. I was nursing a fresh squeezed lemonade and dipping some of the homemade breads ino a mix of olive oil and balsamic vinegar. He looked up at me and fixed me with his best detective look.

"Your brother," he said flatly.

"We're back to your theory already? Pretty easy, isn't it? Blame it on him. He can't do anything about it and it gets you and Dolan off an uncomfortable hook. You're a lazy asshole," I said looking him squarely in the eye. "I mean that in the nicest possible way."

"Hear me out. We have three written confessions all executed on the same day, cross-witnessed. If these guys were still alive, besides this Osaka character, who isn't long for this world according to his son, they'd have some smart-ass defense attorney, your younger brother for instance, and I mean that in the nicest possible way, they'd have some lawyer making the case that there was reasonable doubt about which of them might actually be guilty, so charges would probably never be filed against any of them. If your brother was alive and charges were being considered against him, any one of the confessions, let alone all three, would create enough reasonable doubt to make a D.A. think twice. And even if he were willing to file, chances are they'd be tossed. The only thing that would stick is a conspiracy to obstruct justice, and if these guys were smart enough to set this up, they were smart enough to figure even if the body was ever found, one or more of them would probably be dead by then, or so old that no one would want to pursue it. No, they knew what they were doing. What's missing is one more confession."

"What confession?" I asked. "Whose?"

"Your grandfather's."

"My grandfather? What's he got to do with it?"

"I told you," Phillips said with what I knew was misplaced certainty, "he wouldn't sell the lot that made the project on the Rathbone property possible. He must have been a part of their little conspiracy right from the beginning to keep the body from being found. To protect your brother, his grandson. His first grandson, right?"

"Right," I conceded, "the first."

"There's always a lot of emotional investment in a first child or a first grandchild. We see it all the time. So I figure there's a confession from him floating around somewhere, witnessed by one of the others. I don't suppose you've seen anything of it, have you?"

"No."

I was weighing whether this was a good time to point out that Pop died eight years before the original project was scuttled because the owner of 437 wouldn't sell. Iyama wouldn't sell. It seemed pointless not to set him straight, but somehow his not knowing intrigued me. How could he not know? The Quit Claim Deeds and the Life Estate that Pop and George Bowen and Mr. Avery used to return the property to Hiroki from Sullivan were just unusual enough to cause some confusion, but it would take some pretty sloppy police work on top of that, and Phillips just wasn't sloppy. I'd found it easy enough. Something else was involved, and until I understood it, I wasn't ready to alert him to the gap in his reconstruction of the events he was basing his theory on. I returned to the heart of his theory instead.

"You don't feel the need to supply a motive, or even a solid connection between Marty and Kevin Doyle?"

"I was sort of hoping you could," he smiled, with mock anticipation.

"There isn't one. And even if there were, as they say, when pigs can fly."

He shrugged it off, untroubled.

"Now, if it had been this Ron Baylor guy instead of Doyle, the guy your brother was arrested for assaulting, we'd pretty much have it locked up."

"But it wasn't."

"No, but like I told you on day one, I think there's maybe a pattern here. A tendency to hold things in until they just explode. First Baylor, then Doyle, then turned against himself. I just need to find the connection between your brother and Doyle. Come on," he smiled, "not even a little something?"

Listening to him, I'd quickly gone through anger, amazement, contempt and even amusement, but the upshot was he didn't have a connection.

"You don't have a thing, besides your theory, do you?"

"No, not yet."

"I get the impression you don't care. That you're not going to try, at least not very hard."

He didn't say anything. He busied himself with the food.

"That's it, isn't it?"

"That's what?" he said, looking up, his face the picture of innocence, as though he had sort of lost track of the conversation.

"You'll just lay out your theory, unsubstantiated of course, maybe do a little soft-shoe to gloss over the lack of evidence or motive or even a connection to Marty, but basically uncontested, so you can make it stick with the police brass and the D.A. that the case can be closed. You can return to expanding your already very impressive wardrobe, and Dolan heads to the finish line in the mayor's race. Neat. Except I'm still here."

"And?" he said, unconcerned.

"I'll contest it."

"Oh? Really? And just how would you do that?" he said with a confident smirk.

"Talk to Salter and the mayor. Complain about the police department being used to protect Dolan and unfairly tarnish Marty."

"Good luck. They may hate Dolan, but that's the kind of political manuevering that usually backfires, and they're smart enough to know it, even if you aren't. I don't think they'd want any part of it. You'd make them look like witch-hunters, and that's what we've all been trying to avoid from the beginning."

"Maybe I could raise their level of interest. Give them a little incentive."

"Yeah? How might you do that?"

"I've been reading the Times most mornings," I said, tapping a finger on today's paper on the window sill next to me. "I like the way that guy, what's his name...?" I picked it up and found what I was looking for, "Evan Morris, their local political writer, I like how he gets his teeth into something and just sort of hangs on until he's satisfied he gotten to the bottom of it. You seen his stuff?"

"Don't."

"Why not? Isn't that ultimately what investigative reporting is for? Besides selling papers, of course, lots and lots of papers, to turn up the heat and get public officials, like you, all of you, to do your god damn jobs? Make it more uncomfortable not to than to do it?"

"You don't want Dolan turning his attention to you. You really don't."

"Geez, can't I count on you to protect me? Protect and Serve, right?"

"That's LAPD," he said dryly.

"And your motto here in Beverly Hills is what, Kiss Ass and Dress Well? Are you working for him or the city? You know, I was almost willing to believe your story about the department and the mayor, and even Salter, wanting to show him some consideration, to keep the investigation circumspect, given the 'delicacy' of his position, and theirs, but this is different. You're either protecting him at Marty's expense, or just too comfortable and lazy to do your job and rock a few boats. Either way, I don't care. Let's see which way the mayor and Salter jump when the pan starts getting hot."

His face had grown dark, and his eyes bored into me, but surprisingly, he didn't either contradict or argue with me. I got up to go.

"You take care of this one," I said pointing to the check. "Maybe Dolan will reimburse you."

I wished Vann were still around. I missed her. But more to the immediate point, I would have liked her take on Phillips. Much as I hated to think he'd gotten himself entangled with Dolan, much as it seemed to make sense, I couldn't quite bring myself to sell him that short. Vann would have a better read on it. On him. I was sitting in the rental car outside Il Fornaio. I could see him at the table, still poking at his lunch, occasionally muttering to himself, swearing, from the look of it. I don't think he noticed me there. He was too pre-occupied. He quit eating and sat for another three or four minutes, just staring into space, thinking. He snapped out of it, getting to his feet, suddenly energized and committed to some new plan, or at the least, seemingly happy about the direction his thoughts had taken him. He was all smiles. It looked like he even paid in cash, throwing a bunch of bills on the table and heading for the door. He crossed the street, going east on Dayton, probably to Rexford and back to City Hall and the police station. That could be back to his office, to the mayor's office or Salter's, or maybe even Dolan's. I was going to get out of the car, feed the meter, and follow him on foot. But the problem was, once he entered the building, I'd have no idea where he'd gone anyway, so that was pointless. With nothing better to do, and no real plan of my own, I decided to give him a head start and then follow in the rental. I opened the file folder Vann had put together and Miriam McDermott's name jumped out at me. I had a lot of questions for her. She had to be next, I thought. I'd given Phillip's enough time. I closed the folder. I started the car, pulled to the corner and caught the light. I turned left when I got to Rexford and when I got a little past Burton Way, I could see him heading for the police parking lot, not the building. I pulled to the curb and watched as he drove out of the lot, heading east on Civic Center. I followed at a safe distance. When he turned right onto Oakhurst, I slowed, letting him get a little farther down the street before I entered it. I parked in front of Shelly and Norma's place. He was getting out of his car in front of the project at Rathbone's, where construction had apparently been allowed to resume. I couldn't see it, but I could hear the diesel drone of the backhoe. Victor Osaka and John Dolan met him at the sidewalk. Dolan's Limo was parked at the curb, and the driver, a burly guy that even from the top of the block looked like a former linebacker, his thick arms and chest bulging beneath the black material of his suit or uniform, stood a respectful distance away. It looked like Phillips was talking more to Victor than Dolan. The driver stood statue-like, occasionally shifting his weight from one foot to the other, inert, but inert like a coiled spring. He wore sunglasses, had short hair, and if Dolan had been running for President instead of mayor, I would have taken him for Secret Service. Victor smiled, nodding repeatedly, apparently relieved by whatever Phillips was telling him. Dolan, not. Phillips reached into his inside pocket and took what I guessed must have been the copies of Kenny Lester's and Maurice's confessions. He showed them to Victor and Dolan. He and Victor shook hands. It appeared Iyama's last days would be untroubled by any of this. Phillips must have concluded that Iyama wouldn't tell him anything beyond his confession anyway, which, because of the others, rendered it meaningless. Victor went back onto the job site, out of view. Dolan stayed to talk to Phillips. Phillips must have been making it clear to Dolan that the multiple confessions would have simplified things, and he might have been able to close the investigation, if it weren't for me. That I was complicating things. Watching them, I was pretty sure Phillips was well aware of whatever Dolan had had for breakfast and lunch, since he was sending wave after wave of angry, close-up and in your-face breath washing over him. Dolan crowded Phillips, leaning his bulk into him, his fists clenched, his face red, the words not clear, but the sound of them reaching me all the way up the block. If Phillips hadn't been a cop, in his anger and rage, Dolan looked like he would have beaten him to a pulp. I wandered down the block. Dolan was still yelling at Phillips when I got close enough for them to notice me.

"Trouble in River City?" I asked.

They both looked at me like I'd materialized out of thin air. The burly guy let his arms drop to his sides.

"Christ," Phillips said.

Just when things were going so well, I thought, smiling at him.

"What do you want?" Dolan said, turning his attention, his wrath, towards me.

Ham, maybe sausage, coffee, grapefruit juice and possibly a croissant, was my guess.

"A fair question," I said. "How about the truth?"

"Whose truth? Yours? Don't make me laugh. I don't think you give a flying fuck about your brother or his somewhat questionable reputation. I've looked into him. Into you. I think I had you pegged from the very first moment. You want to twist me around for some money. You're a two-bit builder with too little construction money to complete your projects. You bite off more than you can chew, then scratch around to find enough money to finish. It looks like that's your story, one under-funded project after another. I know guys like you, you're no mystery to me. Now you're looking to twist me around for enough scratch to bail your sorry ass out of whatever current trouble you're in. Plain and simple. And your sainted brother was just another Hebe shyster who pulled the cord on himself when it looked like he was cornered about some bogus deal he concocted. Phillips here's got his number. Beats the crap out of some guy, gets the records sealed 'cause of his age. He's as good a candidate for Doyle's death as anyone."

"If you'd really looked into Marty's life, or his death, you'd know that's a load of shit. How about we let this Evan Morris guy just sort of run with the whole thing?"

"What'n the hell 're you talking about?" he said to me, drawing back slightly. He turned to Phillips, "What's he talking about."

Apparently, Phillips hadn't gotten that far.

"The reporter for..." Phillips began.

"I know who he is, what the hell is he saying?"

Before Phillips could find the words that would ease Dolan's alarm, I jumped in.

"I think it's time to air the whole thing out. Let this guy Morris do his thing and get to the bottom of it. I don't have anything to hide and neither does my brother."

Not exactly true, but close enough. Enough to shake him up. His face went from alarm to calculation to resolve in quick succession. If looks could kill. I hadn't seen anything like this in anyone's eyes since I'd helped send Marty's law partner, John Mason, and the studio head, Faustini, to jail for their attempts to kill Marty. Dolan turned to Phillips.

"Take a hike."

"Beg your pardon?" Phillips said, like he couldn't have heard him right.

"I said, take a hike."

"Hold on, partner," Phillips protested, "I'm not taking that kind of crap from you or anyone..."

"Councilman," Dolan reminded him, softening it with the kind of smile a serial killer must, when he's charming and lulling a victim. Or someone running for office. "Sorry, Detective. Forgive me."

He put his thick paw on Phillips shoulder in a gesture of goodwill.

"Would you leave me and Mr. Goldman to discuss some City business? I'm going to put on my hat as a councilman, and would appreciate your understanding. And absence, for a little privacy."

Phillips wasn't particularly mollified, but didn't seem to want to antagonize Dolan further. He stood there with his hands on his hips, looking at me and Dolan. He seemed to conclude that whatever it was Dolan had in mind, I had coming.

"Don't be a stranger," he smiled to me. I'll be back in my office in an hour if you're lookin' for me or your return ticket."

He got in his car and started it. Victor joined us just as Phillips pulled away.

"Hello again," he said to me. Then to Dolan, "They'll be done with the drainage Saturday and we can start drilling the piers Monday." he told Dolan. "Don't worry, we'll get back on schedule in two or three weeks."

"Good," Dolan said. "I'm counting on you to keep this moving. I've got too goddamn much on my plate, with the election and all."

He shot me a look. I figured I was the 'and all'. Victor shook hands with me and wished me well, his expression, I imagined, meant he might not see me again. He got in his car and took off. Dolan watched him go. With his back to me I could see what looked like a cow-lick at the back of his head. His hair was slicked back uniformly until it was forced to make a detour around the fat scar. I wasn't sure if he connected me to that or not. It didn't seem like the best time to ask and remind him. There was no one out and about and the hum of the backhoe was the only sound on the block. With his back still to me, watching as Victor's car turned west on Beverly Boulevard, there was the slightest nod of his head as he said, "Don't call Morris."

Dolan turned towards me as I was about to reply, only before I could, the burly guy hit me so hard in the face that the words that had gotten as far as my lips just evaporated into the blackness that overwhelmed me. As the darkness began to lift, I had this dizzy, exhausted feeling like I'd been drugged. The pale blue sky filtered through the jacaranda leaves came and went as I struggled to keep my eyes open. Just when I thought I'd succeeded, Dolan's face replaced the sky and leaves. He had a hard time grabbing my hair to lift my head off the grass because I kept my hair cut pretty short when I was building - it made it easier to wash out saw dust or concrete splatter - but he managed. With his face close to mine, his breakfast and lunch still in evidence, he clarified his position.

"I got lots of people, like Doug here, to take care of scrawny-little-piece-of-crap problems like you, but this time's a little different. Don't fuck with me. Hear? You let this go away, you go away, or I'll see to it you do. And don't think Phillips is going to be of any help. He's not. You got crazy and attacked me, and Doug stepped in. End of story. Unless you can get my knuckle prints off your face, you got no proof. None. Besides, Phillips knows better than to fool with me."

I wasn't going to ask him about it, but I was wondering why he'd said his knuckle prints, when he should have said Doug's.

"This one's for J.T.," he said, and hit me in the face himself.

I don't know how long I was out, but the next thing I knew, the back-hoe operator was kneeling next to me on the parkway.

"You okay? Hey, man, wake up. You okay?"

The sky and jacaranda leaves flickered in and out again, then returned to stay when I was able to keep my eyes open. The guy was a skinny, wiry type with bad teeth and an L.A. Dodger's baseball cap. He tried to help me sit up, but I couldn't manage it, so he dragged and I tried to help, and we got me to the base of the jacaranda tree a couple of feet away.

"Man, what happened? How long you been here? "

"What time is it?" I mumbled through a fat mouth, thinking, what month, as long as I'm asking.

"Quarter after five. I just shut down over there," he said, motioning to the Rathbone project, "and came out to my truck and here you were. What happened? You get mugged or somethin'?"

"Somethin'," I said.

"You need any help? Need a ride somewhere?"

"No thanks. I'll be okay."

"You should call the cops. Man, this ain't right."

"Kurt? Kurt Goldman? Is that you?"

I tried to shift around to see her. My vision was blurry and I was having trouble keeping my eyes open, but concluded it was Joanne Stuckey. I waved. Motioned, anyway. She put down a bag of groceries on the sidewalk at her feet and ran across the street.

"My god! What happened?" she said, kneeling next to me.

I was about to explain, but my body seemed to think a little snooze was a higher priority, because I passed out. When I woke, I was on the couch in her living room below the big window that faced the street. It was dark outside. I could hear lowered voices from the direction of the dining room table. I craned my neck and could see Joanne, her kids and husband at the table. Another woman sat facing them with her back to me. Joanne saw my eyes had opened.

"How are you feeling?"

"Okay," I mumbled, but even that much hurt to say.

The other woman turned around.

"I can't leave you alone for a minute, can I?"

It was Vann.

It was a little after nine as we were leaving. Being on my feet for all of five minutes was taking a toll. I felt woozy, and wanted to sit down, even if it was in the car. I thought I would be okay to drive the rental back to the Pacific Hotel if I got started pretty soon. I returned the original of Kenny's confession to Joanne.

"I'll treasure it," she said. "We all will. I've told them about it, not everything, but enough, to get them ready in case it becomes public. Whatever he was up to, they were up to, I'm so proud of him," she said, thanking me.

I told her it was unlikely to come to anything with Phillips, but he had a copy and knew it had come from her, in the unlikely event he wanted to pursue it.

"I wish we could have met again without all this," she said, her hands floating around without anything to grab hold of, sort of defining the whole mess. "I wish I could be of more help."

"You can," I said.

"I can? What?"

"Don't vote for Dolan."

"I don't know what I'm going to do about you." Vann said.

I didn't remember getting in the car, but we were driving somewhere, the powerful rumble of the Fury lulling me as I drifted in and out. I hadn't asked and didn't really care where. I was having trouble keeping my eyes open and my teeth hurt. Other parts of my face did too, but the teeth were making the most noise about it.

"Just don't hit me," I said, my eyes still closed.

"Funny."

I managed to get my eyes open, but it was an effort. She was examining me. I let them close again. Let might be an exaggeration.

"I think you should go to the emergency room. You might have a concussion."

"If I feel like this in the morning, yeah, maybe, but there's proabably not much they could do about it if I did. Right?"

"I suppose," she said.

We were heading west on Pico, a little past the Beverly Hills Country Club. We could be heading for her place or the Pacific Hotel. I was hoping for her place, but in my current shape, it probably didn't really matter. We drove in silence, her leaving me to snooze, and I could feel myself drifting in and out, but somewhere between them, the thought occurred, she'd come. In spite of everything, she'd come. That she always would. Before I passed out again, I remember hoping we were going to her place, no matter.

I don't know how she got me in, because I don't remember being able to help, but somehow Vann had gotten me up the stairs and through the living room to her bedroom. It was on the east side of the house, and the morning sun was streaming in so brightly, when I opened my eyes, it made my head ache. Or at least reminded me my head already ached and probably would for the foreseeable future. She'd gotten me undressed to my underwear and tucked into her bed. She was asleep next to me on my left, on top of the sheets and blanket, but under the bedspread. She cuddled against me, her left arm across my chest. Her breathing was regular and smooth, her sleep as peaceful and untroubled as a well-loved child's, interrupted occasionally by the slightest snore. The thoughts that usually came to me only in quiet times at night, alone, in the privacy of my head, were bouncing around in full force now. Next to Jason, my son, and my ex-wife, Jane, Vann was the best thing that had ever happened to me. If ever there was a chance to trust someone, it was she. But could I trust myself to be as good to her as she deserved? Could I inoculate her against the poison I carried like a virus, ready to infect anyone I let get too close? The fear and anger and rage, the helplessness, all of it, never more than the blink of an eye away, was woven into a shroud, wrapped tight around me, pinning my arms, muffling my screams, as I'm lowered, alive, into the ground, believing someone will come. But they don't. I wait and wait and they don't. Not my mom or dad, not Marty or Pop. Not George Bowen or Kenny Lester. Not Maurice or Miriam. Was it her face in the window, or did I imagine it? No matter. No one came. I clawed my way out like a trapped animal determined to live, determined to have my life. Changed, but still mine. Max promised me we'd get away. He calmed me. Made me stop screaming, even though, for the most part, it wasn't out loud. He said he couldn't think with all the noise. The trick was not to expect help. Assume there won't be, there can't be, there never will be. Do what you can by yourself. Whatever it takes, promise yourself you won't wait for someone to help, to come for you, because they won't, they can't, they don't even know where you are. You're alone. That much as some of them might want to, they won't come they can't come there's no time no chance no way no anything you can expect, you just have to do what you can. I know I have to do it myself. I promise myself, I promise Max or he promises me, one of us will kill Kevin Doyle. I'll chew off my foot to escape. I'll do what I have to do. I did what I had to do. It's a poisonous brew, but it serves me. I just don't want it spill over onto anyone else. Not Jason, not Jane, not Vann. Same problem, same conclusion, except I had to admit, given every reason not to, Vann came, and I had to believe, always would. Sort of makes a fellow think. Which is what I'd been doing, watching her for the ten or twelve minutes before her eyes fluttered open. She smiled, a little sheepishly.

"I could have taken advantage of you last night."

"Then you're a better man than I, Gunga-Din."

"How do you feel?"

"Okay," I said.

She gave me a skeptical look.

"Really?"

"My head feels like someone's standing on it and my teeth hurt. Other than that, I'm fine."

"Let's make coffee here," she said. "If you're up to it, we can take a stroll on the beach. You can take it easy today. Why don't you get in the shower, and I'll walk up to the bakery on Ocean. What would you like?"

It was a little after seven and I could hear the coffee at Il Fornaio calling. On the other hand, not only had she come, but I didn't have the rental and it was clear she wasn't going to fire up the Fury so I could have my way. Ever gracious in defeat.

"If they have anything that looks like the homemade breads and jam at Il Fornaio; if not, a couple croissants or a Brioche."

She leaned across and gave me a gentle little kiss on the lips.

"That was easier than than I thought it would be," she chirped.

"Only because I couldn't find the keys to the Fury before you woke up," I said.

Her smile faded, like a kid going from happy to uncertain.

"Really?"

"No, I was kidding."

Her face tightened and she started to get up off the bed, if not mad, definitely miffed. I grabbed her wrist. I pulled her closer to me. She resisted, definitely mad, not miffed, with a look like I'd blown her good-will all to hell for the last time. Again. Well, maybe just the second to the last. Again. And for nothing. Her face was close, her eyes searching mine for some reason to be here with me, other than the inconvenient fact it was her place. I thought about the poison. Keeping it away from her. Keeping me away from her. About her sweetness.

"Vann..."

"What."

She was still annoyed, still pulling away, but only half-heartedly.

"Thank you for last night. For coming. I know you didn't have to and probably think now you shouldn't have. But thank you anyway. It means a lot to me."

She quit pulling altogether. She was shaking her head, warning herself she was heading for trouble, but going willingly. She kissed me again, gently, making allowances for the aching, puffy side of my face and mouth.

"One of these days you're going to get it right. Whatever the demons are, you're going to get free of them or past them or whatever, and I want to be there. I love you," she said.

A few minutes after eight we were sitting in the sand above the high water mark, drinking the coffee and eating warm, soft Brioche, little rollers coming in off a mostly flat steel blue-green sea. The coffee was only a little better than so-so, but it was hot and the Brioche was good. The bright sun made my head hurt and my teeth ache, but I managed the food. I filled Vann in on the multiple confessions, Phillips', Dolan's and Victor's reactions, and of course, my new friend, Doug. She listened.

"What's Dolan afraid of? What could be serious enough for him to risk the election by having his thug pound you?"

"And taking a shot or two himself," I reminded her.

"That too. I'd like to call Ron."

She looked at me for consent. I thought about it, but didn't say anything. I shrugged. On the one hand, I didn't want to bother him with this, particularly after he'd helped so much before, but more importantly, I wanted to keep the investigating and poking around as limited as possible. On the other, if Dolan had a small army of Doug's, I could use his help. Ron and his crew, Vann included, had saved me more than once when my looking into Marty's death put me in the cross-hairs.

"If Dolan and his gang are getting physical, or willing to do even worse, I'd feel better if he was involved."

"I'm not quite there yet, but the idea is gaining appeal. Let's wait until the next phase of my little investigation has played itself out."

"And what might that be?"

"When you found Miriam, did you call her? Did you speak with her?"

"Yes. Both."

"What did you tell her?"

"Not much. I said I was doing chain-of-title searches on properties on Oakhurst, and her name came up. Was she the same Miriam McDermott?"

"And?"

"She is."

"She didn't want to know more about who you were or what you were looking for?"

"She asked."

"Did you mention me?"

"No, I didn't have to. She said she's briefly taken title for a friend, then transfered it back. I let it go at that and thanked her. That's where we left it."

"Perfect."

"Why?"

"She's next. I want to see her. Talk to her. But I'd like it to be a surprise."

"As in a nice little surprise, or heart-attack-surprise? How old is she?"

"She must be close to seventy."

"You're going to just show up?"

"That's the plan. I don't want her to have too long to think about it, just answer a few questions as they're asked."

"You think she will? It sounds more like the third degree than a reminiscense of old times. What is it that you think she knows?"

Back to square one again and we both knew it. I listened to the water wooshing over the sand as the waves came in, paused, then slid back. I thought it about it a little too long, so I don't think she had particularly high expectations for me to do much better than I'd managed up to that point. Maybe I surprised her. Maybe I surprised myself.

"Why don't you come with me and we'll find out together?"

We landed in Oakland at ten the same morning. We'd picked up the rental from Oakhurst, I dropped it off at the Burbank Airport, and Vann put the Fury in the long term lot in case we stayed in Berkeley overnight or longer. The idea of never going back crossed my mind.

"What's this? It's cute," Vann said, as we approached my car in the Oakland Long Term Parking lot.

"The much maligned and ridiculed Pontiac Fiero V-6. An interesting idea that was nicely executed in most ways, except for the never-ending little built-in problems that drive you nuts," I told her.

"But you like it?"

"I've had a love-hate relationship with it since the day I got it. I think I've stuck with it long enough to have worked out most of the problems, so more love than hate these days. You see a lot of them on used car lots. The faint of heart," I said.

"But not you, of course?"

"No, not me. We're a match made in heaven."

"It's a test of wills," she said.

"Exactly. Except I don't look at it like it's me against the car. The car and I are on the same side. I'm liberating it. It's me and the car against the morons that undermined what it was supposed to be. What it was meant to be. When we get there, we'll get there together, and it will be a thing of beauty. A sight to behold."

"Sort of like me and you?" she teased. Sort of.

"Exactly," I said. "Anyway, it may not be the Fury, but it is a muscle car. Powerful and fun to drive. And I bet it handles a lot better."

"That depends on who's driving, buster, you or me. You didn't sell the truck, did you?"

"Never. Want to drive? My head still hurts."

"You're on."

We got in.

"Buckle up," she smiled.

It was going to be a warm day, not Southern California warm, but for up here, anything in the eighties or above was considered hot. It was clear, the air fresh, definitely not L.A. I pointed that out to Vann.

"Air you can breathe. Pretty nice, eh?"

"It's beautiful," she agreed, avoiding our old argument about where we might locate when there was a we to be considered.

She was zipping along the 880, keeping the speed down to seventy, which by L.A. standards was keeping it way down. We went through the Bay Bridge-880-580 maze heading west on 580 towards Berkeley and the San Raphael Bridge. Traffic was thick, but moving well. When we got a little past Ashby, my eyes locked on the Campanile, the Berkeley Hills, at least my part of the Berkeley Hills, the Panoramic Hill. I'd wanted Jason to be my main helper on the new project. He had other ideas. I might have forced him, assuming it would be a good time to teach him something that was both creative and financially productive. He was no longer thinking about college. His heart was into music to the exclusion of everything else. Since he didn't buy my notion that there was nothing wrong with being an educated musician, I thought teaching him to build might give him a way to make a living while he tried to make a go of his music. He's wonderfully talented, but in that business, that's never enough. I was wondering if I'd done him any favors by not insisting, or just taken the path of least resistance for myself. After Marty's death, the idea of pressing anyone about anything became unbearable. A part of the reason Vann was in L.A., me up here. Only a small part, I had to admit, but a part. Before, I would have pressed and pressed, until I forced things to be the way I wanted, willing to run the risk of breaking whatever it was I was pressing on. After, I was afraid to. You never know where someone's breaking point is. I was simultaneously both guilty and relieved I hadn't forced him. He was a strong sweet guy, and he'd find his own way. It hurt to think about what a difficult and frustrating path he'd chosen for himself and how young he was to choose it, since it might dictate the course of his whole life. On the other hand, therein lies the beauty and mystery and excitement. There was no protecting Marty, not really, so I suppose it was illusory to think I could protect Jason. On the other hand, there was nothing wrong with making sure he had the tools to succeed. And he did. Does. Maybe not college, or a trade, but drive and stubbornness. All things considered, the best I could pass on. The talent was his own.

"Homesick?"

"A little. I was thinking about Jason. He's helping me part time on my current project."

"How's that?"

I shrugged. "He's not very interested in anything but music, but he's willing to work hard."

"Well, that's something."

"Right now, that's everything."

"Are you going to stop and see him?"

"If we stay over tonight, yes. Otherwise, I call to say hello, and see him when I get back."

We went through the toll plaza. Vann seemed content to feel out the Fiero and leave me to my thoughts. For the most part, I was trying not to have any beyond it was a beautiful day, Vann was with me, and Jason and Jane were both fine. My thoughts about them were never completely without regrets, never without the realization that the poison seeps and spreads and washes over the innocent and wicked alike. The best I could do was love them and help them whenever and however I could. For the wicked, it was another story.

I directed Vann to the overpass off 580 towards Larkspur Landing and 101 South. She pressed the little car through the long curve, then past the back side of San Quentin, caught both lights, and blew by a stream of cars under the old railway trestle and at the last possible second merged onto the ramp for traffic heading south towards the City. Once on the 101, she immediately moved to the fast lane and started to sprint to who-knows-where. She was having fun blasting along in the little car and I was sorry to reign her in, pointing to the sign for the Tamalpais exit. She cut across a few lanes and approached the stop light at the bottom of the exit. If we'd been in L. A., horns would have been blaring at her cavalier ways. On the other hand, in L.A. they wouldn't have been unusual or cavalier.

"Which way?"

"Right."

We drove along Tamalpais, until at the east end it became Redwood Avenue.

"Stay on Redwood across Corte Madera and pull over up there," I told her.

I'd drawn a map of the maze of streets leading to Miriam's place on Summit Drive. My teeth still ached and the side of my face felt a few sizes too big for the skin covering it, but I thought I'd drive the rest of the way. Vann thought otherwise.

"You don't look so good," she said, apparently trying to flatter me, "just give me the map and I'll figure it out."

Her hand was outstretched, waiting. I would have argued, but the bright sun was making my head hurt more, and the desire to close my eyes for a while suddenly seemed irresistible. I handed her the map.

"I want you to know I know you know I know you're bullying me."

I barely got the words out when my eyes closed on their own. I think she said right as I drifted off. I tried to keep my eyes open, but they wouldn't cooperate. They'd open for a few seconds, then close. The ride up the hill seemed to take a long time. I caught glimpses of street signs for Redwood Avenue, Edison, Morningside, Sunrise, and Marina Vista. Vann was muttering to herself, annoyed at not finding Summit, but enjoying whipping the car around the sharp hillside curves.

"Taking the long-cut?" I asked her.

"Go back to sleep. I'll find it," she said.

"Miriam's pretty old," I warned her. "We gotta get there before she croaks."

We were headed back down the hill on Crescent Road, which didn't seem like a good sign. I was about to point that out, when my eyes closed again.

The next thing I knew Vann was parked next to an aging, rusting Carmen Ghia, getting out of the Fiero on a parking structure next to the house at 57 Summit.

"You found it," I complimented her. "And it's not dark yet."

"Are you okay? I don't think you're up to this. You should see a doctor, Kurt. You haven't been able to stay awake for more than fifteen minutes."

"No reflection on the company," I told her.

"Thanks, but I'm serious. I'm worried."

"Let's do this and maybe I'll see someone in Berkeley. Do you mind if we stay overnight?"

"No, that's fine. I'd love to see Jason."

"Good. Let's go see Miriam, then see about a doctor if I'm still feeling lousy."

The house overlooked Corte Madera, Larkspur, Sausalito and a nice Marin perspective of the San Raphael Bridge. It was a little more than half way up on one of the smaller hills south and east of Mount Tamalpais, patches of Redwood trees scattered here and there, not in numbers great enough to suggest the forest that once covered them, or even the remnants of it, but more like survivors of some distant devastation, having snuck over here to hide among these out-of-the-way houses, hoping to be left alone. Her house was perched on the downside of the hill, close to the narrow road, distressed looking, but not ready to fall down any time soon. It must have started out as one of those little cottages built in the twenties and thirties, owned by San Franciscans who wanted to exchange the summer fog there for the warmer days here in Marin, only it had been added onto in an eclectic way, the dominant theme being the half-timbering and stucco and slate roofing of a Swiss mountain chalet. Dormers popped out of the roof for no apparent reason, cantilevered out over the previously existing roof with enough ginger-bread detail to make them interesting, in spite of their awkwardness. It occurred to me, even back in the fifties, this would have been expensive. I wondered if Miriam had been renting it all these years or had bought it. There were about ten or twelve steps down from the parking structure to the door. I wasn't sure I could manage them. The more or less constant headache I'd been having hurt, but worse, I couldn't keep my eyes open when it came. I paused at the top, Vann watching me. She looked worried, and I smiled and was going to say something to reassure her, but before I could, I passed out again.

I woke up in Marin General Hospital. Vann was sitting in a chair next to me, listening to her little tape recorder, one hand across her mouth, her knees drawn up to her chest, her other arm wrapped around them. It was dark outside and she was crying.

"What happened?" I asked her.

Her eyes fluttered and she wiped away the tears and shut off the recorder. Her smile was suddenly radiant. Tear filled, but radiant.

"What's the matter? I didn't die, did I?"

She put the recorder in her bag on the night stand next to the bed and lay down next to me, snuggling close, her arm across my chest. She gently turned my face towards hers, and ever so gently kissed my lips.

"No. You've got a concussion," she said, "a bad one. They scanned you last night for any blood clots. There weren't any," she said, smiling. "We were so worried. Waking up is a very good sign."

"Considering the alternative, I'd say so. What we?"

"Jason and Jane were here last night for a few hours. They'll be back later this morning."

While I was digesting that, Miriam came to mind.

"What happened with Miriam?"

"After you passed out, she helped me get you back in the car and led me down the hill to the hospital."

"So much for surprising her."

"Oh, she was surprised alright, but we can talk about that later. You've got to get some rest."

"Did you talk with her?"

"Just rest, Kurt."

"No! Tell me, did you talk with her? Did you tell her I had some questions I wanted answered?"

Vann pushed herself up onto one elbow, resting her head on her hand and stroked my forehead and face with the other.

"She doesn't want to talk to you. She won't."

"God damn it! God damn her! Why not?"

Vann continued to stroke my face. Her eyes began to tear. She kissed my forehead.

"She spoke with me. She let me record it, but she won't see you. She said she can't. She said she's sorry, but what's past is past. Whatever you did, you had to do."

Vann began to cry, burying her face next to mine, hugging me to her.

# Chapter 28

### *Summertime On The Wings of The Red Rider*
### Monday, June 18 to August 2, 1951

IT WAS THE FIRST REAL day of summer vacation and Sarah and the Oakhurst Irregulars were going to the Stars game at one. I wasn't invited, but I couldn't have gone anyway since Ron had said he'd drop the papers on the parkway then. I practiced until my thumbs started cramping, but I wasn't getting much better than that first paper. At that rate, I'd be lucky to get them all folded by six, let alone delivered. When Marty got home from the gas station that night, he laid out the best way to go. He drew a map of all the streets in the neighborhood and used the list Ron had given us to mark deliveries. Pretty soon you could see a pattern. Marty figured out the best way so'd there be lots of houses taking the paper close together, so I could get rid of more papers, and the weight of them, sooner.

"Pretty smart," I told him. "I wouldn't have ever figured that out."

"Sure you would have, squirt," he joked me, "after about four or five days of carrying most of the load over most of the route. You'd have figured it out too."

He showed me the route should be sort of a crazy corkscrew. I'd go all the way down Oakhurst to Burton Way, and zig-zag back and forth on each side of it, first on Weatherly, then Doheny, Oakhurst, Palm, Maple, Rexford, Elm and Crescent. By the time I'd done that I'd be down to twelve papers, and work my way back up to our side of Burton Way, then back and forth between our side of Beverly Boulevard and Lower Santa Monica on Crescent, Elm, Maple, Palm, then Oakhurst and home. On the map, it looked pretty easy.

I was sitting on our front steps. It was about eight o'clock and I wasn't sure what to do. I wanted to be here the minute Ron dropped the papers off so I could start folding them right away. I started thinking, what if I couldn't fold them right? What if they flew apart as soon as I threw them? What if it took me so long to fold them there wasn't any time left to deliver them before six and everyone on the route complained and I had to pay for them? What if I got a flat tire? Geez, I hadn't thought of that before. I'd be dead! What do you do if you get a flat? I wished I'd asked Bill about that, but now it was too late. Or too early, depending on how you looked at it. Either way, that would be a disaster. Then I thought maybe I should take a ride over to Bill's Bike Shop right now so that the minute it opened I could ask him what to do if I got a flat. That seemed like a pretty good idea. The only trouble with that plan was, what if riding back and forth to the bike shop got me too tired to do the route?

Man oh man, how did everything get so complicated? Since I still had five hours to go, maybe I could ride to the bike shop and have enough time to rest up before the route. But the longer I sat here thinking about it, the less time I'd have for that to work. Maybe I should just think of something else to do besides think of things that could go wrong. But once it got started, it just took over, and every thought I had was a new way for trouble to ruin me. I had to think about something else or I'd go crazy. I tried to think about what everyone else was doing. My mom and dad and Nick had left at seven-thirty to go downtown. Marty had left on his bike about seven forty-five to get to the Standard Station by eight. Sarah was in the house on the phone organizing everybody for the game. I pictured them all doing what they were doing. That helped until I noticed I had the map Marty had made and the list Ron had given me on the step right next to me. I didn't want to look, but I couldn't help it, hoping Kevin Doyle wasn't on it, but he was. The way the route was laid out, he'd be the very last delivery, so if I was the least bit late, he'd probably be the guy to complain. On the other hand, I'd be rid of all the other papers by then, so I could throw his and go like heck before he could say or do anything crazy.

"Today the big day?" George asked me, coming up our walkway. He was wearing his usual army pants and a white t-shirt and hard black shoes.

"Uh huh," I said, like everything was under control.

"You all set? Need any help with anything?"

"Nope."

"I was thinking, since the Times is a morning paper and lots of things happen during the day, maybe I should subscribe to the Mirror too and have an afternoon paper. Rathbone and Avery were thinking the same thing. What d'ya think?"

"Yeah, sure," I said, really not so sure.

It was nice of them to want to help me, but I was thinking, just what I need, more papers when I'm not sure I can even lift the thirty-five I've already got. And as much as I didn't want to disappoint George and Rathbone and Mr. Avery, or Sharon and Julie or Norma, man oh man, I'm not Superman.

"You don't look so sure," George said, blowing a cloud of smoke from his cigarette towards the street, away from me.

"I'm not sure I can lift the papers I've already got, George."

I wasn't complaining, not really, just telling the truth.

"Well, in that case, waiting might make more sense," he said. "Let's wait and see. Once you get used to it, you let me know when you're ready to add some more deliveries."

I showed him the route the way Marty had laid it out to change the subject before anything could slip out by accident.

"See? Marty figured this out for me. It gets rid of lots of paper quicker so I don't have to ride around with them for too long."

"That looks good," he said. Then he said, "You know what?"

"What?"

"I just thought of this. What if you got your papers ready and before you even got on your bicycle, you just walk on over to my place and Avery's and toss the paper? You could have the extra subscriptions and not have to worry about carrying the extra weight. You think that might work?"

"It might. Yeah, that's a great idea! I could just run up the block a couple of houses and just like that, they'd be done."

"Well, it's just an idea. After you get used to this, let me know."

"Thanks George."

"Anything else worrying you?"

"Well...."

"What?"

"Kevin Doyle's on the route."

George didn't say anything. He smoked the cigarette down almost to his fingers, put the butt out against the bottom of his shoe, then put it in his pocket.

"If you left a paper for me before you ride off, I could take it over there for you."

I thought about it. Suddenly everything felt okay and I wanted to say yes yes yes, and I almost did, but then I thought about Pop and my dad and it seemed like just another part of taking care of the locks and doing what I said I'd do, even if I didn't want to and was afraid of being anywhere around Kevin Doyle. I felt trapped into saying no, even when yes was all I could hear in my head.

"No thanks, George. I guess it'll be okay."

"Are you sure?"

"Yeah....I guess."

"If you need any help getting started, come get me. I'll be around."

"Thanks. I will."

George went back to his place and I sat on the step a while more. Almost as soon as he was gone, my brain started bugging me about all the things that could go wrong, and on top of that, now I was thinking about Kevin Doyle. What the heck, I thought, I couldn't sit here all day just waiting for Ron to drop off the papers. If I did, I'd go nuts for sure. I'd go to the bike shop and find out about flats and just figure on resting enough before the route, maybe take a snooze in the bamboo patch. That sounded like a good plan. I got the Red Rider out of the garage and took off. Before I even got to Lower Santa Monica, the magic of it wiped out everything else. I was free as a bird, like they say, and no one could take that away.

Near the top of the block, Kenny Lester had the Buick running at the curb. The driver's door was open but he wasn't in it. As I passed, he called to me as he came down his stairs. I stopped next to his car.

"Kurt, where're you off to so early?"

"Bill's Bike Shop. I gotta find out what to do when you get a flat. I forgot to ask."

"You get it fixed," he laughed.

"But how?"

"You take it to the bike shop. It's pretty hard to do it yourself."

"So, if you get a flat, you're just stuck there? Maybe in the middle of nowhere?"

"No. Usually a nail or some glass will puncture the tire and it'll lose air slowly, not all at once. If you check it every time you go for a ride, or at least pretty often, and it seems a little soft, you just go to the gas station and put more air in until you can take it to get fixed."

"How much air is it supposed to have?"

He put his briefcase on the seat of the Buick and put the Red Rider on the kickstand. He knelt down and rotated the front tire until he could read what he wanted.

"See here," he showed me. "50-65 psi?"

"Yeah. So what's that mean?"

"It means these tires should have between fifty and sixty-five pounds of air pressure. You know the air hoses they have at the gas stations, right next to the water hoses for the radiator?"

"Yeah, I guess..."

"Well, you take this cap off the stem and there's a little valve in there. See?"

I took a look. He pushed it with his fingernail and let some air escape.

"See?"

"Yeah, that's neat."

"Well, you push the air hose over the valve there, and hold it on tight and push the handle and air goes into the tire. If you stop putting new air in but keep the hose on the stem real tight, a little thing pops out of the top of the air hose. It has numbers on it, so when you get above fifty but less than sixty-five, you're done. If you put in too much, you take some out like we just did. If it's not up to fifty, you add some more. You can practice when you're at the carwash. Or maybe you could go up to the Standard Station where you're brother works and he could help you."

"You just saved me a trip to Bill's. Thanks, Kenny."

"Just you be careful about parked cars and driveways, okay?"

"Okay."

He got in the Buick and headed up the street to the top of the block and turned right on Lower Santa Monica, heading towards Doheny. Since he'd let a little air out of the tire, I thought I'd better go to the carwash and put some back.

Joseph's Hot Dog Stand was open and there were a couple of guys on the stools at the counter. I pulled up to the gas pump islands and put the Red Rider on the kickstand and found the air hose Kenny was talking about. I gave the handle a couple of squeezes to make sure I had the right one. If I filled the tires with water, that could really be bad. It was the air hose, alright, and boy, I thought, if you had one of these things at the beach, you could make a fortune blowing up rafts for people. I unscrewed the cap on the valve stem and put the hose over it. No matter which way I tried to push it on, air kept leaking out, so I squeezed the handle to try and put some back in but it just spilled out all around the stem. I don't think any got in. I tried again and the same thing happened. At this rate, I'd have a completely flat tire in no time. I gave the tire a squeeze. It still felt pretty hard, but if I didn't get some air in pretty soon I'd probably be the first kid in the world to make a flat tire out of a full one right at a gas station without a nail or glass anywhere in sight. I was about to try again when Joseph came over.

"Got to hold it on tighter," he said, "like this."

He held the hose onto the valve stem for me.

"You press for the air. Gettin' ready for the paper route?"

"Uh huh"

I pressed and the air went right in.

"Stop for a minute and let's see where we are."

When I quit pushing on the handle, the little thing with the numbers popped out.

"Whatcha got?"

I shifted around, trying to get a better look.

"Fifty and two lines," I told him.

"That's about fifty-four pounds. What's it supposed to be?"

"Kenny said fifty to sixty-five."

"Let's run it up to sixty. It'll ride a little faster. Give it another shot."

I gave it a long squeeze and stopped again. The thing was above sixty by one line. When I told him, Joseph said to bleed a little out. He took the hose away and I did what Kenny had done and let some air out. Joseph checked it and let me see. It was right on sixty.

"Wanna do the back?"

"Sure."

When we were done he went back behind the counter.

"Thanks, Joseph. See you Saturday."

"So long. Good luck with the route."

As I was leaving, Miss Rimes pulled into the station. She waved and called hello to me as I was riding off the lot. I waved back, but didn't stay to have hot chocolate with her since I figured she came to see Joseph. Besides, I didn't have any money. I thought about going to the Wonder Bread Factory to see Helen and maybe get some rolls or something to eat since I hadn't had breakfast, but it was getting close to nine and the boss guys would be around and that might spell trouble, so I didn't. I felt the tires and they were both hard as rocks and I still had four hours before Ron was supposed to drop off the papers and didn't know what to do so I wouldn't start thinking about things that might go wrong. Before I started to ride again, just to make sure it was there, I checked my pocket for the propeller medal Kenny had given me. I always took it with me no matter what. It was right there where it was supposed to be. I should have thought of that sooner. I could rub it for good luck and maybe quit worrying about all this stuff. I gave it a squeeze and rode off towards the little park with the fountain where Kenny had given it to me. It was sunny and getting warm, so I thought I'd go there and sit close enough for the spray to cool me off even though I wasn't that hot yet. When I got to the park there was a woman with a baby in a stroller already at the fountain, so instead of getting the spray, I laid the Red Rider down on the grass and sat at the base of a tree on the north side of the park, away from the fountain.

I fell asleep right there under the tree. When I woke up, the woman and baby in the stroller were gone and I had no idea what time it was, but it couldn't be past one. What if it was way past one and I'd slept a really long time? It was hot, like middle of the day hot, but I tried not to think about that, because there's no way I could have slept that long. That was impossible. I rode the Red Rider around by Carl's Market and over to Oakhurst on Lower Santa Monica, then started peddling fast down the block. Even from high up, near Kenny's house, I could see the parkway was empty. No papers at all. What a relief! I put the Red Rider on the kickstand and headed for the house to see what time it was. The screen door was closed but the front door behind it was wide open so I thought Sarah would still be here.

"Sarah?" I called.

No answer. That was bad. The Stars game was at one, so if she was gone, it had to be getting close to that. Or maybe she and the Oakhurst Irregulars had taken off early. The question was, how much early? I went through the living room and dinning room to the kitchen. The clock on the stove said one-o-five. That wasn't too bad, I thought. I wasn't too late. Then I realized it was after one and the papers weren't here. Where were the papers? How could I start folding them if they weren't here? At the rate I folded them, I'd need every possible minute. Why weren't they out on the parkway? Then I thought, what if Ron came by at exactly one and saw I wasn't here and didn't drop them off? Maybe he thought I wasn't responsible enough to be a paper boy if I wasn't here right exactly when the papers were dropped off? My stomach began to ache. Not like I was sick, just ache like I forgot to get dressed and went outside anyway. Why did I ever say yes to being a paper boy? This was going to drive me crazy

I went outside and sat on the curb, waiting just in case he was late. A Yellow Cab came down the block from Lower Santa Monica and stopped across the street. Miriam got out and paid the driver. She smiled when she saw me and waved and I waved back. I had that funny feeling again and it almost made me forget all about the papers and the paper route and everything else. It was hard to explain, even to myself, because she wasn't as young and pretty as Julie and Sharon, and she definitely wasn't as pretty as Norma, but the feeling came like a good stomach ache and that was that.

I waited and waited, but no Ron. George came out.

"No papers yet?" he asked.

I didn't want to tell him I'd probably missed Ron, so I just shook my head no, which was true and wasn't lying. I'd never lie to George, even if it seemed like a good idea at the time, which now when he asked me, it didn't. He sat with me there on the curb for awhile. When he finished a new cigarette he went back inside.

I was just about to give up, thinking about having to explain to everyone how I'd ruined the chance to pay off the locks faster. Just the thought made me feel like crying. How could I tell Kenny Lester and Pat Mahoney I didn't have the paper route because I fell asleep under a tree at the little park? How could I tell my dad and Pop when they stood up for me and said I could do it and I'd take care of it? I was thinking of lies I could tell to make it sound better, but I couldn't think of anything good, and besides, they might pretend to believe me, but they'd probably know I was lying, and then it would be even worse, because I'd be a liar and an irresponsible lock stealer. Just when I thought I should probably run away from home, Ron's truck came down the street. He pulled up to the curb and jumped out and grabbed a bundle of papers from the back and dropped them next to me on the parkway grass.

"Sorry I'm late kid," he said looking at his watch. "You better get started. Gotta run."

"What time is it?" I called to him.

"Three-fifteen," he said as he got back in the truck and took off.

Three-fifteen? How in the heck could I fold all the papers and deliver them by six? And besides, the stack of papers looked huge, much bigger than I imagined thirty-five of them could possibly look. All of a sudden, being irresponsible and not showing up and having him not drop off the papers didn't seem so bad. Looking at the papers, the whole thing seemed impossible. What if I didn't deliver the papers at all? I wondered what they would do to me. I bet if you added all the papers together they weighed more than I did. I went to the front porch and got the route bag and rubber bands from where I'd left them.

I knelt down in front of the stack of papers which was tied up with some scratchy looking rope going around in both directions. I tried to untie the knot, but it wouldn't come loose. I wondered if I was allowed to cut it. What if I wasn't and I did? I sat there worrying about that for way too long, because for all I knew it might be three-thirty already. Out of nowhere, there was a big clock inside my head, just ticking away, second by second, until it would be six o'clock and I'd be doomed. Heck, if I didn't figure out how to get the rope off pretty soon, I be so far behind before I even started folding, I wouldn't have any time to deliver them, once they were folded. I thought I should try at least one more time to untie the rope in case I was supposed to save it.

I'd give it to fifty. I tugged and pried and even tried with my teeth to get the knot loose, but it wouldn't budge. At fifty-five, I ran into the kitchen and got a big knife. I came back and put it on the parkway grass right there next to me, but still thought I shouldn't cut the rope. I got to fifty twice more and was thinking about giving it a third count. Actually, it would be the fourth, but...

"Want some help?" George said.

"I can't get it untied, and it's really late," I said.

"So, cut it," he said, nodding to the knife.

"I don't know if I'm I allowed to. What if I'm supposed to save the rope?"

"Well, I wouldn't have thought of that, but I'm pretty sure they tie it up like that so they can drop them off the truck onto the ground and not worry about the papers flying all over the place. I think they'll use new rope every day. That's my guess, anyway."

"Are you sure?"

"Pretty sure," he smiled.

I wasn't convinced he was right, but the longer I sat around worrying about it, the later it was getting so I picked up the knife.

"Here goes," I said.

I started sawing the knife back and forth across the rope but the knife was too dull and didn't cut past the first few threads. George took out his pocket knife.

"Here, let me help you."

He took one little swipe at it and there was a pop sound as the tight rope was cut in two. He cut the one in the other direction and the same thing happened, and there they were, all thirty-five papers waiting for me to fold them. I took the first one off the pile and hooked my thumbs the way Ron had and done it, first right, then left. It looked pretty good until I reached for the rubber band and it started to move around like it was alive. By the time I had the rubber band stretched big enough to go around it the way it had been, it wasn't that way anymore and it wouldn't go. It was like trying to get the Lester's puppies to do what you wanted. They just did what they felt like and that was that. George was watching me, which made me a little more nervous than I already was going to be if I was all by myself, but I was glad he was there because he came up with a great idea.

"I think you've got the folding part down just right. The problem's getting the rubber band on before it moves around, and your hands just aren't big enough. How 'bout like this?"

He put the cigarette in the corner of his mouth and squinted his eyes and tipped his head away from the smoke. He knelt down beside me and took a paper off the pile and folded just the way I had. Only when he had it right, he put it on the ground and put his knee over the end of it. His weight kept it folded tight while he had both hands to spread the rubber band big enough to go over the other end away from his knee. Just like that, he had one all ready.

"You give it a try," he said.

I didn't do it as fast as he did but it worked, and now we already had two folded.

"How about if I help you with the folding, since it's your first day?

Four hands are better than two."

"That would be great. Thanks George."

We worked side by side on the parkway until the stack of papers became a pile of folded ones. George probably did two papers every time I did one, but mine looked almost as good and tight as his did. The knee-trick was the answer to all my problems. I started standing the papers up in the route bag, but as soon as I put the first ones in, they tipped over and blocked the next ones or made them stand up too high so I knew they'd fall out when I was riding, so I had the idea to stand the bag next to Mumps, the jacaranda on our parkway, and let the first papers in the bag rest against the tree until there were enough in it so they held each other up.

"Nice," George said.

I kept putting papers in until I had seventeen in front and eighteen in back. The full bags were puffed out and looked huge. George was watching me and waiting to see how I was going to get the bags up and over my head. His guess was as good as mine, because I had no idea. I couldn't expect that he'd be around every day, so I needed to figure out how to do it alone. I think he was thinking the same thing because he just started smoking a new cigarette and kept watching me. I tried lifting the bags from the middle, at the neck hole. I got them off the ground but only about to my waist. I put them back down. George didn't say anything, but I could tell, he was thinking, well, that's not going to work. I kept thinking about it getting later and later while I was just standing there doing nothing. Finally, I moved the two sides of the bag as far apart as the middle cloth area with the neck hole would let them go. I got down on my stomach and crawled beneath the middle part, which was above the grass a little more than a foot, like a bridge between the two bags, and poked my head through the hole. I twisted around so the bags were front and back instead of side to side. I used the tree to help me stand up, lifting the bags as I went. When I'd made it to my knees, the bags were barely off the ground. When I was all the way up, they came more than half way down between my waist and knees, which would definitely be a problem once I got on the bike, but getting on was the next problem. At least the tree idea had worked. I was up and the bags were on me. George was nodding, but still didn't say anything. We both knew getting on the Red Rider with the bags might be worse than getting the bags on in the first place, before the bags-hanging-down-too-far problem could even be one.

"I've got a step stool I think will help. I'll go get it."

He didn't run, but he moved a lot faster than usual, probably because the weight of the bags was beginning to pull the neck hole over my shoulder and down my left arm. If it went much further, the weight would be too sideways and I'd either fall over, or the bag might slip over my right shoulder too, and then the whole thing would end up around my waist or back on the ground. George came back with a wooden stool with two steps, if you counted the top. He put it as close to the edge of the curb as he could. He moved the Red Rider into the street next to the stool and put it on the kickstand.

"See if you can go up the steps and swing a leg over the bike."

Before I could, the route bags made it over both shoulders and was headed for the ground.

"That won't do," he said, laughing.

I didn't think it was so funny, but in a way, I guess it was. I was standing in the neck hole like the bags had been on the ground the whole time and I'd just stepped into the middle of them. George shoved the cigarette to one side of his mouth and squinted the eye close to it almost shut. He lifted the bags over my shoulders and got them centered. Even when I was perfectly in the middle, the sides of the hole were trying to sneak over the edges of my shoulders again. George picked up a couple of the fallen purple jacaranda blossoms off the grass and used them to mark where the neck hole should be to fit me. He lifted it off and put it back on the ground.

"I think I've got just the thing to fix this," he said. "Come on back to the garage."

He carried the route bags and we walked down the path between his house and Mr. Avery's to the back door of his garage. There were work benches on the three walls that didn't have the big garage door to the alley. I'd never seen him drive a car, so I don't think he even had one, and I'd never seen him ride this, but there it was, a big motorcycle, right in the middle of the garage, up on a back-wheel stand. It was a deep shiny black with sparkling chrome on the fenders and spokes of the wheels and parts of the motor and the pipes going to the back. It looked brand new, but also, at the same time, looked old fashioned. The gas tank had a curved brass plate on both sides that said, Vincent, in raised up letters. On the chain guard, in dull silver letters, it said, Black Shadow, and over the back fender were two leather bags, one on each side like saddle bags on a horse.

"That's my Red Rider," he said, winking at me. "I wanted that almost as much as you wanted yours. I thought about it almost every day I was overseas, and almost every day since I got back. I was sure it would have been the first thing I'd buy when I got home, but I kept putting it off, waiting and waiting. I don't know why or what for, " he said. "I bought it at the beginning of this year."

He put out the cigarette against the bottom of his shoe again, put the butt in his pocket and started another one. I bet his pockets were full of them.

"Do you ever ride it?"

"I haven't much. Once in a while. And I kick it over from time to time to keep a little oil going through it," he said, "but it's pretty loud. Don't want to get the neighbors in an uproar."

"Does it go fast?"

"Like a bat out of hell, Kurt, like a bat out of hell," he said smiling, then added, "if you'll pardon the French."

"What French?"

"The expression....'bat out of hell'."

"Is that French?"

"Never mind. This is what we're looking for."

He took an old leather belt from a box under the back-wall work bench. Then he took some fat scissor-looking things off a hook on the wall and cut off two pieces about a foot long. There was the kind of sewing machine bolted down at one end of the work bench they had in shoe stores where you pushed a wheel and the needle went up and down. George emptied the papers out onto the floor and then, one at a time, sewed the two leather straps to the purple marks on one side of the neck hole where they'd pass over my shoulders half way to my neck. He had these rivet things that had little mushroom-like heads, and he attached them to the front side of the neck hole right across from the two straps. He put the bags over my head and tested to see where the straps should button over the rivet bumps. He marked it with his pocket knife and took the bags off me. He had another tool that looked like pliers, but really they were for punching holes in things. They had a bunch of different sized spokes on a wheel you could put in the place to do the punching, then you just punched. Two quick squeezes and the holes were done. George took his pocket knife and made little slits above and below each of the holes.

"That oughta make them go on and off pretty easy," he said, showing me how to push the holes over the mushroom bumps. "You try."

I put the empty bags over my head and buttoned the straps over my shoulders onto the rivet buttons. It was perfect.

"Let's fill it back up and see how it hangs," he said.

While I stood there he loaded the papers front and back until the bags were full again. It was pretty heavy and I was thinking it was a good thing I wasn't planning on walking the route because the bags hung down against my legs and the weight made waddling the best I could do, and when I did that, the bags started swaying back and forth sideways, pulling me with them, making the waddling worse.

"Even if you can get on the bike with the stool, I don't see how you can ride with the bags hanging that low."

I knew he was probably right, but I didn't want to give up on the thirty bucks a month before I even got off Oakhurst, so I didn't say anything.

"Well, let's give it a try."

I started to waddle across the garage to the back door.

"Let's take those off," he said.

He carried them back out to the curb. He kept a hand on the Red Rider so it wouldn't tip over while I was trying to get on from the stool. I got on okay, but the route bags did hang down too far. In back, they rested on the fender just a little, and would probably be okay, but in front they rested on the bar so much the papers were pushed up and were getting ready to spill out. As soon as I pedaled it would be all over.

"I think were going to need to make a frame for the back of your bike so you can hang the bags back there. Like the saddles bags on the Vincent. But that won't help for today. Let's try this," he said.

He forced all the papers away from the center of the each bag, half to each side, then laid down two in the middle to keep the halves separated where the bar would hit so the weight of the papers would make the bag droop down over each side and the two papers in the middle wouldn't be forced up so high they'd spill out. It looked like it would work.

"Give it a try."

I pushed off from the stool and rode down towards Beverly Boulevard. Every time my knees came up they hit the bottom of the bag and lifted papers up, but not high enough to push them out. Turning was hard, but I managed, and came back to where George was standing. I was afraid to ask, but I needed to know.

"What time is it?"

He looked at his watch.

"Four thirty-five."

"Oh no. Really?"

"Really."

"Then I'm doomed."

"Doomed? Are you sure?"

"Completely. I'm supposed to have everything delivered by six. Even if I already knew the route, I don't think I could do it by six. But I've got to figure out Marty's map one house at a time. Oh brother, I'm double doomed."

He put out his cigarette on his shoe and put it in his pocket again. He helped me get off the bike and lifted the bags over my shoulders and put them back on the parkway.

"I've got an idea," he said. "Wait here."

He disappeared between his house and Mr. Avery's. He was gone for about a minute when I heard a loud explosion, then a roar coming from the alley. A minute later he was coming down the block on the Black Shadow and pulled up to the curb. He was wearing big round goggles strapped around his head over a helmet that looked like something the old fashioned football players wore.

"Go put your bike away," he yelled over the engine noise. "We'll do your route on this since it's so late."

"Really?"

"Sure. It'll be a lot faster, and besides, it ought to be fun."

I put the Red Rider in the garage and came back to the street. George had put the Vincent on it's side kick stand and took one paper out of the route bags and walked across the street and tossed it onto Kevin Doyle's front steps. He came back and lifted the route bags off the grass and put them over the leather saddle bags. He took a leather strip, like a fat shoe lace, and tied the route bags on over the saddle bags. The Vincent had a double black leather seat, double so the driver's front part was separated by a little bump from the passenger part, I suppose so the passenger wouldn't slide forward and mess up the driver's driving, and it rested on the back fender, just in front of the saddle bags, and on the back of the gas tank in front of the driver's part. George flipped down foot pegs for my feet to rest on. He put out the cigarette he'd been smoking because it was almost finished anyway, and lit another, I suppose so he could have a new one and not have to try and light it while we were driving along. He added the old one to the collection in his pocket and then swung his leg over and got comfortable on the driver's seat and told me to get on. When I climbed on, I wiggled around like he did to get comfortable. It was much higher off the ground than the Red Rider and the noise of it was scary and exciting. I realized I was smiling even though I hadn't meant to and couldn't have stopped even if I'd wanted to.

"You got your delivery map and the address list?" he shouted over his shoulder.

"It's in the route bag," I shouted back.

"Get 'em out and let's have a look."

I reached back and felt around until I had them and gave them to him. He shifted the cigarette to the corner of his mouth and looked them both over. He tucked them between his leg and the gas tank.

"You all set?"

"I guess," I said, not so sure, but still smiling, feeling like I'd gotten to the top of a roller coaster and was about to drop down.

"Hang on," he said.

I wrapped my arms around him as tight as I could.

"I won't be able to breathe like that, Kurt," he said. "Hang onto by belt instead."

I wrapped the fingers of both hands around his belt, squeezing as hard as I could, bending the leather to the shape of my curled up hands. It felt okay, but I thought holding around his waist was better.

"Okay, then, we're off," he said.

As quick as he said the words the Vincent shot forward like a rock out of a noisy slingshot, kaboom! and the next thing I knew we were at the corner of Beverly. I didn't actually see us get there because I had my eyes closed, but when we stopped at the sign I opened them and there we were. Even with my eyes open I couldn't see ahead, around George, but I could see to both sides and partway behind if I turned my head far enough. There wasn't much traffic, so after a car or two went by, George shot across Beverly and we roared down Oakhurst headed for Alden. Part way down, he stopped and nodded towards a pale yellow house on the right with white trim around the windows.

"That's our first stop. 331."

I got off the motorcycle and walked to the front door and dropped the paper on the mat and came back and got on again and took hold of George's belt. About as soon as I got settled, I heard someone call my name and saw Julie standing on the sidewalk across the street in front of her house. I let go with one hand to wave and she waved back, but as quick as I could I grabbed back onto George's belt because the Vincent was already roaring down the street again. We got to the end of the block so fast it was like as soon as you thought about the next place to go, you were already there. When he stopped at Alden, he checked Marty's map, then put it back, and headed for West 3rd. He stopped part way down the block and showed me which house was next. I put the paper on the mat and we were off again. We made two more stops before we got to Burton Way. He turned left then left again onto Doheny. We got to the next house on the map and he yelled back over his shoulder to me.

"That's it there," he said, pointing. "You should try to memorize the addresses and the houses they go with, Kurt. It'll make your route go a lot faster once you do."

"Okay," I yelled back.

I got off the Vincent and took a paper with me and ran up to the porch. There was one entrance, but six buzzers for six different apartments. I went back to George.

"There's six apartments there. Am I supposed to take it inside?"

George looked at the route list, shifting the cigarette, tipping his head away from the cloud of smoke.

"It says Apartment 2, front steps."

"Okay," I said.

I ran back and set it down as carefully as I could on the top step. When I got back to the motorcycle, George was smoking away at his cigarette.

"That was good," he said, "that was just fine. Only I think we're going to have to do it a little differently if we're going to get done by six. Get back on."

When I was settled back on the seat, he roared off again towards West 3rd, slowing down about six houses before we got there. He pulled up close to the curb and stopped.

"Hand me a paper," he said.

I reached into the bag and handed it to him. Since the house was on the right, he drew his arm across his body to the left and flung the paper towards it. It flew all the way onto the porch.

"Hang on," he said.

We went up the block, crossed 3rd and he stopped at the next address.

"Give it a try," he said.

I couldn't fling it like he had because his body blocked me, so I invented a left-handed overhead toss. It got part way up the walkway to the house, but not really close enough to count as delivered, so I got off the motorcycle and ran and got it and threw it farther up. When I got back on, we went up the street, almost to Alden to the next delivery. It was on the right again, so I tried the left-handed overhead toss and the same thing happened. When I was back on, we went to Alden and turned left to the next address. Same thing. I just couldn't throw it far enough, especially if all of the houses were going to be on the right and I had to use my left hand. I was right-handed and that was that.

"Okay then," he said, "I think I know what we have to do. Get back on."

I got on and off we went. We turned left and started down Palm.
George went up a driveway right onto the sidewalk and stopped in front
of the house.

"That one right there," he called back to me, "let 'er fly."

This time I had to invent the right-hand overhead toss because the
house was on the left side. It plopped right onto the first step on my first
try, partly because I got to use my right hand, and mostly because we
were so much closer.

"Perfect," George said.

"Are we allowed to go on the sidewalk?" I asked him.

"Today, we are," he said. "When you're on your bike, it's okay to go
up on the sidewalk to get closer anytime you need to. We'll just do it for
today on the Vincent. It'll be okay," he said.

With each house I was getting better at the right and left-handed overhead throw and most of them got on either the steps, or even once in a
while, twice anyway, all the way to the porch. My arms were getting as
tired as at the carwash on a busy day, which made me think Saturdays
were going to be really hard if I worked at the carwash then had to do this
and pedal the Red Rider too. But that was Saturday and this was Monday, so I figured I wait to worry about that until Saturday. Today, doing
it on the Vincent, was better than a rollercoaster ride, and I was going
to get paid for it. How's that for luck, I was thinking. We crisscrossed
back and forth between Burton Way and Alden Drive like Marty's map
showed, and little by little the route bags were emptying out. I had been
trying to memorize the addresses and the houses they went with like
George had suggested, and also, I was also trying to keep count in my
head of the number of deliveries we'd made. I was pretty sure we were
up to either twenty-two or twenty three by the time we stopped at Burton Way. George checked Marty's map and the route list, put them back
under his leg and turned left to catch one last house before we'd head
up Crescent to Alden and above to stay. We pulled up in front of a big
apartment house with a black iron fence and gate. There was a double
iron arch over the gate going from one side of the fence to the other, and
in between the two arches, black letters said, Maple-Burton Arms.

"You've got to go inside for this one," he yelled over the Vincent.
Apartment 16."

"Okay," I said.

I took a paper from the route bags, opened the creaky gate and went to
the front steps. The building used to be white, but was now a dirty white
and sort of shabby looking. Arched over the doorway it said, Maple-Burton Arms again, this time in faded gold letters outlined in black. Below
that in a straight line were the address numbers, also gold with a black
outline. The front door was huge and mostly glass, with a heavy dark
wood frame, and the door handle was a giant brass thing, an elephant
head, with the elephant's trunk going in a half circle from his face down
to below where his chin should be, making the handle you'd push or
pull. The thumb lever was his tongue sticking out of his mouth. At least

it wasn't wet and slimy, I thought when I pushed it down. At first the door wouldn't budge. It wasn't locked, it was just too heavy to move, so I tucked the paper under my arm so I could push the tongue thing down and lean into the door with my shoulder, using all of my weight against it. It opened about a foot but as soon as I relaxed and quit pushing with my shoulder, it pushed me back to where I'd started. I put the paper down and pushed as hard as I could again and got it to open more than enough to get in. The problem was, I knew if I let go it would probably close before I could pick up the paper and get in, so I pushed it open all the way to the wall behind it, grabbed the paper as fast as I could, and ducked back inside before it could swing shut. Inside, the lobby wasn't very big, maybe ten feet across from the door to a wall with a big mirror on it. I was surprised to be looking at myself and the closed door behind me in the mirror. There was a fancy wooden table below the mirror with lots of mail and magazines on it. There was a funny smell, a bad smell, that at first I thought was coming from the carpet that covered the floor and the stairs too, but it seemed more like it was coming from every direction, even from out of the walls. It gave me one of those feelings, like on Halloween, when you go up to a house, ring the bell, then suddenly wish you hadn't. You know you should probably run away, but since you already rang the bell, you were sort of stuck. There were stairs on each side of the entry, up against the wall, going to the two separate sides of the upstairs. I tried to hold my breath. When I realized I couldn't hold it that long, I tried to breathe as little as possible. The lobby went left and right past the stairs to hallways that ran the long way away from the street, so I knew the building was like a 'U' shape pointed away from Burton Way. There were numbers on each side of the mirror, showing Apartments 1-8 downstairs to the left, 9-16 upstairs to the left, 17-24 downstairs on the right and 25-32 upstairs on the right. It seemed simple enough, so I went up the stairs on the left. By the time I got to the top it was so dark I could hardly see. And the smell was even worse. What little light there was coming up from the lobby seemed to disappear altogether when I started down the hallway. There was one light bulb hanging from a wire coming out of the ceiling half way down the hall, but it was so dim you could hardly see where the doors to the different apartments were. There was a window at the very end, but it had a shade pulled down and dark curtains over that shutting out all but a tiny little bit of orange-brown light that managed to get through. I could just barely make out the number on the door closest to the stairs and it was 8, so 16 was going to be at the far end of the hallway. It looked like about a mile away. I waited for a few seconds, hoping my eyes would adjust better, but they didn't, at least not much. When I took the first step, there was a creak in the floor I bet George could hear out on the street even over the noise of the Vincent. It was so loud I was afraid to pick up my foot and have it un-creak. When the hallway was quiet again, I took another step and it was almost as bad. At this rate, it'd be six o'clock before I got halfway down, so I decided to just go. Even through the thick smelly carpet, creak, creak, creak with each step. It was almost better when they came one right after the other than when there was one, then quiet, then another. At least that's what I thought until a door that I didn't even know was there popped open right next to me. Out of nowhere, there was an old woman in a ratty robe and she had gray hair standing up and sideways like she'd stuck her finger in an electrical plug and when I saw her face, a face with no teeth and eyes looking in different directions and hair on her chin, I screamed. I'm not sure if I did it out loud or not, probably I did, but she didn't seem to notice or care, because she was busy yelling at me.

"Who's making that racket? Who's there? What do you want? Who said you could come in here? Get out! This is private property!"

Her face was looking right at me, but her eyes were looking left and right, so maybe she just missed me, or maybe she was blind or something, because I knew that if I didn't move, it didn't seem like she'd could see where I was. Whatever, I came so close to peeing right there, it was a miracle I didn't, so it was a really good thing I hadn't stopped to have a coke with Miss Rimes at the carwash, that was for sure. Since no one answered her questions, she slammed the door closed and the hallway got even darker. Inside my head, someone was yelling run run run, and I almost did, but down at the end of the hallway another door opened and another old lady stuck her head out. She had a nice gentle old lady voice and looked like Larry See's grandmother, Mary See on the See's Candy boxes. White hair and glasses and a black dress. He was in my class at school and said his grandmother really looked like that.

"Is that my paper?" she said.

"Yes, mam," I said.

"You can call me Mrs. Gunther, if you like, young man," she said. "I'm sorry it's so dark."

I went down the rest of the way to her door, creak creak creak all the way. I handed her the paper.

"I'm sorry to make you come all the way up here, but I have trouble with the stairs."

"That's okay," I said.

"Oh my, you're so small. Are you big enough to deliver papers?"

"I think so. Today's my first day."

"What happened to the other young man?"

"Ron?"

"I think that's his name. The only time I ever see him is when he collects the money. He's supposed to bring me the paper but he usually just leaves it on the table in the lobby. That's not much help for me."

"He's the route master. I guess he figures he doesn't have time to come upstairs."

"I hope you will."

"I will. I promise."

"You take this for your trouble," she said, handing me a dime.

I didn't think I should take it. I wanted to, but it was sort of like the tips at the carwash. It didn't seem right since I was already getting paid.

"That's okay," I said. "It's just part of the route."

"I'd feel much better if you did. Please," she said, pressing the coin in my hand.

"Well....okay," I said.

"Thank you," she said, closing the door.

It was so dark I couldn't see it, but I could feel it in my hand. I was going to tell George about the smell and the dark and the scary lady, but I didn't think I'd tell him about the dime. When I looked back down the hall towards the stairs there was more light than there'd been looking the other way. I took a deep breath and ran all the way to the stairs. The creaking was mixed with the thumping of each running step I took and by the time I got to the stairs a couple of doors had opened and there were old people shouts, like, 'Who's there?' and 'What's that noise?' but I pretended I didn't hear them and just raced down the stairs and out the big door and out the gate and back to the Vincent.

"Everything go okay? You were in there pretty long."

"It smells bad and it's dark and hard to see but I found 16 alright."

"Good," he said, and off we went.

By the time we got to the part of the route between Beverly Boulevard and Lower Santa Monica my ears were ringing from the sound of the Vincent and I had this funny vibrating feeling in my bottom and legs and even my feet, but when we made the final turn onto Oakhurst I was about as happy as I could ever remember. Except for getting the Red Rider, of course. Norma and Shelly were in their front yard playing with Snowball and I waved to them. It was sort of showing off, but I was too happy to care. Sometimes being happy just seems like showing off, so I thought it didn't count against the rule. I waved to Kenny Lester and Mrs. Lester too, who were also in their front yard. If there'd been anyone else to wave to I would have, but there wasn't so I didn't. There was one more paper to deliver a few houses down from Kenny's place on his side of the street. 440 was the apartment house where Jeff Schumur and Dick Goldsmith lived. George pulled up onto the sidewalk and I let 'er fly. It didn't land close enough to the steps, probably because even my right-handed overhead toss was too tired to get it there, so I had to get off and was going to toss it again, but before I could, a tall skinny window opened on the second floor and a guy stuck his head out. It wasn't either Mr. Goldsmith or Mr. Schumur because I knew what they looked like, and they both had jobs that they drove off to in the morning and the guy sticking his head out of the window looked like he hadn't gotten dressed at all that day and maybe never did. The window came down close to the floor and there was a little white iron balcony in front of it and he stepped out wearing only baggy underpants and an under-shirt and a robe that was untied and way too open. He had a cup of coffee in his hand.

"See if you can get it up here through the window," he said.

"I'll try."

I threw the paper and it hit the bottom of the balcony.

"You'll have to do better 'n that," he said.

I tried again, throwing harder and the paper went higher and hit the wall to the left of the window, dropping back down into the bushes below. I picked it up and was about to try again when George came up to me and took the paper from my hand.

"Try this," he said.

He stood with his back to the building, facing the street and brought the paper up from between his legs with both hands like he was going to throw it over his head backwards, but he didn't. He was just showing me how. He handed me the paper. I stood where he'd been and did what he did except I let go and it flew right past the man on the balcony through the window and into his apartment. George put his hand on my shoulder.

"Perfect," he said.

"Hey! Not so hard," the guy said. "You knocked stuff off the kitchen table."

"Sorry," I said.

"Listen," George said, checking the route list, "Duffy," "if you want it through the window, move stuff out of the way. If that's a problem, the front steps will have to do."

"Delivery's 'sposed to be inside," he said. "I'll leave the window open for you. Just try to go a little easy, that's all I'm askin'."

He didn't wait for any more talk. He stepped back inside and closed the window.

"Some people," George said, shaking his head and putting his hand on my shoulder.

We got back on the Vincent and went the rest of the way down Oakhurst and pulled up in front of my house. Marty and Sarah were sitting on the top step of the front porch. Sarah jumped up and opened the screen door and called inside.

"He's back, mom!"

My mom came out and stood on the porch with Marty and Sarah as George and I got off the Vincent. Nick came out too, and held onto my mom's leg. George shut it off and put the goggles up on his forehead and put the map and route list in the route bags, then untied and handed them to me. Marty and Sarah and my mom came down to the parkway. Nick was still attached to her leg.

"We were worried," my mom said, "we saw your bike in the garage and didn't know what to think."

"I'm sorry, Lara, we should have left you a note," George said. "It was getting late and it looked like the only way to go."

"Ron, the route guy dropped the papers off way too late and then the route bags wouldn't stay on me so George fixed them but by that time there was no way I'd get done by six on the Red Rider so we went on the Vincent instead. Boy oh boy, Marty, you wouldn't believe how fast it goes! George, do you think you could give Marty and Sarah a ride? Sometime, I mean. Not now. Unless you want to."

"We could do that. Can I offer them a ride?" George asked my mom.

"Can we mom, please?" Sarah asked, "he got to," she said, pointing at me.

"It's not too dangerous?" my mom asked him.

"Heck, he went," Sarah said, pointing at me again.

"Okay," my mom said, "if George has time."

Marty was walking around the Vincent, gently touching it here and there, trying not to look too excited, but I could tell he was.

"How about you, Marty? Want to go for a ride?" George asked.

"You bet!" Marty said, all smiles.

"Ladies first," George said to Sarah.

George got on and gave the kick-starter a few big kicks, bringing all of his weight down on the steel pedal, and the Vincent exploded to life again. He got comfortable and pulled the goggles down from his forehead to cover his eyes. My mom had her hands over her ears, but she was smiling. She couldn't help it. No one could.

"Climb aboard," George shouted to Sarah.

I showed her the foot pegs, pointing to them.

"I'm not blind, I see them," she told me, pushing my hand away.

She got settled and George told her to hold onto his belt like I'd done.

"All set?" he asked her.

"Uh huh," she said.

She wasn't smiling at all now. Over the noise of the motorcycle, I told Marty, "She's afraid."

"I heard that," she said. "I might pound you when I get back. Think about that for a while."

That seemed to make her feel better, because the worried look mostly disappeared and she was back to being Sarah.

"Sarah, just pay attention to holding on and enjoy the ride," my mom told her.

They roared off down the street, stopped, but not completely at Beverly, and turned right. While we were standing there, my mom and Marty asked a lot of questions about the route and I told them what there was to tell, about the creepy Maple-Burton Apartments, but mostly I told them about riding around on the Vincent. About five minutes later, George and Sarah and the Vincent came down the block from Lower Santa Monica. As they pulled up to the curb, Sarah was all smiles, and I think she'd forgotten about pounding me.

"That's the most amazing experience in the world! Mom, you should go for a ride."

"Not me!" my mom laughed. "No thank you!"

Marty got on and got comfortable and they took off. Marty was so tall he could see right over the top of George's head, so he should have had goggles too, I thought, but he probably didn't care at all. This time George went across Beverly and down Oakhurst headed for Alden. Even two blocks away, we could hear the Vincent pull away from the stop sign down there.

"I've got to finish making dinner," my mom said.

She and Nick went back inside. Sarah and I stood there on the parkway waiting for Marty and George to come back.

"Who won?" I asked her.

"The Stars. Sort of a boring game, though."

"All of the Oakhurst Irregulars go?"

"Yep."

"How many?"

"Ten."

"How come so many? I didn't think there were so many."

"There are now."

"Any other plans to do something?"

"Maybe."

"Can I do it too?"

"Maybe."

"If I'm not doing the paper route or the carwash, can I?"

"I said, maybe. How's the route?"

"It was really fun with George and the Vincent, but it's going to be hard on the Red Rider. The route bags hang down too far and when I start out, they're too heavy. Marty's plan to get rid of as many papers as soon as possible worked pretty good, but if that Ron guy is late again, I'm doomed. It took almost an hour and a half on the motorcycle. It's going to take at least three hours on my bike."

"If you have trouble, maybe I can help."

"Really? You would?"

"It's a possibility. Remote," she said, "but possible."

"Really?"

"Possible," she said, "but don't push your luck."

Marty and George were gone a lot longer than he'd been with Sarah, but she didn't seem to care. They came up from Beverly from the direction of Doheny. They pulled up to the curb and Marty got off.

"Thanks George, that was great."

"Thanks, George," Sarah said.

"Kurt, maybe tomorrow you could come over and we can fix a permanent divider so the bags can hang down over the bar of your bike," George said.

"What's wrong with the bags?" Marty asked.

"They hang down so far they reach the bar on the bike and the papers would spill out."

"Because you're a runt," Sarah said.

"Why don't you get a fender-rack," Marty said.

"What's that?"

"Like that," he said, pointing to the saddle bags on the Vincent. "They make a rack that connects to the post below the seat and has legs that attach to the bolts on each side of the back wheel. The rack is held just above the back fender. You could tie the route bags on it and just reach back for a paper when you need one."

"That would be perfect."

"Bill's Bike Shop should have one."

"How much do you think they cost?" I asked him.

"Three or four dollars," he said, "something like that."

"I don't have that much. I gave Mr. Mahoney everything I had."

"I could loan it to you," Marty said.

"I'll pay you back, I promise."

"I know," he said. "I leave it on my desk for you. You could go to the bike shop before the route tomorrow."

"Is it okay if I pay you when I get paid the paper route money?"

"Sure."

"'cause I promised Mr. Mahoney the two-fifty every week from the car wash."

"That's fine. I think I can trust you."

"What a relief! I didn't know how I was going to ride around with those route bags around my neck."

"If you need help putting the rack on the bike, I've got a lot of tools back there," George said. "Just come on over."

"Thanks, George, that would be great. And thanks for taking me on the Vincent. I'd never have made it by six. Never."

"You're welcome. I hope you had as much fun as I did."

"Boy, you can bet I did!"

George stood part way up, straddling the Vincent so he could reach into his pocket. He took something out and handed it to me. It was his little pocket knife.

"You keep this. I've got another one. You'll need it to cut the ropes," he said, over the noise of the engine. "Just be careful with it. It's sharp."

"Isn't it your favorite?"

"It's a good one, alright. But I'd like you to have it. I've got a bunch of favorites."

He sat back down and rode off up the street and around to the alley and down to his garage. We could hear the Vincent every inch of the way until he shut it off. Marty and Sarah headed for the house. I stood there looking at the little knife. It was about three inches long and had dark sides held on by silvery rivets and polished steel ends and two small blades and one longer one. There was a little oval metal plate on one side that said, KA-BAR. I put it in my pocket with the propeller medal from Kenny Lester. I decided I'd keep both of them with me every day from now on for the rest of my life and I'd have double good luck. I went into the house holding the knife and the medal with my hand in my pocket.

At dinner they all asked me more questions about the first day, except for Nick, who was mostly interested in eating, and if he had any questions about the route, was saving them for some other time, but what I really wanted to do was tell my dad all about the route and George and the Vincent, but he got home late, and I didn't see him and he was gone in the morning before I got up, even though I got up at six.

I had a hard time sleeping. I was excited and tired from doing the route on the Vincent and worried about doing it on the Red Rider. I kept trying to picture all the houses and the addresses I was supposed to deliver to, but they sort of ran together and the harder I tried, the more confused I got until pretty soon, I couldn't remember any of them, but just before I did finally fall asleep, I decided I'd ride my bike along the route with the map and the address list, but without the route bags or any papers, and try to memorize the houses all over again. Since I had a long time before Ron was supposed to drop off the papers, I thought I could do it and go to the bike shop and put the rack on the bike and rest up before I had to do it for real. I had Marty's four dollars, but there wasn't any lunch money on the kitchen table for me and I didn't want cereal, so I just went out. I thought I'd check to see if George was up early too so I could tell him what time I'd be back from the bike shop. I crossed his grass to the walkway and looked into the Courtyard, but his L.A. Times was still on the step. I'd hate to deliver those things, I thought. This early in the morning? And they were a lot bigger and heavier than the Mirror. I'd never given it much of a thought before, but now, the Times looked huge. You'd have to be at least as big as Marty to deliver them. Probably someone did it from a car. I'd never noticed, but I'd bet no one could do it from a bike. Imagine doing them on Sundays. Impossible.

I went down our driveway and got the Red Rider. It had to be at least quarter to seven by now, so I decided to go up to the Wonder Bread Factory and Joseph's Hot Dog Stand. I had the dime Mrs. Gunther had given me, so I could buy hot chocolate. I didn't want to make the Red Rider feel bad, but in my head, I was pretending it was the Vincent. The wind pushed my hair back and I tried to make the roaring noise it made. I got to the carwash pretty fast, considering it wasn't really the Vincent, and parked my bike on the Elm Street side of Joseph's stand.

"Be right back," I told him, and ran for the Wonder Bread Factory.

Helen was in the pastry room. They were pretty busy, busier than I'd ever seen them, so when Helen saw me, she wiped her forehead and smiled, but kept on working.

"Got a special order to get out, honey. You could help by gettin' rid of the irregulars. Could you do that?"

"Sure," I told her.

The sorting table was a mess of bent and squished cinnomon rolls and bear claws and some new thing they'd never made before, and as fast as they all came out of the oven, Helen and Marie were sorting and packaging them and needed the extra help to keep making room on the table, so that's what I did. I ended up working for about half an hour. I hated to do it, but most of the bad ones ended up in the big garbage cans. I filled three big paper bags, some for me, maybe for Marty and Sarah and Nick too, and some for the carwash guys, but most of them ended up in the cans. By the time they had four of the rolling metal racks filled with packages of perfect ones ready for the trucks, things slowed down and Helen gave me a hug.

"You were a big help, baby. Got here right in the nick of time. Sweet Lord, if they want to double the morning order, you'd think they'd know enough to double the help, but that ain't gonna happen, not in this lifetime!"

"Is it okay if I take one of the bags?"

"You take whatever you can carry, honey. Sooner that stuff's outta my sight the better."

I took the biggest bag. It must have had twenty or thirty pieces in it. I was thinking it would have been better if I'd brought the route bags. I could have taken two or maybe all three of the paper bags and put them in the route bags to get them home. This one would never fit under my t-shirt so I didn't know how I'd get it home. I thought I'd wait and see what was left over after I gave some to Joseph and the carwash guys and maybe Norma if she showed up. Maybe Kenny Lester on his way to work if he stopped by. I took the bag and headed back to the Hot Dog Stand.

"Quite a haul," Joseph said.

"Want some?"

"Watcha got?"

I put the bag on the counter and let him take a look.

"What are those things?" he asked me.

"I don't know. I forgot to ask Helen. I think they're something new. At least I've never seen them before."

"What's the squishy stuff in the center?"

"I don't know. Try it."

"You first," he said, like he was afraid it was poison or something.

"Better get me a hot chocolate to wash it down, just in case," I joked him, putting my dime on the counter.

He pushed it back to me.

"Told you, your money's no good here."

He made the hot chocolate while I tried to separate one of the new pastries from the squishy mess in the bag. I was going to put it on a paper napkin, but he shoved a plate in front of me before I could.

"Oh no you don't. That sticky stuff would go right through the napkin and onto the counter. Use this."

I got my fingers around what I was pretty sure was one of the new things, and as I pulled my hand out of the bag, part of it came. I put it on my plate and took a taste off my fingers. It was some kind of lemon custard stuff and boy was it good!

"Well?" he asked, his hands on his hips.

"It's great! You try."

He looked in the bag and came up with what was probably the other half of what I taken out. He put it in his mouth all at once.

"Mmmm, you're right, that's pretty good."

"You should buy some from the Wonder Bread Factory that aren't squished and sell them here with your coffee. Not everyone has time for pancakes or eggs, you know. Look at Norma. She barely has time for the coffee."

"I was thinking the same thing. That might work out pretty well."

Kenny pulled into the station at the pumps. He waved when he saw me and got out of the car and came over. Randy started pumping his gas.

"Kenny, you gotta try these things. It's something new Helen's making at the Factory."

I handed him my plate with the chunk on it. He looked at it funny.

"Helen gives me the squished ones they can't sell," I told him.

"I wondered," he said.

He picked it up like he still wasn't sure he wanted to put it in his mouth.

"Go on," Joseph said. "They're good."

Kenny pinched off a piece of the piece and put it in his mouth, then smacked his lips and licked them with his tongue. His face lit up and he smiled and took the rest of the piece and ate that too.

"Damn good. What do you call them?"

"We don't know, but Joseph may buy fresh ones and sell them here. With coffee. For when people are in a hurry and can't stay for pancakes or eggs. Pretty neat, huh?"

"That so?" he said to Joseph.

"Thinkin' about it. Seems like a good idea to me. Might start openin' earlier on weekends and weekdays too. What do you think?"

"Just give 'em lots of napkins for the rolls," he said, licking his fingers. "Why early?"

"Got a lot of regulars comin' in before the wash is open, hopin' for coffee. I'm usually here anyway. Might as well."

"You got another one?" Kenny asked me.

"Sure, you just have to fish around for it."

I handed him the bag. He took a look in trying to spot another of the custard things.

"I don't see another one," he said, sort of disappointed.

"You want coffee?" Joseph asked him.

"Sure," Kenny said.

He was dressed up for work in a fancy suit and tie, so he put the tie over his shoulder to keep it from getting spilled on. Joseph put a steaming-hot mug of coffee in front of him and Kenny added cream and sugar. He took another look in the bag, moved things around, and came out with a cinnomon roll instead.

"How 'bout this? Can you spare a cinnomon roll?"

"Sure," I said.

He sipped at the coffee and ate the roll in about four bites.

"How'd the route go? That was a real surprise seeing you on the back of George's motorcycle. How'd that happen?"

"The route master dropped the papers off way late, so George took me on the Vincent. It was the most fun thing ever. We got done on time too."

"So, everything's going okay?"

"Yeah, mostly."

"Problems?"

"A few, but George is helping put a thing on the bike to hold the route bags, so that'll take care of that."

"What else?"

"I can't remember which houses I'm supposed to deliver to."

"Well, geez, it was the first day. You'll figure it out."

"I suppose. I'm going to take a practice ride this morning. See, I've got the map and addresses," I said taking them out of my shirt. "That should help."

"There you go. You've got the right idea. Don't worry, you'll do fine. Let me know when you're ready to add me to your route."

He looked up at the clock on the wall across from the counter.

"Geez, I've got to run."

He put a couple of dimes on the counter for Joseph, went to his car and gave Randy money for the gas. He waved as he drove off.

"I like that guy," Joseph said.

"Me too."

The clock behind Joseph said a little before eight. Even without the clock you could tell it was getting late because the traffic was getting heavy. Every time the light changed, there were at least three or four cars waiting to go in each direction by the time it went to green. I told Joseph to eat whatever he wanted from the bag and give William and Maurice and Dennis and Jackson whatever they wanted too. There was no way I could get them home on the bike anyway, so what the heck.

"See you later," I told him and took off.

I went down to Oakhurst and turned right heading for Alden, but stopped as soon as I turned. I took out the map and the addresses and looked it over. If you didn't count Kevin Doyle, the first house was the one across from Sharon and Julie. 331. I said it about a dozen times with my eyes closed then went looking for it. I remembered it as soon as I saw the pale yellow with white trim. I stayed there in front of it staring at it, repeating the numbers and opening my eyes wider to sort of take a picture of it. It was 331 alright. There were black numbers, a 3 and a 3 and a 1 next to the front door. I looked at each one separately, then all together. 331. From behind me, Julie called.

"Kurt? What're you doing? How's the route going?"

"It's going okay, but I don't remember the houses I'm supposed to deliver to, so I'm going around to memorize them."

"That's a good idea. Sharon and I are ready to take the paper whenever you're ready to add us."

"Could we wait a little? I've got to try it by myself on my bike. The route bags are pretty heavy already."

"Sure, just let us know. Bye."

"Bye."

Boy, was she pretty, I was thinking as I watched her go up the walkway to her apartment. It was going to make memorizing the house numbers harder if I was thinking about her instead of them, so I closed my eyes and tried to picture the 331 numbers and the pale yellow house. I opened my eyes to take one more look at 331 before I left, and just about had it memorized when she called to me again.

"Did you ever see, you know who again?" she pretend whispered.

"Yes, and I told her you guys liked her work."

"You did? Oh my God! You did?"

"You said to. Right?"

"Of course! What did she say? Did she say anything?"

"She said if you really want it, don't give up and one day it'll be your turn. Something like that."

"No! Really? She said that?"

"Uh huh."

"I could just kiss you! Wait until I tell Sharon! Bye!"

She ran back into her apartment. I rode the rest of the route memorizing the house numbers and the houses they went with the best I could, but mostly I kept thinking about the kiss, so I thought I might have to do it all over again.

It took almost as long to ride around memorizing as it did to actually deliver the papers, but it wasn't as hard and it was fun to be buzzing around on the Red Rider doing it. By the time I got to the top of Palm and Lower Santa Monica, there were only four houses left on the list. I went down Palm and memorized the one house there. That left only one on Beverly, one on Doheny, and that Duffy guy in the upstairs window on Oakhurst. I could picture all three of them without any extra memorizing, so I headed for Bill's Bike shop. I didn't know what time it was, but it had to be around nine-thirty, so he should be open. I rode up Beverly and past the carwash and waved at the guys as they were getting ready to open. In next to no time, I pulled up in front of the bike shop. Bill was washing the big front windows.

"Hi. How's the bike?" he asked me.

"Perfect, Bill, just the best."

"You stop by to say hello, or is there something I can help you with?"

"I'm doing a paper route on the bike and the route bags are too big for me and hang down to the bar, so Marty suggested a fender rack. Do you have one?"

"Sure."

"How much are they? Marty loaned me four dollars. Is that enough?"

"You know what?"

"What?"

"I'm pretty sure I've got a used one that looks like new. I could let you have it for, say, a dollar-fifty. How would that be?"

"That would be great! Does it really look like new?"

"Pretty much, I'd bet."

"'Cause I'd hate to spoil the Red Rider if it was sort of beat up, if you know what I mean. 'Cause it's really nice of you anyway, but if...."

"I know exactly what you mean. I'd feel the same way. Let's go take a look. You decide."

He put down the window washing stuff and we went through the shop to the work area. The fender rack was in a box that he had to open, so I knew he took good care of even the used stuff.

"Are you sure that's used?" I asked him. "It looks brand new to me."

"Didn't I tell you? Just like new. A dollar-fifty sound okay?"

"You got a deal!" I said, and whipped out two of Marty's dollar bills and handed them to him.

He took the money and we went to the cash register and he rang it up and gave me a fifty-cent piece.

"Want to put it on? It'll only take a few minutes."

It was bigger than I thought it would be and getting it home either in or out of the box would be a problem, but I was worried that George might be disappointed if I did it without his help. On the other hand, he might have other things to do and if I walked the bike home so I could carry the rack, it might get really late, and then we might have to take the Vincent again, only maybe he couldn't, maybe he was going to be busy, and if he had to say no, even though he knew I couldn't finish before six, he'd feel really bad, so this was probably better.

"Okay."

In about ten minutes Bill had the rack on the back of the Red Rider. It looked new and shiny alright, just like he said it would, like the bike might have come that way in the first place, but it hadn't, and because it hadn't, I didn't like it very much. The Red Rider didn't look as free anymore. I stood there looking at it. I felt like I'd taken a wild animal and put it in the zoo. But then I could hear the Red Rider telling me it was okay. We'd do the route together because that was our job. We'd pay for the locks and then off it would come. We'd both be free then. We made a deal right there at Bill's Bike shop, and we were both good with it.

Since I had saved so much money with the used fender rack, I thought about going to Whalen's for a milkshake, but then I'd just have to pay Marty anyway, so maybe that wasn't such a good idea. While I was deciding, I decided to go in just in case. Also, Sarah and the Oakhurst Irregulars might be there planning something, so I could check on that while I was making up my mind about the milkshake, but they weren't. No one was at the soda fountain. Ozzie was fiddling around behind the counter with his back to me cleaning stuff. I was standing over by the candy shelves to the left of the counter when in came Kevin Doyle and Miriam. He was wearing his fancy army uniform with all the medals on it and Miriam was all smiles. His face was still a little puffy and you could see the strings in his face where they sewed the stitches in, but they were laughing and acting all lovey-dovey. Didn't she know he was bad news? Why was she laughing and holding hands with him? That's what I wanted to know. How could she? When Miriam saw me her smile sort of drifted away, and as soon as it was gone, Kevin Doyle noticed, and when he saw me, he knew it was my fault, and his face got mean.

"Hi, Kurt," Miriam said.

"If you're going to deliver the goddamn paper, maybe you should deliver it ," he said. "Maybe George has better things to do."

"Leave him alone, Kevin," Miriam said.

Ozzie turned around to see who was there and saw Kevin and made a face, then turned back to what he'd been doing before any of us got there. I thought Ozzie had told Kevin to get out and stay out. Whatever happened to that? And what about him going the other way whenever he saw me, like Maurice had told him? What happened to that? I never believed he would, but at the same time I'd sort of hoped it would be true. I'd hoped at least at school and the carwash and Bill's Bike Shop, and maybe Whalen's, I could forget about him. But right now, none of it was going to do me any good. I didn't know what to say to him and I was pretty sure whatever I said would just make him go from mean to crazy, so I didn't say anything, which made him go crazy anyway.

"And another thing, god damn it, don't put the paper on the front steps," he said, "bring the god damn thing around back."

His face was getting scary, like when he seemed ready and glad to fight all of the carwash guys at once. I could feel my legs shaking. If it had been a month before, I would have been crying for sure. I was still afraid of him, but not in the same way. It was a funny feeling. I'd have given almost anything if the fender rack had cost the whole four dollars so there wouldn't have been any money left over, or if I hadn't thought about a milkshake or looking for the Oakhurst Irregulars, but here I was and here he was and I couldn't do anything about it. When he'd been on the ground after Maurice had put him down and he kept looking at me to let me know it wasn't over, I'd had the feeling no matter how much Maurice or Jackson or Dennis or William or George wanted to protect me, he might get crazy and kill me anyway. I had that feeling again. I wondered if I should tell the carwash guys about this? I wondered if I should tell George or my dad. He hadn't really done anything, and besides, what good would it do? They'd told him to leave me alone and that didn't work, and if someone got in a fight with him about this and got hurt or put in jail, that would just make things worse, and all because I didn't like him yelling at me. He was crazy and that was that. My legs were shaking and there was a big ache in my stomach and I could feel tears rolling down my face, but it didn't feel like crying, because at the same time, I had a sort of calm feeling, like I'd just have to wait, that one way or another, I'd either sink down to the bottom and drown or I'd come back up to the surface, to fresh air, like body surfing the big waves at Will Rogers. There just wasn't anything anyone could do, I thought. He might kill me. He might. But maybe, just maybe, I might kill him first.

"Are you listening to me? ARE YOU?" he shouted.

"STOP IT KEVIN!!" Miriam yelled at him, trying to pull him to the door.

He shook her off. He kept looking at me and pointing a finger. He could point all he wanted, I was thinking, and as I thought it, he began to disappear from my sight. He was there okay, but I just stopped seeing him. I pictured the Red Rider instead. I had it and was free to ride away anytime I wanted. It was going to be the best summer ever. Me and the Red Rider had a deal and we'd deliver the papers and pay off the locks and ride around wherever we wanted. Maybe I'd go to the beach again with Norma. Maybe we'd both ride bikes there. Maybe, maybe not. But for sure it was going to be the best summer ever, Kevin Doyle or no Kevin Doyle.

"On the back porch, god damn it! Bring it around back and leave it on the back porch!"

He came back into view. His face was turning purple, he was so angry, maybe because I'd stopped paying attention to him. I don't know where he'd come from because I hadn't seen him in the store, but Iyama Osaka was standing there next to me with one arm around my shoulder, the other keeping Kevin an arm's length away.

"Take your hands off me you dirty Jap! I've killed dozens like you, don't you know that?" Kevin said, with a nutsy grin, "I looked them right in the eye and spilled their guts all over my shoes."

Iyama didn't say anything, and he didn't take his arm away from me or Kevin, but kept a steady push against Kevin's chest and backed him towards the door with me huddled against his leg. For a minute, Kevin had this worried look, like he wasn't so sure he wanted to fight Iyama, and he kept backing up. But then he got crazy again and he tried to reach past Iyama to grab me, but Miriam pushed his hand away and knelt down between us.

"STOP IT KEVIN! WHAT'S THE MATTER WITH YOU?! Are you okay?" she said, wiping away the tears that had been running down my face, stroking my face with her long fingers.

That's all it took. As calm as I'd felt only a minute before, something came loose inside and I started crying and yelling at Kevin and trying to hit him. It didn't really feel like it was me, and I didn't sound like me to me, but it was coming from me, okay. I couldn't pull free from Iyama, but I wasn't hiding behind him anymore, either.

"I not afraid of you! I'm not going to be afraid of you any more! I'm sick of being afraid of you! I wish you were dead! Do you hear me? I wish you were dead!"

"Shhh, honey," Miriam said, trying to calm me down. "It's going to be okay."

She was trying to stroke my forehead, but all I could see was that behind her, Kevin Doyle was smiling like he'd just found something, looking at me like he wanted me to know he found it and knew it was mine and he wasn't going to give it back.

"And what are you going to do about it?" he said to me and Iyama Osaka, "either of you?"

"Kill you!" I shouted at him, crying and not crying. "I'll kill you and spill your guts all over my shoes, that's what I'll do about it!"

Iyama pulled me back against his leg tighter. Maybe because Miriam was there, Kevin didn't start a big fight with Iyama. Or maybe he was afraid of Iyama. It was hard to tell. But either way, all of a sudden, he seemed calm and happy. He kept pushing Iyama's hand off of him as fast as Iyama put it back, but every step was backwards and towards the door and the next thing I knew, Kevin and Miriam were outside. That's when Ozzie remembered how to talk.

"You're a whacko, Doyle, a nutcase! I told you before, keep outta here!"

"Fuck you, Ozzie. Fuck you, altogether," Kevin said from just outside the door, but he said it with a smile, like he was saying, thank you, instead.

Iyama stood in the doorway holding me to his leg, blocking Kevin from coming back, just in case he wanted to, but he didn't, and he and Miriam walked around the corner and out of sight on Burton Way. Iyama looked down at me, his hand resting on the top of my head, the expression on his face asking me if I was okay, then he winked at me and messed my hair. He stood there for a moment or two, until he was pretty sure I was okay and maybe to make sure Kevin was really gone, then he left. Ozzie was already back to doing whatever he'd been doing and didn't say goodbye when I left.

I walked towards the Red Rider feeling like I hadn't slept for a month, but just seeing it there waiting for me, the chrome sparkling in the sunlight, the perfect dark red paint, the words The Red Rider Special in white with black outlines, made me feel better, and I reminded myself, if I wanted, we were free to go anywhere. Anywhere at all. No matter what, we were going to make it the best summer ever. I promised myself and the bike it would be the best summer ever, no matter what. Amen to that, I thought, picturing Maurice always making the best of everything.

"Amen to that," I said out loud to the Red Rider.

I wanted to stop at the carwash on the way home, but if I did, and if I told Joseph or the carwash guys about Kevin, who knows what might happen? And besides, I thought I should let George know I got the fender rack and already put it on, and be back to get a fast start on the folding. But since I hadn't had the milkshake I thought a Coke might be good. It might settle my nerves, like Jackson said sometimes, only he was talking about coffee and a cigarette. So I decided to stop at the carwash after all. I just wouldn't mention Kevin Doyle.

"What's the matter?" Joseph said, as soon as I sat on a stool. "You were pretty upbeat this morning."

"I'm okay. Could I have a Coke please?"

"Coming right up," he said.

There weren't any cars on the lot for the carwash guys to wash and William came over for coffee. The others were coming a little behind him.

"Thanks for the sweet rolls," William said, sitting on a stool.

Joseph put the coke in front of me and I started to sip at it as Jackson and Dennis and Maurice sat down. Just having them near, I felt better. But at the same time, I thought I was going to cry and I could feel myself wanting to tell them about Kevin. It was about to pop out.

"Be sure and thank Helen for us," Dennis said. Those things hit the spot."

He looked at me.

"You okay?"

"Uh huh," I said. "I gotta go tell George I already got the fender rack."

"Don't you want to finish your Coke?" Joseph asked.

"No thanks."

I got on the Red Rider and took off, thinking I'd go see George right off and tell him about the rack, but when I got back to Oakhurst, after I put the bike away in the garage and without really thinking about it or planning it, I went through our back yard and slipped into the alley. I didn't see anyone and no one saw me, and I snuck under the fence into the bamboo patch. I fell asleep before I remembered having laid down.

When I woke up the sun was high and it was hot. I went back through the alley and into our yard and took the Red Rider out to the street. The papers were already there. I got the route bags and rubber bands from the place on the porch where I was always going to leave them, and started folding. It was going pretty well, I thought. I didn't know exactly what time it was, and wasn't planning on looking. It was whatever it was. I'd just fold as fast as I could and deliver as fast as I could and hope for the best. George came down his walk.

"You okay?" he asked me. "I thought we were going to put the rack on your bike."

"Sorry," I said, "Bill put it on at the bike shop. I didn't know how I'd carry it home otherwise. I was going to come tell you..."

"That's okay. I'm glad you got it all taken care of. That's the important thing."

He stood smoking, watching me fold the papers.

"I was thinking, it might be easier if you tied the route bags onto the bike first, then filled them with the papers, rather than filling them and trying to lift them on."

"That's a good idea," I said.

"Can I make another suggestion?"

"Sure."

"Try to remember to take papers from each side as you go. That way, one side won't get light while the other one stays heavy. Otherwise, your bike might be harder to control."

"I didn't think of that. That's a good idea too. Thanks."

"You okay?"

"Uh huh."

"I've got that piece of rawhide we used yesterday. Want me to tie them on with that?"

"Sure."

He put the route bags over the rack and tied them in place. As fast as I could fold the papers he put them in the bags for me, half on each side to keep the bike balanced.

"Want help folding?" he asked me.

"No thanks. I kind of want to see how long the whole thing takes me by myself."

"You got your map and the addresses?"

"Uh huh. I went around the route this morning to help memorize the houses."

"That's the ticket. You'll have it all figured out in no time."

"I hope so."

When I finished folding and he had the bags full, I was ready to take off. George took a paper out of the bags and nodded towards Kevin Doyle's house.

"Never mind, George. I'll do it," I said, taking it from his hand.

"You sure?"

"Uh huh."

I walked across the street and down the driveway between Kevin's house and Miriam's. A few wooden steps led to a small porch by his back door. I noticed an ashtray and a cigarette lighter right there on the railing waiting for Kevin any time he wanted to smoke out back instead of on his front steps. I tossed the paper on it and went back across the street to my bike. George was waiting for me, still puffing away on his cigarette.

"What's that about?" he asked me.

If I looked him in the eye, it would be all over, so I just looked at my feet. After I paid Marty back for the fender-rack and paid off the locks, if I had enough money left over, I thought I should buy some new sneakers. The holes in mine were getting so big my toes were down on the ground at the same time the front of the shoes were a little up in the air because the tops were separating from the bottoms. It was a good thing it was summer and warm.

"Kevin said so."

"When?"

"This morning."

"Where?"

"At Whalen's."

"At Whalen's? The drug store?"

"Uh huh. At Ozzie's Soda Fountain. After I was at the bike shop getting the rack."

"Why?"

"I don't know why, George, that's just what he said."

My eyes were starting to cry. Not me, really, because it didn't feel at all like crying, just my eyes, leaking tears out.

"He just wants it in back. I gotta get started."

"Be careful, Kurt. Watch out for parked cars and ones backing out of driveways, okay?"

"Okay."

He stood there smoking. He waved as I rode off but when I stopped at the stop sign at Beverly Boulevard and looked back, he was crossing the street to Kevin Doyle's place.

I could feel the weight of the route bags making the Red Rider want to tip one way or the other if I didn't keep it almost exactly in the middle. I just about tipped over when I started up again to cross Beverly. I wobbled and had to jump off the seat and put my feet down to balance, then start over, but at least the bike didn't fall and the papers didn't spill. And one great thing was I didn't even have to look at the list or the map for the first house. 331 popped into my head like magic! I rode down the street and up onto the sidewalk a couple of houses before I got to it and stopped right in front. I reached back and got a paper and used George's across-the-body-fling. It smacked up against the front door and dropped right on the mat. Perfect! It was going to be a great day, after all. Like Kenny Lester says, sometimes you can tell by the way things fall into place. And here it was, kerplop!

"Kurt!"

I looked across the street. It was Sharon.

"Did you see that?" I shouted. "Did you?"

"What?"

"I got the paper right on the mat!"

"That's great," she said, coming across the street.

When she got close, she kept pushing the hair out of her face, only it wasn't really in her face, so I didn't know why she was doing it so much.

"Julie said you talked to," she whispered, "Norma...."

"Uh huh."

"I'd like to hear all about it."

"There's not much to tell. I told Julie what she said. Sort of, 'don't give up' stuff."

"I know, but, well I'd like....we'd both like to hear more about it. We thought you might like to have some cookies and milk with us."

"Now?"

"Well, it could be now."

"I've got to do the route. I just started."

"Well, it could be later. Maybe after you're done. How would that be?"

"Great, I guess."

"Well, it's a date, then," she said, pushing the hair away again.

"A date? I'm only eight. Actually, I'm still seven until August."

"Not a date type-date," she laughed. "Just a social date. A get together for friends. Is that okay?"

"Sure, I suppose. And Julie will be there too?"

"Of course."

"Okay, but since this is the beginning of the route and I'm not sure how long it's going to take on my bike, I don't know when I'll be done."

"You just come when you can. If not today, anytime. Cookies and milk. Okay?"

"Okay."

"And say hello to you-know-who for us if you see her."

"Sure," I said.

Things were going pretty well, I thought, and pretty fast. I checked the map and the list when I had to, but I knew at least a quarter of the houses as soon as I saw them, without having to check. I got to the Maple-Burton Arms and leaned the bike against the iron fence. I took a paper and headed through the gate. I got lucky because someone was coming out just when I got to the big heavy front door, so I didn't have to struggle with it. The smell hit me in the face like driving past the Beverly-Ponyland, only the Ponyland smell was better. I tried not to breathe too much and ran up the stairs and into the dark hall and down to number 16. I wasn't sure if I should just leave the paper on the floor in front of the door or knock on it so Mrs. Gunther would know it was there. If I just left it, she might not find it for hours, or maybe not at all, thinking I hadn't delivered it. On the other hand, if I knocked and handed it to her, she might think she had to give me a dime everytime I brought the paper, and that would be a big gyp to her, even if she didn't care. So I put the paper down, knocked on the door and ran back down the hallway. The thumping and creaking was just as loud as yesterday, but no one opened their doors to yell at me, so the good day was still falling into place. If I had cookies with Julie and Sharon, that would be the best proof. I hid behind the wall at the top of the stairs and peeked around into the darkness of the hall. Her door opened and she looked around and didn't see anyone and started to shut the door. I thought I might have to do it all over again, but at the last second, she spotted the paper and took it inside.

As the papers emptied out of the route bags and they lost their puffy shape, the bags kept sagging around the legs that went down from the rack to the back wheel bolts, and rubbed against the spokes. I was afraid they'd get caught and jammed and make me crash, but they never did. I thought I'd ask Marty or maybe George if they had an idea about it. If I were zipping along fast and they got caught, I'd be a goner. Or if I was crossing the street and they got caught and it made me stop suddenly, a car, or jeez, a bus, might be coming and squish me flat. For sure I was going to ask Marty or George.

The rest of the route just happened. After worrying abut the route bags getting caught, I don't remember thinking about anything at all and the next thing I knew, I was coming down Oakhurst. Shelly was in the front yard with Snowball, but no Norma. I stopped there in the street.

"Hiya, kid. What's up with you? How's the route going?"

She was wearing jeans and a sweatshirt and you could tell they both should have been a bigger size, but I suppose they might have been old and fit her better when she bought them, or maybe she bought them too small by accident. It was just the opposite with me. My mom got everything way too big so I'd grow into them, but I never did, because they got worn out before that happened.

"Good, I think. Do you know what time it is?"

"A little before six."

"Yikes, I got one more paper to deliver before six."

"See ya."

I started to pedal off.

"Hey," she called after me.

I stopped again.

"If you think you can handle another paper, we're ready to sign up. Okay?"

"Yeah, I think I can. It wasn't as hard as I thought it would be on my bike."

"Good. If you start throwing it here, see if you can get it outside the fence by this gate. Keep this fuzz ball from chewing it up before we get a look at it. Right over there, okay?"

"Sure. I have to ask Ron, the routemaster, for extra papers, so it might be a day or two."

"Whenever," she said.

I started up again. In about three seconds I got to Mr. Duffy's place, only the window was closed. I checked the route list. It didn't say inside, but Mr. Duffy had, and the list said, upstairs, 2A, which might mean maybe I was supposed to deliver it inside even if his window wasn't open. I parked the Red Rider on the sidewalk and took the last paper from the bags and went to the door expecting to go into a lobby, like at the Maple-Burton Arms, only the door didn't have glass, so I couldn't see if there really was a lobby, and besides, it was locked. There were buzzers for eight apartments but it was almost impossible to read the faded numbers. Faded or not, I was pretty sure the four buzzers on the top row would be for the first four apartments, 1A, 1B , 1C and 1D; the bottom row should be 2A, 2B, 2C and 2D. I pushed what I thought was the 2A buzzer. I waited and waited, but nothing happened. Just in case I had it wrong, I pushed the one I thought should be 1A in case it was really 2A, but no one answered that one either. I could leave the paper on the steps since the window was closed and that wasn't my fault, but since he said he wanted it through the window, I thought I'd try to get it onto the balcony in front of the window. It took four tosses and finally it plopped down where I was trying to get it. I walked back to the Red Rider. Across the street, Rathbutt was watching me. He was standing on the sidewalk, smoking a cigarette, one hand holding it, the other in the side pocket of his dark red jacket. His hair was slicked back and his thin face and long nose and pale skin looked like an older version of the man in the Robin Hood poster. He nodded his head towards me and put the cigarette in his mouth and made the motion of gentle, slow clapping, I suppose for getting the paper up on the balcony. I smiled at him and put my arm across my stomach and bowed. He laughed and called to me.

"Well done, young man. Bravo."

I waved to him and rode for home. That's when I remembered Julie and Sharon and the cookies.

I pulled into our driveway and untied the route bags from the rack and put them on the porch. Sarah came out.

"Is mom home yet?" I asked her.

"No. She and dad are still downtown and I'm stuck here with Nick. Why don't you come in and stay with him. I want to go over to Megan's. She can't leave the phone."

"Can't." I told her.

"Why not? That's not fair. I've been stuck here for hours. Why can't you?"

"Some people on the route asked me to stop by when I was done."

"What for?"

"They might want to take the paper."

"Either they do or they don't. What's the big deal?"

"How should I know?"

"I don't see why I have to watch Nick all the time. You're big enough."

"Well, mom told you to, so that's why."

"It's still not fair!" she called as I rode off.

I figured I might ask Sharon and Julie if they could spare a cookie for her and maybe one for Nick too, but it probably wouldn't have been a good idea if I told her that's why I was going. Besides, when I got to Julie and Sharon's apartment, no one was home, so that was that. No cookies. No milk. No kiss.

After dinner I called Ron and told him some extra people maybe wanted the paper and asked him what to do. He asked how many and I counted up Sharon and Julie, George, Mr. Avery, Mr. Rathbone and Kenny Lester and Norma and Shelly and told him six. He said he'd leave me the extra papers from now on.

"Weekdays or weekdays and Sunday too?"

"I'm not sure."

"I'll leave you extra Sunday papers too, just in case."

"I said they maybe want it. What if they all don't take it? Or don't want Sundays?"

"We'll work it out. Don't worry about it. Just get the ones that want it to fill out and sign the subscription slips. It says right on the slip weekdays or weekdays and Sunday."

"What slips?"

"They're proof that they asked for the paper and are going to pay for it."

He said he'd leave a big bunch of the slips since we had a subscription night coming up on Saturday, anyway.

"This Saturday? So soon?"

"Saturday's gonna be June 23. We try make the subscription nights about a week before the end of the month. That way, there'll be time to record the subscriptions and start the paper by the first of the next month. And you'll still have the following Friday and Saturday for the end of the month collecting. I'll pick you up at seven. Be ready."

"Okay," I said.

The next couple of days went better and better, just like George and Kenny Lester said they would. And George must have been right about the rope on the bundles too, because Ron didn't complain about me cutting it off, and every day there was brand new rope holding the papers together just like the day before. By Friday, I hardly had to look at the map or route list at all. Even the Maple-Burton Arms wasn't a big deal. It was still a big stink and I didn't like how dark it was, but no one bothered to yell at me when I creaked down the hall on tiptoes, or when I ran thumping and creaking back after I dropped the paper and knocked on Mrs. Gunther's door. The only weird thing on the whole route was Mr. Duffy. The window was never open and the front door was always locked, and even though I managed to get the paper on the balcony okay, they weren't piling up like maybe he was out of town or something. Someone was taking the papers in alright, just not leaving the window open.

It was six o'clock Saturday morning, and everyone was asleep. My mom and dad got back late, so I thought that's why they were sleeping late too. I'd put the left over two-fifty of Marty's money on his desk when I finished the route Tuesday, but it was still there, so maybe he hadn't seen it yet. I used a piece of his school paper and wrote him a note that said, 'I only owe you $1.50 because Bill had a used rack and here's the left over ------------>" with an arrow pointing to it. He didn't work until ten, so he'd be asleep as long as possible, but he couldn't miss that, I thought. Sarah wasn't up yet, for no reason that I knew of, except if my mom was going downtown again, and if she expected Sarah to watch Nick all day, maybe that's why she was staying in bed as long possible. And Nick was just being Nick. All week, getting ready for the route and doing it and coming home and eating dinner and going to bed and getting up the next day to do it again became all mixed together, like a one long day that never ended. Today was going to be different, I thought. Harder! Mr. Avery had already said it would be okay for me to leave the carwash right at four, so if I hurried home and folded fast, I could probably get the papers delivered by six. Maybe. Thursday had taken an hour and twenty-four minutes and Friday, only an hour and nineteen. George was there both days and I asked him what time it was when I was ready to start and checked the clock in the kitchen when I got back. I was going to subtract three minutes for the time it took to put the route bags on the porch and the Red Rider in the garage. It probably only took one minute, but if I'd gone slower, it would have taken two or maybe three, so I thought I should subtract three just in case I was extra tired from the carwash and put things away slower. But then I couldn't decide if I should subtract or add, so I decided to forget about that and figured if I got started folding by ten after four and was ready to ride by four-forty, I had an hour and twenty minutes, which meant I had a minute to spare, that is, if everything went just right. Then I thought, maybe I should have asked Mr. Avery if I could leave at quarter to four. But if I did, maybe he'd think I wasn't doing enough work for the two-fifty. What if he thought because I wanted to leave at exactly four I wasn't doing enough work period, and fired me? That would be a disaster. Even with the paper route money, I had to be sure I could pay Mr. Mahoney at least the two-fifty. What if Ron took the paper route away? I could tell Marty didn't trust him and I didn't either, not really, so I needed to make sure I had the carwash job. Maybe I could fold faster and start delivering sooner and get done more than one minute before six. Folding faster was the answer to all my problems. I wasn't going to even think about mentioning quarter to four to Mr. Avery.

On the way through the kitchen I saw fifteen cents on the edge of the table and figured my mom probably had left it for me, so I took it. Things were falling into place again, already. I went out the back screen door into the driveway to get the Red Rider. I didn't know where I wanted to go, but just plain riding around for the fun of it sounded good to me, and with the fifteen cents in my pocket, when I got to wherever it was, I could get something to eat. When I got to the garage, Pop was there. He was wearing his Saturday morning stuff, the tan pants and an undershirt and his old black shoes. He hadn't shaved, which was unusual for him, even if it was Saturday. He was knelt down in front of the lawn mower, sharpening it with this tool he dragged slowly from one end to the other a few times for each blade, then he felt the edge to see if it was sharp, then started on the next one.

"Hi, Pop."

He looked up, surpirsed to see me.

"Are we talking now?"

"Sure."

"That's good. I was afraid you weren't ever going to speak to me again. How's the paper route going?"

"Pretty good. I've got most of the houses memorized."

"In just one week?"

"Uh huh."

"That's pretty good. You're working at the carwash and the route today?"

"Uh huh."

"Think you're up to that?"

"I think so. I get to leave the carwash at exactly four, so it should be okay."

"Well, if you get pressed for time, I could take you around in the car."

"Thanks, Pop, but I think it'll work out okay."

"Alright, but remember, if you need the help..."

"Okay. Thanks. Did you know George Bowen took me on his Vincent the first day?"

"His what?"

"Vincent."

"What's that?"

"A big motorcycle. Haven't you ever heard of a Vincent? The Vincent Black Shadow?"

"I must have missed that one. How come he took you?"

"The route guy was way late dropping off the papers, so George took me. He gave Sarah and Marty rides too. Just for the fun of it. Boy, is that thing fast!"

"That was nice of him. He's a good neighbor, okay. Always has been."

"You can say that again. He helped me fix the route bags and all kinds of other stuff. Pop?"

He looked up from the mower.

"Did he ever have kids of his own?"

"Not that I know of. He was married before the war, but when he got back, she'd already made other plans, and was gone. I don't think he wants to try it again."

"That's too bad. I think he'd be a good dad."

"Maybe so."

"Pop?"

"What?"

"Are you and my dad ever going to be friends again?"

He stopped sharpening the mower. His eyes were magnified behind his glasses when he looked up at me.

"I hope so, Kurt."

"Then stop being mean to him," I suggested. "See you later, Pop."

He snorted the funny way he laughs, and said, "So long, kiddo."

I took the Red Rider down the driveway and out into the street. I was about to get on when I saw Miriam watching me from her window. She looked tired and sad, but still so pretty it made my stomach ache. She waved and tried to smile, but seemed like she couldn't get rid of being sad. Probably thinking about Sean, I thought. I wanted to cheer her up again, but then I thought about her and Kevin Doyle together at Whalen's. I just waved back and headed for Joseph's Hot Dog Stand, hoping he was going to open early, like he said. When I got to where our alley met Beverly Boulevard, Norma was just getting there in her little

MG car.

"Are you going to the Hot Dog Stand?" she called to me.

She was wearing sunglasses and a scarf over her head and a gray sweatshirt with cut-off sleeves. I kept peddling so I wouldn't have to start up again, but I called to her as I went past.

"Yes."

"I'll meet you there. There's something I'd like to ask you."

"Okay."


She was on a stool at the counter drinking coffee by the time I rode up, so he was doing it, okay. I parked the bike and sat down next to her. Joseph put a plate of pancakes in front of her and asked me what I wanted.

"Hot chocolate," I told him.

"How 'bout a pancake?"

"No thanks."

"I've got one left over from hers," he said, nodding at the plate. "She asked for a short stack and I made the regular one out of habit. Come on, otherwise I'll have to throw it away. I hate that," he said.

"Okay, I guess."

"They're delicious," she told me, "you'll be glad you did."

She put more syrup on them than I did, and that's really saying something.

"If you're not careful, they're going to float away."

That's what Pop always told me.

"Mmmm," she smiled, "I just love them with lots of syrup!"

"Me too," I said.

Joseph put the extra pancake and my hot chocolate and a glass of water in front of me. I poured a ton of syrup on the one pancake until the plate was almost like a lake and wiggled off a bite with the side of the fork. Steam came out of it it was so hot. I put my fifteen cents on the counter, but Joseph gave me his 'your money's no good' look, and pushed it back to me. He started cleaning the edge of the grill. Norma had chewed her way through about half of her pancakes already, but I was blowing on mine to cool if off before I put it in my mouth. I can't even remember how many times I'd burned my mouth because I was so hungry I forgot to, so this time I was going to be more careful. It still had a little steam coming off it, but it looked okay so I put it in.

"Yeow!" I said, spitting it out onto my plate.

"Are you okay?" Norma said.

"Still too hot," I said, drinking some water.

She wiped some syrup off the corner of her mouth and sipped at the coffee.

"The thing I wanted to ask you is, how would you like to be in the movie I'm working on?"

"The Love Nest movie? Are you crazy? I don't know how to be in a movie!"

"It's not very hard, sweetie, really. I think you'd be perfect. We need a little boy about your age and I thought it might be fun for you."

"Are you serious or are you just joking me?"

"Completely serious, she said. "The little boy they had planned to use got the chicken pox, so all of a sudden, they need someone. I thought of you, and told the director you were my first choice and I wanted to ask you before they found someone else. What do you think? "

"What would I have to do?"

"Well, the movie's about a young couple who've bought an apartment house just after the war and have lots of trouble with it. They have some interesting tenants in the building. One old man in particular. The young man's wife is surprised to find out that his wartime buddy, me, Roberta, is a woman, when the he lets her, me, become one of the tenants. It's silly, but in this business, like Shelly says, you just try to keep working. Anyway, you'd only be in a couple of scenes. You'd be a boy who lives in an apartment building a few doors up. In one scene, Jim, the young man, is taking some old mail boxes off the outside wall and tosses them to you for scrap metal. In another scene, you're about to run a stick across a picket fence they've just painted and Jim's wife, Connie, tells you not to. I think there's another scene where you and some other boys are playing on the sidewalk."

"Do I have to say anything?"

"I don't think so. Or maybe your supposed to say something to Jim, like 'yes', or 'okay', if he asks you if you want the metal for scrap. We'll figure all that out when the time comes."

"Beats the heck out of working in the carwash the rest of your life," Joseph teased me.

I didn't know what to say. I tried, but I couldn't picture it at all.

"We'd have to ask your mom and dad, of course. That is, if you think you'd like to."

"I suppose I could do it. But I'm supposed to work at the carwash and do the paper route today, so I don't think I can."

She smiled and touched my arm and told me, "Oh no, honey, not today! We'd have to plan ahead a little. I was thinking, maybe you'd like to come to the set with me one morning next week. You could watch how a movie gets made and see if you like the idea of being in it. Then you could decide. I could bring you back at the lunch break so you'd be home in time to do your paper route. If you decided to do it, they'd pay you for it."

"Really?"

"Not very much, of course, but you'd get paid something. More if you say something."

"Really? Hello, hello, good-bye, I'll take all the mail boxes you got, hello good-bye. That oughta be about five bucks worth, right?"

"Could be," she laughed. "I think you're catching on pretty quickly."

"You need a Hot Dog Stand cook in your movie?" Joseph asked her, "Or a horn player?"

"If we do, you're my first choice. I promise."

"Good enough," he said. "Sounds like fun to me, Kurt, but what do I know?"

I took a careful bite of the pancake. It was cool enough now. As I chewed it, I tried to picture the whole thing. I thought about how hard it seemed to be for Julie and Sharon, just trying to get in a movie, and how this was just falling into place like I'd planned the whole thing, even if it wasn't part of any plan I ever thought of. Heck, my only plan was to pay for the locks and ride the Red Rider. But this might help pay them off faster.

"You'll be there the whole time?"

"Of course I will. You and me and Shelly can be the Oakhurst Players. Only the three of us would know, but that's what we could be."

"Shelly's in Love Nest too?"

"No, but we'd still be the actors from Oakhurst, so we could be the Oakhurst Players."

"What about Julie and Sharon?"

"Who?"

"The girls that live down the street on the next block of Oakhurst. They're actors too, at least they're trying to be, the ones that said they liked your work, remember?"

"Yes. What about them?"

"Well, since they live on Oakhurst, maybe they should be in the Oakhurst Players too."

"I hadn't thought of that. We'll make them Oakhurst Players, too. If they want to be."

"And Joseph will know, even if he isn't an actor," I pointed out.

"I think we can trust him to keep it our secret."

"This is going to get bigger than the Oakhurst Irregulars."

"The what?" she asked me.

"A club my sister started to keep me out," I said.

"That's not very nice."

"It's okay, because I'm getting too busy to be in it anyway. Especially if I get in your movie."

"So, you're interested?"

"I guess. Sure. I'll ask my mom."

"That's wonderful! I'll tell Joe. He's the director. And if your mom says it's okay, one of Joe's assistants will come by your house with a few papers for your parents to sign and then we'll pick a morning and we'll just see. Oh, I'm so glad you'll do it!"

"I said I'll come see about it," I reminded her.

"Maybe you should skip the acting and become a lawyer," Joseph said.

"Well, coming to the set is the first step," Norma said. "I think you'll have fun and want to do it. I really do."

"Maybe," I said.

I finished my pancake and the hot chocolate. The clock on the wall over the grill showed it was only a few minutes after seven.

"Gotta run," Norma said.

She got off the stool, left some dollar bills for Joseph, sipped a little more coffee and leaned over and kissed the top of my head.

"Bye sweetie. I'm so excited! Bye, Joseph," she said as she headed for the MG.

As she drove off the lot, Joseph told me again, "If only you could bottle those kisses."

I rode back to Oakhurst and home, hoping my mom was still there so I could ask her about the movie. I still had about two and a half hours before I had to be at the carwash and was also sort of hoping George would be outside by now. I wanted to tell him about Norma and the movie. Maybe Kenny Lester too, if he was around. I thought I could do it without it being bragging, but by the time I turned the corner, I knew it would be, so I figured I'd just wait and see if it really happened or not before telling anyone. Kenny would understand about things falling into place when you didn't expect them to, but because it was Norma, it would automatically be bragging even with him. George probably wouldn't think it was a big deal one way or the other, but he might tell Kenny or someone else, and I'd be right back to the beginning. If George was there, I should just find out if there was any trouble with Kevin Doyle when he went over to his house after I started the route yesterday. Movie or no movie, I wanted to know about that. Well, not really wanted to know, but needed to know. Because if my yelling at Kevin was going to make him crazy against me all the time now, or if George got in a fight with him about him bothering me at Whalen's and that was going to make him crazy all the time, I had to know even if I didn't want to. I didn't know what I could do about it, but I should know if he was going to be crazy anytime he saw me. When I pulled into our driveway, Sarah was sitting on the bottom step, reading and watching Nick, who was on his back on the grass, happy as can be, with a book held up over him. He was dressed in a t-shirt and short pants, but barefoot.

"Where's mom and dad?"

"Downtown," she told me.

"Already?"

"Already, alright. And guess who's got to watch Nick? You can scratch Marty and yourself off the list, so guess who that leaves?"

"Let me think," I said, trying to joke her.

"It's not fair! Megan's stuck with the phone and I'm stuck here. My whole life is coming and going and all I do is watch Nick."

Nick put the book to the side, and was lying there looking at the sky. He was pinching together the thumb and first finger on both hands and putting them together, making a little square. He had one eye shut and was looking through the hole where all of the fingers came together. Whatever it was he was looking at or thinking about, because with him, you just knew he was thinking about stuff, I knew if he had food and his blanket and one of his books, he was the happiest kid on the block. Just watching him made you feel good. It also made me wonder what he was thinking about.

"If you want to go over to Megan's, I'll stay with him," I said

"What's the catch?"

"Nothing. You said you'd help with the route if I had trouble."

"Yeah, but you didn't."

"But you offered. I'll watch him for a while. I've got to leave here about nine-thirty, okay?"

"Thanks," she said coming off the step. "I'll be back before then. If he gets tired of fooling around out here, mom said I could take him for a walk up the block."

"Maybe I'll take him up to see if Snowball's outside."

"Sure. Whatever," she said as she dashed across the street to the Weis's house. "Thanks."

"Nick," I said.

He rolled over so he could see me but didn't say anything. His eyebrows went up to show me he was listening.

"Wanna go see Snowball?"

"Mmmm hmm," he mumbled.

I was pretty sure he was saying yes, but since he didn't make a move to get up, I wasn't positive. If he thought I was going to pick him up, he was crazy. Sometimes he'd hold his arms up waiting for someone to get him started. He could do it himself, of course, but usually he just waited to see what would happen. He was four years old and two months and was way too heavy for me to pick up, so if he wanted to go see Snowball, he was going to have to get up on his own. While I was standing there, I heard the door open and close across the street. Kevin Doyle came out onto his front steps in his usual dirty looking pants and shirt and some slippers instead of shoes. He coughed a bunch of times, then lit a cigarette. He stared at me. His hair was sticking up and his face was dark from needing a shave and it seemed like I could smell him, even though he was too far away. Maybe just seeing the cigarette made me think I was smelling it and him too. I knew he saw me, but he didn't show it. He just stood there smoking. Then, all of a sudden, with a little smile, he nodded at me, like we were old pals. Sort of, 'good morning', or 'howya doin'? So I thought maybe he wasn't going to be crazy all the time after all. It wasn't the crazy smile or the nasty one. Just a smile. That's a relief, I thought. Nick had stood up and was holding his hand out for me to take it, which I did. We were heading up the street when George came down his walkway.

"Where're you guys off to?" he asked Nick.

Nick mumbled something to George," pointing up the street

"What was that?" George asked me.

"Snowball. You know, the puppy Norma and Shelly got from the Lesters.

"Oh, I see."

George saw Kevin across the street on the steps. He motioned for him to come over. Oh no, I thought, Kevin might not be smiling nasty, but that doesn't mean I want to see him up close. What was George thinking?

"Kurt, can you wait a minute before you go?" he said.

I didn't answer. I just stood there frozen like a statue as I watched Kevin cross the street. I had the feeling go through me that if I ran right now, I could get away from him. Maybe I could drag Nick with me and maybe make it into the bamboo patch far enough ahead of him so, even if he was chasing after us, he wouldn't see where we'd gone. Maybe. Even with George there, the idea of running was all I could think about. It had worked its way down from my head to my feet. They were ready to go, except just then, Nick took hold of my hand again and sort of hid behind me like I'd been behind Iyama Osaka at Whalen's, and I knew there was no way I could get away fast enough with him and no way I could leave him behind, so I stood there, my legs beginning to shake, then my whole body. When he got to us he spoke to George.

"Hey, George," he said.

Most of the puffiness was gone from his face, but the stitches looked like little railroad tracks.

"Kevin's got something to say, Kurt," George said.

Kevin looked at me then at George.

"Go on," George told him.

"Kid, I'm sorry I got mean yesterday."

He looked at George.

"Okay?"

"Okay," George said, "what else?"

"It won't happen again."

He looked at George, waiting for George to let him know that was good enough.

"And?"

"Oh yeah. You can throw the paper on the front steps."

He looked at George again.

"Okay?"

"Okay, then," George said. "I think we're all square now."

George patted Kevin's shoulder. Then he took hold of mine. My legs were still shaking, but the rest of me had settled down. Nick had been holding onto my hand so tight the tips of my fingers were getting white. I was going to tell him to let go, but with Kevin there, I knew how he felt, even if he didn't know why, so I didn't.

"Mind if I come with you guys to see this Snowball character?" George asked.

"Sure. Do you know my brother, Nick?"

"Well, we've never formally been introduced."

"This is Nick. He's four. Nick, this is George."

George reached down with his hand out to Nick. Nick stood there looking right at George, looking him right in the eye, not about to shake since his one hand was busy both holding the blanket, and the other was holding mine. Most kids would have been looking at the ground, I bet.

but Not Nick. He might not say much, but he didn't plan on missing anything either.

"You probably don't want to shake with him anyway, George. His fingers are usually gooey."

"Thanks for the tip," George said. "See you later, Kevin."

"Later, George," Kevin said, and started back across the street.

Mr. Avery came down his walkway on his usual walk to the carwash and said hello and said he'd see me there later.

"Mr. Avery?"

"Yes, Kurt?"

"If you still want to subscribe to the Daily Mirror I can start it today. If you want to. You don't have to or anything, but George said you wanted it. You too, George."

"You're ready to handle the extra papers already?"

"Sure. With the route bags on the fender rack, it's not too hard."

"Okay, then, sign me up."

"Me too, Kurt," Mr. Avery said.

"I'm supposed to do a subscription night tonight, so I'll have the slips you need to fill out, but I could start the paper today and leave the slip under the rubber band and I could come get it tomorrow. Do you want the Sunday paper too?"

"No. It takes me all day to read The Times on Sunday. That's about as much as I can handle," Mr. Avery said.

"I'm afraid that's true for me too," George said.

"Don't feel bad. Those Sunday papers are huge and I've already got seventeen. That's plenty, believe me."

When we got to Mr. Rathbone's place, Iyama Osaka's truck was already there, so he must be in the back garden, I thought. I wondered if I should tell George he'd been at Whalen's and made Kevin leave me alone, but I figured since George had talked to Kevin and Kevin had said he was sorry, that was that. Well, maybe.

"If you're going to be adding papers to your route, remember Basil said he'd like to have the Mirror too."

"You think he'd be up this early?"

"Knock and see."

"Maybe I'll do it on the way back down."

Across the street, Kenny Lester was under the hood working on the Buick and called when he saw us.

"Where're you guys off to?"

"To see if Snowball's in the yard," I called back.

"Don't see you up here too often, George."

"I've heard a lot about Snowball the wonder-dog. Thought I'd see for myself."

"Maybe see Snowball's new mommy?" Kenny joked him.

"Never gave it a thought," George said.

If you thought about it, it seemed odd okay, but I believed him, even if they were joking around. I bet he hadn't even thought about Norma one bit.

"She's not even there," I told Kenny. "I had pancakes at Joseph's with her before. She's already gone to work."

I almost told them about me maybe being in the movie, but stopped just in time.

"Maybe next time, eh George," Kenny teased him.

"Maybe," George said, puffing away on his cigarette.

"See you at the carwash, Kurt. I'm gonna get this boat washed."

"Do you still want the paper?" I called to him.

"Sure. You ready?"

"Uh huh. I could start leaving it today. If you want."

"Good, let's get it started."

"I'll put a subscription slip under the rubber band, okay? Just fill it out and give it to me."

"You got it." See you at the carwash."

"Sundays too or no Sundays?"

"Sundays too. That okay?"

Oh brother, I thought, but told him, "Sure."

When we got to Shelly and Norma's place, Snowball was in the yard all alone. Actually, she was on the porch all alone, and quiet, but when she saw us, she came into the yard and over to the fence and began yipping and jumping up and around in circles all at the same time. Nick was smiling and laughing as soon as he saw her. He let go of my hand so he could touch Snowball through the fence. Snowball was going crazy for Nick. Then Shelly opened the door and yelled at her.

"Hey! Fur-ball! Knock it off! What the hell's the matter with you? Some of us are still sleeping!"

Her face was angry and scrunched up unitl she saw us. George, mostly.

"Oh," she smiled. "Kurt. Nice to see you. A little early, as usual, but nice just the same."

She wrapped her pink robe more tightly around and held it closed as she came down the steps to the yard.

"Who's this?" she nodded at Nick.

She was looking at George though.

"He's my brother, Nick," I told her.

"He might wanna find some shoes," she said.

Nick didn't pay any attention to Shelly about the shoes. He kept his fingers through the fence so Snowball could keep licking.

"You guys can come in the yard if you like," she said to me and Nick.

"Who's this?" she finally got around to saying about George.

"That's George," I said.

"Of course," she said.

"George Bowen," he said, reaching out to shake hands.

"Shelly," she said. "Nice to meet you."

She was running her hand through her hair, trying to comb it with her fingers. Nick and I went into the yard and I showed him about throwing

the ball with the bell for Snowball. She'd bring it back and one of us
would throw it again. I let Nick do most of the throwing since Snowball
seemed crazy for him anyway. Shelly and George stood at the fence,
talking. George stayed outside, Shelly inside, but every once in a while
she'd laugh at something and reach over the fence and touch his arm.
He put out what was left of his cigarette against the bottom of his shoe
and put the butt in his pocket. He lit another one and offered one to her.
He lit it for her then lit his own. He had a big smile on his face, that's
for sure. Maybe Pop was wrong, I was thinking. Nick and I played with
Snowball until she got tired and went back on the porch for water and
just stayed there. Then we went out through the gate and stood next to
George for a while. It didn't seem like he was ready to go, but I thought
I should get back in case Sarah came back from Megan's and wondered
where we were.

"I'm going to take Nick home," I told him.

"I'm coming with you," George said.

That's what he said, anyway, but it didn't look like he really wanted to.

"Don't be a stranger," Shelly told George. "You, I know I'll see," she
said to me.

"If you and Norma still want the paper, I could start it today."

"Sure, kiddo. But like I said, throw it there outside the gate
so the fur-ball doesn't chew it to pieces before we get to it."
"Okay."

"Sundays too?" I asked her.

"Of course. What's a Sunday morning without coffee and more newspaper than you can possibly read?"

Yikes, that made nineteen! I told her about the subscription slip and
then we started down the street. Nick and I did, anyway.

"I'll catch up to you, Kurt," George said.

When we got to Rathbone's, he and Iyama were on the front lawn
inspecting some flowers on bushes against the house. When he saw us,
he stopped talking to Iyama and called to me.

"Just the young man I'm looking for. How are you today?"
"Fine."

"And whom have we here?" he said, nodding towards Nick.

"He's my brother, Nick."

"How do you do, Nicholas? Nice to meet you."

Nick watched him but didn't say anything.

"If you're ready to deliver the paper, I'd be glad to start a subscripiton."

"Thank you. I am adding some new customers. George told me you
might like it too."

"Indeed I would. Especially after seeing you place it with such aplomb
on yonder balcony," he smiled.

"Where would you like it?"

"The front porch will do nicely, young man. Thank you."

I was almost afraid to ask, but I had to.

"Sundays or no Sundays?"

"I think not. I hope that's okay. I could, if you like."

"No, really. That's fine," I said.

I told him about the subscription slip. Nick was tugging at my hand to go. Iyama was looking at me, sort of asking me with his eyes if I was okay. If everything was okay. I smiled at him and he smiled back. Rathbone followed my eyes and saw Iyama and then looked at me, like he knew all about it.

"In this life, it's the friends you can count on that make all the difference," he said.

He smiled and touched my hair and then Nick and I headed home.

We got back to our yard and Nick got comfortable on the grass and started to look at his book again, but pretty soon he was sort of snoozing until Sarah came. George didn't show up before I had to leave for the carwash.

The carwash was the busiest I'd ever seen it. We must have washed thirty-five cars by lunch. Maurice put the rope up across the driveway and he and the other guys went down to their tree for lunch and I sat at the counter and started on a coke, but before I'd gotten halfway through it, there were so many cars backed up waiting to get on the lot, Maurice and the guys decided to cut their lunch time short and get back to work. He took the rope down and started letting a new group of six come on. He called to me.

"Kurt, you finish up your lunch. We'll be fine."

But since all I was having was the coke, I took a few more big gulps and got back to work too. Since I was going to be leaving half an hour early, that is, a half an hour if they got out of here on time, which didn't seem very likely since there were cars backed way up Elm, and Mr. Avery might not want to give a Rain-Check free ticket to a million cars, they might be here until five-thirty or six and then I would have left much more early that just the half-hour, so I figured I'd better get back to work too. By four we must have done another twenty-five cars. Maybe more. Even cutting the lunch break time in half, even then, we could hardly keep up with all the cars. I only had the half a coke the whole day. I knew we washed Hop-A-Long Cassidy's car and Kenny Lester's Buick and Pop's car and some other people that I knew because I saw them or they said hello, but it was just one car after another and I wouldn't have know who's car any of them were if they hadn't said hello. The next thing I knew Mr. Avery was handing me my two-fifty. I felt bad about leaving when there were still so many cars to wash, but if I didn't get started folding right away, six o'clock was going to happen whether I was ready or not.

I raced home and the papers were right there where they were supposed to be. I leaned the Red Rider against Mumps and got the route bags and the leather string and the rubber bands. I tied the bags onto the bike. I took out George's pocket knife and popped the fuzzy rope off.

That little knife was sharp, alright. The good thing about Saturday papers was that they were smaller and easy to fold. Even with the extra six, I was ready to go and it couldn't have been worse than four-twenty, four twenty-five at the worst. I didn't use up time going in the kitchen to look, but I was pretty sure. I put six of the subscription slips inside my shirt and put a rubber band around the rest and put them and the rubber band box on the porch. I was trying to decide if I should do George's paper first or last. I decided first. I took one of the slips out and put it under the rubber band. I walked into the Courtyard and dropped it on his front step. It was still pretty hot out, and when it was and he was home, he usually left his front door open, but it was closed, so he must be gone. I took another paper from the bags and walked across the street and tossed it on Kevin Doyle's front steps. I'd invented a new way to get on the Red Rider when the route bags were full that worked great. I walked it into the street next right next to the curb, got the pedals in the right position, and using the extra height, got on from the parkway side. When I was ready, I just pushed off and pedaled. It worked every time. When I got to Beverly I could do it again. In fact, anytime I had to stop and start up again, I could do it.

I went up on the sidewalk a few houses before 331 so I'd have time to reach back and get a paper and toss it when I got there. That all went fine, and I went off at the next driveway to cross the street to Sharon and Julie's place. I was sort of wobbling since the bags were full and heavy and I had to make the turn to go down the driveway so soon after the doing the right-hand George fling, so I didn't see or hear the car coming. The next thing I knew there was honking so loud my ears hurt and it made my eyes not work right either, because I crashed right into the curb on the other side of the street and down I went and the Red Rider and all of the papers too. Luckily, only some of them spilled out. And luckier still, I didn't see one scratch on the bike, and believe me, I looked expecting to see one. The guy that almost hit me was yelling about me not looking where I was going, which was true, but it didn't seem like he was either or he would have seen me, so it was his fault as much as mine, and I figured we were even. Julie came out, probably because of the honking.

"My God! Are you okay?"

"I'm fine. So's the Red Rider."

"He came right out of the driveway and across the street, just like that," the man said, snapping his fingers.

"You're sure you're okay," she asked me.

"I'm fine. I've got your paper and the subscription slip."

"You've got to be more careful. It's like crossing the street on foot. Look both ways, right?"

"Right," I agreed. "Do you still want the paper?"

The man told me to be more careful and drove off.

"Of course."

I handed her the paper and a subscription slip from my shirt.

"I've got to get going," I told her.

"Be careful!"

"I will."

I sort of wanted to tell her about the movie, but it probably wouldn't have been a good idea, it falling into place and all, and besides, I didn't really have time to hang around. Julie helped me stand the bike back up and held it while I put the spilled papers back in the bags. Sharon came down the walk and Julie told her what had happened.

"That's terrible! Are you sure you're okay?"

"I'm sure."

"Well, if you want some cookies and milk, stop by," Sharon said.

"Maybe," I said.

I got the bike in the right position by their curb and got on and used my new way to start up again. The two of them waved to me as I rode off. I waved but without looking back so I didn't run into anything else. I was thinking, all in all, it turned out pretty good. Imagine what could have happened? The Red Rider could have been creamed and I'd lose the route, or I might have gotten banged up and not been able to work at the carwash and then what? How could I pay off the locks? The movie might not happen, and besides, Norma said they probably wouldn't pay me very much even if I was in it. The whole thing could have been a disaster. But it wasn't. And even though I didn't tell Julie and Sharon, I knew it was because of the luck of the Red Rider and the double extra good luck of Kenny's propeller medal and the pocket knife.

I raced around the route faster than ever, partly because I knew all of the houses now, and partly because the Saturday papers were so much easier to throw. I turned the corner onto Oakhust and angled across the street for Shelly and Norma's. I knew I'd have to get off the bike to put a subscription slip under the rubber band, so I came to a stop in the street in front of her parkway. Shelly's didn't have a driveway, since her carport was in back, facing the alley. The route bags were almost empty. Just three more papers. Four, counting Norma and Shelly's. Only that Duffy guy's didn't need a subscription slip, so when I got off the bike, I put slips on all but his, getting them ready. When I got to the gate in the fence where Shelly told me to leave the paper, the front door was open and George and Shelly were sitting on the top step with coffee cups in their hands. Boy, were they all smiles. Instead of leaving the paper by the gate, I went inside and handed it to Shelly. She was wearing the too tight jeans and a blue and white checkered shirt and a scarf that matched and the kind of boat sneakers Norma and the northsiders wear.

"Hiya kid. How'd it go?"

"Good. A car almost hit me, but it didn't."

"You call that good?"

"Well, it didn't. So that's good, right?"

"You got a positive outlook, I'll say that for you. Doesn't he, George?"

"He does. That's a fact," he told her. "But you've got to be more care-ful," he said to me, lighting another cigarette.

"Thanks for the coffee, Shelly. I enjoyed it. I'm going to have to make a point of trying to see your movies."

He stood up and handed her the cup.

"You do that, George. Maybe sometime we could go see one together. Mine or not."

"I'd like that."

Shelly got up too. George looked at his watch.

"You made good time. It's only five forty-five."

"Are you sure?"

He looked at his watch again.

"Five forty-five on the nose. Wanna walk the rest of the way down? I'll push your bike, you can toss the papers."

"Sure."

I took two papers and ran across the street and dropped the one with the slip at the top of Kenny Lester's steps and then went to Duffy's place. The window was closed again. I did the backwards overhead toss and got it on the balcony on the first try. When I came back to George, he asked me about it.

"It's never open. The papers are always gone by the next day, but the window is never open. I just toss it up there anyway since that's where he asked for it."

"That's strange," George said, puffing on the cigarette.

He stood there looking at the window, thinking about it, but there was nothing to see, so he shrugged and we walked down the street to Rathbone's place. I took the last paper and put it on his porch.

"I already delivered yours," I told him. "First."

"Thank you. I'll go take a look. See what's new."

"Since this morning's Times?" I joked him.

"Might be something. You never know."

When we got to his house, he walked up into the Courtyard and I walked the bike up our driveway and put it in the garage. I left the route bags on so it would be all ready for the Sunday paper. I even thought I might leave the route bags on all the time except when me and the Red Rider took a trip other than the route. That way I wouldn't have to put them on and take them off over and over. It would save time, that's for sure, so it seemed like a good idea to me and it was okay with the Red Rider.

When I came in through the back porch, my mom was in the kitchen and had dinner ready. The clock on the stove said six-fifteen. My dad was still downtown and wouldn't be home 'til late again, but I might see him anyway, since I'd be on the subscription night and wouldn't get home until late myself. We had spaghetti and meatballs for dinner and rootbeer floats for dessert so I was really full and sleepy after dinner, but by the time me and Sarah and Marty cleaned up the kitchen, which was our job after dinner, Ron showed up and it was time to go. He didn't come in but just stood on the porch. The screen door was closed, but the real front door was open, so that when he rang the bell, we could see right away it was him. I went to the door and my mom and Marty came too.

"I'll have him back by nine or nine-thirty at the latest," Ron told my mom.

She asked me if I wanted a jacket but it was warm out and I didn't usually wear one, and besides, I couldn't think of one I had that I could wear if I wanted. I used to have one, but I was probably about Nick's age back then, so it wouldn't fit now anyway, even if I knew where it was. Marty leaned against the wall, watching. He sure didn't like Ron one bit, and Ron didn't like him either, because he made sure he didn't look at Marty or say anything to him. As I was going through the door, Marty came off the wall.

"Is there some number of subscriptions Kurt's supposed to get?"

"As many as possible."

"But no minimum?"

"No, just as many as he can. Anything else?" Ron said in an impatient way.

"Nope," Marty said.

"You got the subscription slips I left?" Ron asked me.

"There in my rubber band box on the porch."

"Get 'em, and let's go. The others are waiting."

Sure enough, there were eight other boys in the back of his pick-up truck and two more inside. They were all older than me by a lot. I didn't ask, but just looking, I'd guess they were all at least twelve, some of them even more.

"Get in back," Ron said.

I climbed up using the back wheel as a step and one of the guys pulled me in.

"You got a route?" he asked me.

"Uh huh."

"Aren't you a little small."

"I don't know. I don't think so. I did it all week."

"Any Sundays yet?"

"No. Tomorrow's the first."

"Oh, boy, you're in for it! Sunday's are a bitch! How many you got?"

"I was going to have seventeen, but I added some neighbors on my block, so it's up to twenty."

"That's not too bad. I've got twenty-eight, and believe me, that's a back-breaker. My name's Brian. What's yours?"

"Kurt."

"Those pants and shoes are a nice touch, but you should have brought a jacket. It's gonna be cold back here on the way home. Maybe even before. The two guys who get the most new subscriptions the month before get to sit in the cab with Ron. I've never made it yet, but I was close a couple of months ago. In the winter it's a big deal because there's the heater up there."

"What's his name?" I asked about the boy on the other side of Brian. He was all huddled up like it was snowing or something, and the sun hadn't even gone down all the way yet. His knees were pulled up to his chest with his arms wrapped around them and his head was down resting on top of them. He had on a thick leather jacket with a sheepskin collar, a flyer's jacket, like one of my mother's brothers, my uncle Myron had, who was a flyer in the war. I supposed Kenny Lester had one too, some-where. In fact, I bet this one probably came from the war too, because it was way too big for him.

"Jim," Brian said. "Say hello, Jim."

Jim looked up and said, "Hello," and put his head back down.

"He's not trying to be mean or anything," Brian told me, "he just gets carsick back here."

Ron pulled away from the curb and we were off. It was windy in back, but not cold, at least not yet, so that was good, since all I had on was the t-shirt and my better jeans. They had small holes at the knees anyway but it was my sneakers that got the prize for holey. The three biggest boys were sitting with their back to the window of the cab where Ron and the other two boys were, and including me, there were three of us sitting across from three other kids with our backs against the two sides. The three bigger boys under the cab window were talking and laughing, but I couldn't hear what they were saying or what was so funny, and I wondered how they could, because the best the three guys across from us could do was nod hello. Even if they wanted to say anything, the wind noise and the old truck noise would have made it impossible, so they didn't try, so I wondered how the bigger boys could.

I'd always thought the streets in Beverly Hills were so smooth. They were dark black, like new, and the white crosswalk stripes and STOP written on the ground at the stop signs always looked like someone had just painted it, fresh and bright, so it seemed like the streets were perfect. And on the Red Rider, going to school and even all the way to Will Roger's State Beach and on the paper route, they all seemed smooth as can be. But sitting in the back of Ron's pick up was a completely differ-ent story. It found every bump for miles around and banged over them like they were all railroad tracks. I bet we hadn't even gone a mile and my bottom hurt. Brian noticed me making a face every time the truck bounced over something.

"Just wait 'til it's cold!" he laughed. "That's a real bitch!"

We bounced around for fifteen minutes or so before we came to whereever we were, which was no where I'd ever seen before.

"Where are we?" I asked .

"Who knows? he said.

One of the bigger boys by the cab window heard us.

"Ron figures out a neighborhood where there's not many subscrip-tions and that's where we go. We've been as far as Santa Monica and once to Watts. Boy, was that a waste of time!"

"Why?" I asked him.

"How many niggers are gonna subscribe when they can probably steal it!" he laughed.

"Why do you say that?" I said. "Just because they have a rough time of it in this town, doesn't mean they steal things."

Brian reached over and squeezed my leg.

"What are you, some nigger lover?" the boy said.

All of a sudden, all of the bigger boys were standing up and the one boy who didn't like Negroes got up from his side of the truck and was standing over me, like he was going to punch me. I stayed sitting. Brian moved away from me and stood up too. Jim didn't get up because his head was still down, still too carsick, I supposed, to care.

"I work at the carwash with some Negroes and they wouldn't steal anything," I said. "Never."

"That's how much you know, you jerk."

He looked me over a little more closely.

"You're not even big enough to hit. Forget you!"

He and the others climbed out of the back of the truck onto the sidewalk laughing at what a jerk I was. At least I was too small of a jerk to hit. That was something. Too bad Sarah didn't see it that way. Ron and the two guys from the cab got out and everyone stood around together on the corner. While we were standing there the street light came on.

"You all got subscription slips and two pencils, right?" Ron said.

"I don't," I said.

"Figures," the boy who didn't hit me said.

"I thought you said you had the slips," Ron said.

"I do. I just don't have a pencil."

"So how did you think you'd fill out the slips, jerk-o?"

"Leave him alone, Will. It's his first night," Brian said.

"Here," Ron said, handing me two short pencils.

At least they were both sharpened.

"You don't want someone to say yes to subscribing, then change their mind 'cause you don't have anything to write with. If one pencil breaks or wears down, you've got another. Get it?" Ron told me.

The others knew all about it and looked bored and mad at me for making them stand around while Ron explained.

"Everyone got their story?" Ron asked.

They all muttered yes, like they knew what he was talking about, but I didn't. I was afraid to say so, because they'd all get mad at me again, but what story, I wondered. I tugged on Brian's jacket sleeve and whispered to him.

"What's a story?"

"Oh, boy! Ron didn't tell you anything, did he?"

"Not much, I guess."

"Listen up!" Ron shouted. "Stop talking you two," he said to me and Brian. "We're going in two's again."

He looked up at the street sign.

"Take a good look. This is where we'll meet up."

We were at Beverly Drive and Monte Mar. It might have been the moon for all I knew. I'd never been around here before.

"Brian, you and Kurt can take Monte Mar, Kirkside and Oakmore between Beverly and Beverwil. Got it?"

"Yep," Brian said.

"Take opposite sides of the street and work your way down and back."

He looked at his watch.

"It's seven-twenty. We'll meet back here at nine. Use whatever story you want, but the baseball mitt's probably the best this time of year. Some of you are falling a little behind with your subscriptions, so if you want to keep your routes, tonight's your chance to catch up. Don't waste it."

The other boys had already chosen each other in two's, and Ron told them what streets they had. When everyone knew where they were supposed to go, they jumped in the back of the truck again and Ron drove off, leaving me and Brian there alone.

"Now what?" I said.

"Ron's going to drop them off at their streets."

"No. I mean, what do we do now?"

"Oh brother! At least our subscriptions don't count as a team. Man, how come he stuck me with you?"

"Sorry," I said.

"Oh, don't worry about it. Just don't expect me to hold your hand all night, okay? I got almost enough subscriptions for a twenty-dollar bonus, and tonight could put me over the top."

"How many does that take?"

"Fifty."

"Fifty? How many more do you need."

"Six."

"How many do you usually get?"

"Three or four. Sometimes five. Six once. It's easier in the spring and summer, like now. When it's cold out, people don't want to even hear your story. They just want you to go away so they can close the door and keep the cold out. Man, that's brutal! You walk around all night in the cold and they can't wait to close the door in your face."

"You think you're going to get six tonight?"

"If you don't slow me down too much. That's not a cut against you, just the way it is. Let's get goin'."

"But what's a story?"

"Oh yeah, the story. There's lots of them, see? It's what you tell people to make them feel sorry for you. So they want to help you out, see? Like your pants and shoes. Did Ron suggest that?"

"No."

"Well, it's a nice touch, like I said."

"I still don't get it."

"Well, like the mitt story. It's a beaut! Ron made it up. He made up most of them, but you're allowed to make up your own too. Here's the mitt one: you go to the door. You ring the bell or knock. Whatever, that's up to you. Someone opens the door. You say, 'Excuse me mam, or mister, but I'm a delivery boy for the Daily Mirror and I was hoping you could help me. It's important you tell them you want them to help you. That way it's not for the Mirror, it's for you, the kid that's right there in front of them. Not some company a million miles away. Or downtown, in this case. But anyway, you say you want them to help you and they say something like 'how?' and you don't say anything about taking the paper. Not right away, because that might cool the whole thing. Get it?"

"Sort of."

"Okay," he said, "then comes the mitt part. You say, 'I have a chance to play on a little league team but I need a mitt. I can't play unless I have one, but I can't afford it. You see the beauty of it?"

"Not really."

"Just listen. You will. So they say something like, 'maybe I can give you a buck or two'. Most people are pretty nice and will offer to help, but you just wave them off, like this.

He showed me, holding up his hands, saying, "'No no no, no thank you. That's really nice of you to offer, but I couldn't take any money. No. Really'. Then they get this puzzled look, like 'what then?'. That's when you come in for the kill. Now you've got 'em."

"I do?"

"You do. You say, 'If I can get another two subscriptions, I'll have earned enough for the Rawlings G-600. It's the best mitt there is'. Even if they've never heard of it, it sounds good, and if they have, they'll know you're telling the truth, because it is the best mitt in the world. Most of the real players use them."

"Why do you tell them you still need two more subscriptions?"

"That's a good question. I'm glad you're paying attention. If you told them you only needed one more, that might sound a little phony. So two sounds better. If they ask how many you need altogether, you tell them fifteen and you've got thirteen. If they don't ask, you can tell them or not. That's up to you. But the real beauty of telling them you need two is that they might have a friend or neighbor and call them and get them to take the paper too! Get it? Two new subscriptions just like that!"

"I think so. But isn't it lying?"

He looked at me funny.

"Well, that's not the point. The point is you're a poor kid who can't afford a mitt and they can help you by subscribing to the paper. That's the whole idea. That's what the story's for. Anyway, if you don't like that one, make up one of your own. I gotta get started or I'll never make six. You take that side and I'll take this. Same on the other two streets, okay?"

"Okay."

"I'll meet you back here at nine. Good luck."

"Thanks."

I crossed the street and looked back. Brian had gone up the walk to his first house. He turned around and motioned for me to go to mine too.

I walked up the walkway about as slow as I could. The house didn't face the street straight ahead, but at an angle, which was sort of neat. I spent a while looking at that. Before I even got to the door, Brian was already coming out of his first house. He waved a slip over his head. He must have gotten one.

"Go on!" he whisper-shouted. "Give it a try. Knock on the door!"

Since he was standing there watching, I figured I had to. I went up the stairs slowly, too slowly for him.

"Hurry up! I haven't got all night!"

I got to the door and rang the bell. There was no answer so I started to leave.

"Jeez, you've got to give them time to answer! Stay put!"

From inside a man's voice said who's there. I didn't know what to say or how to explain. So I didn't say anything. Maybe he'd think he heard the bell wrong or something and not answer it, but no such luck. He opened the door. It took him a second to see me because it was getting dark and he hadn't turned his porch light on, and also he was looking too high and looked over me. Then he saw me.

"Hello. What can I do for you?"

"Wanna take the Daily Mirror?"

"No thanks."

"That's okay."

He shut the door. When I turned around, Brian was waiting on the sidewalk on my side of the street.

"Did you give him the story?"

"No."

"What did you say?"

"I asked him if he wanted to take the paper."

"And?"

"He said no."

"Big surprise! That's why we give them the story! It's a favor to them, for pete'sake. They get to feel good that they're helping some poor kid. Your way, they don't get that. See?"

"I suppose."

"Well, you're on your own now. I got to make up time. Good luck."

"Thanks."

He ran across the street to his next house. I sort of poked along, looking at the houses, trying to decide if any of them looked friendlier than any other. It they didn't have a lot of lights on, I didn't even think about going to the door. If they did, I tried to imagine who lived there and if they really might want the paper. Most times, I thought they probably had all the newspapers they needed, so I might as well not bother them. I'd passed about three or four houses. Maybe five. Brian was already so far up the block I couldn't see him any more, which was good, because that way he wouldn't keep bugging me about going up to all the houses I was skipping. Since I'd gotten six new subscriptions already, without even being on a subscription night, that should be good enough, I thought. But Ron hadn't even mentioned it that way. When I asked for the extra papers he just said he'd leave them. Maybe it didn't count unless you got them on a subscription night. And he was telling the other boys some of them were falling behind and might loose their routes. And they'd had them for a long time. What would he do to me if I didn't get any subscriptions at all? Oh brother, I was doomed again! I figured I'd better try harder. I looked for a house with a lot of lights. Two houses farther up was perfect. Every light in the house must have been on. I got to the front door and it was open. There was loud music playing and I could see some kids about Marty's age dancing in the living room. I rang the bell but I don't think anyone heard it. I waited for a while, like Brian said, but still no one came. I even knocked on the open door. A boy came from the right with a coke bottle in his hand and saw me.

"Hi," he said. "You're not here for the party, are you?"

"No."

"I didn't think so. You're too small."

"Do you want to take the Daily Mirror?"

"No. I don't live here. I'm just here for the party."

"That's okay."

"I'll get Jenny's mom or dad. It's her house. Her party."

"You don't have to bother. It's okay."

"Stay there. They're not doing anything anyway. They're just hanging out in the kitchen."

He went away and came back with Jenny's parents. The boy went back to the party.

"Can we help you? Are you lost or something? Can we call your parents for you?"

I thought about telling them the story, but Jenny's mom had this really nice friendly face and was trying to help me, so lying would have been extra bad.

"No, I'm not lost. It's subscription night for the Daily Mirror and I have a route and one night a month we're supposed to try and get new people to take it."

She looked at her husband. For a minute, I thought they might, but he put the ka-bosh on it.

"No, I don't think so, but thanks for stopping by."

"Would you like a coke before you go?" Jenny's mom asked me.

Before I thought about it I said yes. Her husband went to the kitchen and brought me a bottle.

"Thank you," I said.

"Good luck," she said.

I walked up Monte Mar drinking the coke. There wasn't any point in going up to houses with the coke in my hand, so I thought I'd just keep walking and drinking until I finished it. I was close to the end of the block by the time I did, and by then I was ready to give it another try. Maybe

Brian was right. Maybe it was better for the people if I used the story so they could feel good about helping me get the mitt. The next building was an apartment house with lights on in the upstairs. There wasn't a front door to a lobby, just stairs going up, sort of like at Miriam's. I left the coke bottle at the bottom of the stairs and started climbing them, practicing the mitt story in my head. When I got to the door, I thought I had it memorized just the way Brian had told it to me. I knocked on the door. Just before it opened, I almost ran away, but before I could, it opened. I don't even remember seeing who'd answered it. I just started telling the story about the mitt. I told it as fast as I could to get it over with. When I was done I noticed that the girl who'd opened the door was only about Sarah's age. Maybe a little older.

"Just a minute," she said. "I'll get my mom and dad."

She walked into the apartment and I could hear her telling her parents about some kid that needed two more subscriptions to get a mitt so he can be on a little league team. I heard the mom say something like, 'Oh my'. Now I really wanted to run away, but by the time I decided I would, it was too late because they were coming to the door. Just the mom and the girl. The mom knelt down in front of me and took my hand.

"You only need two more for your mitt?" she said.

I nodded.

"Well, we can help you with one. How would that be?"

I just stood there. All of a sudden I had an ache in my stomach. I think she thought maybe one wasn't good enough and that's why I didn't say anything.

"That would be some help, wouldn't it?" she said.

I was going to say fine and thank you but something else came out before I could stop it.

"The whole thing is a lie!" I said, crying. "It's not true at all! It's a lie I'm supposed to tell you so you'll feel sorry for me and subscribe. You don't have to take the paper at all. It doesn't matter one bit. I'm sorry I lied. Really, I am."

I was crying pretty hard but I felt better just the same. She put arm around me.

"Shhh, that's okay. You told the truth. That's the important thing."

She was trying to make me feel better, but she and the girl were both laughing. Not in a mean way, but laughing just the same.

"Why don't you come in and have a glass of milk? Would you like that?"

"Uh huh," I said.

I stopped crying and she led me by the hand to their dinning room table. I was too embarrassed to say anything, so I just sat there and sipped at the milk while they watched me. Finally, the girl said something.

"Aren't you a little young for a paper route?"

"Maybe," I said, "but I've been doing it for a whole week now."

"How come?"

I told them about the locks.

"Well, I'd still like to take the paper," the mom said.

"You don't have to. Really," I said.

"I'd like to."

She filled out a slip while I finished the milk. They walked me to the door.

"Good luck, Kurt," the mom said.

I already knew from the locks I hated going door to door and this was just as bad. Maybe worse. There had to be a better way to make a living, I thought. I picked up the empty coke bottle at the bottom of the stairs and took it with me for the deposit. Three cents was still three cents, after all.

I went down Beverwil to Kirkside and started down my side. Brian might already be on Oakmore by now for all I knew, and for all I knew it could be nine o'clock. What if it was nine already and I was out here wandering around and everyone else was meeting up and going home. What then? I'd have to ask what time it was at the next house that answered the door. Most of the houses were too dark for me so I passed them up. In the middle of the block one was lit up so I went to their door and rang the bell and a whole song played, not just a ring or a bong, but a whole long song. A lady came to the door. She had white hair in a neat twist on top of her head and a fancy black dress and a necklace with more pearls than you could count and they were the size of medium sized marbles. I knew they might not be real, but brother, if they were, she was rich for sure. She had a fur coat on too, even though it was summer and not cold, so she probably was rich and the pearls were probably real too.

"Oh Charles!" she said. "Come see!"

Me, I supposed.

A man came up behind her. He was wearing fancy clothes too, the kind of black suit you got married in. His shirt was so white it had to be brand new, and it had fancy ruffles on the chest. He was gray-haired and had a trimmed mustache, like Pop, and was probably about Pop's age.

"Hello there," he said. "Can we help you?"

"I'm supposed to lie and tell you I need two more subscriptions to get a mitt so I can play on a little league team, but it's not true, so would you like to take the Daily Mirror anyway?"

The lady laughed and put her hand to her mouth, but the man, wrinkled up his face.

"Who told you to lie?"

"The routemaster makes up good stories for the boys to use. Everyone likes the mitt one, but I don't think it's worth the stomach ache, so I'm not going to use it."

"Good for you," he said.

I hated to admit it, but since I was telling the truth, I told him anyway.

"I tried it once, but it's just not worth it."

"Well, good for you," he said again. "We were just going out, but we've got a few minutes. Would you like to come in?"

"Do you know what time it is?"

He looked at his watch.

"Eight-twenty."

"Okay," I said.

It was better than going house to house, even if I didn't get any more subscriptions. We went through the entry into a huge living room and then into a room like a den or something, only it was bigger than our living room and dinning room combined. It had bookshelves on all of the dark wood walls and a big black piano on one side and Television set on the other side, and a big leather couch facing it. The TV was bigger than Pop's, by a lot. They invited me to sit down on the couch. The man sat at the piano and the woman stood next to him.

"Do you recognize Charles?" she asked me.

"No."

"Do you go to the movies or watch Television?"

"Sometimes movies at the Bugs Bunny Club, but not much Television because we don't have one. Pop does, and sometimes we get to watch with him, but not much."

"Who's Pop?" the man asked me.

"My grandfather."

"Well, Charles is going on Television. Aren't you dear?"

"Indeed, I am."

"Charles is an actor, dear. He was in the movies, but is making the jump to Television. It's going to be bigger than the movies, we think. Don't we, dear?"

"Maybe," he said, not as sure as she was, I thought.

"What's your name, dear?" she asked me.

"Kurt."

"Well, Kurt, you ask Pop if you can watch a show called, My Little Margie, and you'll see Charles. It's going to start next year and it's going to be socko!"

"We're all hoping," he said with a smile. "Now, back to the Mirror. I'd like to take it, and I think Gale and Phil might too."

"You think so?" she said.

"I do. Let me call them."

He went to a phone that was on one of the bookshelves and called someone.

"Would you like a coke, dear?" the woman asked me.

"Sure," I said.

She brought me a glass with ice and coke. Charles talked about me to Gale and Phil and the Daily Mirror and I guess they needed it too, because he said they were coming over.

"We were on our way to dinner with Gale and Phil. Instead of picking them up, they're going to come here so they can subscribe too," Charles said.

"Thank you," I said.

I should have asked them if I could use their bathroom, but I didn't and the two cokes and the milk were beginning to be a problem. The door bell rang and the whole song started over. The woman answered the door and in came Gale and Phil.

"Kurt, this is Gale Storm and her husband, Phil. Gale is going to play my daughter, Margie on the Television show we told you about."

"My Little Margie?" I said.

"Yes, exactly," Charles said.

"Can I get you two a drink?" the lady asked them. "Charles?"

"Yes, dear, please."

"Yes, Lorraine, I'd love one," Gale Storm said.

Her husband nodded a yes but didn't say the word.

Charles told them about the lie I was supposed to tell but didn't, which was why they all decided to take the paper, I thought.

"Isn't that precious?" the lady said.

Gale Storm looked a lot like my mom, but younger, maybe about Norma's age, maybe a little older, but not much. Not as pretty, as Norma, but pretty enough. She didn't wear glasses like my mom, but she had pretty eyes like hers, and short dark curly hair with a little red underneath the dark brown, like my mom's. She had a tiny nose that wasn't like my mom's at all. But all in all, she looked like her anyway. Phil must have been an actor too, because even though he didn't say much, he stood around like any minute someone was about to take his picture.

"You don't have to take the paper just because I didn't want to lie," I said. "Really, if you don't need it, it's okay. I already got some extra subscriptions from six people on my block. Some of them are actors too," I said without thinking about it.

"Oh? Really?" Lorraine said.

"Sharon and Julie," I said.

"You don't know their last names?" Gale Storm said.

"No. They're just trying to be actresses. I don't know if they've gotten any jobs yet."

"It's a very rough road," Charles said. "Many are called, few are chosen."

"Norma and Shelly have been," I said, and as fast as I said it, I wished I hadn't.

"You don't mean, Norma Jean, by any chance, do you?" Gale Storm said.

"Just Norma."

Which was true. That's all I knew, other than Marilyn Monroe, but that was our secret. If Norma meant Norma Jean whoever, and if that was supposed to mean Marilyn too, I didn't know about that, so that was the end of that.

"Probably not," Gale Storm said.

"Well, you wish all your actor friends well for us. It's a wonderful profession but a difficult choice," Charles said. "God bless us all!"

He raised his glass and the others did too and they all had a drink. I did it too, and sipped some more of the coke. They filled out the subscription slips for me and then we all went to the door. I asked Charles what time it was again.

"Eight forty-eight," he told me.

"I gotta go or I'll miss the pick-up truck," I said.

"We can't have that. Do you need a ride somewhere?" he asked me.

"No, I just gotta get going."

"Well, it was a pleasure meeting you, Kurt."

"You too. If we ever get a Television, I'll watch your show."

"We can't ask for more," he said, "can we Gale?"

"That would be very nice of you," she said.

She shook hands with me and so did Lorraine. Phil was still waiting for the photographer as far as I could tell.

I had three new subscriptions and the six from Oakhurst. If that wasn't enough, too bad. The people on my side of Oakmore would just have to wait 'til next month because I wasn't going to even one more house. And besides, it was getting too close to nine for comfort, so if it took me about five minutes to get back to Monte Mar and Beverly Drive, I figured it would still be a few minutes before nine. Nine at the latest. When I got there, no one else was back yet. I stood under the street light waiting. After about five minutes, I started to worry. After about fifteen, I started thinking about the fact that I didn't know where I was or which direction home was. I couldn't even see one house that still had lights on. At least it wasn't very cold. That was something. Almost as bad as being lost and alone, I had to pee so bad I was afraid I'd wet my pants. I thought about sneeking behind a bush and doing it, but what if I was hidden when Ron's truck came and they didn't see me and left? Then I thought, what if it's later than I thought and they were already here and left without me? The whole thing might have made me cry, except the peeing was a bigger problem, so I didn't. Ron or no Ron, I had to find a big bush. I looked around and saw just what I was looking for. I got behind it and peed and peed and peed. Just as I was finishing I heard the truck coming down the street and the boys all making noise. They drove right past. I ran out from the bush and got under the street light and yelled.

"Hey! Here I am!"

The braked lights came on half way down the block and then the trucked backed up under the street light.

"Man, where have you been?" Brian said. "Ron's been blowin' a gasket!"

"God damn it, get in!" Ron yelled at me across the two boys in the cab.

"We've been looking all over for you!" Brian said as I climbed in.

"I had to pee bad, so I went behind that bush," I said, pointing , "but just for a minute. I've been here since a little before nine."

"Yeah," he said, "but this is the wrong corner. Beverly's down there another block."

I looked up at the sign. I was at Monte Mar and Reeves.

Ron stayed mad at me for not being in the right place. He didn't ask how many subscriptions I'd gotten and didn't say goodbye when we pulled up in front of my house. Brian did, though. I climbed out of the truck and headed for the door.

"Long day?" George asked.

He was standing at the bottom of his walkway at the sidewalk.

"Boy, you better believe it."

"How'd it go?"

"Pretty good, except I didn't go back to the right place to get picked up and they almost left me behind and I didn't even know where we were."

"That must have been a little scary. Were you all by yourself?"

George was smoking as usual and blew the smoke away from me.

"Me and a boy named Brian were supposed to work together."

"Did he help you?"

"Sort of, but he needed to get six subscriptions and I was slowing him down so he took one side of the streets and I took the other and he got way ahead of me."

"'So you didn't really work together?"

"Not really."

"It's better when you do. When you can count on someone being there for you."

"I suppose. Like Gung Ho?" I said, pointing to his tattoo.

"Exactly," he said. "Is that why you almost got left behind?"

"No, not really. I just wasn't paying good enough attention to the street signs. But you know what?"

"What?"

"I don't even care. I'm too tired to."

"Well, get some rest. I'll see you tomorrow."

"Good night, George."

"Good night, Kurt."

When I closed the door my dad was there in the living room.

"Hi!" I said. "I was hoping I'd see you."

"Me too," he said. "Come sit on my lap."

He leaned back into the chair and I sat on his legs.

"How's the route going?"

"Pretty good. And I got three new subscriptions tonight and six from people on the block."

"That's great. Can you handle all those papers?"

"Uh huh. Marty loaned me some money to buy a fender rack to hold the route bags and it's easy-breezy," I told him.

"Easy-breezy," he said, "And you worked at the car wash today too?"

"Uh huh."

"You must be bushed."

"You can't believe how much," I told him.

He kissed the top of my head.

"I'm glad I got to see you tonight. I'm going to have to leave early again tomorrow. Go get some sleep."

"Good night, daddy."

"Good night, Kurt."

When the Sunday papers came I was there waiting by the curb. I was studying the route list, memorizing which house took the Sunday and marking them on Marty's map. Ron got out of the truck, lifted the bundle of papers out of the back and dropped them on the parkway.

"You get any subscriptions last night?" he said.

I couldn't believe how big the pile of twenty Sundays was. It was as big or bigger than a regular day even with six new deliveries added in.

"Well?" he said.

He was crabby and I supposed still mad at me.

"Well what?" I said.

"Geez! Did you get any subscriptions last night while you were wandering around all over the place?"

"Three," I said.

He seemed surprised.

"Three? Really?" he smiled. "That's pretty good."

"Plus six, right?"

"Six?"

"The six I got on my block. They count, don't they?"

"Yeah. Right."

"So nine. Right?"

"Right," he agreed. "Ain't that a kick in the butt."

"What?"

"That makes you high man for the night."

"Really?"

"Yeah, really. You get to ride in the cab next month. How 'bout that? You got the slips?"

I handed him the three from last night.

"What about the others?"

"I'll get them today when I deliver these," I said pointing to the pile of Sundays.

"Better get started," he said.

He got in the truck and took off. I brought the Red Rider down the driveway and leaned it against Mumps, then got the rubber band box from the porch. I cut the ropes off the bundle with my KA-BAR knife. They must tie them even tighter on Sundays, I thought, because the pop was bigger than on any of the other days and the bundle changed sized like a seed of popcorn opening up when you heated it. Now the pile looked even huger. I counted, and no wonder. There were twenty-three, not twenty. I told Ron only three of the six new subscriptions wanted Sundays, but he must have forgotten. I took the first one and tried to fold it in the usual way. I couldn't begin to make it go in thirds. I tried a couple more times to make sure, but I couldn't do it. I didn't think anyone could. George came down his walk and over to me.

"You know how the LA Times does it on Sundays?" he asked me.

"I never paid attention to it."

"Like this," he said.

He knelt down next to me and folded it in half the long way instead of in thirds the other way. He put a rubber band on it, but it wasn't going to hold, so he put a second one on.

"That might do it, but three would be better."

He slipped a third rubber band on and it looked tight enough to stay together.

"You should really have a thicker, stronger rubber band for Sundays," he said. "Are they all the same in your box?"

"Uh huh," I said.

"Well, it might take a little longer, but I think you should take the time to put on three. Two might be okay, but three holds it pretty well."

"I'll do three, for sure. If it falls apart it would be a big mess."

"These guys are going to be too heavy to throw. Do you think you've got enough time to walk each one to the door?"

"I think so. What time is it now?"

"Ten-thirty."

"I'm supposed to be done by two, so I think so."

"You don't want me to fire up the Vincent?" he said. "We could."

He had a big smile like he wanted to even more than me.

"You don't have to. Unless you want to."

"Well, why not? If you get done a little early, you can take the rest of the day off, right?"

"Right."

"Good. I'll go get it. You try folding these and I'll help when I get back."

He went up the walkway to his apartment and I started folding. I used the same knee trick he'd taught me to squish the fatter Sunday down the long way and slid the first rubber band over it. Once I got it that far, getting the next two rubber bands on was pretty easy. George came down the walkway with a different shirt on and his hair slicked back.

"I'll be right around," he said and went along the side of his house to the garage.

I heard the roar of the Vincent and this time he'd gone down the alley and was coming up from Beverly Boulevard. He left the Vincent running and moved the route bags from the Red Rider to it. By then I had six or seven folded.

"Why don't you put your bike away and I'll do some of these," he said.

When I got back he was almost done.

"We don't have to fold the last three," I told him.

"We need twenty and the route guy left twenty-three."

"How come?"

"I don't know. I told him only three of the six new subscriptions wanted the Sunday but he didn't pay attention, I guess."

George counted to make sure we had the twenty.

"What should I do with those?" I said, pointing to the three left overs.

"You could give them to someone. It might make them want to take the paper," he said. "Like advertising."

I was up to forty-one on the regular days and twenty on Sundays. That was plenty, I thought. I picked up the three extras and hid them on our front porch.

"Hop on," he yelled over the noise.

He was wearing the goggles, but not the helmut this time.

"All set?" he said.

"All set."

"You know the houses now, right?"

"Right," I shouted. "But I've got the list just in case."

"Okay, so just tug on my shirt when we need to stop."

With a roar we were at Beverly. With another, we were to 331 and I tugged on his shirt. I hopped off and dropped the paper by the door. I ran back to the Vincent and told him over its noise the next paper was just across the street. I took one out of the bags and went up the steps to Sharon and Julie's and dropped it on the door mat and headed back to the Black Shadow. Behind me, the door opened.

"Hi, Kurt. Coffee and the Sunday paper. Perfect!"

"Hi," I said to Sharon. "Guess what?"

"What?"

"I met some other actors last night. This town's full of them."

"Really? Who?"

"An older guy named Charles and Gale Storm. They're going to be in a Television show, where he's the father and she's his daughter. My Little Margie."

"Charles Farrell?"

"I suppose."

"Julie auditioned for that!"

"Well, like Norma said, you guys' turn will come."

"It better hurry up," she said.

She saw George and the Vincent.

"Who's your friend?" she said.

I followed her look.

"That's my friend, George."

She waved at George and he waved back.

"If he'd like milk and cookies sometime too, bring him along," she said.

"Sure," I said.

I only had to check the map twice. Of course Mrs. Gunther wanted the Sunday. What else? I had to stretch my t-shirt to slide it under so I could use both hands to push open the front door at the Maple-Burton Arms, and once inside, I had to hold my breath and lug the paper up the stairs and down the dark hall and knock and run, but it worked out okay. When George and I turned the corner for the final three papers on Oakhurst he stopped in front of Norma and Shelly's and shut off the Vincent. He looked at his watch and told me it was only twelve-fifteen.

"I'll take this one. Why don't you run the other two across the street? They go to Kenny Lester and that Duffy guy, right?"

"That's right. How did you know?"

"Stuff like that just sticks in my head."

He took off his goggles and hung them over one of the handle bar grips. He slicked his hair back with his hands. He took one paper and I took the other two.

"You can just drop it outside the gate there," I told him. "That's where she said she wanted it."

"I thought I might hand it to her, since we're right here."

If he wanted to, that was fine with me. I went across the street to the Lester's place. I dropped a paper at the top of their steps. I went three houses down to Duffy's place. The window was closed again, but that wasn't the real problem. The real problem was the Sunday was too big and heavy to throw up to the balcony no matter what was open or closed. Just for the heck of it, I tried the door. It was locked again, of course. I stepped back to the sidewalk to see if anyone was just inside the window. No luck. I looked up the street. The Vincent was still there, so George was probably talking to Shelly again. I looked back at the closed window. How in the heck was I supposed to get the paper up there? It didn't seem like the best idea in the world, but I couldn't think of anything else, so I went back to the front door and rang all of the bells. At first nothing happened then a buzzer buzzed. By the time I realized it was probably unlocking the door for me, it was too late. So I did it again. This time it buzzed twice and I pushed the thumb thing and the door opened. Inside, there were two doors on the left and right of the stairs, 1A and 1B, then 1C and 1D. 1A opened and a man asked me who I was. Then 1B opened and a woman saw me talking to the man and closed her door.

"I'm supposed to deliver the paper to Mr. Duffy, upstairs, but the window's closed and it's too heavy to throw anyway, and he never answers his outside doorbell."

"So you rang mine?"

"Yes sir."

"Well don't!"

"Yes sir. Sorry."

He started to close his door but changed his mind.

"A friend of Dickie's are you?"

"Dickie who?"

"The boy that lives upstairs in 2C."

"Sort of. He's my sister's age, but I know him. He's in her club."

"He's a good boy. Quiet, like he should be. So," he said, a little nicer, "if you don't get an answer from that mumser, Duffy, it's okay to ring mine. But just once, okay?"

"Okay. Thank you."

"You're welcome."

He closed the door. I went up the stairs. 2A was on the left. I put the paper down in front of the door. There was an inside doorbell too, so I rang it. I was pretty sure I could hear someone moving around in there, or maybe it was just the radio, but whatever it was, it seemed like someone was in there alright. Since they didn't answer, that was that. I went back down and outside and back to Shelly and Norma's.

George and Shelly were standing next to the Vincent. She was running her hands over it like it was a racehorse, sort of petting it. George was smoking a cigarette and letting her.

"How'd it go?" he asked me.

"Okay with the Lesters, weird with that Duffy guy."

"What?"

"Well, the window was closed again, and besides, the Sunday's too heavy to throw but he didn't answer the bell so I rang another one and a man let me in okay."

"And?"

"I rang Duffy's inside bell and I think he was there, but he didn't answer so I left it in front of the inside door."

"Well, he can't ask for more than that. You did what you could."

He looked at his watch.

"It's only twelve-thirty. What are you going to do the rest of the day?"

"I don't know. Maybe take a ride on the Red Rider."

"I'm going to take Shelly for a ride on the Vincent. Let's take you and the route bags home and I'll come back for her."

"Just untie them and I'll walk home."

"You sure?"

"Sure. Thanks for doing it again on the Vincent. It's great. You're gonna love it, Shelly."

"It looks sort of scary, but what the heck, no one lives forever, right?"

"Right," I said.

"Is George a pretty good driver?" she asked me.

She sort of looked like Sarah had, excited but scared at the same time.

"The best."

"Well, that's reassuring. Snowball's in the house now, but Norma should be back in an hour or so if you want to come back and play."

"Maybe," I said.

George handed me the route bags and I started down the street.

"Have fun," I called to them. "And hang on Shelly!"

"You better believe I will!"

She climbed on and was hugging her arms around George so tight I bet he couldn't breath, but he didn't make her hold onto his belt. They roared off past me towards Beverly Boulevard with Shelly screaming the whole way.

When I got to our house nobody was home. I put the route bags on the porch and got the Red Rider. I rode up to the San Vicente Hardware store and put the bike on the kickstand. Mr. Mahoney was standing on the sidewalk smoking.

"Look who's here," he smiled.

"I've got another two-fifty for you," I said, handing him the money. "Sorry I didn't give it to you yesterday, but after the carwash and then the paper route, I had to go on the subscription night. I didn't get home 'til almost ten."

"Sounds like a long day. No problem. I know you're good for it. Did you deliver today, already?"

"Uh huh. Just finished. George Bowen took me on his Vincent Black Shadow motorcycle. Boy, is that fun!"

"Kenny said something about that."

"He helped me on the first day because the papers were late and today because the Sunday papers are so big and he felt like going for a ride anyway."

"Good guy."

"He sure is."

"So what's on for the rest of the day?"

"I'm not sure. I was thinking about riding down to the Watts Towers. I saw them once and want to see them again."

"That's a little far, isn't it?"

"Probably. The worst part is I'm not sure how to get there."

"Maybe best to wait until you can go with your parents, huh?"

"Maybe. So long."

"So long."

I rode back home still thinking about riding all the way to the Towers, but Mr. Mahoney was probably right, it was too far, and besides, I had no idea how to get there anyway. I remembered we'd gone on Beverly Boulevard until it ended in downtown Los Angeles, and I could do that part okay, but after that, I'd be lost. I'd had a bunch of dreams about the Towers and wanted to see them again. Maybe when my dad wasn't working so much he'd take me. I thought he'd like them too. When I got home, no one was there still. What if Joseph and Miss Rimes were going to Watts today? Maybe I could go too. I decided to ride up to the car wash and find out. I got back on my bike and was about to go when Norma came up from Beverly Boulevard. She pulled over to the curb next to me, pointed towards Lower Santa Monica, but on the wrong side of the street. She was wearing jeans and the old sweatshirt and a white scarf over her head tied on under her chin.

"Hi sweetie, how are you?"

"Fine."

"Where are you off to?"

"I was going to the car wash to see if Joseph and Miss Rimes were maybe going to Watts."

"Who's Miss Rimes?"

"She's my art teacher. She was my art teacher until school ended. And I think she will be next year too."

"And she and Joseph are...?"

"I think he has a crush on her or something. We went together in her car to Watts to see Dennis' foundry and then the Watts Towers. Have you ever seen them?"

"No. I've heard of them, though."

"They're the most amazing thing you've ever seen! This guy Sabato has been working on them for twenty years. More, I think. And he's just this little guy, not much bigger than me."

"Do you know how to get there?"

"No. I was thinking about riding there, but it's too far and I don't remember all the streets you have to take. That's why I was going to the carwash. Maybe Joseph and Miss Rimes are going to go again."

"How 'bout if we go to the car wash together and get this washed and ask Joseph for directions. I'd love to see them. Is your mom home so we can ask her if it's okay?"

"No. No one is. I got back from delivering the Sunday papers and no one was home. I suppose they all went downtown. Except Marty's probably working at the Standard Station."

"Maybe we could tell your friend, George you're with me. Do you think that would be okay?"

"It would be, except he took Shelly for a ride on the Vincent."

"He did?"

"Uh huh."

Norma smiled.

"He'd better watch out. When Shelly sets her sights on something, not much can stop her."

"I think George has his sights set too. Maybe Pop's home. I could ask him if it's okay."

"That's a good idea. I'll come with you."

She shut off the car and got out. I put the Red Rider on the kickstand and she took my hand and we went up to Pop's door. It was open, so he was home, alright. I knocked on the screen door and he answered it with a huge glass of V-8 juice in his hand. He was wearing his tan pants and an undershirt and was barefoot. I could hear the Television and it sounded like he was watching wrestling. He'd probably been in his big chair that was pointed right at the TV. He saw me and was about to say something, but then he saw Norma and whatever it was, he forgot.

"Kurt? You're not in any trouble, are you?" he asked me.

"No. Why?"

"Well, I don't know. I...Who's this?" he said.

"Pop, this is Norma. She lives up the block and I went to the beach with her last Sunday and we were going to go to the Watts Towers, but no one's home to tell. Can we just tell you?"

"Hello Mr. Goldman," Norma said.

Pop opened the screen door. He didn't seem to know what to do. He wasn't really dressed to come out on the porch, and I guess he'd been having lunch in the living room in front of the Television and felt funny inviting her into that. Norma reached out to shake hands with him, so he switched the V-8 juice to his left hand and shook.

"Sometimes Kurt and I have hot chocolate at Joseph's Hot Dog Stand, and we did go to the beach last week, and I met his mother and sister and brothers, so I'm sure it would be fine with his mom, but we wanted to tell someone where he'd be. Could you tell her?"

"I think it'll be okay," Pop said.

"We'll be back by three or three-thirty. If it gets any later, we'd call."

"You live here?" Pop said. "On the block?"

"Yes. With my friend, Shelly. The last house on this side before Lower Santa Monica."

"She's the lady with Snowball. One of the Lester's puppies."

"Oh," Pop said. "That Norma."

"That's me," Norma said. "So it's okay?"

"Sure. Have a good time."

"Thanks, Pop."

"Nice to meet you, Mr. Goldman."

"Abe."

"Abe," she said.

When we got to the carwash it was crazier than ever. Not just because of all the cars that needed washing, but because none of them were getting washed. That Dolan guy, John's father and Kevin Doyle's too, was there trying to get votes again. Kevin was in his fancy uniform with all the medals like before, only this time they weren't in the Cadillac convertible, and there was a big crowd of guys around, and Dolan and Kevin were standing on one of Joseph's tables and Joseph didn't look too happy about it. There was a lot of shouting back and forth between Dolan and the guys who wanted their cars washed, or maybe they just didn't want to see him be the mayor. Or maybe both. Kevin's face wasn't very puffy anymore, but he still had the stitches below both eyes and over the right one too. He wasn't saying anything. He kept giving Maurice and Jackson and Dennis and William a look. It was hard to say if it was a nasty look, or an angry look, or an afraid look, or just some other kind of look, but whatever it was, they were standing shoulder to shoulder and Kenny Lester was there with them, and if Kevin even thought about starting trouble, they'd need a mile of string to stitch him up this time. Since he'd just had his car washed yesterday, I wondered why Kenny Lester was here again, but maybe he wanted to talk some more about the war. Whatever he was there for, I knew I just wanted to get out of there.

"What's all this?!" Norma said. "It doesn't look like they're washing cars at all."

"That Dolan guy's trying to be mayor," I said, pointing to him, "and he keeps coming here and messing up the whole car wash business. Mr.

Avery was pretty nice to him the first time, but I guess everybody's tired of him and would rather just get their cars washed and talk about the war. They do that a lot, too."

"This is just the kind of thing I don't need," she said.

She looked a little worried, and so was I. If we stayed around, and somehow the car wash guys and Joseph and Kenny Lester found out about Kevin yelling at me at Whalen's, there might be real trouble. And since George had settled him down, and he said he was sorry, I thought he was maybe going to stop. I hoped he was. I guess I didn't really believe it, but I didn't want any one to go to jail for hurting or killing him because he might. Just because someone might do something, doesn't mean you get to kill them before they actually do it. It didn't seem fair that you might have to wait until they did it before you could, but in a way it made sense. Anyway, I could see why the Marilyn Monroe part of Norma wanted to get out of any big mess that might happen, so that's why I told her, "Let's go somewhere else, okay?"

"As fast as we can," she said.

We got back into the MG and drove off the lot before anyone noticed us. Her, really. When we were at Beverly and Palm she pulled over to the curb.

"We could go to another gas station and get a map and ask for directions to Watts. How about that?"

"Sure. Let's go to Marty's station, okay?"

"Why not?" she said, taking off the scarf from around her head and fluffing up her hair.

She put the scarf in a place in front of me that should have been the glove compartment, only it didn't have a door.

"I can fill up the car, you can say hello to Marty, and then we'll go on our adventure. Which station does he work at?"

"The one at Wilshire and Canon," I told her.

"I know that one," she said.

She moved the little gear shifter that came out of the floor between us and turned down Palm. The MG was almost as much fun as the Vincent when she zoomed around corners. When we got to Wilshire she turned right again, and after four long blocks we were at the Standard Station. She pulled up to the pumps and ran over the hose that makes the bell ring in the office so they know you're there. Sure enough, out came Marty. He had on the bright white pants and shirt, the black shoes and black belt they made him wear, but what he hated was the little hat. It was white too, only the shape of it was like the army hats from the war. Not the bucket kind to keep you from getting a bullet in your head, but the soft kind that were long and skinny from the front to the back. Marty's hair was thick and wavy and the hat never made it to his head because it just sat on top, all set to fall off the first chance it got. I don't know if the Standard Station company did it on purpose to make their stations and workers look like they were part of the war too, but since the war had been over for so long, it seemed pretty silly, especially to Marty. Whenever any of his friends from school came in for gas with their parents, he told me he slipped it off, but on the days he was working in the shop changing tires, they didn't care and didn't make him wear it. On the gas pumps they made a big deal out of it. As soon as he saw the car, he knew it was us and he slipped the hat off and tucked it around his belt. I don't think I'd ever seen his face so completely happy. He was looking at her, but put his hand on my head and messed my hair.

"Hiya, squirt. Whatcha doin'? Hi, Norma."

"Hi, Marty," she said.

"Me and Norma are going down to see the Watts Towers."

"Really? I've heard of them, but never seen 'em."

"I did."

"Right. George told us you went with your art teacher, huh? What are they like?"

"With Miss Rimes. They're...they're...well, there's no way to describe them. You just have to see them. That's the only way."

"Well, someday I will. What do you need?"

"Fill it with Regular, please," Norma said. "And do you have maps for sale?"

"Sure. Beverly Hills or LA?"

"Is there one that has both?"

"Sure. I'll get you one as soon as I'm done here."

While he was filling the gas tank, Norma took the squeeze bottle and rag for washing the windshield from a shelf next to the pumps and started to do it herself.

"I'll do it!" another boy said, running from the office.

He looked older than Marty, but smaller.

"Oh no you don't!" Marty said. "Just go get her an LA County Map."

"I'll wash the window, then get the map. Here," he said, "let me do that!"

He took the rag and bottle from Norma and washed the little window. It was so small it only took about half a minute, but he made a big fuss about getting every speck off. He did the little side mirrors and the inside one too.

"There. How's that?" he said.

He looked as excited as one of the Lester's puppies trying to get you to pay attention to them.

"That looks perfect," Norma said. "Thank you."

"Oh, it was my pleasure. Really. I'll get you the map."

"Thank you," she said.

Marty finished with the gas and looked at the pump. Four gallons and a little and it was sixty-eight cents.

"Would you like me to check the oil?"

"No, I think it's fine. How much do I owe you?"

"Sixty-eight for the gas and ten cents for the map, so seventy-eight cents."

She gave him a dollar and said to keep the change.

"I couldn't. Really," he said.

"How about if you two split it?"

Marty looked at the other boy and shrugged.

"Sure," the other boy said. "Thank you."

"Thank you, Norma," Marty said.

"Norma?! the other boy said, "I thought she was Marilyn Monroe, for pete'sake! Boy, she sure looks like her, don't she?"

"Kinda," Marty said, smiling at us, "but not that much."

The other boy went back into the office, disappointed, but at least he had half the tip. Norma gave Marty a kiss on the cheek.

"Thank you. You're a real gentleman. Both of you," she said, meaning me too.

Sarah'd thought Marty wasn't going to ever wash his hand again because she shook it the day we went to the beach, so now he'd probably never wash his face again. We got back in the car and Norma unfolded the map. Marty was leaning in over her shoulder and traced a path to Watts and the Towers with a dark pencil.

"Thank you, Marty," she said and started the car.

When we were finally on our way, she reached over and took an envelope from under her scarf in the almost glove compartment.

"Those are papers from the Love Nest company. If you'd like to come with me to the set on Tuesday or Wednesday, let me know, and have your mom or dad sign at the bottom. Do you still want to?"

"Sure."

"Wonderful!"

"Just to see though, right? I'm not promising yet."

"Joseph's right," she said, "you should be a lawyer."

"That's what Marty's going to be."

"Really? He knows already?"

"Marty knows just about everything about everything, and for sure about being a lawyer."

"I can see he's working hard."

"He's saving for college. And a car."

"Good for him. And you're working hard too," she said, patting my knee.

"Yeah, but I'm just paying back for the locks."

"Now it's the locks, later, maybe for college or a car. Who knows? Anyway, if you decide to work on the movie, you'll make a little money and have a lot of fun. I'm sure of it."

"Do you know how much? If I decided to do it? If whoever gets to decide decides it's okay for me to be in it?"

"I don't. Not really. But even if you don't say anything and you're in at least one scene, and you're not just an extra, you'd get maybe ten dollars."

"Ten dollars?! Are you kidding me?"

"No. I'm not sure, but I think that's about right. Doesn't that sound fair?"

"Fair? Boy, I'd do it for half that! But you don't have to tell them I said so," I said, just in case. "What's an extra?"

"The people you see in the background. Like if it's a street scene, they might have a lot of extras pretending to be the people on the sidewalk or in stores."

"How much do they get paid?"

"I'm not positive, but I think around five dollars a day."

"That doesn't sound like much for a grown up."

"It's not. But sometimes actors take the work hoping they'll be seen by a director or producer who might use them in something else. They just want to stay involved in any way they can. It's a rough business."

"That's what that Charles guy said."

"Who?"

"I had to do the subscription night last night and one of the houses I went to belonged to an actor named Charles. He's going to be on Television with a woman named Gale Storm. I met her too. He said it's a tough business too."

"Charles Farrell?"

"Yeah, that's it. Do you know him?"

"No, just the name. It's a small town that way. I heard he was going to try television."

"My Little Margie. That's the name of it. He's the dad, she's his daughter."

"Well, I hope it goes well for them. Anyway, I think you'll like it and have fun and make a little money to help with the locks."

"Maybe," I said.

We drove for a long time with Norma pulling over once in a while to check the map. Finally we got to the Towers. She parked and we got out.

"You were right. They're amazing! So crazy beautiful!!" she said.

High up, I could see Sabato. It was sunny and even hotter than it had been the last time. He was wearing the same clothes and the same straw hat. He was adding pieces of metal to take the towers even higher. He was using some kind of wire and twisting it to hold things in place until he could weld it. He had two skinny hoses going up to a nozzle that was hanging over the little rail of his scaffold. He looked around and then threw up his hands and was mad about something and was maybe swearing to himself, but he was too far away and I couldn't hear the exact words, but he started down the ladders. When he got part way down, he saw us and smiled and waved.

"Another pretty girl! How nice!"

When he got all the way down he picked up a welder's mask from one of the work benches scattered around the yard.

"I forgotta this!" he said holding up the mask, "I go allada way up and hava comma allada way down!"

He looked at me.

"Ain't choo da boy came wit' Dennis?"

"Yes sir. Kurt. Dennis is at the carwash today."

"Calla me Sam. Thisa the same pretty girl again?"

"No. That was Miss Rimes, my art teacher."

"Who'za this one?"

"Norma. Norma, this is Dennis' friend, Sabato."

"Sam," he said, shaking hands with her.

"Your work is beautiful, Sam, just wonderful. Breathtaking." "T'ank you, t'ank you, thasa nice. I do it jus' 'a for you. You knowa that, right? I do it jus' 'a for you? But you wanna your breath take' away, you go uppa da ladders! That'll taka your breath away! Gotta go back uppa now. Nice to meeta you."

"Nice to meet you too," Norma said.

"So long kid."

He shook hands with me too and then leaned over, but not much, because he really wasn't much taller than me, and he winked.

"You cana pick 'em, kid," he said, "keep uppa da good work."

He started back up the ladders taking the welder's mask with him. Norma and I watched him for another fifteen minutes as he welded, then tied more steel on, then welded again. He kept on working without ever looking down to where we stood. Like Miss Rimes said, he knew what he wanted to do and was going to do it no matter what.

"Are you hungry?" Norma asked me.

"Sort of."

"We passed a place back there that looked nice. Want to see if they make hamburgers?"

I remembered I'd already given my two-fifty to Mr. Mahoney.

"I'm not that hungry," I said.

"Well, I am," she said. "Would you keep me company while I eat?"

"Sure."

We drove this way and that and a couple of minutes later we came to the Albertine Cafe. When we went in, some people seemed to know who she was, but no one made a big deal out of it. She ordered a hamburger, some french fries and two cokes.

"My treat," she said.

Why didn't she say so sooner? I was starved. When the food came, she cut the hamburger in half.

"You take this," she said. I can't eat the whole thing. Besides, I want some room for the fries."

"Okay," I said, like I wasn't very hungry, but just wanted to do her a favor.

There was a jar of mustard there in front of us. I put a lot on my half.

"I guess you like mustard, huh?" she teased me.

"Uh huh."

We ate every bit of the hamburger and fries and shared a piece of apple pie for dessert. I fell asleep in the car on the way home, because the next thing I knew, she was waking me up and we were there.

"That was fun, sweetie. I hope we can go on a few more adventures this summer while you're out of school. Let me know if you want to come to the set Tuesday or Wednesday, and if you do, have your mom or dad sign the papers, okay?"

"Sure. I'll ask my mom tonight. Bye. Thanks."

"Bye," she waved.

She pulled away from the curb and went up the block. When I went inside no one was back yet. The clock in the kitchen said three-twenty.

I was still sleepy and it was still warm out, so I thought I'd sneak into the bamboo patch and have a snooze. I went out the back porch and through our yard and into the alley. When I passed in front of George's garage he was inside, polishing the Vincent. The alley was all wet in front of his garage, so I suppose he'd washed it too.

"Hi George. How was your ride with Shelly?"

"Fine. Nice girl. Did you know she's an actress?"

"Sure. Didn't I tell you that? I thought I did."

"Maybe you did. Maybe I just forgot. Where've you been?"

"Norma, the other actress, in case you forgot that too, Norma and I went down to the Watts Towers. They are so amazing, George! You've got to go see them."

"Maybe we could take a trip down there on the Vincent, sometime? Interested?"

"Sure. Sam, Sabato, the man making them, remembered me from the last time, but at first he thought Norma was Miss Rimes."

"I guess he doesn't go to the movies much," George said.

It was probably the first time I'd ever seen him that he wasn't smoking. He had the Vincent shining like crazy.

"That Black Shadow is a beauty," I told him, "almost as pretty as the Red Rider. Did Shelly finally quit screaming and like it?"

"She never quit completely, but she seemed to like it anyway."

"Well, that's something I guess."

"I think so."

"I'll see you later," I told him.

"Where're you off to?"

"I was going to take a snooze."

"Headed up the alley?"

He gave me a look like he knew exactly where I was going.

"Maybe up to the little park with the fountain," I said. "Maybe."

"Mmm. That so?"

George was the last person I wanted to lie to, even if I'd said maybe. I suppose I could go to the little park instead, and that would make it true.

"You know, I don't think Basil would mind you being in the garden if you asked him. It might not be as much fun as sneaking in, but it might work out better in the long run. Just a suggestion," he said, still polishing the Vincent.

"Mmm, that so?" I said. "See you later, George."

"See you later, wise guy," he smiled.

I headed up the alley.

Rathbone had been nice enough to subscribe and nice about saying Bravo for the paper toss to Duffy's place, so I thought maybe George was right. I should just ask him. I decided I would, for sure, but next time. I'd sneak in one last time. When I got to the garbage can that covered the hole under the fence, I checked to see if George was still in his garage or had come out into the alley. I couldn't see him, so I moved the can and went under. I crawled into the clearing and got comfortable, laying on my back with my ankles crossed, my fingers locked together, my hands resting on my stomach. That was the best position for a snooze in the bamboo patch, believe me. The inside of my eyelids were a bright pink-orange color from the sun above, but that wasn't going to keep me awake. I could feel this snooze coming a mile away. There were the ususal sounds of bees buzzing and the humming, beating sounds of the dragonfly wings as they jumped from one part of the gardens to another. It was amazing what you could hear when you weren't doing anything else. I was almost asleep when I heard the crunching of footsteps on one of the gravel paths. I might be able to ignore it, I thought, maybe, if I just lay there real still and didn't open my eyes, I might fall asleep anyway. I didn't want to open my eyes because if I did, and saw it was Rathbone walking around, I'd have to worry about whether he would be mad, or worse, what if he thinks I'm sort of cheating on his being friendly? It was okay to sneak in when he was Rathbutt and Iyama was his killer slave, but none of that was true anymore. I didn't want to, but I opened my eyes anyway. I sniped through the thinned bamboo so I could get close enough to the garden to see, and sure enough, it was him. He was at the top of the grassy hill by the pond sitting on the little concrete bench that faced it, throwing pieces of something, probably bread, into the water for the Garibaldi. I watched him for a minute or two. He'd throw a piece out onto the water and watch for the big fish to take it, but before it happened, he'd tip his head back to get the sun on his face, so even if a fish came, he probably wouldn't have seen it take the bread, but he didn't seem to care. He looked completely peaceful and relaxed. He usually did. It seemed like he was the only one on the whole block who was. I was tempted to crawl the rest of the way out of the bamboo and tell him about the best way to feed the Garibaldi, to make them come in close and even take the bread from your fingers, and while I was at it, tell him I was sorry for sneaking in, but that would just disturb him. Since this was going to be my last sneaking in, I thought I might as well just leave him be peaceful.

"Hello, young man," he said without looking around. "Can't sleep?"

He turned around smiling. I didn't know how he could see me. I was pretty sure the bamboos were still thick enough to hide me, even here where I'd thinned them, so how could he know I was here?

"Would you like to join me?" he said.

"Okay, I guess," I said.

I crawled out of the bamboo onto the rock path and made my way over to the pond.

"Sorry," I said. "This was going to be the last time. Really. I promise it's true. I'd already decided."

"One for the road, yes?"

I wasn't sure what he meant.

"One last time. One last one before you put your new plan into place?"

"Yes, sir."

"It so beautiful here, don't you think? You may sit if you like."

I sat on the end of the bench.

"That's why I like to sneak in. It's more beautiful than any park. And it's quiet. It's so quiet you can hear the bees buzz and the wings of the butterflies and dragonflies thumping against the air. Sometimes I can even hear the Garibaldi when they come to the surface."

"You can hear that all the way from your bamboo hideout?"

"Sometimes," I said.

"And you dug that hole under the can?"

"Yes sir."

"Very clever," he said. "I used to wonder how you were getting in."

"Do you want me to go now?"

"No. You can stay if you like. Do you mind if I smoke?"

"No. It's your garden."

"True."

It didn't seem like he was mad, so that was good, but I still felt bad, like I'd cheated on him being nice lately, but even if he was mad, as long as he didn't get Kevin Doyle crazy at me, what the heck.

"Would you like to feed the Garibaldi?"

"Sure."

He handed me some bread crumbs. I knelt by the concrete lip of the pond and threw a piece about three or four feet out. Sure enough, a few bubbles came to the surface and a few seconds later the gold and black one took it. I tossed three more pieces in different places. It didn't take long for the orange and white one and the black and gold one to come for them. I threw two more pieces to the left and when I could see the two Garibaldi go for them, I threw another to the right. I looked back at Mr. Rathbone. He was smoking away, but watching.

"Watch this," I said.

Nothing happened at first. Then the gold and black and the orange and white headed for the new piece on the right. But before they could get to it, the all gold-orange one came and got it. He must be the boss of the pond, I thought, because when he headed for the piece, the other two turned away and let him have it. I tossed another piece, closer this time.

In he came and got it. Then another even closer. He came right for it and swallowed it up. I dropped a piece right next to the edge of the pond and he came for that one too.

"Are you watching?" I said, looking over my shoulder.

"Indeed I am," Rathbone said.

I held a piece in my fingers just above the water. The big orange-gold guy came past once, rolled onto his side so he could see me better, went right on by, but made a short circle to come past again, and sure enough, took it from my fingers.

"Did you see that?! Did you?!"

"Absolutely amazing! How on earth did you ever get him to do that?"

"Practice," I said.

"Lots of practice, no doubt," he smiled.

"Yes sir," I admitted.

"Isn't that something?" he said, smoking the last of his cigarette. "You think he'd take one from me?"

He squished the butt out on the bottom of the concrete bench and put it in his pocket, like George always did.

"Sure. Wanna try?"

"Indeed I do."

He knelt down beside me. He took another chunk from his shirt pocket and held it above the water. The solid colored Garibaldi passed by but not near enough to take it. Rathbone seemed disappointed.

"Just wait," I told him, "and maybe hold it a little closer to the water."

He lowered his hand until it was just above the water.

"That should do it."

And sure enough, the big gold-orange one took it.

"Ow!" he laughed. "He bit me!"

"That happens all the time. I don't think he means it though."

"Probably not," Rathbone said, "but it comes as a bit of a shock. Isn't that something?" he said, shaking his head like he didn't believe it, even though he'd just done it himself.

"Do you know how old they are?" I asked him.

"I'd think eight or nine years, by now. Maybe a little older."

"Boy, that's older than me."

"And just how old are you?

"I'll be eight in August."

"Isn't that something?" he said.

"I suppose. Do you know how long they live?"

"I'm not positive, but I believe they can live to be twenty or twenty-five."

"Do they have babies?"

"All three of these are females. That was recommended to me so they wouldn't overpopulate the pond. Iyama agreed. I trust his judgement when it comes to the garden and the pond."

I was going to tell him that everyone thought he captured Iyama in the war and let him live if he'd keep kids out of the garden, and Pop had told me it wasn't true, but I changed my mind. We sat silently for a while. I still wanted a snooze, but figured the bamboo patch was out.

"I guess I should go," I told him.

"You know, now that you're both my neighbor and my paper boy, I suppose you could come in to enjoy the garden when you like. You could use the front or back gate, for that matter. Unless you prefer your private little entry," he said nodding towards the alley.

"Really?"

"Why not? You seem to enjoy it so. You've always been quiet and careful not to damage anything. Why not, indeed?"

"But it's your private place. Right?"

"That's true. Perhaps we could agree that you'd confine your trips to early in the morning or afternoons later than three. I seldom come here those time. How would that be?"

"Too good to be true," I said. "Thank you."

"You're welcome. Just be sure the gate latches when you come and go."

"I'll make sure."

I started to go.

"How did you know?"

"What?"

"How I was coming in?"

"Once in a while I could see just the top of your head going up the alley from my window and then you'd suddenly disappear without going farther up. Then, the next thing I knew, you'd be crawling through the bamboo there. When my curiosity was sufficiently piqued, I looked around in the alley pondering it. I saw the can and it dawned on me, some of my comrades had escaped from the camps that way. Tunnelling under fences, hiding the entrance under cans. I took a look, and sure enough, there was your little tunnel."

"Sorry," I repeated.

"No need. Not, really. See you, Kurt."

"See you, Mr. Rathbone."

I went out through the front gate. I closed it quietly. As the little thing that kept it shut clicked into place, I could see him still sitting there, starting on a new cigarette. On my way home, I was thinking, it already was the best summer ever. Just everything falling into place.

The next Saturday was June 30th, so it was collection day. The night before, Marty sat down at the kitchen table and helped me figure out who owed how much. There were the regular customers and new customers that had only had the paper a few days and some of those who took the Sunday and some who didn't. Unless there were more new customers in July or some of the regular ones who didn't take the Sunday all of a sudden decided they wanted it, it would be easier to figure out the next time, but this month, I needed Marty's help for sure. He asked me what I was going to put the money in and I told him I hadn't thought of that. My mom was listening to us while she was cleaning up and wanted to give me an old tan leather purse of hers that had a snap thing on the top edge. She said I could put the money in after I collected it and keep it safe, but to me a purse was a purse, so I didn't want to use it.

Marty said, "How about this?"

He cut off the shoulder strap, and since the purse was skinny and flat and only about the size of a big envelope and now it didn't have a strap, you couldn't really tell it was a girl's purse for sure anymore. I still didn't want to use it, but Marty had another great idea, and took a pen and wrote, DAILY MIRROR, in big letters on both sides below the snap, like on the route bags.

"That looks pretty official, doesn't it?" he asked me.

It did! It was amazing. Just like that, it went from being a purse to a DAILY MIRROR money collection gizmo.

"That's great. But there's another problem."

"What now?" he said.

"What am I supposed to say?"

"To who?"

"The people. To make them give me the money."

"Just go to the door, hand them the Saturday paper, and say, 'Hi. I'm also collecting today for the month."

"That's all?"

"That should do it. If they ask you how much, just look at our list. Take this with you and put the money in right away. In fact, you could keep the list in here too. Then when you get back to your bike, slide it down to the bottom of the route bags where it's safe and won't fall out."

"That doesn't seem too hard."

"It shouldn't be."

"Good. I was worried about that. One more thing."

"What?"

"What if no one's home?"

"That's a good question," he said.

He thought for a minute, then went to our room and came back with some school paper and folded two sheets into quarters and tore them along the lines.

"What's that for?" I asked him.

"You'll see."

When he had eights squares, he wrote the same thing on each one.

"How 'bout this?," he said turning them towards me. They said, 'Sorry I missed you. I'll be back tomorrow. Kurt, collecting for the Mirror.'

"I think eight should be enough. Just put them in there with the list and leave one at any house where you can't collect."

"Great! Thanks Marty.'

"And remember to check off the houses you collect from. Maybe draw a line through them. And as soon as you get home, count the money. When you know how much you have, write it down on a piece of paper and put it in with the money. That way you won't forget and have to do it all over."

"How can you think of so many things?"

"Genius," he said, "pure genius. It runs in the family."

He handed me his pencil.

"Here, put this in there too. If you put a mark by the ones where no one's home, they'll show up easier and you'll know who you still have to collect from. Get it?"

"Okay, I get all that," I said, "but one more thing."

"What now?"

"What can I call it?" I said, pointing to the purse.

"What do you mean?"

"I don't want it to be a purse."

"Oh. Okay. How 'bout a money pouch?"

"Is there really such a thing?"

"Yeah, of course."

"Okay then, perfect! It's a money pouch."

I had an hour before I was supposed to be at the carwash, so I thought I'd wash and dry the Red Rider. I parked it on the sidewalk and untied the route bags and put them far enough away so they wouldn't get wet. I pulled the hose down and got Pop's wash bucket and rag and put in a dash of dish soap. The bike had collected lots of dirt on it from all the riding around I'd been doing, so I washed and washed until I was sure it was clean as new. I dried it the way George had dried the Vincent. When I was done, it sparkled like the day I got it. I put everything away and waited until about quarter to ten, then headed for the salt mines.

It was pretty busy, but not crazy busy and before I knew it, it got to four. Mr. Avery paid me the car wash money and also for the paper since he wouldn't be home later and I left and got home a few minutes later. I had the shiny Red Rider and the rubber bands and the money pouch all ready to go, but no papers. He was hours late and it was going to be a slow delivery day already because of the collecting. Then I wondered if George was around, just in case, but finally Ron came. He pulled up to the curb and left the engine running, jumped out and dropped the bundle on the parkway.

"Don't forget, it's collection day. You all set?"

"Yeah, but you're late."

"Couldn't be helped."

"But how am I supposed to deliver before six and collect?"

"Well, for one thing, you should quit yakking with me and get started folding. If you don't collect from them all today, hit the ones you didn't tomorrow while you're doing the Sunday."

"What if they don't take the Sunday?"

"So what? If they don't pay today, you want them to pay tomorrow. I'm going to collect from you on Monday, so make sure you've got it all. Okay?"

"Okay," I said. "I suppose."

"There's nothing to suppose," he said, getting back into the truck. "It's the most important part of the job and it's your responsibility."

He drove off and I got busy folding. I was getting pretty good at it and in about ten minutes I was ready to go. I had the papers in the route bags and the money pouch pushed way down. In my head I was picturing the 331 Oakhurst house, going to the door and asking them for the money. No matter how I thought of to say it, it sounded like begging. Why didn't the people just mail the money to the Daily Mirror Company, like my mom did with the telephone bill and the gas and electric bill? What was wrong with that, I wondered. Then I realized I'd forgotten about Kevin Doyle. Maybe I'd go there last. I could just drop his paper now and collect from him at the end. The trouble with that was I wouldn't want to do it then either. But if he gave me trouble at the beginning, it could ruin the whole rest of the day, but on the other hand, if I waited to do it, I'd probably worry about it the whole time, so even if he didn't make any kind of fuss, I'd waste the whole day worrying about it for nothing. I decided I might as well get it over with. I checked the list then put it back in the pouch and crossed the street with the paper in one hand and the pouch in the other. Since his doorbell was still broken, I knocked, like the note said. Kevin pulled the door open. He smelled bad again, but not as bad as the other time. Before I could say anything, he took the paper from me.

"You collecting today?"

"Yes."

"Two-fifty?"

"Two forty-eight," I told him.

"Close enough. Just a minute."

He closed the door and was gone about half a minute. The door opened and he handed me two dollars and a fifty cent piece.

"I don't have any change yet, but I'll bring it to you later, okay?"

"Keep it," he said and closed the door.

When I got to 331, I didn't even have to knock. They must have seen me coming or something, because by the time I'd gone up to the door, it just opened.

"Here you go, young man," the lady said handing me a bunch of money.

She handed me the money and I put it in the money pouch. She seemed to know how much so I didn't even have to look at the list.

"Thank you for getting the paper on the porch. The young man in the truck had it all over the yard. We never knew where to look next. So, thank you."

"You're welcome."

She closed the door and that was that.

I went across the street to Julie and Sharon's. The door was open and I could hear music. I knocked. I doubted if anyone heard it because the music was pretty loud, so I knocked again on the open door and then rang the door bell. I was about to go when Julie walked through the living room from somewhere in the back of their apartment. Her hair was wet and she had a towel wrapped around her. Her legs were long and tan and smooth. Just seeing her made me feel funny. Not bad funny, just funny. I didn't know what to do. I was going to call to her to let her know I was there but thought she might be embarrassed about not being dressed. On the other hand, if I just stood there, it was sort of like being sneaky when all I was doing was trying to collect for the paper. On the other other hand, the longer I stood there doing nothing, it was like being sneaky anyway. Then I thought since I'd only been delivering the paper a few days, maybe I should just skip collecting from them for this month and get out of there before she saw me. Maybe I could add it on to next month. Except Ron would still collect from me on Monday no matter what, so that seemed like a gyp to me. While I was thinking about it she turned around and saw me.

"Oh!" she said, "you scared the life out of me!"

I couldn't think of anything to say. Right at that moment she was at least as pretty as Norma and even prettier than Miriam. There were drops of water on her shoulders and some dripping from her hair, running down her front between her bosoms and underneath the towel where it only came part way up and part way down.

"How long have you been there?" she said.

"I knocked and rang the bell," I said.

"Have you been there long?"

"Not very."

"Come in. Sorry, I didn't hear you. The music's too loud." She turned it down.

"Maybe I should come back later."

"No, it's okay. What's up?"

"Here's your Saturday paper and I need to collect for this month even though you've only taken the paper a week. Okay?"

"Sure. Let me get some money. How much do we owe you?"

I opened the purse, the money pouch, and took out the list.

"Sixty-six cents. That's for seven regular days and one Sunday. Okay?"

"Sounds right to me."

She went into the back of the apartment and came back with her purse. She took out a little coin purse that had the same kind of snap at the top that my money pouch did. I hoped she wouldn't notice. She handed me three quarters.

"You keep the change," she smiled.

"Are you sure? I think I might have change, and if I don't, I could come back later when I've got more money. You guys are only the third house, so I don't have much collection money yet."

"I'm sure. I should finish drying off. I'm supposed to meet Sharon."

"Okay. Thanks. Bye."

"Bye," she said and closed the door.

I had the funny feeling for about six more houses and then forgot about it, or at least I thought I had, because then without even trying, I started thinking about it and felt funny all over again and she wasn't even anywhere around. Ron was right about one thing at least, Saturday was a good day to collect. Almost everyone was home and had money. A lot of them forced me to take extra. I kept telling them they didn't have to, but after a while, I figured it probably made them feel good, so I should let them if they really wanted to. So far, there'd only been two houses I'd had to mark down where no one was there to collect from. I left the notes Marty had thought up. I got to the Burton-Maple Arms and took a paper and the money pouch and went to the door. I got lucky again because someone was coming out and I didn't have to struggle getting in. When I'd creaked my way down to Mrs. Gunther's door, I knocked a couple of times in a row, and harder than usual, since she never seemed to hear me on the first knock when I left the paper and ran for the stairs and hid to make sure she'd heard me and opened the door and found the paper. This time, she opened up almost right away.

"Hello," she said. "Collecting?"

"Yes mam," I said.

"I wish there was a way I could pay you and not the other young man for the first part of the month. You've made it easy for me and I appreciate it."

She handed me the money.

"There's a little something extra for you."

"That's okay," I said. "You already gave me the extra dime. That's plenty."

"No, I want you to have it."

She put three dollar bills in my hand. I checked the list to make sure.

"You only owe two dollars and forty-eight cents. I've got plenty of change now."

"No, please dear, you keep it for yourself. Thank you," she said, closing the door.

"Thank you," I said through the door.

I hadn't tried to count it up, but on the way back to the Red Rider, I was betting I had about two dollars or maybe a little more in extra money. Boy, that was almost like a whole day at the carwash. I was going to figure out how many hubcaps that would be, but decided not to. Instead, as I headed for the next house on Crescent, I tried to do the math in my head like Marty did for something else. Since I'd done the route half the month and on a full month I was supposed to get around thirty dollars, that meant I should get around fifteen. And if I was right about the two bucks extra money, that was seventeen. And I'd already paid Mr. Mahoney the first two-fifty a week early, since Mr. Avery gave me the extra money to pay off the Red Rider a week early, and paid him the second last week, and I had the third two fifty from today at the carwash, so if I gave him all the seventeen new dollars, then... I got to the house on

Crescent before I figured it out. I hardly remembered going to the door or asking for the money or getting it, because I was still trying to figure out how much money I'd have paid Mr. Mahoney with the seventeen added in and subtracting out what I owed Marty, but by the time I got back to my bike, the number just jumped into my head. Two-fifty two times was five bucks plus two-fifty was seven-fifty and seventeen more would be twenty-four fifty and subtract for Marty and I'd be up to twenty-three for the locks. Man oh man, that was almost half of what I owed him. I might be able to pay him everything by the end of July. Then whatever I made in August would be for me. Talk about the luck of the Red Rider! This was too good to be true!

I finished the collecting on Doheny, turned onto Lower Santa Monica and turned down Oakhurst. Shelly and George were fooling around with Snowball, sitting on the front steps, both of them smoking, tossing the ball with the bell.

"Hiya kid," she smiled, "lookin' for the dough?"

"Uh huh."

I leaned the bike against the fence and took her the paper.

"Hi Kurt," George said, "how'd it go?"

"Pretty good. So far, I only had three places where no one was home."

"How much do we owe you?" Shelly asked.

I checked the list so she'd know I was being careful about it, but I already knew because it was the same as Julie and Sharon.

"Sixty-six cents."

"Sixty-six?"

"Uh huh."

"You sure?"

She frowned like it sounded like too much. I checked the list to make sure. What if Marty made a mistake? Oh boy, that would be a disaster! Then she smiled.

"Just foolin', kid. That sounds right. I'll go get it."

She got up and went in the house.

"She's a nice girl," George smiled at me, "but she's got a scratchy side to her, too."

He put out the butt of his cigarette on the bottom of his shoe and put it in his pocket again. Shelly came back with the money. She handed me a dollar. I fished around in the money pouch and found a quarter and a nickel and four pennies. I fished around a little longer than I had to while I was trying to do the subtraction. I was pretty sure I had it right, so I handed it to her.

"Naw," she said, "you keep it. A little contribution from me and Norma for the Greater Oakhurst Lock Fund."

"But you've only been taking the paper a week."

"Hey, you want it or not?" she said like she was mad or something, but just as quick, she reached out and messed my hair, and said, "I'd be honored to contribute to the fund. Believe me, you put on quite a show with that little trick. I can't remember when I had such a laugh. Worth every penny, eh George."

George was lighting another cigarette and smiled, but didn't say yes or no. He stood up and reached in his pocket and took out three quarters and handed them to me.

"Same for me?"

"No. You don't take the Sunday, so it's only fifty-six cents this month."

"Well, you keep the difference. That's my contribution to the Fund."

I collected from Kenny Lester of course, but not that Duffy guy. He was home alright, but out of money or something. I rang his bell but, as usual, no answer. So I rang Mr. 1A. It took a while, but he buzzed the door and I went in. He opened his door and saw me.

"Mr. Duffy's not answering," I told him.

He made a face, not at me, at least I didn't think so, but about Duffy.

"He's up there, I can tell you. I hear him banging around all day, got the radio on like he's deaf in both ears. I call him on the telephone and ask, politely, mind you, can you please not be banging the floor all day? And can you turn the radio down? And what does he say?"

He looked at me like I was supposed to answer, so I did.

"I don't know," I told him.

"He says, 'turn off your hearing aid!' That's what he tells me, the mumzer! You should pardon the French. Can you imagine?"

"No, sir."

But I was wondering how come everyone around here knew French.

"The man has no consideration. None at all."

"Thank you for buzzing the door for me," I told him.

"You're welcome. Thank you for ringing the bell just one time. You remembered."

"Yes sir."

He closed his door. I went up the stairs to 2A and listened at the door for a second. I thought I could hear someone moving around and for sure I could hear a baseball game on the radio. I rang the bell. All of a sudden the radio went off and the moving around stopped. I rang the bell again, but nothing happened. I waited a minute or so wondering what to do. If I didn't collect, Ron would want the money from me anyway, which didn't seem fair, like Marty pointed out, but if that was the rule, that was the rule. I didn't like the idea of asking the people for the money in the first place, but standing around in the empty hallway here was making me sort of mad. I wasn't some kind of beggar, for pete'sake. I delivered like I was supposed to. Why couldn't he pay like he was supposed to? He never left the window open like he said he would or answered the door bell when I rang it so I could go in and leave the paper without bothering the other man, and now this. I thought maybe I should just leave and try to collect tomorrow. But then I'd just have to ring 1A again and bother him all over. The whole thing made me even madder and before I knew it, I was knocking on the door really hard and ringing the bell at the same time.

"Holy Christ!" he shouted through the door, "stop that pounding. Who's there? Whatever it is, we don't want any!"

"It's me," I said.

"Who?"

"Kurt Goldman."

"Who?"

"The paper boy."

"My god, and you're pounding on the door like that?!"

"Sorry."

"Just leave the paper by the door," he shouted.

"I'm collecting today."

There was a long quiet before he said, "I'm not dressed."

"You could put on your robe," I suggested.

I looked at the list to make sure. Weekdays and Sundays, two forty-eight. For a long time he didn't say anything. Maybe he thought I went away.

"You owe two forty-eight," I shouted through the door.

"It's not convenient now. Come back another time."

"When?"

"How the hell should I know! Another friggin' time!" he shouted.

His yelling came through the door like he was standing right there in front of me, probably in his baggy underwear with his stomach hanging out, but it didn't scare me or make me feel like I was going to cry at all. Kevin Doyle has that job all to himself, I thought, and that made it seem funny. The sound of the baseball game came back on, louder this time. I put the paper down on the floor at my feet. I stood there looking at it for at least a minute and the whole thing was making me mad all over again. I thought about picking it up and taking it with me.

"I'll be back friggin' tomorrow!" I shouted through the door.

By the time I got to the Red Rider, I wished I had taken the paper.

Rathbone paid and Mr. Avery and George already had, so I was done. I put the Red Rider away and went in through the back porch to the kitchen. No one was home. I unsnapped the money pouch and dumped all of the money onto the table, stacking the bills, the fifty-cent pieces, the quarters and dimes and nickels and pennies in separate piles. I got a pencil and some of Marty's school paper and made a list for how many of each thing there was. I was pretty sure I had eighty-seven dollars and fifty-one cents. That was more than enough to buy the Red Rider. I added up the three deliveries with Sundays and the one without and there would be another nine dollars and fifty-two cents when I finished collecting. I had a bad feeling about collecting from Mr. Duffy, but I was almost positive the other guys just happened to be not home, and would pay tomorrow. Since Duffy took Sundays and owed the full two forty-eight, Ron probably would take that out of my pay. Then I suddenly realized what Marty was talking about when he asked Ron who paid how much. It was two forty-eight for the customers, but less for me, so I wouldn't get stuck for as much! It was still a gyp, just not as big a gyp as I thought it was going to be. Ron had told Marty the papers cost me five cents for the weekdays and six cents for the Sundays. I fooled around with adding this and subtracting that, and decided I'd get Marty to help me to make sure, but the way I figured it, Ron should only take away a dollar fifty-four if Mr. Duffy didn't pay. It was complicated, and Marty said he'd help me figure it out, since some were Sunday guys and some weren't, and some just started a week ago and some of those were Sunday and some not, but the whole mess together added up to at least fifteen dollars for me for the half of the month I been delivering. The heck with Mr. Duffy, I was rich anyway. I put the money and the paper with the amount written on it back in the money pouch and put it on the corner of Marty's desk. I hoped he'd check it for me before I had to give it to Ron. I wondered if Ron would give me my money right then and there on the parkway when he dropped off the papers. I pictured him counting it out, one, two, three all the way up to fifteen or a little more. Well, fourteen anyway, because of Mr. Duffy. Heck, with the luck of the Red Rider, maybe Mr. Duffy would pay up after all. He might. Then it would be fifteen. With the carwash money, I'd give Mr. Mahoney seventeen-fifty. If no Mr. Duffy, about sixteen. Then I thought maybe I should keep just a little. Like in case Norma was at the carwash or Gert's with me and I wanted to pay for her coffee or a coke or something. I didn't want to gyp Mr. Mahoney though. Maybe I should just give him everything. Maybe I'd get the job on Norma's movie and have some extra money I could buy cokes with. Except that should probably go to Mr. Mahoney too. Boy, I wished Allen and I had never gone in Mr. Erwin's garage to look at those planes! It would be smooth sailing all the way to the bank if we hadn't. But we had, and that was that. And besides, if we hadn't, I wouldn't have needed the money and probably never would have gotten the paper route in the first place.

I heard my dad's car in the driveway. I looked at the clock on the stove. It was almost seven. I wondered what time I'd finished the route, but bet it was after six.

My mom and Sarah and Nick came in through the back porch and into the kitchen. Nick was holding my mom's hand. His eyes were sort of droopy. Too much downtown, I bet. Sarah and my mom were each carrying a big bag of groceries and put them on the counter next to the sink. My dad came in and had a bag in each arm and put them down next to the others. They were all laughing and joking about something.

"Kurt, my boy! How'd the route collecting go?" he asked.

"Pretty good. Three houses weren't home and one guy didn't want to pay."

"What do you mean?"

"He said it wasn't convenient."

"Is that so?"

My dad's face changed from laughing to that look like he might pound someone.

"It's okay," I told him. "I'm going to go back tomorrow with the Sunday paper and try to collect again."

"It'll be fine," my mom said, patting my dad's arm.

"If that deadbeat gives you any more excuses, let me know. Okay?"

"Okay."

"I mean it. Let me know."

"Dave, let Kurt handle it."

I could tell my dad was getting worked up thinking about it and he got started on an argument with my mom about deadbeats cheating little kids, but my mom reminded him about whatever they'd all been laughing about, and he quit getting worked up about Mr. Duffy, or whoever the deadbeat was, since he didn't know it was Duffy, and sort of forgot about it as quickly as it had gotten started. My dad could get madder, then unmadder, faster than anyone I'd ever seen. I was glad I hadn't mentioned who the deadbeat was, or he might really end up beat-dead.

"What's everyone laughing about?" I asked.

"Let me tell him," Sarah begged.

"Okay," my mom said.

"Dad got some big orders for the new line!"

"Really?"

My dad looked really happy.

"We got our first two good orders today."

"Very good orders," my mom said.

"Good enough so were going to pick up Marty and go out to dinner!" Sarah said.

"At a restaurant?"

"No, stupid, at Ozzie's Soda Fountain."

"Really?"

"No," my mom said, "she's teasing you. Sarah, cut that out. Yes, a real restaurant. A nice one, too, for a real celebration. You guys go get washed up and find the best clothes you can. I'll help Nick get ready. Kurt, pick out something for Marty. He can change at the station."

When we were walking down the hall, I stopped Sarah.

"What if the guys that made the orders are deadbeats and don't pay? Should we be going out to dinner before he gets paid?"

"What makes you say that?"

"Pop's always talking about the mumzers who cancel orders or only pay for part of them and make getting the rest like pulling teeth. I've heard that a million times, I bet."

"That's what mom's afraid of, but she doesn't want to spoil it for dad. He's been working so hard, and this is the first really good news we've had, so keep just your fingers crossed."

We gave Marty his dress up clothes and waited in the car while he changed. He came out of the rest room and off we went. Me and Sarah and Marty were pretty excited, and so was Nick, but except for Nick, we were nervous about the whole thing too. Sarah and I hadn't said anything to Marty, but it looked to me like he was thinking the same thoughts. Anyway, it had been a long time since we'd gone out someplace for dinner. My mom and dad and Marty and Sarah looked dressed up enough to go out to a fancy restaurant okay, but me and Nick just looked clean. If we went to a fancy restaurant, I wondered if they'd let me and Nick in. Maybe because we were littler kids, they wouldn't care too much. I was wearing a pretty nice shirt, I thought. It was white and had a collar. It was too small, but not by that much. Nick had one too, but his fit better, too big, but better. I think it must have been one of mine from when I was smaller, but since it was the kind of shirt I hadn't had much of a chance to wear, it didn't wear out before I got too big for it. He was wearing tan shorts that had a built-in belt. I was wearing my brown corduroy pants that weren't too worn out for the same reason as the shirts. They were still too big to give to Nick but really too small for me, but since I'd cut off the bad jeans for the beach, all I had were the not-as-bad ones or these, and these were much more dress-up than jeans, any day. They fit in the waist okay, maybe a little too tight, but okay, but the legs came up too high. At least my socks were clean and in good shape. Maybe if the orders were good enough, and got paid for, I could get some new jeans. If not, maybe with the next order. If not then, I still figured I should have enough money by the end of the summer to get a new pair of jeans and sneakers after I paid for the locks. If the restaurant checked your shoes before they let you in, I was a goner. I hadn't been paying attention, but now that I did, it seemed like we were headed right back home after we'd picked up Marty. We were headed down Beverly Boulevard going right back to Oakhurst. For a minute I was sure they'd been joking me and my mom was going to cook a special dinner at home and we'd just pretend it was a fancy restaurant. That would be okay too, I thought, because maybe we should just save the money we would have spent at a restaurant in case whoever made the big orders turned out to be deadbeats like Mr. Duffy. It was sort of a relief thinking we weren't going to go spend a bunch of money we might not have anyway. But I got fooled. We went past Oakhurst to Doheny and across it and my dad turned into the parking lot at Chasen's. Oh, brother, that was about as fancy as you could get. At Chasen's, they might not let me in, little kid or not. Nick would be okay, I supposed, because he was really little and even Chasen's wouldn't make a big deal out of it, but I was in-between. Sarah, and Marty for sure, would be expected to be dressed up. I could just see them telling our whole family we couldn't come in because my pants were too high and my sneakers were too worn out. I'd never hear the last of that from Sarah. My mom and dad were talking and laughing and Sarah and Marty were talking about something, and I could tell Nick was excited about being at a fancy restaurant. I decided with the luck of the Red Rider, it would be okay. I closed my eyes and crossed the fingers on one hand and put the other hand into my pocket so I could touch the knife and the propeller medal just to make sure. It was going to fall into place and that was that.

Sure enough, they let us in.

Chasen's had the guys in the parking lot that wanted you to let them park your car for you, so we all got out right in front of the entry and my dad handed the guy the keys and a quarter, even thought he wasn't a Negro or a Mexican. We went in and another guy in a really fancy suit asked my dad for his name and looked on a list and we were on it! They took us to a table and the guy pulled the chair out for my mom and even Sarah. When we were all sitting down, another guy, who I thought was a Mexican, but Marty told me was an Italian when I had a chance to ask him, poured water with ice in it from a fancy glass pitcher into big fancy glasses. Someone else brought a basket of warm bread and a plate of butter and we were allowed to start eating that before we'd even ordered anything. If we'd changed our minds and left without having dinner, we'd have gotten the bread and water for free, but we didn't. Another guy came and he was our waiter. They must have had a million guys working there. He handed each of us a menu, except for Nick, who he figured probably couldn't read, but Nick kept his hand up until the guy finally gave him one. I asked Marty why it was only partly crowded, and he said it was because it was a little early, but even so, there were twenty or twenty-five people there, mostly couples, and as I was looking around at what kind of people came to a place like this, other than us, one of them was Norma! She was at a table with two men. One of them was about Pop's age, maybe even older, and the other was about the same as my dad. When she saw me she waved. I waved back and she got up and came over to our table. I was glad I was sitting down and my pants and sneakers were hidden. Marty was so shocked she came over to us, the smile he had on his face looked like it was painted on. It didn't change the whole time she was standing there.

"Hi! How nice to see you all," she said. "Is this a celebration? It sure looks like it is."

"Hello, Norma," my mom said. "It is. This is Kurt's father, Dave. Dave..."

My dad stood up to shake hands with her, and said, "I know who she is. You're the woman who's got one of the Lester's puppies, right?" he said, joking her. I think.

"DAD!" Sarah said. "You know who she really is, don't you?"

"If I'm known only as Snowball's mom, that's good enough for me, honey," Norma told her. "I don't want to intrude on your celebration, but did you get a chance to ask your mom and dad about Love Nest?" she asked me.

"No. No one's been home all day and then I forgot with the going out to dinner stuff."

"That's my agent, Louie, and the director I was telling you about, Joe Newman. He'd love to meet you."

"What's Love Nest?" my mom asked.

"There's a little boy that was scheduled to be in the movie I'm work-

Berton D. Garey

ing on, Love Nest, but he got the chicken pox. I told Joe I thought Kurt
would be perfect, if he wanted to try it. Kurt said he might. He made it
very clear it was just a maybe, but he was going to ask you if it would be
okay to come to the set with me on Tuesday or Wednesday to see if he
likes the idea. I gave him some papers you'd have to sign, saying it was
okay for him to be there."

"I left them on the kitchen table," I said.

"Would you like to?" my dad asked.

"I think so," I said. "Maybe."

"Maybe? Are you crazy?! This could be your big break!" Sarah said.

"Well, knowing you, maybe not. You'd probably mess it up anyway."

"Sarah," my dad said, giving her a look to cut it out.

"If," Norma said, then looking right at me, "If he wants to do it, he'd
be on the set for three or four days off and on. I could drive him back at
the lunch break in time for his paper route. I thought it might be fun for
him. What do you think?" she asked my mom.

"I hardly know what to think. Dave?"

"It sounds like a great experience. Why not?"

"Why does he get to?" Sarah said.

"Chicken pox," I reminded her.

"Just don't tell me he gets paid. That would be too much!"

Norma laughed, "Sorry, sweetie, he does. Not a lot, but something.
But mostly, I think it would be fun. Could I steal Kurt for just a minute?
I'd like Joe to meet him. I'll bring him right back, I promise."

"Keep him," Sarah said.

"Sure," my mom said.

I didn't see how I could say no, but the idea of my too high pants and
ratty sneakers being seen by all the people in the place who'd already
been looking at Norma the whole time she was standing at our table,
made me wish I could think of something. What the heck, I thought,
maybe they'll be so busy looking at her they won't notice. I stood up and
she took my hand and we walked over to her table.

"Joe, Louie, this is my friend, Kurt, the little boy I was telling you
about."

The Joe guy stood up, then reached down to shake hands. The Louie
guy shook hands but didn't get up, probably because he was older and
it was too much trouble. He had a fat cigar in his mouth that reminded
me of Max's at Carl's, only Louie's wasn't down to a stub, it was more
like a foot-longer at Gert's, but it was just as wet and gooey at the end
in his mouth.

"So," Joe said, "you're the little lockmaster?"

He said it with a smile, so I guess he thought it was funny.

"Yes sir."

"Well, Norma and Shelly said it was quite a scene. Oughtta be in a
movie, that's what Shelly said. If not that, then you. You interested in
being in our little production?"

"Maybe," I told him.

"That's the ticket, kid," Louie said, taking the cigar out of his mouth and pointing at me with it, "play hard to get. We'll have him beggin' you. Push your price through the roof!"

"They're just teasing," Norma told me. Then she said to Joe, "What do you think?"

"Perfect," he said.

"Tuesday?" she said.

"Fine," he said.

"Is he represented?" Louie said.

"Take it easy, Louie," Joe told him.

"Just kiddin', just kiddin'," he said, but then he leaned over to me, took the cigar out again, and said, "don't sign with anyone 'til you talk to me. Hear?"

"Okay," I said, but I didn't know what he was talking about.

"Let's get you back to your dinner," Norma said. "I'll be right back," she told them.

Louie was staring at my sneakers. His eyes moved from them up to mine without his head moving at all. His eyebrows lifted up and the corners of his mouth turned down and the smoke curled and drifted around his head from the long cigar. He sort of nodded and winked at me.

Norma took my hand and I said, "Okay."

When we got back to our table and I'd sat back down, my mom told Norma she'd sign the papers and I could go with her whatever day I wanted.

"Oh, that's wonderful!" she said. Then she said to me, "I'll tell you on Monday if Tuesday or Wednesday is better, but I think Tuesday. Okay?"

"Okay," I said.

"Happy celebration!" she said. "Enjoy your dinner."

And, boy, did we.

Our dinner party lasted 'til eight-thirty. It would have gone on longer, but Nick was falling asleep at the table and my mom wanted to get him home and to bed. I think it was the best dinner I'd ever had. My mom's a good cook, but the cook at Chasen's was even better. We all got to order whatever we wanted. I had some lamb chops that were cut at least twice as thick as any I'd ever seen before. Well, at least tasted before, because they were about the same size as the ones Norma got from Carl. They didn't just taste good, or even great, they tasted like a whole new thing. Like I'd never had lamb chops before in my life, but I had, pretty many times, before we got broke. My mom used to buy skinny ones at Carl's market and cook them and they were good, but not anything like these. Marty and Sarah had Prime Rib and so did my dad. My mom had some fancy chicken thing. Nick had a kid's sized Prime Rib. Everyone kept saying the same things, like they never tasted anything so good, so the cook didn't just get lucky with the lamb chops. But the other thing was they didn't just put the food on the plate. They arranged it so you saw it in a new way. Like a painting or the Watts Towers or the green horse. The cook at Chasen's was making art out of eating. I wished I could tell Miss

Rimes about it or show her. So if all that wasn't enough of a celebration, my dad said we could get dessert too. The waiter rolled out this little cart with all kinds of stuff and we each got to choose. My mom and dad split a chocolate thing that looked like a thin flat cake where the frosting wasn't soft, like usual, but more like a shell. Marty and Sarah got hot fudge Sundays. Nick was too tired to choose, so he had a bite of this or that from everyone else, when he could keep his eyes open, that is. I chose last because I couldn't decide. We might not be back here for years, I thought, so whatever I chose, I wanted it to be the best thing of all. Marty let me take a spoonful of his sunday to test it. It was great, okay, but not the right thing for me. Not this time. My mom broke off a piece of her and my dad's thing, and since I love chocolate, she thought I'd choose it, if I wasn't going to have the hot fudge Sunday. But it wasn't the right thing either. There was this thing on the bottom shelf that seemed to be calling to me like the Red Rider had at Bill's Bike Shop. I tried to ignore it since I liked chocolate the best, but it wouldn't give up.

"What's that?" I asked the waiter guy.

"That's a very special choice," he said. "My personal favorite."

"What is it?"

"A lemon-cranberry tart," he smiled. "If you chose that, I promise you you'll remember it forever. It will be the most intense experience of your young life."

"In a good way or a bad way?" Sarah teased him.

"Young lady," he said, "it's an event. A tour de force. A gift from the Gods."

"I'll have it," I said.

He gave me the tiniest fork you ever saw so you couldn't take a very big bite even if you wanted to. But that was a good thing, it turned out, because the taste was like a flood, so with a big fork you might have drowned or been washed away. I put these little tiny fork bites in my mouth and sucked them tight between my tongue and the top of my mouth. It was the most amazing and wonderful thing I'd ever eaten. It went right up to the point where if it was any more, you probably couldn't stand it. But in a good way.

When everyone was done, the waiter brought the bill in a little black folder thing and put it on the table near my dad. We'd all had such a good time and such good food, I think we'd all forgotten about having to pay for it. Or were afraid to think about it. My dad opened it and took a quick peek. His face lost its smile and his forehead wrinkled up like he didn't believe it. He closed the folder and closed his eyes and was breathing through his mouth in gasps like someone had punched him in the stomach. He sighed a big sigh and after a second or two opened his eyes and was ready to take another look. This time, he sort of pretended he was sneaking up on it, tipping his head back, like the minute he opened the folder the bill would leap out and strangle him or something. He opened it slowly and let the cover fall open onto the table cloth with the bill starring up at him. I took a peek at Sarah and Marty. They both looked like they'd just found out our house burned down while we were at dinner. I had the same sort of feeling, except I was most worried that Norma would see us get kicked out for not being able to pay. He made some more faces of shock and surprise and horror at the bill. My mom was rolling her eyes at him. Nick was leaning against her, almost asleep.

"We might have to wash dishes to pay for this," my dad whispered, his eyes real wide and sad.

Marty and Sarah just stared at him with their mouths open. I thought Sarah was going to cry. If I hadn't been so happy about the lamb chops and the lemon-cranberry tart, I might have too, but the way I saw, it would have been worth washing dishes. As long as Norma didn't see, that is.

"Dave, you're upsetting them," my mom said. "He's just kidding you guys. Look at Sarah, Dave. Tell her you're kidding."

He started laughing, "I'm sorry, honey, I'm kidding."

He paused for a few seconds, then said, "I think."

Then he took another look at the bill and made a face and grabbed his chest like he was having a heart attack. He kept kidding around like that until both Sarah and Marty were laughing.

"Daaaad!" Sarah said.

He counted out a ton of money and put it on top of the little folder thing and we left. The guys that gave my dad the orders better not be a bunch of deadbeat mumzers, I was thinking.

When we'd gotten home and we were getting ready for bed, I told Marty I had the two-fifty from the carwash and could pay him back the one-fifty I owed him, but was it okay if I wanted to give it all to Mr. Sullivan.

"That's fine. There's no hurry," he said.

"As soon as Ron pays me on Monday, I'll have plenty to pay you back with."

"Don't worry about it. What are you going to with the rest?"

"Give it to Mr. Mahoney."

"Maybe you should keep a little for yourself. A little spending money."

"Yeah, I thought about that, but the sooner I pay off the locks, the better. If I actually work on Norma's movie and get any money for it, maybe I could keep some from that."

"It just boggles the mind," he said, shaking his head and smiling at me.

I opened the money pouch on the corner of his desk and took out the paper I'd written on.

"I counted the money and I'm pretty sure there's eighty-seven dollars and fifty-one cents right now. And guess what?"

"What?"

"I think about two bucks is extra. Tips! Even though I told them they didn't have to, some of them insisted. Really."

"I believe you. That's great."

"Anyway, if I collect from everyone else tomorrow, that's another nine fifty-two. One guy might not pay up, so it would be nine fifty-two minus," I looked at the sheet, "two forty-eight, so..."

"Seven oh-four," he said, "plus the eight-seven fifty-one, so ninety-four dollars and fifty-four cents."

"How can you do that?"

"Pure genius," he said.

"Anyway, could you help me make sure I counted right and then figure out how much money out of all this Ron should get?"

"Sure, but can we do it tomorrow? I'm beat."

"Sure. Goodnight, Marty."

"Goodnight, kiddo."

I woke up pretty early on Sunday. Marty was in his bed still conked out and no one else was up either, so I went into the kitchen thinking I'd see if my jeans were dry. Before we'd gone to dinner, my mom had washed them, but it was too late to hang them on the clothesline in the back yard since the sun was most of the way down, so she hung them in the back porch, near the water heater, so that maybe they'd dry overnight. Since they were the only ones I had, because I'd made cut offs out of the bad ones to go to the beach with Norma, I had to wear them all week, and when they were really dirty, they had to be washed, which meant they might not get dry in time for the next day, and if they didn't, I might have to wear the cords, but since they were supposed to be my dress pants, even though they were too small and too tight, I shouldn't, so I'd probably have to wear the cut offs instead. And if I was wearing the cut off and took a spill on the Red Rider, I'd scrape a whole lot more skin off than if I was wearing pants that came all the way down. Just the thought of it made my knees hurt. I'd seen kids at school who'd taken a fall off their bikes and even through long pants had scraped a whole bunch of skin off, so I was hoping the water heater had done the trick. But one more thing had fallen into place, okay, and it wasn't the water heater drying my jeans. It was a brand new pair. There they were, on the kitchen table, and they weren't by themselves. There was a new pair of underwear, a new t-shirt and new socks. On top of the folded pile of clothes was a note from my mom that said, For Kurt. Next to it was a new skirt and shirt and socks and on top of them a note that said, For Sarah. And next to that was a pair of shorts and a striped t-shirt and underwear and socks for Nick. If we weren't Jewish, it would be Christmas in July. I put them on and buttoned them. They were stiff as cardboard and too big, as usual, for me to grow into, but they were brand new. I figured they'd shrink some after they were washed, but I'd still have to roll them way up and I'd need my belt for sure until then and maybe even after, but boy, I couldn't believe how dark blue new jeans were. I guess I'd forgotten, but the blue was so dark, they made my old ones look only about sky-blue. I rolled them up until I had these thick cuffs to just about where the new socks came above the ratty sneakers. I had to hold them up even with all the buttons buttoned. I went back into our room to get my belt.

"Pretty nice, huh?" Marty said.

"It's great. Where'd they come from?"

"Mom and dad stopped at The Broadway on their way home. They wanted to surprise you guys."

"It worked. I can't believe it. Do you think we can really afford all this? The dinner and the clothes too?"

"Let's hope so," he said.

But he didn't seem too sure. I was afraid to ask, but I did anyway.

"Didn't they get you anything?"

"A new pair of cords. See? Hanging in the closet."

I took a look.

"Nice ones," I said.

I strung my belt through the loops, but when I was pulling it tight, it broke. It was old and the leather was cracked, but I never thought a belt could break.

"Rats!"

"What?"

"The belt broke. Now what am I going to do? They won't stay up without it."

"They'll be better after they're washed, but you can have the old cowboy belt for now."

"What cowboy belt?"

"You know, my old cowboy belt. The one with the rhinestones and silver things on it."

"Really? The special one?"

"Sure. I'm not really saving it any more. It's just there."

"Where?"

"In that box on the floor of the closet."

There was a cardboard box on the closet floor that had the top flaps folded so that they sort of locked it closed. I pulled and they popped opened. I dug around through some stuff of Marty's from when he was little, a cowboy hat and some cowboy chaps and a holster and cap guns and finally the belt.

"This one, right?"

"Yeah, that's it."

"I'll give it back when the pants fit better."

"Keep it."

"Really?"

"Sure. Why not?"

"Thanks."

On the inside it said 'Goldman' in gold letters. Marty watched me while I strung it through the belt loops and pulled it to the last hole. It was still too big.

"Wait a sec," he said. "We'll do what we did with the other one."

He got out of bed and in his underwear went out to the garage. He came back with a tool of Pop's, called an awl, and a little block of wood and put them on his desk. He pulled the belt tighter against my stomach and marked the spot by scratching the leather with the point of the awl. He slid the belt out of the loops and flattened it out on top of his desk. He put the block of wood under the spot he'd marked and twisted the point of the awl until he'd sort of drilled a hole.

"Let's try it now," he said, working it back through the loops.

He pulled it tight to the new hole and put the peg thing in and it was just right. The jeans sort of bunched up all around me in little puckers and there was a lot of extra belt hanging down, but the pants were staying up.

"We could cut off the extra again if you want," he said.

"No, that's okay, we'd lose all those silver things. I'll just tuck it in."

"You sure?"

"Yeah. Could I write my name on it too?"

"Sure."

"Thanks."

I'd been using that cuff thing that Bill had given me with my old jeans but with the new ones I really had to. Even with it, the new jeans got so close to catching in the sprocket thing, I thought I was a goner a bunch of times. Without it, I'd have been doomed for sure. Just like I thought, the three houses that weren't home Saturday paid right up on Sunday, but of course, not Duffy. The old man in 1A let me in again and I went upstairs again and rang Duffy's bell and knocked again, but this time he didn't even answer through the door. The radio was on and I could hear another baseball game. I knocked once more, louder, but he ignored it. I started to put the fat Sunday paper down anyway, but just like that, I changed my mind. The heck with him, I thought. It was the first day of a new month and he hadn't paid for the last one. Why should I keep leaving him the paper if he wasn't going to pay for it? Ron would just make me pay for it anyway. I'd tell Ron to leave off one less weekday and one less Sunday from now on, starting tomorrow. I looked at the paper in my hands. I'd have to pay for this one no matter what, so on my way out I rang the bell for 1A. It opened and the old man stood there with a magazine in one hand and little glasses down near the end of his nose.

"Would you like a Sunday paper?" I asked him.

"I don't know," he said, sort of wrinkling up his face. "Do I really need it?"

He said it like a question, but I don't think he was asking me. More like talking to himself.

"For free," I told him.

He smiled, taking off the glasses.

"Duffy's?"

"Not any more," I said.

He smiled again.

"I'd like that very much," he said, nodding and taking it from me.

"Thank you."

"You're welcome. Bye."

I started for the front door.

"Little boychick," he called to me, "if I wanted to take the paper from you, as a regular thing, what would I do?"

"I can leave a subscription slip with you, if you want. I have some in my route bags. Do you want one?"

"Sure. You give me one and I'll think about it."

"Okay."

I went out to the Red Rider and fished around in the bottom of the empty route bags and found one. He'd come to the outside door and was waiting for me on the front steps.

"Here," I said, giving it to him. "If you want the paper, just fill it out and give it to me and I'll start as soon as the routemaster guy adds you on."

He looked at the slip.

"I'll let you know."

"Okay."

"Thank you for the paper," he said, holding it up, "that's a very nice thing of you."

I went back to the Red Rider and got on. When I looked back, Mr. 1A was gone and the outside door was clicking closed. I glanced up for just a second and saw Duffy was at the closed window in his baggy underwear. He looked mad, but I pretended I didn't see him.

When Marty got home Sunday night, he recounted the money and sure enough, I had ninety-four dollars and fifty-four cents with the money I'd collected that day.

"There's three seventy-five in tips. You should get twelve thirty-eight for delivering ten weekdays and one Sunday. Ron should take seventy-eight sixty-six from this," he said, pointing at the pouch.

"Hey! How come I get so little? That's a gyp! I thought I was supposed to get fifteen bucks. Whatever happened to that, huh? That's what I want to know."

"Take it easy, squirt. You started on the 18th, so you delivered less than half the month. We figured about fifteen for a half month. So, it's less money for fewer days. Get it?"

"Yeah, but it still seems like a gyp."

"Well, at least you have the three seventy-five in tips. Altogether, you should get fifteen eighty-eight."

"So I get more than fifteen after all?"

"Yeah, because of the tips," he said.

"That's pretty good, huh?"

"Sure it is. And if you become a movie star, who knows?"

He messed my hair and handed me the paper he'd worked it all out on and I put it in the pouch with the money. Marty took a rubber band from his desk drawer and counted out the seventy-eight dollars for Ron and bound them together.

"Give him this and count out the sixty-six cents change," he said.

It was six on the nose and I was hungry. I put on my new jeans and new t-shirt and took the fifteen cents and the signed papers my mom had left for me and got the Red Rider and took a ride to the hot dog stand with a side trip to see Helen.

"Sweetie," she said. "Don't you look nice in your new clothes! It been your birthday or somethin'?"

"Not yet, but we got some new money and my mom got us each a new set of clothes."

"Ain't that nice. Wanna help a bit?"

"Sure. I've got lots of time before the paper route."

"How's that goin'?"

"Pretty good. I got one guy that hides from me when it's time to pay. But everyone else is nice. Some of them even gave me tips."

"Ain't that nice. Wanna run that cart out for the trucks, honey?"

"Sure."

I pushed the rolling cart with the trays of packaged sweet rolls out to the loading dock.

"I didn't see you come in," Jesse said.

"I'm helping Helen."

"I see," he said. "How's the bike?"

"Great. The greatest."

"Good. Enjoy it."

I waited while he loaded the trays from the cart into the closest truck. I took the empty cart back to the pastry room and got another full one and rolled it to the docks too. When I got back, Helen had put a bunch of sweet rolls in a bag for me.

"You go get you some milk or hot chocolate to go with these," she said. "I put some extra of the new custard rolls in there for you."

"Thanks, Helen."

Joseph made me hot chocolate and I started with a custard roll. Norma pulled into the station but didn't need gas so pulled up closer to the Hot Dog Stand instead of the pumps.

"God, I need some coffee! I overslept and I can't keep my eyes open."

"Comin' up." Joseph said.

He set a mug in front of her. She put a plop of cream and some sugar lumps in and stirred it up and blew on it and sipped.

"Ahhh, that's good! How are you, sweetie?"

"Fine. I got the papers for you."

"Wonderful!"

I reached into my shirt and pulled them out. She noticed my new shirt and pants and smiled but didn't say anything, like it didn't need mentioning.

"I've got to run. I'll let you know tonight, but I'm pretty sure tomorrow will be best. Is that still okay for you?"

"I think so. As long as I'm back in time for the paper route."

"I'll make sure you are.

"Want a sweet roll? There's custard ones."

"Oh, that would be scrumptious."

She reached into the bag and took one.

"Thanks, sweetie," she said. "Bye."

"Bye."

She kissed me on the cheek. Joseph didn't say it this time, but we both knew he was thinking the stuff about selling her kisses.

I'd been waiting on the parkway since quarter to twelve. I didn't want to miss Ron because I couldn't wait to get paid. Since he probably couldn't wait to take the money away from me, there wasn't much chance he'd just drop the bundle and take off like most days, but why take the chance? The Red Rider and the route bags and rubber bands and my money pouch were right there next to me all ready to go. A little before one, Ron's truck pulled to the curb and he shut the engine off. That was a good sign, I thought. He grabbed a bundle from the back of his truck and dropped it on the parkway.

"I hope you got something for me," he said.

"Right here," I said patting the money pouch."

I opened it, and was getting ready to hand him the seventy-eight bucks in the rubber band, but he took the whole thing from me.

"What's this?" he asked me.

"That's your part. Plus you get another sixty-six cents."

"Got it all figured out, huh?"

"My brother did."

"Who? The Einstein?"

"Marty."

Ron flipped through the rubber-banded bills, counting them.

"Well, old Marty miscalculated."

He went through the money pouch and mumbled some stuff I didn't understand and couldn't really hear anyway and handed me nine dollars and fifteen cents and the money pouch. He put the rest in his pants pocket. I looked at the money in my hand.

"What's this?"

"That's your part," he said.

I had an odd ache in my stomach. It didn't really hurt like being sick and having the kind of ache or pain just before you throw up, but whatever it was, it was the kind of ache that made you feel like crying, even if you didn't want to. And I wondered if it counted as complaining if I told him it wasn't fair. I looked at the paper Marty had figured on.

"I'm supposed to get fifteen dollars and eighty-eight cents," I said, showing him the paper.

"Is that so?"

"Because of the tips."

"Really?"

"Marty said...."

"I don't give a rat's ass what Marty says. Did he subtract the four dollars for the route bag?"

He looked at me. I didn't know what he was talking about.

"No? I didn't think so. And the buck and a half for the rubber bands? Who do you think pays for them? Huh? Me? No, not me. You! And I told you, any missed papers, and you pay for those."

"I didn't miss any. Except Mr. Duffy because he didn't pay...and besides, that was yesterday, and yesterday was the new month, so it doesn't count."

"That's not what Mr. Duffy says. That's not what Mrs. Gunther says."

He looked at a piece of paper.

"We got here thirteen missed weekdays and two Sundays."

"That's wrong! I didn't...the window was closed...but I tossed it...just Duffy...and that Sunday doesn't count and I'm not going to deliver to him anymore anyway. Mrs. Gunther?"

I was getting sort of dizzy.

"Mrs. Gunther? What about Mrs. Gunther?"

"Hey! I got to go by what the customer says. I not going to argue with you. I know you're a little small, but you got to be responsible, just like the other boys. As for Duffy, you don't decide when to stop a paper, I do. So until I say stop..."

"I didn't miss any," I said again.

I started to cry. I couldn't help it. I probably would have complained too, but I couldn't think of anything else to say.

"You'll do better next month. Geez, don't cry about it. Nine bucks ain't bad for half a month, a kid your age. You oughta be grateful."

He got back in the truck and off he went. It wasn't fair and me and the Red Rider knew it and my stomach still ached and I thought he was a bigger deadbeat than Mr. Duffy was. Marty was right, okay, not trusting him, but if I told Marty about it and he told my dad, just when things were getting better and we'd sold part of the new line, my dad would beat him up and get in trouble and all the good stuff that was happening would be ruined because of me, since I had the paper route in the first place to pay for the locks I'd switched, so I decided it was just one thing falling out of place, and I shouldn't tell anyone. The Red Rider was telling me it would be okay, and that seemed good enough to me. I stopped crying and started folding. I wondered why would Mrs. Gunther say I'd missed any papers? She even gave me tips. Twice. About the time I'd finished folding, it came into my head like a flash, Ron had been delivering the first half of the month and almost never brought the paper in for her. I bet that was it. They were Ron's misses, which made it an even bigger gyp, but I felt better anyway.

Norma came at about six-ten. She'd called the night before to tell me she was supposed to be at work early, and did I still want to come if it was so early, and if I did, I'd have to be ready to go a little after six. Since I was up early most of the time anyway, that was fine with me, so I was on the front steps at six and she came down the block in the MG a few minutes later. The street was completely empty and quiet. There was a little dew on the grass, and it was a tiny bit foggy, the kind that would burn off early. I was betting it would get good and hot. So far, this had been the hottest summer of my life. Maybe it just felt that way because I was riding around and delivering papers every day with the sun beating down on me, or maybe it was hotter and I was delivering papers, but either way, it was hotter than I'd ever seen it. I still had the nine dollars and fifteen cents from the route and the two-fifty from the carwash and the fifteen cents my mom left me yesterday and today, so altogether I had eleven ninety-five in my pocket. I figured it in my head, just like Marty, which I thought was pretty good, especially if I was right. If I got back from the movie making with enough time before the route, I'd go give it all to Mr. Mahoney. If not, I'd do it at the end of the route. Either way, by the end of the day, I'd be broke again. It was exciting having almost twelve dollars, even if it was only for a few hours, so I figured I should enjoy it while I can. I was sort of daydreaming about what I might buy with it if it were going to stay mine. New sneakers would be first.

"Ready to go?" she called to me.

I snapped out of my sneakers dream. She'd pulled up at the curb in front of our house. She was wearing a fluffy short dark coat over her sweatshirt, and jeans and a dark blue knit hat, sort of like the one George wore, left over from the War, pulled down so it covered her ears, probably because of the fog and the open car. I had my new jeans and a different white t-shirt, an older one, but it was clean and as usual, smelled like bleach, which I liked.

"Have you had breakfast?" she asked me.

"No. Have you?"

"No. Want to go to Joseph's? We'll have to take it with us. We're supposed to be on the set at six-thirty. I hate being late. I'm late a lot and I hate it. Oh well, we'll be there as fast as we can. Right?"

"Right." I said.

We pulled into the Station and up close to the Hot Dog Stand.

"What'll it be, guys?" Joseph said.

Norma sat on a stool and I sat next to her. There was no one else there and the streets around the station were empty. All of a sudden I felt like I was in the middle of nowhere, like I'd been dropped in a strange city and didn't know where I was or know anyone and no one was around anyway. It seemed like Joseph and Norma weren't even there, or worse, like they were strangers. I didn't know how to be in a movie. I was thinking in my head ways to tell her maybe I shouldn't do it. They could probably find a kid who already knew how. And I'd walk home so she wouldn't have to drive me and make herself late. She could just go to the movie without me. That would be best. She and Joseph were laughing about something, and he said something about sixty-five cents. She sure had a pretty smile, I thought. But if I told her I didn't want to go, they'd be without a kid, and since she'd sort of convinced the director they should use me, they might hold it against her like it was her fault for choosing me. How did I get myself into these things, I wondered. Things were finally going along pretty well, except maybe for that deadbeat Ron, and now, boom, just like that, it was getting ready to fall apart. I was trying to picture the Red Rider, but I was looking at her instead. There was something about her eyes that seemed both happy and sad at the same time, like she might be about to laugh or cry and you couldn't tell which for sure. That's probably why she was good in movies, I thought. She'd gotten a hot chocolate for me and coffee for herself and two cinnomon rolls and two custard rolls, so Joseph was giving selling fresh ones from the Wonder Bread Factory a try, and the next thing I knew, I was taking money out of my pocket. With it, came the knife George had given me and the propeller medal from Kenny. I separated out sixty-five cents and paid Joseph.

"This one's on me," I said, so Joseph wouldn't say my money was no good.

I'd just pay Mr. Mahoney sixty-five cents less this once.

"That's so sweet," she said, "but I can't let you do that."

"I want to. Really."

I was going to do it so when I told her I didn't want to go to work on the movie she wouldn't feel so bad, but all of a sudden seeing the little knife and the medal in my hand made me feel better and the feeling that this was going to be the best summer ever came back, so I changed my mind again. It was going to work out okay after all, I thought. I put the knife and medal back in my pocket. What the heck, if some kid was going to be in a movie, it might as well be me. Besides, if they paid me for it, I'd get more than sixty-five cents, so I'd come out ahead.

There was a guard in one of those little boothes at the entrance to stop cars from going into the Twentieth Century Fox Studio on Pico, unless they were supposed to. There was a car in front of us and the guard was talking to the driver and checking a list he had, then he let him drive in. When it was our turn, the guard just smiled at Norma and said hello and in we went. We drove around through fake city streets with fake houses, and even a fake cowboy town and then parked behind a huge building. There was a sign on the wall next to the parking space that said, Miss Monroe. Seeing the sign made the whole thing seem real, because before that, it was just talking about it. I had the feeling again like this might not be a good idea, but at least I wasn't shaking in by boots, just a little worried. She shut off the motor and patted my hand.

"It's going to be fine," she said. "Don't worry, just have fun, okay?"

"Okay," I said.

We got out of the car and walked around the side of the building. When we turned the corner there was a crowd of people in front of the door, maybe seventy-five or a hundred, mostly young men and women, around Norma's age, and some of them older, more like my mom and dad, and a few even Pop's age, and in front of them, there was a man with another list in his hand. I thought he was another guard, until I saw a second guy with a guard uniform, so the first guy was something else. Norma and I had to walk through all of the people crowded around the door, and when the guard saw her, he asked them to make room for us to walk, and they did, especially when they saw who it was. The whole crowd seemed pretty excited just to see her and some of them called her name and said they thought she was wonderful and things like that. We got to the door and the guard opened it for us. He nodded and said good morning. He looked at me a little funny, I suppose because he didn't know me and was supposed to stop people he didn't know from going in, but since I was with Norma, he didn't. Just before we went in, someone called.

"Kurt! Kurt!"

I don't know who was more surprised, me or Norma, but we both looked around. It was Julie and Sharon. I waved to them and then we went in.

"You've got a fan club already?" she teased me. "Who was that?"

"Those are the actresses I told you about. Maybe part of the Oakhurst Players? Remember? How come they're out there? All those people?"

"They're trying to get chosen as extras for a couple of scenes we'll shoot this afternoon."

"Unbelievable!" the director guy called. "Right on time! This is a first!"

"Good morning to you too, Joe," Norma said.

He was standing with three men and two women. They all had coffee mugs, so I figured that's what they were drinking. We walked over to them and Joe bent down to shake hands with me and introduced them.

"Welcome to our little family," he said, shaking with me, but looking at Norma. "I see you're a good influence on Marilyn."

"Heck, she got us here."

"Kurt, this is June and Bill and Frank and Jack Parr and Leatrice."

They all shook hands with me.

"If you like, you can look around, while we get ready. This is the set for the inside of the apartment house that Bill, Jim in the movie, and June, who's Connie, and Marilyn, who's Roberta, and Frank, who's Eddie, and Leatrice, Eadie all live in."

"Who's he gonna be?" I asked about Jack.

"We're never sure," Joe joked him. "Anyway, you'd have two or three scenes outside. We'll try to get over to that set before lunch so you can see it. Marilyn tells me you have to be back for your paper route, right?"

"Right."

"If you want to give it a try, maybe you could do one of the run throughs."

"What's that?" I asked him.

"A rehearsal, like a practice. We go through the scene like we're going to film and everyone does what the story calls for and if it goes well, we do it for real with the cameras running. If someone flubs a line, or comes in at the wrong time, we practice a little more, then try it again."

"You mean, I'm supposed to be an actor today?"

"Not unless you want to," he said, looking at Marilyn.

"Kurt only said he'd come see. He didn't promise he was going to do it," Norma reminded him.

"I understand," he said, looking at her. "That's fine. I just thought as long as you're here, if you feel like it of course, you might want to fool around to see what it's like. How would that be?"

"Okay, I suppose."

"Great. You look around and get a feel for things. Geri!" he shouted.

"Coming!" a young woman called back.

Marilyn whispered something to Joe.

"Sure," he said. "Why not?"

Then this girl, Geri, came over.

"Kurt, this is my assistant, Geri. Geri, Kurt. Kurt may be our next Tommy. May be," he said, nodding at me. "I'd like you to show him around the interiors and then look over 146 and 148. Maybe go over the lines Tommy has too. Okay?"

"Sure."

"Kurt?"

"Yes, sir?"

"You can call me Joe, okay?"

"Okay."

"Marilyn says there are some friends of yours who've come for the extras' call?"

"Julie and Sharon," Norma said.

"Yeah, they're right outside. We just saw them."

"Why don't you and Geri go tell Vic I said to sign them in and tell them to stick around."

"You mean they get to be in your movie?"

"Sure. If they're friends of yours, why not?" he said.

Norma leaned down and whispered to me.

"The Oakhurst Players have to stick together, right?"

"Right," I whispered back.

Geri and I went to the door and she told Vic and I pointed them out and he called to them and signed them up, just like that. I waved to them as Geri and I went back inside. She took me around the whole place and showed me just about everything. I met all kinds of guys with different jobs and they showed me what they did. Then we sat down in the fake hallway and she read from a Love Nest book like the one Norma had. She skipped around so I sort of got the idea of the whole story even though the kid, Tommy, was only in a little part of it. Norma's part wasn't the biggest one either, but Geri said whenever she was in a scene, she stole it, which was a good thing, the way she described it, that is, unless you were Bill or June, because they were supposed to be the stars. She showed me the part where Julie and Sharon and a bunch of other extras would be in a fancy hotel, called Pierrot's, having dinner and some of them would be dancing. I was thinking, no matter how fancy it was, the food couldn't be as good as at Chasen's. Anyway, Julie and Sharon would get to dress up in fancy clothes. The whole thing was funny, because in one way it was just a job all these guys were doing, walking here or there, saying this or that, dancing or pretending to eat, turning on or off lights, helping with clothes or running a camera or moving wires out of the way, a million things, but when it was all done, it was going to be a movie, and in that way it was exciting. By the time Geri had read all the stuff to me she wanted, she asked if I wanted anything to eat or drink.

"No thanks. Are you an actress too?"

"No, not me."

"How come?"

She was pretty enough to be. She was about the same age as Julie and Sharon, not quite as pretty, but if she wanted to, she could be, I bet. It looked like she didn't care about it one way or the other.

"I want to direct. Write and direct."

"Do they let girls do that?"

"Not usually, but I'm going to. Believe me. I'm Joe's assistant now, but I'll be a script supervisor on his next project and an assistant director on the one after that. Joe's generous and encouraging and willing to give me a chance."

"He was pretty nice to Julie and Sharon too."

"You bet your boots. He did that to make you more comfortable."

She winked at me, "And partly to help you decide to play Tommy. But really, he's a sweetheart. You wait here, okay? I'm going to get coffee. I need coffee."

"Okay."

I flipped through the Love Nest book to the places Tommy was in. It didn't seem too hard. I was pretty sure I could do it.

By eleven forty-five I'd done two of the run throughs, and even though no one told me until later, they'd had the camera going on one of them, so I'd been acting and didn't even know it. Joe thanked me and said Geri would give me a contract before we left for my mom and dad to sign, so it would be official. He said he'd need me for five or six more mornings. If I ended up doing everything they planned on, I'd get fifty-five dollars! If they did it without the lines I was supposed to say, it would only be forty. Only forty, I was thinking, is he crazy? Either way, I felt like a thief. But in a good way. On top of that, he gave me a five dollar bill. He said it was a thank you for coming today. Boy, I was thinking, that guy really knows how to thank you.

Norma got me back a little after noon. No one was home, so I made a balogna sandwich with a ton of mustard on some of the odd shaped bread from the Wonder Bread Factory. It was so good I made a second one, this time, a double-decker. I made cold Ovaltine to wash it down. I pulled all of the money out of my pocket and put it on the table in front of me. I counted it while I ate. I had sixteen thirty-five. If I hurried, I could ride up to the hardware store before Ron dropped off the papers and pay Mr. Mahoney thirteen-fifty. I'd keep one-fifty to pay Marty what I owed him. I planned on keeping the other one-thirty for myself.

I rode up Oahkhurst and over to San Vincente. Mr. Mahoney was out on the sidewalk with his hands behind his back, his face tipped up to the sun coming from down San Vicente, away from me. His thick head of hair was silhouetted, so it looked like a crown.

"Hi," I called.

He opened his eyes and looked at me.

"How're things?" he said.

"Great."

I didn't want to brag about the movie or the extra five dollars, but it was hard not to. The more I thought about it, the more fun it had been. Getting paid so much boggled the mind, like Marty kept saying, but being a part of it, even just a tiny part, was even better. It was hard to say why, exactly, but it was. I put the Red Rider on the kickstand and pulled the money out of my pocket. I counted out the thirteen-fifty onto the top of one of the new garbage cans by the front windows. I felt a little funny putting the one-thirty back, like I was cheating him, and almost changed my mind and gave it to him anyway. But I didn't.

"You're way ahead of schedule," he said. "That makes eighteen-fifty so far. Are you sure you don't want to keep a little more for yourself?"

"No, this is fine," I said, patting my pocket. "See you next week."

"So long, Kurt."

The papers were there when I got back. I got the route bags and rubber bands and checked the kitchen clock before I started folding. Ron had been early, because it was only ten to one. The route went well the whole way. I sort of flew through it. I didn't even have to think about which house to throw to and peddling seemed easier than ever before. If I got done early, I thought I might take a trip somewhere. I rounded the corner onto Oakhurst and did a left handed overhead toss for Shelly and Norma, crossed to the other side and did a right hander for Kenny Lester. I was crossing back to our side to do Rathbone's, when the door opened at 440.

"Boychick!" Mr. 1A called, "boychick, I'm calling to you."

I stopped the bike in the middle of the street.

"Hi."

"I've got here for you the slip," he said, waving it at me. "The paper can start when?"

"You can have one starting today."

It was Duffy's paper, but if Duffy wasn't going to pay, and Ron was dropping one off for him anyway and didn't care one way or the other because he was going to make me pay for it no matter what, so why not? I had my own plan.

"Wonderful. Thank you."

I rolled the bike to the curb and put it on the kickstand and took a paper and walked it over to him.

"Where should I leave it?"

"Right here. Right here on the steps."

"You don't want it inside?"

"No, no, I'll come get it. You don't have to get off your bicycle for me. It's no big schlep to come to the door. A little exercise to get the blood going. I'm not your Mr. Duffy in my underwear all day."

He smiled like we had a secret, and in a way, we did.

I got back on the bike and started across to Rathbone's. He'd come out and was standing on the sidewalk smoking a cigarette. I pulled to the curb in front of him.

"Good afternoon," he said.

"Hi."

I got off the bike and took a paper out of the bags and handed it to him.

"Thank you."

He took the rubber band off right there and looked at the front page.

"Did you see this?" he asked me.

I'd just folded forty-one of them and had no idea what was in it. Not even what was on the front page. From now on, I thought, I'd at least look over the front page while I folded.

"No," I said.

"Well, it's a sorry commentary on us all," he said. "What a world."

I didn't know what he meant exactly, but I guessed it was bad news one way or the other. As I watched him read, I thought, if I could tell anyone without it being bragging, other than George, and even with George it might be, it would be him.

"Guess what?" I said.

He looked up from the paper. He had very dark eyes, and since his nose was long and thin and his dark hair was slicked back, they looked right into you like he knew what you were going to say before you said it.

"I'm in a movie. That's what you used to do, right?"

"Yes, that's so. What movie? How did this come about?"

"Well, you know Norma, from up the street? Right?"

"I know who she is, yes."

"Well, a kid on their movie got the chicken pox and she wanted me to take his place. I tried it this morning and it just sort of worked out."

Just telling made me smile so much it was about to turn into laughing. I don't know why. It wasn't funny at all, and it wasn't the five bucks or the forty or the maybe fifty-five bucks either, it just made me happy to think about it. To say it. He smiled.

"Well, isn't that something? We'll have to form a little neighborhood company, won't we?"

"What's that?"

"An actors group."

"We sort of did already. Wanna be in it?"

"You did? Who's we?

"Me and Norma. Shelly. Then there's two girls down the street, Julie and Sharon, and they're trying to be actors too, so they might be in it. They even got to be extras in Norma's movie today."

"Isn't that something?" he said. "I'd be honored," he smiled.

"Perhaps we should invite Miss Hamilton."

"Who's that?"

"Margaret Hamilton? Also an actress. She lives in one of George's apartments."

"Really?"

"I believe she's retired now, but she's a wonderful talent. Have you seen The Wizard of Oz?"

"Sort of."

"How do you sort of see a movie?"

"The monkeys scared me and I cried and Marty had to take me out to the lobby, so I missed a lot of it. So did he."

"Well, Margaret was the Wicked Witch of the West."

"No! Really? Right on our block?"

"Indeed."

"Well, she should probably be in the Oakhurst Players, alright. I'll ask Norma."

"You do that, and you let me know when the first meeting is."

"I don't think were going to have any. Are we supposed to?"

"I was joking with you."

"Oh," I said, "Well, if we do, I'll let you know."

"I'll look forward to it."

I rode down the block and threw the paper for Mr. Avery and was done.

I put the route stuff away and checked the kitchen clock. It was only two-forty and it was sunny and hot and I had the Red Rider and was ready to go. The question was, where? I was sitting on the front steps thinking about it. The beach was too far, especially this late in the day, and so were the Watts Towers. Those were the two places I really wanted to go, but even with just the route, there wasn't enough time. Now, with the movie added on, it was completely impossible. When that was done with, I thought, I'd get a map and figure out how to get to the Towers. If I got started really early, I was pretty sure I could get there and back in time.

"Can I have your autograph?"

It was George. He came down his walkway to the sidewalk, a cigarette in his mouth, wearing his tan army pants and a white t-shirt. He came up our driveway to the side of the steps.

"Shelly told me today was the day. How'd it go?"

"Pretty good. At the Hot Dog Stand, I almost told Norma I didn't want to do it. I was worried I didn't know how, but when we got there, things just sort of fell into place, like Kenny Lester says, and we did this run through thing, a sort of practice, and without saying anything about it, they were running the cameras and I was acting and didn't even know it, and that was that. They said it was what they wanted, so I'm supposed to go back for a few more mornings."

"Was it fun?"

"It was different than fun."

"Scary?"

"I thought it would be, but it wasn't. Something else."

"Exciting?"

"Kind of all of them. Scary and exciting and fun, but just normal too. A different normal. A whole bunch of people doing regular jobs, just like delivering the paper or something, except it ends up being a movie. It's pretty neat, George."

"Sounds like it. No wonder Shelly and Norma like it."

"And they pay a lot. Guess how much they want to give me?"

"How much?"

"Well, to start with, the director, Joe, gave me five bucks as a thank you. Just extra. Can you believe that? And at least forty bucks more for the rest and maybe even fifty-five if I do some talking. Boy, if I tell Sarah, she'll kill me."

"What are you going to do with it all?"

"I gave it to Mr. Mahoney for the locks. Almost all of it, anyway. I kept a little, but he didn't mind, because I'm ahead of our schedule. Anyway, I don't get the rest until the end of the month. When I get it, if I get it, I'll be able to pay him off way early. Is Shelly your girlfriend now?"

He smoked to the end of the cigarette and lit another one with it. He put the first one out on his shoe and into his pocket.

"That's a good question. I hadn't really thought about it. I'll let you know, okay?"

"Sure."

"So, what's on your schedule?"

"I was thinking about taking a ride somewhere, but it's sort of late and the places I was thinking of are too far."

"Which places?"

"Maybe the beach. Or maybe the Watts Towers."

"Pretty far for a bike ride."

"If I had the whole day, or at least most of it, I could."

"I bet you could. Wanna show me the Towers if we go on the Vincent?"

"Really?"

"Sure. I've heard about them. Never seen 'em though. Seems like a nice afternoon for a ride. Is there anyone home to tell? Your mom or dad?"

"Nope, but maybe Pop's home."

"Why don't you check."

The front door to Pop's was open. I knocked on the screen door. Nanny came to the door. She was all dressed up, ready to go out somewhere too.

"Can you tell my mom I'm going with George on the Vincent?"

"The what?"

"His motorcycle."

"Miriam and I are going shopping," she said. "When will your mom be back?"

"I don't know. No one was home when I got done with the route. But I suppose they'll be back pretty soon. Or maybe Sarah will be. You could tell her."

"I'll be back around five. I'll tell whoever's here."

"Thanks, Nanny."

I ran back to George.

"I told my grandmother."

"Okay. I'll go get the Vincent."

"I'll put the Red Rider away."

When I came back from the garage, Nanny and Miriam, who was all dressed up too, were standing on the sidewalk in front of Miriam's place, probably waiting for a Taxi Cab. As pretty as she looked, I pretended I didn't see her. George came roaring down the block. He reached back and flipped the foot pegs down for me.

"Climb on," he yelled over the noise, "we'll go to the Standard Station and get some gas and a map."

I got on and got settled and grabbed onto his belt and we took off. George waved at Miriam or Nanny or maybe both, but I didn't.

Sabato was high up on the Towers. George and I got off the Vincent and stood on the sidewalk and watched him for pretty long, about two cigarettes worth. It gave me that same magic feeling it had the other two times. I knew I was looking at something that couldn't be. No one could do that, but there it was, and that was magic. Once, he waved. I don't know if he recognized me or not, or just waved whenever he noticed someone was watching, but I waved back. A couple of times George said, 'where does something like that come from', not like a real question, but like he couldn't believe it either. When we'd had a good long look, he said we should head back.

My mom and dad came back from downtown together, so he was home for dinner again, and Sarah got home about the same time George and I did from some secret meeting of the Oakhurst Irregulars, and Marty got home a little after six, so we all got to eat together.

"Well," Marty said, "how'd it go?"

"What?" I said, joking him, like I didn't know. "The route? It was fine."

"Funny. No, with Marilyn. The movie. Are you going to do it?"

"Who cares?" Sarah said. "He'll probably mess it up. They should pay him not to do it."

"Sarah," my mom warned her. "How was it, honey?"

"Well, after this girl Geri took me for a look around, we were supposed to do this practice thing, a run through, but they were running the camera in secret, so I ended up acting without knowing it, so it was pretty easy."

"So does that mean you're going to be in it?" Marty asked.

"I already am. They said what they filmed was what they wanted so I'm supposed to go back for a few days. Maybe five. That's okay, isn't it?"

"Dave?" my mom said.

"Just like that?" my dad said.

"You guys have to sign a contract thing. Here." I reached into my shirt. "I almost forgot about it," I said, handing it to my dad.

He read it. His eyes got big and he looked at me and smiled. He must have gotten to the part about the forty or fifty-five bucks.

"Nice work, if you can get it," he said.

"What?" Sarah said, like maybe she knew she didn't want to hear.

He passed the contract to my mom.

She started reading it from the top, but my dad pointed to the money part.

"Oh my goodness," she said, her hand over her mouth. "That's wonderful, honey. Good for you!"

"What?" Sarah said again.

My mom handed it to her and she started reading. Marty was looking over her shoulder.

"Unbelievable," he said, his hand going to his forehead. "It boggles, boggles, just boggles the mind!"

Sarah didn't say anything. She put it down on the table making a big show of groaning and rolling her eyes.

"Good for him? That's completely ridiculous! We should tell them their gyping themselves. I can't believe you're going to let them pay him that. What a racket! It's like stealing!"

My dad was looking at her, getting ready to tell her to knock it off, but she started shaking her head and groaning, but more like in a playful way, so he didn't have to.

"You're worth about a buck and a half. Not a penny more." she said. Then, "Does this Tommy character need a sister?"

"Guess what else," I said.

This was pretty close to bragging, but since it was my family, I thought it was okay.

"I don't think I want to hear," Sarah said.

"What now?" Marty said.

"The director guy, the younger guy that was at Chasen's the other night with Norma..."

"What about him, honey?" my mom said.

"He gave me five bucks extra as a 'thank you' for coming today."
Everyone was looking at me like I made it up.

"Really." I said, "it's true."

They kept looking at me. Then at each other.

"What?" I said. "It's true. I'd show you, but I already gave it to Mr. Mahoney for the locks."

I don't know why, but they looked at each other some more and started laughing. My dad was laughing so hard he had tears in his eyes. Having him home for dinner was great.

We had a morning routine now. Norma came down the block at ten to six and I would be waiting on the steps and we'd go to the Hot Dog Stand. She said it was going to kill her getting up so early, but that way we could eat. Pancakes or pancakes and eggs or eggs and a sweet roll and coffee and hot chocolate or sausage and hash brown potatoes. We tried it all and still got to the movie on time. Since I'd paid the sixty-five cents the first day, she paid the next two in a row. I still had the dollar thirty cents in case I needed it, and even though I was going to get rich from the movie, my mom was still leaving me the thirty-five cents each morning, which was a good thing, since I wouldn't get paid 'til the end of the month. On the second day I found out if I hung around with Norma a little after the lunch break got started for the movie guys, they had this huge table completely full of all kinds of food. A million different things to make sandwiches with and hot things like lasagna, and also desserts and drinks, and they gave it to you for free. Norma liked the hot dogs the best, so that's what she got, but I had them make me sandwiches with so much stuff in them I could hardly get my mouth over it. It was sort of a joke between me and the guy who stood at the table making things. First he'd ask what kind of bread. There were lots to choose from. I'd tell him one, then we'd get to the meats, the pickles, the peppers, the different cheeses and lettuce and tomato. And of course, the mustard. By the time he'd finished putting it together, it was huge. Since I didn't usually eat much at lunch, I wasn't as hungry at dinner, which was my plan. If I didn't eat all the stuff I had them put in the sandwich, they'd probably just have to throw it away, so this way we saved on dinner and they didn't waste as much. Norma and I got lunch from the movie and then she took me home for the route. In a way, like Sarah said, it was sort of a racket, but that's the way they did it and I wasn't going to argue with them as long as they had plenty of mustard. I did the movie stuff for another five days. They did the same thing every day. We'd do the run through, sometimes more than once, and they'd film it one time or another without saying so, and if they got what they wanted, we were done. If not, if someone messed up, they'd just do it again. On the last day, Joe thanked me and said if I wanted to do it again, I should talk to that guy, Louie.

The route was getting easier and easier and it was getting so I could open the door to the Maple-Burton Arms without too much trouble. I'd drop the paper for Mrs. Gunther and knock on her door and run back down the hall before she opened it so she wouldn't feel like she had to give me a tip every time. But the best part of the whole route was leaving the paper for Mr. 1A, whose name was really Irving Rothman, instead of Mr. Duffy. Every day, I was scared and nervous and then happy doing it. Lots of times I saw him in the window in his baggy underwear watching me as I rode past and threw the paper, and every day I expected him to open the window and yell at me, but he didn't. He looked like he wanted to okay, but he didn't. Most days I went somewhere on the Red Rider before the route. They were only little trips, but nice ones, ones that gave me that feeling of being completely free over and over again. I was supposed to get the check for the movie in the mail, but Norma said it probably wouldn't be come until sometime in the first few days of August. I sort of hoped it would come on my birthday, August 1st, but I knew that would be even more luck than the Red Rider could manage. I kept checking the mailbox by our front door anyway. All through the rest of July the carwash seemed to be getting busier and busier every Saturday. And that Dolan guy never missed a chance to clog up the works by barging in front of everyone who was waiting for a wash with his big Cadillac convertible with all the election signs on it, like he had an appointment or something. I don't know how he expected to get any votes by making everyone mad at him, because that's what was happening. Mr. Avery told us carwash guys he was sick and tired of him coming in and stopping the car washing. And after that first time, Kenny Lester sort of made a point of arguing with Dolan about stuff. Then other guys got into it too. Once Kenny had shown them how, it seemed like lots of them didn't like what Dolan was saying or wanted to do as mayor, and they let him know it. Even though me and the carwash guys couldn't vote in Beverly Hills, it was still fun to watch. Dolan had started out coming in like he owned the place and pretty soon he was lucky to get out of there alive. Dennis and Maurice especially had a good time watching things turn from this to that. It made them like Kenny Lester even more.

"That big shot's takin' a whuppin'," Maurice would laugh as Kenny argued him to death.

"Don't have the sense of a sick dog," Dennis said. "Thinks showin' up's enough. If I had a spare fiver I didn't know what to do with, I'd bet he ain't gonna be the mayor of nothin'."

If I had a spare fiver I didn't know what to do with, I was betting Dolan would find another carwash pretty soon. The bad thing was, he kept bringing Kevin with him. The good thing was Kevin didn't pay any attention to me. Or to Maurice and the other carwash guys. He didn't even pay any attention to Kenny Lester or any of the guys arguing with his dad. He looked like he didn't care one way or the other and wasn't going to vote for Dolan either. Before I knew it, July just sort of disappeared. We had another subscription night coming up on Friday, which was the twenty-seventh, and Ron had mentioned a few times when he'd dropped off the bundle that I got to sit up front with him because I'd had the most subscriptions in June, since he was counting the six I'd added before the subscription night, along with the three from it, like that was the best thing in the world, like I couldn't wait to sit up there with him, when really, I was trying to figure out a way not to. When he came to pick me up, I climbed into the back and told Jim, the kid that got carsick, he could go up front if he wanted. Jim jumped out of the back like he thought I might change my mind, but really, he could have taken all the time he wanted.

"Hi," Brian said as I got settled in. "How come you let Jim go up front? You won it."

"He gets carsick back here. He might as well."

"But you got the most subscriptions."

"Yeah, well, I'd rather be back here."

"You're crazy! But if you feel like that in the winter, and you've got a spot in the cab to give away, how 'bout giving it to me?"

"Sure."

We got rolling along to wherever Ron was taking us, bumping along for miles, farther away this time. There were the same boys in back with us, three of them sitting under the window of the cab and another three across from us and one more in the cab with Ron and Jim. Brian was quiet, hunched over like he was trying to stay warm, like that's why he wasn't talking, but it wasn't cold at all, and I figured he was just worried Ron was going to stick him with me again and didn't like it but didn't want to say anything about it.

"Did Ron charge you for your route bag and rubber bands when you started?" I asked him.

"Started? He gets us all with that. Every month."

"Every month? Are you crazy? I thought it was just once and that was that."

"In your dreams! It's more like we're renting them from him."

"That's not fair! Four bucks every month? They probably don't even cost that much altogether! Every month?"

"He only charges me three. And a dollar for the rubber bands."

"Then why did he charge me four? And one-fifty for the rubber bands?"

"Quiet down a little!" he shushed me. "He'll hear you. He charges what he charges. If you want to keep the route, just shut up about it."

We drove about ten or twelve minutes more and got to another neighborhood that I didn't recognize. This time not everyone piled out. Ron told Brian to team up with me again, so just the two of us got out. As soon as Ron drove off, I told him he didn't have to.

"You sure?" he said.

"Yeah, I'll be fine. Good luck," I told him.

"Thanks!" he said and took off, probably sure he'd get ten not being stuck with me.

It didn't matter much one way or the other to me, because I knew I wasn't going to get any new subscriptions at all, and I didn't care. To tell the truth, I just sort of wandered around until it was time to go home. And I made sure I was on the right corner this time.

I was glad the subscription night had been Friday, not Saturday, so I wouldn't have to carwash and deliver and collect all on the same day again, then do that too. One thing I had to admit, John's dad was stubborn. That's probably where John got it. Stubborn and mean, like his dad. Even though he'd worn out his welcome, like Dennis said, Dolan kept coming back looking for votes. If there had been anyone who'd ever planned on voting for him in the first place, it was a good bet they'd changed their mind by now. This time, Mr. Avery saw him coming and he and Jackson got to the car before it could cut in front of ones waiting for a wash. They directed him off to the side, out of the way of the marked boxes where we did the washing. Dolan stood up in the back of the car, shouting and motioning, trying to get a crowd around to talk to, but I think everyone had pretty much already heard what he had to say and weren't very interested, and since his car wasn't in the center of things, it was easier to ignore him. For some reason, that got Kevin started. Or maybe Kevin was just getting back to being Kevin. Even from across half the length of the lot I could tell. He got out of the car and walked up to a few guys who were standing around close to where their cars were in the boxes being washed, which got him much closer to me than I wanted. He never stopped moving. He never stood still. He smoked and pointed, telling them they should go listen to his dad. He had that crazy look, so I didn't blame the guys who obeyed him and wandered over to Dolan's car. They'd might just pretend to listen, but at least they'd be there, so maybe Kevin would leave them alone. Kevin looked right at me once. Maybe he was looking at Maurice, or maybe me, or maybe both of us, because Maurice was working right next to me, but I looked away and kept washing the same hubcap over and over, four or five times. Maurice had noticed and got tired of it and threw his wash rag into the soap bucket and stood up and looked straight at Kevin, sort of daring him to start something. Kevin smiled that nutso smile and wandered over to the convertible, happy as can be. Maurice went over to Mr. Avery and said something to him, but Mr. Avery shook his head no and patted Maurice on the back and Maurice came back and continued washing with the rest of us. He'd look over his shoulder to check on Kevin every once in a while, mumbling to himself, but he kept working. I didn't see when Dolan left. One minute they were there, and the next, gone.

Mr. Avery paid me for the carwash and the paper at the same time again because he wouldn't be home this time either when I was collecting. When I got home, it was almost quarter after four, so there wasn't enough time to go pay Mr. Mahoney before the route. I figured I'd do it tomorrow before I started. But when I did, I'd have paid him twenty-eight fifty so far. If no one else asked for a new lock, I'd only owe him another twenty-one. Sixty-six people had asked for new locks. That seemed like more than I'd switched, but I couldn't say for sure, so I couldn't complain. Besides, there was no one to complain to. And besides that, there was the no complaining rule, so it was sixty-six and that was that. I started folding. But still, it seemed like a gyp. I was starting to get mad about it, but I began to laugh instead, because even if it was a gyp, I was going to get paid fifty-five bucks from the movie and about thirty from the route in just a few days. That was eighty-five. 'It boggles the mind!' I said out loud. Even after I subtracted the twenty-one it was sixty something. Hello new sneakers, I was thinking, when I noticed the front page. CRAZED GUNMAN SHOOTS 2 AND PERILS 50 OTHERS. Like Rathbone said, 'What a world'. Then I thought, some crazy guy's shooting people and I'm thinking about new sneakers. I started to feel bad about that. But on the other hand, I still needed the sneakers. Maybe reading the front page every day wasn't such a good idea after all. I'd give it a few more days and see how it went. The bags were full and I was ready to go. I walked over to George's place with a paper in one hand and the money pouch in the other. There was an envelope on the top step with my name on it. It had the money for the paper in it. I left the paper and took the money and went back to the Red Rider. I had a funny feeling about delivering the paper to Kevin Doyle and collecting for it since it seemed like he was back to crazy, but I thought I'd rather do it now and get it over with. I'd gone through the whole thing last month, whether it was better to get it over with at the beginning of the route and maybe spoil the whole rest of the day if he was mean, or spend the whole day worrying about it whether I had to or not. I took a paper out of the route bags and headed across the street. The door opened and there he was, still wearing the fancy army clothes from the vote getting.

"Put it in back," he said.

"George said..."

"I don't care what George said. Why does everything have to be a load of trouble with you? You want to get paid, you put it where I tell you. Got it?"

"Okay," I said.

He came down the steps and across the grass to the driveway that separated his house from Miriam's. I thought he was going to follow me all the way around to the back porch, to make sure I did it the way he wanted, but he didn't. I put the paper by the back door and headed back to the street. He was standing in the middle of the driveway. It was wide enough, so I could have walked around him, but it seemed like if I went one way, he'd go that way too, so I just walked slower, hoping he'd move. I was wishing George had been home. When I got closer to him, he put his cigarette in the corner of his mouth and reached into his pants pocket and took out money.

"Two-fifty, right?"

"Two fifty-eight this month. There was an extra Sunday."

"Close enough."

He held the money out towards me, but didn't hand it over. It sort of dangled above me.

"In the back, right?"

"Right," I said.

"Without any goddamn arguments, right?"

"Right."

He handed me the money. I didn't know how much he'd given me and I didn't care. If it was two forty-eight or two fifty-eight or two-nothing, I just wanted to get out of there. I put it in the pouch and crossed the street to the Red Rider and tried not to look back to see if he was watching me. When I got back to the bike and got on, I finally took a peek. He wasn't there anymore.

The pale yellow house at 331 was one of my favorites. The house and yard looked like the people enjoyed taking care of it. The walkway and steps were always swept clean and the door mat said 'Welcome' and I think they meant it. Like the last time, the woman must have been watching for me and seen me coming, because she opened the door and handed me the money before I had a chance to knock or ring the bell.

"There's a little something extra there for you," she said handing me three dollars.

"You don't have to," I said. "I've got change. "

"That's for you," she smiled, closing the door.

I walked the bike across the street to Julie and Sharon's. I put it on the kickstand, in the street, right next to the curb, and took a paper and the pouch and headed for the door. It was open and I could hear music again, but not so loud this time.

"Hello?" I called.

I rang the bell too. Julie came to the door.

"Hi!" she said. "Stay right there."

She went back into the apartment, calling to Sharon, "He's here."

They came back to the door together and out onto the porch.

"Can you sit down for a minute or two?" Julie asked.

"Sure. I guess. But I've got to deliver and collect today. It's two fifty-eight this month since there was five Sundays."

"Right," Sharon said, counting out the money.

I put it in the pouch. They sat down on the top step. Julie patted the spot next to her for me to sit, so I did. I was waiting for them to tell me whatever it was they wanted me to wait for, so I could get going with the route and collecting. On the other hand, I had that funny feeling in my stomache just being there with them. Uncomfortable-funny, enough to make me want to go, but good-funny, enough to make me want to stay.

"We want to thank you, but were not sure how, and just a tip for the paper didn't seem right."

"What for?"

"Love Nest."

"Oh, that. That's okay, it was Joe's idea."

"Geri told us that, but he wouldn't have known about us being there for the call if you hadn't told him, so we'd like to do something for you. We just don't know what. Can you help us think of something?"

"Really, you don't have to. Norma says the Oakhurst Players should stick together. Right?"

"The what?"

"The Oakhurst Players. It's sort of a club Norma made up since she and Shelly and I all live on Oakhurst and she wanted me to be an actor in her movie since that kid got chicken pox. I said you guys should be in it too, since you were trying to be actors and lived on Oakhurst. That's how come she told Joe about you being outside trying to get a job. Get it? The Oakhurst Players sticking together? Mr. Rathbone might be in it too. And Margaret Hamilton...only she doesn't know about it yet."

"Basil Rathbone?"

"He used to be an actor too. He lives in the Pink House up the street from me. He's pretty nice after all. But I should get going, okay?"

"Okay," Julie said, "but we want to do something."

I got up to go.

"If I think of something, I'll let you know, okay?"

"Okay," Julie said.

I got on the bike ready to go. They were still sitting there and they waved and I waved back. How about the kiss, I was thinking.

The delivering and collecting went better and faster than I could have hoped for. By the time I turned the corner to come down Oakhust, there had only been two people not home and one of them had left the money for me in an envelope, like George had. Shelly and George were sitting on the bottom step having a smoke. The Vincent was on its kickstand in front of her house.

"You find the money okay?" he asked me.

"Uh huh. Thanks."

Snowball went crazy when she saw me come through the gate. I guessed George and Shelly had been talking and had been ignoring her, because she got the ball with the bell and dropped it at my feet for me to throw. I threw it and she was back before I got to the steps where they were sitting.

"Let me get you the moola," Shelly said.

She went in through the open door.

"Everything go okay?"

I wanted to tell him about Kevin wanting the paper in the back again. It might be complaining and it might not. I wasn't sure. But it seemed like he was still trying to decide if Shelly was his girlfriend or not, and that was his main problem at the moment, and he didn't need to be bothered with paper route stuff. On the other hand, he'd said if Kevin bothered me, I should tell him. I was trying to decide if this counted. Then Shelly came back.

"Here you go," she said. "The extra's for the fund."

"You don't have to. I'm going to be able to pay off the locks when I get paid from the movie."

"The check's in the mail?" she said, like she didn't believe it.

"That's what Norma said. A few days into August."

"I'll keep my fingers crossed for you, kid."

"What's that supposed to mean?" George asked her.

"It'll probably be fine," she said.

But she didn't sound very convinced.

"They might not?" I asked.

That would be a disaster. I had it all figured out how I was going to pay off the locks faster.

"What?" George asked her again.

"The studios are pretty..." she stopped to think about it, blowing the smoke from her cigarette in little puffs, just for the fun of it, I guess, until she decided, "...lax. That's it, they can be pretty lax about getting the checks out."

"What's lax mean?" I asked.

"Unreliable, slow," George said.

"They do it when they feel like it. When they're good and ready to part with the money, but not a minute before. The checks should go out on the first, but you're lucky to see it by the tenth."

"But you'll see it, right?" I said.

"Don't worry, honey, you'll see it. Eventually."

"I better," I said.

Geez, I thought, a whole new thing to worry about. There were deadbeats wherever you looked.

"I got to finish up. See you guys later."

"Bye," George said.

"So long," Shelly said.

I'd forgotten all about Kevin Doyle because I was too busy picturing the check in the mail, just sort of floating around, getting close, but not quite making it to my house.

Kenny Lester wasn't home, but Joanne was there and had the money for me.

Mr. 1A, Mr. Rothman, was standing on the sidewalk when I came from the Lester's house. While he was giving me the money, he kept looking up to Mr. Duffy's window. He paid me in change, so he took a long time counting it out, and with almost every coin, he'd look up to make sure Mr. Duffy was watching, then hand me another one. By the time he'd counted out the whole two fifty-eight, Mr. Duffy looked like he might explode.

I rode across the street to Rathbone's place. I was headed up the walk when Iyama Osaka came out of the little white gate from the garden. Why was he here so late, I wondered?

"You good?" he asked me.

"Uh huh. How 'bout you?"

"Good, good," he said. "But no more trouble?"

He nodded in the direction of Kevin Doyle's place. I wasn't sure what to say. It was another chance to tell someone, and I wanted to, but Kevin hadn't really done anything. If it started a big fight for no reason, whatever happened would be my fault.

"It's okay," I said. "Is Mr. Rathbone home?"

"He's in the garden. You go in," he smiled.

Mr. Rathbone must have told Iyama that it was okay for me to go in there. Even through the front gate.

I took a paper with me and the money pouch and went through the gate. I checked to make sure it clicked shut behind me. It gave me an odd feeling, not sneaking in, not having to worry about whether anyone was watching me. I still had the feeling someone might, but I guess it was just left over from the old days of sneaking in. Rathbone was sitting on the little concrete bench near the pond with his eyes closed and his head tipped back like he wanted the sun on his face, but it was already too low to get much. He was wearing tan pants and a silky looking shirt, not white, but sort of cream colored, and his bedroom slippers. It had to be close to six, so that seemed odd. On the other hand, it was his garden.

"Hi," I said.

He opened his eyes.

"Ah!" he said. "A plenary meeting of the Oakhurst Players. How are you?"

"Fine."

"Collecting?" he said.

"Yes sir."

He stood up and took three one dollar bills out of his pocket and handed them to me. I started to give him change.

"You keep the rest for yourself."

He sat back down.

"Would you like to sit?"

"Sure." I sat on the little bench and opened them money pouch to show him. "I've got plenty of change. Besides, since you don't take the Sunday, it's only two o-eight."

"No, you keep it."

"Are you sure?"

"I am."

"Okay. Thank you. Can I ask you something?"

"Whatever you like."

"When you were an actor, did they pay you on time?"

He laughed.

"What brought that on?"

I told him what Shelly said.

"You needn't worry. It will come. The studios can be a little lax," he said, "but if the director and producer are on top of things, the checks typically go out when they should."

"Whew, that's a relief."

"Would you like to stay in the garden a while? I'm going in now, but you're welcome to remain."

"I'd like to, but I have to deliver Mr. Avery's paper," I said.

"Well, whenever you like," he said.

"Thank you."

I clicked the white gate into place and headed down the block, leaving a paper for Mr. Avery. I didn't have to collect, since he'd already paid at the carwash.

### There'll Be Days Like This

Sunday morning was a beaut. Warm and fresh and clear even at six-thirty. Marty was conked out, and Sarah was sleeping too, but Nick was awake for some reason. My dad was gone and my mom wasn't ready to get up because she'd been downtown with him 'til late and Nick was trying to get her out of bed. He'd found her arm under the covers and was pulling.

"Nickie, please. Just a little longer. Can't you go back to sleep for a while?"

"I'm hungry," he said.

He was standing next to her bed in his underwear. He dropped her arm, standing there trying to figure out what he should do. His hair was the usual mess of curls. No matter what, they always looked the same. When he just woke up or had been playing or had a bath and they'd had a chance to dry, they covered his head like a bunch of new strawberry-blond daisies popping up in a garden. He pulled on her hand again.

"Nick," I whispered to him.

He turned around and looked at me. He didn't say anything, but looking at me was his kind of answer.

"Leave her alone. I'll make you something."

"Thank you, honey," she mumbled.

As she went back to sleep, she mumbled something about toast and keeping him quiet. He dropped her hand and he followed me into the kitchen.

"How 'bout Ovaltine and toast?"

"Hot."

"You know I'm not supposed to use the burners."

"But I like it HOT!" he insisted.

"Shhh, Nick. Come on. Cold is just as good. I'll put in extra."

"Why can't I have it hot?" he said.

If I used the burner it would be big trouble. If I didn't, and he kept yelling, she'd have to get up, so I had another idea.

"Go get dressed. And be quiet, for pete'sake."

"What?" he said.

"You'll see."

"I'm hungry."

"I know. We're going to take care of it. Just get dressed."
He put on his tan shorts and a blue and green striped t-shirt.

"Where are your shoes?" I asked him.
He shrugged.
"How 'bout your sandles?"
He shrugged again.
"You've got to wear something. Come on, I'll help you find 'em."
He couldn't find his sandals, but his Keds were under the bed. His were in pretty good shape, I noticed, as I tied one and he did the other. We went out through the back porch. I let him go first so I could close the screen door without the return whack against jamb.

"Leave your blanket," I told him.

I was going to explain why, but before I could, he got this shocked look on his face that I knew meant he wouldn't come if he couldn't bring it.

"Okay, okay," I said. "Bring it."

We went down the driveway to the garage and he followed me as I rolled the Red Rider to the sidewalk. I got on and stood over the bar. I had to stand on my tiptoes to be above it. I braced myself from side to side.

"Get on," I told him.

He stood there looking at the bike like he didn't have any idea what I meant. He raised his eyebrows to ask me.

"Sit on the fender rack," I told him. "Just keep your feet out of the spokes. They could take your toes right off," I warned him.

He still had his blanket in his hand and wasn't sure what to do with it, which is why I wanted him to leave it in the first place. He stayed right where he was, looking at the bike, holding the blanket, not planning to try, especially if he didn't know why.

"I'll take you to the Joseph's Hot Dog Stand. You can have pancakes and hot chocolate."

His eyebrows went up like he couldn't believe it. He looked around for a place to leave his blanket, but couldn't see anything good, so he held onto it and tried to swing his leg over, but he wasn't tall enough.

"Hang on," I told him.

I got off and rolled the bike into the street next to the curb and got back on and braced myself again.

"Try it now."

With the bike lower than the parkway, he put the blanket on the rack just behind me and wiggled himself on.

"Ready?"

He didn't say yes or no, but I could feel his fingers grabbing at my t-shirt, so I figured he was all set. He was trying to hang on with one hand so he could hold onto the blanket with the other, but as soon as I got going, he stuffed it between us so he could hold on with both. I wobbled a little when we started, but he wasn't any heavier than the twenty Sundays, so I was pretty sure I could do it. The only problem was the Sundays didn't wiggle around like he did.

"Stop wiggling. You're going to make us crash!"

What we really needed was foot pegs, like on the Vincent. Maybe I shouldn't have mentioned loosing toes if he got them into the spokes, because he was trying to keep his feet extra far away, which was good, except that his legs would get tired being held out like that, and they'd start to droop down close, and then he'd suddenly jerk around to get them farther away and it would make me lose my balance. After Crescent, he settled down, or probably just got tired, and let his legs hang just wide enough to keep them away from the back wheel. The last block and a half to the carwash was more uphill. By myself, I hardly noticed, and on the route with the bags full, I never came this way, but with him on the back, it was a struggle. On top of that, now that he was used to it, he kept telling me, faster, faster, laughing like we were on a merry-go-round or something.

"Maybe on the way back. It'll be downhill," I told him.

We came onto the lot and I stopped in front of the Hot Dog Stand and jumped off the seat to my tiptoes to balance him and the bike.

"Get off, Nick, quick!"

He sat there trying to figure out what to do with his legs. I started losing control and the bike tipped over to the side. I didn't let it hit the ground, but it got close enough so his feet reached, and he got off. Joseph was watching us, and he seemed to think I'd planned it like that to help Nick off, but that's just the way it happened.

"Nice," he said. "Who's this?"

"This is my little brother, Nick. He's hungry."

While I was putting the bike on the kickstand, Nick stuffed the blanket between the bars on the rack, close to the seat, so you could hardly tell what it was. I helped Nick onto a stool. Joseph leaned over, close to him.

"Well, you've come to the right place. What'll it be?"

Nick didn't say anything, but he kept his eyes on Joseph like he was figuring him out.

"Does he talk?"

"Not much," I said. "How about pancakes and a hot chocholate?"

"For both of you?"

"For him. Just hot chocolate for me."

"How 'bout if I make an extra big stack and you guys split it?"

I looked at Nick. He didn't seem to care as long as food was on the way.

"Okay. Will a dollar thirty-five be enough?"

"Remember, your money's no good here," he smiled at me.

"Yeah, but this is different. He doesn't work here."

I was looking at the menu on the wall behind Joseph, trying to figure out what it should cost. He followed my eyes.

"How about if we make it fifty cents? That's roughly half. Would that be okay?"

I was still trying to figure out how much two hot chocolates and an extra big stack of pancakes should cost, but it wasn't on the list, so fifty-cents seemed about right, and it was easier than adding and dividing and whatever.

"Okay."

He put the hot chocolates in front of us. Nick started sipping at it. A minute later, Joseph put a stack of steaming hot pancakes in front of each of us. It looked like if you added up both plates, it would be a lot more than two short stacks or even two regular ones, so it seemed like he was gyping himself. I planned on leaving him sixty cents instead of fifty to make it more fair. Nick poured the maple syrup all over his pancakes, his plate and half the counter, then just sat there, looking at it. My mom usually cut up stuff like this for him, so he was waiting. Joseph watched him and Nick watched back.

"What's he waiting for?" Joseph asked me.

"My mom cuts up stuff for him. If you've got a knife, I can do it."

"I got it," he said.

He took a big knife and cut up Nick's pancakes. There was so much syrup on the plate, even careful cutting pushed more onto the counter. Joseph sort of groaned at the mess, but didn't say anything. He got a rag and wiped it up. I'd never eaten much for breakfast, but since Norma and I had been doing it all of the movie making days, I'd gotten used to it, and the short stack or regular stack or whatever it was, was gone before Nick really got going on his. I sipped at my hot chocolate, waiting to see if he could finish his. If he didn't, I was planning on helping him.

There was a toot on a horn and when I looked around, Dennis was there in an old truck, all smiles. It looked a lot like Ron or Iyama Osaka's, but even more beat up. He waved and I waved back. He parked and came over to the counter.

"Coffee," he said, doing a little drum beat on the counter.

Dennis looked around like he was a kid on the first day of school, excited and nervous all at the same time. Joseph nodded but didn't say anything. He just put the mug of coffee in front of him, then went back to cleaning the grill, even though it looked clean already.

"Who's this?" he said, looking at Nick.

"My brother, Nick."

"Hey, Nick, how ya' doin'?"

Nick said, "Hi," and kept eating.

"Don't talk much, eh?"

"Not much. How come you're here so early?" I asked him. "The car-wash doesn't open for hours."

"Connie, Miss Rimes, got Mr. deWitt to take a few of my pieces," he said, nodding at his truck.

There were some big things under a tied-down canvas that made a tent over the whole back.

"She's gonna meet me here and we're going to deliver them to the

gallery. I took the day off from the 'wash. Mr. Avery's good with it."
He sipped at the coffee and kept fidgeting around.
"Great," I told him. "Guess what?"
"What?" he said.
"I've been back to see Sabato twice since you took us there."
"No, kiddin'? How'd you get there?"
"The first time with my friend, Norma, in her car. And then I went
with George, my neighbor, on his Vincent."
"A Vincent? A Black Shadow?"
"Yeah. You've heard of them?"
"Oh yes! Sweet Jesus!" he said. "No kiddin'?"
"No kidding."
"Do you know what that thing is?"
"Yeah. A motorcycle."
"Naw, man, it's sculpture, plain and simple. Beautiful. And it's the
biggest, fastest, meanest machine ever built! He ever come in here?"
"Sometimes. We got gas here before we went to the Towers."
"You think you could get him to bring it some day when I'm here?
I've never seen one in person."
"Sure. I guess. I can ask him, anyway."
"Who'd you say he is?"
"My neighbor. George. You met him."
"I did?"
"Yeah. The day Maurice got in the fight with Kevin Doyle. Remem-
ber?"
"Oh yeah, sure. Well, if he'd bring it down sometime, I'd be grateful.
Man, I thought I'd never ever see one up close."
"I'll ask him."
"That'd be nice. Thanks."
Nick had eaten his way through most of his pancakes and was finish-
ing his hot chocolate. There wasn't much left on his plate, and what
there was was so soggy with syrup I didn't want it anyway, and besides,
I'd gotten the rest of the way full just waiting. I handed Nick a napkin
and pointed to his chin. He wiped it and climbed down from the stool. I
counted out sixty cents and sort of hid it under the corner of my plate.
"Good luck with the gallery," I told Dennis.
"Thanks. I got a good feelin' 'bout it."
"Let's go," I told Nick.
"That was good, Joseph," Nick said. "Thank you."
Joseph turned from the grill.
"He can talk," Joseph said.
"Bye Joseph. Bye Dennis," I said.
I got on the bike and braced myself for Nick to climb on. Without the
curb height to help, he couldn't do it. Dennis got off his stool and lifted
him on.
"All set?" he said to me and Nick.
"I think so," I said.

As we were leaving, Miss Rimes came into the station. I waved and she waved back. I sort of wanted to stay and tell her about the food at Chasen's being art, but since we'd gotten started, and Nick wasn't wiggling around much, I figured we should just keep going. When we got out onto Beverly Boulevard, Nick tugged at my t-shirt.

"You promised," he reminded me, "faster!"

I pedaled as fast as I could, and pretty soon we were roaring down towards Oakhurst. He was laughing and I was making noises like the Vincent and before I knew it, we'd gone past Oakhurst almost to Doheny. Since I still had seventy-five cents, which was more than enough, I thought I'd take him to the Beverly Ponyland and get him a ride or two. It was that kind of day, that kind of summer, just like I'd planned, and if this was going to be the perfect day, Nick might as well be in on it too.

We got home a little after ten and the Sundays were there waiting for me. I pulled up next to the curb so Nick could get off easier. He ran ahead to tell my mom and Sarah about going to Ponyland. They were home but Marty was gone to the Standard Station. I got the route bags and the rubber band box off the porch, cut the rope off the bundle, and started folding. Nick came back out without his blanket and sat on the parkway and watched. I'd folded one and put my knee on to hold it down and reached over to get a few rubber bands, then slid three of them over the end. Two might have been enough, but like George said, why take a chance? With three, there was no way the paper would fall apart, so it was worth it, even if I was paying for them. He was sitting cross-legged, watching me. He wiggled closer, and when I got the next paper folded and had my knee on it and was reaching for a rubber band, he handed me three.

"Thanks," I said.

He smiled. I started on the next one and just as I got my knee on again, he was ready with another three rubber bands. He timed it just right, getting the rubber bands for me and then watching until it was just the right time again. The papers were ready to go and I don't think it could have been ten-thirty yet. I got the route bags tied onto the Red Rider and he helped me load the papers in. One by one we got them evenly divided into the bags. It looked liked there was an extra one. I counted a couple of time to make sure.

"Thanks for the help," I told him again.

He smiled and his eyebrows went up a little, which I figured, meant, you're welcome. I took the extra paper out of the bags and walked it over to George's. Nick followed me. When we got to the back of the Courtyard, George was there on his step, smoking.

"Morning, boys," he said.

"Hi, George."

I handed him the paper.

"I had an extra Sunday. I thought you might like it."

"Sure, why not?" he said. "Thank you."

"There might be something different than in the Times," I told him. "You never know."

"Could be," he said.

"Guess what?" I said.

"What?"

"One of the carwash guys, Dennis, he was there the day Maurice was fighting with Kevin, the sort of smaller guy, the guy with the foundry in Watts? He thinks the Vincent's sculpture."

"I never thought of it that way, but I suppose it is."

"He's a sculptor, too, like Miss Rimes, so he thinks about things like that."

"I suppose he does."

"The day we went to his foundry, he showed us some of his sculptures, and took us over to the Towers and introduced me and Joseph and Miss Rimes to Sabato, so that's how I knew about Sabato and the Towers. Anyway, he asked me to ask you if you'd bring it to the carwash sometime. He's never seen one in real life."

"Well, we'll have to do something about that, won't we?"

"Would you?"

"Sure. Why not?"

"Thanks, George. I think he'll be completely amazed."

"What's he sculpt?"

"Well, he sculpts clay, then makes molds and then casts them in bronze. I think that's how it works, anyway."

"What sort of pieces?"

"Faces, you know, heads. And some whole figures too. War stuff, in a way. But not scary or gory. More like the pain from war."

"Did he tell you that?"

"No."

"Your teacher? Miss...?"

"Rimes. No, you look at them, and after a while, that' how they make you feel."

"Hmmm," he said. "Sounds interesting."

"Miss Rimes helped him get some pieces into an art gallery on Canon. Today's the first day, so he was up there at the carwash this morning with some on his truck. Me and Nick went there for breakfast and Miss Rimes came in as we were leaving. He took the day off from the carwash to put them in the gallery."

George smoked away.

"Maybe I'll take the Vincent up there for him to see."

"They've probably already left for the gallery, and on top of that, like I said, Dennis took the day off from the carwash, so he won't be there today at all."

"The gallery's on Canon?"

"Uh huh."

He got up.

"Maybe I'll swing by there, then," he said. "I think I will. Maybe they'll need some help getting them off his truck. You don't mind if I save the paper for later?"

"Heck no."

"Good. You boys take care."

He stood up with the paper under his arm and opened the door to his apartment.

"Bye," I said.

Nick and I went back to my bike. Kevin Doyle was sitting on his front steps smoking a cigarette and watching us. I heard the Vincent start up and could tell George had gone up the alley towards Lower Santa Monica.

"Why don't you go in now?" I told Nick. "I'm going to get started after I take one across the street."

He shook his head no, and stood there, leaning against the jacaranda, like it was my mom's leg or something, keeping his eyes on Kevin. I took a paper out of the bags and crossed the street and headed down the driveway to the back. Kevin watched me cross the street, then, when I was about to go out of his sight anyway, he stopped looking at me and watched Nick instead. I got past where I could still see him, and I put the paper on the back porch and came back down the driveway. I looked over my shoulder as I got back to where I could see him again, and where he could see me. He shifted his look from Nick to me and back to Nick, who was still just standing there against the tree waiting for me. I crossed the street back to my bike, and took another look. Kevin had his eyes on me again and gave that 'okay' sign where you make an 'o' with your thumb and first finger with the rest of your fingers sticking up. I supposed that was because I obeyed him and put the paper in back.

"Go on in now," I told Nick. "I'm going."

He turned and headed up our walk. When he was in and the screen door closed behind him, I got on the bike and headed towards Beverly Boulevard. I took a peek across the street and Kevin was gone.

When I got to the corner, the Oakhurst Irregulars, about seven or eight of them, were on their bikes on the sidewalk between the alley and Doheny, waiting for someone. Maybe Megan, because I saw Allen, but not her. Probably another Stars game, I thought. I hadn't even been told that I wasn't invited, but all in all, I didn't really care. Allen saw me and waved and Jeff Schumur said 'hi' and that was that. I crossed Beverly before Megan or whoever they were waiting for got there, so they were still there waiting right up to the time I couldn't see them anymore.

I collected from the one house that I'd missed Saturday, so I was all set for Ron on Wednesday. He wouldn't care, but since it was my birthday, I was going to pretend the route money was a present. I'd heard my mom and dad talking and it was beginning to look like the guys that made the big orders for my dad's line were deadbeats. All that work, then delivering the goods on time to those mumzers and only getting paid part of what they owed. What a gyp. We weren't supposed to hear or know, but me and Marty were lying in bed and did. My mom said something to my dad about tightening our belts. I was used to that, just to keep my pants up, but I knew she meant not spending too much money, which it seemed like we didn't do anyway, except for Chasen's, and if you were going to be broke the rest of your life, you might as well have at least one dinner like that you could remember. I was also glad they got us some new clothes before we found out we were going to be broke again, because I'd never have made it to the end of summer on the pair I hadn't cut off.

Even with the heavy Sundays, the route was getting so easy I could just daydream while I was doing it. I could pretend me and the Red Rider where going across the country to famous places like the Grand Canyon or Yellowstone Park, or the place where they had the Presidents heads carved into a mountain, or the place where they had the cracked Liberty Bell, all things I'd heard of, mostly in first and second grade, but might never see. I could picture them, even if I was making it up, so it seemed real, like that's the way they'd look, even if in real life they were completely different. It didn't matter to me, since, for all I knew, my way might be the real way, just by luck.

I finished the route and put the bags on the porch. I still had fifty-five cents left over after the Beverly Ponyland. I was sitting on the bottom step thinking about where I could go. The Red Rider was resting up from the route, but ready to go if I could make up my mind where. Norma came up from Beverly in the MG.

"Hi. All done?"

"Uh huh."

"Whatcha gonna do?"

"I'm thinking about a trip."

"Where?"

"I don't know. Maybe to the art gallery on Canon."

"How come?"

"My art teacher helped Dennis, one of the carwash guys, get some of his sculptures in there. Me and Nick were at the Hot Dog Stand this morning and they were all set to take them. George was going to take a ride on the Vincent to go see."

"That sounds fascinating. Wanna jump in and we can go together?"

"You don't have to work?"

"No, we wrapped!"

"What's that mean?"

"We finished. I've got three weeks off before I start on Let's Make It Legal. I thought maybe we could go to the beach a couple of times. What do you think?"

"That would be great."

"How about the gallery? Is there someone home to tell?"

"I think Sarah's here. I'll see."

I ran into the house and Sarah was back from the Stars game, watching Nick. They were on the floor in the living room listening to the radio and she was helping him with one of those coloring books with a lot of words in them to teach kids to read. It was amazing how many words he could read, especially since he didn't bother to talk very much. She said my mom was downtown with my dad again.

"I'm going to the art gallery on Canon," I told her.

"What for?"

"Dennis's got some stuff there."

"Dennis who?"

"Dennis from the carwash."

"What stuff?"

"Art stuff. He's a sculptor."

"Carwash art?"

"Ha ha," I said.

"You'll be back before dark, right?"

"Uh huh."

"So why tell me? If you're back by then, no one cares."

"I'm going with Norma, so she wanted me to tell someone."

"You've told," she said.

She went back to Nick and the coloring book and I went out and put the Red Rider away.

The deWitt Gallery was half way down Canon, a little above Dayton Way. It was three, or close to it, and downtown was pretty busy for a Sunday. From half a block away, I could see Dennis's truck parked in front of the place and the Vincent a half a dozen parking places farther down. The truck was parked with the back wheels up against the curb so the bed could hang out over the sidewalk towards the gallery to make unloading easier. The truck was already empty.

"Over there," I pointed to Norma.

"Look," she said, "there's Shelly."

Norma waved. I'd wondered why George had gone up our alley instead of down to Beverly, which was closer and more on the way. Maybe he'd decided she was his girlfriend after all. We parked across the street and went over. George and Dennis were folding up the canvas that had covered the sculptures.

"Kurt, Norma," George said, nodding.

"Hi," we both said.

"Hello," Dennis said. Mostly to Norma, since he already knew me.

"This is Norma," I told him, and to her, "this is Dennis. He's the sculptor."

"I can't wait to see your work," she said.

"Well, they're in there," he said.

They shook hands. George had a cigarette in the corner of his mouth and had his head tipped in that way that kept the smoke out of his eyes. Dennis had a grin on his face that wasn't coming off for anything. Getting the sculptures in the gallery must have been a bigger thing for him than he'd admitted, since he'd acted like it would be okay either way, if Mr. deWitt didn't want them or did. It could have been because of Norma, but I thought it was more about having his stuff in the gallery. Shelly was sitting on the curb having a cigarette. I could see Miss Rimes inside talking to two men. Norma stopped to talk to Shelly and I waited there with her. George and Dennis finished folding the canvas and put it on the back of the truck, then went down to where the Vincent was parked so Dennis could get a good look at it.

"Well, lookit here," Shelly said to us, "it's the Love Nest duo."

"What's the matter?" Norma asked her.

"If you guys came for a little culture, you're gonna leave with an aching gut instead."

"What?" Norma whispered to her. "Not very good?"

"Oh contraire, honey. Oh contraire. I thought we were goin' for a little Sunday ride, a little art gallery browsing, but this Dennis guy's determined to twist your heart 'til you can't breathe. 'Til he breaks it. I could only take so much. By the time George and this deWitt character and his assistant and Dennis had the stuff off the truck, I'd had it. No, he's very good. Too good."

She sucked on her cigarette and shook her head.

"Take a look. Just exercise a little restraint. Too much of a good thing, you know?"

She raised her eyebrows and opened her eyes real wide, like that explained everything. I suppose it did, in a way, but if she liked it, she should just say so. If she didn't, like my mom tells you, 'if you don't have anything nice to say, don't say anything at all'. If Sarah paid any attention to that, she'd never speak to me, but maybe Shelly never heard of it. I thought she was making it too complicated and I was afraid she'd hurt Dennis' feelings if he heard her. At least she wasn't talking as loud as she usually did, not whispering, but not so loud that Dennis would hear down by the Vincent.

"Now I don't know what to think," Norma said. "It sounds so... so?..."

"That's about the size of it," Shelly said, blowing cigarette smoke.

"I saw them at his foundry and I like them," I said and started for the door.

"The lockmaster has spoken!" Shelly said.

"Shelly!" Norma said.

"Oh Christ. What the hell," she grumbled as I passed her. "Sorry, kid," she called after me.

Norma came in behind me. Miss Rimes saw me, then Norma. Her eyes got wide, like she couldn't believe it.

"Hi," I said.

"Hi. Are you going to introduce me?"

"Sure. Miss Rimes, this is my friend Norma. She lives up the block with Shelly there. And this is Miss Rimes, my art teacher."

"Connie," Miss Rimes said.

They shook hands. The two men took one look at Norma and it was like they couldn't wait another minute to meet her, couldn't wait for it to be their turn.

"Is she all right?" Miss Rimes asked about Shelly.

"I think so. She wasn't prepared for this," Norma said, pointing to Dennis's stuff.

"Come see for yourself," Miss Rimes said. "This is James deWitt, the owner of the gallery, and Donald, his assistant."

They just about jumped forward to shake hands with her.

"A pleasure," Norma said.

"Oh!!!! The pleasure is ours! Completely ours!" Mr. deWitt said.

"Completely," Donald agreed.

"We're trying to figure out the most natural and advantageous way to display them and neither overwhelm the room, nor deprive clients access to the walls. Feel free to browse," he told her.

"Thank you," she said.

The walls were covered with paintings with bright lights from the ceiling pointed at them. They were pretty good, I thought, better than I could do, that was for sure, but when I saw the price on a small tag hanging from the corner of the one closest to me, I thought they were nuts! Fifteen hundred dollars! And it wasn't even that big. That was more than half the cost of a car. I'd seen an ad in the Mirror for a brand new Oldsmobile Super 88 for $2328. How could they hope to sell a painting for that much, I wondered. Even in Beverly Hills? I guess they figured all they had to do was sell one. I took a closer look at one of the bigger paintings. The price tag was flipped the wrong way so I turned it around slowly and took a peek. When I saw the price, I felt like my dad, at Chasen's, when he pretended to be shocked, except I didn't have to pretend. Just for the fun of it, I made a few faces like he had, and grabbed my chest like it was giving me a heart attack or something. No one could see because I was facing the wall with the painting and everyone was behind me. That's what I thought, anyway. When I looked over my shoulder to make sure, they were, except from sideways, outside the window, Shelly saw me. She smiled and shook a finger at me, then grabbed her chest and made a face like she was dying too, making a bigger deal out of it than I had. They wanted twenty-five hundred bucks for the bigger one. That made me wonder how much they'd try to sell Dennis's sculptures for. His stuff was much better than the paintings, I thought, and just by size and weight alone, they had to be worth a lot more. Boy, talk about boggling the mind. If he sold even one, he'd never have to wash another car the rest of his life. Norma moved around the room looking at his sculptures. She looked at the paintings too, but came back to Dennis's stuff and ran her hands over them the same way Miss Rimes had at the foundry.

"How long have you known her?" Miss Rimes whispered to me.

She was pretty excited about it.

"Pretty long," I said.

I wanted to tell her about having hot chocolate and sweet rolls and breakfast lots of times and going to the beach and the movie stuff too, but it would have been bragging no matter how careful I tried to be so I told her about Chasen's instead. Which I wanted to do anyway, and almost more, besides. But I don't think she really heard me, because she was too busy watching Norma. She pretended to listen, but I don't think she did. Mr. deWitt had one of those hand trucks and he and Donald struggled to move one or another sculpture here or there. Since Dennis had brought four full size and three smaller ones, and the gallery wasn't that big to begin with, they kept experimenting. It might have been better if Dennis had brought only one or two of the big ones, I thought. Finally, that's what Mr. deWitt decided. He told Miss Rimes they'd set up two big ones and the three small ones and move the others into the back.

"If there's interest in these," Mr. deWitt told Miss Rimes, "and I'm sure there will be, if they sell, and I'm sure they will, we'll bring the others out. I don't want to overwhelm the room. They're very powerful."

"And big," his helper said.

"That makes sense," Miss Rimes said. "Only, you might want to run pictures of them all in the ad."

"We hadn't..." the helper started.

"No, no," deWitt said, "she's right. These pieces are going to generate a lot of excitement. We need to make it known that they're here right off. All of them. An ad. Definitely."

Miss Rimes was smiling.

"I think Joe would love these," Norma said outloud, but mostly to herself.

"Joe?" Miss Rimes said.

"Joe Newman. He was in the service during the war, too. He directed the picture Kurt and I just finished," she smiled, winking at me. "I'll tell him they're here."

"Oh, please do," Mr. deWitt said.

"You and Kurt?" Miss Rimes said.

I could tell she didn't believe it by the way she looked at me, like I was supposed to explain before she would.

"It's true," I said, which definitely didn't count as bragging.

George and Dennis and Shelly came in. Mr. deWitt explained to Dennis what he planned.

"Sounds good. You know best," Dennis said.

"Truth to tell, my boy, your agent provocateur, Connie here, is masterminding the whole thing," Mr. deWitt said. "She's trying to let me believe I'm in charge, but we know better, don't we Donald?"

Donald waved his hand and rolled his eyes, but in a friendly way, agreeing I guess, and Miss Rimes suddenly had a big, sort of embarrassed smile on her face and was turning red. Her skin was so white normally that it was easy to see the change. Dennis took her hand and she kissed him on the cheek. I was sort of shocked. Whatever happened to her and Joseph? It seemed like a gyp to him. I think it surprised George too, because even if he didn't say anything, you could tell, if you knew him, he had a funny feeling about it. On the other hand, Mr. deWitt and Donald and even Shelly thought it was the most normal thing in the world. I couldn't tell if Norma thought much about it one way or the other, but Shelly put her arms around Dennis and Miss Rimes.

"You kids are at the beginning of a real adventure," she said. "Art-wise and other-wise. You're gonna break a lot of hearts and make a lot of others grow stronger. Those that can, anyway. Good luck to you both. I mean it. You're gonna need it," she said with a sad smile.

She was looking at George. He was smoking and his head was tipped and his eyes were squinted to avoid the smoke, but it was hard to tell what he was thinking. He began to wander around the room looking at Dennis's stuff. Dennis and Miss Rimes looked happy together, which made me feel bad for Joseph, and glad for them all at the same time. George was running his hands over one of the sculptures. It was a soldier on his knees, hunched over, his clothes muddy and torn and his face in his hands, his rifle and helmet on the ground next to him. I couldn't tell what George thought of it because he had his back to me and I couldn't see his face. But he stayed there like that for a pretty long time.

"We should have some Champagne!" Norma said.

"Precisely! This is a momentous occasion. Donald, do we have any? Chilled?"

"No, just ginger ale, I'm afraid," Donald said.

"It will have to do," Mr. deWitt said, happily. "Get the glasses."

Miss Rimes went with Donald and brought back these tall skinny-stemmed glasses and two big bottles of ginger ale. She and Donald filled them up and passed them out. I got one too.

"How 'bout you take this one to George?" Shelly said.

"Okay," I said.

I came up behind him and bumped him with my elbow since I had a glass in each hand.

"Here, George," I said.

He turned and looked at me, but more, through me. It took him a second to see the glass in my hand and take it. His lips were pressed tight, squishing the end of his cigarette, which he'd let get shorter than usual. His eyes were wet, maybe from smoke getting in, or maybe not.

"Thank you," he said.

"To powerful, beautiful art," Mr. deWitt said, raising his glass.

"To the power of art to change us," Miss Rimes said.

"To life and love," Shelly said, "and to change."

"I think I'm going to cry," Norma said.

"To Dennis," George said, holding up his glass and nodding towards him.

"To ginger ale," I said, holding mine up.

George and Shelly were sitting on the bed of Dennis's truck having a smoke when Norma and I said good-bye to everyone and headed for the MG. George let Dennis take Miss Rimes for a ride on the Vincent, and as they were pulling away from the curb, I could see the huge smile on Dennis's face, and Miss Rimes holding on so tight I bet Dennis couldn't breathe. The noise of the Vincent filled the whole block. It had to have been just about a perfect day for him, I thought. Except for a little too much of Kevin Doyle, I was thinking, it was for me too, or at least very close. Probably not for Joseph, though.

After dinner I counted the route money a couple of times to be sure. I'd collected ninety-eight dollars and eighty-eight cents. Marty helped me figure out that Ron should get fifty-eight thirty and the rest, which included three-sixty in tips was mine. I was supposed to end up with forty dollars and fifty-eight cents. I didn't tell Marty about switching Mr. Rothman for Mr. Duffy, but the money came out the same either way, so it didn't matter. I wrote it on a piece of paper and then counted out Ron's part into one pile and mine into another. I subtracted four dollars for the route bags and another one-fifty for the rubber bands from mine and added it to Ron's and wrapped the paper with the amounts around each pile and used a rubber band to hold them. It was a gyp, but I still had thirty-five dollars and eight cents. Marty was watching.

"What's that?"

"What?"

"You moved money from your side to his. What for?"

"It's okay," I said.

"What's okay? What's that for?"

I didn't answer. I was hoping he'd just forget about it.

"Come on, what's that about?"

"It's the rule."

"What rule? What's that supposed to mean?"

"It's okay," I said again.

"What's okay? Come on, you can tell me."

"I have to pay for the route bags and the rubber bands," I shrugged.

"What are you talking about? Who says?"

"Ron."

"Did he make you pay that last month?"

If he kept talking about it, I was going to cry, even though I was trying not to.

"Yes."

"You're kidding, right?"

I shook my head no. Marty stood there with his hands on his hips. His face got red.

"That rotten bastard!" he said, throwing his hands up into the air and sounding just like my dad. "And you think he's going to charge you again? Those bags can't cost more than a buck or two!"

"He does it every month, that's what Brian says. He's one of the other paper boys. Only Ron doesn't charge them as much. Only three dollars."

That did it. I couldn't hold it any more, and fat sobs hiccupped out of me. It was just too much of a gyp.

"Hey, come on, kiddo, we'll get it straightened out. Don't cry."

"Just don't tell daddy," I said, crying harder now. "He'll kill him and go to jail and it'll be all my fault because of the locks."

I could hardly see because of the tears, but I could see enough to see he thought it was funny.

"You're right about that," he laughed, trying to get me to laugh too. "Jeez, if dad heard about this, oh brother! He'd completely lose control! Let's me and you handle it, okay? He's got enough trouble with his deadbeats. He doesn't need this too."

"Okay," I said. "But if that's the rule, that's the rule. Brian said if you want to keep the route, that's just the way it is."

"We'll see," he said. "He drops the papers off at one, right?"

"Yeah. Sometimes a little before, sometimes a little after, but about one."

"And he's going to collect from you on the 1st?"

"Yeah."

"That's Wednesday."

"Uh huh."

"So if you see him tomorrow or Tuesday, don't say anything about the money or the route bags or anything. Okay?"

"Okay."

"I'll ask at the station if I can take my lunch from twelve-thirty to one-thirty or two on Wednesday."

"Will they let you?"

"I think so. And I'll meet you here and we'll wait for him together and straighten it all out, okay?"

"Okay."

I was putting the two stacks of money back in the pouch.

"Here," he said, taking them from me. "Let's fix them first."

He moved the five-fifty back into my stack.

"I'll talk to him about the first five-fifty, too," he said.

Wednesday morning I couldn't sleep any more. I woke up and knew it was too early so I tried to close my eyes and go back to sleep, but it was hopeless. Once they knew it was a new day, and my birthday, they were going to stay open no matter what. It was five on Marty's clock, and he was snoring away and the rest of the house was quiet, so I didn't think even my dad had gotten up yet, which was good, because then I could get dressed quietly and slip out the back door without anyone seeing me. It wasn't completely light, but not really still dark, sort of in-between, and the jacarandas had this funny look like they weren't ready to be awake yet either. I went up the street on the sidewalk because my sneakers were getting so bad, if I tried making tracks on the damp grass, my socks would get soaked for sure. When I got to Rathbone's and crossed the grass to the gate, I went from stepping stone to stepping stone so they'd stay dry. I opened it just enough to slip through, and I didn't close it all the way either, so there wouldn't be the little clanking-shut. Iyama wouldn't be here for another three hours and Mr. Rathbone would never be up this early, so I knew I had the place to myself. That was going to be my birthday present. I sat on the concrete bench in front of the pond. If I got the thirty-four bucks from the route and the fifty-five bucks from the movie, I could pay off the locks and still have almost seventy-five dollars left over. Even after new sneakers, I'd be rich. I was trying to imagine that much money at once, but it was impossible. I didn't even know what you were supposed to do with that much. I was trying to think of things, but the only thing I thought of was maybe I'd start saving for college, like Marty, only earlier. Or maybe if my dad's deadbeat problem didn't get better, I'd give it to him like Marty did. But after the new sneakers.

Little by little, the sun was coming up and the garden became a mix of bright spots and shady ones, then, pretty soon after that, a bird started chirping from somewhere. He kept it up for a long time, like he was expecting an answer, but the other birds were still asleep, and after a while, he gave up. I knew it would take a lot more than the seventy-five dollars, but I tried to imagine what it would be like to own a place like this. Not the house so much, which was nice okay, and bigger than anything else on the block, but just the garden. You couldn't even see the fences that separated it from the alley or the houses on either side or the wall closing it off from the street. They were pretty far away, and besides, they were hidden by stuff growing in front of them or on them, except for the gate, so everywhere you looked, it was just garden garden garden as far as you could see. When you were back here the rest of the world didn't exist. Nothing out there mattered. Like I'd told Mr. Rathbone, it was peaceful and quiet, but inside the quiet, even the sounds were different. You might know there were cars and motorcycles and trucks out on the street and people might be laughing, or shouting, or fighting about a barking dog or one pooping on someone else's lawn, or all the honking and shouting about the locks, or the guy next to Shelly and Norma, or Mr. Duffy or Ron or Kevin Doyle yelling at me about something, but in here the only sounds were the bees buzzing and crickets and birds chirping and butterfly wings thumping, and sometimes a couple of squirrels barking at each other, so it was its own world. You could close your eyes and be sure nothing bad would happen while you weren't looking. The bird was giving it another try. I closed my eyes and pretended it was mine. All of it. I wondered if I'd be as nice as Rathbone and let me come in whenever I wanted. With my eyes closed, I knew it was a perfect quiet, not perfectly quiet, but a perfect quiet, quiet and separate from the rest of everything, so I could understand why he'd tried to keep it to himself and keep us kids out. Even if Iyama wasn't really captured during the war and ordered to kill anyone that snuck in, I could see how he might have done that. How I might have done that. Kenny Lester could use a place like this, I thought. All of the war guys could. If it were mine, I'd let them in. Maybe not a bunch of kids, but them. On the other hand, they had the carwash.

"Good morning," Rathbone said.

I opened my eyes. It was him alright. Maybe he couldn't sleep either. Maybe it was his birthday too. Wouldn't that be something?

"Should I go?"

"Where?" he said.

He was wearing the maroon robe and crushed down bedroom slippers and the striped pajamas that let the white skin on his ankles show. His hair was slicked back, though.

"I don't know. Somewhere. So you can have your garden to yourself."

"No, no. Perish the thought."

"I didn't wake you up did I? I left the gate unlatched so it wouldn't clank. But I planned to latch it when I go. Should I go?"

"Oh lord, no. You're fine. It was that bird. May I join you?"

"Sure. It's yours, you know."

He sat on the bench with me.

"And what's on your schedule that has you up so early and so pensive?"

"What's that mean?"

"Thoughtful. Lost in thought."

"Oh. Lots of stuff."

I was going to tell him about Ron and the route bags and rubber bands, but it would have been complaining, so I didn't. Then I thought about telling him it was my birthday, even though I'd already decided we had too much trouble to be thinking about birthdays and I wasn't going to mention it to anyone, even if they might have remembered on their own. Since he wasn't in my family, it wouldn't matter much, and it wouldn't be bragging, exactly, but it would be something like it, so I didn't do that either. He lit a cigarette and blew out the smoke and looked at me. It seemed like he was waiting for me to say something, so I did.

"Is it your birthday?" I asked him.

"No, why?" he said.

"I thought maybe that's why you couldn't sleep. That and the bird."

"No, it's not. Is it yours, perchance?"

"Yes! It is! How did you know?"

"A guess," he said.

"A pretty good guess, I'd say."

"Any special celebratory plans?"

"You mean like a party or something?"

"Yes."

"No, not really. I think were going to skip it this year."

"That's too bad."

"It's okay. Too much other stuff's going on."

"Well, I'm sure it will all work out for the best."

"I hope so. I should probably go."

"Why don't you stay? I'm awake now. I'm going to shower and shave. You stay and think your thoughts. Iyama won't be here for quite a while. Stay as long as you like."

"Are you sure?"

"Consider it a birthday present. Happy Birthday," he smiled.

"Thank you."

He took a few more puffs of his cigarette and snuffed it out against the underside of the bench and put the butt in his robe pocket and stood up.

"You're welcome," he said.

He wandered a little here and there through the garden, picking a few flowers as he made his way back to the house.

At first I thought I should go, but since I didn't know where, and since both of us thought the garden was a good birthday present, I stayed. I laid back on the bench and stared at the sky. It was completely light and just starting to get bright. I stared up at the blueness and could see the little things that float around in your eye like tiny tadpoles in a puddle. The next thing I knew, Iyama was waking me up.

"Ohayoo gozaimasu," he said

I opened my eyes and it took a few seconds before I knew who he was and where I was. Out of habit, I jumped up like I was going to run for the bamboo patch to escape, but before I did, he sat down next to me.

"Mr. Rathbone says it's your birthday today. Yes?"

"Uh huh."

"How old?"

"Eight."

"Ah! A good age. I remember eight."

"You do?"

"I do. Any plans?"

"Do the route at one," I shrugged.

"That's all?"

"I guess."

He frowned. No birthday was okay with me, but if Mr. Rathbone and Iyama made a big deal out of it, it would start to feel like a gyp.

"Goin' to start work," he said and patted my knee.

"Can I help?"

He looked at me like he wasn't sure what I meant.

"Not for pay or anything, just for the heck of it. Since I get to be in here."

He nodded okay.

He took a pair of scissor-looking things from a leather holster on his hip and showed me how to open them.

"This way," he said, motioning.

We went to one of the big flower beds where all the flowers were almost as tall as me. He showed me how some of the flowers were still brightly colored and some were turning brown at the edges. Snip, snip and the first brown one was gone. He nodded to the bed and handed me the scissors.

"Now you."

"Where should I put the cut ones?"

"On the canvas," he pointed.

There was a tan canvas tarp spread out on the grassy knoll. He left me there clipping away while he began weeding over by the garage. As the air warmed up, the bees and birds and butterflies showed up and hopped around the place. If I was a bee or a bird or a butterfly, I was thinking, this would be heaven. Even being me, it was.

I worked my way through that bed and two more while Iyama weeded and then cut the grass and did some stuff to clean the pond. When the tarp was covered with the cuttings I'd done and the grass and weeds he'd cut, he folded the corners and made a bundle out of it and took it to his truck. It was hot by then. Mr. Rathbone came out the back door with a tray and a pitcher of lemonade and three glasses.

"Take a little nourishment," he said.

He put the tray on the concrete bench and poured. The three of us had a drink together. I was glad he didn't say anything more about it being my birthday. We just had the lemonade and enjoyed the garden together.

"Do you know what time it is?" I asked him.

He checked his watch.

"Twelve-forty."

"Yikes," I said. "I better get ready for the route. Thank you for letting me stay."

"You're quite welcome."

I was sitting on the curb and had the route bags and rubber bands and the Red Rider and the money pouch all ready to go. Since my mom didn't have to work downtown, she'd left me a note saying she'd taken Sarah and Nick and Megan and Allen and Wyatt to the beach and they'd be back before five. I was worried that Marty wouldn't get home before Ron came. Then I was worried that he would. Either way, I wished the whole thing would just go away. But it wouldn't and Ron showed up first. He dropped the bundle on the parkway.

"Got the money?" he said.

"Yes," I said, reaching for the pouch.

I did it as slowly as I could, hoping Marty would show up, but he didn't.

"I ain't got all day," Ron said.

I took out his part and handed it to him.

"Got it all figured out again, huh?" he said.

"Yes."

"You and your genius brother?"

"Uh huh."

"And I supposed you subtracted for twenty-six dailies and five Sundays?"

"Yes."

"You did?" he said, surprised.

"Yes."

"You sure?"

"Yes."

"I told you...I warned you, didn't I?, you don't get to decide when to stop or start a paper. I do. Remember that?"

He'd leaned down close to my face to boss me around. He thought he was scaring me, and he was, a little bit anyway, but not even close to Kevin Doyle, so it wasn't so bad. I didn't say anything. He sort of smiled, like he'd proved himself right and me wrong forever.

"And you decided not to deliver to Mr. Duffy?"

"Yes.".

"Well, smart guy, I'm going to keep dropping off the papers and keep on charging you for them. So if you don't deliver to Mr. Duffy, you're still paying for it. Got it?"

I was looking at him, just not saying anything. He got mad.

"Are you listening to me?"

I nodded yes.

"Good. Now, for the money."

He took off the rubber band and looked at the paper with the amount on it. He made a face like it was okay.

"Hmm," he said.

He looked up at me.

"That's right. Good for you."

Then he counted it. He looked at me like he'd caught me again.

"You're five-fifty short," he said.

"I already paid for the rubber bands and route bags last time," I said.

"No, no, no," he said. "You're not getting the picture. It's every month."

He grabbed the money pouch. I tried to hold onto it, but he just pulled harder and took it away from me. He reached in and took my part out. He flipped thorugh it and counted out twenty-four o-eight and handed it and the money pouch back.

"I'm taking out the next two months worth of rubber bands and route bag money, eleven bucks, so we don't have to argue about it. This way, it's all taken care of, right?"

He crossed out the forty fifty-eight and wrote twenty-four oh-eight instead, then, below, wrote, eleven dollars, three months rb/rb paid in full. He held out the paper for me. When I didn't take it, he shoved it into the pouch.

"We all set?"

My rules or not, I would have complained or cried or both, except I knew he wanted to make me, so I didn't. On the inside I was, but I didn't let it out. Where was Marty? Ron got in the truck, happy and whistling, and drove off.

I cut the rope off the bundle. My eyes were dripping. Not crying, exactly, just some left over from holding it in, but I was thinking, if Mr. Duffy didn't pay and I stopped delivering to him, shouldn't I not deliver at all if Ron was cheating me? He was a bigger dead beat than Mr. Duffy, for sure. I started to cry after all. Not a lot, but some, because I realized the problem with that was I'd be gypping all the nice people on the route that didn't do anything wrong and expected the paper. I pictured Mrs. Gunther coming to her door and looking for the paper and it wouldn't be there and she'd have to decide if she'd go downstairs to look for it, even though it was hard for her to go up and down, and even if she did, it wouldn't be there, so I started folding. I had the bike and bags ready to go. I took a paper and dropped it on George's steps and another and crossed the street and went down the driveway and tossed it on Kevin Doyle's back porch. I did the route, not fast and not slow. At first, all I could think about was Ron the dead beat. And Marty. He said he'd come, but he didn't. But pretty soon I was thinking about being free on the Red Rider. Then about being in Rathbone's garden. After a while, Ron and the money didn't matter as much. I'd have enough to pay Mr. Mahoney what I owed him for the locks and still might have enough for sneakers, so all in all, it wasn't too bad a birthday.

Since I'd sort of poked along the route, when I got home and put thngs away, it was already quarter after three. I rode up the street planning on going to the hardware store to pay off the locks, but sort of hoping to see George on the way, but I didn't. In a way, that was for the best, since he might make me accidently tell him it was my birthday. When I got close to his house, I wanted Kenny Lester to be home, but I knew he'd be at work this time of day. Before I got there, the door opened at 440.

"Boychick, boychick!" Mr. Rothman called to me.

I stopped in the middle of the street.

"Hi. Your paper's right there," I said, pointing.

"I see it, I see," he said, picking it up. "But some other thing."

He came down his walk to the parkway.

"Come to talk," he said, waving me over.

I rolled the bike over to the curb.

"Your bags go on and off the bicycle?"

"Yes, sir."

"It's not so big a problem?"

"No. It's easy. I just put them over the rack and tie them on, then take them off when I'm done. Sometimes I just leave them on."

"That's very clever. So. I have question," he said.

His eyebrows went up high, like he'd already asked the question and was waiting for the answer.

"What?" I asked him.

"If you have the time, and if you don't you can say no, that will be okay, but if you have the time, would you like a little job?"

"What?"

"I don't like to drive any more, and Carl's is close enough to walk, but I can't carry much, so I have to go every other day."

He made a face and motioned with his hand, like it was a big waste of time.

"If you had those bags on your bicycle and we went to Carl's, I could bring back enough groceries for the whole week. We could pay you something for your trouble. You think?"

"Sure," I said, "I guess."

"And are you too busy now?"

"Well, I was going to the San Vicente Hardware store."

"Perfect!" he said. "Carl's is right on your way! If you go get the bags we could go now together, no?"

"I suppose."

"That would be wonderful!" he said, clapping his hands

"Okay, I'll be right back."

I turned the bike around and rode home. On the way down the street, I was thinking maybe I should have asked him how much he was going to pay me, but I hadn't thought of it, and it didn't matter that much anyway, but really, I wished he'd told me because I hated to have to ask. It was too much like collecting, and I hated that, so it would have been better if he'd just told me. Whatever it was would be fine, I decided, just as long as I didn't have to ask. I'd just do it, and if he didn't pay me or forgot or something, that would be that, because then I'd only do it this once. I'd had enough of deadbeats to last me forever. I put the route bags back on the bike and rode up the street. He was waiting for me by the curb. I wasn't sure what to do. If I rode, he'd have to walk too fast, and if I tried to ride as slow as he walked, I'd probably tip over, and if I got off the bike and walked it, it sort of made having the bike a waste, but he'd already figured it out.

"You'll go on ahead to the market," he said, "and if you leave the bicycle by the door on the liquor store side, I can shop and load it up while you're at the hardware store. How's by that?"

"That's a good idea. Just remember to load stuff on both sides so it stays balanced and doesn't tip over. I don't want it to get scratched or anything."

"Of course, boychick. That goes without saying. I'll be very careful," he said. "Thank you."

I rode up the block and turned towards Doheny. I parked the bike at the top of the parking lot on the liquor store side where he'd said. I walked up to San Vicente and around the corner and down to the hardware store. Mr. Mahoney wasn't in front, so I went in. Considering how hot it was outside, the hardware store was staying pretty cool. He was at the counter ringing up a garden hose some guy was buying. He saw me and waved.

"I'll be right with you," he said.

The guy paid and they talked a little more, then he left.

"What's up?"

"Sorry I didn't get here over the weekend, but things got sort of crazy again."

"I wondered about it, but your way ahead, so, no problem."

"But guess what?"

"What?"

"I have the rest of the money for the locks," I told him.

I put all the money I had on the counter. We both looked at it.

"Really? So fast?"

"Uh huh. I got paid from the car wash on Saturday and the paper route today."

I didn't tell him I got gyped, and good, but I was thinking it. There was the twenty-four o-eight from the route and the two-fifty from the carwash and fifty-five cents left over after the rides at the Beverly Pony-land. He got the card with what I'd paid and what I still owed.

"We were down to twenty-three fifty," he said, "but four more came in this week, so that puts it back up to twenty-six fifty."

Great, I was thinking, there go the sneakers. Mr. Mahoney had this look like he thought I thought it was his fault the extra guys showed up for more locks, but I knew it wasn't his fault at all, I just wondered what took them so long? Just when it looked like it was under control, these guys showed up out of nowhere. Since we'd given them to September 15th, there could even be more.

I watched while he moved bills and change around until he'd separated out the twenty-six fifty. He watched me while I put the left over sixty-five cents in my pocket.

"Are you sure you want to pay it all off now? You're way ahead. Why not keep a little more for yourself. There's no hurry, you know."

I was tempted, that's for sure. Without really thinking about it, I was looking down at my feet, wiggling my toes and I could see them looking back at me from the torn fronts of both shoes. New sneakers were calling to me from somewhere, but they'd have to wait.

"No. I might as well get it over with."

He wrote paid in full on the card and handed it to me.

"I'll keep the account open and let you know if anyone else comes in for a lock, but it's not very likely."

"Good," I told him, "I never want hear about another lock as long as I live."

"I don't blame you," he laughed.

"Thank you for helping me with the account and everything."

We shook hands.

"Take care. And enjoy your bike."

"I will. Bye."


Mr. Rothman was waiting for me when I got back to Carl's.

"I'm all ready, boychick. And you?"

"Me too," I told him.

He handed me a dime.

"It's hot out, so you go get for yourself a soda pop and I'll be walking. When you finish, you ride the groceries home and I'll be there waiting. No?"

"Okay, thanks."

He headed home and I went into the liquor store. Max was behind the counter, leaning against the booze shelves behind him, reading the horse paper, the same old cigar in the corner of his mouth. He looked up for just a second, made some sound, then went back to reading. I figured it was supposed to be hello, or hi or something so I said hi back.

"How ya doin'?" he said without looking up.

"Fine," I said.

"Good," he said, still without looking up.

I opened the soda pop cooler and folded the left-side lid onto the right side. There weren't very many bottles left in there and the ones that were, were mostly RC Colas, which I didn't like. Maybe because it was late in the afternoon and it had been hot all day and he'd probably sold a lot and no one else like the RC Colas either, I thought. But he should have put new ones in. How could he sell them it they weren't in there getting cold? I flipped the lids the other way and felt around under the cold water on the right side and found a hidden Nehi Orange that had tipped over. That's more like it, I thought.

"You need to refill this thing," I told him. "It's almost empty."

"I should do a lot of things, kid. I'll make a note of it."

He looked up, folded the paper and put it to the side of the counter.

"Hey, howya doin'?" he said, recognizing me. "How's our girl?"

"You mean Norma?"

"You bettcha."

"She's fine. Here," I said, handing him the dime.

"You gonna drink it here or take it?"

"Here," I told him.

He shrugged and gave me a nickel back.

"Okay, here. Just take it out to the parking lot so you don't drip all over the place. Make sure you bring the bottle back, right?"

"Right."

Every time I saw Big Max, I couldn't help noticing the size of his forearms and the tattoo of the mermaid on one, and ship's anchor on the other. The mermaid was a girl with no shirt on top and a fish tail on the bottom and a big smile on her face. She had her hands behind her head, sort of showing off her bosoms. He caught me looking at them.

"Watch this," he said.

He held the mermaid arm out towards me and made and un-made a fist so the muscle made the bosoms move like she was alive.

"Keep that under your hat," he winked and smiled. "And bring the bottle back."

I went out to the parking lot and sat on the wooden thing that stopped cars from bumping into the back wall of the liquor store. The Nehi was so fizzy it tickled my tongue, but in a good way. Pop pulled into the lot and parked a few spaces from me. He got out of his car and put his hat on. He didn't see me until he was almost to the door.

"Hey, look who's here!" he said.

"Hi, Pop. How come you're not downtown?"

"Sometimes enough is enough, right?"

"Right. Guess what?"

"What?"

"I paid off the locks today."

"No!"

"Really. I did. Unless someone else asks for one, I'm all done with it."

"Good for you. Did Sullivan get one?"

"I don't know. I gave him a card, so he could have if he wanted to. Actually, six."

"Next time I see that crook, I'm going to make sure he knows you took care of it."

He saw the bike.

"What's that? You doin' the shopping now?"

He had his hands on his hips and laughed that snort-laugh. I followed his look to my bike.

"No. That's for Mr. Rothman. Up the block. He's on my route and asked me to help him get more groceries home than he can carry."

"Is he going to pay you?"

"He bought me the soda," I said, holding it up.

"That's all?"

"I'm not sure."

I could tell he wanted to tell me about how I should have found out all about getting paid before I said I'd do it, and he was probably right since there were so many deadbeats around, but I figured sometimes you just went where things steered you and figured out what to do from there. Besides, I'd already thought about it as much as I wanted to.

"It'll be okay," I told him. "Don't worry."

"You're right. I'll let you handle it."

"What are you here for?" I asked him.

"My pal, Johnnie," he said.

I knew that meant a kind of Whiskey he liked.

"Yuk," I told him.

He'd given me sips of it. I'd stick to the Nehi, I thought. I'd finished mine and we walked into the store so I could return the bottle.

"Abe," Big Max said.

"Max," Pop said. "A fifth of Johnnie. Anything look good?"

Max looked at me.

Pop said, "I'll see you later, Kurt. You better run those groceries home for that guy before they spoil out there in the sun."

I hadn't thought of that.

"Yeah, so long, Pop."

"See you, kiddo."

As I got to the door, Big Max was telling Pop something about Hobson's Choice in the eighth at Hollywood.

Mr. Rothman had balanced his groceries pretty well and the Red Rider wasn't any harder to ride than when it was filled with the Sundays. I got back to his place and he was waiting on the bottom step.

"So, it was not too difficult?" he asked, coming to meet me at the parkway.

"Smooth sailing," I said, moving my hand like George did.

"Good, good."

I put the bike on the kickstand and held onto the handle bars while he took the grocery bags out from one side, then the other. He set them down one by one on the parkway until he had all four off the bike.

"So, now, the pay," he said. "Is fifty cents and the soda pop enough?"

"Sure," I said. "That sounds fair."

"Are you sure? I don't want to cheat you. I want you to do this again, if you will."

"Yeah. Fifty cents and the soda is fine."

"Good," he said.

I remembered the nickel change from Big Max. I reached into my pocket.

"Here," I said, handing it to him, "the soda was only a nickel. Max didn't charge the deposit since I drank it there."

He reached out and closed my fingers around the nickel and patted my closed hand.

"You're a good boy. No, you keep that. Thank you for doing it."

"You're welcome."

I put the nickel back in my pocket.

"You want help carrying them in?"

"No. A little exercise to get the blood moving. Remember?"

"Uh huh."

His saying it reminded me of Duffy. I looked up expecting to see him in the window with his baggy underwear and a crabby look on his face. He wasn't there, but just the thought of Ron making a big deal about warning me and charging me for the missed papers that I was delivering to Mr. Rothman instead, and collecting from him so it came out even, the whole thing made me happy.

"Okay," I said. "See you later."

I started peddling down Oakhurst. Before I'd gotten as far as the Pink House, Pop pulled up along side me. He slowed to the same speed as me and the Red Rider.

"Happy Birthday," he called across the seat through the passenger window. "It's your birthday, right?"

"Right. Thanks."

"Doing anything special?"

I didn't know what to say. If I said yes, it'd be lying. If I said no, he'd think my mom and dad...well, whatever he'd think, it wouldn't be good.

"Maybe," I said.

"What's that mean."

"Maybe means maybe!"

"Well, is the maybe anytime soon or later?"

"Later," I said. "Maybe."

"How would you like to go to the races with me. A little birthday present?"

"Horse races?"

"Yes."

"When?"

"Now. If we hurry, we can get to Hollywood Park for the last two or three races of the day. How about it?"

"Just me and you?

"Just me and you."

"I've never been to the races," I said.

"Yes you have," he said.

"No I haven't."

He laughed.

"I've got the picture to prove it. Santa Anita. I took you when you were two and a half or three. We bought you that Camel Hair long-coat and beanie from the track shop and had a picture of the two of us taken by the wishing well. You don't remember that?"

"Really?"

"Really. How about it. Wanna go?

It sounded pretty good to me. Kind of like the old days when Pop took me lots of places, but I knew I probably shouldn't. We were still supposed to be mad at him. On the other hand, everyone else got to go to the beach today.

"We'll be back by six or six-thirty. Before dark for sure."

"No one's home to tell, so maybe I shouldn't. I'd like to, but if we might be back after six, maybe I shouldn't."

"We could leave a note. That would do, wouldn't it?"

"I suppose."

"Come on. You're only eight once."

"That's true."

"So, we're on?"

"Okay, I guess."

By then we were all the way down to our house. Pop parked his Oldsmobile out front by the parkway and I turned into the driveway and put the route bags back on the porch and the Red Rider in the garage. He went into his part of the duplex and a minute later came out with an envelope and tucked it into the screen door on our side for my mom or dad.

"That should do it. All set?"

"All set."

We got into the Olds.

"Watch out for the hat," he said.

Pop's hat was on the seat between us. On off, on off. I wondered why he wore it at all. My dad used to wear one too, but he'd stopped. I didn't really remember it, just from pictures.

"How's it feel being eight?" he asked.

"About the same as seven except seven had the lock problem, and eight won't, so eight's going to be better."

"That's a good way to look at it."

He turned on the radio. There was some stuff about Korea, but he didn't seem to be listening. I'd heard of it and seen stuff on the front page of the Mirror, but no one talked about it much, which was sort of funny. At the car wash, all they talked about was the war that was over, but hardly mentioned the one that was still going on. Pop changed the station. The announcer was doing an ad for The Smiling Irishman, Jack's Fine New and Used Cars. He mentioned the Olds Super 88 for only $2328.

"Did you hear that?"

"What?"

"About the brand new Super 88?"

"What about it?"

"I saw a painting that cost almost as much. Can you believe that?"

"Not really," he said, making a face like that was terrible. "Where'd you see that?"

"At the deWitt Gallery on Canon. You know Dennis, right? From the car wash?"

"Sure. Maurice's friend. He and the others worked in the yard."

"Right, that's him. He's a sculptor and my art teacher helped him get some of his sculptures into Mr. deWitt's Gallery."

"Really?"

"It's true. And there were a bunch of paintings for a ton of money, one of them was more than the Super 88. It was good, but not that good. "

"Hmmm," he said. "You never know about people, do you?"

"Sometimes yes, sometimes no," I said.

I was thinking about George and Kenny Lester and Ron and Mr. Duffy and Rathbone and Iyama. Sometimes you thought you knew, but you really didn't.

We drove down Beverly all the way to La Brea and turned right. After a while, it looked like we were heading towards the Towers.

"Pop?"

"What?"

"Have you ever seen the Watts Towers?"

"No. I've heard of them, though. Some crazy guy's been working on them for years. Why?"

"Nothing. I just wondered."

In another fifteen minutes we were pulling into the huge parking lot at Hollywood Park. It was still sunny and still pretty hot, and it was only about half full, but even half was a lot of cars, which had to mean a lot of people, especially for a Wednesday during work time. Close to the building, the lot was blacktop. farther away, it was dirt. We drove around close to the entrance but couldn't find an empty spot, so we ended up in the dirt part. Pop took his hat and got out his side and I got out mine. The ground was covered in dirt-dust and as soon as my foot hit it, the flap at the front of my sneaker flopped open and closed, like a mouth spitting it out in a puff. After a couple of steps, Pop's shiny black shoes were covered in it too. He looked at my sneakers but didn't say anything.

"He's not crazy," I said.

"Who?"

"Sabato."

"Who?"

"The guy that's making the Towers."

"What makes you so sure?"

"I know him. He's not crazy, he's an artist."

"Same thing," he snorted. "Let's hurry."

I could see why my dad got mad at him sometimes. We paid at the Main Admissions Gate and went in. Pop had given the guy a quarter for himself and a nickel for me.

"That's all?" I whispered to him.

"That's it. They let you in cheap because they expect to make it up on bets."

"Are you going to bet?"

"Damn tootin'," he said.

We walked through a wide tunnel under the Grandstands. When we got to the end of it you could see the track. And smell it. The whole place had a smell, sort of like Beverly Ponyland, only not as bad. Not good, but not bad. In fact, I sort of liked it. When we stepped back into the sun, it seemed much brighter and hotter than it had in the parking lot. Pop was looking at a big green board with names and numbers all over it. He went to the left and I followed him.

"Hurry up, Kurt," he called to me. "We've got to place our bets before they go to the post."

I ran to catch up to him. He took my hand and we walked as fast as we could up the stairs through the stands to a place at the back of them and went inside where there were lines of mostly men and a few women waiting in front of a long row of windows. We got in line. Pop tapped the man in front of him on the shoulder. The guy was reading one of the horse newspapers like Max had. I looked around. Most of the other people in the lines were too.

"Is this the fifth or sixth?" Pop asked him. "We just got here."

The guy looked over his shoulder.

"Sixth," he said, and turned back to his paper.

Pop took a folded up paper from the side pocket of his suit jacket. He flipped and refolded it until he found what he was looking for.

"Anything look good to you?" he said to me.

"What does Big Max say?"

Pop put his hands on his hips and looked right at me.

"What do you think he knows about this?"

"He reads the race papers all the time. He ought to know."

"Well, he gave me a tip in the eighth. But for six and seven we're on our own."

"Let me see."

He handed the paper to me and pointed to the list of names for the sixth and seventh races. He'd already circled Hobson's Choice in the eighth. None of the names made much sense. Why would someone name a horse Sir Greek, or Hellowise? Or Bloody Step? Yuk.

"How about this one?" I said pointing.

"Pensive Lady?"

"Uh huh."

"Do you even know what pensive means?"

"Uh huh."

"Really? What?"

"Lost in thought, right?"

He put his hands on his hips again and looked at me like I was making it up or got lucky or something.

"That's right. How'd you know that?"

"Mr. Rathone told me."

"Hmm. Well, I was going to put a bet down on Grand Sunbeam, but Pensive Lady's fourteen-to-one to win, ten-to-one to show. We'll give her a try. Take a look at the seventh."

We were still pretty far from the window. I looked over the list. It was a lot more crowded. I wondered why they didn't balance it out better since there were only seven horses in the sixth race but eleven in the seventh. Compare, Desert Ruler, Loyal Brigand, Bold Knot, Little Millie, Bleu Martha, Chelsea Cat, Jiminy Cricket, Raffle House, Pistol Packer and Land's End. I kept going over the list, thinking I'd tell Pop I liked Jiminy Cricket the best, but my eyes kept going back to Loyal Brigand. I'd never heard the name before, and if it was supposed to mean something, it was a mystery to me, but my eyes kept going back to it so that's what I told him.

"Loyal Brigand? Why that one?"

"I don't know."

"How about Pistol Packer instead? Besides, I think that might be a typographical error. I think I've seen the name before and it should be Royal Brigand."

"I like it as Loyal Brigand."

"I don't think there is a Loyal Brigand."

"There is today," I said, pointing to the paper.

"I suppose," he said.

We were almost to the window.

"So, Pistol Packer?" he said, like we'd already agreed.

I shrugged, okay.

"It's your birthday."

"Pistol Packer's okay."

"Alright, then," he said, rubbing his hands together.

We got to the window and Pop bet Pensive Lady to show, Pistol Packer to show and Hobson's Choice to win. He gave the man two dollars for Pensive Lady and two more for Pistol Packer and twenty dollars for Hobson's Choice and got twelve tickets.

We went back into the stands. Down on the track the horses for the sixth race were getting ready and I could feel the crowd getting excited. It was like all these separate people became one alive thing, all of its attention on the track and the seven horses getting ready to run. Pop pointed out Pensive Lady. She looked smaller that the other horses so it didn't seem fair. They got lined up in the starting gate and the bell rang and off they went. It started out slowly, but by about half way through, the crowd noise got loud, then louder, then crazy. I got excited and started yelling at Pensive Lady to hurry up, but from the very beginning, she looked like she was lost in thought and not very interested in racing. Or even running. All the other horses were across the finish line and were ready to go home by the time she crossed it. Pop made a face and tore up the ticket.

"That's why she was fourteen-to-one," he said.

He sounded sort of crabby, but then he messed up my hair, and laughed, so I knew he wasn't mad about it. It took about twenty minutes before they were ready to run the seventh race. There were so many horses there weren't enough spots in the starting gates for them all. Three horses had to line up at the far end, outside the gate. One of them was Loyal Brigand. He was beautiful. If the story about Black Beauty was true, he'd be it. All of the other horses were big and strong looking and could probably run fast, but even if I didnt' know his name and like it, I'd have chosen him anyway. He was big and strong too, but he looked like he wanted to run. Like he couldn't wait to get started. The three horses outside the gates didn't have anything to stop them from moving around so there was a couple of what Pop told me were false starts. By the time they were settled down and the bell rang, those three had gotten a slower start and were at the back of the crowd. With so many horses running, their hoofs hitting the ground sounded like thunder, the kind that keeps up and up, steady and rolling, not too close, but not too far away either, and you could feel it coming up off the track and into the stands and into the seats and into your feet and legs and your stomach, like a vibration or rumbling that might go on forever. In the sixth race, I hadn't heard or felt anything like this and I could feel it getting the crowd more excited. Me, for sure. I felt like I was on Loyal Brigand's back, I was riding him and could feel his hooves pounding against the dirt, feel him pulling to catch up. In a way, it was like being on the Vincent, if you could make yourself believe the Vincent was alive, or the Red Rider, which was alive, for me at least, but here I could see and feel Loyal Brigand, completely alive, his chest swelling up as he tried to get more air, and I could feel him sucking it in and pushing it out in a determined way, the way Miss Rimes described artists that knew what they wanted and did it no matter what. That was Loyal Brigand. He was determined to win just because he wanted to and knew he could. They went into the first turn staying bunched together, but by the time they'd gone into the second, they'd ended up in more of a long line. Except for Loyal Brigand. He'd stayed outside, going wide on the two turns. On the straight part on the back side, some of the horses in back started trying to get to the front. With so many horses ahead of him it seemed hopeless. He'd gotten a bad start and was running what Pop told me was a longer race by staying outside. Pistol Packer was in second place and only half a horse length behind Land's End, but Loyal Brigand started passing a bunch of the other horses. One, then two, then three and pretty soon, going into the third curve he was in front of as many horses as he was behind. He stayed on the outside of both the third and fourth curves, so if Pop was right, he was running a really long race. He didn't seem to mind, though. Even before he came off the last part of the last curve, he was charging harder, then down the straight part to the finish. Pistol Packer had slipped into third place, behind Chelsea Cat and Land's End. He passed them both. At the finish he was less than half a horse behind Land's End. If the race had been a little longer, I bet he could have won. He'd run a really good race, but I could tell he was disappointed.

"Can we go down there?" I asked Pop.

"Where?"

"Down there on the field."

"The track?"

"Yeah, the track."

"What for?"

"I want to see him up close."

"Who?"

"Loyal Brigand."

"Why?"

"Just because."

He looked at me. I could tell he was going to say no.

"For my birthday present," I said. "You're only eight once," I reminded him.

He put his hands on his hips and tipped his hat back on his head and laughed.

"Sure. Why not?" he said, "you're only sixty once, too".

We walked down through the stands to the little low wall that separated the seats from the track. There were openings in front of different sections of the Grandstands, so by the time we got to the bottom of our area we just stepped through the closest one. The horses were all walking around catching their breath. Across the main dirt track, inside of it, there was a grass track they called the Turf Course, and just inside that, the Winner's Circle. There was another whole course for jumping horses in the middle of the two tracks, with a couple of small lakes, and the fence things they were supposed to jump over. There were a lot of people on the track, not other customers like us, but the riders and owners and guys who took care of the horses and led them around. The horses from the seventh race were being led away and the ones getting ready for the eighth, the last race, were just coming on. Land's End was a pretty horse too. He was sort of a dark red-brown. Up close he wasn't just big and strong, he was huge. They all were. He'd won fair and square, but if

Loyal Brigand had been in one of the regular gates, I was sure he would have won. They were leading Land's End to the Winner's Circle to give him his prize. I could see Loyal Brigand across the track. Some of the other horses were already being led all the way around to the back side of the track where the barns were. There was a guy holding Loyal Brigand's leash, getting ready to lead him away too, so I let go of Pop's hand and ran across the track.

"Can I say hi to him?" I asked the guy.

The guy leading him didn't seem to care. He looked at me and shrugged, but the rider slid down off his back. He was a grown up, but pretty small. Like Sabato.

"Ran a hell of a race, didn't he?"

"I thought he was going to win," I said. "He got gyped starting outside the gate."

The rider patted my back just as Pop got there.

"Dam tootin', kid, damn tootin'," he said. "He's got more heart than the whole bunch of them together. Wanna sit on him?"

I was so startled and scared, I didn't know what to say.

"Can I just pet him?"

"Sure."

"Jim," the guy holding the leash said, "we gotta get off the track."

"Yeah, yeah, we got time. They're still jawin' over there in the circle."

Pop took hold of one of my hands. The rider took my other hand and spread it out flat. He put a sugar cube on it and held it out for Loyal Brigand. He snorted and his lips flapped and he shook his head up and down and turned and found the cube. His big lips sort of plucked it right off. I didn't know whether to laugh or cry, I was so excited.

"How 'bout it," the rider asked Pop, "can he sit up top?"

Pop looked at me.

"It's up to you, Kurt. You want to? It'll be a hell of a birthday present."

"It's your birthday?" Jim asked.

I nodded.

"Well, that settles it! You ready?"

"I guess," I said.

Pop and the rider lifted me up and up and up. I was so high up I couldn't believe it. It was like being on top of a two-story Vincent. The saddle was tiny and since Loyal Brigand's back was so wide, my legs stuck out past it almost straight out to the sides. The rider reached up and bent my knees so they were pointed forward and my feet were pointed back. It was a lot more comfortable.

"That's how we do it," he said.

He held on to the metal thing in Loyal Brigand's mouth that the leash was attached to but took the long leather straps from the other guy and handed them to me.

"Now lean forward and hold the reins in tight, like this."

He showed me how to cup them up close in front of my chest.

"Ready?" he said.

"For what?"

"A little trot."

"I guess," I said.

I looked at Pop. He shrugged like it was okay with him if it was okay with me. I was too excited and scared to say anything or to smile, but on the inside I was.

"Okay," Jim said, "we're coming down the stretch."

He took off running down the track and Loyal Brigand trotted along beside him. It was like riding over a bumpy road in the back of Ron's pick up truck, only a lot more fun. I petted Loyal Brigand's neck and whispered to him he'd win next time. Jim brought him to a stop and helped me off.

"How was that?"

"Great! Thank you."

"Happy Birthday, Kurt," Jim said.

I was going to ask him if it was Loyal Brigand or Royal Brigand, but decided not to. He took off his cap and handed the reins to the other guy who had to trot around to the back side of the track in a hurry since they were getting ready for the eighth race. Pop caught up and took my hand.

"How was it?"

"Great. Thanks Pop."

"Happy Birthday."

Hobson's Choice won in the eighth. It seemed like Big Max knew before it even happened. Anyway, Pop was happy and so was I. We got home a little after six-twenty.

"Sorry, kiddo," Marty said at dinner. "It got busy and they needed me to stay. I never even took lunch. I just ate bites of my sandwich between changing tires all day."

"It's okay."

My dad had made it home to eat with us and my mom made a special pot roast dinner for my birthday and we were going to have Root Beer floats for desert instead of a cake, since she hadn't been home all day to make one. For a birthday present, they'd gotten tickets to the Sunday Bugs Bunny Club for me and Sarah and Nick for the morning matinee before I'd have to do the route. We hadn't been there since last summer, so that was pretty neat.

"So, how'd it go with Ron?" Marty asked.

My dad wasn't really paying attention, and I tried to tell Marrty with my expression that he should forget about it, before my dad heard. That was some trouble we definitely didn't need.

"What?" Marty said. "Why are you making that face?"

"What's the matter?" my dad said.

"Nothing," I said. "Guess what?"

"What?" my dad said.

"I paid off the locks today. I'm all done."

"No!"

"Really. It's true. There's a little chance someone might still come in for a lock between now and September 15, but Mr. Mahoney said it's not very likely, so that's that."

"Good for you, Kurt," my mom said.

"What did you do the rest of the day?" Sarah asked.

"Well, I finished the route and a guy I deliver to, Mr. Rothman, wanted me to help him get groceries from Carl's to his house, so I put the route bags back on my bike and went to pay off Mr. Mahoney and went back to Carl's and took the groceries back to his house."

"That was nice of you," my mom said.

"He paid me," I said.

"Well, it was nice of you and nice of him."

"He wants me to do it some more times, too."

"Good."

"Anything else?" Sarah asked.

"Like what?" I said.

"Like the note we got from Pop."

"What note?" my dad said.

He was getting all set to get mad. My mom patted his hand.

"It's nothing. It's fine," she said.

"What?" my dad said right to me.

"Pop took me to the horse races."

My dad looked at my mom, then at me, like I'd spoiled his party, even if it was my birthday. Like I wasn't supposed to do anything with Pop, and to tell the truth, I knew it. I knew it when I said yes to Pop. If it hadn't been for my dad's deadbeats, I was pretty sure it would have been okay. But they were making money a big problem again, and that made Pop a problem again, so I shouldn't have gone. I'd never have seen or sat on Loyal Brigand, but one look at my dad's face and I wished I just said no. He didn't say anything, but I could tell. Everyone was quiet. We kept eating, but the fun was sort of gone out of it. At least Marty quit asking about Ron. That was something. If I'd had to tell about that dead beat, there'd be big trouble for sure. But almost as quick as he got mad about it, my dad changed his mind. He smiled at me.

"Good for you. I wish I could have taken you, but I'm glad he did. How was it?"

I checked his face to make sure he meant it. When I was sure he did, I told them about Pensive Lady and Hobson's Choice, but especially about Loyal Brigand.

"You got to sit on him?" Sarah asked. "I don't believe it!"

"Ask Pop," I told her. "He'll tell you."

"What was that like?" Marty asked.

"High. Unbelievably high! So far up, the ground looks like it's in another world. He was sweaty from the race and tired, but mostly disappointed because he didn't win."

"Horses don't get disappointed," Sarah said.

"That's what you say. I know he was. You should have seen how hard he tried. Anyway, he would have won if he'd started inside the gate. That's for sure."

"Sounds like you had a pretty good birthday after all."

"It was."

"Who wants Root Beer Floats?" my mom said.

Everyone said me at the same time. Even my dad.

When we were in our room, Marty asked me about Ron again.

"He agreed with our numbers?" he asked.

"Yeah. Sort of."

"What's that mean?"

"He agreed. It's okay."

"What's okay? Either he did or he didn't. Which is it?"

"Both. But it's okay."

"How can that be? Come on, tell me. I'm sorry I wasn't there, but I want to take care of this. Remember? We want me to deal with it, not dad, right?"

"Right," I said. "But can't we just forget about it? It's okay. Really."

"Kurt? Do you want me to go get dad and ask him to ask you?"

"No."

"Then tell me. What happened?"

"He agreed with the numbers and the missed papers..."

"What missed papers?"

I told him about Mr. Duffy being a dead beat and that I'd stopped delivering to him and added Mr. Rothman instead and it was coming out the same even if Ron didn't know about it and thought he was charging me for missed papers. Marty shook his head .

"Will wonders never cease?" he laughed. "Good for you. But what else?"

"Well, he said we didn't subtract for the route bag and rubber bands."

"That's garbage," Marty said, raising his voice. "That's complete garbage. He overcharged you the first time. That's more than enough."

"He said he was sick of arguing about it with me, so he subtracted for three months in advance."

I took the piece of paper out of the money pouch and showed it to him. He looked at it and shook his head like he couldn't believe it. When he looked up, he looked so much like my dad it was scary.

"That bastard!" he said. "He cheated you out of sixteen-fifty? And he thinks he's going to get away with it? Never!"

I might as well have told my dad. He mumbled a few more things, then calmed down and went to brush his teeth. When he came back ready for bed, he messed my hair.

"Happy Birthday, kiddo," he said, "we'll take care of this tomorrow. I've got to get some sleep. Good night."

"Good night," I told him.

I had a hard time getting to sleep. When I finally did, I dreamed I did my route on Loyal Brigand.

At twelve thirty-five Marty came blasting around the corner on his bicycle from Beverly. He was wearing his Standard Station whites, the pants and shirt, and they were already smudged black from the tires he'd changed. He skidded to a stop next to the parkway where I was sitting waiting for Ron, the route bags, the rubber bands and the Red Rider all set to go. He had this look that made me think, brother, oh brother, we should just forget the whole thing. He looked around and was relieved to see the bundle hadn't been dropped off yet.

"Hi," he said. "I see I made it in time. No Ron yet, right?"

"Right," I said.

"I'll be back in a second," he said, "I'm gonna get a glass of milk. You want any?"

"No thanks."

He went into the house. When he came out, he stood on the porch drinking the milk. I could see he'd washed his face and hands and combed his hair.

"Where's mom and Sarah and Nick?" he called to me.

"Mom's downtown and left Nick with Sarah. She's doing something with the Oakhurst Irregulars at Hawthorne and took him with her."

"Like what?"

"I don't know. She never tells me. She kicked me out, remember?"

He shrugged. I heard Ron's truck coming down the street.

"Here he comes," I shouted to Marty.

Ron pulled to a stop by the curb, jumped out, grabbed a bundle and dropped it on the parkway.

"How's it goin'?" he said, but I could tell he didn't care and wasn't expecting an answer one way or the other.

Before I could answer, even if I'd wanted to, which I didn't, he'd already turned to get back in the truck.

"See ya."

He had the door open and one foot in.

"Hey! Wait a minute!" Marty called, coming down the walk.

Ron looked up at me, then realized it was Marty talking to him.

"Hey, Einstein. What's up?"

Marty was to the parkway. Ron still had one foot inside the cab and started to get the rest of the way in, so whatever he thought Marty had on his mind wasn't of much interest to him. He was ready to go and that was that.

"You owe Kurt some money. Let's take care of that before you go anywhere."

If I was guessing from the look on his face, Ron was thinking, are you kidding me? Not in a million years. But Marty came around the front of the pick up and stood there so Ron couldn't leave. He shook his head from side to side to let Ron know he wasn't moving until it was taken care of.

"Get out of the way before I run right over you," Ron said.

Marty put his hands on the hood.

"Move!" Ron shouted at him.

Marty just shook his head no.

Ron jumped out of the truck and charged around to the front and stood eyeball to eyeball with Marty, trying to scare him. The sleeves of Marty's Standard Station shirt, which had his name on it on the left side above the pocket, were rolled up to his elbows. I noticed the veins in his arms, then just his arms. They reminded me of Iyama Osaka's. They weren't as big and strong, but you could tell he used them for hard work. And he was taller than Ron, skinnier, but taller, so Ron had to look up at him.

"Listen, kid, you're bitin' off more than you can chew. Get out of the way and we'll forget about the whole thing. Got it?"

"Not until you pay him what you owe. Fork over the sixteen-fifty and then we'll forget about how you cheated him the first month. There's no way the bags should cost four dollars and the rubber bands a buck-fifty. I hear you're cheating all of your other delivery boys too. Does the Mirror know about that?"

"Get lost!" Ron said. He started back for the cab of the truck.

Marty came around right behind him.

"You're not going anywhere until you pay up!"

Ron spun around and smashed Marty in the mouth. He lost his balance and went down to one knee, blood coming out of his mouth. Ron started to turn back to the truck, but Marty grabbed his leg and wouldn't let go. Ron turned back and reached down and took a handful on his just combed hair and lifted him to his feet. He hit him in the stomach and Marty crumbled back down to his knee again. Ron was all set to finish him off with another hit, but I'd come off the parkway and dropped down behind him and grabbed a leg and bit him as hard as I could. He screamed and kicked me away, but by then Marty was back on his feet. When Ron turned to face him, out of nowhere, Marty brought a punch up under his jaw. It lifted Ron off the ground and he went down straight backwards, hitting the pavement and smacking his head sort of like John Dolan had at school. Marty didn't even look mad. His mouth was bleeding and his clothes were all twisted around and his hair was standing straight up and his fist was still balled up, ready to hit Ron again if he had to, but he was calm as could be. Ron got to his feet and took a swing at Marty, but it wasn't much of a punch. His eyes had a far away look, like he wasn't sure where he was, and Marty just pushed his arm away as it came towards him. Then he pushed Ron against the fender. Ron put one elbow on it to hold himself up.

"Sixteen-fifty," Marty said.

He held his fist close to Ron's face. Ron was trying to catch his breath and figure out where he was, but at the same time he reached into his pocket and put a bunch of money on the fender. Marty picked out sixteen-fifty and tossed the rest into the cab on the seat.

"Thank you," Marty said.

Ron sort of slithered back into the truck. He sat there behind the wheel with his head tipped back resting against the rear window. Finally, after about a minute, he sat up, pulled the door closed and drove off. Marty handed me the money.

"That's that," he smiled through a bloody mouth. "What's the matter?" he said, looking at me.

"Should I deliver these or do you think I'm fired?" I said, nodding at the bundle.

He smiled and put his hands on his hips, sort of like Pop.

"You go ahead and deliver. We'll see what we see. I've got to get back to the station."

He got on his bike and headed for Beverly. I guess it was better than if my dad had handled it, but it probably wasn't that much different. I folded the papers and delivered them. The good thing was I was much faster than usual. I suppose knowing I had the left over sixty-five cents from paying off the locks and the sixteen-fifty Ron tried to gyp me out of must have given me extra energy. The bad thing was Marty got arrested as soon as he got to the Standard Station.

By the time I got home from the route and put the bags and my bike away, it was only ten to three. Sarah and Nick were back but not my mom. Whatever the Oakhurst Irregulars had been doing, it tired Nick out because he'd fallen asleep on the living room floor listening to the radio with Sarah with his blanket pressed to his cheek. He wasn't exactly snoring, but something pretty close. I wasn't sure if I should tell her about Marty and Ron, even though I wanted to, because if she told my mom or dad, my dad might go after Ron too, and then we'd be right to the place me and Marty had been trying to avoid in the first place. Before I could tell her or not tell her, the phone rang.

"You get it," she told me. "I'm listening to this."

I went into the kitchen, which is where our phone was.

"Hello?"

"Kurt?"

"Marty?"

"Yeah. Is mom home?"

"Not yet."

I could hear him breathing but he didn't say anything. He sounded funny, like he was trying not to cry.

"What's wrong?" I asked him.

"I got arrested."

"What? What for?"

"What?" Sarah called from the living room.

"Ron. He called the police," Marty said.

"Marty's in jail," I called to her.

"What for?" she called back on her way to the kitchen.

"When's she coming home?" he said.

He sounded scared. Sarah was next to me.

"When's mom coming home?" I asked her.

"Five-thirty or six. In time for dinner, she said."

I looked at the clock on the stove. Three o'clock.

"Will they let you come home?" I asked him.

"Only if mom or dad come get me."

"What'd he say?" Sarah asked me.

"Only if mom or dad go get him," I told her.

Nick had woken up and come into the kitchen and stood next to Sarah. She whispered to him that Marty was in jail. At first his face pouted up like it didn't make sense or he couldn't understand what she was talking about, but as he got awake enough, he looked like he was going to cry, so I knew he got the idea.

"Do you know the number downtown?" he asked me.

I didn't, so I asked Sarah. She shook her head no.

"Neither of us do. Is it written down anywhere?"

"I don't think so," he said.

"What about Pop?" she said. "Would they let Pop get him?"

"What about Pop?" I asked him.

He was quiet for a long time. I knew he must be thinking if we had to get Pop into this my dad would go nuts for sure, because that's what I was thinking. On the other hand, if I was Marty I wouldn't want to be a jailbird the rest of my life. That's what he decided too.

"Is he home?" he asked me.

"I think so. His car was here a few minutes ago when I put my bike away."

"Let me ask them," he said.

I could hear him asking someone if his grandfather was okay. He told them we shared the duplex with Pop. The someone said, sure.

"He says okay. Would you ask Pop?"

"Sure. Stay on the phone with Sarah. I'll be right back."

I ran out to the front porch and over to Pop's side. Since the front door was open I could see through the screen door that he was in his easy chair reading the paper. It looked like another day where enough had been enough since he was home so early. I knocked on the screen door.

"Hey Pop, come here, it's important!" I called to him.

He got up carrying the paper with him.

"What's the matter? What's so important?"

He pushed the screen door open for me but I didn't go in.

"We have a big problem and we need you to help. Can you?"

He put his hands on his hips and snort-laughed, like what could be that important.

"Come in and tell me about it."

"There isn't time. Can you help us get Marty out of jail?"

"What? What in Christ's name are you talking about? Where's your mom and dad?"

"They're downtown and we don't have the phone number. Marty got in a fight with my routemaster who was cheating me out of money and got arrested. They'll let him out if you come get him."

His face went from the amused look, like nothing could be that important, to angry, but I wasn't sure about what. It could have been that he was being bothered with it when all he wanted to do was read the paper, or that my mom and dad should be taking care of it, especially since all of us were supposed to be mad at him since my dad was, or that Marty shouldn't be getting in trouble or maybe it was that Ron was a jerk and that made him mad. I was hoping it was that one. And I hoped he hadn't thought of one other thing, because I already had. It was my fault. I switched the locks and wanted the paper route and that's why Ron was a problem now. Marty was just trying to help me. And now he was in jail.

"Please, Pop."

"Of course. Let me get my shoes."

He sat on the ottoman and laced up his shoes and grabbed his keys and hat. I walked with him to the garage.

"You're not coming, Kurt. I'll take care of it."

He still seemed mad, and I still wasn't sure why, but it didn't matter much. I just wanted him to get Marty out of jail. After that, we'd all just have to go where things pushed us.

"Please, Pop, let me go with you."

"Yeah, okay. Marty will probably be glad to see one of you if your mom and dad aren't coming."

We got in the Oldsmobile and backed down the driveway.

"Hold on a second. I want to tell Sarah I'm going with you."

I popped out of the car and up our steps and into the living room.

"Is Pop gonna do it?" she asked me.

"Yeah, and I'm going with him."

"What'd he say?"

"Not much, but he's mad."

"Mad? Why?"

"I don't know. Could be a lot of things, but at least he's going. See you later."

I got back in the car and we headed for the Beverly Hill Police Department.

Marty was waiting, but not in jail. He was sitting outside the office of the Chief of the police. We'd gone up the stairs and talked to a policeman at the counter and he pointed to Marty. Pop went into the Chief's office. I sat next to Marty on a wooden bench. He didn't seem too upset. More thoughtful. Pensive.

"Are you okay?"

"Yeah. I'm fine."

"You're not scared?"

"Not any more. I was. I admit it, but not now."

"I'm sorry."

"What for? You didn't do anything."

"I switched the locks and took the route and that got Ron into things. It's all my fault."

I started to cry.

"I'm really sorry," I said.

He patted my hand.

"Hey. Really. It's not your fault. Don't cry, for pete'sake. Ron's a thief. Period. I'd do it again. I would."

He smiled at me, but he still looked like he was worried about something.

"What's the matter, then?"

"Well, besides having to call Pop, and Pop probably making dad feel like he failed at something and rubbing his face in it, and dad going nuts about that and me not using very good judgment, I was thinking getting arrested might keep a college from letting me in."

I was so shocked I couldn't speak. I felt this pounding in my chest like my heart was falling apart. He said it like he was just rolling it around in his head, maybe yes, maybe no, but it crashed on me like the end of the world. Just when I'd thought the whole lock business was over, it got worse than ever. I had a picture of all the tires he'd changed, all the odd jobs he'd been doing for so long, saving for college, and all of a sudden, it would be for nothing, and because of me. Pop and the Chief were shaking hands. Pop came out of the office with the Chief right behind him.

"I'm releasing you into the custody of your grandfather, but I expect you to show up for the arraignment next Monday. With one or both of your parents. Agreed?"

"Yes, sir," Marty said.

"You okay?" Pop asked Marty.

"I'm okay. Thanks for coming, Pop."

"Let's get out of here before he changes his mind," Pop whispered to us.

I got in the back seat and Marty rode up front with Pop, but no one said anything at all on the way home. When we got there, my mom and dad were on the porch waiting. Pop pulled into the driveway, but not down it, stopping just past the sidewalk so me and Marty could get out. My mom came running to Marty as he got out.

"Oh honey, are you okay?" she said.

"I'm fine," he said.

My dad came up and hugged him. Pop stood there watching. Over Marty's shoulder, he and my dad were looking at each other. Pop was shaking his head. That's all it took.

"What?!" my dad said, getting mad. "What now?"

Pop just shrugged, but his expression was telling my dad, this is what happens when you don't do things the way you should, the way I do, which was what Marty expected, and I was afraid of, and my dad had been hearing most of his life, I guess, because he went nuts.

"Say it! You're dying to say it. Go on, god damn it! Get it off your chest!"

"Dave," my mom said, trying to calm him down, "it's okay. Marty's home, that's what's important."

Nick and Sarah had come out on the porch and were watching. Nick took one look at my dad and started to cry. Sarah had this blank look, like she was too shocked to cry.

"And I wasn't there to get him. That's what he wants to say! Look at him! He's dying to say 'I told you so'. About something! About anything! God damn it, it never changes!"

Pop had a sad smile on his face and just shrugged again, like he didn't have to say anything. Which just made may dad madder. He turned on Marty.

"What the hell were you thinking? I gave you more credit than to do something so god damn stupid. Do you hear me? Do you?!"

When Marty didn't answer, he shook him by the shoulders. My mom tried to stop him but it was way too late. He'd gone past the place where you could talk to him. Once he went nuts, he was going to stay there for a while. If it was about money that was bad enough, but if it had anything to do with Pop or uncle Bernie or brothers fighting, that was the worst. If Nick and I got into even the smallest argument, and he heard us, he'd go nuts for sure.

"Answer me?! What the hell were you thinking? You think I've got time for this? What happened?"

Marty was taller than my dad, too big to be shaken like he was some kid my size, but Marty stood there with tears in his eyes saying he was sorry, getting shaken so hard his head was snapping back and forth. He wasn't crying and he didn't complain, tears just slipped out.

"Dave!" my mom shouted at him, "stop. You're hurting him!"

"God damn bastards! The whole bunch of you!" he growled, first looking at Marty, then me and then Sarah and even Nick. He threw up his hands, like it was so hopeless he didn't know what else to say or do.

Sarah and Nick were both crying now.

"It's my fault!" I yelled, crying, pulling at him. "Stop hurting Marty! Please! It's my fault!"

My dad looked at me like he'd never seen me before. His eyes were still crazy, but at least he'd snapped out of it enough to hear me.

"What are you talking about?" he yelled.

I was crying so hard I could hardly get it out, but I told him about Ron subtracting for the route bags and the rubber bands and then doing it again and for three months this time and Marty making him pay me back and that we didn't tell him because we were afraid he would have beat Ron up and gone to jail and it would have been more trouble that we didn't need but it ended up the same anyway, only Marty in jail, instead of him.

"It's all because of the locks and then the route and Marty trying to help me. I'm sorry. Don't blame Marty. And anyway, Ron started the fighting part. Not Marty."

I was hugging his leg.

"Please," I begged him.

My dad stood there perfectly still. It was like he had this on and off switch and first it was on and the next thing you knew it was off. He put one arm around Marty and held me to his leg with the other.

"I'm sorry, Marty. I didn't understand. I should have known better," he said, crying, big sobs choking his voice, "I'm sorry."

He hugged us tighter and I could feel his sobs vibrate through me.

"I'm proud of you both," he said. "I am. We'll deal with the court, but I'm proud of you for looking out for each other and trying to look out for me."

Then he looked at Pop, and the switch flipped back on.

"This is what brothers do!" he yelled. "This is what families do! They look out for each other! Can't you understand that? God damn you, can't you?"

Pop turned and started across the grass towards his side of the duplex. He looked like a dog that'd been yelled at, when they tuck their tail down and drop their head and walk away before you can yell at them some more. My dad was still crying. I was crying too, but I couldn't decide for who. I felt bad for Marty and my dad and Pop all together. I couldn't separate anything from anything else.

"Go inside, all of you. We'll talk about it some more later," my dad said to me and Marty. "Wait, dad, wait a minute," he said to Pop.

Marty and my mom and Sarah and Nick went in. I got as far as the porch and turned to see.

My dad caught up to Pop and put his hand on his shoulder. I heard him say he was sorry. He hugged him, but Pop just stood there, stiff, then put his hand on my dad's chest and pushed him away. He went inside, leaving my dad standing there. I was supposed to be inside and not see, but I did, and when my dad saw me, he just held up a hand, like he couldn't say anything and I should go in. He covered his face with his hands and started to sob, then began walking up the street.

"Go inside," he said as he passed. "Go on."

On Monday, the judge put Marty on a kind of probation where if he didn't get in any more trouble they'd forget about the whole thing. They'd seal up the records so no one would know and the colleges wouldn't ever find out and they'd let him in after all. I didn't get to go, partly because no one would let me or wanted me to, and also because I had to do the route, but Marty told me about it at dinner. It was the biggest relief of my life. My dad wasn't at dinner since he'd had to spend half the day in court and went back downtown 'til late. In fact, he wasn't home for dinner much at all, and I hardly saw him the rest of August because he'd leave too early and get home too late, trying to make the new line and sell it and deal with the deadbeats. Even though the whole thing only lasted twenty minutes once they finally got started, we had to pay a lawyer thirty-five dollars just for going to court and being there with Marty, and the guy hardly had to say a thing because the judge did most of the talking. The thirty-five bucks was bad news, okay, but I gave my mom the sixteen-fifty Marty had beaten out of Ron, so that helped. She gave me back one-fifty, so really, I only gave her fifteen. I didn't tell her, but as soon as I got the money from the movie, I was going to give her the other twenty. Easy come, easy go, as someone said. I didn't know who, but I'd heard it, and boy was he right.

The second biggest relief to come after Marty's fight with Ron was I didn't get fired but Ron did. My mom called the Daily Mirror Monday afternoon after court and talked to the boss of circulation. It didn't take her very long to convince him. I don't know how they broke the news to Ron, but by Wednesday, someone named Jingo was dropping off the papers. Jingo was kind of a wild man, but I liked him. His eyes looked like they were on fire, and he had this white hair that stood up like he'd put his finger in an electric socket, and he must have been close to Pop's age, but he acted younger and more alive and was friendly and told me no more using stories on subscription nights, just see if they want the paper or not, which was my story anyway, and no more charges for the route bags and rubber bands, and if someone didn't pay up when they were supposed to, I was supposed to tell him and he'd take care of it. And I wouldn't get charged for the papers at all until it was settled. Where was this guy all my life, I wondered. Anyway, I didn't plan on missing Ron one bit.

### *The Star Shopper*
## Wednesday-Thursday, August 8 & 9, 1951

When I delivered to Julie and Sharon on Jingo's first day they came down the walk and met me at the curb. They told me they were going to Carl's the next morning, on Thursday, for The Star Shopper Show and would I come.

"What's that?" I asked Julie.

"A show on television," Sharon said.

"We don't have one," I admitted. "But Pop does."

"No television?"

"Nope."

"Well," Julie said, "a man named Bill Welch has this television show where he goes to different grocery markets and they set up a camera and choose contestants from the crowd that gathers and they race through the store for fifteen minutes gathering up as much as they can into a cart. They try to team an adult with a child. At the end of the fifteen minutes, they ring up what's in the carts, and the team that has the most money's worth of groceries wins."

"What do you win?"

"The groceries! Or, if you want, a coupon for the amount they rang up."

"That's pretty neat."

"And you're on television," Sharon added, "and that can't hurt an actor now, can it?"

They both did this little excited dance, like they were sure they'd be chosen and couldn't wait.

"Wanna come? We need a kid." Julie said. "Please? We figure with you, we're a shoe-in."

"What time?"

"Ten. If you're coming, we thought we should be there twenty minutes early. Maybe if they see us before the show goes on, while they're setting up, they might be more likely to choose us," Julie said.

"How could they resist?" Sharon said.

"Sure. I could meet you at nine-thirty or nine-forty, okay?"

"Oh, would you? That's perfect."

"Sure. I'll see you tomorrow. Bye."

"Bye."

I took off on the Red Rider with both the free feeling from the bike and the floating on a cloud feeling too.

That night, I told Sarah and Nick about The Star Shopper Show being at Carl's, and me meeting there with Julie and Sharon from the route and the Love Nest movie, and asked them if they wanted to come see. Sarah had heard of the show and thought it would be fun, so the three of us were going to go together. The next morning, Thursday, when we went outside at nine-thirty, the whole Oakhurst Irregulars gang was waiting on the sidewalk. Most of them, anyway. Somehow they'd heard about it and decided to come along too. Jeff Schumur, Dick Goldsmith, Robbie Ganz, Donna Hooper, Megan, Allen, Wyatt, Sarah, and Nick, and even though he and Wyatt didn't count as Oakhurst Irregulars, that made nine kids that might be racing against me, and all of them except Nick and Donna and Wyatt were bigger. I'd sort of pictured me and either Julie or Sharon getting chosen and Sarah and Nick watching us race through the store getting stuff. Maybe one or two other kids that I didn't know, teamed up with one or two other grownups that I didn't know either. I never pictured that even if I got chosen, they might choose some other kid and grownup that I knew. All the way up Oakhurst and around the corner onto Lower Santa Monica and to the light at Doheny, the whole bunch of them were talking about getting chosen and what stuff they'd put in the cart to make sure they won. It wasn't the way I'd pictured it at all. They seemed to have it all figured out, knowing which aisle they'd go to first, then second and third, filling the cart up with as many expensive things as possible, even if you knew you'd never shop for them if you really had to eat the stuff. I'd never thought of that, either. In a way, it sort of seemed like cheating. It would ring up for a ton of money, and when you won, you'd just ask for the coupon instead of the groceries in your cart. It didn't seem fair, and I thought about turning around and going home, but on the other hand, it was pretty smart, and besides, I'd told Sharon and Julie I'd go, so I did.

When we crossed Doheny, I could see there was a huge crowd gathered in the parking lot, spilling out onto the sidewalk. On the window next to the front door, there was a sign saying to use the parking lot, liquor store, side. The front door was blocked with two big television cameras on wheels, and cables, and workers settings things up and some people who didn't want to wait with the crowd, or maybe just wanted to hang around closer to The Star Shopper guy and his helpers. Or maybe they'd just come to do some shopping and found this big mess instead and were waiting to see if they could go in and buy what they'd come for. When we got to the corner of the building, I could see the whole parking lot was filled, not with cars, but people, kids and grownups. Dozens and dozens of them. Maybe more than a hundred. All of a sudden, the idea of actually getting chosen, seemed pretty ridiculous, to say the least. All the sneaky plans the Oakhurst Irregulars were dreaming up to win made me smile to myself. I bet all these other people had their own sneaky plans to win, and were sure they would. I was glad I'd come. This was like a circus and all these people, these kids and the grownups too, were clowns for the television, only they didn't know it. I was too, but at least I knew it.

"Kurt! Over here!"

It was Julie and Sharon. They tried to wave to me, but I could see it wasn't easy because they were being bumped around by the crowd surrounding them. Everyone wanted to make sure they got in the store and had the best chance possible to get chosen, so they pushed and shoved trying to get or stay close to the door. Sarah and the Oakhurst Irregulars were squeezing into the crowd. Nick and Wyatt and Donna Hooper stayed on the sidewalk, close to me, since I was the oldest one around now. Julie had worked her way over to us.

"Boy! What a scene!" she said. "This is worse than an open call!" she laughed.

She noticed Nick and Donna and Wyatt standing there with me. She gave them a long look.

"Who're these guys?" she said, gently brushing at Nick's hair with her hand.

"That one's my little brother, Nick. That's Wyatt and Donna. They live on our block."

"Is your mom here? Is theirs?"

"No."

"Who's watching them?"

"No one," I shrugged. "Me, I guess. My big sister and her friends went in there," I said, pointing to the crowd.

Julie may not have seen which one Sarah was, or known who her friends were, but she could see there were a ton of kids all over the place, bigger and older than me and Nick and Wyatt and Donna, most of them about eleven or twelve or thirteen. Julie took a look at me and Nick and Wyatt and Donna.

"Hmm," she said, looking at the crowd. "I've got an idea."

She waved until Sharon saw her, then motioned for her to come. Behind us, one of the two cameras had been rolled onto the sidewalk and was pointed at a sign that said The Star Shopper Show, held by one of the show's workers. Another guy that was dressed up in gray pants and a dark blue sports coat had a microphone and began talking quietly. As he spoke, the worker took the sign away and then the camera was looking at him and Carl and Jan.

"We're here today with Carl and Jan Harvey, owners of Carl's market, at Doheny and Melrose. Your Star Shopper host, Mr. Bill Welch is about to address the crowd that's gathered here for today's show. Let's listen in and watch!"

Right then, the door to the liquor store opened and the Star Shopper guy stood there while another of his helpers waved his arms and kept shouting for everyone to be quiet. It took a long time before the people at the back of the crowd even knew he was there and even longer before they got quiet enough for him to tell them anything.

It took Sharon a lot of squeezing and twisting, but she made it to the sidewalk.

"What?" Sharon said, out of breath, when she got to us. "Now we're out of position. Look. We'll never get back there!"

"Good," Julie said. "Sharon, meet Nick and Wyatt and Donna. Nick is Kurt's brother. The others are neighbors."

Sharon smiled and said hello. She frowned at Julie for making her give up a good spot to come meet some kids. Julie smiled at her.

"Take a good look," she told Sharon.

Sharon took another look, but didn't know why she should. Wyatt and Donna were standing there watching the crowd, but looking like they were lost. Nick might have felt a little lost, but he hadn't taken his eyes off of Julie unless it was to look at Sharon. He had that Nick look. He wasn't going to speak, but he seemed on his way to figuring something out. He was barefoot and wearing tan shorts and a tan pullover sweatshirt, both of them washed so many times they were closer to white. His hair kept falling back across his forehead. I didn't know when he'd last had a haircut. Me either. It wouldn't have been at Raleigh's Barbershop anytime recently, because he charged pretty much, so when we were broke, my mom did it, only I couldn't remember when the last time that was. Sharon smiled.

"You're a genius," she told Julie.

"We'll just stand here with these guys, away from the crowd. Kurt in front of one of us, Nick in front of the other. If that doesn't get us noticed and chosen, nothing will. Is that okay with you guys?" Julie asked us.

Nick didn't say anything, but he shifted his eyes to me. I leaned over and explained it to him.

"They're actors and want to get seen on television. Get it?"

He shook his head no.

"If they get chosen for The Star Shopper Show, they'll be on television. So will we. It might help them get acting jobs. If they have a cute kid with them, they have a better chance of being chosen. Get it now?"

He nodded yes.

"So, is that okay?" I asked him.

He stood there thinking about it. Finally, he nodded yes again. He pulled me down to whisper, but he kept his eyes on Sharon.

"If I'm with her," he said.

"Okay."

I turned to Julie and Sharon.

"He'll do it," I said, "if it's with Sharon."

They both laughed.

"Men!" Julie said.

"It's a deal," Sharon said.

The Star Shopper helper had finally gotten the crowd quiet enough for Bill Welch to tell everyone the rules. He was younger than Pop and older than my dad. He wore dress pants and a white shirt and tie and his sports jacket looked like a checker board, except it was blue and white, not black and white. His hair was wavy, part brown and part gray, and slicked back. He wore glasses with black frames, and when the lenses reflected the sky it made his eyes disappear and turn into circles of bright light. All the crowding around had been for nothing, because he was going to choose out here in the parking lot. Anyone not chosen could come into the store to watch, or watch through the front windows if there wasn't enough room inside. If you were a grownup, he said, and had a kid with you, you should stand together. If you didn't, you should find one in the crowd and pair up. Ten pairs would be chosen for the contest. You could go anywhere in the store and put anything you wanted in the cart for fifteen minutes. No pushing or shoving other teams out of your way. If you had to be served, or if two teams were after the same item on the same shelf, they'd have to take turns. You couldn't just stand there and take every box of expensive chocolates if another team wanted some too. You'd take one, then them, then a third team if they were there too, or back to the first if there were only two. You could pile stuff up, but you couldn't hold it on, so if the cart got so full things were falling off, you were done and that was that. At the end, they'd ring it up and the cart with the most money's worth of stuff won. You could either have what was in the cart or get a coupon for that many dollars. The coupon would go to the adult if they were related to the kid, or split between them if they just paired up to be a team. All the losing teams would get a five dollar coupon just for being chosen and trying. He didn't say whether it was five dollars for each team, or each person in the team, but I thought it didn't matter that much since the whole thing was supposed to be for the fun of it.

"Does everyone understand?" Bill Welch asked.

Lots of people yelled yes. He held his hand to his ear and tried again.

"I can't hear you! Does everyone understand?"

This time the crowd roared YES!, and he smiled and held his hand to his ear again.

The crowd yelled even louder, YES, YES, YES!!! until he seemed satisfied.

"Okay, then. A few tips," he said. "If the child pushes the cart, the adult can reach the higher shelves; on the other hand, a kid may not manage the driving chores that well, and that can create problems. And fun! It's up to you. But once you decide on who pushes the cart and who selects the items, you can only change back once, no back and forth," he warned, shaking his finger at the crowd like he was scolding them. "Okay, is everyone ready for the selection?"

Another huge yes came from the crowd, but before he said or did anything else, he held up his hands asking the crowd for quiet. He stood quietly like that and passed his eyes over just about every face there. His eyes came our way, swept over us, and kept going. The crowd was restless and wanted to get started, but he took his time. Watching him, I could tell that he was making a map in his head of all the faces while he was taking that look. And even though he made a big deal in the next few minutes out of trying to decide who to choose, like it was painful and killing him to make up his mind, I think he knew who he was going to choose right after that first long look.

"Okay!" he shouted suddenly, "does anyone want to volunteer?!"

The place went nuts. Grownups and kids shouting and yelling, I do! and choose me! or we do! Over here! He just smiled and held his arm out ready to point to somone, but not doing it, letting the crowd get wilder. Even though the contest hadn't started yet, the camera behind us on the sidewalk had been putting the whole thing on television. If we had a set at home, it was probably on it right now. I wondered if Pop was watching. When it looked like the crowd couldn't get any crazier, he pointed to Jeff Schumur and some lady that wasn't his mom. Jeff and the lady jumped up and down holding each other. That drove the crowd even crazier, because now there were only nine spots left. Bill Welch swung his arm and outstretched pointing-finger this way, then that, and stopped at Megan and a young guy who couldn't have been more than twenty. Bill Welch motioned for them to come up through the crowd. He picked another pair then another and another. Julie and Sharon looked a little disappointed like their plan hadn't worked, and when he picked two more pairs, it looked hopeless. But sure enough, he turned our way. He turned off his smile replaced it with a look of surprise or maybe shock.

"Who's that over there?" he said. "How could I have missed them?!"

The crowd followed his look. One of the cameras rolled around so it could look at Julie and Sharon from the side. I couldn't tell if me and Nick were even in the picture. Julie and Sharon smiled and waved at Bill Welch, but they didn't go crazy. Julie was standing behind me and had her hands on my shoulders. Sharon was holding Nick's hand..

"I think those two beautiful girls and their little boys are are eighth and ninth pairs!" he said.

"Thank you!" Julie said.

"You're quite welcome," Bill Welch said. Then, "And now, for our last pair."

He made a big show of looking the crowd over, up and down, left and right, front and back, but his eyes had found what they were looking for and when I followed them, parked on Rangley, the side street at the bottom of the parking lot, was the Cadillac convertible with the DOLAN FOR MAYOR sign on it. I hadn't seen them there, but if I had one, I would have bet a spare fiver Bill Welch had. The chauffer was holding the door open and J. T. Dolan, Kevin Doyle in his fancy army clothes, and John Dolan, from my school, had just gotten out. They stood there leaning against the side of the car until J. T. Dolan sort of pushed Kevin to one side and John to the other so they weren't blocking the DOLAN FOR MAYOR sign. The camera behind us had swiveled around to follow Bill Welch's look. When I turned to see that, I also saw that Big Max was leaning against the corner of the building, his thick forearms folded across his chest, the soggy chunk of cigar in the corner of his mouth. The frizzy skirt of hair around the sides of his head was even frizzier than usual. He was shaking his head, speaking to Carl and Jan and Raleigh, from Raleigh's Barber Shop, who was standing there in his white barber shirt watching the whole crazy thing. When we had enough money, which we used to, that's where we got our haircuts before my mom started cutting it. It was a few buildings down Doheny from Rangley. Raleigh sort of reminded me of my uncle George with sandy red-brown hair and about the same size and quiet like him. He'd been in the war too and when he cut your hair, you could see the tattoo on his arm. He never talked about the war, but when some of the men in his shop did, and if they asked him something about it, he'd just smile and say, I really wouldn't know about that, and keep cutting.

"That sonofabitch don't miss a trick, does he? Shows up here and all of a sudden he's a man of the people. What a crock," Max said.

"It's a million bucks worth of free publicity for his campaign," Carl said. "If the camera shows his sign for even half a minute, he's way ahead."

"He's going to keep that poor kid of his in uniform ten years after the war's been over," Jan said.

"Only four more to go," Raleigh smiled.

"You two!" Bill Welch said, pointing. "The highly decorated, and no doubt, brave defender of our Liberty and his little companion there! Come on forward!"

Then, he acted surprised, like he'd just noticed J. T. Dolan, even thought the letters on the DOLAN FOR MAYOR sign had to be a foot high.

"Oh my! Look who's here! It's our very own councilman and candidate for Mayor, Mr. J. T. Dolan! It's an honor to have you here this morning...your Honor, if I may be a little so forward looking!"

J. T. Dolan smiled a fake embarrassed smile and waved at Bill Welch and the crowd, like they'd all come to see him. Max couldn't stand it.

"Good Christ," he said to Carl, "the whole god damn thing's a set up."
Carl and Jan looked at each other.

"I think he's right," she told Carl.

"If I'd know that, I'd never agreed to let them use the store, even if it is good advertising for us. What's Bill Welch and The Star Shopper got to do with Dolan?"

"Money," Big Max said, "simple as that. I'd make book on it."
He was shaking his head as he went back in.

"Of course you would," Jan said.

Kevin Doyle and John Dolan came through the crowd. J. T. Dolan stood next to his sign waving to everyone. Especially the camera.

The rest of the crowd had calmed down now that they knew they weren't going to get chosen and they let us pass through to the door without squeezing or bumping or pushing, in fact they were pretty good sports about it, and opened up a path so we just walked in. The camera that had been on the sidewalk had been rolled back through the front door and was set up near the check out tables so it could see us come through from the liquor store. Max was already back at his counter reading the racing paper. He watched as we all trooped through his part of the store. He just grunted and kept reading. He wasn't going to sell much of anything until The Star Shopper Show was over and done with, and he knew it. When we got inside the grocery part of the store, the other camera had already been set up along the far side of the vegetable tables where it had a good view of most of the aisles from front to back, so if the one closer to the front door couldn't see the teams, it would. They already had ten carts ready and waiting. They safety-pinned paper numbers to our shirts. Me and Julie both got eights pinned to us because we were team eight, Nick and Sharon team nine, Jeff Schumur and the lady he was with were one and Megan and the guy she was with were two. Kevin Doyle and John Dolan were ten. Kevin was smoking and fidgeting. His eyes were getting that crazy Kevin Doyle look, like he was going to win no matter what anyone else did, but at least it wasn't the crazy-mean look. Just crazy. It was hard to tell what John Dolan was thinking about. I knew he'd seen me, because I saw him point me out to Kevin, touching the back of his head at the same time, which was something I figured I didn't need, Kevin knowing I'd cracked his brother's head open. I waved, but he didn't wave back or say hi. Then again, after the crack on his head, I didn't expect he would. On the other hand, he'd started it, so I figured we were even and he could at least say hello. He didn't seem to want to stand too close to Kevin, and who could blame him, but he had his own crazy-eyed look, like he was getting ready to beat someone up, and that's all that was on his mind. Maybe that's it, I thought. Me. Maybe since he's seen me here he's planning to get even now. That would sure take the fun out of the whole Star Shopper business. No, probably not, I thought. Not with so many people around. Besides, it would be bad publicity for his dad trying to be mayor. But seeing him and Kevin Doyle together made me kind of nervous. But since I wasn't afraid of John any more, if he started a fight it was going to be his problem as much as mine. What the heck, maybe they were just here to have fun too. But with Kevin and John on the same team, I had the feeling the rest of us were wasting our time. Sharon was trying to convince Nick to take his hand out of his pocket so both hands would be free to push the cart. He was so small he wouldn't able to reach much, so they were better off with him pushing and her taking things off the shelves. He took the hand out, but probably not for good.

"Do you want to push or take things from the shelves?" Julie asked me.

"I'll push," I told her.

Sarah and Dick Goldsmith had taken charge of Wyatt and Donna Hooper and had made it into the store along with another twenty-five or thirty people from the crowd. The rest were out on the Doheny sidewalk looking through the windows. Sarah was trying to remind Megan about their secret sneaky plan to get expensive stuff, but without giving it away to anyone else, except for Jeff Schumur, who already knew.

"Remember," Sarah called to her, "the you-know-what stuff!"

Megan shook her head like she knew, but she looked so nervous I thought she was just pretending to remember, because the more Sarah said, the more nervous she got, and I think she just wanted Sarah to leave her alone to be nervous without any help.

Jeff Schumur had a smile on his face like he'd already won. He was stretching and jumping up and down like a runner before a race. He was big for his age, fat really, and not a guy who would run anywhere unless he was being chased, but he was loosening up like this was the Olympics. The lady with him watched with a friendly, calm smile on her face. She reminded me of Mrs. Gunther, except younger. If I were deciding for their team, I don't know which one I'd have push or grab. If she did the pushing, I could see she was going to take her time going down the aisles, like she was just doing the week's grocery shopping, with that nice smile on her face. Jeff would be pulling things off the shelf the length of an aisle waiting for her to catch up. If he pushed, he'd probably run her over trying to get to the next aisle while she took her time picking and choosing.

Kevin was going to push the cart. He already had his hands wrapped around the handle and was all set to go. John Dolan would grab and toss and they'd probably fill the basket before any of the rest of us got out of our first aisle. Most of the other teams were smiling and laughing and looked like they were there for the fun of it and going to have a good time no matter how they did.

"Is everyone ready?!" Bill Welch asked.

We all said yes.

"Team one? Are you ready?" he asked.

"Yes!" Jeff answered.

"Team two?"

"Yes," the guy with Megan answered.

It went on like that through all the numbers.

"Grab your carts! On your marks! Get set!"

He paused. I could see his lips sounding out one, two three, four, then he shouted, "GO!" and we were off. It was a little like the races at Hollywood Park, the horses anxious to go, and as soon as the bell rings, they all crowded together and bumped into each other trying to get to the front, except here it was carts banging into each other and getting jammed up so no one could move. It was fun and kind of funny at the same time.

Jeff Schumur knew exactly what he wanted to do and started for the meat counter, but his partner had wandered down the closest aisle and was looking over stuff on the shelves from high to low. She took reading glasses from her purse and put them on and reached to get something, looked at it, I guess, checking the price. Jeff called to her.

"This way! Come on!" he yelled.

She looked at him, her hand on her chin, wondering if she should take the item in her hand or put it back before going with him.

"Come on!" he begged her.

Julie told me, "Let's go to the Foreign Foods, over there," she said, pointing. "They have Russian Caviar. It's horribly expensive!"

"Good idea," I said.

I pushed the cart. When we crossed in front of the camera near the check out tables, she turned and smiled. She looked at me and winked. When we got there, Kevin Doyle and John Dolan were clearing the shelf.

"Our turn," Julie said.

Kevin ignored her, blocking me from pushing the cart past them, while John kept taking stuff from the shelves and filling up their cart.

"Excuse me," Julie said. "It's our turn."

"In a minute," Kevin said, leaning on his cart, taking the cigarette out of his mouth, then putting it back.

By then, John had pretty much cleared the shelf and he and Kevin raced down the aisle headed for what I guessed was a date with Jeff and the nice lady and Carl at the meat counter. Meat was one of the Oakhurst Irregulars sneaky plans.

"What a jerk!" Julie said.

"You can say that again."

"Do you know him?"

"He lives across the street. He's kind of nuts."

"He's rude, that's for sure. Oh well. Let's see what's left."

She was picking and choosing and putting things in the cart.

"They missed a lot of the most expensive things," she smiled. "Poetic justice!"

I could hear an argument coming from in back at the meat counter. Over the other voices, I could hear one, and it sounded like Carl's. He was telling someone, and if I had another spare fiver, I would have bet it was Kevin, he had to take turns, probably with Jeff and the lady. I'd thought the meat counter was a good idea too when I heard the Oakhurst

Irregulars talking about it, but when Bill Welch said you'd have to take turns with whoever else was where you were, it would just even out, so it didn't seem like such a great idea after all. Julie and I rounded the corner of our Foreign Food aisle and could see back to the meat counter and sure enough, Kevin and John and Jeff and the lady were already fighting it out and Carl was shouting at Kevin to wait his turn.

"Let's skip the meats," Julie said. "Any ideas?"

I looked in our cart. We only had a few things in it. The wire floor wasn't even covered. Some of the other teams weren't looking for the most expensive things they could find, they were just filling theirs up with bread and mustard and cereal and cheese and ordinary groceries, but lots and lots of it, and their carts were nearly full.

Because he was so short, Nick had to reach up over his head for the handle and it made steering hard. I saw him start out one way and veer off another, banging into the shelves on each side of an aisle, like the Bumper Cars at the Santa Monica Pier. Sharon thought it was pretty funny, and laughed about it, but after he'd also crashed into a few other teams, she'd decided to avoid the crowded aisles and more banging together of carts. Instead, they stayed up near the candy counter, and Nick pointed to all his favorites and Sharon took whole boxes of Tootsie Rolls and Wrigley's Gum and Tootsie Pops and Ju-Ju Bees and put them in their cart. Nick had a huge smile on his face as the candy piled up in front of him. They were right in front of the camera the whole time, so Sharon was happy to stay there and let him choose as much as he wanted.

"Any ideas?" Julie said again. "We're running out of time."

Everywhere I looked, some other team was already there grabbing stuff, or waiting their turn to grab. Kevin Doyle and John Dolan were tossing a few more items in their cart, but they'd pretty much filled it with meat and the Foreign Food aisle stuff and were just using up the rest of the time topping it off. Kevin saw me and gave me a smile. He was pretty sure he and John were going to win. They looked at me, then each other and pretended to click glasses together, like at the deWitt Gallery when they made the toast with ginger ale instead of Champagne. That's what made me think of it.

"Let's go this way," I said.

I raced the cart down the ramp into the liquor store. Big Max looked up from his paper, sort of surprised.

"The contest's in there," he said, nodding at the main part of the store.

"They said 'anything from anywhere', right?" I asked Julie.

"Right!" she said.

"The expensive wine's up there," I said, pointing to the shelf Max had told Norma about for when she got an Oscar. "Get as many bottles as you can reach."

"Hey, just a damn minute," Max said, coming from behind the counter.

He came towards me, but when he passed the ramp to the store, he saw Kevin Doyle and John Dolan pushing their cart to the check out table to ring up their stuff, and so did I.

"Here," he said, "use this."

He put a wooden stepping stool in front of the very good stuff shelf so Julie could reach higher and get it.

"Be careful with those," Max smiled, "they cost an arm and a leg."

Julie went up and down over and over, bringing two or three bottles each trip. Our cart was filling up. It could have held even more, but the next thing we heard was Bill Welch yelling time was just about up.

"One minute!" he shouted.

He started counting down, fifty-nine, fifty-eight, fifty-seven, and one by one the teams made they're way back to the check out tables to be rung up. Kevin and John's cart was first in line. When me and Julie came up the ramp with the cart full of wine bottles, he was going from seven to six to five to four to three to two to one and then shouted to stop.

"Time's up my friends. Bring your carts to the front of the store!"

Max stood leaning against the jamb at the top of the ramp, his arms folded again, nodding towards me and Julie's cart, smiling at Carl and Jan.

"Hey!" Kevin complained, "they can't get liquor!"

"That's not fair!" John said.

"Anything anywhere in the store, right?" Julie said to Bill Welch.

He had a funny look on his face, like he was trapped.

"Well....I...don't know...I suppose....it's never come up..."

"It's part of the store," Max said from the jamb. "Like it or not."

"It's part of the store, alright," Carl agreed, "always has been."

"All in all, I have to agree," Bill Welch said smiling to the camera. "Let's ring 'em up and see where we stand, shall we?"

Kevin's face went from regular crazy to crazy-mean just like that. He whispered something to John and pointed. I watched John go outside to Doheny and push through the crowd that was still on the sidewalk. He went to the Cadillac, which had pulled around the corner and was parked now right in front. The big DOLAN FOR MAYOR sign was ready for the camera to see it some more. John was telling his father something.

"What!" J. T. Dolan shouted.

It was muffled, but I could hear it over everything else.

"How could you be so stupid?"

He stood with his hands on his hips leaning forward towards John, more angry than he'd been in the Principal's office. I thought he was going to hit him. If there hadn't been a crowd of maybe-voters watching, I bet he would have. Kevin lit another cigarette and watched. He seemed to calm down.

"You're both goddamn useless!" Dolan was shouting, throwing up his hands and getting into the car.

John stood there on the sidewalk, not knowing what to do. His father yelled at him to get in, and when he did, the car drove off in a hurry. I sort of felt sorry for Kevin, standing there all by himself in his fancy army clothes. At least it wasn't a long walk home.

Max was smiling as he went back down the ramp into the liquor store.

When they finished ringing up, Julie and I had a hundred and fifteen dollars worth of stuff, mostly the wine. Kevin and John had seventy-six dollars and forty-two cents. Jeff Shumur and the lady had forty-five something and the others had less than that. Since we won, me and Julie got to talk with Bill Welch in front of the camera. He seemed to like her, and kept talking to her for a long time, and when she said she was here with her friend, Sharon, and they were both actors, he invited her to come talk too. They were on televison for a pretty long time, because Bill Welch let them hand out the five dollar coupons to everyone on all the other teams. Five bucks for both guys on a team, it turned out. Kevin left before he got his and John's.

When I got home, a little before one, Jingo had already left the bundle on the parkway. I got the Red Rider, the route bags and rubber bands and started folding. I was about half done when Kevin came out and sat on his front steps and lit a cigarette. I kept folding. The Thursdays were fatter than every other day except the Sundays, and I was using two rubber bands, so I concentrated on that.

"Pretty neat trick," he called across the street.

When I looked up at him, he didn't seem mad, but I didn't say anyting back and kept folding.

"The wine," he said.

He kept smoking and watching me.

"Got the old man in an uproar, you did," he said. "He was counting on me and Johnny winning and getting a little more TV time for the campaign. That was the plan, okay, but you sure fixed that. You can bet ol' Johnny's gettin' ridden pretty hard."

He still didn't seem mad, not really, but his voice had a different sound than when he said, neat trick, so just in case, I decided I'd deliver his paper at the end of the route instead of the beginning, so maybe he wouldn't be around. I took a paper over to George's place dropped it on his step. I rang his bell, but he didn't answer. I was hoping he'd be home. Since he wasn't, I decided maybe I should give Kevin time to finish his smoke, so I sat on George's step and unfolded the paper and read the front page. There was a lot of stuff about Korea and drafting 41,000 more soldiers and something about a boy they thought got lost on a freight train but was really just hiding in a lumber yard near the train tracks and some Girl Scouts that got killed by lightening on a church camping trip. You could ruin the whole day just reading the paper. When I'd read most of it, I went to the front of the Courtyard and peeked around the corner. Kevin wasn't there anymore so I folded the paper back up and left it on the step and went back to my bike and took off for Beverly.

When I tossed the paper for Julie and Sharon, their front door wasn't open and I couldn't hear any music, so they probably weren't there. I was sort of hoping to see them and talk about The Star Shopper Show, but no luck, so I just buzzed through the route thinking about how happy my mom would be when I gave her the Carl's Market coupon for fifty-seven fifty, my half of our cart's money's worth. When I came down Oakhurst, Norma was in the front yard with Snowball.

"Hi," I said.

"Hi, sweetie! Wanna play with me and Snowball?"

"Sure, but just for a little while. I've got a few more papers to deliver."

I took her and Shelly's paper into the yard and dropped it on the bottom step. While we took turns tossing the ball with the bell for Snowball, I told her about The Star Shopper Show and Julie and Sharon getting on television.

"That's wonderful," she said. "It's bound to help them get noticed. As a matter of fact, Joe mentioned the dark haired one...."

"Julie," I said.

"Julie. He might contact her."

I was going to say, what about Sharon, but I didn't. Like Joseph at the Hot Dog Stand said, things go where they go and you just have to make the best of it. At least she got on television.

"I'd better finish up," I said.

"See you later. Maybe at the Hot Dog Stand tomorrow?"

"Sure," I said. "I've been there most mornings but I haven't seen you. How come?"

"Since we wrapped on Love Nest, I've been sleeping late. Getting caught up. But I'm supposed to finish reading Gentlemen Prefer Blondes. It's a wonderful script. God, I hope I get it!"

"I bet you will," I said. "See you later."

"Bye."

I tossed the papers for Kenny Lester, Mr. Rothman, Rathbone and rode down the street and into our driveway just off the sidewalk and parked the bike. I took the last paper out of the bags and crossed the street. Miriam was in her window. I saw her and she saw me but neither of us waved. I walked down the driveway and tossed the paper on the back porch. It sort of whapped against the back door. Almost as fast as I turned to go, the door opened and Kevin stood there like he'd been waiting the whole time.

"God damn it," he said, "why don't you see if you can knock the god damn door down?"

"Sorry," I said.

I turned to go.

"Hold on, buddy. That's not the end of it. Get over here!"

"What?" I said, not moving.

"Get your ass over here," he said pointing at the porch, "and try that again. This time, without trying to wake the dead. Okay?"

I went up the stairs and picked up the paper. The ashtray on the railing was full of ashes and cigarette butts and there was smoke coming up from one. He had a new cigarette in his mouth, like ususal, but he smelled bad again, and not just the cigarettes. His eyes looked funny too, sort of mean, sort of crazy, but sort of sleepy or dizzy or something, and angry on top of everything else. I bent down and put the paper gently at his feet. Before I could stand up, he grabbed the back of my t-shirt and lifted me back to standing. He put his face close to mine. The cigarette smoke made my eyes burn.

"The old man's really not happy about this morning," he said, "not happy at all. I think we should give him a call and you can tell him how sorry you are. You're always sorry, aren't you?"

He pulled me inside. The back door was to a little room with a water heater, sort of like ours. He pushed me through ahead of him to a dark hallway and then left, into his bedroom. It was sort of dark too, but not completely, because even with the shades down, the light that came through from one window that faced the back yard, and another that faced the house next door towards Beverly Boulevard, filled the room with a dirty yellow-gold color. I didn't see a phone. The smell was everywhere and I supposed that was what was making me dizzy. He pushed the door closed. When I told him at Whalen's that I was tired of being afraid of him and wasn't going to be any more, I thought it was true. But inside my head I was afraid of him again, more than ever. I didn't want to cry and make him get crazier, but little sobs were getting close to coming out, so I squished them down, like holding in hiccups. He sat down on the edge of his bed.

"Come sit down," he said, patting the bed next to him, "right here."

He was smiling, like we were supposed to be friends. I shook my head no.

"Come on. We'll figure out what you're going to tell the old man. You don't have to be afraid."

I was looking down at the floor, but keeping an eye on him at the same time. It was a wood floor and there was a long skinny rug on it next to the bed. The floor and the rug were dirty with cigarette ashes because next to the bed there was a table with an ashtray that was so full of butts and ashes, it was spilling over onto everything else. The bed wasn't made and the sheets weren't white any more.

Tears were leaking out and plopping down and were mixing with the cigarette ash making it a worse mess. I hoped he wouldn't notice and get mad because of that too. The room seemed like it was getting smaller and smaller and he'd be able to reach me without even getting up no matter where I was, but I backed up anyway, as slowly as I could, hoping he wouldn't notice that either, until my back was against the door. He just stared at me. He crushed his cigarette out in the ashtray, spilling more of what was already there at the feet of a statue of a man in a long robe. It was about a foot tall and looked like it was made out of ivory and the base was brass, I thought.

"Come here," he said. "Come on."

I shook my head no.

"Get over here!" he yelled, his face suddenly angry, and before I knew it, he'd come off the bed and grabbed my hand and pulled me away from the door. He sat back down on the edge of the bed with me right in front of him. He let go of my hand and smiled, not angry anymore.

"Nice belt," he said.

I wondered where George was. Maybe with Shelly someplace.

"Let me see it."

When I didn't move he reached out and unfastened it. The extra long part, past the hole Marty had punched for me, dangled down close to my knees.

"I want to go home," I said, sort of in a whisper.

He was playing with the silver things on the belt and I wasn't sure if he'd heard me.

"You do, do you?" he said without looking up, "Well, then, sure. Why not?"

For a minute, I thought he meant it, but when he looked at me, I could see in his eyes it was a lie. I was getting dizzy and could feel my heart banging and I wanted to yell for someone to help me but I just stood there afraid to move, afraid to breathe, afraid until I didn't think I could get any more afraid. But I was wrong. He started to pull my pants down. I tried to hold onto them, but he bent my fingers away and they dropped down on top of my sneakers. Inside my head I was starting to scream. I tried to keep it in because it would just make him crazier. He kept a hold on my hands. Behind him, on the wall over his bed, was a picture of a man with a halo around his head, the same man as the statue. He had a sad smile on his face, like he knew how scared I was and wanted to help, but couldn't. No one could. Kevin pulled on my hands and forced me down onto the dirty rug and held me there, his hand in the middle of my chest, his knees on either side of me. The screaming started to come out so he put his hand over my mouth. I was kicking and wiggling but I couldn't get free. I bit his hand.

"Oww! God damn you!"

He slapped me. I saw his hand coming, but I barely felt it. I was there and not there.

"I want to go home," I begged him, crying, "please, just let me go home. I'm sorry about the locks and the wine...the paper banging, please...I want to go home, please, let me go home now."

He reached to unbuckle his belt. I was getting so dizzy that keeping my eyes open was making the room feel like it was spinning. I wanted my dad. Or Marty. Or Maurice, or George. Someone. Anyone to come. I wanted the door to open and someone to come pull him off, someone to help me. To save me. Where were they? They said they'd make him leave me alone! They promised! Why wouldn't anyone come? I knew no one was home at our house, that no one was around, that no one knew where I was anyway, but still, someone should come. I kept thinking they'd come anyway, someone would come and find me. But no one did. The noise inside my head was going to split it open if I didn't let it out.

I started to scream out loud again and Kevin pushed his hand against my mouth again. I was going to scream and scream until someone came or I couldn't scream any more.

"Shut up! Shut up" he said. "I can't think!"

I thought it was Kevin, but it didn't sound like him, and it wasn't. It was Max.

"If you scream, he's going to kill you. Don't you know that? Stop it! Calm down."

"I can't! I'm afraid," I cried, still wiggling to get free.

"Stop wiggling! I'm not going to hurt you," Kevin said, "just lay still. You don't have to be afraid."

I kept wiggling and screaming. Kevin pushed his hand harder against my mouth.

"Stop it!" Kevin yelled.

I kept twisting and turning and screaming. Kevin put his hand on my throat and squeezed.

"Stop it!" Max said. "Stop it, he'll kill you! Stop!"

The more I tried to fight him, the madder Kevin got, and the madder he got, the more he became crazy-mad and his face began to look like when he was fighting Maurice and ready to fight all the carwash guys at once, happy, like it was the best thing in the world.

I couldn't breath and couldn't wiggle or twist anymore. Kevin pulled his pants down and closed his eyes and wasn't really paying attention to me. His hand was still on my throat, but he wasn't squeezing and I could breath. I was quiet and still on the outside, but I was screaming inside and another one was about to come out.

"Look at the blinds," Max said. "See? The pattern the light makes? What's it look like?"

I looked at it but didn't see anything. Then Kevin moved his hand from my throat to my chest and was leaning on it and I could hardly breathe again. He was moving on top of me, groaning. The scream that had been waiting was about to come out, but before it did, I could hear Max begging me not to let it, to look at the shade again and when I did, I finally saw what he was talking about. The worn place on the shade to the back yard looked like a horse. It looked like Loyal Brigand. I tried to picture him, and when I did, when I could see him clearly, I tried to picture the seventh race at Hollywood Park from the beginning to the end.

"That's better," Max said. "That's good. Just take one breath, then another. Watch the race. You're doing fine."

Loyal Brigand got his slow start and was way back. The horses were all crowded together going into the first turn and he was on the outside, still far behind all the others. Coming out of the second turn onto the backstretch they weren't bunched up any more, but were in a long line. He was way back, but began moving up, to pass horses, one, then two, then three. He was going into the third curve, staying outside, running his longer race, sure he could win. Sure he wanted to. I could feel his heart pounding, feel him wanting to run, wanting to race, wanting to suck in the air, to feel the sun beating down on him, wanting to stay alive.

"That's better," Max told me, again. "Just a little longer."

Loyal Brigand came down the final part, the last stretch, his heart pounding, his lungs burning, fighting to get past Pistol Packer and Chelsea Cat and Land's End, past them all to the finish line. He fought with ever bit of strength and energy he had, stretching and reaching, more determined than ever, and this time, he did it. He won. I was riding him and he won. When we got past the finish line and he'd slowed down to a walk, he twisted his neck around to see me and shook his head, like he knew we could do it all along.

Kevin started crying. He got off me and and pulled up his pants and sat on the edge of the bed. Then he stood up and took some Kleenex from a box on his dresser and wiped my hip and threw it in a wastebasket. He sat back down on the bed, still crying. I didn't move. Max told me we should stay where we were. Laying there, I reached down and pulled up my pants. Max decided, I decided to stand up. Kevin watched me. I buckled the cowboy belt.

"I'm sorry," he said, still sort of sobbing. "It won't happen again."

I backed slowly towards the door, keeping an eye on him. He reached for his cigarettes and tried to light one but his hands were shaking and he couldn't. After a few tries he got it lit and took a few puffs. He stopped crying and his face went back to normal. Kevin normal.

"If you tell anyone, I'll kill you."

I wasn't going to say anything to him. I just kept backing little by little for the door. The cigarette smoke was filling up the room. Then he smiled.

"If I tell you to come in here with me, you come. Understand?"

I didn't say anything. His face started getting mad again.

"Understand?"

I reached behind me for the doorknob.

"Whenever I say. Understand? Or I'll have to kill you."

"No you won't," Max said.

"You don't think so?" Kevin said.

I was dizzy and sleepy all of a sudden. I just wanted to get out of there. I didn't think he'd try to stop me. Let's just go, I tried to tell Max. I just want to leave. But Max wouldn't let me or couldn't hear me.

"No," Max said.

"And why's that?"

"Because I'm going to kill you first."

He laughed at me because he didn't think I was serious. Or that I could. I suppose he was right about me, but not Max.

"Don't bet on it," he said, sucking on the cigarette. "Get outta here. And remember, if you tell anyone, ever..."

"You'll kill me," Max said. "So what? Do it! Do it now! I dare you!"

I didn't know how to talk to Max the way he did to me, but if I could, I wanted to tell him to shut up so we could just go.

"I've killed more times than I can count. You think you'd be a problem? Or your mother or father or big brother? Your sister? Do you understand me?" he said, looking at me to make sure I did. "You'll come when I say."

"I'm never coming in here. Never. You'll have to kill me outside where everyone will see you." Max said.

"Don't be so sure."

I didn't say anything and neither did Max. Kevin stared at me.

"What about that little kid brother of yours?"

"What?" I said, a new ache in my stomach, a new weight crushing me down.

"Maybe I'll invite him in if you're too busy. How'd that be?"

I turned the knob and stepped out into the hallway, backwards. He didn't make a move to get up and stop me. I closed the door.

"How'd that be? Think about that," he called throught the door.

I could hear him crying again as I went down the hall, through the living room and out the front door. I closed it as quietly as I could.

The air outside was warm, warm and fresh, but it made me so dizzy I almost fell over. And the sun was so bright, my eyes hurt. As suddenly as he'd come, Max was gone. Just not there. My stomach hurt and I had the feeling like when you need to throw up and it won't come. I sat on the curb, next to the shared driveway between Miriam's and Kevin's. I looked across the street and could tell no one was home yet. Besides, I didn't want to go there. I didn't know where to go. I tried to think, but I couldn't hold on to thinking. Things sort of floated past and disappeared before I could think them. Maybe I could go somewhere on the Red Rider. It was there, waiting for me, right where I'd left it, but I couldn't think of anywhere to go. I should put the route bags and the bike away, I thought. But I didn't. I looked at the bike and couldn't find the feeling about being free. I wondered where it had gone, but I was too tired to care. If only I could think of someplace to go, a place where I could close my eyes and not be afraid to be asleep. There were a bunch of the fallen jacaranda blossoms in the gutter at my feet. I picked one up and twirled it in my fingers and started crying. I looked up at the sky, pale blue, filtered through the fern-like leaves and the blossoms still in the trees, hanging on until they couldn't hang on any longer. I stood up and put it in my pocket. The bamboo patch, I thought. I'd be safe there. I crossed the street to our side, going at an angle, so when I got to the parkway, I was already to Mr. Avery's house. I was going to go around to the alley and go in under the fence, but it seemed too far, so I went through the gate instead. I closed it without the clank. I thought I was going to go to the pond to see the Garibaldi, but I ended up going straight to the bamboo instead. I crawled through the part I'd thinned to the opening in the center. I curled up even though it wasn't cold. I threw up and fell asleep.

It was dark when I woke up. I heard Marty and my dad calling my name. There wasn't much throw-up but it smelled bad and I crawled away from it towards the alley. I had to push the trash can aside from underneath. It was hard to move and I almost tipped it over, but after a few tries, I'd moved it far enough to come out into the alley. I put the can back over the hole and headed down to our yard. It was too dark to see more than just a shape, but Marty must have seen mine, because he called from the top of the alley by Shelly's carport.

"Kurt? Is that you?" then, "Dad! He's down the alley."

I went through the opening in our hedge where the gate used to be into the yard. My mom and Pop came running down the driveway from the front.

"My God!" she yelled, "where have you been? We've been frantic!"

I couldn't think of anything to say. Pop was looking at me over her shoulder. My dad and Marty came into the yard from the alley. The screen door opened and Sarah came into the driveway holding Nick by the hand.

"Are you okay?" my dad said.

I nodded, pushing my hands down into my front pockets.

"Where were you?" Marty asked me.

I shrugged. My mom grabbed my shoulders and shook me. Sarah and Nick came down the driveway into the yard.

"Answer, where were you? We've been worried sick!" my mom said

I started crying but couldn't say anything.

"You left your bike right out there like that? I almost ran it over. We couldn't imagine what happened. What have you got to say for yourself?" my dad said, starting to get mad. "God damn it, answer me!"

"I fell asleep in the Pink House Garden," I finally said.

"Rathbone's place?" Pop said.

I nodded.

"You're sneaking in there? Christ, that's all we need, another neighbor up in arms," Pop said. "Dave, you've got to take care of this."

"I will."

"For sure. No ifs ands or buts," Pop said.

"I will, I said, and I will. Kurt, get in the house."

"He said I could."

"Could what?"

"Go in there."

"Who?" my dad said.

"Mr. Rathbone."

They were all quiet for a minute. Pop knelt down in front of me.

"Is that true?"

"Uh huh."

"You promise?"

"Uh huh."

"Well," Pop said, standing up and looking at my mom and dad, "that's a little different."

"Not after dark, it's not," my mom said. "That's no excuse for worrying us to death. Go in the house and get ready for bed."

"What about his dinner? Dinner's all ready" Sarah said, holding

Nick's hand.

"He's going to bed without it," my mom said.

"You think that's really necessary?" my dad said.

"Don't start," my mom said to him. "He knows the rules. Everyone's working so hard and doing the best they can and we don't have the time or energy to be running around about locks and lawyers or worried to death on top of all that because he's taking a nap in the Pink House Garden. I don't, anyway. Maybe this will teach him a lesson. Go on," she said to me.

I started to go, but my hands felt the folded up paper. I took it out and handed it to her.

"Here," I said holding it out.

"What's this?"

"A coupon for Carl's," I said.

She took it from me and looked it over.

"It's for fifty seven-fifty."

I shrugged.

"Where'd you get this?" she asked, mad again, like I'd stolen it or something, "My god, what now? What have you done now?"

I started to cry again. She held up her hand to stop me if I was going to say something, only I wasn't.

"I don't want to hear. Whatever it is, don't say a word. Just go get ready for bed."

Everybody was looking at me. Pop and my dad and Marty and my mom, and all of a sudden, everything was hopeless again. Everything. I was still tired and afraid to go to sleep and hungry and wasn't supposed to eat and there was nothing I could say, like they would be mad at me no matter what, so I started down the driveway and got to the corner of the house.

"He won it," I heard Sarah say.

"What are you talking about?" my dad said.

"The Star Shopper Show was at Carl's and Kurt and this lady won."

When I got to our room, I got ready for bed, but before I got in, out of nowhere, it seemed important to do this one thing, so I put the leather attachment on my wood burner and let it heat up. I burned an 'M' into the belt in front of the gold letters spelling 'Goldman' that Marty already had on it. When Marty came in, I was in bed with my face to the wall.

"It's okay, don't cry, they're not really that mad about it. They were just worried about you. And they know how you got the coupon. Sarah told us. But geez, sneaking into the Pink House Gareden? What about the Jap?"

"He's not a Jap! He's Japanese and he was born here and he's not mean at all," I said, "just ask Pop."

I slept late, which was sort of funny, because I was having the kind of dreams you can't wait to wake up from. I couldn't remember them, but I knew they were bad, so waking up was a relief. I knew for sure I'd slept later than eveyone else in the house, because when I woke up, no one was there. I took a long shower and found my newest jeans and the cowboy belt and a t-shirt and socks and was perfectly clean until I had to put on the sneakers. They were falling apart and were dirty on the inside as well as the outside, but there wasn't anyting I could do about it so I put them on and tried to ignore them, but worse than that was my stomach was growling and I was so hungry it hurt. Maybe almost starving to death. But the good thing was, even though my mom was mad at me, and even though it wasn't a school day, she'd left me thirty-five cents for lunch, and I still had the dollar-fifty left over from the money Marty made Ron give me back, after the fifteen dollar part of it I'd given my mom for the lawyer, so the way I felt, I planned on using every bit of it at Joseph's for breakfast. I was trying to picture how much food I could get for a dollar eighty-five. Really a lot, I bet. If it weren't so late, I'd go see Helen for some sweet rolls too, but it was too late for that. The boss guys would be around and they'd throw me out and she'd get in trouble.

I got my bike and went up the block instead of down to Beverly. I thought I was hoping to see George or Kenny Lester, but when I passed George's house and he wasn't around, I realized I was glad, and by the time I got to his place, I didn't want to see Kenny Lester either. I didn't want to see anyone. Maybe Snowball. I passed Shelly and Norma's, but no Snowball, so I turned the corner and went all the way on Lower Santa Monica to where it met Beverly at the carwash. I parked the bike and climbed up on a stool.

"Keeping banker's hours today?" Joseph said.

"What's that mean?"

"Banks open late and close early, so bankers...."

"I get it," I told him. "No, I just slept too much."

"What can I get you?"

"How 'bout a big stack and two eggs over easy and hot chocolate?"

Joseph made a big deal out of being surprized.

"What's this? From a banker to a lumberjack in less than a minute. You sure you can eat all that?"

"Positive. I want to pay you for it too."

"You know your money's no good here," he smiled.

"I want to pay. Really. I should, since even if I work here, that's a lot of food."

I put the dollar eighty-five on the counter. Joseph looked over his shoulder and studied the price list. He took fifty-five cents and pushed the rest back to me.

"That'll do it," he said.

"Are you sure? Is that enough?"

"Just right."

He started cooking. A couple of minutes later, Norma pulled into the station and stopped at the pumps for gas. I was glad to see her, even though I didn't want to before. Randy came out of the office and said hello to her without making a fuss and started filling up the MG. She came over and sat next to me.

"We meet at last," she laughed. "How come you're so late?"

"I slept too long," I shrugged.

"And he's eating a real breakfast," Joseph told her. "Look at this."

He put the plate in front of me. It was beautiful. I could hardly decide where to start. Joseph put the maple syrup in front of me and I poured a lot of it over the pancakes. I put the eggs on top and broke the yokes so they'd soaked in. Joseph made a face like I'd ruined his artwork, but Norma just laughed.

"That's certainly one way to do it," she said.

"What'll it be?" Joseph asked her.

"The same as him," she said, "only a short stack, and put the eggs on a separate plate, please, and coffee."

"You got it."

"Did you get your check yet?" she asked me.

"Nope. Did you?"

"No, but I expect they should come today or tomorrow, or Monday at the latest. I hope so. I owe Shelly some rent. What are you going to do with yours?"

I wiggled my sneakers at her.

"Get new ones," I said. "That's first. After that, I owe my mom twenty dollars for Marty's lawyer. Whatever's left over, maybe save it for college."

"That's a wonderful idea!" she said, then, "What lawyer? What's that about?"

I told her about Ron and the route bags and rubber bands and Marty getting the money back for me and getting arrested and the Daily Mirror firing Ron. Joseph was putting her coffee on the counter, listening too.

"That's terrible!" she said. "What a terrible person, cheating you kids like that. They should have fired him ages ago. He's probably been cheating all the route boys for a long time. You should be proud of your brother."

"I am," I said.

"Damn right," Joseph said, turning back to the grill.

I don't know why, but tears started leaking out of my eyes. I tried to make them stop, but I couldn't. Joseph put her food in front of her and reached over and patted my shoulder.

"What's the matter, kiddo? It can't be that bad, can it? Sounds like it's all taken care of."

Norma put her arm around my shoulder and leaned in close.

"But they fired him, right? He can't bother you anymore, right?"

I nodded. As quickly as it came, it went. We both ate without talking. Joseph cleaned the grill. I was getting full but had eaten most of my stuff.

"I'm full," I said, pushing the plate away.

"I was thinking about going to the beach. Wanna come with me?" she asked.

I nodded yes. If I said anything, I was afraid it might start again.

"Oh, honey, it's okay," she said, looking at me. "The beach will be fun and I'll have you back in time for your route. Okay?"

I nodded yes again. I told her I'd get a head start and ride home and get my cut offs and a towel.

I was waiting for her on our front steps when she came down the street. I tried not to look, but as I got into the MG, I checked to make sure Kevin wasn't around, and he wasn't and off we went.

The waves were small or only medium at best, no monsters, and the beach was mostly empty, but we had a good time. I had a lot of good rides and tried to teach her how to too, but she said she was hopeless and she was right. She splashed around while I rode, and after a while we got out. She went back up to our towels to dry off. I fooled around watching for bubbles in the wet sand when the water drained away and then, as quickly as I could, dug down with my hands looking for the crabs that had made them. I caught a few, watched them crawl around on my hand, then put them down and watched as they dug themselves back under. The sun was bright and the sand was hot when I crossed it. I laid down on my towel next to her. I wasn't quite asleep when she took my hand and held it and then we both snoozed. She woke me up at twelve-fifteen.

"We better get going," she said. "If we hurry, we've got time for a hot dog. Do you want one? I do."

"Okay."

I suppose I was still hungry from no dinner last night, but whatever it was from, I wasn't sure one was going to be enough. We went across the street to Gert's.

"Look who's here," Pete said.

I wasn't sure if he meant me or Norma.

"You ride your bike again?" he asked.

"No. Norma drove us in the MG."

"MG?" he said. "Nice."

"What'll it be?" Gert said.

"Two foot-longers and two cokes?" Norma said, sort of asking me at the same time she was telling Gert.

"Okay. I can pay," I said.

"No, you save it for your sneakers or college," Norma said.

"Really, I want to."

I put the dollar on the counter. I figured for two foot-longers and two cokes it should be seventy cents and the rest would be for Gert and Pete.

"Thank you, sweetie, it'll be my turn next time, okay?"

"Okay," I said.

Gert picked up the money and started to hand me the change.

"That's for you and Pete," I said.

"Naw," she said, "that ain't necessary."

"I want to," I said.

Gert nodded okay. Pete stopped cleaning and looked right at me and nodded and smiled. He didn't say anything, but there was something about that sad, friendly smile of his that almost made me cry, not in a bad way, but like it wasn't all hopeless after all. Gert served them up and we ate the hot dogs and washed them down with the cokes and headed for home. I think I fell asleep on the ride because I didn't remember any of it.

We got back at ten to one and the bundle was already there. I got the bike and the route bags and rubber bands and started folding. I cut the rope on the bundle with one quick swipe of the KA-BAR knife and it really popped. I kept checking to see if Kevin was there, but if he was, he didn't come outside. I took a paper to George's and Mr. Avery's, even though I didn't really need to anymore, because I could handle the extra papers in the route bags now, but I'd sort of gotten in the habit of walking their papers over first, so I just did it that way. I got back to the bike and started to take out a paper for Kevin. I even had my fingers on it. I looked across the street and thought, I'm not going there. Not even to deliver to his front steps. Never. I don't care what he says or if they charge me for his papers or not. I got on the Red Rider and pedaled towards Beverly. By the time I got to the stop sign, I'd found it. The free feeling had come back. Being on the Red Rider was like flying again. I could go anywhere and do anything and no one could take it away. I could feel Norma's hand holding mine and see the smile on Pete's face, and I knew I was free again. Kevin might be able to make me afraid, but I wasn't going to let him take that away, not again, not ever.

When I got close to home, I could see Kevin was waiting for me. He was standing on the sidewalk in front of the Courtyard with George, smoking, both of them, but I could tell he was waiting for me. I pulled into our driveway and planned on going all the way to the garage without stopping. George waved when I passed in front of them. As I turned, Kevin called to me.

"Hey, buddy," he said, "hold on there. You missed me."

I stopped and put the bike on the kickstand, just past the sidewalk. I stood next to the bike. My legs were starting to shake as he came over to get it. I didn't get it for him so he reached into the route bags and took the one left over paper. He leaned a little closer to me, and with his back to George half whispered.

"You see how much help George is going to be?"

He smiled and walked back to finish smoking. Right then, I knew Max was right.

# Chapter 29

## *Dominoes*

"YOU'RE UNDER ARREST," he said, hands on hips, snazzy suit jacket open, a less-than-apologetic smile on his lips.

"How ya doin', Vann?"

"Just swell, Detective. This couldn't wait?"

"'Fraid not."

It would have been nice if he'd at least waited until I was fully awake. When my eyes opened it took me several seconds and the plastic strip below the screen of the TV across from my bed that said, Marin General, to remind me where I was. It took a little longer to remember why.

"What are you talking about?" I said, my head still throbbing, "Did Dolan put you up to this? Take a closer look. It's me in the hospital."

"Not Dolan. Doyle."

"What are you talking about?"

"I've got a witness says you were there. That you came out splattered in blood. She saw Doyle come out feet first a little later, carried by that platoon of your neighborhood pals. It's you they were trying to protect with their confessions, not your brother. That ought to be more than enough for the D.A., even after thirty-eight years."

"What are you talking about? What witness?"

"Miriam McDermott."

How had he gotten to her, I wondered?

Vann looked at me. It was hard to read, but I had the unhappy feeling that she believed him. Believed Miriam, whatever it was she'd had to say. I wished I could have stayed awake long enough to listen to the tape.

"Here's the deal," Phillips said. "Your under arrest for the murder of Kevin Doyle. You have the right to remain silent. I should be so lucky, but you have the right..."

"I know my rights," I said.

"While you're laid up here, consider it a house arrest. You don't go anywhere farther than the bathroom over there, got it? As soon as you're fit to travel, we'll get you back to L.A. and get you arraigned. I'm sure your brother can get you an OR. Even though it's a murder charge, you were a minor and it's been a long time. I don't think you're much of a flight risk."

He smirked. Given my current condition, I couldn't argue with that.

"I'll be in touch with the doctor that's treating you. As soon as he says you're good to go, I'll come get you and we'll just wing our way back down to the real world. How's that sound?"

"Like you're out of your mind."

Before I could say anything more, Vann put her hand on mine.

"I'm sure Nick would tell you not to say a thing," she said. "So don't."

She was right. But since Nick wasn't here, I felt I had a little leeway.

"What the hell did Miriam say?"

"You'll have a chance to sort all that out with your attorney. Just sit tight, enjoy a little TV and get well."

"Tell me one thing."

"What's that?"

"Have you determined the exact cause of death?"

"We got the report back yesterday."

"And?"

He hesitated.

"Well?"

"The belt. Strangulation. Asphyxiation. Okay?"

"Just strangulation?" I pressed.

"You don't think that's enough?"

"I'm just asking."

"Well, it was asphyxiation, but his neck was broken in the process."

"His neck was broken?"

"Yes."

"Anything else of interest?"

"Hey, your brother can go through it with a fine-tooth comb. That's what lawyers do. That's what you pay them for. Or in your case, don't."

"You're here and I'm here. Anything else?"

"He probably died with a hell of a headache."

"Why's that?"

"He had a dent in the side of his skull the size of a quarter," Phillips said, pointing to his left temple. "Maybe a fifty-cent piece. Broken bone."

"Not an old wound? Not from the war, maybe?"

"No. There wasn't any healing. It all happened at the same time."

"And you're charging me with murder because you think I strangled him and broke his neck and dented his head? Keeping in mind I'd just turned eight."

"I can't say how it all happened, but that's the way it looks. We know he was shootin' up. Maybe you caught him at a weak moment. Hey, when you and your brother get together, I'm sure he'll propose more than one possible defense."

He gave me an altogether too knowing look that made me squirm.

"It's pretty wide open. I'm sure he and the D.A. will sort it all out. I've done my job. Let them do theirs. How are you feeling, by the way?"

"Great. Thanks for asking."

"So, now the good news. Dolan said he's not going to press charges."

He was enjoying himself immensely.

"He what? Are you out of your mind? Why aren't you arresting him? How do you think I got here? First his thug blind-sides me, then he decides to take a couple of free shots while I'm on my back. Talk about doing your job, arrest that sonofabitch. I'll press charges."

"Don't even think about it. You've got enough trouble. Besides, I tried to warn you about fooling with him. They've already signed affidavits saying you got a little crazy and started swinging first."

"That's bullshit."

He shrugged.

"Says his driver, Doug, intervened to protect him from your assault. They're sort of stressing the 'pattern of violence' they see in you. He mentioned some old scar on the back of his head you're supposed to be responsible for."

"Christ, I suppose he wants you to charge me with that too?"

"No," he smiled. "We're letting that one slide. He brought it up as more of the 'pattern'."

"Sounds familiar, though, doesn't it? Like he took a page from your book? Or maybe you from his? Trying to pave the way for the D.A.? First with Marty, now me?"

He shrugged again. It was their word against mine. Two of them, one of me. Him a candidate for mayor, me a candidate for a long stretch in San Quentin.

"You know this is wrong, Dave. All of it. If you've learned anything about this Doyle character, you know how wrong this is," Vann said.

"I've learned what I've learned. Look, someone got killed, someone killed him. The guy was a war hero, fer Christ's sake, and connected to the Dolan family. We've got a credible witness. What do you want me to do?"

"Do your fucking job," I yelled at him from the bed, "not the one Dolan's paying you to do. That would be nice for a change"

"I'm doing it, cowboy. This has nothing to do with Dolan. I've got a body, a witness and you. She may have kept her mouth shut all these years to protect you since you were a kid and all, but once I confronted her, she was glad it get it off her chest. And by the way, she remembers you as having been the one that wore that belt. It may have been your brother's at one time, but she definitely remembers it on you. And now I've got an explanation for the multiple confessions. It's pretty well wrapped up. I'd like to thank you for all your help," he smiled. Then to Vann, "I'm staying at the Hyatt Regency, in Embarcadero Center. I'll check with the doctor in a day or two. He says you should be ready to go in three at the most," he said to me.

"Don't miss Fisherman's Warf and Pier 39 while you're here. Christ, they give any high school drop-out a badge, a gun and an expense account and he thinks he's a fucking detective."

"Get well soon," he said with a nod.

Vann closed the door behind him.

"You should call Nick. Right now."

"Later," I said.

I looked at her, hoping to see something other than the same odd look, a look that seemed to say she was prepared to love me no matter whom I killed, which was nice, reassuring even, but not quite the vote of confidence I was hoping for.

"They'll never convict you. Never."

Her face seemed to lose focus and tears started running down her cheeks. She sat down on the edge of the bed and held my hand.

"I want to hear the tape you made of Miriam."

"Not now, Kurt. It'll keep. You should rest."

"Vann, I want to hear it now. Right now. Please. I'll probably have fifteen-to-life to rest."

She got the tape recorder out of her purse. She rewound and started playing it. She laid down beside me and we listened together. By the time it was over, I was almost convinced I'd done it. I could see how Phillips might buy it. Maybe Vann too, for that matter. But it was too pat. Way too pat. The details were pretty convincing, most of them accurate as far as I could remember, but there was something about her conclusion that made me think it had been arrived at before the narrative had been constructed. It was a cover story. But there's no way she'd be covering for George or Iyama or Kenny Lester. Far less for Maurice, since even if she'd seen him on the block working for my grandfather, I'd bet she'd never even exchanged a word with him. So if it were me they thought they were trying to protect, who was she protecting? And why? Listening to the tape again, Vann was in agony. I figured Joanne Lester-Stuckey must have filled her in about Kevin Doyle's little idiosyncrasies and their connection to the suicides on the block. It was hard to hear, but oddly enough, it didn't trigger the usual flood of fear and anger and dispair in me. Or the rage. Instead, it filled me with such a wave of love for the friends that thought they were protecting me, my eyes were tearing. Vann took it for a reaction to thoughts of Kevin, and hugged me.

"I'm so sorry," she said.

But I wasn't thinking of Kevin at all. I was picturing them. Maybe I'd seen them together at the carwash, or maybe it was just an imaginary gathering, but I could see them so clearly, standing around, not saying much, except maybe Kenny Lester telling a story, all of them probably smoking, but enjoying each other's company, enjoying the certainty of being able to rely on each other, doing whatever they thought needed doing. George and Iyama and Maurice and Kenny Lester. Rathbone and maybe Pop. They all had to have played a part.

"What a crew," I said. "Rathbone was right."

"What?" she said.

"He once told me, 'in this life it's the friends you can count on that make all the difference'. God, I love them. And you," I said, taking her hand.

We sat there holding each other for about a minute, maybe a minute and a half, which is about my limit when my mind is already heading for the exit.

"Help me get dressed," I said, swinging my feet off the bed to the floor.

I tried to stand but somewhere between my head and feet the message was lost or scrambled and I had to ease myself back to a sitting position.

"You can't go anywhere, you're under arrest, remember? Besides, you can't go anywhere. Look at you."

"That was my first try," I said. "I'll do better this time. Just find my clothes. Please."

"Where do you think you're going to go?"

"To Miriam's."

"What for? She won't talk to you. She made that clear. Besides, what more do you expect her to say?"

"The truth. The whole truth. There's more. There's got to be. I know you think you're supporting me. That I had good reason to kill Kevin – and I did – but I need you to trust me. At least for a little while longer."

Phillips had just about taken care of any remaining doubts. If I could talk with Miriam I was sure I could dispel the shadow that remained. I looked at Vann. I wasn't sure if it was doubt or confusion in her face, but I didn't want or need either. What I wanted was more than her loyalty, I wanted her conviction and certainty. Her trust. Maybe it was her faith I was looking for. I wanted to be able to trust that. She came to the same conclusion. It was what I wanted okay, but the question was, was it what she believed? What she felt? Given the circumstances, I figured I'd have to settle for a suspension of disbelief. Her face softened.

"I asked Ron to have someone keep an eye on Dolan and his gang. If they head up here, someone will follow. If they're up to something down there, we should know about it. Even if Phillips is giving him a pass on assaulting you, there's something desperate in the way he's putting himself out on a limb with this. He must think he's got his reasons, and that makes him all the more dangerous. We just need to keep tabs on him to find out what they are."

"Good. So, from the philosophic to the mundane. Where are my pants?"

"I'll take you, but you're making me an accessory to something, you know. I'm not sure what, but something. So, for the record, I'd just like..."

"I know," I said, not quite ready to say anything, not quite sure that it would be of help to her or to me if I did. I wanted Miriam's story to sink in, to paint a picture whose missing parts would somehow materialize for me.

"She's so certain. How can she be so certain if she's so wrong? I believe in you. I absolutely do. But if you did it, and I've already come to terms with that possibility, it was an act of self-defense if ever there was one. My god, seven years old. To tell the truth, I was proud of you. I am. Either way."

"Eight," I corrected her with a smile. "You're one of those women who go after the bad boys, huh? The killer-types?"

"Not really, but I'm prepared to make an exception in your case."

She stood there with my clothes in her hand. I kissed her on the lips as gently as I could. Even that hurt my banged up mouth.

"Hang in a little longer," I said, "just a little longer."

She handed me my clothes and helped me into them.

"Excuse me a minute."

I went into the bathroom and closed the door. I took a much needed piss, washed my hands and face and pushed my hair around like it made a difference. My face was black and blue, but the swelling was lessening, so it wasn't as distorted as it felt. It occurred to me Jason and Jane might return. I went back into the room and wrote a note on a pad Vann had. 'Back Soon, or maybe not. I'll be in touch'. I left it on the pillow.

"Who's that for?" she said.

"Jason and Jane, if they come back. Phillips too," I smiled.

"Somehow, I don't think he'll be amused."

We got in the Fiero and Vann started for Summit Drive. I took the recorder out of her purse and rewound and played it again. If Phillips came away from this with the feeling Miriam had been protecting me all these years, I had a bridge or two I'd like to sell him. A sense of urgency engulfed me. I could feel some sort of resolution was within reach. Thirty-eight years is a long time to hold your breath.

# Chapter 30

## *Brotherhood*
## August 10 to 18, 1951

I SET THE FIRE THAT NIGHT, or the next morning, depending on how you count it. Maybe it was Max or maybe me or maybe both. I don't know and I don't care. I was in bed and was afraid to go to sleep. It seemed like it was Max talking to me, but it wasn't the same as before. I could hear him, but it sounded more like me, but not me, but more like me. He was telling me we had to do something about Kevin. That we shouldn't wait. If we waited it would be too late. I wasn't sure what, and he didn't suggest it, but then the idea came and I just did it. I got out of bed and got dressed. Marty was snoring away, and I could hear my dad snoring and my mom grinding her teeth where they slept all tangled up together on the Davenport. I snuck out through the kitchen and back door as quietly as I could. I went through the back yard and down our alley to Beverly, crossed towards Doheny and then up the alley on Kevin's side and came into his yard and tiptoed up his back stairs. Sure enough, the ashtray with the cigarette lighter was on the deck rail. I took it and flipped it open and spun the little wheel and lit the cardboard boxes and newspapers that were under the porch. I put the lighter back and ran through his yard to the alley and all the way up to Lower Santa Monica and around past Norma and Shelly's to our alley and down to our yard and came in through the back door. I was out of breath and panting, but Marty didn't wake up. I got undressed and back in bed and listened for fire trucks, but none came. I pictured his whole house burning all the way down to the ground and nothing left but a chimney sticking up in the air from a pile of ashes like you see in the newspapers after a big fire like the ones in Malibu or Big Bear. I didn't even know if Kevin's house had a chimney. I'd never noticed it if it did, but whether it did or didn't, I fell asleep and didn't dream about anything.

The next morning was Saturday and the carwash and the paper route. I got up early and got dressed and took the Red Rider to Joseph's for breakfast. I still had thirty-five cents and figured it was early enough to go see Helen. She was glad to see me and I was glad to see her, but I didn't feel much like talking and neither did she, so we just worked sorting out the bad custard and cinnamon rolls and then she filled up a bag for me and she hugged me and I went to Joseph's for a hot chocolate to go with them.

Joseph was quiet too, which was good, since I didn't want to talk about anything. I didn't even want to think about anything. I helped

Randy pump gas for a while and I cleaned the counter for Joseph a few times and before I knew it, Maurice and William and Jackson showed up and opened the storage room with the carwash boots and rags and soap. I was wondering where Dennis was, but I would have bet a spare fiver that was the problem with Joseph, because I thought he probably knew. A little while later, Miss Rimes drove up and Dennis got out of her car. Joseph pretended he didn't notice, but he did for sure. Jackson and Maurice and William did too, but it was more like they already knew and this just proved it. They liked Miss Rimes, Connie, but I think they felt a little funny about her and Dennis being in love or whatever. I felt bad for Joseph all over again, but it seemed like he was getting used to it. She didn't get out of the car, but waved and drove off. I passed out squished sweet rolls to all of them and they had their coffee and we got started.

The carwash wasn't as busy as usual, so even though we worked hard, it wasn't crazy hard and the time seemed to go slower. When it finally got to four, Mr. Avery paid me. Two-fifty and it was all mine. No more locks, no more Red Rider payments, no more anything. With a little more I could get new sneakers. I was hoping the check for the movie would come today. It was August 11th and that should have been plenty of time for them to write it and mail it and for the mail man to bring it, but you never knew, so like Shelly said, it would get there when they were good and ready to part with the money. Lax, she'd said. More like deadbeats, I'd say.

When I got home the bundle was there waiting for me like usual. I popped the rope off first, then got the route bags and rubber bands from the porch and started folding. George came down his walk.

"Just get back from the carwash?"

"Uh huh."

"Hear about the fire at Kevin's?"

I kept my head down and shook it no and kept folding. He came over and stood on the sidewalk, close to me on the parkway.

"The ashtray on his back deck overflowed onto some cardboard. Apparently there was a butt that wasn't out. A little fire got going. No real damage, it just blackened the back of the building, but it could have been bad. His mom's not well and she's been staying in the upstairs apartment and couldn't have gotten out if the fire had taken off and the building had gone up. That would have been the end of her. Need any help?"

"No thanks."

I didn't know that about Kevin's mom. Then I had the feeling that maybe George knew I'd done it. Then I was sure of it. I wanted to tell him I was sorry, but except for maybe killing Kevin's mom, I wasn't.

"Is everything okay?" he asked.

I wanted to tell him about Kevin, no matter what Kevin said he'd do if I did, but then I thought of Nick. That was bad enough, but then all of a sudden I knew the idea of telling him at all was impossible, Nick or no Nick. I was ashamed to tell him. And if I couldn't tell him, I couldn't tell anyone. Ever. It seemed like a gyp that Kevin got his way no matter how come. While I was thinking about it, George was smoking and the street was quiet and out of nowhere, Max was talking to me again. 'That's just the way it is. We'll figure out something else.' I finished folding and loaded the bags and got on the Red Rider.

"How's the bike?" George asked me. "Still the greatest?"

"Better than ever, George. Like flying. See you later."

"See you," he waved.

I did the route that Saturday and all the next week without leaving a paper for Kevin. I didn't see him and he didn't complain to Jingo, so I figured he didn't care that much. I got paid the following Saturday at the carwash and had enough for the new sneakers, but never found the time to go all the way down to The Broadway or even into Beverly Hills to Rudnick's. It had become kind of a joke between me and Norma and Shelly, and Joseph too, that my feet were more out of than in the old sneakers. The weather was warm, so it didn't matter much, and the longer I waited to buy the new ones, the newer they'd be when school started, so that was a good reason for not getting the new ones right away. Marty's birthday was the following Wednesday and we had a special dinner with roast beef and potatoes and spinich and a chocolate cake my mom had had time to make. Little by little, my dad's deadbeats were starting to pay up, so money things were looking better. Then on Thursday, more than two whole weeks late, an envelope came in the mail with my name on it. It was the movie check. That was the good news. The bad news was it wasn't for fifty-five dollars. It was only for thirty-five. There were a lot of numbers on an attached part, but I still couldn't figure out what happened to the other twenty. You couldn't trust anyone these days. When I showed it to Marty, he figured out they'd subtracted for SAG dues, which was a group they forced you to join if you were an actor, even if it was only for one time. That was ten bucks, gone, just like that. Marty showed me where it said it was for a whole year, but if I never acted in another movie again, who needed a whole year? So it was a big waste. Or if I did, and it was after the year was up, I'd have to pay them all over again. The next thing was taxes. Even if I was a kid, they took out taxes and social security and some studio payroll deduction that Marty didn't understand either. But it added up to twenty bucks and that was that. On the other hand, I had thirty-five dollars. On the other other hand, I still owed my mom twenty for the lawyer, so it was down to fifteen. I'd saved five from the carwash and Saturday was coming up again, so I'd have twenty-two fifty and it was half way through August, so I'd be collecting again, and without Ron to cheat me, I'd have another thirty or so from the route, so I'd be back up to around fifty-two, which was pretty close to the fifty-five I thought I'd have from the movie, so it was working out okay any way you looked at it.

When we finished at the carwash on the next Saturday, and Mr. Avery had paid us, Maurice said he'd see me Monday.

"How come?" I asked him.

"I'm gonna do some yard work for your grandpops," he said.

"Not the others?"

"Nope. Just me. Dennis' and Connie got art gallery plans and Jackson and William and Joseph goin' to San Francisco to play. Just me."

"I'll probably see you then."

"So long," he said.

I said good bye to Joseph and told him to have fun in San Francisco, and headed home to do the route. I left the papers for Mr. Avery and George in the bags to deliver last instead of walking them over first, not for any particular reason, but that's just the way I felt. The whole thing went faster than ever before and it was only about quarter past five when I came down Oakhurst. I tossed the paper for Norma and Shelly and crossed over to Kenny Lester's. I hadn't seen him for a while and wanted to. At the same time, I didn't. It seemed like Kenny and George could read my mind and there was stuff I didn't want them to read, so I was both glad and worried when I saw him having a smoke on his bottom step.

"Hey, stranger, howya doin'?" he waved.

"Pretty good."

"I was watching you pedal. I bet we could take those blocks off now. I bet you've grown at least an inch since you got the bike. Maybe more. Wanna try?"

"Sure."

I parked the bike next to the curb and put it on the kickstand. He came over and took his pocket knife out, and slit, just like that, he'd cut the tape and had them off.

"Give it a try."

I got back on and rode up towards Lower Santa Monica. My legs reached fine without them.

"Looks about right to me. How's it feel?" he called.

"Perfect. I can reach all the way to the bottom without having to go to my toes."

"Pretty soon we'll probably have to start raising the seat."

I stopped in front of his parkway.

"Thanks, Kenny."

"You're welcome. You okay?"

"Yeah."

"You sure?"

"Yeah. See you later."

"Okay. See you later."

I rode down the street and delivered to Mr. Rothman and then Mr. Rathbone. It was really too late for him to still be there, but Iyama's truck was out in front of the Pink House. I tossed papers for Mr. Avery and George and turned into our driveway and put the route bags and the bike away. No one was home yet, so I decided I'd go up to the Pink House gardens. I'd just make sure to stay out of Iyama's way.

I could have just as easily gone through our back yard to the alley and up to the garbage can and under, but I didn't. I wished I had because Kevin was on his front steps smoking when I came down our driveway. He nodded at me like pals saying hello without the words. I looked away so I wouldn't see his eyes and headed up to the Pink House. Iyama's truck was still there and it looked like all his tools were back on, so he must be about ready to go, I thought.

I went through the iron gate and straight for the pond. Iyama saw me and nodded hello. He had finished all his work and was using a grass rake to make swirly patterns in the crushed rock pathways. I came part way over and watched. He'd do it carefully, but if it didn't turn out the way he wanted, he scratch it out and start over. It was like painting or sculpting or maybe both at the same time. As soon as someone walked on it, it would get ruined, but until they did, it was something to see. I looked down to make sure I wasn't walking on one of his designs, but he hadn't gotten this far yet. That was a relief. He was working his way from the far side, the alley side of the garden, to the gate, one path at a time. I got off the one I was on and walked up the grassy hill to the pond hoping to fool around with the Garibaldi. I didn't have any bread crumbs, but sometimes if I gently tapped the surface of the water with a stick, they'd come. At least the solid gold-orange one would. Even if there wasn't any treat for him, he seemed to like to watch me watching him. I knew he was really a she because Rathbone told me they all were, but he still seemed like a boy one to me, so that's what he'd stay. I didn't see anything like a stick or a long stem to use. If there had been one, I knew Iyama would have already taken it away as he cleaned up. I kneeled down on the concrete lip and leaned forward and tapped the water with my finger. Little circles floated away and spread out, bumping into the Lilly pads and pond grass stalks, getting wider and wider and flatter as they went, making the sparkles of light on the water change and dance. He came. Slowly and without any fear, he swam past, rolled on his side and looked at me.

"Is it okay if I say you're a boy?"

I knew he couldn't say anything back, but he might understand, he might slap the water with his tail if he didn't like the idea. If he didn't slap the water, he'd stay a boy. If he did, it would be a she. That seemed fair enough. And if he didn't understand, it couldn't matter one way or the other, so he'd just stay a boy. He passed by at least three times with no slap, so that was that. Iyama was getting closer so I decided I should leave before he got to the path near me and I'd have to walk on his design to get to the gate. I bet Rathbone liked seeing it all finished with no footsteps on it, so I wouldn't come in the morning, even if I wanted to. I hadn't planned on it anyway, but in case I wanted to, I wouldn't. If he did an early morning walk tomorrow, his would be the only prints on it, like he was the first one, the only one in his world back here. It was worth cutting this visit short so he'd have that. I waved to Iyama and ran out ahead of where he was raking.

For some reason the Sundays were especially fat and it was hot and I just took my time. It had been a long time since it had taken me three hours to deliver the Sundays, but that's how long it took. Part of it was Julie and Sharon invited me in for lemonade and to tell me about both of them getting acting jobs, Julie on television and Sharon in a new movie. They were both small jobs and they both said it was because they'd been seen on The Star Shopper Show. By the time I'd finished the lemonade, two glasses worth, and we'd talked about being actors and stuff, I didn't really want to go. It was cool in their apartment. The door was open and a breeze was coming in and we listened to music for a while. I could have stayed there like that all day, so if I didn't get going, I never would, so I told them I had to go and I did. But I thought about them the rest of the route. Especially Julie.

On Monday, my mom was going downtown, which she'd been doing less lately, but she was going to leave Nick with Sarah, and I was supposed to watch him when I was done with the route so Sarah could be free to do something. I didn't know what and I didn't ask, but it was probably something with the Oakhurst Irregulars. It seemed fair enough since Sarah had to watch Nick almost whenever my mom went downtown. Sometimes I did, and sometimes Marty did, but not very often, either of us. I thought maybe I'd surprise him and take him to Beverly Ponyland again. As long as I kept an eye on him, my mom didn't care where we went as long as it wasn't too far from home and as long as we beat the summertime before dark rule.

I finished the route and pulled into our driveway and left the bike out in case we went somewhere. Nick was on his back, holding the Paul Bunyon book above him, sounding out the words. He looked at me and smiled hello, but didn't say it, and went back to his book. I passed Sarah where she was sitting on the bottom step when I went to put the route bags away behind her on the porch. Sarah put her book down.

"What took you so long?" she said, closing the book and standing up.

"I thought it went pretty fast. What time is it?"

"At least two-thirty. Maybe two forty-five. Geez, I gotta get outta here. He had lunch and stuff to drink since then. He hasn't been to the bathroom yet, so remind him or he'll keep reading 'til it's too late."

"Okay. When are you coming back?"

"That's none of your beeswax. Anyway, what do you care? It's your turn to watch him, so watch him. I've been doing it all day. All summer! Mom and dad should be back around six."

She ran off up the block. I was betting to Julie and Jeryl's house for some big Oakhurst Irregulars meeting.

"You need to use the bathroom?" I asked Nick.

He shook his head no. His curly hair moved lower on his forehead, getting pretty close to his eyes and he pushed it back so he could see his book.

"Is Maurice here?"

He shook his head yes and pointed to the back yard.

"Wait here. Don't go anywhere, okay? Stay right there. I'm going to go say hello to him."

I went down the driveway and into the yard. Maurice was up in the bigger apricot tree. We had two of them and sometimes built rope bridges between them. Pop didn't like it because he thought we'd fall and get hurt, but he didn't make us take them down, so Maurice was using what was left of the last one we'd made, really, mostly Sarah, to get from one tree to the other up in the air. He was cutting away the dead scruffy branches with Pop's limb saw, letting them drop to the ground. The hedge that ran along the alley and the south side of our yard had already been trimmed and the cuttings were on the ground along the whole length of it. When he was all done cutting stuff, it would end up on Pop's compost pile on the south side of the house just inside the stucco arch to the front lawn.

"Hi, Maurice," I called to him.

"Hey, howya doin'?"

"Good. How 'bout you."

"I'm good. Nice day, got a little work here, just gettin' on fine."

"I'm supposed to be watching Nick, my brother, out front," I told him, "so, see you later."

"You take care."

He went back to work and I went through the house and got some of the left over movie money from my drawer in case we went to the Ponyland. I looked at the money and thought, what the heck, and took a little more. I planned to take me and Nick to Raleigh's Barber Shop before Ponyland. When I got back, Nick was crying.

"What's the matter?"

He wouldn't tell me, but I could see and smell he'd wet himself.

"Because you peed?"

He nodded yes.

"Well, geez, why didn't you go inside?"

"You told me to stay right here."

"Oh, brother, not if you have to pee!"

He looked like he was going to cry again, but before he got to that, I tried to calm him down.

"It's okay. I'm sorry, okay? It's not your fault. We'll go in and find you some clean stuff. Okay?"

He nodded.

"Get over here."

It was Kevin's voice. I looked from Nick to him. He was standing on the parkway on his side, dressed in his fancy army clothes with the medals on his chest. His dad was probably going to take him to look for more votes again, but whatever, he was talking to me. I didn't move, though. I had this funny feeling like I couldn't have. Like I was frozen.

"Get over here and make it quick!"

I looked around hoping to see someone out on the block, but there wasn't anyone. Out of nowhere, I had a feeling like I couldn't breathe, and then the light got yellow and I was dizzy.

"What?" I said.

"I don't want to shout. Get over here."

"Just leave me alone," I said.

"We've got some paper route business to straighten out, buddy. You been cutting me off. Not nice. Not nice at all. And maybe a little fire we should discuss?"

He smiled one of his nastiest smiles. He pointed at the ground, motioning for me to cross the street. When I didn't move, he quit smiling.

"You coming?" he said to me, but he was looking at Nick.

Nick was standing there on the grass, the big wet spot on his shorts, drips of the pee working their way down his leg to his bare feet. He wanted to get cleaned up and I knew he wanted to complain to make sure I took him in for some new clothes, but one look at Kevin and the sound of Kevin's voice, and Nick knew not to. He stood there, unhappy and uncomfortable, but quiet.

"Go sit on the porch, Nick. Wait there. Don't go anywhere, okay? No matter what."

"I'm wet," he complained, but quietly.

"I know. I'll help you get you changed as soon as I can. Just stay there, okay?"

He nodded and went up the steps and sat on the porch, his feet on the first step down. I started across the street walking as slowly as I could, hoping someone would see me. I thought about yelling for George. Or Maurice. I don't know why I didn't. I should have, but I didn't. I should have told Nick to go get Maurice, but I didn't do that either. Maybe because my throat felt like it was squeezed shut. Maybe because I thought Max would tell me what to do.

"Move it," Kevin said.

I looked up the street and down. No people, no cars except for parked ones, no anything but Kevin. I got to the curb on his side but stayed in the street. For just a second, I thought I saw Miriam in her window. Maybe yes, maybe no, but if she had been there, she moved away and let the curtain fall closed. I think it fell closed. Maybe it was closed the whole time and she wasn't there. But I think she was.

"You set the fire, right?"

I didn't say anything.

"You little fuck, right?!"

Tears started running out of my eyes but without sounds and I didn't answer and he got mad and grabbed my t-shirt on top of my shoulder and started pushing me down his driveway, almost dragging me.

"I want you to see the mess you made."

"No! Let me go!" finally came out.

I started to scream, the kind they say would wake the dead, because that's how it sounded in my head, but he put his hand over my mouth.

"It's you or him," he said, nodding towards Nick. "Your choice."

But he didn't wait for me to choose anything. He just marched me down the driveway to the blackened back porch and steps, steering me by my t-shirt. The back door was already open. He sort of half pulled, half lifted me up the stairs and into the house, kicked the door shut and pulled me down the hall into his bedroom. He let go of me, pushing me forward at the same time, and backed against the door, closing it. He walked past me and sat on the edge of his bed, like the other time. The yellow light that I'd seen outside on the street was blocking everything else out. I could hardly see him as he lit another cigarette. My chest was pounding so hard I thought he could hear it too. I stopped breathing, holding my breath, trying to make the pounding calm down, but it only got worse and I had to take air in gulps. Screams were beginning to echo inside my head like car horns in a tunnel, blocking everything else out, like the other time too, but this time Max didn't tell me to shut up or be quiet or calm down or anything. I couldn't get them to come out. They were stuck inside and the noise in there was so loud whatever Kevin was saying was drowned out. I knew no one knew where I was, except Nick, and no one would come, just like before. Now, not even Max. Why wouldn't he come? I thought he would when no one else would or could. Without him, I felt like the blood was draining out of me, like Kevin was probably going to kill me anyway, but before he did, I'd die from the blood leaking out. Whatever it was that makes you alive can just leak out, and the next thing you know, you're dead. Then I was thinking about Nick all alone out there on the step, the Red Rider waiting to take us to Raleigh's Barber Shop and the Beverly Ponyland. Why did I have to go say hello to Maurice? If I'd just told Nick to go pee and then we'd go, he'd have been really happy and we'd have left before Kevin came out. That made me think about the Red Rider and the free feeling coming back that day when I got to Beverly. I remembered thinking I wasn't going to let him take that away again. The next thing I knew, I wet my pants and I didn't even care. I just wanted to be outside away from him. I wanted to be free before everything leaked out and there was nothing left of me.

"Oh Christ," he complained.

Then he smiled, like it was funny, or like he thought my wetting my pants was a good thing.

"Come here," he said. "We don't have all day. My old man's coming. Wouldn't he just love to get his hands on you?" he smiled. "Then again, he's got his little Johnny. Come here," he said, getting angry.

When I didn't move he reached out and grabbed me. His fingers hooked around the cowboy belt and my pants. He pulled me closer and unbuckled the belt. Somewhere inside me something exploded, and the next thing I knew, I was hitting him as hard and fast as I could. He laughed at me, but I kept hitting him until he pulled me so close I couldn't. I burned the palm of my hand on his cigarette trying to push away, my hands against the side of his face, as I wiggled and struggled to get free. His cigarette fell onto the long skinny carpet, and as I was pushing, he got mad and yelled something and pushed back, the buckle side of the belt still in his hand, and it suddenly came out of my too big pants with the too big loops and I lost my balance and spun part way around and fell into the little bedside table, knocking the ashtray onto the floor and making the statue of the man in the robe rock back and forth. The belt coming out so suddenly made Kevin fall sideways, away from me, and he tried to scramble back before I could get away. He lunged and the skinny rug came out from under his feet and the next thing he was on his face on the floor.

"Now!!" Max yelled. "Now! Get out the door! You can do it!"

But I was still trying to get my balance back, using the table to keep myself up, so I didn't know if I could get to the door before Kevin. Maybe I could have. Maybe. But before I could even think about it, Kevin's hand wrapped around my ankle and he pulled. He was still on his face so he couldn't pull very hard.

"Yank your foot free!" Max yelled. "He doesn't have a good grip. Pull free and run for it!"

As I was trying to pull away and keep my balance, I clawed at the edges of the table trying to get a better hold and the statue fell. Then Kevin was changing his grip on my foot, and for a second it came loose, and I pulled free and stood up. He pushed himself up off the floor to his knees, on all fours. Then he rocked back so he was sitting on his heels. He looked at me and smiled. I was looking back at him, but my right hand had found the statue and I wrapped my fingers around it. I could feel the man's chest in my hand, his outstretched arms and head and shoulders just below my fingers. Kevin kept smiling at me like he had all the time in the world, like I had nowhere to go, like he was in control and could do whatever he wanted before my life leaked away. He stayed like that for a second, like he wanted to make sure I knew it. When he made a move to stand up I swung the statue like a baseball bat, like the Stars catcher, Malone, swinging for the fences. I caught him on the side of his head with the heavy base. Blood squirted out and sprayed all over me. His eyes rolled back and he fell forward on his face. I just stood there looking at him, the statue hanging by my side.

"Geeez! Why didn't you just run?" Max yelled. "I think you killed him."

Or maybe it was me. It all seemed like a dream, me, Max, Kevin. I put the statue back on the table. I started to pick up the ashtray I'd knocked over but changed my mind and left it on the floor. I started to cry.

"I don't want to be afraid anymore," I told him.

Or maybe he told me. I looked at the statue. There was blood and some skin on the corner of the base, but the man had the same sad smile. But kind and peaceful, like he was glad he could help. Kevin groaned and tried to roll over onto his back. I walked to the door, opened it and went down the hall to the living room and out the front door. I thought I was going to throw up, but I didn't.

The light outside seemed too bright, then, after a second or two, it was nice. The air was nice too, warm and clean smelling. I looked up at the sky through the jacaranda leaves and blossoms expecting to see the smell, and I think I did. I looked across the street and saw Nick curled up on the porch, close to the front door. He was asleep. I saw the Red Rider and it seemed like it was asleep too. Maybe we were all asleep. Maybe it was all a dream, a bad one, but a dream, and then Max was telling me it wasn't my dream, it was his dream and I could forget about it if I wanted. I looked at the Red Rider waiting for me and knew I wanted to be free, and I was, to have the free feeling, and I did. I left Nick to dream his dreams and went up to the Pink House gardens. I saw Iyama's truck and didn't see it. I went through the white gate and closed it. Maybe I saw Mr. Rathbone on the bench next to the pond, or maybe it was part of the dream I was about to have. I thought I wanted to sleep in the bamboo patch but I guess I didn't, because I went into the room at the back of the garage and crawled under the table with all the swords on it, hidden by the rug that hung down almost to the floor, and curled up and slept. Max kept his promise and I didn't dream his dream, just my own, and I was on the Red Rider somewhere near the beach in Santa Monica, then near Gert's, and I could hear the waves crashing on the wet sand and see the sun sparkling on the water, and Pete was in front of the Hot Dog Stand and he waved. I wondered how far it was to Malibu and how long it would take to get there and he said he didn't know and to just take my time and enjoy the ride whether I got there or not. Then I thought I heard Mr. Rathbone and Iyama. I thought someone changed my clothes and wiped me with a wet towel, but it was just a part of the dream. It was part of the dream I shared with Max because I knew I couldn't let him have to dream it alone. We'd share it. That would be fair, I thought. When I woke up, that's what I'd decided. I felt free. I was free. Then I was walking through the garden, floating really, and I saw Maurice and Iyama in the bamboo patch, like magic spirits, not solid, but more like smoke, and I could see through them. They waved and went back to their work. Then Kenny Lester and George Bowen were walking me home. I didn't know where they'd come from, but they were on either side of me, each of them holding my hand. They walked me almost all the way home and said it was just a dream. That I was safe now. That he was gone and wouldn't come back. When we got to our driveway, they let go of my hands and nodded that I should go in. Nick wasn't on the porch anymore. I walked up our steps and opened the screen door. My mom heard me come in. I didn't really hear what she was saying, but she was so mad she didn't notice that my new jeans weren't too long and fit good enough so that I didn't need a belt to hold them up and the t-shirt still had the fold lines from being new. I got spanked and sent to bed without dinner for leaving Nick alone and wet when I was supposed to be watching him, but that was okay. I reached into my pocket and felt the KA-BAR knife and the propeller metal. I kept them both in my hand as I took off my clothes and got into bed. Max and I could never tell anyone, ever, but we would share the dream, even though we knew it was real. We were free. We didn't let Kevin take that away.

I didn't. It was me. I held on to the knife and propeller medal and fell asleep.

I dreamt about taking Nick to Joseph's for breakfast and Raleigh's Barber Shop and to the Beverly Ponyland on the Red Rider. When I woke up the next morning, I decided that's what I was going to do. Maybe we could make it a perfect day. Maybe yes, maybe no. But we were free and we could try, so that's what we did.

A few days later, Pop changed his mind and said we could take the last of the Lester's puppies, the boy one that liked to bite my leg, and we did. So that made it a pretty good summer after all.

# Chapter 31
### *A Perfect Day*

"HE WAS ALIVE when you left?" she asked.

Most of the time I'd been in the hospital I'd been adrift, somewhere between awake and asleep, dreaming about that summer. It was strange, because I'd never dreamed about it before. Maybe the concussion. But the dreams coincided with my recollections, and I told Vann everything. All of it. I have to confess, it was both harder and easier than I would have thought, but mostly it was a relief, a weight lifted. Vann had insisted on driving to Miriam's. My head still ached and the light hurt my eyes, so I didn't argue. On the other hand, the sense of urgency had intensified, the feeling that the last piece of an old puzzle was within reach and I didn't want to have it slip away at the last moment, and that would have been better served if I'd been driving. Not that I would have gotten us there any faster, but it would have felt like it to me. Vann whipped the Fiero confidently around the curves, knowing where she was going this time.

"Yes," I told her, "I think so. He groaned, then tried to roll over onto his back. If he didn't die from the hit on the head, I didn't kill him."

"You don't think one of your friends, Kenny Lester or Maurice or Iyama, went in, after they found you, and finished him off?"

"It's possible, but no, I don't think so."

"Why not?"

"Because it would have been the easiest thing in the world for Miriam to say that or to suggest that at the outset and she didn't. She was focused on something else. Someone else. Hurry up, okay?"

She gave me one of her Vann looks, annoyed, but not planning to dignify my impatience with a response, other than a patented roll of the eyes. We worked our way up the hill and rounded the last curve and she pulled onto the parking structure at 57 Summit Drive.

Phillips was sitting on one of those tire stops that keep you from pulling too far forward, or in this case, crashing through the rail and toppling down the hillside. He was smiling and shaking his head as he stood to greet us.

"Detective," Vann said. "What a surprise."

"Vann," he said. Then to me, "Predictable. Completely predictable."

He looked at his watch.

"Your house arrest lasted all of three hours. To tell the truth, I thought you'd be here sooner."

"If you're going to re-arrest me, it'll have to keep. I want to talk to

Miriam. Her story's a cover. There's more. That's what we're here for."

"Well, cowboy, you're too late. That's sort of how I figured this would play out. You'd crawl out of the hospital, come up here and squeeze the rest of the story out of her. I was counting on it. Tie it all up in a nice package with a bow on it. But, be that as it may, I've got some good news and some bad news," he said. "Or maybe it's all good, depending on your point of view."

"What are you talking about? She isn't dead, is she? Don't tell me she died."

Coming this close and not getting there seemed impossible. Too outrageous and unfair to contemplate. I had a wave of something go through me. Not panic, not exactly, but something close. Like the times I've misplaced the KA-BAR knife or the propeller medal. Everything stops until I find them. I don't care where I'm supposed to be or who's waiting for me. Finding them, getting them back in my pocket where I can feel them, comes first.

"Not that I know of, but she done flew the coop."

"What do you mean?" Vann said.

"She's gone. For good, from the look of things."

I don't think it had anything to do with my current physical condition, but I was suddenly dizzy and lightheaded and felt like my legs weren't going to hold me up much longer.

"Sit down before you fall," Phillips said.

I sat on the tire stop where he'd been.

"Where?" I asked.

"Who knows? But first, this just in: Dolan won't be mayor after all."

"Why's that?" Vann asked.

"He drove himself off a cliff a little north of Malibu about two hours ago."

"Oh my god. Dolan? Why?" she said.

"Who can say? It's a mystery. Life's just one big mystery after another," he said, looking at me.

"Let me guess," I said. "He talked to Miriam. She told him she'd talked to you, or was about to. Again. The whole story this time. That his brother, his father, him, the whole thing would go public. Then Miriam took off."

"That's about the size of it. You're off the hook for Doyle. She told me another story on the phone and left this to confirm it."

Phillips waved a letter at me that Miriam had had notarized and handed it to me. I read it and handed it to Vann.

I almost felt sorry for the bastard. I was picturing little Johnny Dolan, not the Dolan of today. In a way, I figured he'd just become a sort of honorary Oakhurst Irregular.

"Know who owns this place?" Phillips asked.

"Dolan," I said. First J. T., then John William. Right?"

"Good guess."

Vann handed me back the letter and I handed it to Phillips.

"Do you remember what happened in the mayoral race when his old man was running?"

"No."

"I looked it up. He dropped out of the race towards the end of August. Cited health reasons. He'd been running in large part on Doyle's war record and suddenly there was no Doyle and no explanation for his disappearance and none he could give. So he just dropped out to avoid questions."

"You believe this?" Vann asked Phillips. "Do you?" she asked me

"Why would she protect J.T. all these years?"

"For love? Or money? Who knows?" Phillips said. "Miriam sees Dolan show up just after Kurt, here, left. They were supposed to go out campaigning but Dolan finds Doyle's been clobbered. Finds out a little more than he's prepared to forgive and forget. They get in an argument over it, whatever it might be, which covers a lot of ground, and Dolan kills the bastard. Uses the belt you've so conveniently left behind. Miriam sees Dolan come out, he sees her see him, and maybe after a little persuasion, he seems to have been a pretty persuasive guy, they strike a deal. He leaves. Your friends find you, go to deal with Doyle, find him expired, and think somehow you managed to kill him. The dent in his head? Blood all over you? A reasonable assumption. They haul him out and bury him. Leave the confessions just in case. Dolan sets her up here and life goes on. I don't think our Dolan, J.W., knew anything more than he was supposed to take care of Miriam, let her live here and send her money according to his father's instructions."

"Wouldn't Dolan think he had to take care of Doyle's body? Do something to cover his tracks?" Vann asked him.

"Sure. Maybe he was going to send someone back to deal with it. Or come back himself at night. Maybe in the alley. No witnesses. But maybe when Miriam saw your gang go in and come out with Doyle she told Dolan. Problem solved. If the body was found, it would be easy enough to point a finger at them. Or, if necessary, through them, at you. Something like that."

"I suppose," Vann said, not completely convinced. "And you think all that's enough for a guy like Dolan to toss in the towel? That that becomes public? Because he's running for mayor?" Vann said, unconvinced. "It doesn't sound like the bruiser we've all come to know and love." She shook her head. "I don't believe it. Do you?" she asked me.

I shrugged. I was at a loss and couldn't wrap my head around it. The whole thing seemed just out of reach, like a name you're trying to remember, but it won't come.

"From what I've seen and heard, the old man was a very sick sonofabitch. Kevin Doyle didn't come out of nowhere. And my guess is, our Dolan had them both in his nightmares. He was running from, not for. Sometimes, you just can't run fast enough."

"And how much of this did you know or suspect before you called me?" I asked him.

Phillips smiled.

"Some."

"And you got Kurt involved? Risked Dolan going after him?" Vann said.

"Well, I didn't plan on that. At least not the details. I'm sorry. Truly."

"What did you think was going to happen?"

Vann was getting madder at Phillips than I was.

"I was a stalking horse, right?" I said.

"Well, that was the plan in the beginning. I did believe it might have been your brother. But from the very first, Dolan was wrong. He wasn't telling the truth. I just didn't know why and I couldn't press him, what with the campaign and all, but he wouldn't let it alone. From the minute the body showed up, he wanted to control things every step of the way. I figured your having lived on the block was a start. If nothing else, the more you found out, the closer you got to things, the more it would provoke him. We'd get to the truth, you and I, or he'd tip his hand about his all too passionate interest in it. Then it started to look like it was you. Either way, I'd get to the bottom of it. I'm sorry it ended like this for him, but there's only so long you can keep things like he did inside. It takes a toll."

He shrugged. He looked past me, past the canyon, past Corte Madera below us, across the Bay and the Golden Gate Bridge to the City. Vann reached out her hand and helped me up. The dizziness had passed. I noticed what a beautiful day it was. The sun was bright, the air clean. I smiled at Vann as she put her arm around my waist. I could feel the knife and propeller medal in my pocket. I was alive, and in a way, freer than I'd ever been.

"It's nice up here," Phillips said. "Not Beverly Hills, but nice."

He looked at Vann.

"You ever think about moving up here?"